Language

Its Structure

and Use Fourth Edition

Edward Finegan

University of Southern California

THOMSON
™
WADSWORTH

Australia Canada Mexico Singapore Spain United Kingdom United States

Language: Its Structure and Use, Fourth Edition

Edward Finegan

Publisher: *Michael Rosenberg*
Acquisitions Editor: *Stephen Dalphin*
Development Editor: *Leslie Taggart*
Production Editor: *Samantha Ross*
Director of Marketing: *Lisa Kimball*
Executive Marketing Manager: *Carrie Brandon*

Senior Print Buyer: *Mary Beth Hennebury*
Compositor: *Datapage Technologies*
Project Manager: *Christine Wilson*
Cover Designer: *Gina Petti*
Text Designer: *Carol Rose*
Printer: *Banta Book Group*

Cover Images: *all © Index Stock Imagery: IT Stock International/David Marshall/Don B. Stevenson*

For more information contact Wadsworth, 25 Thomson Place, Boston, Massachusetts 02210 USA, or you can visit our Internet site at http://www. wadsworth.com.

For permission to use material from this text or product contact us:
Tel   1-800-730-2214
Fax   1-800-730-2215
Web   www.thomsonrights.com

ISBN: 0-8384-0794-3

Library of Congress Control Number: 2003110245

Preface

A SPECIAL WORD TO STUDENTS

For hundreds, even thousands, of years, philosophers, rhetoricians, and grammarians have analyzed the uses to which people put language in their everyday lives and the linguistic and social structures supporting those uses. The nineteenth and twentieth centuries proved rich in linguistic insight, as philologists at first and then linguists and cognitive scientists broadened and deepened our understanding of the singularly human trait that is language. In recent decades, as space explorers revised our views of the satellites of Uranus and microbiologists plumbed the recesses of DNA in the Human Genome Project, linguists too have generated a burst of insight into the representation of language in the mind and into the interactions between language use and community social structures. In this book you will uncover a glimpse of language as we now understand it.

Despite the impressive pace at which investigators have gained insight into human language, tough questions remain unanswered and many arenas remain unexplored or underexplored. Far more remains to be discovered about language than is now known, and an abundance of intellectually exciting and socially useful work remains to be achieved by today's college and university students, who are tomorrow's investigators. Today, we understand a good deal more about the structures and functions of languages than we knew when you were born. For those of you wanting to contribute to our understanding of the human mind and of human social interaction, rest assured that what is now known will be dwarfed by what is discovered during your lifetime—and some of you will make those discoveries. For those wanting simply to grasp what we now know about language, this book will be equally useful. You are invited to dive in and raise your own questions about language and its role in your life and the lives of people around you.

"A stitch in time saves nine" is one of the helpful proverbs I first heard in school, and "Look before you leap" was another. One proverb involving language proved false. It said, "Sticks and stones may break my bones, but words will never hurt me." Most of us learn early in life how powerful a tool language is and how it can be used for good or ill. It can delight and enlighten us, and it can also inflict injury. Pivotal in all human lives, language is as central to your social interactions as it is to your cognitive pursuits. You'll want to learn as much about it as you possibly can.

In reading *Language: Its Structure and Use*—LISU for short—you'll see occasional words in **boldface** type. When an important concept is first discussed (not necessarily when it is first mentioned), the term for it is set in boldface to highlight its significance and alert you that the term is defined in the Glossary. There, you'll find definitions or characterizations of terms whenever you need to refresh your memory. To learn more about topics that interest you, check out the Suggestions for Further Reading at chapter ends. You'll also find lists of videos and Internet addresses. For more, go to the LISU Web site at http://english.wadsworth.com/finegan-frommer/.

A WORD TO INSTRUCTORS

LISU includes more chapters than can be covered in a one-semester course. Typically, instructors cover the first six chapters and then select among the others according to their students' needs and interests. In this edition, as in the previous one, the chapter on morphology appears before those treating phonetics and phonology. That organization succeeds partly because novices find words more tangible and accessible than sounds and partly because morphology can be discussed without phonetic symbols, whose alien character at the gateway can be daunting. The existing chapter sequence invites instructors to teach morphology before phonology, but to teach phonetics and phonology before morphology, simply postpone the section on "The Interaction of Morphology and Phonology" (pages 129–134) until you've completed your morphology unit.

Each chapter contains sections on computers and language, Internet and other resources, and separate exercises for English and for other languages. Aiming prospectively to engage students with quotidian situations in which a chapter's contents may play a role, each chapter opens with a few puzzlers under the rubric, "What Do You Think?" Then, preceding the exercises at the end of the chapter, there are brief responses to the puzzlers in "What Do You Think? Revisited." You may wish to encourage your students to think about the puzzlers and check the "Revisited" section *before* studying the chapter. The questions and nontechnical answers may whet some students' appetite for what lies ahead in each chapter.

In other ways, too, I've tried to make LISU more interactive. The new "Try it yourself" sections straightforwardly apply what has just been explained in the text and encourage students to check their own understandings. Exercises designated "Especially for Educators and Future Teachers" may be of special interest in pedagogical contexts, but most will also prove helpful to students aiming for careers in other professions—as professionals and as parents of tomorrow's school children. Probably all students have experienced highly effective and less effective approaches to language analysis and language teaching in their own schooling, so dialogue between experienced students and future teachers may prove stimulating to both.

In this edition, all chapters have been revised for greater clarity, and whole sections sometimes omitted in the interest of a trimmer presentation. At the suggestion of reviewers, I have replaced the discussion of ideal languages in the introductory chapter with other topics of interest, including the important matters of standard and non-standard language varieties, multilingualism, and English-only or English-plus programs. At the same prompting, I have eliminated discussion of syntactic constraints from Chapter 5 and expanded on syntactic functions. Chapter 11 on dialects omits several maps from older atlas projects and incorporates treatment of the major vowel shifts affecting English in North America. It draws on the *Atlas of North American English* to illustrate the Northern Cities Shift, the Southern Shift, and mergers in the *cot~caught* and *pin~pen* word classes. I hope students will be drawn into analysis of dialect variation by examining these familiar North American features.

A WORD ABOUT PHONETIC TRANSCRIPTION

Settling on a phonetic transcription in an introductory textbook is complicated. For one thing, custom in the United States favors a modified version of the International Phonetic Alphabet. For another, the considerable variation in published and Internet sources makes it desirable for students to recognize that in any given treatment they must determine just what the symbols stand for. Of course, it is precisely to avoid that problem that many linguists favor the IPA, more or less strictly. Still, there is variation, and from time to time, the IPA itself also changes. As in all matters linguistic, prescription yields to practice. For the tables in this edition, I have adhered closely to IPA representation. While generally preferring IPA symbols once they have been introduced in Chapter 3, I sometimes use alternative symbols after that and indicate what the symbols represent. It is my hope that in this fashion students will be better prepared for real-world practice, including the ordinary use of dictionaries.

WORKBOOK AND ANSWER KEYS

To accompany this edition of LISU, a third edition of *Looking at Languages: A Workbook in Elementary Linguistics* has been prepared by Paul Frommer and me. It is useful in helping students review, apply, and extend basic concepts. New spoken-language files to accompany many of the exercises in the workbook are available on the LISU website: http://english.wadsworth.com/finegan-frommer/. The textbook and workbook have separate answer keys, which, besides answers to exercises, contain occasional suggestions on other matters. The keys are available only from the publisher.

ACKNOWLEDGMENTS

I have relied on many scholars whose work provided a footing from which to address the topics taken up here. References in each chapter only hint at the range of scholarship I've invoked, and I am indebted as well to the many whose work is not cited. I am grateful to colleagues and student readers of earlier editions who have offered helpful comments, including Michael Adams and his students, John Algeo, Joseph Aoun, Anthony Aristar, Dwight Atkinson, Robin Belvin, Doug Biber, Betty Birner, Dede Boden, Larry Bouton, Leger Brosnahan, William Brown, Paul Bruthiaux; Ron Butters and his students, Allan Casson, Steve Chandler, Bernard Comrie,

Jeff Connor-Linton, Janet Cowal, Marianne Cooley, Carlo Coppola, John Dienhart, David Dineen, Sandro Duranti, Paul Fallon, Andreas Fischer, Paul Frommer, John Hagge, Jim Hlavac, John Hedgcock, Kaoru Horie, José Hualde, Larry Hyman, Yamuna Kachru, Christine Kakava, William A. Kretzschmar, Juliet Langman, Peter Lazar, Audrey Li, Ronald Macaulay and his students, Joseph L. Malone, Erica McClure, James Nattinger, John Oller, Doug Pulleyblank, Vai Ramanathan, Gregory C. Richter, La Vergne Rosow, Robert Seward, Trevor Shanklin, Harold F. Schiffman, Deborah Schmidt, Chad Thompson, Gunnel Tottie, Edward Vajda, Robert R. van Oirsouw, Heidi Waltz, Rebecca Wheeler, Roger Woodard, Anthony Woodbury, and Thomas E. Young. I appreciate the helpful data provided by Marwan Aoun, Zeina el-Imad Aoun, Dwight Atkinson, Liou Hsien-Chin, Yeon-Hee Choi, Du Tsai-Chwun, Nan-Hsing Du, Jin Hong Gang, José Hualde, Yumiko Kiguchi, Yong-Jin Kim, Won-Pyo Lee, Christopher Long, Mohammed Mohammed, Phil Morrow, Masagara Ndinzi, Charles Paus, Minako Seki, Don Stilo, and Bob Wu. Min Ju indexed the third edition, and Susan Leeming, the current one. Eric Du contributed the photograph on page 84, Julian Smalley, the one on page 54, and Bill Labor the map on page 384.

I received first-rate recommendations from the commissioned reviewers for this edition, and it would be impossible to give adequate thanks, so a simple acknowledgment must suffice, along with an expression of regret that time and circumstances did not permit me to incorporate all their excellent suggestions. My gratitude goes to Charlotte Webb of San Diego State University, Michael Newman of Queens College, Timothy J. Pulju of Dartmouth College, Johanna Rubba of California Polytechnic State University at San Luis Obispo, Barbara Speicher of De Paul University, Ingo Plag of the University of Hannover, Nicole Dehé of Braunschweig University, and Rüdiger Zimmermann of Philipps-Universitat Marburg.

To Steve Dalphin, Editor; Steve Marsi, Editorial Assistant; Samantha Ross, Production Editor; and Christine Wilson, Project Manager, go my appreciation for intelligent editorial supervision and attentive production. Publishers increasingly acknowledge their staff and the freelancers who contribute centrally to making a textbook all that it can be. I applaud that acknowledgment. A special word of thanks to Leslie Taggart, who served as development editor for this and the previous edition; she has helped make the contents more amenable to the needs of instructors and more accessible to student readers.

For hauling me over assorted word-processing challenges and for a generous dose of patience, almost endless good cheer, and countless unspoken blessings I am especially thankful to my partner Julian Smalley.

A FINAL WORD TO ALL READERS

From students, instructors, and all other readers, I welcome comments and suggestions at Finegan@USC.edu.

—Edward Finegan
Los Angeles

Contents in Brief

Contents in Detail

Part One
Language Structures 37

Chapter 6 The Study of Meaning: Semantics 179

Part Three
Language Change, Language Development, and Language Acquisition   443

Chapter 13 Language Change over Time: Historical Linguistics   445

Chapter 1

Languages and Linguistics

- ❖ Two roommates who'll argue over anything are debating the number of languages in the world. One says thousands and the other says there's no way to count 'em. What do you say?

- ❖ A friend in Los Angeles opens her utility bill and says with alarm, "Look at this—in five languages: Spanish and Chinese and who knows what else! Isn't English supposed to be the official language of the USA?" What's the answer to her question?

- ❖ Watching TV one night, your family sees an investigative report stating that, depending on a caller's accent, landlords respond differently to telephone inquiries about apartment vacancies. Callers with some accents more frequently found advertised vacancies still available than those with other accents. Your mother says you can't always tell someone's social identity from an accent—and that housing discrimination is illegal. Your brother says it's easy to identify ethnic groups on the phone. What's your view?

- ❖ While reading a newspaper, your ninth-grade sister Nan looks up and asks what the word *note* means. You figure Nan knows its meaning in expressions like *love note* and *thank-you note,* so you ask her to read the sentence aloud. Once she does, you say it means 'bill,' as in "$20 bill." Nan asks how hearing the whole sentence helped you know what the word meant. Your explanation?

❖ Your classmate Claire complains that her history instructor corrected the word *snuck* to *sneaked* on a paper she submitted. Claire claims everyone she knows says *snuck*, and she wonders where the prof gets her information! The complaint reminds you of other discussions—about *who* and *whom, nuclear* and "nucular," "ee-ther" and "eye-ther." What have you heard people citing as authoritative in deciding what's right and wrong in English usage, and where can Claire find reliable information about *sneaked* and *snuck?*

❖ At a family picnic, fifteen-year-old Frank is teasing his seven-year-old cousin Seth and asks, "Do you know when your birthday is, dude?" When Seth answers, "September ninth," Frank retorts, "I didn't ask you <u>when</u> your birthday was! I asked if you <u>knew</u> when it was!" What does seven-year-old Seth understand about language use that fifteen-year old Frank pretends not to understand?

❖ You and your roommate, Rod, see a TV show about communication among porpoises. At the end, Rod says, "Well, maybe not porpoises, but what about chimpanzees? Isn't their language like ours?" You suggest checking the Internet together. What do you learn?

HOW MANY LANGUAGES ARE THERE IN THE WORLD?

Some dictionaries include language names among their entries, and you've probably seen lists that provide information about the number of speakers of various languages. When the U.S. Census Bureau compiles its census data each decade, it asks residents what language they speak and publishes that information. Most countries are represented at the United Nations, and the ambassadors to the U.N. must know which languages are spoken in their home countries. With all that information, you'd think it would be easy to answer the question, *How many languages are there in the world?*

Actually, enumerating the languages spoken on Earth is not a straightforward task. First, it's not always clear whether to call two "language varieties" *dialects* of the same language or *different languages*. (In fact, the very criteria for distinguishing between languages and dialects are complicated.) Then, more often than you might think, new languages are discovered in the Amazon, Papua New Guinea, and other remote parts of the world. Some compilations of languages may be limited to spoken tongues, while others also include signed languages. Finally, languages disappear when their last speaker dies, and sadly that, too, happens more often than you'd think.

Even when the criteria for inclusion on a list of different languages are established, compiling the information may not be easy. For one thing, a given language may have different names, as with *Hebrew* and *Ivrit* or with *Irish, Erse, Gaeilge,* and *Irish Gaelic.* For another thing, a name may be spelled in different ways, not all of them obvious variants of one another. Uyghur, a language spoken mainly in China (but not related to Chinese), has been spelled *Uighur, Uighar, Uygur, Uigur, Uighuir, Uiguir, Weiwuer,* and *Wiga,* among others; among its speakers, Uyghur isn't spelled with the Roman alphabet but with Arabic script, and it has also been represented in Cyrillic.

Possibly, some languages die and others are born during most periods. Some that die may later be revived, as Hebrew has been. Similarly, the last speaker of Cornish, a Celtic language, died in 1777, but the language was revived recently and is now in use among a couple thousand speakers in the southwest of England. Manx, another Celtic language formerly spoken on the Isle of Man, is now extinct as a first language, but some second-language speakers are endeavoring to revive it. In 1996 in Worcester, Massachusetts, Red Thunder Cloud died and with him died Catawba, a Siouan language. On the flip side of the coin, pidgins are spoken as second languages in some places in the world, and when children start speaking a pidgin as their first language it develops into a full-blown language called a creole. Creoles must be counted among the world's languages (even when their users still call them pidgins).

One trusted source of information, *The Ethnologue,* lists 6809 languages in its latest edition. But don't think there are exactly 6809 languages in the world as you read this number. Consider that in this book we sometimes refer to "Chinese" and that the U.S. Census Bureau allows residents to identify themselves as speaking "Chinese," but *The Ethnologue* does not list Chinese among its languages. Instead, it lists thirteen languages with names such as Hakka Chinese, Mandarin Chinese, Wu Chinese, Xiang Chinese, and Yue Chinese, each of which may have dialects of its own. In the English-speaking world, Mandarin Chinese is known as Mandarin and Yue Chinese as Cantonese. Also worth bearing in mind is that a good number of the 6809 languages are sign languages. Except for their mode of expression, most sign languages are like spoken languages and share with them the challenges of how to be identified and counted. For example, in the city of Chiangmai in northern Thailand, Chiangmai Sign Language is known in the deaf community but only among older signers, while younger signers use a distinct language called Thai Sign Language.

It seems safe to stick with the conventional wisdom that there are between 5000 and 7000 languages in use in the world. You should note that only Arabic, Chinese, English, French, Russian, and Spanish have official status at the United Nations, and French does not rank among the top 10 languages in terms of numbers of speakers, while Bengali, Hindi, Portuguese, and Indonesian-Malay have greater numbers of speakers than some of the official U.N. languages. Of course, deciding which language to use in any situation may be a matter of some delicacy and diplomacy, reflecting historical and political realities. It is also interesting to note that for the year 2000 the U.S. Census Bureau names 30 individual languages in use in the United States (and many unnamed others under labels such as "Scandinavian languages," "African languages," "other Indic languages," "other Native North American languages," and "other Asian languages"). Given the 30 named languages (which include no sign languages and count Chinese as a single language) and given those other broad categories, would you be confident estimating the number of languages spoken even in the United States? Imagine coming up with an exact number for the whole world!

DOES THE UNITED STATES HAVE AN OFFICIAL LANGUAGE?

It's not uncommon for Americans to think of English as the official language of the United States and to believe this has always been the case. In fact, though, the United States does *not* have an official language and never has. Some states have designated official languages: Spanish in New Mexico and English and Hawaiian in Hawaii, but not the nation.

Some Americans also believe the United States is essentially a monolingual nation, albeit with large numbers of Spanish speakers in three corners of the "lower 48"—the Southwest, Southeast, and Northeast corners. Actually, in the United States, nearly 47 million residents over the age of 5 speak a home language other than English. That's almost 18% of that age group (an increase from 11% as recently as 1980). Twenty-eight million of them speak Spanish, with more than half of these Spanish speakers reporting that they also speak English very well. Additionally, youngsters between the ages of 5 and 17 who speak a home language other than English number close to 10 million, and the vast majority of them also report that they speak English very well. In seven heavily populated states, at least one of every four residents over the age of 5 speaks a home language other than English, and only in five states do fewer than 5% of the population speak a home language other than English. Languages that are spoken in all 50 states include Arabic, Hindi, Hungarian, Korean, Tagalog, Thai, Urdu, and Vietnamese. The indigenous languages of North America are spoken by some Native Americans in all 50 states, and Navajo, with

Los Angeles, California. Voter information pamphlets are available in English, Spanish, Tagalog, Korean, Vietnamese, Chinese, and Japanese.

For General Election Information, please call 1-888-873-1000

Under federal law, voter information pamphlets are available in English as well as in the following languages:

Si Ud. desea obtener una copia de la pamfleto en español por favor llame al teléfono 1-800-994-VOTE (8683)

Kung kailangang ninyo ang kopya ng pamplet sa Tagalog, tumawag po lamang sa 1-800-994-VOTE (8683)

이 팸플릿을 한국어로 원하시면 다음 전화번호로 연락하십시오. 1-800-994-VOTE (8683)

Nếu quý vị muốn có tập sách bằng tiếng Việt xin gọi cho số điện thoại này. 1-800-994-VOTE (8683)

若您希望索取本手冊的中文譯本，請撥此電話號碼。 1-800-994-VOTE (8683)

このパンフレットの日本語版をご希望の方は、お電話ください。 1-800-994-VOTE (8683)

more than 175,000 speakers, is used at home in 47 states. According to figures given in *The Ethnologue,* 176 living languages are spoken in the United States today. They range from Abaza and Adyghe through Eastern Kanjobal, Khuen, Mezquital Otomí, Carpathian Romani, Upper Taoih, Uyghur, and Yatzachi Zapoteco. At the moment, then, the United States is rich in languages, and even election ballots come in many linguistic flavors. That's significant when you recall that the privilege of voting in the United States is limited to American citizens. In Los Angeles, ballots are available not only in English and Spanish, but also in Vietnamese, Chinese, Japanese Korean, and Tagalog.

Still, the great linguistic diversity of the United States is not a stable and reliable richness. Clearly, the survival of most Native American languages is threatened, in part because speakers tend to be older and in part because insufficient resources are allocated to support these heritage languages, which yield to English among younger Native Americans. Moreover, English aside, no language spoken in the United States comes close to Spanish in number of speakers. The 28 million speakers of Spanish far exceed the 2 million who speak Chinese and the 1.6 million who speak French. With few exceptions, the children or grandchildren of immigrants can no longer comfortably speak or readily understand the language of their grandparents, and this is true even with Spanish. Moreover, for all the richness of languages other than English throughout the United States, the 2000 Census data report that 215 million U.S. residents above the age of 5 speak English at home. That's a whopping 80%.

Try it yourself: Using your knowledge about current and past immigration patterns, say what you think are the ten most popular non-English languages spoken among U.S. residents aged 5 and over: Spanish, Chinese, French, and then what? For the record, Polish and Arabic are ranked ninth and tenth.

English-Only, English Plus, Multilingualism

Many people in the United States do not regard its great linguistic diversity as an asset and seem to prefer that English alone be used, at least in public discourse. Their reasons are many, and there has been a spate of legislation, ballot initiatives, and court rulings on the matter. The "English-only" movement arose in recent decades to push for legislation that would outlaw the use of non-English languages in certain circumstances and is particularly concerned about the use of non-English languages in schools. While much of the concern about using languages other than English seems unwarranted and perhaps xenophobic, much of it is also prompted by legitimate concern over widespread failure of school-aged youngsters to master standard English. Other Americans, concerned about loss of the great social, cultural, and political treasure that linguistic diversity represents, have wanted to preserve heritage languages and have advocated bilingual education and "English plus."

There has also been considerable controversy surrounding bilingual education in the United States. As an example of a recent development, California voters in 1998 endorsed a ballot initiative (a citizen-sponsored law) requiring that "all children in California public schools shall be taught English as rapidly and effectively as possible." Proposition 227, as it was called, did away with bilingual education except in specific circumstances. In California, many think that Proposition 227 is the right way to go, while others think that bilingualism and multilingualism are invaluable resources that should be cultivated.

In reading this book, you will become familiar with a good deal about what is known of human language and be in a position to analyze these important social and political issues. You will also be able to make informed decisions about what is suitable policy for students in your community and for the nation as a whole in language-related matters. While much of what is said in the first few chapters relates mostly to the structure of languages, much else in subsequent chapters relates to language use.

WHAT IS HUMAN LANGUAGE?

The academic field of linguistics is relatively young and holds promise for advancing our knowledge in the twenty-first century, but the modern study of language is rooted in questions that were asked millennia ago. As old as speculation on any subject, inquiry into the nature of language occupied Plato and Aristotle, as well as other Greek and Indian philosophers. In some areas of grammatical analysis, the ancients made contributions that have remained useful for 2000 years and in some cases established the very same categories of analysis that we will use in this book. In the nineteenth and twentieth centuries, the field of linguistics emerged to address certain questions, among them these:

- What is the nature of the relationship between signs and what they signify?
- What are the elements of a language, and how are they structured into words, sentences, and discourse?
- What enables speakers to produce and understand sentences they have never heard before?
- How do languages achieve their communicative goals?
- What is the origin of language?
- In what ways do languages change and develop?
- What does it mean to say that languages are related to one another?
- How are languages and dialects related?
- What enables a young child to learn a language so efficiently?
- What makes it so challenging for an adult to learn a foreign language?
- Are there right and wrong ways to express things, and, if so, who decides?

This book provides a modern context for asking and addressing those questions.

Three Faces of a Language System

Language seems to face in two directions, for the fundamental function of every language system is to link meaning to expression—to provide verbal expression for thought and feeling. A grammar can be viewed as a coin whose two sides are *expression* and *meaning* and whose task is to provide a systematic link between them. But there is far more to the successful use of language than the linking of expression and meaning. Language has a third face, which is so important in communicating and interpreting utterances that it can override all else. That face, of course, is *context*. It is only in a particular context that the meaning of an expression can convey a speaker's intended content and correctly be interpreted by a hearer/addressee.

Imagine a dinner-table conversation about the cost of living in which a guest asks, "Is there a state income tax in Connecticut?" Among the replies that this question could elicit are "Yes," "No," and "I don't know." In other words, in this context the question is likely to be taken as a request for information. Now consider an equally straightforward inquiry made by the same guest at the same dinner: "Is there any salt on the table?" In this instance, a host who earnestly replied "Yes," "No," or "I don't know" and who let the matter rest there would seem insensitive at best.

Is there a state income tax in Connecticut?

Is there any salt on the table?

The form of the salt question resembles the form of the income tax question, but the point of the questions—their intended *content*—and the expected responses could scarcely be more different. In a dinner context, a guest inquiring about salt naturally expects a host to recognize that it's *salt* that's wanted, not *information*! A host who ignored the *context* of the question and took it as a request for information would be regarded as rude, or perhaps a tease. By contrast, in a related context, say, with the host standing in the kitchen, pepper mill in hand, and asking a guest who's just come from the dining room, "Is there any salt on the table?" the host is likely to be understood as seeking information even though *the form of the question* and the meanings of its words are exactly the same as those asked by the guest at the table. In answer to the question asked in the dining room, a reply of "Yes" or "No" would seem bizarre. In the kitchen, it would be altogether appropriate.

You can see from these examples that conversationalists cannot interpret an utterance from expression alone. To grasp the intended content of an expression, hearers must examine it *in light of its context*. At the same time, when uttering expressions, speakers routinely rely on their hearer's ability to grapple with and recognize their intentions in uttering an expression in a specific context. In other words, effective language use is partly a guessing game in which a hearer must calculate what a speaker intended by uttering a given expression in a given context.

Besides meaning and expression, then, the base of language use is *context,* and language can be best viewed as a three-sided figure comprising expression, meaning, and context.

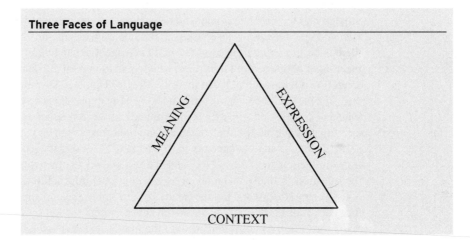

Three Faces of Language

MEANING

EXPRESSION

CONTEXT

Expression encompasses words, phrases, sentences, and pronunciation, including intonation and stress. **Meaning** refers to the senses and referents of these elements of expression. **Context** refers to the social situation in which expression is uttered and includes whatever has been said earlier in that situation. It also relies on generally shared knowledge between speaker and hearer. **Content** refers to the intended message of an expression uttered in a particular context. What links expression and meaning is grammar. What links grammar and interpretation is context. Without attention to both grammar and context, we cannot understand language or how it works.

Language: Mental and Social

Language is often viewed as a vehicle of thought, a system of expression that mediates the transfer of thought from one person to another. In everyday life, though, language also serves equally important social and emotional functions.

Linguists are interested in models of how language is organized in the mind and how the social structures of human communities shape language, reflecting those structures in expression and interpretation. The main goal of this book is to provide an understanding of how human languages are structured and how they function in social interaction.

SIGNS: ARBITRARY AND NONARBITRARY

In everyday conversation, we talk about *signs* of trouble with the economy, no *sign* of a train arriving at a railway station, a person's vital *signs,* and so forth. **Signs** are indicators of something else. In the examples mentioned, the indicator is inherently related to the thing indicated. Nonarbitrary signs have a direct, usually causal relationship to the things they indicate. Smoke is a nonarbitrary sign of fire, clouds a nonarbitrary sign of impending rain.

Arbitrary Signs

Nonarbitrary signs such as clouds and smoke differ crucially from partly or wholly arbitrary signs. Arbitrary signs include traffic lights, railroad crossing indicators, wedding rings, and national flags. There is no causal or inherent connection between arbitrary signs and what they signify or indicate. No property of the color red is inherently associated with stopping, but red lights are *conventionally* used to indicate that traffic must stop. Arbitrary indicators can be present even when the thing indicated is absent (as with a bachelor wearing a wedding ring). Because they are simply conventional representations, arbitrary signs can be changed. If a national transportation department decided to use the color blue as the signal to stop traffic, it could do so. By contrast, no one is able to change the relationship between smoke and fire. But the relationship is generally arbitrary between words and what they represent. Language is a system of *arbitrary* signs.

Representational Signs

To make matters interesting, some essentially arbitrary signs are not entirely arbitrary. Sometimes an arbitrary sign suggests its meaning. Poison may be suggested by a skull and crossbones ☠, while an icon such as ☼ may suggest the sun, and the Roman numerals II and III represent the numbers two and three. Because these signs suggest what they indicate, they are partly iconic. Still, though, there is no inherent connection: The sign can be present without the signified, and the signified without the sign. Signs that are basically arbitrary but partly iconic are called **representational signs.** Linguistic examples in English include *meow* and *trickle*, at least insofar as the words suggest what they signify. Besides the kind of iconicity that words occasionally capture, as when the sound of the word *meow* echoes the sound of a kitten to an English speaker, iconic expression can appear spontaneously in ordinary speech. I once telephoned the home of a friend, and her four-year-old son answered. He reported that his mother was showering, and when I said I'd call back in a few minutes he indicated that calling back too soon would do no good. His explanation was this:

> My mother is taking a *long, loong, looong* shower.

By stretching out his pronunciation of the vowel sound in *long,* the boy directly captured his intended meaning and demonstrated the potential for spontaneous iconicity in human language. By making his vowels longer, he directly suggested length of time. He iconically emphasized the salient part of his meaning. Representational (or iconic) language is linguistic expression that in any fashion mimics or directly suggests its content.

Try it yourself: Besides stretching out the vowel in *long* as a way to represent length, the boy's utterance was iconic in a second way. First, identify this second way. Then, identify another very, very common example in English in which this second mechanism conveys a meaning different from extended length.

Iconicity can also be expressed in grammar. Consider that English has two ways of organizing conditional sentences. The condition (the "if" part) can precede the consequence or follow it.

If you behave, I'll give you some M&Ms. (condition precedes consequence)

I'll give you some M&Ms if you behave. (condition follows consequence)

English permits placing the condition (*if you behave*) before or after the consequence (*I'll give you some M&Ms*). Although contextual factors can influence the choice, speakers and writers show a strong preference for the condition to precede the consequence, a preference also found in many other languages. The reason has to do with the order of occurrence of real-world events described by conditional sentences. In our example, the addressee must first behave, and then the speaker will provide the M&Ms. These real-world events are ordered in time with the condition preceding the consequence, and this real-world order is reflected in the preferred linguistic order. There is thus an iconic explanation for preferring the condition-preceding-consequence order over the reverse. With the condition-preceding-consequence order, the expression iconically mimics the sequencing of real-world events. Some languages allow *only* the condition-preceding-consequence pattern; others permit both; but no language appears to limit conditional sentences to the noniconic order, consequence before condition.

Language—A System of Arbitrary Signs

Despite occasional iconic characteristics, human language is basically and essentially arbitrary. The form of an expression is generally independent of its meaning except for the associations established by convention. We can illustrate the arbitrary nature of linguistic signs with a simple example. Imagine a parent trying to catch a few minutes of the televised evening news while cooking dinner. Suddenly a strong aroma of burning rice wafts into the TV room. This *nonarbitrary sign* will send the parent scurrying to salvage dinner. The aroma is *caused* by the burning rice and will convey its message to speakers of any language. There is nothing conventionalized about it. Now contrast the aroma with the words of a youngster who sees the smoke in the kitchen and shouts, "The rice is burning!" That utterance is also likely to send the parent scurrying, but the words are arbitrary. It is a set of facts about *English* (not about burning rice) that enables the utterance to alert the parent. The utterance is thus an arbitrary sign.

Other languages express the same meaning differently: Korean by the utterance *pap tʰanda*, Swahili by *wali inaunguwu*, Arabic by *yaḥtariqu alruzzu*, and so on. The forms of these utterances have nothing to do with rice or the manner in which it is cooking; they are not iconic. Instead, they have to do solely with the language systems called Korean, Swahili, and Arabic. Because the relationship between linguistic signs and what they represent is arbitrary, the meaning of a given sign can differ from culture to culture. Even words that mimic natural noises are cross-linguistically distinct. Cats don't *meow* in all languages, for example; the Korean word is *yaong*.

As you see, a central characteristic about human language is that the connection between words and what they mean—between signifier and signified—is arbitrary. In England, bakers bake *bread;* in France, *pain;* in Russia, *xleb;* in China, *miànbāo,* in Fiji *madrai.* Not only are things signified differently in different languages, even a single language may use multiple signs to represent a simple notion. We purchase *a dozen* or *twelve* bagels for the same price, and we write 12, XII, TWELVE, twelve, or Twelve. For more complex content, the variety of possible expressions in phrases and sentences can be limitless.

LANGUAGES AS PATTERNED STRUCTURES

Given the arbitrary relationship between linguistic signs and what they represent, languages must be highly organized systems in order to function as reliable vehicles of communication. If there were no pattern to the way speakers voiced their thoughts and feelings, listeners would face an insurmountable task in trying to unravel arbitrary signs for the meanings they encode.

The observable patterns that languages follow we call "rules." Language rules are not imposed from the outside (such as traffic regulations are) and do not specify how something *should* be done. Instead, they capture regularities that can be observed when people use language. In other words, the "rules" described in this book are based on the observed regularities of language behavior and the underlying linguistic systems that can be inferred from that behavior. They are the "rules" that even children have unconsciously acquired and use when they display mastery of their native tongue.

A language is a set of elements and a system for combining them into patterned expressions that can be used to accomplish specific tasks in specific contexts. Utterances report news, greet relatives, invite friends to lunch, request the time of day, make wisecracks, poke fun, argue for a course of action, make inquiries, express admiration, propose marriage, create fictional worlds, and so on in an endless list. And a language accomplishes its work with a finite system that a child masters in a few years. The mental capacity that enables speakers to form grammatical sentences such as *My mother is taking a long shower* rather than "A taking long my shower is mother" (or thousands of other possible ill-formed strings of exactly the same words) is **grammatical competence.** It enables speakers to produce and understand an infinite number of sentences that they haven't seen or heard before. Two hallmarks of this deserve highlighting.

Discreteness

Speakers of a language can identify the sound elements in its words. English speakers can identify the sounds in *cat* as three sounds, namely, those represented by the letters *c, a,* and *t.* Likewise for the sounds in *ship,* which they can also identify as three, the initial and final consonant sounds and the vowel sound in the middle. It is a structural feature of language that words are made up of elemental sounds.

Duality

Another characteristic is that human languages can be analyzed on two levels, one that carries meaning and one that does not. At the higher level, languages can be divided into meaningful units—for example, into words such as *bookshops* and into meaningful word parts such as *book* and *shop* and the *s* that marks *bookshops* as plural. At the lower level, though, these meaningful units comprise elements or segments that do *not* carry meaning. *Book* contains three sounds—the initial consonant sound *b,* the final consonant sound *k,* and the vowel sound in the middle. While none of these sounds carries a meaning by itself, organized into the sequence *book* they form a meaningful unit. Precisely because these elemental segments do not carry independent meaning, they can be combined to form units with different meanings. The same three meaningless sound segments that occur in the word *cat* can be combined variously to form a set of words whose meanings are unrelated to one another, including *cat, tack, act, tact,* and (using just two of the sounds) *at, ack, tat,* and the now obsolete *cack.*

SPEECH AS PATTERNED LANGUAGE USE

Knowing the elements of a language and the patterns for putting those elements together into well-formed sentences falls short of knowing how to accomplish the work that speakers accomplish with language. This requires not only mastery of its grammatical rules but also competence in the appropriate use of the sentences structured by those rules. Among other things, it requires knowing how to link sentences in conversations and how to rely on context to shape (and interpret) utterances appropriately.

The capacity that enables us to use language appropriately is called **communicative competence.** It enables us to weave utterances together into naratives, apologies, requests, directions, recipes, sermons, scoldings, jokes, and all the other things we do with language. Being a fluent speaker presumes both communicative competence and grammatical competence.

Grammatical competence is the language user's implicit knowledge of vocabulary, pronunciation, sentence structure, and meaning. *Communicative competence* is the implicit knowledge that underlies the appropriate use of grammatical competence in communicative situations. Because the patterns that govern the appropriate use of language differ from one speech community to the next, even a shared grammatical competence may not be adequate to make you a fluent speaker in another community. For example, members of one culture may find jokes about other people's misadventures funny, whereas members of another may find them offensive. In fact, the very concept of telling jokes (*Did you hear the one about . . . ?*) as distinct from telling "funny stories" seems not to exist in certain societies. Likewise, what is considered impolite in one place might be routine interaction elsewhere. Differences in interactional customs explain why some visitors to the Big Apple judge New Yorkers brusque or impolite when giving directions, though the same directions may be interpreted by a fellow New Yorker as routinely polite.

THE ORIGIN OF LANGUAGES: BABEL TO BABBLE

A good many people in all parts of the world share a belief that the origin of language can be traced to the Garden of Eden, where the first woman and the first man spoke the language originally bestowed upon them by their creator. Even among people who may give little credence to that story, many are persuaded that language originated in a paradise where its pristine form was perfectly logical and perfectly grammatical. The belief is widespread that, with the passage of time, languages that were once pure have become contaminated with impurities, illogicalities, and ungrammaticalities.

As examples of *impurities,* subscribers to this worried view cite borrowed words such as American *okay* and French *disco,* which have spread into many other languages, making these languages less "pure." Alleged *illogicalities* come in many shapes, with double negatives a commonly cited English example. Here's the claim. Just as two negatives yield a positive in algebra or logic (*It is not untrue* means 'It is true'), *I don't want none* should logically mean 'I do want some' and *He never did nothing* should mean 'He did do something.' Of course, they don't. Ungrammaticalities include use of the personal pronoun *I* in *just between you and I* and of *him and me* as the subject in a sentence such as *Him and me were friends in the army.* The argument offered is that objects of a preposition *must* be in the objective case (thus, *just between you and me*) and that subjects of a sentence *must* be in the common (or subject) case (*He and I were friends in the army*). Another alleged ungrammaticality is the word *snuck,* which many regard as an ungrammatical form of *sneaked.* We all recognize that millions of speakers around the globe use these and many other allegedly impure, illogical, and ungrammatical expressions—and the sun still rises over them each morning and sets each evening, just as it does with those whose language may be deemed more pure, logical, and grammatical.

Try it yourself: If, as a student assistant on a project to produce a dictionary of modern legal usage, you had been trained to search a huge database of legal opinions and discovered that judges and lawyers had written *sneaked* for the past tense of *sneak* about two-thirds of the time and had written *snuck* the other one-third, what would you expect the dictionary to say about modern legal usage of past-tense *snuck?* What if your findings were 60/40 or 50/50 instead of 66/33?

As well as having different views on the origins of languages, people have different ways of explaining why languages differ from one another and why they change. The Old Testament relates that before the Tower of Babel all men and women spoke the same language and could understand one another. Eventually human pride provoked God into punishing people by confounding their communication with mutually unintelligible tongues. According to this story, language differences among people can be seen as a penalty for sinful behavior. Similarly, Muslims believe that God spoke to Mohammed in pure and perfect Arabic, which the Koran embodies. By contrast, the varieties of present-day Arabic spoken in the Persian Gulf, North Africa, and elsewhere are seen as deriving from the subsequent weakness and culpability of their speakers.

Professional linguists take a different approach. They see the multiplicity of languages as resulting from natural change over time, the inevitable product of reshaping speech to meet changing social and intellectual needs, reflecting contact with people speaking other languages. When groups move to new places and mix with speakers of different tongues or settle areas with unfamiliar plants and animals, their language must adapt to new circumstances. Meeting people who use unfamiliar artifacts and hold different views and encountering unfamiliar aspects of nature invite language users to adapt their language. As a result, languages evolve quite differently around the globe.

Still, as more and more languages are analyzed, what is more striking than the differences among them is the extent of their similarity. The differences are all too apparent, the similarities more subtle. But the similarities, when you stop to think about it, are not surprising because, after all, every language must conform to the constraints and limitations of the human brain. Of all the conceivable kinds of language structure, only a relatively narrow band exits among the languages of the world (Chapter 7 examines selected universals of language structure).

As you recognized the first time you heard a foreign tongue, there are marked differences across languages. Not only do Japanese and French sound distinct, but French differs from its close relatives Spanish, Italian, Rumanian, and Portuguese. Different social groups speak even the same language differently, and every social group controls a range of styles for use in different situations; the language of conversation differs from that of sermons and political speeches. Speakers show a powerful tendency toward linguistic diversification, with some language varieties characteristic of groups of *users* (Burmese and Brooklynese) and others characteristic of situations of *use* (legalese, computerese, motherese). Each language variety marks the social identity of those who speak it and the situation in which it is used.

LANGUAGES AND DIALECTS

Along with physical appearance and cultural characteristics, language contributes to defining nationality. But even within one nation's borders, people may speak different languages. Ethnic French-Canadians in Quebec maintain allegiance to the French language, while ethnic Anglos maintain loyalty to English. Citizens of Switzerland speak French, German, Italian, and Romansch. In India, scores of languages are spoken, some confined to villages, others used regionally or nationally. Papua New Guinea has hundreds of languages, and an English-based language called Tok Pisin is used for communication across groups.

Wherever speakers of a language are separated by geographical or social distances, considerable linguistic variation is likely. Striking differences can be noted between the varieties of French spoken in Quebec and Paris and between the varieties of Spanish spoken in Madrid and Mexico City. English speakers from Sydney, London,

Dublin, and Chicago speak notably different varieties. Even countries thought largely to be monolingual, such as Germany, Japan, and England, have linguistic variation from group to group. Americans acknowledge regional variation when they speak of a Boston accent or a Southern drawl.

Try it yourself: Identify a characteristic of your own *pronunciation* that others have commented about when you've traveled outside your region. What about a *vocabulary item* of yours that others have found unusual or even odd? Any characteristics of *grammar?* Do the same for a roommate or classmate whose speech you've noted as being different in pronunciation, vocabulary, and grammar.

Some people seem to believe that only *other* people speak a **dialect,** but that *they themselves* don't. Instead, they think of themselves as speaking a *language* or even *the* language. The truth is that everyone speaks a dialect. American English, Australian English, and British English are national dialects. But everyone also speaks a regional dialect. What else could you have learned growing up? Since a language can be thought of as a collection of dialects, anyone who speaks a dialect of English speaks the English language, and anyone who speaks the English language can do so only by using one of its dialects.

What Are Social Dialects?

Language varieties differ across borders and from region to region within a nation. They also differ across age groups, ethnic groups, and socioeconomic boundaries. In the United States, communities of white Americans and communities of black Americans speak differently even when they live in the same city. Similarly, middle-class speakers and working-class speakers can often be distinguished from one another by the language variety they speak. You know that women and men may differ in how they use language and that the speech of your grandparents differs from that of your friends. The characteristic linguistic practices of ethnic groups, socioeconomic groups, and gender and age groups also constitute dialects. You speak a dialect that is characteristic of your nationality, your region, your sex, your socioeconomic status, and other characteristics as well. And so does everyone else.

Different Dialects or Different Languages?

The Romance languages developed from regional dialects of Latin spoken in different parts of the Roman Empire. Those dialects eventually gave rise to Italian, French, Spanish, Portuguese, and Rumanian, now the distinct languages of different nations. While these tongues share certain features of grammar, pronunciation, and vocabulary, the nationalistic pride taken by the Italians, French, Spaniards, Portuguese, and Rumanians supports the view that they speak separate languages rather than dialects of a single language. The opposite situation characterizes Chinese. Not all Chinese dialects are mutually intelligible (for example, speakers of Cantonese and Mandarin cannot understand one another), but speakers regard themselves as sharing a single language and highlight that unity with a single writing system.

Whether two varieties are regarded as dialects of one language or as distinct languages is a social matter as much as a linguistic one, and the call may be influenced by nationalistic and religious attitudes. The Hindus in northern India speak Hindi, while the Muslims there and in neighboring Pakistan speak Urdu. Opinions differ as to how well they understand one another. Until a few decades ago, Hindi and Urdu constituted a single linguistic unit called Hindustani, and the fact that professional linguists have written grammars of "Hindi-Urdu" reflects a judgment that the two language varieties required only a single grammatical description. Naturally, with the passage of time, Hindi and Urdu—whose different names proclaim that their speakers belong to different social, political, and religious groups—will become increasingly differentiated, as the Romance languages have become over the centuries.

What Is a Standard Variety?

No single variety of English can be called *the* standard. To begin with, there are different national standards—for British, American, Australian, and Canadian English, among others. But there are several standard varieties of each of those. Suffice it to note that many varieties of standard English can be identified.

What then is meant by a **standard variety?** There are at least two useful ways to address the question. We could identify as standard the variety used by a group of people in their public discourse—newspapers, radio broadcasts, political speeches, college and university lectures, and so on. In other words, we could identify a standard variety as the one used for certain activities or in certain situations. Alternatively, we could identify as standard the variety that has undergone a process of *standardization,* during which it is organized for description in grammars and dictionaries and encoded in such reference works.

A standardized variety does not differ in character from other varieties. It certainly isn't more logical or more grammatical. Nor is there any linguistic sense in which it could be said to be better, even if for some purposes it may be more useful. For example, this book is written in a variety of English that has been standardized, and that fact makes it possible to read it in many parts of the world. Instead of using spelling that reflects my own pronunciation, I have used standardized American spellings, and of course they differ from British spellings in a few familiar ways.

Typically, varieties that become standardized are the local dialects spoken in centers of commerce and government. In such centers the need arises for a variety that will serve more than local needs, for example, distributing technical and medical information, proclaiming laws, and producing newspapers and books. These centers are also where dictionary makers and publishers are likely to be located. Samuel Johnson lived in London while he wrote his dictionary, and Noah Webster in New England. Had circumstances been different, the varieties represented in their dictionaries might well represent the dialects of other groups. Dictionaries serve to describe (and then enshrine) a variety of the language that can be used for public discourse across regions and countries. Not all situations are typical, of course. With Basque, authorities combined forms from various regions into a single standardized variety so as to be socially and regionally inclusive. The same thing happened with Somali.

Is There a Right and a Wrong in English Usage?

Is there a right way and a wrong way of saying and writing things? Of the two spellings *honor* and *honour,* which is correct? In pronouncing *schedule,* is Canadian "shedule" or American "skedule" right? Should the break between theater acts be called an *intermission* (as it is on Broadway) or an *interval* (as it is in London's West End)? Americans, Canadians, and Britons may prefer their own expressions, but all these alternatives are correct, depending on who and where you are and what you want to accomplish. If you say "shedule" in Detroit, you identify yourself as Canadian. If you say "skedule" in Toronto, you identify yourself as a Yankee. What about within a country? Are *sneaked* and *snuck* both okay? And isn't grammar a different matter? Aren't some things (like posted signs that say *Drive Slow* instead of *Drive Slowly*) just downright wrong?

To answer that question, it helps to think of grammar as a *description* of how language is organized and how it behaves. In that case, ungrammatical sentences of English include these:

> Experience different something allergy season this.
>
> Season experience something different allergy this.
>
> Somerience diffthing seaserenton thallergyis exper.

These strings of words are *ungrammatical* variants of the grammatical sentence *Experience something different this allergy season,* which appeared in a print ad promoting an allergy medicine. No one who speaks English would normally say or write any of the three, and in that sense they *are* ungrammatical.

Another view would count as ungrammatical any violation of a relatively small set of prescriptive "rules" such as these:

- Never end a sentence with a preposition.
- Never split an infinitive.
- Never begin a sentence with *and* or *but.*
- *It's me* is ungrammatical; *it is I* is grammatical.

Prescriptions like those arose in the eighteenth century, but even then they did not accurately describe the language people used in their ordinary interactions or even when they wrote books. Commentators in this prescriptive tradition have formulated rules for what they regard as the "proper" use of *shall* and *will,* condemned phrases like *between you and I,* and tried to ban the use of *ain't.* More recently, they've been poking fun at *like* when it's used to mark quoted speech or thought (*And I'm, like, "Do I really wanna do this?"*).

Partly from this prescriptive tradition, judgments were accepted that some common expressions are ungrammatical, as with *Me and him would sit and talk all day* and *He don't like to cook* or *It don't matter*. These sentences are not standard English, but they are perfectly grammatical in some varieties and are the ordinary forms preferred by millions and millions of English speakers.

One way in which varieties of English differ from one another is in their rules, and different rules lead to different structures. It isn't reasonable to judge the sentences permitted by the rules of one variety as ungrammatical simply because they don't follow the rules of another variety. By that logic, any expression permitted in standard American English but not in British English would be ungrammatical.

All functioning varieties are thus fully grammatical. It's as simple as that, but that's not to say that all functioning varieties have been standardized. They haven't. When Ebonics was a hot topic in the United States in 1997, some newspaper and radio commentators judged its sentences ungrammatical, and some Ebonics sentences are ungrammatical as judged by the rules of other varieties. But by that measure, all varieties of English, including standard English, would be ungrammatical if judged by the rules of any other variety. African-American English, like all other varieties of English, is perfectly regular and perfectly grammatical. Sure, it's different. But each variety differs from every other. Differences are precisely what make for language varieties. (As we'll see in Chapter 7, there is also striking sameness across language varieties.)

Because language relies essentially on arbitrary signs to accomplish its work, there is no justification for believing that there is only one right way of saying something. From a linguistic point of view, there is no basis for preferring the structure of one language variety over another. Judgments such as "illogical" and "impure" are imported from outside the realm of language and represent attitudes to varieties or to forms of expression within particular varieties. Often they represent judgments of speakers rather than of speech itself.

Try it yourself: Given the premise that, say, Japanese and Italian are grammatical, Parisian French and Montreal French are grammatical, and American English and British English are grammatical, make an argument that it is equally logical to regard Brooklynese, Bostonese, and African-American English as grammatical.

In this book we apply the word "ungrammatical" only to utterances that *cannot* be said by native speakers of a language. We limit the term "ungrammatical" to an utterance like *One that reading am I right now* (compare *I am reading that one right now*) because it does not occur in the speech of those who know English (except as an example of an ill-formed sentence made up for use in textbooks like this one). We do not call an expression such as *just between you and I* "ungrammatical."

MODES OF LINGUISTIC COMMUNICATION

There are three basic **modes** of linguistic communication, corresponding to different modes of perception: oral communication, which relies on the use of speech and hearing organs; writing, which is a visual representation; and signing, which is a visual or tactile representation.

Speaking

The most common vehicle of linguistic communication is the voice, and speech is thus a primary mode of human language, with some advantages over other modes. Because it does not need to be viewed, speech can do its work effectively in darkness and in light, as well as around corners. Although in its natural state speech cannot span time, its physical reach is longer than arm's length. During the development of the human species, when hands and eyes were occupied in hunting, fishing, food gathering, and other manual activities, speech was free to report, ask for and give directions, explain, promise, bargain, warn, and flirt.

Speaking has still other advantages. For one thing, the human voice is complex and has many channels. It has variable volume, pitch, rhythm, and speed; it is capable of wide-ranging modulation. Besides a set of sounds, speech takes advantage of the organization of those sounds, their sequencing into words and sentences. Like writing and signing, speech can take advantage of word choice and word order.

Writing

Long before the invention of writing, people painted stories on cave walls and exploited other visual signs to record events. Such *pictograms* were independent of language—a kind of cartoon world in which anyone with knowledge of the lives of people but without specific linguistic knowledge could reconstruct the depicted story. When shown to adult speakers, depicted stories can be told in Tagalog, Japanese, Arabic, Swahili, Vietnamese, Spanish, English, Indonesian, or any other language. Pictograms (☺ ⃓ ☼) can be understood in any language because they are a direct, nonlinguistic symbolization, like a silent film or the road signs used internationally to indicate a curved roadway or the availability of food and lodging. Perhaps the most popular icons now in use are the "emoticons":) and : (that are so common in e-mail correspondence.

If icons come to be associated not with the objects they represent but with the words that refer to the objects, we have a much more sophisticated system. Written representation becomes *linguistic* when it relies on language for its organization and communicative success. For example, while it is difficult to use pictograms to express a message about abstractions (such as hunger or danger), the task becomes manageable if the graphic signs represent existing words. The moment some imaginative soul first recognized that the written sign ☼ could represent not only the sun itself but also the word for 'sun' in his or her language, the initial step was taken toward the development of writing. Writing was invented about 5000 years ago by ingenious people who chanced upon an occasion to use pictograms to represent spoken words instead of the objects they customarily represented.

Speech and writing are related in different ways to the world they symbolize. Speech directly represents entities in the world—things such as the sun, the moon, fish, grain, light, and height. Writing represents the physical world only indirectly. A written sentence such as *Chris caught a fish* is a secondary symbolization in which the written signs represent the spoken words, not the entities themselves.

Writing has certain advantages over speech. For one thing, although writing generally takes longer to produce than speech, it can be read much more quickly. Leaving aside recorded speech, writing (in letters or books or on cave walls) endures longer than speech and in many cases has a greater geographical reach. A message can be left on a blackboard for someone to read after its author has left the room. The same cannot be said for a spoken utterance.

Signing

The third mode of linguistic communication is signing, the use of gestures to communicate messages. While all speakers use gestures and facial expressions to convey some meaning, those gestures differ from signing in that they only *support* oral communication. By contrast, signing (also accompanied by facial expression and other gestures) can be used as the sole means of conveying messages and accomplishing the work of language.

There are two primary kinds of signing. One consists of spelling out words by "drawing" with the hands the shape of written signs (such as letters) that are used in writing to represent sounds. This method depends on the prior existence of a spoken language and a form of written representation. Thus, any signing system that relies on the modeling of letters (such as the one used by the deaf and blind Helen Keller) is two steps removed from the linguistic system that hearing and seeing children acquire.

A more common kind of signing is independent of the written and spoken word and can be used cross-linguistically, provided users understand the code. In this type of signing, particular gestures stand for particular words. The fact that these words may be pronounced differently from one language to another does not matter because the gesture does not make reference to the words of any language. Such a system was traditionally in use among certain Native American nations in the western United States and among certain Australian Aborigine nations. It is also what underlies certain signing systems in use today. Signing differs from writing in that signers must be in full sight of one another to communicate successfully.

In this book, we focus on language as represented in spoken and written communication. It is important to keep in mind that, both historically and developmentally, writing is a secondary mode of linguistic communication. Speaking is the primary mode. This priority can be a challenge to students, whose principal focus and context for discussing language in school has been reading and writing.

DO ANIMALS HAVE LANGUAGE?

When you observe animals in groups, it doesn't take long to realize that, like people, they interact with one another. Dogs display their fangs to communicate displeasure or aggression; bees appear to tell each other where they have found flowers; male frogs croak in order to attract female frogs. It's only natural to ask, *How do the forms of communication used by animals differ from human language?*

People sometimes speak of porpoises, chimpanzees, gorillas, dolphins, whales, bees, and other animals as though they had language systems similar to those of humans. Television programs show people trying to communicate through music with apes, alligators, or turkeys (turkeys gobble when a particular note is played on a wind instrument). Doubtless, all species of animals have developed systems of communication with which they can signal such things as danger and fear. We now know a good deal about how and what bees communicate. More recently, chimpanzees, with their extremely limited vocal apparatus, have been raised from infancy and taught sign language.

How Animals Communicate in Their Natural Environment

For a long time people wondered how bees were able to tell one another the exact location of a nectar source and speculated about a "language" of bees. After years of observation and hypothesizing, Karl von Frisch claimed that honeybees have an elaborate system of dancing by which they communicate the whereabouts of a honey supply. Various aspects of the dance of a bee returning to a hive indicate the distance and direction of a nectar source. The quality of the source can be gauged by sniffing the discoverer bee. Although some of von Frisch's interpretations have been questioned, his careful analysis demonstrated that the kind of creativity characteristic of a child's speech is lacking in the bee's dance. Bees do not use their communicative system to convey anything beyond a limited range of meanings (such as 'There is a pretty good source of nectar in this direction'). Analogies between bee dancing and child language are far-fetched and fundamentally misleading.

The same lack of creativity characterizes communication between other animals. Beyond a highly limited repertoire of meanings, even intelligent mammals such as dogs do not have the mental capacity to be communicatively creative. Furthermore, much of the communication between animals relies on nonarbitrary signs. When gazelles sense potential danger, they flee and thereby signal to nearby gazelles that danger is lurking. The communicative function of the act is incidental to its survival function. Similarly, a dog signals the possibility that it might bite by displaying its fangs. These acts are not arbitrary symbols but nonarbitrary signs that accompany desires and possibilities.

Vocalizations that might be construed as symbols of various sorts in different animals are usually accompanied by gestures. One study found that only 3% of the vocalizations among rhesus monkeys were not accompanied by gestures. Whatever animals express through sounds seems to reflect not a logical sequence of thoughts but a sequence accompanying a series of emotional states. The communicative activities of most animals thus differ from human language in that they do not consist essentially of arbitrary signs.

Can Chimpanzees Learn a Human Language?

The situation with chimpanzees is more interesting. In the wild, chimps use a limited nonlinguistic communicative system similar to that of other mammals, though it is more sophisticated. Because the intelligence of chimps comes closest of other mammals to that of humans, researchers have attempted to teach them human language, but there is disagreement about whether and to what degree they can achieve human-like linguistic competence.

The earliest chimp to gain notoriety for her communicative prowess was Vicki. After being raised for about seven years by psychologists Keith and Catherine Hayes, she could utter only four words—*mama, papa, up,* and *cup*—and she managed them only with considerable physical strain. Chimps are simply not equipped with suitable mouth and throat organs to enable them to speak.

Washoe, born in 1965, now living at the Chimpanzee and Human Communication Institute, Central Washington University, Ellensburg.

Though chimps do not have the *physiological* capacity to speak, the question still remained whether they had the *mental* capacity to learn language. After viewing a film of Vicki trying to vocalize human language, psychologists Allen and Beatrix Gardner gave a home to a ten-month-old chimp named Washoe, whom they raised as a human child in as many ways as possible. Eventually, Washoe ate with a fork and spoon, sat at a table and drank from a cup, and even washed dishes after a fashion. She wore diapers and became toilet-trained; she played with dolls and showed them affection. Like human children her age, she was fond of picture books and enjoyed having her human friends tell her stories about the pictures in them.

Ingeniously, the Gardners arranged to conduct all communication with Washoe in American Sign Language (ASL), which they also used to communicate between themselves and with members of their research team whenever Washoe was present. ASL consists of both representational and arbitrary gestural signs that can be combined, in accordance with rules such as the grammar rules of ordinary spoken language.

The Gardners were keen observers of the kinds of simplified communication that human parents commonly provide for children, and like many parents talking to human babies they used repetition and simplified signing in talking with Washoe. As a result, during the first seven months in her very human environment, Washoe learned four signs. In the next 14 months, she mastered an additional 30 signs. After 51 months, she had acquired 132 signs describing objects and thoughts, and she understood three times that many. Washoe used the signs not just for particular objects but also for classes of objects. She used the sign for 'shoe' to mean shoes in general; she used the 'flower' sign for flowers in general, and even for aromas like the smell of tobacco. She signed even to dogs and trees. She asked questions about the world of objects and events around her. After mastering only eight signs, she started combining them to make complex utterances: YOU ME HIDE; YOU ME GO OUT HURRY LISTEN DOG (when a dog barked); BABY MINE (referring to her doll); and so on. After just ten months in her foster home, she made scores of combinations of three or more signs, such as ROGER WASHOE TICKLE and YOU TICKLE ME WASHOE.

In subsequent work with four other chimps (Moja, Pili, Tatu, and Dar) who arrived at the Gardners' laboratory within days of birth, the Gardners demonstrated that chimps who are cross-fostered by human adults replicate many of the basic aspects of language acquisition characteristic of human children, including the use of signs to refer to natural language categories such as DOG, FLOWER, and SHOE. Remarkably, when these chimps subsequently took up residence in another laboratory, an infant chimp named Loulis acquired at least 47 signs that had no source other than the signing of his fellow chimps.

In cross-fostering Washoe and her chimpanzee playmates, the Gardners made the simple but crucial assumptions that human language is acquired by children in a rich social and intellectual environment and that such richness contributes to the child's cognitive and linguistic life. The Gardners' research with cross-fostered chimpanzees has persuaded some observers that there is no absolute difference between human language and the communicative system that chimps can learn. They believe there is a continuum between human and nonhuman communication.

The language activities of other celebrity chimps were not vocal like Vicki's nor gestural like Washoe's, but visual. Sarah used plastic chips as symbols for words and showed considerable ability putting them in sequence. Lana used an appropriately marked computer terminal to create series of symbols similar to the plastic ones used by Sarah.

Did Project Nim Fail?

Certain psychologists have voiced skepticism about the various projects to teach chimps human-style language. Some critics believe that the individual words the chimps select in the various modes could have been triggered in some instances by inadvertent clues from the researchers. As a result, they claim, the sequences of strings produced by chimps are not productive sentences that parallel those that human children create. Other critics doubt that chimps have the ability to use language to make comments, ask questions, and express feelings as humans do.

In an attempt to provide more control on the effort to teach language to a chimp, a rigorous experiment sought to avoid many of the objections to previous research (though, inevitably, it introduced problems of its own). The chimp in this instance was named Nim Chimpsky, after the well-known linguist Noam Chomsky, a proponent of the hypothesis that the nature of human language differs fundamentally from that of animal communication. In the course of his education, Nim had several linguistic accomplishments, in part repeating the achievements of his predecessors. But after five years of work with Nim, psychologist Herbert Terrace concluded that chimpanzees are incapable of learning language as children do. Even with elaborate training, Nim produced very few longer utterances and displayed little creativity and spontaneity in his use of signs. Unlike Washoe, Nim would sign only when researchers prompted him, and he never initiated interactions. These characteristics, Terrace contends, clearly distinguish between what Nim was able to learn and what children can do with language.

Critics of Project Nim note that Terrace employed more than 60 research assistants over the five years and believe that fact may have contributed significantly to the limitations in Nim's linguistic achievements. Moreover, the assistants were instructed to treat Nim not like a human baby but in a detached fashion, and they were forbidden to comfort him even if he cried during the night. The question arises as to how similar Nim's learning environment was to the environment in which a normal human child acquires language. Critics maintain that the research conditions of Project Nim had a crippling impact on Nim's emotional and linguistic education.

WHAT IS LINGUISTICS?

Linguistics can be defined as the systematic inquiry into human language—into its structures and uses and the relationship between them, as well as into the development and acquisition of language. The scope of linguistics includes both language structure (and the *grammatical competence* underlying it) and language use (and its underlying *communicative competence*).

Language is often defined as an arbitrary vocal system used by human beings to communicate with one another. This definition is useful as far as it goes, but it downplays writing and signing. It also downplays an important fact that philosophers have emphasized about language, namely, that language is more than communication. It is social action, with work to perform. It is a system that speakers, writers, and signers exploit purposefully. Language is used to *do* things, not merely *report* them or *describe* them or *discuss* them. "That shirt looks terrific on you!" is not a mere report (whereas "Halloween falls on a Tuesday this year" might well be). More likely, it is a compliment. "Out!" is a mere opinion or conjecture when a fan shouts it at a baseball game, but said by the umpire, "Out!" is a call, and as such it can end an inning or a game.

As we said earlier, people have been interested in analyzing language for millennia. Plato and Aristotle discussed language in the fourth and third centuries B.C., and we have inherited several categories of grammatical analysis from them. More than a century earlier, Pāṇini wrote a description of Sanskrit that is one of the finest grammars ever produced for any language. Today, the empirical study of language has taken on additional importance in an age in which communication is critical to social, intellectual, political, economic, and ethical concerns. Now augmented by insights from neurology, computer science, psychology, sociology, anthropology, philosophy, and rhetoric, as well as from communications engineering and other sciences, linguistics has become a prominent academic discipline in universities and research centers throughout the world.

What Are the Branches of Linguistics?

Historically, the central focus of language study has been *grammar*—patterns of speech sounds, word structure, sentence formation, and meaning. More recently, attention has also focused on the relationship between expression and meaning, on the one hand, and context and interpretation, on the other. This field is called *pragmatics*. Some linguists describe particular languages; others examine universal patterns across languages and aim to explain them in cognitive or social terms.

Some linguists focus on *language variation* across speech communities or within a single community, across time, or across situations of use, such as conversation and sports announcer talk. Linguists studying variation seek two kinds of explanation—cognitive ones having to do with constraints on the human language-processing capacities and social ones having to do with social interaction and the organization of societies.

A third group of linguists applies the findings of the discipline to real-world problems in *educational* matters, to the acquisition of literacy (reading and writing) and of second languages and foreign languages; in *clinical* matters, to understanding aspects of Alzheimer's disease and aphasia; in *forensic* settings, to analysis of conversation for evidence of conspiracy, threats, defamation, and other matters of legal concern, to interpretation of contracts (from rental agreements and insurance policies to agreements for manufacturing airplanes), to clarification of public safety instructions (such as medical labels and dosage directions), and to identification of voices and the authorship of documents. Some applied linguists address problems in *language policy* at national and local levels: what languages to designate for use in schools, courts, voting booths, and so on; what kind of writing system to employ in a culturally diverse modern nation; what regulation of existing language is needed, as in the Plain English movement in the United States or in the development and production of the tools of standardization, such as dictionaries and grammars. As the world shrinks and cultures mix together, linguists are also applying their skills to the challenges of cross-cultural communication.

Computers and Linguistics

 At the end of each chapter in this book, you'll find a section that discusses some aspects of computers and language related to the topics discussed in the chapter. You don't have to be computer literate to understand these sections and benefit from them, and even if your instructor doesn't assign them you'll probably find reading the sections helpful. Seeing the substance of a chapter from a different perspective will help you grasp it. The section below serves as an introduction to the parallel sections in later chapters.

What Is Computational Linguistics?

Computational linguistics aims to test theories of language and to apply linguistic knowledge to real-world problems with the help of computers. To understand how using computers can test theories of language, it's helpful to view linguistics as an endeavor to make explicit exactly what it is that speakers implicitly know about their language. Imagine creating a model of what a child must know in order to use his or her language. Even the simplest model would need a list of elements—words, for example—and a set of rules for combining them into strings that would resemble the child's utterances. To the extent that the implicit knowledge possessed by a fluent speaker can be made explicit in the model, investigators can use computers to test the accuracy of the model. In other words, a program incorporating the elements and rules of the model produces strings of words that can be checked to see whether they are in fact possible sentences. If that program generated strings like "a Chris caught fish" or "caught Chris fish a," you'd know your model was wrong. You may be surprised to learn that, so far, it has proven impossible to make explicit what even a child knows about its language.

Here are two examples of how these programs could be applied. Speech scientists would like to write programs to *synthesize speech* from written text. You could then feed a printed page into a synthesizer that would efficiently and naturally read it aloud. You're already familiar with synthesized music. Well, synthesized speech is related, even though producing modulations of the human voice is far more challenging than producing music. Machines for "text to speech" synthesis already exist, but speech scientists are far from satisfied with their success. (You can hear computer synthesized speech of your written sentences at some Web sites identified at the end of Chapter 4.)

The flip side of speech synthesis is *speech recognition*. Linguists would like to know enough about interpreting speech to enable computers to turn speech into writing, and even to carry out spoken commands. A successful speech recognition program would allow physicians to make oral reports of their findings during a physical examination of a patient and have the oral reports automatically converted to written ones. This task is relatively straightforward for a human transcriber but is so little understood that we have not yet succeeded in enabling machines to do it well. Today, certain speech recognition and speech synthesis tasks can be accomplished in rudimentary ways, and in later chapters you'll see some of what has been achieved so far.

Computers and Machine-Readable Texts

In the middle of the eighteenth century, Samuel Johnson's dictionary provided illustrative citations from books to exemplify how words were used. During his own reading, Dr. Johnson marked sentences whose context made a word's meaning or use especially clear. His assistants then transcribed the passages onto sheets of paper, and he organized them in the entries of the dictionary. In the nineteenth century, essentially the same process was used to compile the *Oxford English Dictionary.* That project required thousands of readers and consumed half a century to complete. (You can read a riveting tale of murder and mayhem by one of the most prolific readers in one of the "Suggestions for Further Reading" listed on page 34.) In the twentieth century, the makers of *Webster's Third New International Dictionary* also mined a collection of several million citations to discover and illustrate different word senses. Dictionary making today is undergoing dramatic change, owing to advances in computers and the availability of machine-readable bodies of texts known as *corpora.*

Corpus linguistics is the term used for compiling collections of texts and using them to probe language use. In this context a **corpus** is a representative body of texts (*corpus* is the Latin word for 'body'), and as a practical matter a computer makes it possible to manipulate a large corpus. You're familiar with the kinds of machine-readable texts created by word processors, and it is the fact that they are machine-readable that enables you to search for a particular word or phrase. At supermarket or department store checkout counters you've also seen scanning devices that read barcodes and translate them into the product names and prices printed on your receipt. The first computerized corpus—the Brown University Corpus—included 500 texts from American books, newspapers, and magazines. The texts were selected to represent 15 genres, including science fiction, romance fiction, press reportage, and scholarly and scientific writing. Each text contains 2000 words, and the total collection contains a million words. Researchers at universities in Europe later compiled a parallel corpus of British English called the London–Oslo/Bergen Corpus, or LOB for short. These two early corpora are parallel collections of American and British writing that appeared in print in 1961. Some data and exercises in this chapter rely on findings from the Brown Corpus.

Since these corpora were compiled, computers have become cheaper and more powerful, and reliable but inexpensive scanners have become available. As a result, more recent corpora contain over 100 million words, and corpora of texts in many languages are being compiled. Corpora are proving essential not only for twenty-first century dictionary making but in many other ways, including speech recognition and artificial intelligence.

SUMMARY

- The total number of spoken and signed languages in the world is between 5000 and 7000.
- In the year 2000, according to U.S. Census data, 47 million United States residents over the age of 5 (18%) spoke a home language other than English.
- The United States does not have an official language and has never had one.
- Human language is an enormously complex system that is easily mastered by children in a remarkably short time.
- Natural processes of linguistic change affect all languages over time, and linguistic change is not linguistic decay.
- All languages are equally logical (or equally illogical).
- Human language is primarily a system of arbitrary signs, but some linguistic signs are representational.
- Grammar is a system of elements and patterns that organizes linguistic expression.
- Rather than being a two-sided coin, a language system is better viewed as a triangle whose faces are meaning and expression and whose base is context.

- Linguistic communication can operate in three modes: speaking, writing, and signing.

- Everyone speaks a dialect, and a language encompasses all its dialects.

- Chimpanzees do not have a suitable vocal apparatus for speaking, but at least in limited ways they are capable of putting together several signs to form a string.

- The degree to which the language of chimps and of very young children is fundamentally alike remains unclear.

- Computers can be used to test models of language as it is hypothesized to exist in the brain.

- In the developing field of corpus linguistics, large bodies of computerized texts called corpora are used to explore natural language use in all its contexts.

WHAT DO YOU THINK? REVISITED

❖ *How many languages?* The question can't be answered exactly, but there are about 6000 languages in the world, give or take 1000.

❖ *Multilingual utility bill.* The United States has never had an official language. Even voting materials are available in several languages, depending on which ones are spoken in particular communities. Utility bills need to be understood by customers, and the only way to communicate with people is in a language they understand. We all feel relieved when we're confronted with an important piece of text in a language we don't understand and then find a translation in a familiar language. The United States accepts large numbers of immigrants, and when they cluster in urban or suburban areas it makes sense for commercial and government establishments to communicate with them in a language they can understand.

❖ *Investigative report.* We grow up speaking like those around us, especially our peers, and familiarity with speakers of other social groups enables us to recognize their characteristic speechways. We don't hesitate to judge whether the voice at the other end of the telephone belongs to a man or a woman, and we readily make judgments about age. We can often, but not always, accurately categorize speakers by their telephone voices. Research has demonstrated that some landlords practice "linguistic profiling" and choose to violate U.S. law by discriminating against prospective renters on the basis of their perceived ethnicity. You can take a linguistic profiling test yourself at abcnews.go.com/sections/wnt/WorldNews Tonight/linguistic_profiling011206.html (see also "Other Resources" at the end of this chapter).

❖ *Nan the newspaper reader.* Any word form may have several senses. *Note* carries different senses in *musical note, bank note,* and the metaphorical *discordant note.* And besides being a noun, *note* may be a verb. So a context of use can sometimes be essential in deciding on the appropriate sense of a word in an utterance. (Read more about this in Chapter 6.)

❖ *Snuck or sneaked?* Traditionally, *sneaked* has been the usual past tense form of *sneak.* But English speakers increasingly say and write *snuck.* Languages change and what's "right" for one generation may not be right for the next generation. When usage changes, judgments about right and wrong also change. Everyone knows that usage varies for *who* and *whom, nuclear* and "nucular," "ee-ther" and "eye-ther." People often cite "the dictionary" as authority for one usage or another, and some dictionaries tout themselves as "authoritative." But even dictionaries differ in their philosophies of right and wrong usage. Dictionary makers know that any authoritative position they hold rests on actual usage—what is being said and written at a particular time. But whose usage should count and under what circumstances it should count may differ from dictionary to dictionary. (This question is discussed further in Chapters 10 and 11, and language change is discussed in Chapters 13 and 14.)

❖ *Young dude's birthday*. Seven-year-old Seth understands that utterances have to be interpreted in context. Fourteen-year-old Frank pretends that utterances have only a literal meaning, irrespective of context. Because everyone knows his or her own birthday, Frank's question is silly if taken literally, so Seth must figure out an interpretation that would make sense of it. "September ninth" is information Seth presumes Frank doesn't have: Why else would he ask the question? (You can read more about this in Chapter 9.)

❖ *Chimps*. You've heard of primatologist Jane Goodall's work with chimps, and you and Rod uncover a recent interview with her on the Internet. "Chimps have a repertoire of at least 30 sounds that mean different things and show emotions. It's not like human language, but these calls help the chimps understand what's going on. Chimps can display fear or pleasure, but they can't show complex language about things that aren't present—as in expressing the idea that there's a poacher two miles away. Chimps are capable of American sign language and use it in the right context. They can learn a few hundred signs." (http://www.emagazine.com/march-april_2003/0303conv_goodall.html)

EXERCISES

1-1 Here's a series of questions that could constitute a basis for your linguistic autobiography. Reflect on them and jot down your answers in bulleted form. (1) When did you first become aware that people judge certain linguistic expressions to be naughty or nice, and what do you think the basis for those judgments must have been? (2) When did you first become aware that some people judge certain linguistic expressions to be grammatically right or wrong, and what do you think the basis for their judgments must have been? (3) For how long have you thought of speech as being more fundamental than writing? (4) Was there ever a time when you judged writing to be the basis for speech, and, if so, why? (5) Which aspects of your current views about language place writing in a superior position to speaking?

1-2 Over the course of two days, write down every instance you hear (on radio or television programs, in your class lectures, or in talk among your acquaintances) of various kinds of representational expression (representing length, loudness, speed, repetition, emphasis, ordering, etc.). (You may find it easier to gather examples from sitcoms or programs for children.)

1-3 Below is a list of characteristics that describe linguistic communication through speaking, writing, and signing. Decide which modes of linguistic communication the characteristic applies to, and provide an example to illustrate your claim. Pay particular attention to the different types of spoken, written, and signed communication because certain of these characteristics might apply to some but not other types of communication. Also note the impact of modern communication technology on these characteristics.

1) A linguistic message is ephemeral—that is, it cannot be made to endure.

2) A linguistic message can be revised once it has been produced.

3) A linguistic message has the potential of reaching large audiences.

4) A linguistic message can be transmitted over great distances.

5) A linguistic message can rely on the context in which it is produced; the producer can refer to the time and place in which the message is produced without fearing misunderstanding.

6) A linguistic message relies on the senses of hearing, touching, and seeing.

7) The ability to produce linguistic messages is innate; it does not have to be learned consciously.

8) A linguistic message must be planned carefully before it is produced.

9) The production of a linguistic message can be accomplished simultaneously with another activity.

1-4 Consider the following quotation from a mid-twentieth-century dictionary (*A Pronouncing Dictionary of American English* by John S. Kenyon and Thomas A. Knott, Springfield, MA: Merriam, 1953, p. vi).

> As in all trustworthy dictionaries, the editors have endeavored to base the pronunciations on actual cultivated usage. No other standard has, in point of fact, ever finally settled pronunciation. This book can be taken as a safe guide to pronunciation only insofar as we have succeeded in doing this. According to this standard, no words are, as often said, "almost universally mispronounced," for that is self-contradictory. For an editor the temptation is often strong to prefer what he thinks "ought to be" the right pronunciation; but it has to be resisted.

a. Make an argument supporting the view that editors should resist the temptation to record their own personal pronunciation preferences in a dictionary. Explain whether your argument also applies to an editor's expressing his or her personal preferences for other aspects of language, such as spelling or usage.

b. Make an argument claiming that the phrase "almost universally mispronounced" is self-contradictory.

c. What do you understand by the phrase "cultivated usage"? How would you determine whose usage is "cultivated"? How do you imagine a dictionary editor would determine whose usage is "cultivated"? Whose usage do you think a dictionary should describe? Explain your view.

1-5 In papers and exams comparing natural conversation with written varieties of English, students sometimes claim that conversation is filled with errors such as those given below. Offer an alternative explanation to the claim that they are errors.

> I was, like, "Hi," and she goes, "Hi."
>
> I said, "Hi Pat," I went, she goes, "Hi Chris."

1-6 Consider the following, said by John Simon (*Paradigms Lost,* New York: Penguin, 1980, pp. 58–59) concerning Edwin Newman's book, *A Civil Tongue:*

> With demonic acumen, Newman adduces 196 pages' worth of grammatical errors. Clichés, jargon, malapropisms, mixed metaphors, monstrous neologisms, unholy ambiguities, and parasitic redundancies, interspersed with his own mocking comments . . . and exhortations to do better. The examples are mostly true horrors, very funny and even more distressing . . . . Worse than a nation of shop-keepers, we have become a nation of word-mongers or word-butchers, and abuse of language whether from ignorance or obfuscation,

leads, as Newman persuasively argues, to a deterioration of moral values and standards of living.

a. Simon seems to equate "grammatical errors" with clichés, jargon, malapropisms, and so on. Which of these can legitimately be called errors of grammar in the linguistic sense? What would be a more appropriate way to characterize the others?

b. Cite two ungrammatical structures that you have heard from nonnative speakers of English. Have you heard similar errors of grammar from native speakers? What do you judge to be the reason for your findings about native-speaker errors and nonnative-speaker errors?

c. The point that Newman and Simon make about "abuse of language" leading to a deterioration of moral values and standards of living is a common claim of language guardians. What kinds of abuse does Simon seem to have in mind when he makes that claim? Are he and Newman correct in claiming that such abuses lead to a deterioration of moral values? Could it be the other way around? What stake could anyone have in advancing the Newman/Simon claim? (Who are the winners and who are the losers if that view prevails?)

d. Do you think that genuine grammatical errors (such as those made by nonnative speakers) could lead to a deterioration of moral values? Explain your position.

1-7 Writing and gesture are visual modes of linguistic communication. What is the relationship between writing and Braille (the writing system used for blind readers)? Is Braille a mode of linguistic communication? How many modes of linguistic communication are there?

1-8 When there is a choice between linguistic modes, as in telephoning a distant friend or sending a letter, what are the advantages and disadvantages of each mode? List some of the circumstances in which each mode of linguistic communication would be preferred over the others.

1-9 List the two strongest reasons you have heard for maintaining bilingual education programs in the schools in your community and the two strongest arguments you have heard for having monolingual programs in English. What's your assessment of these arguments?

Especially for Educators and Future Teachers

1-10 For students whose home language matches the language of instruction in school, do you regard the primary focus of teaching language arts to be reading and writing or speaking and listening? Explain your position.

1-11 For the same group of students, do you think the actual emphasis of the curriculum is on reading and writing or on speaking and listening? Explain the basis for your view.

1-12 For students whose home language differs from that of school instruction (for example, for students who speak Spanish at home but attend an English-language school), would your answers to the previous two questions be different? If so, how?

1-13 For students whose home language is a different dialect from that of school instruction, would your answers to questions 1–10 and 1–11 be different (focus on your local situation or the situation in a district you are likely to work in). If so, how?

1-14 In your early years in school, did your teachers speak the same language you spoke? The same dialect? If they didn't, did they convey different attitudes toward their speech and yours? Was there any discussion of other language varieties, and can you reconstruct what attitudes your teachers fostered toward the language varieties of other students? Can you remember anything that a particular teacher said about other languages or other dialects? Did you feel comfortable speaking up in class? Do you think everyone in your class felt the same as you? Can you recall an occasion in which a teacher discussed the importance of language in every child's life and about how central an aspect of one's personal identity one's speech is?

1-15   At any point in your school and college years, did anyone convey to you an impression of what they thought of your speech? If so, who were they, and what were their attitudes?

OTHER RESOURCES

Internet

Information and the results of considerable laboratory research are available on the Internet. In this section of each chapter you will find addresses that can help you understand the chapter and provide you a laboratory unlike any that was previously available to students of linguistics at even the best-equipped universities. As you know, Internet addresses can change unexpectedly, so the ones given below may have changed by the time you try them. If they have moved, there is sometimes an automatic connection to the new address. Updated addresses can also be found at the first Web site given below. There, too, you may find new addresses that may interest you.

- **LISU Web Site: http://english.wadsworth.com/finegan-frommer/**

  For users of this textbook. Provides updated Internet addresses as well as supplemental material for students and instructors.

- **The Field of Linguistics: http://www.lsadc.org**

  For general information, go to the Web site of the Linguistic Society of America and click on "The Field of Linguistics." You will find brief treatments of language and thought, computers and language, endangered languages, prescriptivism, writing, slips of the tongue, language and the brain, linguistics and literature, and more than a dozen other topics.

- **A Basic Dictionary of ASL Terms: http://www.masterstech-home.com/ASLDict.html**

  Here you can find a large dictionary of American Sign Language signs, including schematics and definitions.

- **An Animated ASL Dictionary: http://dww.deafworldweb.org/asl/**

  You can see animated representations for a substantial dictionary of ASL signs.

- **National Fair Housing Alliance News (March 2002):
  http://www.nationalfairhousing.org/html/Updatearchive/marupdate/Page1.htm**

  You'll find a brief report of the research of John Baugh on linguistic profiling.

- **James Crawford's Language Policy Web Site & Emporium:
  http://ourworld.compuserve.com/homepages/jwcrawford/home.htm**

  Here is a rich source of information and interpretation of language policy in the United States and in various states. You can link to Crawford's "Obituary: The Bilingual Education Act, 1968–2002. " At his "Census 2000: A Guide for the Perplexed," you'll find remarkable facts about language trends in the United States as reflected in Census data, Crawford's interpretation of those facts, and pointers to Web sites treating language diversity, English-only, English-plus, and related topics.

- **Census 2000 Gateway: http://www.census.gov/population/www/cen2000/phc-t20.html**
  At this official site of the U.S. Census Bureau, you can see which languages are spoken and by how many residents in every state and in the entire United States; the tables are easy to read.

Video

- **The Human Language Series**
  An award-winning set of videos, originally broadcast on PBS in 1995: *Discovering the Human Language: "Colorless Green Ideas"*; *Acquiring the Human Language: "Playing the Language Game"*; and *The Human Language Evolves: "With and without Words."* The 55-minute videos are informative and entertaining. Produced by Equinox Films, Inc.; available from Transit Media, 22 Hollywood Avenue, Hohokus, NJ 07423.

SUGGESTIONS FOR FURTHER READING

- **Jean Aitchison. 1996.** *The Seeds of Speech: Language Origin and Evolution* (Cambridge: Cambridge University Press). A basic treatment of language beginnings.

- **Douglas Biber, Susan Conrad, & Randi Reppen. 1998.** *Corpus Linguistics: Investigating Language Structure and Use* (Cambridge: Cambridge University Press). An accessible basic introduction to corpus linguistics.

- **David Crystal. 1997.** *Cambridge Encyclopedia of Language,* **2nd ed.** (Cambridge: Cambridge University Press). Highly recommended; treats topics in a few pages each, usually with illustrations or photographs.

- **Edward Finegan & John R. Rickford, eds. 2004.** *Language in the USA* (Cambridge: Cambridge University Press). Intended for a wide audience, these 26 essays treat such topics as multilingualism, Spanish in the Southwest, Spanish in the Northeast, African-American English, Asian-American voices, the Ebonics controversy, language and education, the language of cyberspace, rap and hip-hop, and slang.

- **Ray Jackendoff. 1994.** *Patterns in the Mind: Language and Human Nature* (New York: Basic Books). Accessible, fascinating discussion of the cognitive aspects of language structure and language acquisition.

- **Donna Jo Napoli. 2003.** *Language Matters: A Guide to Everyday Thinking about Language* (New York: Oxford University Press). A thoroughly enjoyable and accessible introduction to most of the topics treated in this chapter.

- **Edward Sapir. 1921.** *Language: An Introduction to the Study of Speech* (New York: Harvest). An accessible classic that continues to hold interest and yield insight. It's as clear and perceptive a treatment of language as anything written—and that's why it's still in print.

- **Deborah Tannen. 1986.** *That's Not What I Meant! How Conversational Style Makes or Breaks Relationships* (New York: Ballantine). A favorite among students, this best-seller provides insight into the sometimes baffling connection between conversational styles and social and romantic relationships.

- **Simon Winchester. 1998.** *The Professor and the Madman: A Tale of Murder, Insanity, and the Making of the* **Oxford English Dictionary** (New York: HarperCollins). Whether you're interested in the tale of murder and insanity or the making of the OED, this book will hold your attention. It calls into question Dr. Johnson's definition of a lexicographer as a harmless drudge.

ADVANCED READING

Crystal's (1997) *Dictionary of Linguistics and Phonetics* is a useful reference work for a wide set of terms and concepts. Schiffman (1996) has useful and interesting chapters on language policy in the United States and California, as well as other parts of the world. For discussion of the relationship between arbitrary and nonarbitrary signs, consult de Saussure (1959). The papers in Haiman (1985) touch on iconic elements in syntax and intonation. For sources on speaking and writing, see the "Suggestions for Further Reading" in Chapter 12. On standard varieties and attitudes to correctness in English usage, see Finegan (1998) with an emphasis on British and Finegan (2001) with an emphasis on American, as well as Milroy and Milroy (1999) and Wardhaugh (1999). For information on American Sign Language, see Lucas and Valli (2004), and for a survey of sign languages among Native Americans and Australian Aborigines, see Umiker-Sebeok and Sebeok (1978). On the origins of language, see Lieberman (1991). For corpus linguistics, see McEnery and Wilson (1996) or Kennedy (1998); for computers and language, see Barnbrook (1996).

REFERENCES

- Barnbrook, Geoff. 1996. *Language and Computers* (Edinburgh: Edinburgh University Press).
- Crystal, David. 1997. *A Dictionary of Linguistics and Phonetics,* 4th ed. (Oxford: Blackwell).
- de Saussure, Ferdinand. 1959. *Course in General Linguistics,* trans. from French by Wade Baskin (New York: Philosophic Library).
- Finegan, Edward. 1998. "English Grammar and Usage." In S. Romaine, ed. *Cambridge History of the English Language,* Vol. 4 (Cambridge: Cambridge University Press), pp. 536–88.
- Finegan, Edward. 2001. "Usage." In J. Algeo, ed. *Cambridge History of the English Language,* Vol. 6 (Cambridge: Cambridge University Press), pp. 358–421.
- Haiman, John, ed. 1985. *Iconicity in Syntax* (Amsterdam: Benjamins).
- Kennedy, Graeme. 1998. *An Introduction to Corpus Linguistics* (London: Longman).
- Lieberman, Philip. 1991. *Uniquely Human: The Evolution of Speech, Thought, and Selfless Behavior* (Cambridge, MA: Harvard University Press).
- Lucas, Ceil, & Clayton Valli. 2004. "American Sign Language." In Edward Finegan & John R. Rickford, eds. *Language in the USA* (Cambridge: Cambridge University Press).
- McEnery, Tony, & Andrew Wilson. 1996. *Corpus Linguistics* (Edinburgh: Edinburgh University Press).
- Milroy, James, & Lesley Milroy. 1999. *Authority in Language: Investigating Language Prescription and Standardisation,* 3rd ed. (London: Routledge).

- Schiffman, Harold F. 1996. *Linguistic Culture and Language Policy* (London: Routledge).
- Umiker-Sebeok, Jean D., & Thomas A. Sebeok, eds. 1978. *Aboriginal Sign Languages of the Americas and Australia,* 2 vols. (New York: Plenum).
- Wardhaugh, Ronald. 1999. *Proper English: Myths and Misunderstandings about Language* (Malden, MA: Blackwell).

Part One

Language Structures

Words are the centerpiece of language, and when you think about languages you typically think of words. In examining language in this book, words are a focal point, and we begin our investigation of language structures by looking at words from several perspectives:

❖ the meaningful parts of words

❖ the sounds and syllables that make up words

❖ the principles that organize words into phrases and sentences

❖ the semantic relationships that link words in sets

In the first part of this book, you'll see how just a few elements combine into speech sounds, how just a few speech sounds combine to form a larger number of syllables, how syllables combine to produce word parts that carry meaning, and how languages package these word parts and a finite vocabulary into an infinite number of sentences. You'll also see how the systematic principles of language structure help you understand utterances even when you haven't heard or read them before. Finally, you'll examine the semantic relationships that organize sets of words.

Chapter 2

Words and Their Parts: Lexicon and Morphology

WHAT DO YOU THINK?

- Suppose you are the parent of a three-year-old daughter who asks if you "maked" a cake and "speaked" with your friends and "telled" them about it. How would you describe the pattern your daughter uses to mark past time on these verbs?

- You have agreed to make a list of foods that volunteers could contribute to a fundraiser for a college athletic team about to undertake an international tour. All the items must bear a name that English borrowed from another language. Could you name a total of ten foods, dishes, or drinks from at least five different languages?

- If you were to guess the "top ten" words used in printed English, what would they be? Why did you choose these?

- A friend mentions that the state of Washington is named after a famous person, but that most other states have names that don't mean anything in English. "They're just names!" Where do the names Delaware, Missouri, and Illinois come from? What about Virginia and North Carolina?

INTRODUCTION: WORDS ARE TANGIBLE

The most tangible elements of a language are its words. You've heard people say "There's no such word" or "What does the word *lollapalooza* mean?" Someone doing a crossword puzzle may have asked you, "What's a three-letter word for *excessively?*" We say one person likes to use "two-bit" words and another has a preference for "four-letter" words. In these instances people have clear notions of what a word is.

On the other hand, when it comes to meaningful parts smaller than a word, our intuitions are less confident. We readily understand that *car, sing,* and *tall* have one meaningful part each and that *bookstore, laptop,* and *headset* have two each, but our intuitions may be less certain about *bookkeeper, sneakers, women's, sang,* and *impracticality.* This chapter examines words and their meaningful parts, as well as the principles that govern the composition of words and the functions of words in sentences. You will learn what it means to know a word and how languages expand their word stock.

WHAT DOES IT MEAN TO KNOW A WORD?

Consider what a child must know in order to use a word. The child who asks "Can you take off my shoes?" knows a good deal more about the word *shoes* than what it refers to. She knows the sounds in *shoes* and the sequence in which the sounds occur. She knows that the word can be used in the plural (unlike, say, *milk)* and that the plural is not irregular like *teeth* or *children* but is formed regularly. She also knows how to use the word in a sentence.

Using a word requires four kinds of information:

- its sounds and their sequencing (this is called *phonological* information, the topic of Chapters 3 and 4)
- its meanings (*semantic* information, discussed in Chapter 6)
- how related words such as the plural (for nouns) and past tense (for verbs) are formed (*morphological* information, treated in this chapter)
- its category (e.g., noun or verb) and how to use it in a sentence (*syntactic* information, discussed here and in Chapter 5)

For children and adults, using any word requires information about sounds, meanings, related words, and use in sentences, and that information must be stored in the brain's dictionary (called the *mental lexicon,* or *lexicon* for short).

There are some parallels between the kinds of information stored in the lexicon and the kinds found in a desk dictionary. A dictionary contains information about pronunciation, meaning, related words, and sentence use. But it also contains information that is not needed for speaking—including information about a word's spelling and historical development (called its *etymology).* Dictionaries also provide illustrations of how a word has been used by writers or speakers. Obviously, a mental lexicon does not normally contain etymological, illustrative, or spelling information.

LEXICAL CATEGORIES (PARTS OF SPEECH)

The ability to use any word in a sentence requires knowledge of its **lexical category.** That means that even young children know the category of every word they use—they know which ones are verbs and which are nouns or adjectives. Of course the child's knowledge is unconscious knowledge, and even a grammarian's child wouldn't ordinarily know the *names* of the categories.

How To Identify Lexical Categories

There are several ways to help identify the lexical category of a word, and to some extent they rely on principles similar to the ones children use in figuring out the same information. One way focuses on closely related forms of a word. *Fork* and *forks, book* and *books, truck* and *trucks* show parallel patterns of related forms, and words with parallel forms belong to the same category—in this case, nouns. Words such as *old, tall,* and *bright* have a different pattern. Unlike nouns, *old, tall,* and *bright* don't have related forms with *-s* ("olds," "talls," and "brights" are not words). Instead, the related forms have *-er* and *-est* endings: *older/oldest, taller/tallest, brighter/brightest. Old, tall,* and *bright* are thus members of a different category, called adjectives. Finally, words such as *jump* and *kick* appear with parallel endings, including *-ed* as in *jumped* and *kicked, -ing* as in *jumping* and *kicking,* and *-s* as in *jumps* and *kicks.* Other words that share this pattern include *laugh, play,* and *return*—all of them belong to the category of verbs.

Another way to identify categories focuses on which words and categories can occur together in phrases. For example, the nouns above can be preceded by *the* and *a* (or *an*): *a fork/the fork,* and the plural forms in *-s* can be preceded by *the.* Basic adjectives such as *old, tall,* and *bright* can be preceded by *very* or *too,* as in *too bright.* Basic verbs can be preceded by *can* or *will: will laugh.* Below are examples of these patterns for the lexical categories of noun, adjective, and verb.

Nouns

bike	bikes	a bike	the bike(s)
aunt	aunts	an aunt	the aunt(s)
camp	camps	a camp	the camp(s)

Adjectives

old	older	oldest	very old	too old
new	newer	newest	very new	too new
red	redder	reddest	very red	too red

Verbs

look	looks	looked	looking	can look	will look
play	plays	played	playing	can play	will play
camp	camps	camped	camping	can camp	will camp

Knowing the typical related forms in each lexical category enables you to gauge that *sharper* is related to the adjective *sharp* (compare *too sharp, very sharp*), *jackets* to the noun *jacket,* and *missed* to the verb *miss* (*missing/misses, can miss, will miss*). Locating a word in a dictionary requires looking up its base form because dictionaries don't have separate entries for words with endings, such as *sharper, jackets,* or *missed.* To generalize, we can say that from an early age children recognize that words belonging to different categories have characteristic endings or forms and characteristic distributions in phrases. (In more technical terms, different categories have different patterns of inflection and co-occurrence of categories.)

Relying on meaning is a third way of identifying lexical categories, though it is not always reliable and is useful principally in forming an initial hypothesis about a word's category. From the perspective of meaning, nouns name (or refer to) persons, places, or things. Thus, *swimmer, Cleveland,* and *trees* are all nouns. Adjectives name qualities or properties of nouns, as with *tall* and *impressive* in the phrases *tall trees* or *an impressive swimmer.* Related forms of *tall* can be identified in *taller* and *tallest,* but related forms of *impressive* do not occur, although *tall* and *impressive* can both be preceded by *very* and *too,* which makes them adjectives. Verbs describe actions, as with *jumped* and *sang.*

Verbs

English-speaking children implicitly know that **verbs** have a set of related forms (*talk, talks, talked, talking*) and that the basic verb form—the one without an ending—can be preceded by *can* or *will.* This knowledge is implicit, of course; that means the child is not consciously aware of the knowledge.

Subcategories of Verbs   To use a verb, a child must know (without necessarily being aware of) the kinds of sentence structures the verb allows. Because children are thought to store this knowledge in the mental lexicon, it's useful to treat it here. Consider 1 through 6, where an asterisk marks the sentence as ill-formed.

1. Sarah told the joke.
2. *Sarah laughed the joke.
3. *Sarah told at the joke.
4. Sarah laughed at the joke.
5. *Sarah told.
6. Sarah laughed.

You can see that the verbs *told* and *laughed* don't permit the same structures to occur after them. Sentences with *tell* require a noun phrase (here, noun phrase means *the* plus a noun) after the verb, as the ill-formed 5 demonstrates. But as 6 shows, not all verbs require a noun phrase after them. In fact, *laugh* does not permit a noun phrase to follow directly, as 2 shows, but it does permit the phrase *at the joke* to follow. Some verbs permit a noun phrase after them but don't require one, as you can see in 7 and 8:

7. The diva played.
8. The diva played the piano.

Sentences 1 through 8 illustrate that words such as *tell, laugh,* and *play* all belong to the *category* verb but do not permit the same sentence structures because they belong to different *subcategories*. If children didn't have accurate (unconscious) information about verb **subcategorization,** they couldn't avoid uttering sentences like 2, 3, and 5. Verbs that take a noun phrase after them are called **transitive.** Those that do not require a noun phrase are called **intransitive.** In a child's lexicon, each verb is categorized as a verb and subcategorized as transitive or intransitive.

Nouns

Nouns constitute another lexical category. You have already seen that English nouns share certain properties of form. They have a shared set of endings, or inflections. The inflection at the end of *forks* represents information about *number.* **Number** is the term used to cover *singular* and *plural.* In English nearly all nouns have distinct singular and plural forms, as with the "regular" *cat/cats* and *dish/dishes* or the "irregular" *tooth/teeth* and *child/children.* A few exceptions like *deer* and *sheep* have the same form for singular and plural. Not all languages mark number on nouns. Chinese is one that does not.

Adjectives

Many **adjectives** can be recognized by the pattern of their related forms, namely, the endings *-er* and *-est,* as in *larger* and *largest.* But others, especially those adjectives containing more than two syllables, do not permit these endings; **beautifuller* and **beautifullest* are not well-formed (and hence are starred). But *beautiful* is nevertheless an adjective. That is demonstrated by its having co-occurrence patterns like other adjectives. In particular, *beautiful* can be preceded by *very* or *too* (*very beautiful*). Like other adjectives, *beautiful* can precede nouns, as in *beautiful flowers.* As a third frame, the only single words that can fit into "it seems _____" or "he/she seems _____" would be adjectives: *odd, able, sure, funny, sweet.*

Pronouns

Pronouns constitute a small category but with several subcategories. Besides personal pronouns, there are demonstrative pronouns, interrogative pronouns, relative pronouns, and indefinite pronouns. They substitute for noun phrases.

Personal Pronouns   The most familiar pronouns are **personal pronouns,** such as *I, me, she, him, they,* and *theirs.* Primarily, personal pronouns are distinguished from one another by representing different parties to a social interaction like a conversation. This aspect of pronouns is called *person* and is an easy notion to understand: the speaker or speakers are called the first person; the person or persons spoken *to* are called second person; and the persons or things spoken *about* are called third person.

In other words, first person is the speaker, second person the addressee, and third person anyone or anything else spoken about.

First person—speaker: *I, me, mine, we, us, ours*

Second person—addressee: *you, yours*

Third person—spoken about: *she, her, hers, he, him, his, it, its, they, them, theirs*

Demonstrative Pronouns   **Demonstrative pronouns** refer to things relatively near (*this, these*) or, by contrast, relatively far away (*that, those*) when the referent can be identified by pointing or from the context of a discussion. Examples of demonstrative pronouns include *that* in *That really bothers Guy* and *those* in *Those are Guy's.*

Interrogative Pronouns   **Interrogative pronouns** are used to ask questions. *Who* in *Who played the role of Emma?* and *what* in *You told Rose what?* and *What did you tell Rose?* are interrogative pronouns. In the sentence *Whose are those?*, *whose* is an interrogative pronoun (*those* is a demonstrative pronoun).

Relative Pronouns   **Relative pronouns** have the same forms as other kinds of pronouns, but they are used differently. In the sentences that follow, examples include *who* (in 1), *that* (in 2), and *which* (in 3). Other relative pronouns include *whose* and *whom.* Notice that a relative pronoun is related to a preceding noun phrase. In the examples, the relative pronoun and the related noun phrase are italicized, with the relative pronoun underlined.

1. Ellen's *a doctor <u>who</u>* specializes in gerontology.
2. *The show <u>that</u>* won most awards is "60 Minutes."
3. She's *a licensed masseur, <u>which</u>* I am not.

Indefinite Pronouns   **Indefinite** is the name used for a set of pronouns whose referents are not specific: *someone, anyone, everyone, no one, somebody, anybody, everybody, nobody, something, anything, everything, nothing.*

Pronouns are used independently and not as modifiers of other words. For words like *I* and *something,* that's clear enough, but other word forms can be pronouns or another category. In *Whose is this? whose* and *this* are both pronouns. In *Whose book is this red one? whose* and *this* are determiners, as explained in the following section.

Determiners

Another small category, **determiners** precede nouns (*a book, an orchestra, the players, this problem, those guys, which film, whose ball*), although words in some other categories can intervene (*a great book, an acclaimed orchestra, the very best players*). Determiners do not have endings like adjectives or verbs. They fall into several subcategories:

- definite and indefinite articles: *the, a, an*
- demonstratives: *this, that, these, those*

- possessives: *my, our, your, her, his, its, their*
- interrogatives: *which, what, whose*

Unlike nouns, adjectives, and verbs, categories whose members cannot be fully enumerated, determiners can be enumerated, as in the named subcategories above.

Prepositions and Postpositions

Prepositions constitute a class with few members, and the prepositions of English can be enumerated. Prepositions do not have endings or other variations; they are invariant in form. They typically precede a noun phrase, as in *at a concert, on Tuesday,* or *under the table.* Prepositions indicate a semantic relationship between other entities. The preposition in *The book is on* (or *under* or *near) the table* indicates the *location* of the book with respect to the table. Notice the underlined prepositions in *Tina rode <u>to</u>* (or <u>*from*</u>) *Athens* (indicating *direction* with respect to Athens) <u>*with*</u> (or <u>*without*</u>) *Chris* (indicating *accompaniment)* <u>*at*</u> (or <u>*near*</u> or <u>*by*</u>) *her side* (indicating *location* of Chris with respect to Tina).

Instead of prepositions, Japanese and some other languages have **postpositions,** which function like prepositions but follow the noun phrase instead of preceding it. Compare the Japanese-English pairs below:

Japanese Postpositions	English Prepositions
Taroo *no*	*of* Taro
hasi *de*	*with* chopsticks
Tookyoo *e*	*to* Tokyo

The placement of prepositions, which seems natural to speakers of English (and French, Spanish, Russian, and other languages), would not seem natural to speakers of Japanese, Turkish, Hindi, and many other languages that **post**pose rather than **pre**pose this category.

Adverbs

Most **adverbs** cannot be identified from form alone and do not have related forms. Many adverbs are derived from adjectives by adding *-ly,* as with *swiftly* (from *swift), usually* (from *usual),* and *possibly* (from *possible),* but others carry no distinctive marker. Besides that, some *-ly* words are not adverbs; *manly* and *heavenly* are adjectives. The very common words *then, now, here, soon,* and *away* can be identified as adverbs only by their distribution in sentences—by noting where they occur and with which categories they co-occur. The meaning of an adverb can also hint at its category because adverbs often indicate when (*often, now, then),* where (*here, there),* how (*quickly, suddenly),* or to what degree (*very, too).* Grammatically, adverbs play a range of functions, including modifying verbs, adjectives, or other adverbs.

Adverbs Modifying Verbs (Sentences with related adjectives in parentheses)

He talked *loudly.* (He was a *loud* talker.)

She slept *soundly.* (She was a *sound* sleeper.)

She thought *quickly*. (She was a *quick* thinker.)

They studied *diligently*. (They were *diligent* students.)

Adverbs Modifying Verbs

She spoke *often*.

She studied *here*.

They'll arrive *soon*.

She believes it *now*.

Below, the modifying adverbs are italicized, and the modified adjectives or adverbs are underlined.

Adverbs Modifying Adjectives	Adverbs Modifying Adverbs
a *very* tall tree	*very* soon
a *bitterly* cold winter	*unbelievably* quickly
a *truly* splendid evening	*truly* unbelievably fast

Conjunctions

There are two principal kinds of **conjunctions. Coordinating conjunctions** such as *and, but,* and *or* serve to conjoin expressions of the same category or status—for example, noun phrases (*Dungeons and Dragons, tea or coffee*), verbs (*sing and dance, trip and fall*), adjectives (*slow and painful, hot and cold*), and clauses (*she sang and he danced*).

Subordinating conjunctions are words such as *that, whenever, while,* and *because,* which link clauses to one another in a noncoordinate (that is, a subordinate) role, as in *She visited Montreal while she attended Bates College* or *He said that she was ill.* (Subordinate clauses are discussed in Chapter 5.)

Subordinating conjunctions are usually referred to simply as *subordinators* and coordinating conjunctions simply as *conjunctions.*

MORPHEMES ARE WORD PARTS THAT CARRY MEANING

You know that words such as *girl, ask, tall, uncle,* and *orange* cannot be divided into smaller meaningful units. *Orange* is not made up of *o + range* or *or + ange* or *ora + nge*. Neither is *uncle* composed of the parts *un* and *cle*. But most words do have more than one meaningful part. You can find two elements each in *grandmother, bookshelf, homemade, asked,* and *taller,* and in *oranges* and *uncles*. Other words with more than one meaningful element include *beautiful, supermarkets,* and *decomposing*. A set of words can be built up by adding elements to a core element, as the following are built up around *true:*

truer	untrue	truthfully
truest	truth	untruthfully
truly	truthful	untruthfulness

These words share a root whose meaning or lexical category has been modified by the addition of other elements. The meaningful elements in a word are called **morphemes.** Thus, *true* is a morpheme; *untrue* and *truly* contain two morphemes each; *untruthfulness* contains five (UN- + TRUE + -TH + -FUL + -NESS). *Truer* has the two elements TRUE and -ER ('more'). The morphemes in *truly* are TRUE and -LY; in *untrue,* TRUE and UN-; in *truthful,* TRUE + -TH + -FUL.

Most morphemes have lexical meaning, as with *look, kite,* and *tall.* Others represent a grammatical category or semantic notion such as past tense (the *-ed* in *looked)* or plural (the *-s* in *kites)* or comparative degree (the *-er* in *taller).*

Don't be tempted to equate one morpheme with one syllable. Consider that *harvest, grammar,* and *river* contain two syllables but only one morpheme each. *Gorilla* contains three syllables and only one morpheme. *Connecticut* contains four syllables making up its single morpheme, and *hippopotamus* with its five syllables is also just one morpheme. The other way around, a single syllable can represent more than one morpheme: *kissed* is one syllable with two morphemes (KISS + 'PAST TENSE'); so are *dogs* (DOG + 'PLURAL') and *feet* (FOOT + 'PLURAL'). *Men's* actually contains three morphemes in its single syllable (MAN + 'PLURAL' + 'POSSESSIVE').

Morphemes Can Be Free Or Bound

Some morphemes can stand alone as words: TRUE, MOTHER, ORANGE. Others function only as a word part: UN-, TELE-, -NESS, and -ER. Morphemes that can stand alone are **free morphemes.** Those that cannot are **bound morphemes.**

Try it yourself: Identify all the morphemes in these words and whether they're free or bound: *bakery baseball borderlands cider dusty fried outlaw prayer prefabs these*

Morphemes That Derive Other Words

Certain bound morphemes change the category of the word to which they are attached, as with the underlined parts of these words: *doubt<u>ful</u>, establish<u>ment</u>, dark<u>en</u>, fright<u>en</u>,* and *teach<u>er</u>.* When added to the noun *doubt,* -FUL derives the adjective *doubtful;* -MENT added to the verb *establish* derives the noun *establishment. Dark* is an adjective, *darken* a verb; *fright* a noun, *frighten* a verb; *teach* a verb, *teacher* a noun. In English (but not in all languages) derivational morphemes tend to be added to the ends of words (and are called suffixes). We can represent these relationships in the following rules of derivation:

Noun + -FUL	→	Adjective (*doubtful, beautiful*)
Adjective + -LY	→	Adverb (*beautifully, really*)
Verb + -MENT	→	Noun (*establishment, amazement*)
Verb + -ER	→	Noun (*teacher, rider, thriller*)
Adjective + -EN	→	Verb (*sweeten, brighten, harden*)
Noun + -EN	→	Verb (*frighten, hasten, christen*)

A similar process uses morphemes added at the beginning of a word (called prefixes). English prefixes typically change the meaning of a word but do not alter its lexical category.

MIS- + Verb	→	Verb (*misspell, misstep, misdeal, misfire, misclassify*)
UN- + Adjective	→	Adjective (*unkind, uncool, unfair, unfaithful, untrue*)
UN- + Verb	→	Verb (*undo, unchain, uncover, unfurl, undress*)
UNDER- + Verb	→	Verb (*underbid, undercount, undercut, underrate, underscore*)
RE- + Verb	→	Verb (*reestablish, rephrase, rewrite, reassess*)
EX- + Noun	→	Noun (*ex-cop, ex-nun, ex-husband, ex-convict*)

Processes of **derivation** that transform a word into another word that has a related meaning but belongs to a different lexical category are common in the languages of the world. Here's an example from Persian. (Note: æ is pronounced like the *a* in English *hat*, and x like the *ch* in German *Bach*.)

dærd 'pain'	dærdnak 'painful'
næm 'dampness'	næmnak 'damp'
xætær 'danger'	xætærnak 'dangerous'

The suffix -*nak* can be added to certain nouns to derive adjectives. Thus Persian has the following derivational rule:

Noun X + -NAK   →   Adjective 'the quality of being or having X'

Another derivational suffix of Persian creates abstract nouns from adjectives, as illustrated in these word pairs:

gærm 'warm'	gærma 'heat'
pæhn 'wide'	pæhna 'width'

This process of derivational morphology can be expressed by this rule:

Adjective + -A   →   Noun

Not every word belonging to the lexical category can undergo a given derivational process. In English, the nouns *doubt* and *beauty* can take the suffix -*ful,* but *rust* and *book* cannot. Unless words are marked in the lexicon for particular derivational processes, the ungrammatical forms **rustful* and **bookful* would result instead of the grammatical *rusty* and *bookish,* which are derived by other rules.

In Fijian, *vaka-*, meaning 'in the manner of,' is a derivational morpheme that can be prefixed to adjectives and nouns to derive adverbs according to these two rules:

VAKA- + Adjective	→ Adverb
VAKA- + Noun	→ Adverb

The following adverbs exhibit the morpheme VAKA-: *vaka-Viti* 'in the Fijian fashion' (from *Viti* 'Fijian'), *vakatotolo* 'in a rapid manner, rapidly' (from *totolo* 'fast, rapid'); to illustrate the derivation from a noun, consider *vakamaarama* 'ladylike' (formed by prefixing *vaka-* to *maarama* 'lady').

Not all bound morphemes serve to change the lexical category of words. Adding other bound morphemes like English DIS-, RE-, and UN- (*disappear, repaint, unfavorable*) to a word changes its meaning but not its lexical category. For example, *appear* and *disappear* are both verbs, as are *paint* and *repaint; favorable* and *unfavorable* are both adjectives. There is a notable tendency in English for morphemes that change meaning without altering lexical category to be added to the front of words as prefixes, though this is not universal across all languages (and in fact some languages lack prefixes altogether, as Turkish does).

The two types of morpheme we have just examined are called **derivational morphemes.** They produce new words from existing words in two ways. First, they can change the meaning of a word: *true* versus *untrue; paint* versus *repaint.* Second, they can change the lexical category of a word: *true* is an adjective, *truly* an adverb, *truth* a noun.

Inflectional Morphemes

Another type of bound morpheme is illustrated in the underlined parts of the words *cats, collected, sleeps,* and *louder.* These **inflectional morphemes** change the form of a word but not its lexical category or its central meaning. Inflectional morphemes create variant forms of a word to conform to different roles in a sentence or in discourse. On nouns and pronouns, inflectional morphemes serve to mark semantic notions such as *number* and grammatical categories such as *gender* and *case.* On verbs, they can mark such things as *tense* or *number,* while on adjectives they indicate *degree.* They shape the so-called "related forms" we used earlier in the chapter to help identify lexical categories. We return to inflectional morphology in detail later in the chapter.

HOW ARE MORPHEMES ORGANIZED WITHIN WORDS?

Morphemes Are Ordered in Sequence

Within a word, morphemes have a strict and systematic linear sequence; they aren't randomly arranged.

Affixes   Some morphemes, called **suffixes,** always follow the stems they attach to, such as 'PLURAL' in *girls* and -MENT in *commitment:* both **sgirl* and **mentcommit* are ill-formed. **Prefixes** attach to the front of a stem, as in *untrue, disappear,* and *repaint.* (Compare **trueun, *appeardis,* and **paintre.*)

Derivational morphemes can be prefixes (*unhappy, disappear*) or suffixes (*happiness, appearance*). Generally, inflectional morphemes are added to the outermost parts of words. Taken together, prefixes and suffixes are called **affixes.**

Infixes Besides affixes, some languages have infixes. An **infix** is a morpheme inserted within another morpheme. Tagalog (spoken in the Philippines) has infixing. For example, the word *gulay* meaning 'greenish vegetables' can take the infix *-in-*, creating the word *ginulay,* meaning 'greenish blue.'

Morphemes Can Be Discontinuous

Not all morphological processes can be viewed as joining or concatenating morphemes to one another by adding a continuous sequence of sounds (or letters) to a stem. In other words, not all morphological processes involve prefixes, suffixes, or infixes. The technical term for discontinuous morphology is *nonconcatenative.*

Circumfixes Some languages combine a prefix and a suffix into a **circumfix**—a morpheme that occurs in two parts, one on each side of a stem. Samoan has a morpheme FE-/-AʔI, meaning 'reciprocal': the verb 'to quarrel' is *finau,* and the verb 'to quarrel with each other' is *fefinauaʔi*—FE + FINAU + AʔI.

Interweaving Morphemes Semitic languages, such as Arabic and Hebrew, can have **interweaving morphemes.** For example, Arabic nouns and verbs generally have a root consisting of three consonants, such as KTB. The Arabic word for 'book' is *kitaab.* By interweaving K-T-B and various other morphemes, Arabic creates a great many nouns, verbs, and adjectives from this single root. The nouns and verbs in Table 2–1 all contain the same KTB root, with other morphemes interwoven.

Table 2-1
Derivational Morphology in Arabic

kitaaba	'writing'	kataba	'he wrote'
kaatib	'writer'	kaataba	'he corresponded with'
maktab	'office'	ʔaktaba	'he dictated'
maktaba	'library'	ʔiktataba	'he was registered'
maktuub	'letter'	takaataba	'he exchanged letters with'
miktaab	'typewriter'	inkataba	'he subscribed'
kutubii	'bookseller'	iktataba	'he had a copy made'

Incidentally, the English words *Muslim, Islam*, and *salaam* all contain the Arabic root SLM, with its core meaning of 'peace, submission.'

Portmanteau Words Contain Merged Morphemes

Another phenomenon joins multiple morphemes in such a way that the sounds in the word cannot be assigned tidily to each of its morphemes. The classic example is the French word *du,* which combines the two morphemes DE 'of' and LE 'the.' You can see the difficulty of assigning the sounds to one morpheme or the other. Some analysts call blends like *smog* (from *smoke* and *fog)* **portmanteau words.**

Morphemes Are Layered Within Words

Morphemes are organized in highly patterned ways. They have an obvious linear order, and they also have a **layered structure.** *Untrue* is *true* with *un-* prefixed to it (not *un* with *true* added). *Truthful* is composed of a stem *truth* with *-ful* suffixed to it (and *truth* is itself *true* with *-th* added). *Untruthful* would be incorrectly analyzed if we claimed it was composed of *untrue* with *-thful* suffixed. Instead it is *truthful* with *un-* prefixed.

Now consider *uncontrollably.* Could it be *controllably* with *un-* prefixed? Or *uncontrol* with *-ably* suffixed? It's helpful to picture the sequence of layering from the root morpheme *control* as built up by a set of derivational rules that are widely used for other words as well:

control (Verb)

Verb + -ABLE ➜ Adjective

controllable (Adjective)

UN- + Adjective ➜ Adjective

uncontrollable (Adjective)

Adjective + -LY ➜ Adverb

uncontrollably (Adverb)

The root of *uncontrollably* is *control,* which functions as the stem for *-able; controllable* functions as the stem for *uncontrollable;* and *uncontrollable* functions as the stem for *uncontrollably.*

The structure can be represented using the tree diagram in Figure 2–1 or using labeled brackets as follows:

[[un [[control$_{Verb}$] able$_{Adj}$]$_{Adj}$] ly$_{Adv}$]

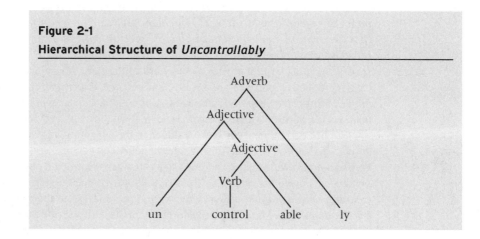

Figure 2-1
Hierarchical Structure of *Uncontrollably*

HOW DOES A LANGUAGE INCREASE ITS VOCABULARY?

Languages have three principal ways of extending their vocabulary:

- New words can be formed from existing words and word parts
- Words can be "borrowed" from another language
- New words can be made up, created from scratch

Some Word Classes Are Open, Some Closed

In some societies, the need for new nouns, adjectives, and verbs arises frequently, and additions to these categories occur freely. For this reason nouns, adjectives, and verbs are called *open classes*. Other categories such as prepositions, pronouns, and determiners are *closed classes,* and new words in these categories are seldom added. Century after century, English speakers have added thousands of new words, borrowing many of them from other languages and constructing others from elements already available.

How to Derive New Words

Affixes   Adding morphemes to an existing word is a common way of creating new words. English has added the agentive suffix -ER to the prepositions *up* and *down* to create the nouns *upper* and *downer* to refer to phenomena that lift or dampen your spirits. More commonly, -ER is added to a verb (V) to create a word with the sense 'one who Vs': *singer* 'one who sings'; *campaigner* 'one who campaigns'; *designer* 'one who designs.'

English adds morphemes principally by prefixing or suffixing. **Prefixes** like UN-, PRE-, and DIS- change the meaning of words, but not usually their lexical category. The prefix UN- added to the adjectives *true, popular, successful*, and *favorable* creates new adjectives with the opposite meanings: *untrue, unpopular, unsuccessful, unfavorable*. Prefixed to a verb, UN- yields a new verb with the opposite meaning: *unplug, unbutton, untie, unscrew, undo*. DIS- prefixed to a verb creates a verb with an opposite meaning: *disobey, disapprove, disappear, displease, dishonor*. PRE- serves as a prefix to several categories: verbs (*preplan, prewash, premix, preallot*), adjectives (*pre-Copernican, precollegiate, prenatal, presurgical*), and nouns (*preantiquity, preaffirmation, preplacement*). PRE- has roughly the same sense in each case, and from an existing word it creates a new word of the same lexical category. Three recently productive prefixes are CYBER- (*cyberspace, cyberpal*), BIO- (*bioterrorism, biotechnology, bioweapons*), and NANO- (*nanotube, nanosecond, nanotechnology, nanoworld*), none of which changes the lexical category of the stems they attach to.

English derivational **suffixes** are added to the tail end of a stem. Unlike prefixes, derivational suffixes usually change the lexical category of the stem—from, say, a verb to a noun. For example, adding -MENT to a verb makes it a noun: *arrangement, agreement, consignment*. The suffix -ATION does the same thing: *resignation, organization, implementation, observation, reformation*. (Despite their appearance, *discrimination* and *alienation* actually derive from the verbs *discriminate* and *alienate*.)

Suffixes are widely exploited in the languages of the world. The Indonesian suffix -KAN changes a noun to a verb, and among the various meanings it can produce are: 'to cause to become X' (*rajakan* 'to crown' from *raja* 'king') and 'to put in X' (as in *penjarakan* 'imprison' from *penjara* 'prison' + -KAN).

Reduplication   **Reduplication** is the process by which a morpheme or part of a morpheme is repeated to create a new word with a different meaning or different category. The Mandarin Chinese word *sànsànbu* 'to take a leisurely walk' is formed by reduplicating the first syllable of *sànbu* 'to walk'; *hónghóng* 'bright red' is formed by reduplicating *hóng* 'red.' Partial reduplication repeats only part of the morpheme, while full reduplication reduplicates the entire morpheme. In the Papua New Guinea language called Motu, *mahuta* 'to sleep' reduplicates fully as *mahutamahuta* 'to sleep constantly' and reduplicates partially as *mamahuta* 'to sleep' (when agreeing with a plural subject). In Turkish, adjectives like *açik* 'open,' *ayrɨ* 'separate,' and *uzun* 'long' are reduplicated (by prefixing the initial vowel followed by a consonant) as *apaçik* 'wide open,' *apayrɨ* 'entirely separate' and *upuzun* 'very long.' Reduplication is not repetition, which does not create a new word but simply reiterates the same word, as in English *very, very (tired)* and *night-night.* English does not have a productive process like the reduplication of Chinese, Motu, or Turkish.

Reduplication can have different functions in languages. It can moderate or intensify the meaning of a word, as illustrated by the Chinese, Motu, and Turkish examples just given. It can mark grammatical categories, as in Indonesian, where certain kinds of noun plurals are formed by reduplication: *babibabi* 'an assortment of pigs' is a reduplicated form of *babi* 'pig.'

Compounds

English speakers show a disposition for putting existing words together to create new words in a process called compounding. Recent compounds include *moon shot, waterbed, upfront, color code, computerlike,* and *radiopharmaceutical,* as well as *V-chip, e-mail, online, Web page, Web site,* and *download.* (Notice that these compounds have heavier stress or emphasis on the first element than on the second element.) To gauge the popularity of compounding, consider that one relatively short piece in an issue of the *Los Angeles Times* contained the following examples.

Nouns			**Adjectives**
petroleum engineer	whistle-blower	pay phone	whistle-blowing
government documents	troublemaker	phone call	baby-faced
government witness	debt ceiling	storerooms	highranking
subcommittee hearing	brain cancer	cover-up	overzealous
aircraft carrier	reserve account	kickbacks	born-again
training course	sea power	breakup	middle-aged

Compounding occurs in many languages. Mandarin, for example, has numerous compounds, such as *fàn-wǎn* 'rice bowl,' *diàn-nǎo* ('electric' + 'brain') 'computer,' *tái-bù* 'tablecloth,' *fēi-jī* ('fly' + 'machine') 'airplane,' and *hēi-bǎn* ('black' + 'board') 'blackboard.' German is famous for its compounding tendencies. The word *Fern-sprecher* (literally 'far speaker') was for a long time the preferred word for what is today usually called *Telefon.* A ballpoint pen is called *Kugelschreiber* ('ball' + 'writer'); a glove *Handschuh* ('hand' + 'shoe'); mayor is *Bürgermeister* ('citizen' + 'master'). Indonesian has exploited compounding in a word made familiar to Westerners from its use as the assumed name of a well-known World War I socialite and spy: *matahari,* meaning 'sun,' comes from *mata* 'eye' and *hari* 'day.' The word for 'eyeglasses' is *kacamata,* a compound of *kaca* 'glass' and *mata* 'eye' (similar to the English compound *eyeglasses* but with a different order of elements).

Bear Encounters at Yosemite National Park. A warning in four languages, including German. Can you spot any likely compounds in the German version? Lebensmittel machen Bären angriffslustig. Schützen Sie Lebensmittel vor allen Tieren im Park.

Shortenings

Shortenings of various kinds are a popular means of multiplying the words of a language. Ordinary shortenings are common: *radials* for radial tires, *jet* for jet airplane, *narc* for narcotics agent, *feds* for federal agents, *obits* for obituaries, *poli-sci* for political science, *indie* for independent film, *rec room* for recreation room, *comp time* for compensatory time, and *app* or *apps* referring to computer application programs. Other kinds of shortenings include acronyms, initialisms, and blends.

Acronyms   **Acronyms** are shortenings in which the initial letters of an expression are joined and pronounced as a word:

UNESCO	*NATO*	*radar* (radio detecting and ranging)
WASP	*NASA*	*yuppy* (young urban professional + -Y)
DOS (disk operating system)		*dink* (double income no kids)

ASCII (American standard code for information interchange, pronounced "ask-ee")

Initialisms   Some shortenings resemble acronyms but are pronounced as a sequence of letters and not as a word. The University of Southern California can be referred to as *U-S-C* and New York University as *N-Y-U*. A grade point average may be called a *G-P-A*. Customers of America Online refer to it as *A-O-L*. The shortening *PC* carries two distinct meanings—'politically correct' and 'personal computer,' but neither is an acronym; given their pronunciation as a set of letters, they are called *initialisms*. While many initialisms (*AI, CD, CNN, DNA, MTV, NHL, PDA*) cannot be pronounced as ordinary words, others could be but are not, as with *CEO* for chief executive officer, *ADD* for attention deficit disorder, and *SUV* for sports utility vehicle.

Try it yourself: Which are acronyms, which initialisms? EU USA FBI CIA WMD GI SARS BSE NYPD ER DARPA MBA VIP IHOP SEC MTV DJ ATM SEC IT

Blends   Blends are words created by combining parts of existing words. *Smog* (from *smoke* and *fog*) and *motel* (*motor* and *hotel*) are older blends. Newer ones include *fanzine* (*fan* and *magazine*), *punkumentary* (*punk* and *documentary*), *infomercial* (*information* and *commercial*), and *biotech* (*biology* and *technology*). *Modem* is well known, though its elements are not (*modulator* and *demodulator*). *Netizens* and *netiquette* blend *net* (a shortened form of *Internet*) with *citizens* and *etiquette*. Combining the existing blend *smog* with the tail end of *metropolis* forms *smogopolis*. Blends like *Spanglish, Franglais,* and *Yinglish* suggest how heavily certain languages have borrowed words from one another. Blends also serve as trade names and as names of related products: *Amtrak, Eurailpass, eurorail, eurotrip,* and *flexipass*. Most blends appear to combine two nouns, but *wannabes* 'persons who want to be something other than what they are' and *gimmes* 'things that aren't earned' combine other categories.

Back Formation

Another type of word formation is exemplified by *pronunciate*, which some university students can be heard to say when searching for the verb corresponding to the noun *pronunciation*. From *pronunciation*, they have "back formed" a new verb. Other back formations include the verbs *typewrite, baby-sit,* and *edit*, which are back formed from the nouns *typewriter, baby-sitter,* and *editor*.

Conversion or Functional Shift

In some languages, a word belonging to one category can be converted to another category without any changes to the form of the word. This is called functional shift. We request someone to *update* (verb) a report and then call the revised report an *update* (noun). We ask a fellow worker to *e-mail* or *fax* the report, both of which are verbs converted from shortened forms of nouns (*electronic mail, facsimile*). Companies *hire* (verb) a group of employees and call them new *hires* (where *hires* is a noun). To promote a product in the *market* we *market* it. Conversion of this type commonly leads to noun/verb and noun/adjective pairs. Table 2–2 illustrates that sometimes the same form can serve as noun, verb, and adjective. Once a form has been shifted to a new lexical category, it conforms to the inflectional morphology of that category: an *update,* two *updates,* she's *updating* the report now, and he *updated* it last month.

Table 2-2
Some English Forms Belonging
to More Than One Lexical Category

NOUN	VERB	ADJECTIVE
e-mail	e-mail	
bookmark	bookmark	
bust	bust	
outrage	outrage	
market	market	
delay	delay	
plot	plot	
play	play	
local		local
inaugural		inaugural
illegal		illegal
average	average	average
model	model	model
blanket	blanket	blanket
brick	brick	brick
prime	prime	prime

Semantic Shift

Existing words can take on new meanings by shrinking or extending the scope of their reference. Two well-known examples have remained popular since the Vietnam War, when *hawk* came to be used frequently for supporters of the war and *dove* for opponents of the war, extending the meaning of these words from the combative nature of hawks and the symbolically peaceful role of doves. Today, computer users utilize a *mouse* and *bookmark* Internet addresses. These new meanings did not replace earlier ones but extended their range of application. Called *semantic shift* or *metaphorical extension,* this phenomenon creates *metaphors.* Over time the metaphorical origins of words can fade, as in the meanings of the underlined parts of these phrases: *to derail congressional legislation, a buoyant spokesman, an abrasive chief of staff, to sweeten the farm bill with several billion dollars to skirt a veto fight.*

Borrowed Words

"Neither a borrower nor a lender be," Shakespeare advised, but speakers pay little heed when it comes to language. English has been extraordinarily receptive to *borrowed words,* accepting words from nearly a hundred languages in the last hundred years. As in most of its history, English borrowed more from French during the twentieth century than from any other language. Following French at some distance are Japanese and Spanish, Italian and Latin and Greek, German, and Yiddish. In smaller numbers, English is now host to words borrowed from Russian, Chinese, Arabic, Portuguese, and Hindi, as well as from numerous languages of Africa and some Native American languages.

In turn, many languages have welcomed English words into their stock, although some cultures resist borrowings. The Japanese have drafted the words *beesubooru* 'baseball,' *futtobooru* 'football' and *booringu* 'bowling' along with the sports they name, trading them for *judo, jujitsu,* and *karate,* which have joined the English-language team. Officially at least, the French are not open to borrowings, especially from English, and have banned the use of words like *weekend, drugstore, brainstorming,* and *countdown.* For using the borrowed term *jumbo jet,* Air France was given a stiff fine by the French government, which had insisted that *gros porteur* was the proper French name for, well, for the jumbo jet. The Americanism *OK* is now in use virtually everywhere, as are terms such as *jeans* and *discos,* which accompanied the items they name as they spread around the globe.

As is true of other languages, most borrowings into English have been nouns, but some adjectives and a few verbs, adverbs, and interjections have been borrowed. You can readily recognize as borrowings such popular words as *paparazzi, karaoke,* and *résumé.* Among borrowed nouns having to do with food and drink are *hummus* (from Arabic), *aioli* (from Provençal), *mai tai* (from Tahitian), and *burrito, enchilada, fajita,* and *taco* (from Spanish). Yiddish has given us the more general term *nosh.* Other popular borrowings include Cantonese *wok,* German *glitch,* Italian *ciao,* Spanish *macho, pronto,* and *mañana,* and Yiddish *chutzpah, klutz, nebbish, schlep,* and *schlepper.*

Borrowed words sooner or later conform to the pronunciation patterns and grammatical rules of the borrowing language. In Los Angeles, a sign draped across a restaurant undergoing a change of cuisine reads "Burritofication in Progress," signaling the opening of a Mexican restaurant by punning on and mimicking the morphological processes that created *beautification.* In time, borrowed words undergo the same processes that affect other words. *Nosh* was borrowed as a verb that could not take an object (*I feel like noshing*) but has since taken on new use as a verb that can take an object (*Let's nosh some hot dogs*). The verb *nosh* with the suffix *-er* produces the noun *nosher* 'one who noshes,' and *nosh* itself can be used as a noun meaning 'a snack.' In Britain, *nosh* has been compounded into the noun *nosh-up,* meaning 'a large or elaborate meal.'

How many processes of word formation can you spot here?
Initialism
Acronym
Borrowing
Blending
Inventing
Prefixing
Suffixing
Compounding

Inventing Words

Inventing words from scratch is not common. The advantages of using familiar elements in forming new words and the ease of borrowing words from other languages are sufficiently strong that languages do not often invent new words. In recent years, invention has contributed such words as *granola, zap,* and *quark* to the English word stock. The popular word *nerd* was invented by Dr. Seuss. Some products and brand names like *Kodak* have invented names. Other words like *gizmo* and *lollapalooza* whose origins are unknown may have been invented.

Jeans and Discos

The *jean* in your favorite blue jeans is a form of the word *Genoa* taken into Middle English (that is, around the time of Chaucer). *Jeans* is a shortening of *jean fustian* 'Genoa fustian,' referring to a coarse cloth once produced in Genoa, Italy. The word *denim,* used for the cloth from which jeans are made, evolved from *serge de Nîmes,* a cloth product from the French city of Nîmes. You might wear your favorite *jeans* to a *disco.* The French word *discothèque* 'record library' is a compound of two French morphemes, *disque* meaning 'disk' or 'record' and the suffix *-thèque* as in *bibliothèque* 'library.' *Discothèque* was first recorded in English in 1954, and as an abbreviation, *disco,* ten years later. *Disco,* the noun, has also undergone a functional shift to *disco,* the verb, meaning 'dance to disco music.' Music buffs may note that *disco,* the verb version, was first recorded in 1979. Both noun and verb can be heard around the world in cities whose inhabitants speak neither English nor French.

WHAT TYPES OF MORPHOLOGICAL SYSTEMS DO LANGUAGES HAVE?

You have now seen examples of derivational morphology and inflectional morphology in several languages. But not all languages have inflectional morphology, and some have little or no morphology at all. Still others have complex words with distinct parts, each part representing a morpheme. These three types of morphological systems have been called isolating, agglutinating, and inflectional. Some languages are mixed in the kinds of morphology they use.

Isolating Morphology

Chinese is a language with isolating morphology—in which each word tends to be a single isolated morpheme. An isolating language lacks both derivational and inflectional morphology. Using separate words, Chinese expresses certain content that an inflecting language might express with inflectional affixes. For example, whereas English has an inflectional possessive (*the boy's hat*) and what's called an analytical possessive (*hat of the boy*), Chinese permits only *hat of the boy* possessives. Chinese also does not have tense markers, and on pronouns it does not mark distinctions of gender (*he/she*), number (*she/they*), or case (*they/them*). Where English has six different words—*he, she, him, her, they,* and *them*—Chinese uses only a single word, though it can indicate plurality with a separate word. The sentence below illustrates the one-morpheme-per-word pattern typical of Chinese:

wǒ gāng yào gěi nǐ nà yì bēi chá
I just will give you that one cup tea
'I am about to bring you a cup of tea.'

Even more than Chinese, Vietnamese approximates the one-morpheme-per-word model that characterizes isolating languages. Each word in the sentence below has only one form. You can see that the word *tôi* is translated as *I, my,* and *we.* Note that to say 'we' Vietnamese pairs *chúng* and *tôi* (the words for 'PLURAL' and 'I'). Like Chinese, Vietnamese lacks tense markers on verbs and case markers on nouns and pronouns, as well as number distinctions (though it can indicate plurality with a separate word).

khi tôi đến nhà bạn tôi, chúng tôi bắt đầu làm bài
when I come house friend I PLURAL I begin do lesson
'When I came to my friend's house, we began to do lessons.'

Some languages that tend to minimize inflectional morphology nevertheless exploit derivational morphology to extend their word stocks in economical ways. Indonesian, for example, has only two inflectional affixes, but it utilizes about two dozen derivational morphemes, some of which we've seen in this chapter.

Agglutinating Morphology

Another type of morphology is called *agglutinating.* In agglutinating languages, words can have several prefixes and suffixes, but they are characteristically distinct and readily segmented into their parts—like English *announce-ment-s* or *pre-affirmed* but unlike *sang* (SING + 'PAST') or *men* (MAN + 'PLURAL'). Turkish has agglutinating morphology, as shown in this example. (Hyphens represent morpheme boundaries within a word.)

herkes ben üniversite-ye bašla-yacağ-ɨm san-ɨyor
everyone I university-to start-FUTURE-I believe-PRESENT
'Everyone believes that I will start university.'

Inflectional Morphology

Many languages have large inventories of inflectional morphemes. Finnish, Russian, and German maintain elaborate inflectional systems. By contrast, over the centuries English has shed most of its inflections, until today it has only eight remaining ones— two on nouns, four on verbs, and two on adjectives, as shown in Table 2–3 on page 61. When new nouns, verbs, and adjectives are added to English or when a child learns new words, the words are extremely likely to be inflected like the examples listed, and the eight inflectional morphemes of English are thus said to be *productive.*

Compare this inflectional system of English with the examples from the Russian noun *žena* 'wife' and verb *pisat'* 'to write' in Tables 2–4 and 2–5 on pages 61–62.

Grammatical Functions of Inflections   Consider the sentences below. They contain exactly the same words, but they express different meanings.

1. The farmer saw the wolf.
2. The wolf saw the farmer.

These sentences illustrate how English exploits word order to express meaning: different orders communicate different scenarios about *who* did what to *whom*. When semantic facts such as *who* did what to *whom* are expressed by word order rather than by inflection, it is not a morphological matter but a syntactic one, and syntax is the subject of Chapter 5.

Table 2-3
Inflectional Morphemes of English

LEXICAL CATEGORY	GRAMMATICAL CATEGORY	EXAMPLES
Noun	Plural	cars, churches
Noun	Possessive	car's, children's
Verb	Third person	(she) swims, (it) seems
Verb	Past tense	wanted, showed
Verb	Past participle	wanted, shown (or showed)
Verb	Present participle	wanting, showing
Adjective	Comparative	taller, sweeter
Adjective	Superlative	tallest, sweetest

Table 2-4
Russian Noun Inflections: *žena* **'wife'**

CASE	SINGULAR	PLURAL
Nominative	žena	zëny
Accusative	ženu	žën
Genitive	ženu	žën
Dative	žene	žënam
Instrumental	ženoy	žënami
After some prepositions	žene	žënax

Table 2-5

Russian Present-Tense Verb Inflections:
pisat' **'write'**

PERSON	SINGULAR	PLURAL
First person	pišu	pišem
Second person	pišeš	pišete
Third person	pišet	pišut

A comparison with Latin is enlightening because Latin had relatively free word order. Given that *agricola* means 'the farmer' and *lupum* 'the wolf,' speakers of Latin could have arranged sentence 1 ('The farmer saw the wolf') in either of these two ways (among others):

Agricola vīdit lupum.

Lupum vīdit agricola.

The word order does not affect the meaning. Obviously, then, Latin speakers did not rely on word order to signal *who* was seeing *whom*. Instead, inflections on the nouns were used to signal such information. The three Latin sentences below all mean 'The farmer saw the wolf'; the different word orders do not alter that meaning.

Agricola vīdit lupum.
FARMER SAW WOLF

Lupum vīdit agricola.
WOLF SAW FARMER   } 'The farmer saw the wolf.'

Agricola lupum vīdit.
FARMER WOLF SAW

To express the 'opposite' meaning, 'The wolf saw the farmer,' different inflections were required:

Agricolam vīdit lupus.
FARMER SAW WOLF

Lupus vīdit agricolam.
WOLF SAW FARMER   } 'The wolf saw the farmer.'

Agricolam lupus vīdit.
FARMER WOLF SAW

The inflectional suffixes *-a* on *agricola* and *-us* on *lupus* identify them as subjects. The inflections *-am* and *-um* on *agricolam* and *lupum* identify them as direct objects.

A loose English parallel to Latin noun inflections can be seen in certain pronoun uses, where the form of the pronouns and the order of the words reinforce one another:

She praised him. (*She* is the subject, *him* the object.)

He praised her. (*He* is the subject, *her* the object.)

In both English and Latin, nouns have inflections for number and case. English nouns exhibit only two cases, called possessive and common. The possessive case (sometimes called genitive) is marked by a suffix (*cat's, robot's*). The common case is unmarked (*cat, robot*) and is used for all grammatical functions except possession. In an English sentence, an unmarked noun can serve as subject, direct object, indirect object, or object of a preposition.

Latin, too, had a genitive case, but in addition it had inflections for several other cases, notably nominative (principally for subjects), dative (indirect objects), accusative (direct objects and objects of some prepositions), and ablative (objects of some prepositions). Latin generally had five or six case inflections in the singular and in the plural, although some inflectional forms were pronounced alike, as can be seen in Table 2–6.

Table 2-6
Paradigms for Two Latin Nouns

SINGULAR	'FARMER'	'GARDEN'
Nominative	agricola	hortus
Accusative	agricolam	hortum
Genitive	agricolae	hortī
Dative	agricolae	hortō
Ablative/instrumental	agricolā	hortō
PLURAL	'FARMERS'	'GARDENS'
Nominative	agricolae	hortī
Accusative	agricolās	hortōs
Genitive	agricolārum	hortōrum
Dative	agricolīs	hortīs
Ablative/instrumental	agricolīs	hortīs

The set of forms constituting the inflectional variants of a word is known as a **paradigm,** and paradigms for nouns are called **declensions.** Latin had several declensions, such as the two given for *agricola* and *hortus* in Table 2–6. The paradigms for the equivalent English words *farmer* and *garden* appear in Table 2–7.

Table 2-7
Paradigms for Two English Nouns

SINGULAR

Common	farmer	garden
Possessive	farmer's	garden's

PLURAL

Common	farmers	gardens
Possessive	farmers'	gardens'

You'll notice that the four written forms in the English paradigms represent only two distinct pronunciations because *farmers, farmer's,* and *farmers'* are pronounced alike, and so are *gardens, garden's,* and *gardens'.* Spoken English usually has only two forms of a regular noun, but irregularly formed plurals may have four spoken and four written forms: *man, man's, men, men's; child, child's, children, children's.*

Some English pronouns have a third form for the objective case. In Table 2–8, you can compare the paradigms for first-person and third-person pronouns in English. First-person pronouns show three distinct case forms in the singular and three in the plural. Third-person pronouns have distinct masculine, feminine, and neuter forms in the singular, but in the plural no distinction is made for gender. The neuter singular *it* does not have distinct forms for common and objective cases.

Table 2-8
Paradigms for First- and Third-Person Pronouns in English

	FIRST PERSON	THIRD PERSON		
		MASCULINE	FEMININE	NEUTER
SINGULAR				
Common	I	he	she	it
Possessive	mine	his	hers	its
Objective	me	him	her	it
PLURAL				
Common	we	they		
Possessive	ours	theirs		
Objective	us	them		

The second-person pronoun (*you*) and third-person singular neuter pronoun (*it*) do not have distinct objective forms, as can be seen in Table 2–9. Instead, they have only two forms, just like regular nouns.

Table 2-9

Second-Person and Third-Person Pronouns Compared to Nouns in English

| | PRONOUNS | | NOUNS |
	SECOND	THIRD	
SINGULAR			
Common	you	it	farmer
Possessive	yours	its	farmer's
PLURAL			
Common	you		farmers
Possessive	yours		farmers'

In English, gender distinctions in pronouns are based on biological sex: reference to males requires the masculine pronouns *he, his,* or *him,* while reference to females requires the feminine pronouns *she, hers,* or *her.* To refer to something neither male nor female, English speakers use *it.* In German, French, Spanish, Russian, Old English, and many other languages, nouns do not have biological gender but grammatical gender. In these languages, certain other word categories such as determiners and adjectives that occur within a noun phrase carry inflections that *agree* with the noun in gender, number, and case.

In contrast to the English definite article *the* (with a single written form representing the two pronunciations "thuh" and "thee"), the German definite article has forms for three genders and four cases in the singular, though there are no distinct gender markers in the plural, as Table 2–10 illustrates.

Table 2-10

Paradigm for German Definite Article

| | SINGULAR | | | PLURAL |
	MASCULINE	FEMININE	NEUTER	ALL GENDERS
Nominative	der	die	das	die
Accusative	den	die	das	die
Genitive	des	der	des	der
Dative	dem	der	dem	den

French and Spanish also exhibit variant forms of the definite article, though neither is as varied as German. French distinguishes only two noun genders; it marks masculine nouns with the definite article *le* or the indefinite *un* and feminine nouns with the definite article *la* or indefinite *une;* the plural form of the definite article for both genders is *les.* Spanish is similar, with two genders, but gender in Spanish is marked in both the singular and the plural. Table 2–11 gives examples in French and Spanish.

Table 2-11

French and Spanish Definite Articles with Nouns

	FRENCH	SPANISH	
Masculine	le chat	el gato	'the cat'
	les chats	los gatos	'the cats'
Feminine	la maison	la casa	'the house'
	les maisons	las casas	'the houses'

There is not always a strict demarcation between agglutinating and inflectional languages, and some languages are difficult to classify. Still, the distinction among inflectional, isolating, and agglutinating is useful in characterizing languages with respect to their morphological systems.

Using Computers to Study Words

A good deal of information can be derived from a corpus like the Brown Corpus (described on page 27 of Chapter 1). The most frequent and least frequent word forms can be identified in the corpus as a whole or in any of its genres, such as science fiction or press editorials. You won't be surprised to know that three of the four most frequent words are *the, of,* and *and*. By contrast, words like *oblong, obstinate, radionic, narcosis,* and *mystification* occur only once.

Information about how general or specialized a word is can also be gauged. As you might guess, *the, and,* and *of* occur in all 500 texts of the Brown Corpus, whereas a proper name might occur often in a single text but nowhere else in the corpus. The name *Mussorgsky* occurs seven times, but all of them appear in the same 2000-word text. Such a narrow distribution is not limited to proper names. The noun *dialysis* occurs twelve times, all in a single text; *radiosterilization* occurs six times, all in one text.

Contrast such extremely specialized ranges of use with a word like *moreover. Moreover* occurs 88 times in 63 different texts and in 13 of the 15 genres

represented in the corpus. The frequency is not exceptionally high but the distribution is wide: *moreover* occurs in nearly all genres of published English represented in the corpus and in nearly as many texts as the number of occurrences.

Table 2–12 on page 68 contains examples of the simplest kinds of information you can derive from the Brown Corpus. Next to each listed word is given the total number of times it occurs and the number of genres (out of 15) and of texts (out of 500) in which it occurs. The four words occur fewer than 65 times each in this million-word corpus, and in each case those occurrences are spread across at least 12 genres. That spread suggests they are not specialized vocabulary items.

You can compare these widely occurring words with others whose distribution is narrower. The words listed in Table 2–13 on page 68 occur in fewer than half the genres of the corpus. That relatively narrow distribution identifies more specialized words that appear in few contexts despite their overall frequency. Consider *anode,* which appears 75 times—more occurrences than any word listed in

Table 2–12. Despite its frequency, *anode* occurs in only two texts, both in the same genre. This illustrates how specialized words may not occur widely but may be used frequently when they are on topic. This is particularly true of technical or scientific writing. As an example closer to home, consider that the word *corpus* appears in this section fifteen times and but not once anywhere else in the chapter. In Table 2–13 *budget* and *fiscal* are also specialized and occur in fewer than half the genres. Which words would you choose to include in the vocabulary of a textbook for international students learning basic English? How could you best determine what those words would be?

In addition to providing word frequencies for the kinds of texts it represents, a corpus enables investigators to determine which words typically occur near one another. These co-occurrence patterns are called **collocations** and are useful for several purposes, one of which is preparing naturalistic teaching materials for language learners; the patterns are also very helpful in distinguishing among word senses, as you'll see in Chapter 7.

For the most part, the information reported in this section relies on simple counts of word forms and not on information about lexical category. In practice, the words in a corpus are often "tagged" with additional information such as a word's lexical category: nouns carry a tag of *noun*, verbs a tag of *verb*, and so on. Such tagging makes it possible to study group characteristics of words carrying a particular tag. Manually tagging a large corpus (by inspecting each word and keyboarding the tag into the corpus) would be enormously time-consuming. (Just imagine adding the lexical category to the words in this paragraph, let alone a million-word corpus.) Consequently, researchers have devised ways to tag a corpus automatically. One way is to have a computerized reference dictionary that lists the lexical category of the most common words or of as many words as possible. Then each word in an untagged corpus can be automatically assigned the tag of the corresponding word in the tagged dictionary. In that way, if the forms *information* and *distribution* appeared in the corpus and in the tagged dictionary, the tag *noun* that accompanied them in the dictionary

would automatically be transferred to their corpus entries. Likewise, the forms *lexical* and *frequent* would automatically be tagged as adjectives (because they are always members of that category), *the* and *a* would be tagged as determiners or articles, *identify* and *weigh* as verbs, and so on.

As you may have already recognized, this process of matching forms in the corpus to forms in the tagged dictionary won't succeed at identifying the category of all forms because some forms can be members of more than one category (as illustrated in Table 2–2 on page 56). In the present paragraph, you can find several words whose form does not uniquely identify them as members of a particular category. For example, *forms, can, use, present,* and *process* can all be nouns or verbs. Because English has so many word forms that belong to more than one category, accurate tagging must rely on more complicated procedures than automatic matching with a tagged dictionary. In context (in actual use) a word form will typically belong to only one category. Consequently, accurate tagging can be helped by identifying the category of the words immediately preceding (and following) a form whose category is ambiguous.

Take *deal* as an example: it could be a noun or a verb. Suppose the corpus contained the phrase *a good deal of trouble,* and suppose that the automatic matching to the tagged dictionary had already assigned the *adjective* tag to *good.* Given a choice between an adjective preceding a noun or preceding a verb, it is a safer bet to assign the tag *noun* because English adjectives typically precede nouns and don't typically precede verbs; thus, *deal* in *a good deal of trouble* could reasonably be judged a noun. As you can see, if you begin a tagging routine by tagging the words that belong uniquely to a single category and then use that information to help clarify ambiguous cases, many unclear cases can be resolved. What often happens in practice is that words are tagged initially for all parts of speech to which they may belong, and then adjacent categories are used to decide the category of forms that carry several tags.

From a tagged corpus, more useful information can be extracted, including how often a particular form occurs as a noun or a verb (if it could be either).

In fact, to know anything about the noun *list,* you would need to group all its possible forms together (*list, lists, list's, lists'*); likewise for the verb you'd need to know its forms (*list, lists, listed, listing*). For reasons that will become clear later in this book, researchers are interested in determining which genres (press reportage or scientific writing or financial news, for example) have frequent adjectives or nouns or verbs or prepositions or pronouns as compared with other genres. This kind of information about the distribution of lexical categories (rather than of particular words) can be helpful in designing teaching materials and in creating automatic speech recognition systems.

Table 2-12

Frequency of Four Widely Distributed Words in the Brown Corpus

WORD	OCCURRENCES	GENRES	TEXTS
establishment	52	12	43
careful	62	14	56
powerful	63	14	54
unusual	63	15	52

Table 2-13

Frequency of Five Narrowly Distributed Words in the Brown Corpus

WORD	OCCURRENCES	GENRES	TEXTS
artery	51	3	5
budget	53	7	23
dictionary	55	3	5
anode	75	1	2
fiscal	115	5	26

SUMMARY

- A morpheme is a minimal unit of meaning or grammatical function.
- Words can contain a single morpheme (*house, swim*) or several (*bookshops, premeditation*).
- In the mental lexicon, each morpheme contains information about sounds, related words, phrasal co-occurrence patterns, and meaning.
- Free morphemes are those that can occur as independent words: CAR, HOUSE, FOR.
- Bound morphemes cannot occur as independent words but must be attached to another morpheme: CAR + -S, LOOK + -ED, ESTABLISH + -MENT.

- Bound morphemes can mark nouns for information like number (e.g., 'PLURAL') and case (e.g., 'POSSESSIVE') or verbs for information like tense (e.g., 'PAST') and person (e.g., 'THIRD PERSON').

- Bound morphemes can derive different words from existing morphemes; for example, UN- (*untrue*), DIS- (*displease*), and -MENT (*commitment*).

- Bound morphemes can be affixes (prefixes or suffixes), infixes, or circumfixes.

- In words, morphemes have significant linear and hierarchical structures.

- The array of morphological processes for increasing a language's word stock may include compounding, reduplication, affixation, and shortening.

- Languages borrow words from other languages and sooner or later submit the borrowed words to their own pronunciation patterns and morphological processes.

- Among the types of morphological systems are inflectional, isolating, and agglutinating systems.

- Isolating systems (e.g., Vietnamese) tend to have one morpheme per word.

- Agglutinating systems (e.g., Turkish) tend to have distinct affixes.

- Corpus study is useful in showing the distribution of categories of words and morphemes as well as particular words and morphemes in different genres of text, information that can be helpful in designing automatic speech recognition systems.

- *Collocation* is the term used to refer to co-occurrences of a word with other words.

- Words in a corpus can be automatically tagged for lexical category, although several rounds of tagging may be needed to tag all words.

WHAT DO YOU THINK? REVISITED

❖ *Maked a cake.* Most English verbs form their past tenses by rule; they are regular verbs. A few, including some of the most common ones, are formed irregularly. Relatively early, children learn the rule for forming past tenses of regular verbs (see Chapter 15), and they show a tendency then to form all verbs the same way, including those that adults form irregularly. Instead of using the irregular past tense forms *made, spoke,* and *told,* this three-year old forms past tenses by the general rule, as though these particular verbs were formed like *baked, leaked,* and *spelled.*

❖ *Food terms.* English has borrowed foods and terms for foods from around the world. A very small sample includes *sashimi, sushi, wasabi* from Japanese; *chop suey, dim sum, wonton* from Cantonese; *alfalfa, anchovy, tortilla* from Spanish; *curry, mulligatawny* from Tamil; *beef, mutton* from French.

❖ *Top ten words.* According to their frequency in the Brown Corpus, the "top ten" words in printed American English are *the, be, of, and, a, in, he, to* (the infinitive marker), *have, to* (the preposition) and the next three are *it, for, I.*

❖ *State names.* Carolina is named after King Charles II; Virginia after Queen Elizabeth, who was known as the Virgin Queen; Missouri takes its name from a Native American people of the Sioux family; Delaware takes its name from an Algonquian Indian people; Illinois takes its name from a confederation of Algonquian Indian tribes.

EXERCISES

Based on English

2-1 Identify the category of the italicized words in the sentences below. Use the abbreviations *N* for noun, *V* for verb, *Adj* for adjective, *Adv* for adverb, *Prep* for preposition, *Pro* for pronoun.

   a. *People who rarely read in bedrooms* can *feel abnormal.*

   b. *Nobody really knows* what *normal reading* is.

   c. *The market for audiobooks* is *very large.*

2-2 For the five words in Table 2–2 (page 56) that belong to three lexical categories, provide a sentence illustrating their use in each category. Examples are provided for *average*.

Is there a difference between an *average* and a median? (noun)

A guide can *average* $75 a day in tips. (verb)

He worked hard but earned only *average* grades. (adjective)

2-3 **a.** For each word listed below, identify its lexical category.

   b. List all the morphemes (each word here contains more than one) and indicate whether they are free or bound.

   c. Indicate for each affix whether it is derivational or inflectional.

heard	tinier	unproductive
toys	saw	bookshops
listened	reassessment	children's
fixer-upper	fatherly	improbable
improbability	repayment	unamusing
tidiest	realignments	calculating
disarms	unremarkable	forewarned
untidiness	realigned	unpretentiousness

2-4 **a.** The three sentences below contain capitalized DEMONSTRATIVE PRONOUNS and italicized *demonstrative determiners*. Characterize the difference in how they are used. (*Hint:* What are the lexical categories of the words they precede?)

   1) THIS is the last time I'm doing THAT.

   2) *This* time I'm not going to make one of *those* fancy pizzas.

   3) I've had enough of THESE; give me one of *those* red ones.

   b. List each pronoun in the passage below and identify its kind (personal, demonstrative, interrogative, relative). For personal pronouns, also indicate the person (first, second, third).

      What about those books? Whose are they? They look like they come from the library, so they should be returned. If you want, you can put them into a shopping bag and I'll return them for you if I can get Pat to take me in her car. It's been in the shop for a few days. I hope it's ready now.

2-5 Consider two popular compounds. *Convenience food* 'food that is convenient to buy, cook, or eat' is a compound made up of a noun and a noun. *Natural food* 'food made with natural ingredients, free of chemical preservatives and pesticides' is an adjective + noun compound. Taken as a whole, each compound functions as a noun. List six compound nouns that contain a noun-noun combination and six that are unmistakably a combination of adjective + noun. (Be mindful that not all adjectives preceding nouns are compounds, and that it is helpful to pay attention to the stress pattern. In the following sentences, the compounds are italicized; say them aloud to see the pattern. Not every white house is the *White House*! Not every black bird is a *blackbird*.)

2-6 From a passage of about 500 words in a weekly newsmagazine like *Time, Newsweek,* or the *Economist* make a list of 20 compounds, marking the lexical category of each constituent word of the compound and of the compound as a whole. Thus, given *telephone tag* you would identify *telephone* as noun (or N), *tag* as noun (or N) and the compound *telephone tag* as noun (or N).

CATEGORY OF:	1ST ELEMENT	2ND ELEMENT	COMPOUND
telephone tag	N	N	N
software	Adj	N	N
bozo filter	N	N	N

2-7 *Cyber-* became a popular prefix in the 1990s. It was attached principally to nouns to form new nouns, as in *cyberlove, cyberland, cyberspace,* and *cybercowboy.* List ten words that use the prefix *cyber-*, identifying any examples of *cyber-* prefixed to a lexical category other than noun.

2-8 Draw trees similar to the one in Figure 2-1 on page 51 for these English words:

revaccinations	recapitalization	unlikelihood	reassuringly
disenchantment	unreasonableness	unshockability	updated

2-9 Consider the two analyses of *untruthful* given below. Give arguments for preferring one analysis over the other.

a. [[[un [true$_{Adj}$] $_{Adj}$] th $_N$] ful$_{Adj}$]

b. [un [[[true$_{Adj}$] th $_N$] ful$_{Adj}$] $_{Adj}$]

2-10 The following terms are associated with computer or Internet use. For each one, identify the kind of formation (compound, shortening, acronym, conversion, and so on) and its lexical category. If you are familiar with the term, provide a brief definition or a sentence in which you use it in its customary way. (Just in case you are unfamiliar with some of the shortenings, *FAQ* stands for "frequently asked questions," *IMHO* for "in my honest opinion," and *WYSIWYG* for "what you see is what you get.")

Example: chatgroup—compound, noun, 'a group of people "talking" together via the Internet'

client-server	cyberizing	FAQ	source code
mouse	cyberspace	PC	programming language
a flame	to flame out	IMHO	to download
info pike	a lurker	to e-mail	code writer
Internetter	I-way	to lurk	newbee or newbie
info superpike	netiquette	netter	domain name
Mac	a remailer	smileys	browser
spamming	a sysop	a thread	cyberenthusiast
a twit filter	WYSIWYG	software	to keyboard

2-11 **a.** Graduates of the University of California at Los Angeles call their alma mater "U-C-L-A", but it is sometimes lightly referred to as "youkla" or "ookla." Which of these three pronunciations would count as acronyms?

b. From the list that follows, identify four acronyms and four initialisms: DNA, STD, AIDS, SIDS, NBA, HIV, NHS, NHL, UNESCO, UN, NATO.

c. What's interesting about the word CD-ROM?

2-12 **a.** As determined by their frequency in a million-word corpus of texts (the Brown Corpus), the 26 most common words in printed American English are listed below. The category of a few of these words has already been specified. For each of the others, specify its category and then answer the questions that follow. Choose your categories from this list: N (noun), V (verb), Adj (adjective), Prep (preposition), Det (determiners, including articles), Pro (pronoun).

the	_____	they	_____
be	_____	with	_____
of	_____	not	adverb
and	_____	that	conjunction
a	_____	on	_____
in	_____	she	_____
he	_____	as	conjunction
to	infinitive marker	at	_____
have	_____	by	_____
to	_____	this	_____
it	_____	we	_____
for	_____	you	_____
I	_____	from	_____

1) List the pronouns that fall among the 26 most frequent words of written English: _____

2) List the prepositions: _____

3) List the determiners: _____

4) List the verbs: _____

5) List the adjectives: _____

6) List the nouns: _____

b. The words listed in the two columns are found so frequently in print that one of every four words in the Brown Corpus ranks among the first eight words on the list (*the* through the infinitive marker *to*). To put it another way, over 250,000 of the million words in the Brown Corpus are the same eight words used over and over. With that in mind, answer the following questions.

1) Which two lexical categories are strikingly absent from the list? What explanation can you offer for their infrequency?

2) What explanation can you offer for the frequency of prepositions in the Brown Corpus? (*Hint:* It may help to think about what prepositions do.)

3) What explanation can you offer for the frequency of pronouns as compared to nouns?

4) The verbs *be* and *have* appear on the list. If you knew that the 27th word on the list was a verb, which verb would you guess it to be? Why?

5) Of the 21 words whose lexical category you were asked to identify in part a, how many belong to closed classes of words and how many to open classes?

2-13 The words or phrases below come from an article discussing electronic commerce (*Newsweek*, July 7, 1997, p. 80). On the line next to each word (or italicized word) write the name of the process by which that word has come to have its use in this discussion, drawing the terms from this list: compounding, affixation, invention, shortening, conversion, derivation, semantic shift, borrowing, blend.

a. cluelessness _____

b. Information *Highway* _____

c. into *hyperdrive* _____

d. the *digital* world _____

e. the *wonky* title _____

f. a *cutting-edge* blueprint _____

g. a cutting-edge *blueprint* _____

h. a virtual *storefront* _____

i. cyberspace _____

j. that will *grease* commerce _____

k. *zipless* electronic commerce _____

l. *CDA* 'Communications Decency Act' _____

Based on Languages Other Than English

2-14 Consider the following pairs of singular and plural nouns for human beings in Persian. How does Persian form these noun plurals? (*Note:* æ represents a vowel sound like the one in English *hat* and x represents a sound like the final consonant of German *Bach*.)

zæn	'woman'	zænan	'women'
mærd	'man'	mærdan	'men'
bæradær	'brother'	bæradæran	'brothers'
pesær	'boy'	pesæran	'boys'
xahær	'sister'	xahæran	'sisters'
doxtær	'daughter'	doxtæran	'daughters'

2-15 Consider the following Persian word pairs with their English glosses. Note the lexical category of the words in column I, and give the complete rule for forming the words of column II from those in column I. (*Note:* x represents a sound like the final consonant of German *Bach*, and š represents a sound like the *sh* of English *ship*.)

I		II	
dana	'wise'	danai	'wisdom'
xub	'good'	xubi	'goodness'
darošt	'thick'	darošti	'thickness'
bozorg	'big'	bozorgi	'size'
širin	'sweet'	širini	'sweetness'

2-16 **a.** Analyze the Turkish nouns below and provide a list of their constituent morphemes, along with a gloss for each. (*Note:* ɨ represents a vowel similar to u.)

kitap	'book'	elmalar	'apples'	saplar	'stalks'
at	'horse'	masa	'table'	adamlar	'men'
oda	'room'	odalar	'rooms'	masalar	'tables'
sap	'stalk'	atlar	'horses'	sonlar	'ends'
elma	'apple'	kɨz	'girl'	meyvar	'fruit' (SINGULAR)

b. On the basis of your analysis, provide the Turkish words for the following English ones: *books, man, girls, end, fruit* (PLURAL).

c. Given Turkish *odalarda* 'in the rooms' and *masalarda* 'on the tables,' provide the Turkish words that mean 'in the books' and 'on the horse.'

2-17 In the Niutao dialect of the Polynesian language Tuvaluan, some verbs and adjectives have different forms with singular and plural subjects, as in these examples:

SINGULAR	PLURAL	
mafuli	mafufuli	'turned around'
fepaki	fepapaki	'collide'
apulu	apupulu	'capsize'
nofo	nonofo	'stay'
maasei	maasesei	'bad'
takato	takakato	'lie down'
valea	valelea	'stupid'
kai	kakai	'eat'

a. Describe the rule of morphology that derives the plural forms of these verbs and adjectives from the singular forms.

b. In the Funaafuti dialect of the same language the process is slightly different, as the following plural forms of the same verbs and adjectives show. (Double consonants indicate that the sound is held for a longer period of time.) How are plurals formed from singular forms in this dialect? How does that process differ from the process of plural formation in the Niutao dialect described in the first part of this exercise?

vallea	nnofo
maffuli	maassei
feppaki	takkato
appulu	kkai

2-18 On the basis of the examples given below, determine whether the following languages have an isolating, inflectional, or agglutinating morphology, and justify your answer.

SAMOAN

ʔua	maalamalama	aʔu	i	le	mataaʔupu
PRESENT	understand	I	OBJECT	the	lesson

'I understand the lesson.'

FINNISH

tyttö	silitti	paidat
girl-SUBJECT-SING.	iron-PAST-SING.	shirt-OBJECT-PLURAL

'The girl ironed the shirts.'

JAPANESE

akiko-ga	haruko-ni	mainiti	tegami-o	kaku
Akiko SUBJECT	Haruko to	everyday	letter OBJECT	write

'Akiko writes a letter to Haruko every day.'

MOHAWK

t-en-s-hon-te-rist-a-wenrat-e?

DUAL-FUTURE-REPETITIVE-PLURAL-REFLEXIVE-metal-cross-PUNCTUAL

'They will cross over the railroad track.'

THAI

kʰruu	hây	sàmùt	nákrian	săam	lêm
teacher	give	notebook	student	three	ARTICLE

'The teacher gave the students three notebooks.'

2-19 Examine the following sentences of Tok Pisin (New Guinea Pidgin English) to identify the morphemes needed to translate the seven English sentences given at the end of this exercise.

a. manmeri ol wokabaut long rot
people they stroll on road
'People are strolling on thc road.'

b. mi harim toktok bilong yupela
I listen speech of you-PLURAL
'I listen to your (PLURAL) speech.'

c. mi harim toktok bilong yu
I listen speech of you-SING.
'I listen to your (SING.) speech.'

d. em no brata bilong em ol harim toktok bilong mi
he and brother of he they listen speech of me
'He and his brother listen to my speech.'

e. mi laikim dispela manmeri long rot
I like these people on road
'I like these people (who are) on the road.'

f. dispela man no prend bilong mi ol laikim dispela toktok
this man and friend of me they like this speech
'This man and my friend like this speech.'

Now, relying on the meaning of the morphemes you can identify in the Tok Pisin sentences above, translate the following sentences into Tok Pisin:

1) These people like my speech.

2) I am strolling on the road.

3) I like my friend's speech.

4) I like my brother and these people.

5) These people on the road and my friend like his speech.

6) You (SING.) and my brother like the speech of these people.

7) These people listen to my friend's and my brother's speech.

Especially for Educators and Future Teachers

2-20 Assume you are teaching young ESL students to change verbs into their "opposites"—for example, *appear* into *disappear.* How would you get them to provide as many different English-language prefixes to turn verbs into other verbs with an opposite meaning?

2-21 **a.** Suppose you are teaching a middle school English class how to figure out the lexical category (part of speech) of the words *newer, books, played,* and *surprise?* Would it be better to present them in isolation or in sentences? Why?

b. Now reconsider *books* and *surprise,* and try putting them into two sentences each, used as a verb in one and as a noun in the other. Any further observations about which way of presenting them is better? What else could you do to provide your students useful tools for deciding the part of speech of these words? How did you determine their part of speech for yourself?

2-22 Imagine you and your students are looking at a map of the United States, examining place names and river names. Concentrating on one side or the other of the Mississippi River, can you anticipate six names your students would rightly guess are borrowed from Native American languages? Examining the whole map, which states or state capitals could they identify as being named after some person? After another country? As using words borrowed from languages other than English and Native American tongues?

2-23 How could you encourage your students to identify the names of food items that English has borrowed from the languages of the students' respective ethnic heritages?

2-24 What would you do to help your students identify three "things" and three "activities" that don't have names in English? If you had your students give names to those things and activities and then use them in a variety of sentences, which sentences would you provide them to help them see the regularities of English inflections on nouns and verbs?

OTHER RESOURCES

A good deal of valuable information is available on the Internet. The addresses listed in this section may be helpful in understanding this chapter or in exploring related aspects of language on your own. Internet addresses often change, so the ones given below may go out of date. If you try an out-of-date address, an automatic connection to the new address is often possible. The Web site for this textbook (see Wadsworth below) will also post updates to Internet addresses as well as new addresses that become available after publication.

• **Wadsworth: http://english.wadsworth.com/finegan-frommer/**
The Web site for *Language: Its Structure and Use,* 4th ed., provides updated Internet addresses as well as supplemental materials for students and instructors using this textbook.

• **Merriam-Webster OnLine: http://www.m-w.com**
Entry to the world of dictionaries produced by the Merriam-Webster Company. Well worth bookmarking for its definitions, which are available on-line.

• **Merriam-Webster New Book of Word Histories:**
http://www.m-w.com/whist/etyterm.htm
A Web page for *The Merriam-Webster New Book of Word Histories.* You'll find a couple dozen fascinating examples of word histories, as well as definitions and illustrations of some terms used in this chapter, including *blends* and *shortened forms.*

- **Tutorial on Corpus Linguistics:**
  http://www.georgetown.edu/cball/corpora/tutorial.html
  Catherine Ball maintains a three-hour on-line tutorial for corpus linguistics. If you're interested in corpus linguistics, this site is a good place to begin your exploration.

- **Corpus Linguistics: http://www.ruf.rice.edu/~barlow/corpus.html**
  Maintained by Michael Barlow, this Web site (with a four-star rating by Magellan) is a goldmine of references to corpora in many languages, as well as to software for exploring corpora and information about many other aspects of corpus linguistics.

- **Bookmarks for Corpus-Based Linguistics: http://devoted.to/corpora**
  Maintained by David Lee, this Web site is another goldmine of information about corpora and corpus-based linguistics, but chiefly for English.

- **LTG Helpdesk: http://www.ltg.ed.ac.uk/helpdesk/faq/index.html**
  Provides a set of frequently asked questions (FAQs) and answers, as well as a large number of links to a wide variety of language technology projects. Among the FAQs to which answers are provided you'll find these: "I'm looking for a tagged corpus of English." "Are there any part-of-speech taggers available for Spanish?" "I'm looking for a list of the most frequent words of English, French, Italian, Russian, Polish." You can also find links here to on-line taggers that will assign part-of-speech labels for texts you submit.

SUGGESTIONS FOR FURTHER READING

- **Jean Aitchison. 1994.** *Words in the Mind: An Introduction to the Mental Lexicon,* **2nd ed.** (New York: Blackwell). An entertaining and accessible treatment of the mental lexicon.

- **Laurie Bauer. 1983.** *English Word-Formation* (Cambridge: Cambridge University Press). A solid, accessible introduction to English word formation.

- **Ronald W. Langacker. 1972.** *Fundamentals of Linguistic Analysis* (New York: Harcourt). An excellent introduction to linguistic analysis and problem solving. Chapter 2 discusses morphological analysis, with illustrations from many languages, including Native American languages. Helpful model solutions provided to some problems.

- **Donka Minkova & Robert Stockwell. 2001.** *English Words: Structure and History* (Cambridge: Cambridge University Press). A book rich in examples and easy to use.

- *12,000 Words: A Supplement to Webster's Third New International Dictionary.* **1987.** (Springfield, MA: Merriam). A list of 12,000 new words added to English in the 25 years after the publication of *Webster's Third New International Dictionary* in 1961.

- **"Among the New Words."** *American Speech.* In each quarterly issue of *American Speech,* you'll find a column that defines the most recent additions to the English word stock. You'll be surprised at how many words that are part of your everyday life are brand-new to English. Look up the most recent "Among the New Words" next time you're in the periodicals room of your library.

- *The Merriam-Webster New Book of Word Histories.* **1991.** (Springfield, MA: Merriam). This exciting book provides word histories for thousands of English words from A (i.e., *assassin)* to Z (i.e., *zombie)* and includes all sorts of interesting words in between such as *jeep* and *OK.* (See the Web page address in the previous section.)

ADVANCED READING

A good general treatment of morphological processes can be found in Katamba (1993). Matthews (1991) is more advanced. Our examples of reduplication in Turkish come from Underhill (1976). Good treatments of morphology can be found in Shopen (1985), especially the chapters by Stephen R. Anderson on "Typological Distinctions in Word Formation" and "Inflectional Morphology," by Bernard Comrie on "Causative Verb Formation and Other Verb-Deriving Morphology," and by Comrie and Sandra A. Thompson on "Lexical Nominalization." Comrie (1987), from which several examples in this chapter are taken, provides valuable descriptions of more than 40 major languages, usually including discussion of morphology. The Vietnamese example is taken from Comrie (1989).

REFERENCES

- Comrie, Bernard. 1989. *Language Universals and Linguistic Typology,* 2nd ed. (Chicago: University of Chicago Press).

- Comrie, Bernard, ed. 1987. *The World's Major Languages.* (New York: Oxford University Press).

- Katamba, Francis. 1993. *Morphology.* (New York: St. Martin's).

- Matthews, P. H. 1991. *Morphology,* 2nd ed. (Cambridge: Cambridge University Press).

- Shopen, Timothy, ed. 1985. *Grammatical Categories and the Lexicon,* vol. 3 of *Language Typology and Syntactic Description.* (Cambridge: Cambridge University Press).

- Underhill, Robert. 1976. *Turkish Grammar.* (Cambridge: MIT Press).

Chapter 3

The Sounds of Languages: Phonetics

WHAT DO YOU THINK?

❖ A whiz at reading, your third-grade niece reports one day that English has five vowels—*a, e, i, o,* and *u,* she calls them. You recall reading that English has two or three times that many vowel sounds. How would you go about figuring out with your niece just how many vowel sounds English has?

❖ A friend says that George Bernard Shaw claimed English spelling is so chaotic that *ghoti* could be pronounced *fish,* and she challenges you to identify words whose pronunciation and spelling could have led Shaw to his seemingly preposterous conclusion. What words can you identify in which <gh> is pronounced "f"? Can you cite any in which <gh> appears at the beginning, as in Shaw's *ghoti*?

❖ Because you're taking a linguistics course, your roommate asks whether English has 26 sounds to match the 26 letters of the alphabet. You know English has more than 26 sounds and, thinking quickly, point out that there's no letter to represent the initial sound in *thus* so English uses two letters. You're then asked for other examples where two letters are required to represent a single sound. What examples can you provide?

❖ Citing *put* and *putt* as a pair of English words that are pronounced and spelled differently but whose spelling difference doesn't correspond to the pronunciation difference, a friend claims English has many similar pairs and challenges you to name just one. Can you do it?

SOUNDS AND SPELLINGS: NOT THE SAME THING

As a reader of English, you are accustomed to seeing language written down as a series of words set off by spaces, with each word consisting of a sequence of separate letters that are also separated by spaces. You readily recognize that words exist as separate entities made up of a relatively small number of discrete sounds. The words *spat* and *post,* for example, are readily judged by English speakers to have four sounds each, while *adult* has five and *set* has three. Somewhat less obvious is the number of sounds in the words *speakers, series, letters,* and *sequence,* which do not have the same number of letters and sounds. This lack of correspondence is common in English. *Cough* has three sounds but is spelled with five letters; *freight* has only four sounds despite its seven letters.

Through with seven letters and *thru* with four are alternative spellings for a word with three sounds. *Phone* and *laugh* have three sounds each, represented by five letters. *Delicacy,* with an equal number of sounds and letters, uses the letter <c> to represent two different sounds—one a *k*-like sound, the other an *s*-like sound.

Because of the close association between writing and speaking in the minds of literate people, it is important to stress that in this chapter we are interested in the sounds of spoken language, not in the letters of the alphabet that represent those sounds in writing.

Same Spelling, Different Pronunciations

Observe the variety of pronunciations represented by the same letter or series of letters in different words. Consider the pronunciations of the following words, all of which are represented in part by the letters <ough>:

cough	"k<u>off</u>"
tough	"t<u>uff</u>"
bough	"b<u>ow</u>"
through	"thr<u>u</u>"
though	"th<u>o</u>"
thoroughfare	"thurr<u>a</u>fare"

Though the precise sounds in these words may vary among English speakers, still the lesson of the distant relationship between sounds and letters is clear. The <ough> spelling represents at least six different pronunciations in English, as indicated in Figure 3–1.

Same Pronunciation, Different Spellings

Other sets of English words are pronounced alike but spelled differently, as school children learn when they are taught sets of homophones (or homonyms) like *there/their, bear/bare, led/lead,* and *to/two/too.*

Figure 3-1

Same Spelling, Different Sounds

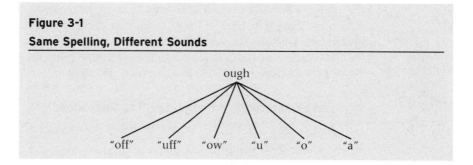

Consider the set of words in Figure 3–2, where nine different spellings represent a single sound, as in the word *see*. Still other spellings for the sound of the word *see* could be cited, including *situ* and *cee* (the name of the letter). Notice that the letter <x>, as in *sexy* and *foxy,* stands for the two sounds [k] and [s] as represented in *folksy.*

Figure 3-2

Different Spelling, Same Sounds

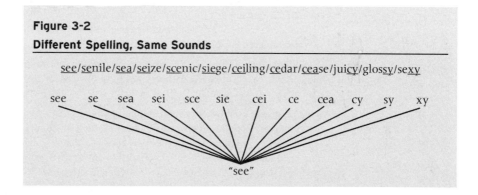

Compare the sound and spelling of *woman* and *women* and you'll note that the difference in the letters <a> and <e> does not represent a difference in pronunciation because the second syllables of these words are pronounced alike. On the other hand, <o>—the letter that does not change—represents two different sounds (in *woman* like the <oo> of *wood,* and in *women* like the <i> of *win*). The pair *Satan* (the devil) and *satin* (the cloth) illustrates the same point: the <a> of the first syllable represents two different sounds, but the <a> and <i> spellings of the second syllable represent the same sound. The same point can be made with *loose* and *lose,* where the only pronunciation difference is in the final sound ([s] vs. [z]), while the only spelling difference is in the identically pronounced vowels.

The playwright George Bernard Shaw was a keen advocate of spelling reform and highlighted the problems in establishing correspondences between English sounds and spelling when he provocatively alleged that *fish* could be spelled <ghoti>:

the <gh> as in *cough,* the <o> as in *women,* and the <ti> as in *nation.* Despite the efforts of Shaw and other reformers, English spelling has remained basically unchanged. You can see very modest success at simplification in such isolated spellings as *thru, nite,* and *foto,* though not even these examples have been widely adopted for the more traditional *through, night,* and *photo.*

Whys and Wherefores of Sound/Spelling Discrepancies

Here are five reasons for the discrepancy between pronunciations and written representations for many English words.

1. Written English has diverse origins with different spelling conventions:

   - *Anglo-Saxon* The system that evolved in Anglo-Saxon England before the Norman Invasion of 1066 gave us such spellings as *ee* for the sound in words like *deed* and *seen.*

   - *Norman French* The system that was overlaid on the Old English system by the Normans, with their French writing customs, gave us such spellings as *queen* (for the earlier *cwene)* and *thief* (for earlier *theef).*

   - *Dutch* Caxton, the first English printer, who was born in England but lived in Holland for 30 years, gave us such spellings as *ghost* (which replaced *gost)* and *ghastly* (which replaced *gastlic).*

   - *Spelling reform* During the Renaissance, attempts to reform spelling along etymological (that is, historically earlier) lines gave us *debt* for earlier *det* or *dette* and *salmon* for earlier *samon.*

2. A spelling system established several hundred years ago is still being used to represent a language that continues to change its spoken form. For example, the initial <k> in words like *knock, knot, know,* and *knee* was once pronounced, and so was the <gh> in *knight* and *thought.* As to vowels, pronunciation change in progress when the writing system was developing and later changes in pronunciation have led to such discrepancies as those represented in *beat* vs. *great* and *food* vs. *foot,* where different vowel sounds are represented by the same spellings.

3. English is spoken differently around the world (and in different regions of a nation), despite relatively uniform standards for spellings. Such spelling uniformity facilitates international communication, but it also increases the disparity between the way English is written and spoken.

4. A given word part may be pronounced differently depending on its adjacent sounds and stress patterns. In *electric,* the final <c> represents the sound [k] as in *kiss,* but in *electricity* it represents [s] as in *silly.* In *senile,* the <i> represents the sound of <I> in *I'll,* but in *senility* it represents the sound of <i> in *ill.*

5. Spoken forms may differ across social situations. The writing system incorporates some degree of variation (*do not* vs. *don't* and *it was* vs. *'twas),* but there is little tolerance for spellings like *gonna* ('going to'), *wanna* ('want to'), and *gotcha* ('got you'), and still less or none at all for *j'eat* ('did you eat?') and *woncha* ('won't you?'). Variable spellings for the same expression would force readers to determine the pronunciation of the represented speech before arriving at meaning instead of reading directly for meaning, as adult readers normally do.

Advantages of Fixed Spellings   Some disadvantages of an inconsistent set of sound-spelling correspondences are obvious. Though less obvious, the advantages are also substantial. Consider Chinese, in which many written characters make little or no reference to sounds but directly symbolize meanings—much as numerals like 3 and 7 and symbols like + and % do for European languages. Using such characters, groups of people whose spoken languages are mutually unintelligible can nevertheless communicate well in writing, as is the case between speakers of Cantonese and Mandarin Chinese. As a parallel, consider that the symbol 7 (or the slight variant 7) has a uniform meaning across European languages, even though the word for the concept is pronounced and spelled differently: *seven* in English, *sept* in French, *sette* in Italian, *sieben* in German, and so on. Similarly, the fact that English spelling is somewhat independent of pronunciation is not altogether a bad thing when you consider that English has exceptionally varied dialects from New Zealand to Jamaica to India, as well as in places where English is used in official capacities alongside indigenous native tongues or as a second language for scientific and other international enterprises. Despite diverse pronunciations around the globe, a uniform written word is associated with a single set of meanings. Moreover, in a language with different pronunciations for the same element of meaning, stable spellings can contribute to reading comprehensibility—as in *musical/musician, electrical/electricity,* and even the <s> of *cats* and *dogs* (pronounced as [s] and [z], respectively).

Independence of Script and Speech   The untidy relationship between sound and spelling occurs in many languages, so it's important to distinguish between the sounds of a language and the way they are represented in writing.

To emphasize the independence of sounds and spellings, remember that a given language may be represented by completely different writing systems. For instance, Hindi-Urdu is written by Hindus living in India in Devanāgarī, an Indic script that derives from Sanskrit. The same language is written with Arabic script by Muslims living in Pakistan and parts of India. Sometimes, too, people adopt a new writing system for their language. Early in the twentieth century, the government of Turkey changed the orthography (the technical name for a writing system) for representing Turkish from an Arabic script to one based on the Roman alphabet.

Sometimes languages use different scripts for different purposes. Imagine sending an international telegram in a language that uses a script other than the Roman alphabet—Japanese, Korean, Greek, Russian, Persian, Thai, or Arabic, for example. Rather than using their customary orthographies, speakers of these languages use the Roman alphabet to send telegrams internationally. Even within a country, an alternative writing system may be needed: In China, each character has a four-digit numeral assigned to it and these numerals are sent telegraphically and then "translated" back into Chinese characters. Sometimes a language uses more than one writing system for different aspects of writing. Japanese draws upon three kinds of writing: *kanji,* based on the Chinese character system, in which a symbol represents a word independent of its pronunciation, and two syllabaries. A *syllabary* is a writing system in which each symbol represents a spoken syllable. Throughout the world there are discrepancies between sounds as they are spoken and as they are represented in writing.

Bilingual Sign, Xinjiang Autonomous Region, China. Written alternately in Arabic script (for Uyghur) and Chinese characters (for Chinese), with Arabic numerals in both. Neither language is related to Arabic.

In Chapter 12 you'll learn more about the written representation of languages. Now, we focus on the sounds of language. The rest of this chapter examines the human vocal apparatus and the sounds it produces; Chapter 4 examines the nature of the sound systems of human language.

PHONETICS: THE STUDY OF SOUNDS

Phonetics is the study of the sounds made in the production of human languages. It has two principal branches.

- *Articulatory phonetics* focuses on the human vocal apparatus and describes sounds in terms of their articulation in the vocal tract; it has been central to the discipline of linguistics.

- *Acoustic phonetics* uses the tools of physics to study the nature of sound waves produced in human language; it is increasingly important in linguistics with attempts to use machines for interpreting speech patterns in voice identification and voice-initiated mechanical operations.

Our discussion will be limited almost exclusively to articulatory phonetics—to the nature of human sounds as they are produced by the vocal apparatus.

Phonetic Alphabets

To refer to the sounds of human language in terms of their articulation, phoneticians have evolved descriptive techniques that avoid the difficulties of describing sounds in terms of customary writing systems. You already know it is impossible to use customary written representations to analyze sound structure because, even within a single language, some sounds correspond to more than one letter, and some letters to more than one sound. Then, too, a single letter can be used to represent different sounds in different languages. So we need an independent system to represent the actual sounds of human languages.

In scientific discussion, the requisite characteristics of symbols for representing sounds are clarity and consistency. The best tool is a phonetic alphabet, and the one most widely used is the International Phonetic Alphabet (IPA). The IPA provides a unique written representation of every sound in every language.

A list of symbols used to represent the consonant sounds of English is given in Table 3–1. It shows the phonetic symbol for each sound and words that have the relevant parts emphasized. In several instances where some American books use symbols that differ from the IPA symbols, we've indicated those symbols in parentheses. The words illustrate word-initial, word-medial, and word-final occurrences of the sounds.

Table 3-1
English Consonants Arranged by Position in Word
(Alternative phonetic symbols in parentheses)

PHONETIC SYMBOL	INITIAL	MEDIAL	FINAL
p	pill	caper	tap
b	bill	labor	tab
t	till	petunia	bat
d	dill	seduce	pad
k	kill	sicker	lick
g	gill	dagger	bag
f	fill	beefy	chief
v	villa	saving	grave
θ	thin	author	breath
ð	then	leather	breathe
s	silly	mason	kiss
z	zebra	deposit	shoes
ʃ (š)	shell	rashes	rush
ʒ (ž)	———	measure	rouge
tʃ (č)	chill	kitchen	pitch
dʒ (ǰ)	jelly	bludgeon	fudge
m	mill	dummy	broom
n	nill	sunny	spoon
ŋ	———	singer	sing
h	hill	ahoy	———
j (y)	yes	beyond	toy
r (ɹ)	rent	berry	deer
l	lily	silly	mill
w	will	away	cow

The Vocal Tract

The processes the vocal tract uses in creating a multitude of sounds are similar to those of wind instruments and organ pipes, which produce different musical sounds by varying the shape, size, and acoustic character of the cavities through which air passes once it leaves its source. Every speech sound you make sounds different from every other speech sound because of a unique combination of features in the way you shape your mouth and tongue and move parts of the vocal apparatus in making it. Examine the simplified drawing of the vocal tract in Figure 3–3. Here we will look at the different parts of the vocal tract and show how these parts work together to produce different sounds.

Figure 3-3
The Vocal Tract

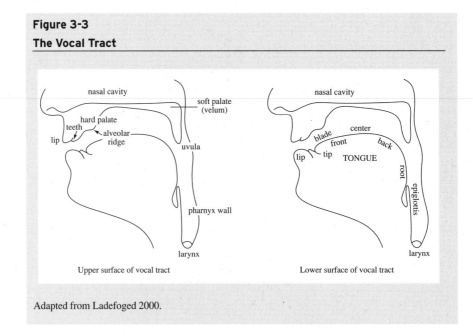

Upper surface of vocal tract   Lower surface of vocal tract

Adapted from Ladefoged 2000.

How are speech sounds made? First, air coming from the lungs passes through the vocal tract, which shapes it into different speech sounds. The air then exits the vocal tract through the mouth or nose or both.

Despite the fact that speakers of all languages have the same vocal apparatus, no language takes advantage of all the possibilities for forming different sounds, and there are striking differences in the sounds that occur in different languages. For example, Japanese and Thai lack the [v] sound of English *van,* and Japanese lacks the [f] sound of *fan.* Thai lacks the sounds represented by <g> in *gill,* <z> in *zebra,* <sh> in *shell,* <s> in *measure,* and <j> and <dg> in *judge.* French, Japanese, and Thai lack the quite different <th> sounds in *ether* and *either.*

Just as some languages lack sounds that English has, other languages have sounds that English does not have. You are probably aware that English lacks the trilled *r* of Spanish and Italian and that German has a sound at the end of words like

Bach 'stream' and *hoch* 'high' that does not occur among the inventory of English sounds. Arabic has a sound similar to the German <ch> of *Bach,* but in Arabic it can occur word initially. A similar (but not identical) sound occurring word finally in the German word *ich* occurs in English (for those dialects that pronounce the <h>) in the initial sound of *human* and *huge.* Still, it can be tough for English speakers learning German to pronounce the sound in a word like *ich* because English doesn't permit that sound to occur at the end of a word.

The Vocal Cords and Voicing

Human beings have no organs that are used only for speech. The organs that produce speech sounds have evolved principally to serve the life-sustaining processes of breathing and eating. Speech is a secondary function of the human "vocal apparatus"—and in that sense it is sometimes said to be parasitic on these organs. The vocal cords offer an illustration of the "parasitic" nature of speech: the primary function of these two folds is to keep food from going down the wrong tube and entering the lungs.

With respect to speech, vibration of the vocal cords is what distinguishes voiced and voiceless sounds. You can perceive the difference between voiced and voiceless consonants by alternating between the pronunciations of [f] and [v] or [s] and [z] while holding your hands clapped over your ears. See whether you can tell from pronouncing the words *thin, thirty, then,* and *those* whether [θ] or [ð] is voiced; take care not to confuse the voicing of the vowels following the consonants in question. In English, vowels are always voiced. Check your conclusions against Table 3–7 on page 100.

DESCRIBING SOUNDS

As you explore the inventory of sounds, use your vocal tract to produce the sounds that are described. Pronounce them aloud, noting the shape of your mouth and the position of your tongue for each sound. Such firsthand experience will familiarize you with the reference points of phonetics, make the discussion easier to follow, and give you confidence as you master articulatory phonetics.

As in our early discussion, we will continue to use square brackets to enclose the symbols representing sounds. Thus [t] will symbolize the initial and final sounds in *tot,* [d] the initial and final sounds in *did,* and [z] the initial sound in *zebra,* the medial consonant in *busy,* and the final sound of *buzz* and *dogs.*

Speech sounds can be identified in terms of their *articulatory* properties—that is, by *where* in the mouth and *how* they are produced. All English consonants can be described in terms of three properties:

- **Voicing** (whether the vocal cords are vibrating or not)
- **Place of articulation** (where the airstream is most obstructed)
- **Manner of articulation** (the particular way the airstream is obstructed)

Voicing

Begin by distinguishing between [s] (as in *bus* or *sip*) and [z] (as in *buzz* or *zip*). When you pronounce a long, continuous [zzzzz] and alternate it with a long, continuous [sssss], you'll notice that the position of your tongue within your mouth remains the same, even though these sounds are noticeably different. You can feel this difference by touching your **larynx** (voice box or Adam's apple) while saying [zzzzz sssss zzzzz sssss]. The vibration that you feel from your larynx when you utter [zzzzz] but not [sssss] is called **voicing;** it is the result of air being forced through a narrow aperture (called the **glottis**) between two mucosal folds (the vocal cords) in the larynx. It is like the leaf with a slit in it that children use to make a vibrating noise by blowing air through. When the vocal cords are held together, the air forced through them from the lungs causes them to vibrate. It is precisely this vibration, or "voicing," that distinguishes [z] from [s] and enables speakers to differentiate between two otherwise identical sounds.

Using these very similar but distinct sounds enables us to create words that differ by only a single feature of voicing on a single sound but carry quite different meanings, as in *bus* and *buzz, sip* and *zip, peace* and *peas, sane* and *Zane.*

Besides [s] and [z] other sounds are characterized by a voiced versus voiceless contrast. Consider [f] and [v], as in *fine* and *vine:* both sounds are produced with air being forced through a narrow aperture between the upper teeth and the lower lip; [f] is voiceless and [v] is voiced. Other voiceless/voiced pairs include [p] and [b] as in *pet* and *bet* and [t] and [d] as in *ten* and *den.*

Manner of Articulation

Besides having a voicing feature, [s] and [z] can be characterized as to their **manner of articulation.** In pronouncing them, air is continuously forced through a narrow opening at a place behind the upper teeth. Compare the pronunciation of [s] and [z] with the sounds [t] and [d]. Unlike [s] and [z], [t] and [d] are not pronounced by making a continuous stream of air pass through the mouth. Instead, the air is completely stopped behind and above the upper teeth and then released (or exploded) in a small burst of air. For this reason, [t] and [d] are called *stops,* and because the air is released through the mouth (and not the nose), they are also called *oral stops.* Sounds like [s] and [z] that are made by a continuous stream of air passing through a narrowed passage in the vocal tract are called *fricatives.*

Try it yourself: Pronounce the sounds [p], [b], [f], and [v] in order to determine which are stops and which are fricatives.

Place of Articulation

Of the sounds analyzed so far, [s] and [t] are voiceless, [z] and [d] are voiced. All four are pronounced with the point of greatest closure immediately behind the upper teeth. Pronounce *ten* and *den* aloud, feeling where the tip of your tongue touches the top of your mouth for the consonants. Both words start (and finish) at the alveolar ridge. Because [t], [d], and [n] are all articulated at the alveolar ridge, they are called **alveolars.** [s] and [z] are also articulated at the alveolar ridge, as you'll notice by pronouncing the words *sin* and *zen.* (Of course, [s] and [z] are fricatives, whereas [t] and [d] are stops.)

There are three major **places of articulation** for English stops: alveolar ridge, lips, and soft palate (or velum). If you say *pin* and *bin,* you'll notice that for the initial sound in each word air is built up behind the two lips and then released. Thus the point of greatest closure is at the lips, and for that reason [p] and [b] are called **bilabial** stops (*bilabial* means 'two lips').

Try it yourself: Compare your pronunciation of [p] and [t]. Both are voiceless, so what is the difference between them? Pronounce word pairs like *pin* and *tin* or *ripe* and *right* for examples.

Attend to the pronunciation of the first sound of *kin,* and you'll notice that [k], like [p] in *pill* and [t] in *till,* is a voiceless stop, but it differs from [p] and [t] in its place of articulation: [k] is pronounced with the tongue touching the roof of the mouth at the velum (the soft palate) and is called a **velar;** it is a voiceless velar stop.

Corresponding to the three voiceless stops [p], [t], and [k] are three voiced stops: [b] as in *bib* is a voiced bilabial stop; [d] as in *did* is a voiced alveolar stop; and [g] as in *gig* is a voiced velar stop. English has three pairs of stops, with each pair pronounced at a given place of articulation but one voiced and one voiceless.

Try it yourself: Identify the pairs of stops pronounced at the lips, at the alveolar ridge, and at the velum.

Besides lips, alveolar ridge, and velum, English takes advantage of other articulators to produce some sounds. The <th> of *thin* is a fricative pronounced with the tongue between the teeth. It is described as a voiceless **interdental** fricative and has the Greek letter theta [θ] as its phonetic symbol. [ʃ] (the sound represented by <sh> in *shoot* and *wish)* and [ʒ] (the final sound in *beige* and the middle consonant in *measure)* are pronounced between the alveolar ridge and the velum (or palate); sounds produced there are called **alveo-palatals.** [ʃ] is a voiceless alveo-palatal fricative; [ʒ] is a voiced alveo-palatal fricative.

CONSONANT SOUNDS

Consonants are sounds produced by partially or completely blocking air in its passage from the lungs through the vocal tract. If you review the inventory of English consonants given in Table 3–1 on page 85 and pronounce the sounds aloud while concentrating on the place and manner of articulation, you'll perceive how the rest of the tables represent the distribution of English consonants according to their voicing, their place of articulation, and their manner of articulation. Here we describe these consonants, grouped according to their manner of articulation and described in terms of voicing and place of articulation. We concentrate on the consonant sounds of English and mention selected consonants in other languages.

Stops

The principal **stops** of English are [p], [b], [t], [d], [k], [g]. By pronouncing words with these sounds in them (see Table 3–1 on page 85), you can recognize that [p] and [b] are bilabial stops, [t] and [d] alveolar stops, and [k] and [g] velar stops. Stops are formed when air is built up in the vocal tract and suddenly released through the mouth.

ENGLISH STOPS				
		PLACE OF ARTICULATION		
	BILABIAL	ALVEOLAR	VELAR	GLOTTAL
VOICELESS	p	t	k	ʔ
VOICED	b	d	g	

In addition, many languages have a glottal stop. It is pronounced by using the glottis to completely but briefly block the air from passing in the throat. The glottal stop is represented by [ʔ]. In English, the glottal stop occurs only as a marginal sound—between the two parts of the exclamation *Uh-oh!* in American English and in Cockney English as the medial consonant of words like *butter* and *bottle,* for example. In languages like Hawaiian, the glottal stop is a full-fledged consonant that can distinguish two different words: *paʔu* 'smudge' and *pau* 'finished.'

Fricatives

To pronounce the alveolar **fricatives** [s] and [z], air is forced through a narrow opening between the tip of the tongue and the alveolar ridge. English has a large inventory of fricatives, some articulated in front of [s] and [z] and others behind. Fricatives are characterized by a forcing of air in a continuous stream through a narrow opening. In pronouncing the first sound in the words *thin, three,* and *theta* and the final sound in *teeth* and *bath,* notice that the tongue tip is placed between the upper and lower teeth, where the airstream is most constricted and makes its articulation. Represented by [θ], the sound in these words is a voiceless interdental fricative. The voiced counterpart is the initial sound in the words *there* and *then* and the middle consonant sound in *either.* Notice that in English the spelling <th> is used for two distinct sounds: [θ] as in *ether* and [ð] as in *either* or *leather.*

Try it yourself: Pronounce the following words to discover other fricatives and become aware of their common properties and their different places of articulation:

fine/vine; beefish/peevish	[f] [v]	labio-dental fricatives
thigh/thy; ether/either	[θ] [ð]	interdental fricatives
sink/zinc; bus/buzz	[s] [z]	alveolar fricatives
rush/rouge; fishin'/vision	[ʃ] [ʒ]	alveo-palatal fricatives
here; ahoy	[h]	glottal fricative

ENGLISH FRICATIVES					
	PLACE OF ARTICULATION				
	LABIO-DENTAL	INTER-DENTAL	ALVEOLAR	ALVEO-PALATAL	GLOTTAL
VOICELESS	f	θ	s	ʃ	h
VOICED	v	ð	z	ʒ	

Some languages have other fricatives. Spanish, for example, has a voiced bilabial fricative (represented by [β]), as in the <b> of *cabo* 'end.' Japanese has a voiceless bilabial fricative represented by [ɸ] and pronounced somewhat like [f] but by bringing together both lips instead of the lower lip and the upper front teeth. The West African language Ewe has both voiced [β] and voiceless [ɸ] bilabial fricatives. Spanish and many other languages have a voiceless velar fricative [x] and a voiced velar fricative [ɣ], the latter less common. Pronounce [x] as if you were gently clearing your throat. The sound occurs initially in the Spanish word *joya* 'jewel' and the personal name *José* (when borrowed into English, *José* is pronounced with [h], the closest sound to [x] in English). [ɣ] is represented by <g> in Spanish *lago* 'lake.' German, Irish, and Mandarin Chinese have a voiceless palatal fricative [ç], as in the German word *Reich* 'empire.'

You may have noticed that the physical distance in the mouth between the places of articulation for the English fricatives is not as great as for the stops. The bilabial, alveolar, and velar places of articulation for stop consonants are spaced farther apart than are the labio-dental, interdental, alveolar, and alveo-palatal fricatives. This closer spacing of the fricatives can cause difficulty in perceiving them as distinct. The differences may be especially difficult to perceive for speakers of languages with fewer fricatives than English has or languages whose fricatives are spaced at greater distance from one another. For example, French does not have the interdental fricatives [θ] and [ð], so French speakers tend to perceive (and pronounce) English words like *thin* and *this* as though they were "sin" and "zis." One French fricative familiar to English speakers, even though English doesn't have it, is the voiced uvular *r*-sound (as in *Paris* or *rue* 'street'), which is made farther back in the mouth and is represented by [ʁ].

Affricates

Two consonant sounds of English are more complex to describe than its stops and fricatives. These are the sounds that occur initially in *chin* and *gin* and finally in *batch* and *badge*. If you pronounce these sounds slowly enough, you can recognize that they are stop-fricatives, which we'll refer to as affricates. In the pronunciation of an **affricate,** air is built up by a complete closure of the oral tract at some place of articulation, then released (something like a stop) and continued (like a fricative). The sound in *chin* is a combination of the stop [t] and the fricative [ʃ] and is represented as [tʃ] (North American books sometimes represent this affricate by [č]). The sound at the beginning and end of *judge* is a combination of the stop [d] and the fricative [ʒ], represented as [dʒ] (in North American books sometimes represented by [ǰ]). English has only this pair of affricates, and to capture their place of articulation they are called alveo-palatal affricates.

Other languages have other affricates. The most common are the alveolar affricates [ts] and [dz], which occur at the beginning of the Italian words *zucchero* 'sugar' and *zona* 'zone' respectively.

ENGLISH AFFRICATES	
	PLACE OF ARTICULATION
	ALVEO-PALATAL
VOICELESS	tʃ
VOICED	dʒ

Obstruents

Because they share the phonetic property of constricting the airflow through the vocal tract, fricatives, stops, and affricates are together referred to as **obstruents.**

Approximants

English has four sounds that are known as **approximants** because they are produced by two articulators approaching one another almost like fricatives but not coming close enough to produce friction. The English approximants are [j], [r] (IPA [ɹ]), [l], and [w]. The sound that begins the word *you* is the palatal approximant [j]; the word *cute* begins with the consonant cluster [kj]. Because [r] is pronounced by channeling air through the central part of the mouth, it is called a central approximant. To pronounce [l] air is channeled on one or both sides of the tongue to make a sound that is called a lateral approximant. To distinguish them from the other approximants, [r] and [l] are sometimes called **liquids.** (In some Asian languages, [r] and [l] are not contrastive sounds, so native speakers of these languages may find it challenging to distinguish them in speaking or perceiving them in English speech. This is a matter to which we return in the following chapter.)

In pronouncing the approximant [w], the lips are rounded, as in *wild*. For certain dialects, in some words [h] precedes [w] as in *which* or *whether.* When [w] is the second element of a consonant cluster (as in *twine* or *quick),* the initial sound (in these cases, [t] or [k]) is rounded in anticipation of the [w].

ENGLISH APPROXIMANTS			
	PLACE OF ARTICULATION		
	BILABIAL	ALVEOLAR	PALATAL
VOICED (CENTRAL)	w	r (ɹ)	j
VOICED (LATERAL)		l	

Nasals

Nasal consonants are pronounced by lowering the velum, thus allowing the stream of air to pass out through the nasal cavity instead of through the oral cavity. English has three nasal stops: [m] as in *mad, drummer, cram;* [n] as in *new, sinner, ten;* and a third, symbolized by [ŋ] and pronounced as in the words *sing* and *singer.*

ENGLISH NASALS		
	PLACE OF ARTICULATION	
BILABIAL	ALVEOLAR	VELAR
m	n	ŋ

Because of the way it is usually spelled in English, English speakers may think of [ŋ] as a combination of [n] and [g], but it is actually a single sound. You can test this for yourself by comparing your pronunciation of *singer* and *finger.* Ignoring the initial sounds [s] and [f], if your pronunciation of *singer* and *finger* differs (for some speakers of English it does *not),* then you have [ŋ] in *singer* and [ŋg] in *finger* (notice that if you had [ng] in *finger,* you'd pronounce it like "finn-ger"). Most American English speakers have a three-way contrast among *simmer, sinner,* and *singer,* depending on whether the middle consonant is [m], [n], or [ŋ]. By noticing where your tongue touches the upper part of your mouth in articulating these nasal consonants (and by comparing their place of articulation with other sounds identified above), you can determine that [m] is a bilabial nasal, [n] an alveolar nasal, and [ŋ] a velar nasal. If while you are saying [mmmmm] you cut off the airstream passing through your nose by pinching it closed (as a clothespin would), the sound stops abruptly, thereby demonstrating that in producing nasal stops air passes through the nose. Compare cutting off the air passing through your nose while saying [nnnnn] and saying [sssss], and you'll sense how the nasal and oral cavities function in sound production. When you cut off air passing through the nose, there is almost no difference in the quality of the sound for oral consonants; for a nasal consonant the effect is altogether different.

If you have successfully identified the places of articulation for nasals and understood why they fit in their slots in the consonant table, you may have noticed that English has three sets of consonants articulated in the same places and differing only in their manner of articulation: the oral stops [p] and [b] and the nasal stop [m] are bilabials; the oral stops [t] and [d] and the nasal stop [n] are articulated at the alveolar ridge and are called alveolars; [k], [g], and [ŋ] are articulated at the velum and are called velars.

The nasal consonants of English are [m], [n], [ŋ]. Other languages have other nasals. French, Spanish, and Italian have a palatal nasal [ɲ], which you'll recognize in the French word *mignon* 'cute' (which English has borrowed in the phrase *filet mignon),* in the Spanish words *mañana, señor,* and *cañón* (which has been borrowed into English as *canyon),* and the Italian *bagno* 'bath' and *lasagna* (also borrowed into English).

Clicks, Flaps, Trills

Some languages have consonants that belong to the same classes we have discussed but are strikingly different from those in European languages. Several languages of southern Africa have among their stop consonants certain **click** sounds that are an integral part of their sound system. One example is the lateral click made on the side of the tongue; it occurs in English when we urge a horse to move on, for example, but it is not part of the inventory of English speech sounds; it is represented with the IPA symbol [ǁ]. Another click sound that occurs in some of these languages can be represented in English writing by the reproach *tsk-tsk*. This last click is not a lateral but a dental (IPA [ǀ]) or a (post)alveolar (IPA [!]) made with the tip of the tongue at the teeth or the alveolar ridge.

A few consonant sounds are not stops, fricatives, affricates, approximants, or nasals. The middle consonant sound in the words *butter* and *metal* is commonly pronounced in American English as an alveolar **flap,** which is a high velocity short stop produced by tapping the tongue against the alveolar ridge. We represent this flap by [ɾ] (a sound discussed further in Chapter 4). Spanish, Italian, and Fijian have an alveolar **trill** *r*, as in Spanish *correr* 'to run.' In order to keep the familiar symbol [r] to represent the "r" of English, North American books represent the alveolar trill by [r̃] (instead of the IPA symbol [r]).

VOWEL SOUNDS

Vowel sounds are produced by passing air through different shapes of the mouth, with different positions of the tongue and of the lips, and with the air stream relatively unobstructed by narrow passages except at the glottis. Some languages have as few as three distinct vowels; others have more than a dozen. You may have thought English had only five vowels, but a count of five better reflects writing than speech. Pronounce the following words, and you'll realize that English has at least a dozen distinct vowels: *peat, pit, pet, pate, pat, put, putt, pool, poke, pot, part*, and *port*.

Vowel Height and Frontness

Vowels are characterized by the position of the tongue and the relative rounding of the lips. Partly on the basis of auditory perception, we refer to vowels as being *high* or *low* and *front* or *back*. We also consider whether the lips are *rounded* (as for *pool)* or *nonrounded* (as for *pill).*

Try it yourself: You can get a feel for these descriptors by alternately saying *feed* and *food*—the first contains a front vowel, the second a back vowel. To get a feel for tongue height, alternate saying *feet* and *fat*. If you don't feel the difference between high and low vowels with this pair of sounds, look at yourself in the mirror (or look at a classmate saying them); you'll see that the mouth is open wider for the vowel of *fat* than for the vowel of feet. The reason? The tongue is lower for *fat*.

Figure 3–4 indicates the relationship of the English vowels to one another and the approximate positions of the tongue during their articulation.

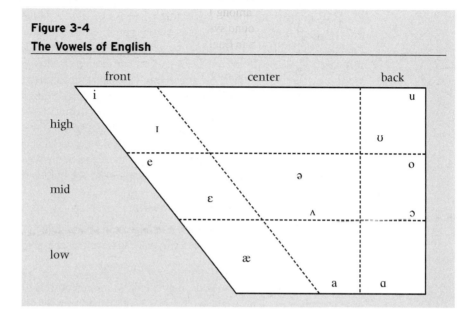

Figure 3-4

The Vowels of English

Here are English words for each of the vowel symbols shown in the figure. Note that these words are chosen on the basis of North American English; British English pronunciations may differ for some:

i	Pete, beat			u	pool, boot
ɪ	pit, bit			ʊ	put, foot
e	late, bait	ə	about, sof<u>a</u>	o	poke, boat
ɛ	pet, bet	ʌ	putt, but	ɔ	port, bought
æ	pat, bat	a	park (in Boston)	ɑ	pot, father

The symbols [ə] (called *schwa)* and [ʌ] (called *caret* or *wedge)* represent similar sounds. Both occur in the word *above* [əbʌv]. We use [ə] to represent a mid central vowel in unstressed syllables, such as the second syllable of *buses* [bʌsəz] and the second and third syllables of *capable* [kepəbəl]. We also use it before [r] in the same syllable, whether stressed as in *person* [pərsən] and *sir* [sər] or unstressed as in *pertain* [pərten] and *tender* [tɛndər]. We use [ʌ] to represent mid central vowels in other stressed syllables, such as *suds* [sʌdz] and the first syllable of *flooded* [flʌrəd]. (Some books use [ɚ] to represent a mid central vowel with *r* coloring. In systems using the [ɚ] notation, *person* would be transcribed [pɚsən], *sir* [sɚ], and *pertain* [pɚten].)

Diphthongs

English also has **diphthongs,** represented by pairs of symbols to capture the fact that a diphthong is a vowel sound for which the tongue starts in one place in the mouth and glides to another. Say these slowly to get a sense of what a diphthong is: [aj] (as in *bite);* [aw] (as in *pout, bout);* [ɔj] (as in *boy, toy).* (Some books transcribe these diphthongs as [ay] or [aɪ], [au] or [aʊ], and [ɔy] or [ɔɪ], respectively.) Diphthongs change in quality while being pronounced, as you can notice by slowly pronouncing the words *buy, boy, bough.* Thus American English dialects have up to thirteen distinctive vowel sounds (plus three diphthongs). In England and in certain parts of the United States, including metropolitan New York City, sixteen distinct vowels and diphthongs exist. In other parts of the United States, fewer distinct vowel sounds exist because no distinction is made between the vowels of *bought* and *pot.* Dialects surrounding the city of Pittsburgh, as well as in California and other parts of the West, do not make this distinction and pronounce word pairs like *caught* and *cot* and *hawk* and *hock* alike.

Other Articulatory Features of Vowels

To create differences among vowels, languages can exploit other possibilities besides tongue height and tongue backness. Vowels can have tenseness, rounding, lengthening, nasalization, and tone.

Tenseness   Languages can make a distinction between vowels that is characterized as *tense* versus *lax.* These labels represent a set of characteristics that distinguish one set of vowels from another. For example, lax vowels do not occur at the end of a stressed syllable, and they tend to be shorter; they also tend to be more centralized than the nearest tense vowel. The contrast between [i] of *peat* and [ɪ] of *pit* is in part a tense/lax contrast; likewise for the vowels in *bait/bet* and in *cooed/could.* The lax vowels don't end a syllable, are shorter than the tense vowels, and are more centralized in the mouth. Thus, English has the lax vowels [ɪ ɛ ʊ] as in *pit, pet, put.* The corresponding tense vowels are [i e u] as in *beat, bait, boot.* The English lax vowels [æ ʌ] do not have corresponding tense vowels.

Rounding   Whereas in English high front vowels tend automatically to be unrounded (and high back vowels to be rounded), some languages have *rounded* and *unrounded* front vowels. French and German have high front and mid front rounded vowels as well as unrounded ones. French has a high front unrounded [i] in words such as *dire* 'to say' and *dix* 'ten' and a high front rounded vowel [ü], as in *rue* 'street'; it also has a contrast between upper mid front unrounded [e] (as in *fée* 'fairy') and upper mid front rounded [ø] (*feu* 'fire'); and between lower mid front unrounded [ɛ] (*serre* 'hothouse') and lower mid front rounded [œ] (*soeur* 'sister'). German has similar contrasts.

Length   German has two of each vowel type—one *long,* the other *short.* The pronunciation of long vowels is held longer than that of short vowels. Long vowels are commonly represented with a special colon after them in phonetic transcriptions or by the vowel symbol doubled. (In dictionaries and some writing systems, a macron (¯) may be used above the vowel symbol.) Thus, in addition to the short vowels [i] and [ü], as in *bitten* 'to request' and *müssen* 'must,' German has words with high front long vowels: unrounded [iː] in *bieten* 'to wish' and rounded [üː] in *Mühle* 'mill.' These examples illustrate how languages can multiply vowel differences by exploiting long and short varieties. English, too, has vowels of differing length, although it does not exploit length to create different words (see Chapter 4). To sense differences in the duration of vowels, pronounce the English words *beat, bead, bit*. You should be able to hear that the vowel of *bead* is longer than the vowel of *beat,* and that both are longer than the vowel of *bit*.

Nasalization   All vowel types can be *nasalized* by pronouncing the vowel while passing air through the nose (as for nasal stops) and through the mouth. Nasal vowels are indicated by a tilde (˜) placed above the vowel symbol. French has several nasal vowels paralleling the oral vowels:

lin [lɛ̃] 'flax'	*lait* [lɛ] 'milk'
ment [mɑ̃] '(he) is lying'	*ma* [mɑ] 'my' (feminine)
honte [ɔ̃t] 'shame'	*hotte* [ɔt] 'hutch'

Other languages with nasal vowels include Irish, Hindi, and the Native American languages Delaware, Mixtec, Navaho, and Seneca.

Tone   In many languages of Asia, Africa, and North America, a vowel may be pronounced on several pitches and be perceived by the native speakers of these languages as different sounds. Typically, a vowel pronounced on a low pitch contrasts with the same vowel pronounced on a higher pitch. An example of a two-tone language is Hausa, spoken in West Africa. In Hausa, the word for 'bamboo' is *górà* with a high tone (´) on the first syllable and a low tone (`) on the second syllable. Compare that with the word *gòrá,* in which the sequence of tones is reversed and the meaning is 'large gourd.' Some tone languages have more complex systems. The Beijing dialect of Chinese has a high level tone (symbolized with ¯); a rising tone (´); a falling-rising tone (ˇ), in which the pitch begins to fall and then rises sharply; and a falling tone (`), in which the pitch falls sharply. There is a four-way tone contrast among the following vowels, which happen to be distinct words.

ī (high level)	'one'
í (rising)	'proper'
ǐ (falling-rising)	'already'
ì (falling)	'thought'

A given accent mark can be used to represent different tones in different languages. Thus, ´ represents a high tone in Hausa but a rising tone in Chinese; in Hausa, ` represents a low tone but in Chinese a falling tone.

Thai has five tones; the standard dialect of Vietnamese six tones; and the Guangzhou (Canton) dialect of Chinese nine different tones. Tone is a widespread and diverse phenomenon.

Tables 3–2 through 3–5 are vowel charts illustrating the sound patterns of four languages—French, Spanish, German, and Japanese.

Table 3-2
French Vowels with Illustrative Words

	FRONT UNROUNDED	FRONT ROUNDED	CENTRAL UNROUNDED	BACK ROUNDED
ORAL				
high	i	ü		u
upper mid	e	ø		o
mid			ə	
lower mid	ɛ	œ		ɔ
low			a	
NASAL				
lower mid	ɛ̃	œ̃		ɔ̃
low				ɑ̃

FRONT UNROUNDED	FRONT ROUNDED	CENTRAL UNROUNDED	BACK ROUNDED
i gris 'grey'	ü mûr 'ripe'	ə chemin 'path'	u fou 'crazy'
e fermé 'shut'	ø jeûne 'fasts'	a par 'by'	o mot 'word'
ɛ frais 'fresh'	œ jeune 'young'		ɔ fort 'strong'
ɛ̃ brin 'sprig'	œ̃ brun 'brown'		ɔ̃ fond 'bottom'
			ɑ̃ faon 'fawn'

Table 3-3
Spanish Vowels with Illustrative Words

	FRONT UNROUNDED	CENTRAL UNROUNDED	BACK ROUNDED
HIGH	i		u
MID	e		o
LOW		a	

FRONT UNROUNDED	CENTRAL UNROUNDED	BACK ROUNDED
i chiste 'joke'	a mar 'sea'	u sur 'south'
e fe 'faith'		o boca 'mouth'

Table 3-4

German Vowels with Illustrative Words

	FRONT UNROUNDED	FRONT ROUNDED	CENTRAL UNROUNDED	BACK ROUNDED
HIGH				
long	iː	üː		uː
short	i	ü		u
UPPER MID				
long	eː	øː		oː
short	e			o
MID				
short			ə	
LOWER MID				
long	ɛː			
short		œ		
LOW				
long			aː	
short			a	

iː bieten 'to wish' ü: Mühle 'mill' ə liebe 'dear' u: Huhn 'hen'
i bitten 'to request' ü müssen 'must' a: Rabe 'raven' u Mutter 'mother'
eː wen 'whom' øː ölig 'oily' a Ratte 'rat' o: Ofen 'oven'
e wenn 'when' œ Röntgen 'X-ray' o Ochs 'ox'
ɛː Käse 'cheese'

Table 3-5

Japanese Vowels with Illustrative Words

	FRONT UNROUNDED	CENTRAL UNROUNDED	BACK UNROUNDED	BACK ROUNDED
HIGH	i		ɯ	
MID	ɛ			ɔ
LOW		a		

i ima 'now' a aki 'autumn' ɯ buji 'safe' ɔ yoru 'to approach'
ɛ sensei 'teacher'

Tables 3–6 and 3–7 summarize all the vowels and consonants introduced in this chapter.

Table 3-6
Vowels Discussed in Chapter 3
(All vowels can be nasalized and either short or long.)

	FRONT UNROUNDED	FRONT ROUNDED	CENTRAL UNROUNDED	BACK UNROUNDED	BACK ROUNDED
high					
tense	i	ü		ɯ	u
lax	ɪ				ʊ
upper mid	e	ø			o
mid			ə		
lower mid	ɛ	œ	ʌ		ɔ
low	æ		a	ɑ	

Table 3-7
Consonants Discussed in Chapter 3

MANNER OF ARTICULATION AND VOICING	BILABIAL	LABIO-DENTAL	INTER-DENTAL	ALVEOLAR	ALVEO-PALATAL	PALATAL	VELAR	UVULAR	GLOTTAL
STOPS									
voiceless	p			t			k		ʔ
voiced	b			d			g		
NASALS									
	m			n		ɲ	ŋ		
FRICATIVES									
voiceless	ɸ	f	θ	s	ʃ	ç	x		h
voiced	β	v	ð	z	ʒ		ɣ	ʁ	
AFFRICATES									
voiceless				ts	tʃ				
voiced				dz	dʒ				
APPROXIMANTS									
voiced central	w			r (ɹ)		j			
voiced lateral				l					
OTHERS									
voiced trill				r̃ (r)					
voiced flap				ɾ					

PLACE OF ARTICULATION

Computers and Phonetics

 You know that alphabetic writing systems rely on the notion of discrete sounds, and it has also proved useful to linguists to think of speech sounds as discrete. But in reality—in conversation, for example—sounds are not discrete and do not occur separately. Instead each sound touches the next sound in a word (and in an utterance), and sounds and words merge into one another.

Imagine a computer that could create discrete sounds that seem natural when spoken in isolation—it could produce the sounds [ɪ], [n], [k], [l], [u], [d], [ə], and [d]. If it put these sounds together in the sequence [ɪnkludəd], you might expect a noise that resembled the word *included*. But there are complications. As it is usually pronounced, *included* does not have the same [ɪ] sound that occurs in *sit,* and the [n] of *included* is often pronounced more like the [ŋ] of *sing* than the [n] of *tin.* So if natural-sounding words are the goal, their production cannot rely on a simple sequence of discrete individual sounds.

Suppose instead that the computer put together the sounds [ĩ], [ŋ], [k], [l], [u], [d], [ə], and [d]. That combination would sound more natural, but it would still be stiff. For one thing, the first and second [d] sounds of *included* differ from one another, and both of them differ from the [d] sound of *dig.* Even further refinement wouldn't go far enough, for the individual sounds would have to run into one another as in natural speech. They couldn't be separated as in print or in phonetic transcription. As a further complication, consider that a word like *photo* could be represented phonetically as [foɾo], but the same morpheme in *photograph* would be pronounced as [forə] and in *photographer* as [fətɑ]. In other words, without some general principles of pronunciation, a computer could not simply combine the sounds represented in spelling and produce synthesized speech that sounded remotely like natural speech. We return to this matter in the following chapter.

SUMMARY

- Sounds must be distinguished from letters and other visual representations of language.

- Phonetic alphabets represent sounds in a way that is consistent and comparable across different languages; each sound is assigned a distinct representation, independently of the customary writing system used to represent a particular language.

- This chapter uses the International Phonetic Alphabet (IPA).

- All languages contain consonants and vowels.

- Consonants can be produced by obstructing the flow of air as it passes from the lungs through the vocal tract and out through the mouth or nose.

- For fricative consonants, air forced through a narrow opening forms a continuous noise, as in the initial and final sounds of *says* [sɛz] and *fish* [fɪʃ].

- For stop consonants, the air passage is completely blocked and then released, as in the initial and final sounds of the words *tap* and *cat.*

- Affricates are produced by combining a stop and a fricative, as in the final sound of the word *peach* or the initial and final sounds of *judge.*

- As a group, fricatives, stops, and affricates are called obstruents.

- An approximant is produced when one articulator approaches another but the vocal tract is not sufficiently narrowed to create the audible friction of a consonant. Examples are the initial sounds of *west* [wɛst], *yes* [jɛs], *rest* [rɛst], *lest* [lɛst].

- "Liquid" is a cover term for [r] and [l] sounds.

- Consonant sounds can be described as a combination of articulatory features: voicing, place of articulation, and manner of articulation. For example: [t] is a voiceless alveolar stop; [v] is a voiced labio-dental fricative.

- Vowels are produced by positioning the tongue and mouth to form differently shaped passages.

- The airstream for oral vowels passes through the mouth; for nasal vowels, the airstream passes through the nose and mouth.

- Vowels are described by relative height and frontness. For example: [æ] is a low front vowel; [u] is a high back vowel.

- Secondary features of vowel production—such as tenseness, nasality, lengthening, or rounding—are sometimes specified, as in "long vowel" or "nasal vowel."

- In many languages vowels (and nasals) can be pronounced on different pitches, or tones.

- Languages differ from one another in the number of speech sounds they have.

- Although linguists find it useful to conceptualize the sounds of speech as separate and discrete from one another, the sounds of real speech are actually connected and overlapping.

WHAT DO YOU THINK? REVISITED

❖ *How many vowels?* An easy way to figure out which vowels exist in English is to take a simple word frame like b_t and see how many different vowels you can set inside to produce a different word: *bit, beet, bet, bait, bat, but, boot, boat, bought, bite, bout.* Still other vowels don't occur in that frame but do occur in a frame such as p_t: *put* and *pot.* There are 13 vowels already, far more than the 5 that seem to be suggested by the vowels in the alphabet.

❖ *Shaw's "ghoti."* Words in which <gh> is pronounced as [f] include *cough, tough,* and *rough.* A word in which <gh> appears at the beginning is *ghost,* but the pronunciation is not as [f]. No English word beginning with <gh> (there are only a few such as *ghetto, Ghana, gherkin,* and *ghee*) is pronounced like [f]. Shaw was exaggerating.

❖ *Sounds and letters.* <gh> for the initial sound in *ghost;* <th> initial sound in *thin* and final sound in *path;* <th> initial sound in *then* and final sound in *smooth;* <ph> initial sound in *physics* or *philosophy;* <sh> initial sound in *shoot* and final sound in *wish;* <pn> initial sound in *pneumonia;* <ps> initial sound in *psalm;* <ch> initial sound in *cheese* and *choir;* and so on.

❖ *Put and putt.* English words that are pronounced and spelled differently but whose spelling difference doesn't correspond to the pronunciation difference include *satin/Satan; bit/bite; lit/light; woman/women.*

EXERCISES

Based on English

3-1 Refer to the tables on page 100 or the inside back cover, and give a phonetic description of the following sounds. For consonants, include voicing and place and manner of articulation. For vowels, include height, a frontness/backness dimension, and (where needed) a tense/lax distinction. *Examples:* [s]—voiceless alveolar fricative; [i]—high front tense vowel

Consonants: [z] [t] [b] [n] [ŋ] [r] [j] [ʃ] [θ] [ð]
Vowels: [ɛ] [æ] [ɔ] [ɪ] [ʊ] [o] [ə] [ɑ] [e] [aj]

3-2 A minimal pair is a set of two words that have the same sounds in the same order, except that one sound differs: *pit* [pɪt] / *bit* [bɪt]; *bell* [bɛl] / *bill* [bɪl]; and *either* [iðər] / *ether* [iθər].

a. For each of the following pairs of English consonants, provide minimal pairs that illustrate their occurrence in initial, medial, and final position. (Examples are given for the first pair.)

		Initial	Medial	Final
[s]	[z]	sue/zoo	buses/buzzes	peace/peas
[k]	[b]	_____	_____	_____
[t]	[b]	_____	_____	_____
[s]	[t]	_____	_____	_____
[r]	[l]	_____	_____	_____
[m]	[n]	_____	_____	_____

b. For each of these pairs of vowels, cite a minimal pair of words illustrating the contrast. *Example:* [u] [æ] *boot/bat.*

[i] [ɪ]; [ɔj] [aj]; [u] [ʊ]; [æ] [e]

3-3 Write out in ordinary spelling the words represented by the following transcriptions. *Examples:* [pɛn] *pen;* [smok] *smoke;* [bənænə] *banana*

[læŋgwədʒ]   [træpt]   [spawts]
[θwɔrt]   [ðiz]   [ðɪs]
[lʌvd]   [plɛʒər]   [kwɪkli]
[mənɑrənəs]   [frænɛrək]   [ɛntərprajzɪŋ]

3-4 The names below are phonetic transcriptions of the names of recent popular movies. Write their names using ordinary English spellings. Example: for bʌɾi you would write "Buddy"; for əvitə "Evita"; for et majəl "8 Mile."

fɑrgo

ʃrɛk

tajtænək

maj bɪg fæt grik wɛrɪŋ

hæri pɑrər ənd ðə tʃembər əv sikrəts

lɔrd əv ðə rɪŋz

ðə pipəl vərsəz læri flɪnt

trajəl ən ɛrər

ðə lɔst wərld dʒəræsək pɑrk

ə bjutəfəl majnd

blæk hɔk dawn

mulẽ ruʒ

dʒɪmi nutrɑn bɔj dʒinjəs

mɛn ən blæk

3-5 The transcription below represents one person's reading of a passage about the actor Will Smith (adapted from *Newsweek,* July 7, 1997). The transcription does not represent secondary features such as vowel length or consonant aspiration, and you'll quickly discover that capitalization and punctuation are not represented, either. Write out the passage using ordinary English spellings, as indicated in the first few lines and the last line.

wɪl smɪθ hæz ə dɑrk ferəl flɔ	Will Smith has a dark, fatal flaw.
ɪts ən əbsɛʃən əv sɔrts	It's an obsession of sorts,
ðə kajnd əv θɪŋ ðæt kən drajv lʌvd	the kind of thing that can drive loved
wʊnz krezi	ones crazy.
ən majt ivən ɪf əlawd tə rʌn əmʌk	
direl ən dəbɪlətet ən ʌðərwajz prɑməsɪŋ kərir	
hi hets bæd græmər	
prənʌnsieʃən ɛrərz mɪsteks əv ɛni lɪŋgwɪstək sɔrt	
ðe mek hɪm nʌts	
hɪz gərlfrɛnd ði æktrəs dʒedə pɪŋkət noz ət	
əkeʒənəli ɪn ðer dʒɛntləst most kærɪŋ we	
ðe traj tə kɔʃən hɪm əbawt ðə sɪriəsnəs əv hɪz əflɪkʃən	
sɪrɪŋ dawn ovər brɛkfəst wʊn mɔrnɪŋ	
ɪn ðer spænɪʃ stajəl vɪlə awtsajd ɛle	
pɪŋkət kæsts ə tɛnərəv glæns ɪn hɪz dərɛkʃən	
wɑt wər jə telɪŋ mi ði ʌðər de ʃi sɛz	
ðæt pipəl se ðə wərd ɔfən lajk ɔf fən wɛn ɪts rili prənawnst ɔf tən	
smɪθ lʊkɪŋ spɔrti ən prɑpər ɪn ə wajt ræl f lɔren polo ʃərt	
wajt swɛtpænts ən najki ɛr ʌp tɛmpoz	
sɛts dawn ə plærər əv bənænə pænkeks wɪθ ə dɪsəpruvɪŋ θʌd	
no no hi sɛz	
ðə rajt we ɪz ɔfən	
pipəl hu prənawns ðə ti ɑr trajɪŋ tə sawn səfɪstəkerəd	
bət ðe dʒʌst sawn rɔŋ	
pɪŋkət gɪgəlz ðɛn əfɛks ə supərmæn ton əv vɔjs	
ɪts ə nawn ɪts ə vərb	
no ɪts kæptən kərɛkʃən	No, it's Captain Correction.

3-6 The following transcription represents one person's reading of a passage about love potions (adapted from *The Encyclopedia of Things That Never Were,* p. 159). Write out the passage using ordinary English spellings.

æz ðə nem ɪndəkets	As the name indicates,
ðiz poʃənz ɑr kəmpawndəd	these potions are compounded
spəsɪfəkli	specifically

tu ətrækt ə sʌbdʒɛkt   to attract a subject

hu ɪz rilʌktənt tə sərɛndər   who is reluctant . . .

    tə wʌnz kɑrnəl dəzajərz

ðə poʃən me bi hæd ærə prajs frəm ɛni ælkəmɪst

ɔr ʌðər pərsən skɪld ɪn ðə prɛpərɛʃən əv majn tʃɛndʒɪŋ kɑmpawnz

wɪtʃəz wɪzərdz ən sɔrsərərz

hu ɑr dʒɛnrəli nɑt ɪntrəstəd ɪn lʌv

ɑr sʌmtajmz ənwɪlɪŋ tə mænjəfækʃər ðə poʃənz

ðə pərtʃəsərz onli prɑbləm me bi ðæt əv pərswerɪŋ

ði ɑbdʒɛkt əv hɪz ɔr hər dəzajər

tə swɑlo ɛni əv ðə poʃən

ə risənt rɛsəpi fɔr ə lʌv poʃən ɪŋklurəd

dʒɪndʒər sɪnəmən drajd ən grawnd grep sidz

ɔjstər ɛlk æntlər ən tel her frəm ə mel ænəməl

ænd ɛni surəbəl ɑbdʒɛkt frəm ðə pərsən

sʌtʃ æz hɪz ɔr hər nel klɪpɪŋz

3-7 Transcribe each of the following words as you say them in casual speech. (Don't be misled by the spelling; it could be helpful to have someone else pronounce them for you.) *Examples: bed* [bɛd]; *rancid* [rænsəd]; *shnook* [ʃnʊk]

changes	mostly	very	friend	teacher
semantics	system	ready	more	musician
crackers	peanuts	palm	music	photographer
pneumonia	attitude	psalm	fuel	photograph

3-8 Examine the following list of consonants as they are represented in four popular dictionaries (the first three are American, the COD British), and compare the dictionary symbols with the IPA symbols. (In parenthesis an alternative symbol sometimes used in North America instead of the IPA symbol is given.) The abbreviation MWCD stands for *Merriam-Webster's Collegiate Dictionary,* tenth edition; WNWCD for *Webster's New World College Dictionary,* fourth edition; AHD for *The American Heritage Dictionary of the English Language,* third edition; COD for *The Concise Oxford Dictionary of Current English,* tenth edition.

IPA Symbol	MWCD	WNWCD	AHD	COD
p	p	p	p	p
k	k	k	k	k
θ	th	th	th	θ
ð	<u>th</u>	*th*	*th*	ð
s	s	s	s	s
ʃ (š)	sh	sh	sh	ʃ
ʒ (ž)	zh	zh	zh	ʒ
tʃ (č)	ch	ch	ch	tʃ
dʒ (ǰ)	j	j	j	dʒ
ŋ	ŋ	ŋ	ng	ŋ
h	h	h	h	h
j	y	y	y	j

Some symbols used by dictionaries are the IPA symbols, but not all. North American dictionaries tend to prefer their own symbols, while the British dictionary leans strongly toward the IPA. Choose three sounds for which at least one dictionary uses a different symbol from the IPA symbol, and discuss why it might have been chosen.

3-9 Examine the following list of vowels as they are represented in three dictionaries; compare the dictionary symbols with the IPA symbols. (See Exercise 3–8 for identification of the dictionaries.)

IPA Symbol	Words	MWCD	WNWCD	AHD	COD
i	peat, feet	ē	ē	ē	iː
ɪ	pit, bit	i	i	ĭ	ɪ
ɛ	pet, bet	e	e	ĕ	ɛ
e	wait, late	ā	ā	ā	eɪ
æ	pat, bat	a	a	ă	a
ə	soda, item	ə	ə	ə	ə
ʌ	putt, love	ə	u	ŭ	ʌ
u	pool, boot	ü	o͞o	o͞o	uː
ʊ	push, put	u	oo	o͝o	ʊ
o	boat, sold	o	o	ō	əʊ
ɔ	port, or	ȯ	ô	ô	ɔː
ɑ	pot, bottle	ä	ä	ŏ	ɒ
aw	cow, pout	au̇	ou	ou	aʊ
aj	buy, tight	ī	ī	ī	ʌɪ
ɔj	boy, toil	ȯi	oi	oi	ɔɪ

In contrast to their practice with consonants, desk dictionaries differ from one another and from the IPA in transcribing vowels. Cite three instances of a difference from the transcription in this book, and discuss the advantages and disadvantages of the dictionary's representation as compared to ours.

3-10 George Bernard Shaw's tongue-in-cheek claim that English spelling is so chaotic that *ghoti* could be pronounced [fɪʃ] 'fish' has been called misleading. That judgment is based on observations like these: <gh> can occur word initially in only a few words (for example, *ghost* and *ghastly),* and then it is always pronounced [g]; only following a vowel in the same syllable (as in *cough* and *tough)* can <gh> be pronounced as [f]; thus, *ghoti* could not be pronounced with an initial [f]. What other generalizations about the English spelling patterns of <gh>, <o>, and <ti> can be used to argue that Shaw's claim is at least exaggerated?

Especially for Educators and Future Teachers

3-11 Your fifth-grade class complains that English spelling is chaotic and that's what makes learning to read more of a challenge than it needs to be. Reading would be easier, they say, if spelling reflected pronunciation. As examples, they claim that *electricity* should be spelled <elektrisity> or <alektrisatee> and *electrical* <elektrikal> or <alektrakal>; likewise, they say, *cats* should be spelled <kats> and *dogs* <dogz>. In what sense could your students' claim be right? On the other hand, what arguments could you offer in support of the view that reading is easier with little or no variation in the spelling of the ELECTRIC morpheme and the 'PLURAL' morpheme even when the pronunciation differs? In other words, what are good arguments for keeping traditional spellings in such cases?

3-12 As a follow-up to the discussion about spelling consistency for the same morpheme in different words, you realize that you have students in your class from different regions, and their vowel pronunciations (and perhaps some of their consonants) differ. Some might have the same pronunciation for *hawk* and *hock* (or *talk* and *tock, walk* and *wok),* while for others these pairs are not pronounced alike. What will the spelling reformers among your students propose to accommodate these pronunciation differences across different groups of speakers?

3-13 Your ESL class notices that you pronounce words like *later, fatter,* and *metal* as though they were spelled with <d> instead of <t>—you pronounce them as in *lady, ladder,* and *medal.* They ask why you don't pronounce them with the [t] sound of the spelling. What's your explanation?

OTHER RESOURCES

- **International Phonetic Association: http://www.arts.gla.ac.uk/IPA/ipa.html**
  At this site you'll find the latest version of the IPA, including vowels, consonants, diacritics, suprasegmentals, tones, and word accents. You'll also find links to sites where you can download IPA fonts for your word processing programs, as well as information about recordings of the sounds of the IPA.

- **The Sounds of the IPA: http://www.phon.ucl.ac.uk/home/wells/cassette.htm**
  A cassette and CD of the sounds of the International Phonetic Alphabet are available. For ordering information, use the link at the IPA home page or go directly to this Web site.

SUGGESTIONS FOR FURTHER READING

- **David Crystal. 1997.** *A Dictionary of Linguistics and Phonetics,* **4th ed.** (Oxford: Blackwell). A rich source of information about the meanings of terms.
- **Peter B. Denes & Elliot N. Pinson. 1993.** *The Speech Chain,* **2nd ed.** (New York: Freeman). An accessible account of the physics and biology of spoken language; includes chapters on acoustic phonetics, digital processing of speech sounds, speech synthesis, and automatic speech recognition.
- **Peter Ladefoged. 2000.** *A Course in Phonetics,* **4th ed.** (Boston: Wadsworth). An excellent introduction to the production mechanisms of speech and to the variety of sounds in the languages of the world.
- **Peter Ladefoged & Ian Maddieson. 1996.** *The Sounds of the World's Languages* (Oxford and Malden, MA: Blackwell). An advanced treatment of the articulatory and acoustic phonetics of the various sounds in the languages of the world.
- **Ian R. A. MacKay. 1991.** *Phonetics: The Science of Speech Production,* **2nd ed.** (Boston: Allyn and Bacon). The most complete elementary treatment of all aspects of phonetics; accessible and with excellent illustrations.
- **Ian Maddieson. 1984.** *Patterns of Sound* (Cambridge: Cambridge University Press). An inventory of the sounds in a representative sample of the world's languages; the inventories vary from a low of 11 to a high of 141 sounds.

- **Geoffrey K. Pullum & William A. Ladusaw. 1996.** *Phonetic Symbol Guide,* **2nd ed.** (Chicago: University of Chicago Press). Discusses the various symbols used in the International Phonetic Alphabet (IPA) and by other writers in their treatments of phonetics and phonology; arranged like a dictionary, with each symbol clearly illustrated.
- **Michael Stubbs. 1980.** *Language and Literacy: The Sociolinguistics of Reading and Writing* (London: Routledge). Contains an excellent discussion of the relationship between sounds and spelling in English and other languages; offers insights into the problems facing spelling reform.

CHAPTER 4

Sound Systems of Language: Phonology

WHAT DO YOU THINK?

❖ Imagine you're a junior high school language teacher and one of your students returns from a visit to Berlin, Paris, and Madrid. She tells her classmates that when she listened to the radio she could not separate the stream of speech into separate words—"It all seemed a blur," she says, "not like English, where the words are separate and easy to pick out." She claims English words are almost as distinct from one another in speech as in writing, but that German, French, and Spanish aren't structured that way. Other students ask whether that's true and, if so, what accounts for the difference between those languages and English. Your reply?

❖ You're visiting Paris with a cousin who has studied French for five years and prides himself on his mastery of the language. He's fluent enough to give complicated directions to a taxi driver taking you back to your hotel, and you're impressed at the ease with which he and the cabbie talk in French. Then, as you're stepping out of the cab, the cabbie asks your cousin whether he's Canadian, American, or English. Crestfallen that the driver recognizes his accent as not native, your cousin asks you which characteristics in his French identify him as an English speaker and why he hasn't been able to eliminate them. What do you say?

❖ At work you get a message from the secretary; it reads "Call Jules Biker," but you don't know anyone by that name. You say it aloud, trying to remember, and you recognize that it refers to your friend Jewel Spiker. You return the call and tell Jewel about the misspelling. She can't imagine what accounts for the secretary's perception of p as b. Can you think of an explanation?

❖ A techie friend claims machines can synthesize speech so well you can't tell whether it's a real person or not. Skeptical, you determine to explore the subject. After half an hour on the Internet, what can you report to your friend about the quality of speech synthesis?

INTRODUCTION: SOUNDS IN THE MIND

This chapter focuses on the systematic structuring of sounds in languages. It examines which phonetic distinctions are significant enough to signal differences in meaning; the relationship between how sounds are pronounced and how they are stored in the mind; and the ways sounds are organized within words.

It's useful to approach sound systems from the point of view of children acquiring their native language. Imagine the task of an infant listening to utterances made by its parents, siblings, and others. From the barrage of utterances it faces in early life, a child must decipher the code of its language and learn to speak its mother tongue. Caregivers in some cultures use slow and careful speech, sometimes called "baby talk," in addressing children, but they don't do so consistently, and not all cultures follow that practice. To make the situation tougher, the utterances children hear are often incomplete, interrupted, or flawed in other ways.

In Chapter 3 you learned to distinguish between the number of letters in a written word and the number of sounds in the word's pronunciation. We have taken it for granted that words have a specific number of sounds. But children in their early months would seem to have no ready access to that simple fact. Attempting to count the number of words in a sample of even a few seconds' duration in a conversation or radio broadcast in a language you don't know will quickly demonstrate how difficult that task is because most words are generally run together. This is true of all spoken languages and all dialects.

Ifwordswereprintedwithoutspacesbetweenthemtheywouldbeprettytoughtoread.

As you recognize, sorting out the individual words would not be easy. Yet that's part of the challenge you faced when you began acquiring your primary, or mother, tongue.

Actually, the task is even more difficult than is suggested by the run-together words in the printed sentence above: whereas the letters in the run-together sentence are discrete and separated from one another, the individual sounds in a spoken word blend together into a continuous noise stream. To take our writing analogy a step further, imagine attempting to spot the beginning and end points of each letter in a handwritten sample: this would more closely capture the challenge that infants face in deciphering the code of distinctive sounds in their language. Consider the following:

In cursive writing, the letters of each word are joined.

Although anyone who knows English and can decipher this handwriting can count the letters in each word, there is no clear separation in their visual representation. Each word is written continuously; the letters blend into one another. No beginning or end can be pinpointed (except for the initiation of the first letter and the termination of the last letter in each word). The same is true of the speech infants hear; there is no separation between the individual sounds of a word, no beginning or end for the individual sounds in the speech stream. And for children the situation is even more difficult because the words themselves aren't separated. Children nevertheless learn the words of their language quickly and efficiently, a remarkable feat considering how much else they have to learn in their early years.

If you examine a physical "picture" of a word as made by a sound spectrogram, you can see that there is no separation between the sounds. One important reason for the continuity between sound segments is that a sound's phonetic features—for example, voicing and nasalization—do not all begin or end simultaneously. If you say *lint,* you don't say [l], then stop and then say [ɪ], and when that's finished say [n] and then [t]. Instead, individual features of one sound can continue into the next sound, and the features of a sound can be anticipated in pronouncing a preceding sound. For example, the nasalization of [n] in *lint* is anticipated in the vowel, which is partly nasalized. Likewise, the voicing characteristic of a particular sound may be discontinued in anticipation of a following voiceless sound—in saying *imp,* the tail end of [m] is devoiced in anticipation of the following voiceless [p]. Figure 4–1 presents a spectrogram that illustrates how the utterance *Weren't you here yesterday?* appears acoustically. There isn't any separation between sounds within words or between one word and the next. In the same way, the acoustic signal an infant's ears pick up is continuous, and part of a child's task is to sort out words within sentences and sounds within words.

Figure 4-1

Sound Spectrogram of Utterance: *Weren't you here yesterday?*

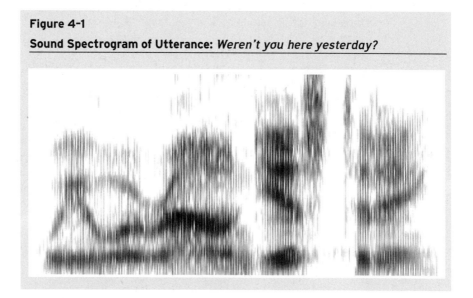

What must a child understand in order to know a word of its language? Well, to know a word is to know its meaning and its sounds. Children pass through stages in learning words, and there is some disagreement about how they succeed at this task. Some children appear to take up phrases and clauses in utterances as whole units and later dissect them into parts (this is called a gestalt approach). Others manage a more analytic approach from the start, taking up words directly and constructing phrases and clauses from them as necessary. All children eventually sort utterances into distinct units of meaning.

Focusing on one crucial ingredient, we can ask what kind of information a child must learn about the sounds of a word. What is needed just to recognize a word? For one thing, children must recognize pronunciations of a given word by different people as the same word. To understand speech it is essential to disregard certain voice characteristics and particularities of volume, speed, and pitch.

A child must observe a word's sounds and the order in which they occur—that *bad,* for example, contains the three sounds [b], [æ], and [d] in exactly that order. After all, *bad* and *dab* have the same sounds but are not the same word.

Phonemes and Allophones

Eventually every child also learns that sounds are pronounced differently in different contexts; in other words, that the "same sound" can have more than one pronunciation. Consider that English speakers aren't generally aware of the fact that the words *cop* [kɑp] and *keep* [kip] begin with different [k] sounds. You can notice the difference if you alternately pronounce the two words. Notice where your tongue touches the roof of your mouth at the very beginning of each word, and you'll see that it touches the velum farther back for *cop* than for *keep.* Here's why: [ɑ] is a back vowel and [i] is a front vowel, and in anticipation of pronouncing the back vowel in *cop* you pronounce the [k] farther back in your mouth than you do for the [k] that precedes the front vowel [i] in *keep.*

Try it yourself: Position your tongue as if to say *keep*. Once your tongue is in position for the initial sound of *keep,* say *cop* instead. You'll find that you must reposition your tongue to do it; if you say *cop* from the *keep* position, it will sound peculiar or foreign. The need to reposition the back of your tongue to achieve a natural pronunciation demonstrates that the *k*-like sounds of *keep* and *cop* are not identical.

As a second example, you should be able to identify differences in the sounds represented by <p> in *pot* and *spot* or *poke* and *spoke*. Hold the back of your hand up to your mouth when saying these word pairs, and you'll notice a considerable difference in the puff of air that accompanies the sounds represented by <p>. The <p> sound in *pot* and *poke* is an aspirated stop, represented as [pʰ]. The sound following <s> in *spot* and *spoke* is not aspirated; we represent it as [p].

Try it yourself: The aspiration accompanying the [p] sound in *pot* and *poke* is strong enough to blow out a lighted match held in front of the mouth. Be careful! The [p] sound following [s] in *spot* and *spoke* is not aspirated and will not blow out the match. You might try saying *spot, spot, spot,* followed by a single *pot.* If everything is positioned correctly, saying *spot* will leave the match burning but *pot* will blow it out.

In discussing these two *p* sounds, we have noted that they occur in different positions within words. Examine the following list of words to identify the positions in which unaspirated [p] and aspirated [pʰ] occur.

pill	[pʰɪl]
poker	[pʰokər]
plate	[pʰlet]
spill	[spɪl]
sprint	[sprɪnt]
spine	[spajn]

Notice in our list that aspirated [pʰ] occurs only at the beginning of words (*pill, poker, plate*), and unaspirated [p] occurs only after [s] (*spill, sprint, spine*). When you have two sounds and neither can occur where the other one occurs in a word, we say they are in **complementary distribution.**

In the words listed above, aspirated [pʰ] occurs only word initially, and unaspirated [p] occurs only after [s]. By definition, then, [pʰ] and [p] occur in complementary distribution; they could not occur in the same position in a word and therefore cannot distinguish one word from another. We conclude that [pʰ] and [p] are not distinctive sounds in English words. Instead, they constitute a single unit of the English sound system; they are called *allophones* of a single *phoneme*—in this case, allophones of the phoneme /p/. A **phoneme** is a structural element in the sound system of a language. **Allophones** are realizations of a single structural element in the sound system of a language. Allophones of a given phoneme cannot create different words, so we say they are noncontrastive. To native speakers allophones are perceived as the same sound despite the physical difference. Given that, in English, aspirated [pʰ] and unaspirated [p] are allophones of the phoneme /p/, there could not be a pair of English words such as [pʰit] and [pit]. Likewise the two [k] sounds of *cop* and *keep* are allophones of the phoneme /k/ in English and cannot make contrasting words.

Note: We have now started using slanted lines / / to enclose phonemes and square brackets [ ] to enclose allophones. We will continue this practice, though sometimes we will have to choose one representation or the other when either would serve as well. (Angled brackets < > enclose letters.)

Besides the aspirated and unaspirated allophones of /p/, there is a third voiceless bilabial stop in English, which can occur in a word like *mop.* This third allophone can occur at the end of a word when that word happens to occur at the end of an utterance:

Where's the mop? In this position, the lips may remain closed so that the <p> sound is not released. We represent this allophone as [p˺]. Now here's a slight complication. In this case we don't have complementary distribution because both unaspirated [p] and unreleased [p˺] can occur in the same position (word finally) in a word. When two sounds can occur in the same position in a word but do not contrast—that is, without creating different words—those sounds are said to occur in **free variation.** At the end of an utterance, English speakers can pronounce *lip* as [lɪp] or [lɪp˺]. Both unaspirated and unreleased voiceless bilabial stops are allophones of /p/, and /p/ therefore has three allophones: aspirated [pʰ], unaspirated [p], and unreleased [p˺]. To repeat, the allophones of a phoneme occur in complementary distribution or in free variation; in neither case can a change of meaning be signaled by the different allophones.

Distribution of Allophones

It may be helpful to view a phoneme as an abstract element in the sound system of a language—a skeleton unit of sound that lacks a fully specified pronunciation but will be pronounced in a specific way depending on where it occurs in a word. For example, while the phoneme /p/ would have the skeletal features *voiceless bilabial stop,* one allophone might be aspirated, another unaspirated, and a third unreleased. The pronunciation of the phoneme /p/ cannot be fully specified unless its position in a word (or utterance) is known. Only then can its aspiration and release be determined.

We have just seen that particular allophones are determined by where they occur. If you examine the sets of words in Table 4–1, you'll see that the picture is a bit more complicated. In these words the accent mark (´) indicates the syllable on which the primary stress falls (as in *rídicule* versus *ridículous*).

Table 4-1
Allophones of /p/ in English Words

A	B	C	D
[pʰ]	[pʰ]	[pʰ]	[p]
pédigree	petúnia	empórium	rápid
pérsonal	patérnal	compúter	émpathy
pérsecute	península	rapídograph	competítion
pílgrimage	pecúliar	compétitive	computátional

All the words have /p/ in syllable-initial position. The words in column A have primary stress on the first syllable, with [pʰ] as the initial sound. Those in column B also have aspirated [pʰ] word initially, though primary stress occurs on the second syllable. The words in columns A and B demonstrate that /p/ is aspirated word initially whether it appears in a stressed or unstressed syllable. In column C, aspirated [pʰ] introduces the second syllable, which carries primary stress in each case. Thus aspirated [pʰ] occurs not only word initially but also word internally when it introduces a stressed syllable. The words in column D demonstrate that unaspirated [p] occurs word internally when introducing unstressed syllables. In summary, the phoneme /p/ is aspirated word initially in stressed and unstressed syllables, but it is aspirated word internally only when it initiates a stressed syllable.

Given these observations, we can be more precise in describing the distribution of the allophones of /p/, taking account of stress patterns in a word. This we do in Table 4–2.

Table 4-2

Two Allophones of English /p/

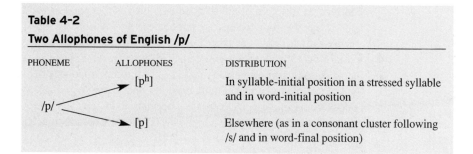

PHONEME	ALLOPHONES	DISTRIBUTION
/p/	[pʰ]	In syllable-initial position in a stressed syllable and in word-initial position
	[p]	Elsewhere (as in a consonant cluster following /s/ and in word-final position)

Contrast these facts about aspirated [pʰ] and unaspirated [p] with the facts about /p/ and /s/. If a child aiming to say the word *sat* said *pat* instead, he or she would have failed to observe one of the significant differences in English pronunciation. That's because /p/ and /s/ are separate phonemes and can distinguish words, as in the word pairs below:

A	B	C	D
[pɪt] pit	[pʌn] pun	[læpt] lapped	[sip] seep
[sɪt] sit	[sʌn] sun	[læst] last	[sis] cease

The words in each pair have different meanings and differ by only a single sound. Two words that differ by only a single sound constitute a **minimal pair.** (Note that the distinction depends on sounds, not spelling.) Minimal pairs are valuable in identifying the contrastive sounds—the phonemes—of a language. Each minimal pair above demonstrates that /s/ and /p/ are separate phonemes of English and not allophones of a single phoneme. Articulatory descriptions of /s/ and /p/ show that they differ in both place and manner of articulation.

	/s/	/p/
VOICING	voiceless	voiceless
PLACE OF ARTICULATION	alveolar	bilabial
MANNER OF ARTICULATION	fricative	stop

To take another example, /s/ and /b/ differ from one another not only in place and manner of articulation but also in voicing.

	/s/	**/b/**
VOICING	voiceless	voiced
PLACE OF ARTICULATION	alveolar	bilabial
MANNER OF ARTICULATION	fricative	stop

/s/ is a voiceless alveolar fricative, /b/ a voiced bilabial stop. The fact that /s/ and /b/ contrast (as in the minimal pair *sat/bat*) proves that they are significantly different sounds. They belong to separate phonemes.

Sounds (allophones) that belong to a single phoneme share certain phonetic features but differ in at least one other feature. This may be related to voicing (voiced vs. voiceless), aspiration (aspirated vs. unaspirated), manner of articulation (e.g., stop vs. fricative), or place of articulation (e.g., dental vs. alveolar). When analyzing the sound system of a language, it is important to take particular note of the distributions of sounds that have similar phonetic descriptions. Consider this list of English words:

[pʰæt]   pat

[bæt]   bat

[tʰæp]   tap

[tʰæb]   tab

[spæt]   spat

[pʰ] and [b] are both bilabial stops; they share those two features. On the other hand, [pʰ] is voiceless and aspirated, while [b] is voiced and unaspirated. Are they separate phonemes or allophones of a single phoneme? We cannot answer that question by examining the phonetic descriptions alone. But, because there is a minimal pair above, we know that [pʰ] and [b] contrast. That is, *pat/bat* demonstrates that [pʰ] and [b] belong to different phonemes. On the other hand, since there are no examples in English in which aspirated [pʰ] and unaspirated [p] contrast (in fact, they occur in complementary distribution), [pʰ] and [p] are allophones of a single phoneme. From the minimal pair *tap/tab* above (two words that differ by just one sound), we know that unaspirated [p] contrasts with [b]; thus aspirated [pʰ] and unaspirated [p]—both voiceless bilabial stops—contrast with the voiced bilabial stop [b].

The phonemes /p/ and /b/ contrast in word-initial and word-final position, as we saw. But sometimes two sounds contrast in some positions but not in all positions. Two sounds are distinctive if they contrast in any position. Consider the position following /s/ as in the word *s__at:* there aren't two words of English like *sbat* and *spat* that carry different meanings. Even though /p/ and /b/ are different phonemes in English, the contrast between them is not exploited in the position following /s/.

Now consider the situation in Korean. Like English, Korean has the three bilabial stops [pʰ], [p], and [b], as in the following words:

[pʰul] 'grass'

[pul] 'fire'

[pəp] 'law'

[mubəp] 'lawlessness'

The minimal pair [pʰul] and [pul] demonstrates that [p] and [pʰ] contrast in Korean. On the other hand, even with a large sample of words you could not find a minimal pair in which [p] contrasts with [b]. The reason is that in Korean [p] and [b] are in complementary distribution: [b] occurs only between vowels and other voiced segments, as in [mubəp], and [p] never occurs in that environment. This demonstrates that [p] and [pʰ] are separate phonemes in Korean, but that [p] and [b] are allophones of a single phoneme.

Table 4-3

Three Sounds of English and Korean Compared

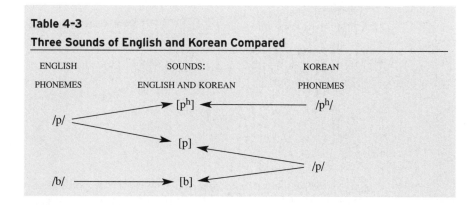

The diagram in Table 4–3 captures the difference in the phonological systems of English and Korean with respect to these three sounds. The same three sounds occur in both languages, but their systematic relationships in those languages are different. In English, [pʰ] and [p] are noncontrastive allophones of a single phoneme and therefore cannot signal a meaning difference. In Korean, [pʰ] and [p] are contrastively different sounds; that is, they *are* separate phonemes and *can* distinguish one word from another (as in [pʰul] and [pul]). We can say that voicing is phonemic in English (the *voiced* bilabial stop [b] is distinct from the *voiceless* bilabial stop [p]). Aspiration, however, is not phonemic in English (no two English phonemes differ from one another solely in aspiration). In Korean, on the other hand, the voiced bilabial stop [b] is an allophone of /p/: [b] occurs predictably between voiced sounds; hence [b] and [p] cannot distinguish Korean words.

To summarize: in Korean, voicing is not contrastive but aspiration is; in English, aspiration is not contrastive but voicing is.

PHONOLOGICAL RULES AND THEIR STRUCTURE

You're probably aware that French has nasal vowels, and you may think that English lacks nasal vowels. In fact, though, English does have nasal vowels. Let's look closely at them. In Table 4–4, the words in column B have nasalized vowels (vowels pronounced through the nose, in addition to the mouth), while those in column A have oral vowels (vowels pronounced through the mouth). When you pronounce the words of column B, air from the lungs exits through the nasal passage; hence when that passage is blocked, the sound of the vowel changes perceptibly.

Try it yourself: Pinch your nose closed while saying the words in each column of Table 4–4. You'll discover that for the words in column A it will make no perceptible difference; for those in column B it will make a striking difference.

Table 4-4

Oral and Nasal Vowels in English

A	B
sit	sin
pet	pen
light	lime
brute	broom
sitter	singer

If you search out nasal vowels in English words, you'll discover that *all* of them precede one of the nasal consonants /m n ŋ/. That's another way of saying that the distribution of nasal vowels in English is regular and predictable: a vowel is nasalized before a nasal consonant. Since the distribution is predictable in English, the occurrence of nasal vowels cannot signal a meaning distinction. (Of course, in French and in other languages where its distribution is not predictable, nasalization can signal a difference in meaning.) Two sounds whose distribution with respect to one another is predictable constitute allophones of a single phoneme; their distribution is describable by a general rule.

Phonological rules have this general form:

A ➔ B / C___D

You can read a rule like that as "A becomes B in the environment following C and preceding D" or, more simply, as "A becomes B following C and preceding D." A, B, C, and D are generally specified in terms of phonological features, although in this book rules will be presented more informally. In cases where it is unnecessary to specify both C and D, one of them will be missing. For example, the phonological process of nasalization can be represented by the following statement:

Nasalization rule

vowel ➜ nasal / ___ nasal

(Vowels are nasalized when they precede nasal sounds.)

We said earlier that in acquiring a word a child must learn the number of phonemes in the word, what those phonemes are, and the order in which they occur. As the English *cop/keep* alternation shows for the allophones of /k/, and as the *poke/spoke* alternation shows for the allophones of /p/, a child must also learn to pronounce particular allophones of a phoneme depending on the phoneme's position in a word and the character of nearby sounds. This is done not by memorizing the sounds in each individual word but by acquiring rules that apply to all words, as with the nasalization rule above.

The situation for a child acquiring Korean [p] and [b] is parallel to that of an English-speaking child acquiring nasal vowels. Since [p] and [b] never contrast in Korean, they are allophones of a single phoneme in that language, and only one form is needed to represent them in the lexicon. Of course, speakers of Korean must also know the phonological rule that specifies the distribution of the allophones: [b] between vowels and [p] elsewhere. The alternative to having a single representation in the lexicon for [p] and [b] in Korean could involve considerable inefficiency. It would require a specific differentiation between these sounds in every word that contains either of them. For example, *pəp* 'law' and *mubəp* 'lawlessness' would have different specifications for [p] and [b]. To speakers of English (which does not have a predictable distribution of [p] and [b] because they are separate phonemes), this differentiation seems natural and necessary. But to have different forms for [p] and [b] in the lexicon of a Korean speaker would be equivalent to an English speaker's having different representations in the lexicon for the different /k/ sounds of *cop* and *keep*, for the different /p/ sounds of *poke* and *spoke,* and for the different /i/ sounds of *seat* and *seen.* Instead, each phoneme is represented in the lexicon by only a single underlying form. Native speakers internalize the phonological rules specifying the distribution of allophones and automatically apply the rules wherever the phoneme appears.

Generalizing Phonological Rules

Until now we have considered phonological rules as though they were formulated to apply to particular sounds; in fact, they are more general. Consider the aspiration that accompanies the production of initial /p/ in English words like *pillow* and *pot:*

1. For /p/:
   voiceless
   bilabial   ➜ aspirated / word initially and initially in stressed syllables
   stop

This rule says that a voiceless bilabial stop is aspirated in specific environments.

Why English Speakers Speak French with a Foreign Accent

In foreign accents you can notice one indication that information such as the differences between allophones is not stored in the lexicon but is determined by regular rules. Consider a native speaker of English who knows no French and has been introduced by a French speaker to a neighbor named Pierre. English speakers aspirate initial voiceless stops like /p/ (they are pronounced with a puff of air) but French speakers do not. So the French speaker introducing Pierre will pronounce his name without aspiration. Despite the fact that the English speaker has *not* heard aspiration in the pronunciation of *Pierre,* he or she will tend to pronounce *Pierre* with an aspirated [pʰ], making it conform to the phonological rules of English (rather than French). This indicates that English speakers have a rule that aspirates initial /p/ (even when pronouncing French names). The subconscious application of the phonolog-ical rules of your native tongue to a foreign language is one main factor that contributes to a foreign accent and marks you as a non-native speaker.

On the other side of the coin, when you speak a foreign language you may fail to make a necessary distinction. English distinguishes between the *k* sounds of *cop* and *keep,* and it does so by rule. English speakers don't have to learn separately for *cop* and *keep* which *k* sound to use. But in some languages—including Basque, Malay, and Vietnamese—these two sounds are contrastive; they are separate phonemes. The initial sound of *cop* is represented by [k] and of *keep* by [c]. In languages like Basque, Malay, and Vietnamese, it is critical to know which velar stop occurs in a word, just as English speakers must know whether /p/ or /t/ occurs, because those sounds are not distributed by rule and are not predictable.

If you examine other English words with stop consonants, you'll discover that, besides /p/, /t/ and /k/ also have aspiration when they are syllable initial. Since /p t k/ have parallel distributions of aspirated allophones, English would appear to need two additional rules like rule 1—rule 2 for /t/ and rule 3 for /k/.

2. For /t/:

    voiceless
    alveolar ➔ aspirated / word initially and initially in stressed syllables
    stop

3. For /k/:

    voiceless
    velar   ➔ aspirated / word initially and initially in stressed syllables
    stop

Because these three rules exhaust the list of voiceless stops in English, they can be collapsed into a single rule of greater generality covering /p/, /t/, and /k/, as follows:

4. For /p t k/:

    voiceless
    stop   ➔ aspirated / word initially and initially in stressed syllables

Notice in rule 4 that the combination of the features "voiceless" and "stop" leaves the place of articulation unspecified. Thus, a phonological rule like 4 will apply to all voiceless stops irrespective of their place of articulation. In particular, it will apply to bilabial, alveolar, and velar voiceless stops—to /p/, /t/, and /k/.

The more general a rule is, the simpler it is to state the rule using phonetic feature notation, and there is evidence that internalized phonological rules are specified not in terms of allophones such as [p] and [pʰ], nor in terms of phonemes such as /p/, /t/, and /k/, but in terms of classes of sounds specified by sets of phonetic features such as "voiceless" and "stop."

Natural Classes of Sounds

A set of phonemes such as /p t k/ that can be described using fewer features than would be necessary to describe each sound individually is called a **natural class of sounds.** A natural class of sounds contains all the sounds that share a particular set of features. For example, /p t k/ constitute the natural class of "voiceless stops" in English. /p t k/ share the two features "voiceless" and "stop," and there are no other sounds in English that have both of those features.

Now consider the set /p t k b d g/. This is the natural class of stops. There are no other stops in English, and all the sounds in the set share the feature "stop."

The sounds /p t k b d/ do not constitute a natural class. These five sounds share the feature "stop"—but so does /g/, which is not included. Whatever feature we use to describe the set /p t k b d/ would also describe /g/. Notice too that /p t k m/ does not constitute a natural class because any feature introduced to specify /m/ would also characterize other sounds. Adding the feature "nasal" to the description in order to accommodate /m/ entails including /n/ and /ŋ/, because they are also nasals. Notice, however, that in order to specify the set /p t k m n ŋ/ we need an "either/or" description: either "voiceless stop" or "nasal." Because there is no combination of features that uniquely specifies just those six sounds, /p t k m n ŋ/ is not a natural class of sounds.

Underlying Forms

Thanks to internalized rules that yield the correct allophones for every phoneme in a given word, children eventually can produce entries in their lexicons like those in Table 4–5 on page 122. Such forms are called **underlying forms;** we will represent them between slanted lines, using the same notation we have used for phonemes. The **surface form,** which characterizes a word's actual pronunciation, results from the application of the phonological rules of English to the underlying forms. In some cases the surface form is the same as the underlying form simply because there are no applicable phonological rules.

Table 4-5

Underlying and Surface Forms for Six English Words

UNDERLYING FORM	RULE	SURFACE FORM	WRITTEN FORM
/kʌlər/	aspiration	[kʰʌlər]	color
/bʊk/	none	[bʊk]	book
/bit/	none	[bit]	beat
/ʌp/	none	[ʌp]	up
/spɪn/	nasalization	[spĩn]	spin
/pɪn/	aspiration/nasalization	[pʰĩn]	pin

Rule Ordering

One additional phonological rule will illustrate a point about the organization of phonological rules in the internalized grammar. Consider the following words:

A	B		A	B
write	ride		treat	treed
neat	need		cute	cued
rope	robe		root	rude
lop	lob		moat	mowed
lock	log		wrote	road
tap	tab		clout	cloud
pick	pig		boot	booed

If you listen carefully while pronouncing these words aloud, you may notice that the vowels in column B are longer in duration than those in the corresponding words of column A. In phonetic symbols, we represent long vowels with a colon after them, as in [aː]. Since English has no minimal pair such as [pit]/[piːt] or [bæt]/[bæːt], vowel length cannot be contrastive in English. Instead, it is predictable; vowel length can be specified by a phonological rule. If you look past the spelling, you'll note that all the words of column A end with a voiceless consonant /t p k/, and all the words of column B end in a voiced consonant /d b g/. English lengthens vowels when they precede voiced consonants. Using V to represent vowel and C to represent consonant, we can state the rule as follows:

Lengthening Rule

V → Vː / ___ C
      voiced

(Vowels are lengthened preceding voiced consonants.)

As a result of this rule, the following processes take place in English:

ε → εː / ___ /d/ (as in *bed* versus *bet*)

o → oː / ___ /g/ (as in *brogue* versus *broke*)

aj → aːj / ___ /d/ (as in *slide* versus *slight*)

(Note that this rule applies to diphthongs like /aj/.) English vowel length is predictable and can be specified by rule; vowel length need not be learned for each word individually. In some other languages, vowel length is *not* predictable and must be learned word by word. For example, Fijian has a minimal pair *oya*, meaning 'he, she,' and *oyaa*, meaning 'that (thing).' *Dredre* means 'to laugh'; *dreedree* means 'difficult.' *Vakariri* means 'to boil'; *vakaririi* means 'speedily.' Thus Fijian vowel length cannot be assigned by a phonological rule. It is contrastive, distinctive, phonemic in that language.

Now consider the following pairs of words, paying attention to how the pronunciation of each word in column A differs from the pronunciation of the corresponding word in column B. You'll notice that the difference in pronunciation is not the one represented by the spellings <t> and <d>. Instead, the difference is in vowel length. For most dialects of American English, the first vowel in each word of column B is longer than that in the corresponding word of column A.

A	B
writer	rider
liter	leader
seater	seeder
rooter	ruder

The medial consonants <t> and <d> do not represent different pronunciations because Americans tend to flap (or "tap") /t/ and /d/ between vowels in these words. In the pronunciation of /t/ or /d/ in words like those above, the tip of the tongue rapidly taps the alveolar ridge. Because the flap allophones of /t/ and /d/ are identical (IPA [ɾ]), the difference of pronunciation that might have resulted from the *t*/*d* distinction is lost, or **neutralized.** The distinction is not lost in the words *write* [rajt] and *ride* [raːjd]. Again using V to represent any vowel, the flapping rule for American English is this:

Flapping Rule

$$\begin{matrix} \text{alveolar} \\ \text{stop} \end{matrix} \quad → \quad \text{flap} \quad \Big/ \quad \begin{matrix} \text{V}\_\_\_\text{V} \\ \text{unstressed} \end{matrix}$$

(/t/, /d/ are realized as [ɾ] between two vowels, the second of which is unstressed.)

Even though the flapping rule neutralizes the *t*/*d* distinction in this environment, many Americans pronounce the column B words differently from those in column A—and the reason is interesting. By combining the flapping rule and the lengthening rule, speakers of American English pronounce the words in column B with a vowel of longer duration, despite the fact that there is no difference in the pronunciation of the medial consonant. Here's one explanation for how it works.

We've specified two rules of English that can operate on the same words. Let's examine how they interact in producing a pronounceable surface form. Consider the pair of words *writer* and *rider*. Assume that the underlying forms in the lexicon are /rajtər/ for *writer* and /rajdər/ for *rider*. We can represent the derivation of the surface forms as in Table 4–6. (When the form of a word does not meet the requirements of a rule, the rule does not apply, so we write *DNA.*) From the underlying forms and the application of the two rules in the order shown (lengthening first, flapping second), the surface forms [rajɾər] and [raːjɾər] are produced. This is the correct pronunciation of these words for some speakers. Let's call them speakers of dialect A.

Table 4-6
Derivation of *Writer* and *Rider* in Dialect A

	WRITER	RIDER	
Underlying form	/rajtər/	/rajdər/	(input)
Lengthening rule	DNA	applies ↓	
Derived form	[rajtər]	[raːjdər]	(output/input)
Flapping rule	applies ↓	applies ↓	
Surface form	[rajɾər]	[raːjɾər]	(output)

If we apply the same rules in the reverse order (flapping first, lengthening second), the results will be different. Here's why: because the flapped sound is voiced, the vowel preceding it is lengthened in both words. As Table 4–7 on page 125 shows, this is precisely what happens for speakers of another variety of English. Call it dialect B.

The two identical surface forms [raːjɾər] and [raːjɾər] that are derived by applying the flapping rule prior to the lengthening rule would not be correct for dialect A. In dialect A (the more common dialect), *writer* and *rider* are not pronounced alike. Instead, *rider* has a longer vowel than *writer*. Even beginning from the same underlying forms and with the same pair of phonological rules, applying them in one order produces correct surface forms for a given dialect; but if applied in the other order, the rules produce incorrect forms. Evidence such as this has led some researchers to hypothesize that rule ordering is part of the organization of phonological rules.

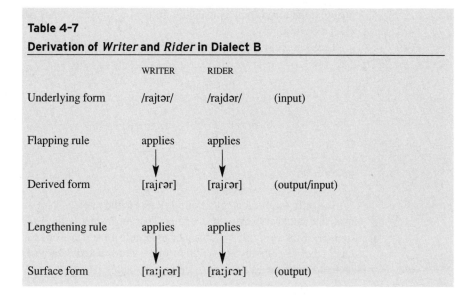

Table 4-7

Derivation of *Writer* and *Rider* in Dialect B

	WRITER	RIDER	
Underlying form	/rajtər/	/rajdər/	(input)
Flapping rule	applies ↓	applies ↓	
Derived form	[rajɾər]	[rajɾər]	(output/input)
Lengthening rule	applies ↓	applies ↓	
Surface form	[raːjɾər]	[raːjɾɔr]	(output)

Note that the forms resulting from the second derivation (Table 4–7), though incorrect in dialect A, are correct in dialect B. This illustrates how speakers of different dialects can share the same underlying forms and the same rules but produce different surface forms as a result of ordering the rules differently. Dialects with lengthening before flapping will have different forms of *writer* and *rider.* Dialects with flapping before lengthening will produce identical forms with a long vowel.

SYLLABLES AND SYLLABLE STRUCTURE

So far we've said little about how sounds are organized within words (although our analyses have presumed a certain organization, as you'll see). It may seem obvious that sounds occur in words as a sequence *abcdef,* but that isn't the whole story. Sounds are organized into syllables, and syllables are organized into words. Each word consists of one or more syllables, and each syllable consists of one or more sounds.

"Syllable" is not a tough notion to grasp intuitively, and there is considerable agreement in counting syllables. But technical definitions have proven challenging. Still, there is agreement that a **syllable** is a phonological unit consisting of one or more sounds and that syllables can be divided into two parts—a rhyme and an onset. The **rhyme** consists of a nucleus and any consonants following it. The **nucleus** is usually a vowel, although certain consonants called sonorants can also function as a nucleus. **Sonorants** include nasals like [m] and [n] and liquids like [r] and [l]. Consider the words *button, butter,* and *bottle,* whose second syllables we represent as [əC], containing a vowel and a consonant. These same words could be represented as [bʌtn̩], [bʌɾɹ̩], and [bɑɾl̩], where the diacritic [̩] under the sonorants [n r l] indicates that they are the nucleus of a syllable. Consonants that precede the rhyme in a syllable constitute the **onset.** Any consonants following the nucleus as part of the rhyme are called the **coda.**

The chart below represents the structure of a syllable as just described.

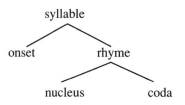

The only essential element of a syllable is the nucleus. Not every syllable has an onset, and not every rhyme has a coda. That means that a single sound can constitute a syllable. Since a single syllable can constitute a word, a word can consist of a single vowel—but you already knew that from the words *a* and *I*. Table 4–8 gives some English words with one, two, three, and four syllables.

Table 4-8

English Words Divided into Syllables

1 SYLLABLE	2 SYLLABLES	3 SYLLABLES	4 SYLLABLES
ton	even	loveliest	anybody
[tʰʌn]	[i-vən]	[lʌv-li-əst]	[ɛ-ni-bɑ-ri]
spin	although	anyone	respectively
[spɪn]	[ɔl-ðo]	[ɛ-ni-wən]	[ri-spɛk-təv-li]
through	consists	computer	algebraic
[θru]	[kən-sɪsts]	[kəm-pʰju-ɾər]	[æl-dʒə-bre-ək]
sail	writer	syllable	definition
[sel]	[raj-ɾər]	[sɪ-lə-bəl]	[dɛ-fə-nɪ-ʃən]

Sequence Constraints

The possible sequences of sounds in a syllable differ from language to language and are limited within each language. If you examine the phrase below, you'll notice that English syllables allow several patterns of consonants (C) and vowels (V). (We use dashes to separate syllables within a word.)

in a pre-vi-ous cap-tion

ɪn ə pri vi əs kæpʃən

VC V CCV-CV-VC CVC-CVC

You can see that English permits several syllable types: VC, V, CCV, CV, and CVC. Some other permissible types can be seen in words of one syllable like these:

past	/pæst/	CVCC		queen	/kwin/	CCVC
turned	/tərnd/	CVCCC		squirts	/skwərts/	CCCVCCC

Not every language allows such a wide variety of syllable types. The preferred syllable type among the world's languages is a single consonant followed by a single vowel: CV. Other common types are CVC and a simple V. (All three types occur in the illustrative phrase above.) Polynesian languages like Samoan, Tahitian, and Hawaiian have only CV and V syllables. Japanese also allows syllables basically of the forms CV and V, as well as CVC (but only when the second C is a nasal). Korean permits V, CV, and CVC syllables. Mandarin permits syllables of the forms V, CV, and (if the second consonant is [n] or [ŋ]) CVC.

It is not common in the languages of the world to have onset consonant clusters—CC—as in the English words *try, twin,* and *stop,* and it is very uncommon to have onset consonant clusters of more than two consonants—CCC—as in *scream, sprint,* and *stress.* Even English has a limited range of consonants that can occur as C_1 and C_2 of a two-consonant onset cluster (C_1C_2) and an extremely narrow range of consonants in each of the positions $C_1C_2C_3$ of a three-consonant onset cluster. (It is no coincidence that all three illustrations of initial CCC begin with /s/.) Likewise, English three-consonant onset clusters have different constraints from those clusters that constitute the coda.

Try it yourself: Cite three English words that have onset clusters of three consonants. What sound do they all begin with? What sounds occur as C_2? What about C_3? Can you think of any onset clusters that have a different C_2 or a different C_3? What are they?

The rules that characterize permissible syllable structures in a language are called **sequence constraints** (or **phonotactic constraints**), and they determine what constitutes a possible syllable. As a result of such constraints, there are—besides the words that do exist in a language—thousands more that *do not* exist but could, and there are thousands upon thousands that *could not* exist because their syllable structures are not permissible sequences of consonants and vowels in that language. The following would be impossible words in Hawaiian and Japanese because they violate the sequence constraints of those languages: *pat* (CVC), *pleat* (CCVC), and *spa* (CCV).

Sniglets

Comedian Rich Hall has compiled lists of "sniglets" for English—words that do not appear in the dictionary but should. Here are a few of those sniglets and their proposed definitions.

charp 'the green mutant potato chip found in every bag'

elbonics 'the actions of two people maneuvering for one armrest in a movie theater' *glarpo* 'the juncture of the ear and skull where pencils are stored'

hozone 'the place where one sock in every laundry disappears to'

spibble 'the metal barrier on a rotary telephone that prevents you from dialing past O'

Sniglets conform to the sequence constraints of English.

Try it yourself: Because the following forms violate the sequence constraints of English, they could not serve as sniglets: *ptlin, brkow, tsmtot, ngang.* Add three more to the list.

Learning a foreign language whose syllable structure differs from one's native tongue, speakers tend to impose the sequence constraints of their native syllables onto the foreign words. For example, neither Spanish nor Persian permits onset clusters such as /st/ and /sp/, which is why speakers of those languages may pronounce the English words *study* and *speech* as /ɛs-tʌdi/ and /ɛs-pitʃ/, pronunciations that conform to the sequence constraints of Spanish and Persian. Similarly, the words *baseball* and *strike* have been borrowed by Japanese speakers as *beesubooru* and *sutoraiku,* forms that obey the sequence constraints of Japanese.

STRESS

A shopworn aphorism among American linguists points out that "Not every white house is the White House, and not every black bird is a blackbird." The point is that *stress* patterns can be significant. In pronouncing the phrase *every white house,* relatively strong stress is given to both *white* and *house: whíte hóuse.* In referring to the official residence of the American president, relatively strong stress is assigned to *White* but only secondary stress to *House: Whíte Hòuse.* The stress pattern assigned to the name of the president's residence matches that in the word *téachèr: Whíte Hòuse.* The stress pattern of the same words in the phrase *(every) whíte hóuse* does not. From the fact that stress can vary and that the meanings of the two expressions differ, it follows that stress can be contrastive in English. Below is a list of several other word pairs. The pairs in column A are distinct words—they constitute noun phrases, comprising an adjective and a noun (as well as an article); the stress patterns of the pairs in column B match the pattern of *téachèr*—they constitute compound nouns.

A	B
a bláck bóard	a bláckbòard
a blúe bírd	a blúebìrd
a hígh cháir	a híghchàir
a réd néck	a rédnèck
a jét pláne	a jétstrèam
an íced téa	an íce crèam
a yéllow jácket (clothing)	a yéllow jàcket (a kind of wasp)

English has variable stress, not fixed stress. So do some other languages, including German. Many others have fixed stress, where stress is assigned to a particular syllable in words. In Polish and Swahili words, stress typically falls on the next to last syllable (called the penultimate syllable). Czech words carry stress on the first syllable. French words usually carry stress on the last syllable.

Try it yourself: Think of three English phrases like *a réd néck* that have matching or near matching parallel compounds (which may be written as one word—*rédnèck*—or two—*íce crèam*).

SYLLABLES AND STRESS IN PHONOLOGICAL PROCESSES

We saw above that certain phonological rules depend for their formulation on the syllable, on stress, or on both stress and the syllable. Aspiration of the English voiceless stops /p t k/ occurs "word initially and initially in stressed syllables" (page 120). Such a formulation assumes that words are organized into syllables. In turn, that means that children must have some grasp of how words are organized into syllables. The flapping rule that produces [rajɾər] for *writer* and [mɛɾəl] for *metal* also relies on stress, and by now you can probably imagine that the flapping rule could be formulated in terms of syllables instead of vowel segments, which is how we formulated it on page 123. Current models of words use multiple tiers to accommodate phonologically significant levels, including segments, syllables, and stress.

THE INTERACTION OF MORPHOLOGY AND PHONOLOGY

Before leaving the subject of phonology, let's examine the pronunciation of the most productive inflectional suffixes of English and see the striking regularity in the patterns.

English Plural, Possessive, and Third-Person Singular Morphemes

Regular nouns have several pronunciations of the plural morpheme, as in *lips* [lɪp + s], *seeds* [sid + z], and *fuses* [fjuz + əz]. The surface forms for these different pronunciations of a morpheme are called its **allomorphs.** As the following lists demonstrate, the allomorphs of the plural morpheme are determined by the character of the final sound of the singular form.

Allomorphs of the English 'plural' morpheme

[əz]	[s]	[z]
bushes	cats	pens
judges	tips	seeds
peaches	books	dogs
buses	whiffs	cars
fuses	births	rays

These lists indicate the pattern of distribution for the plural allomorphs of English.

1. [əz] occurs on nouns ending in /s z ʃ ʒ tʃ dʒ/ (a natural class called *sibilants).*

2. [s] occurs following all other *voiceless* sounds.

3. [z] occurs following all other *voiced* sounds.

You may want to think of arguments for positing one of the three allomorphs as the abstract underlying form of the plural morpheme. We will assume that it is /z/. From this underlying form, all three allomorphs must be derivable by general rules that apply to all regular nouns.

From an underlying /z/, a rule such as the following would derive the [əz] allomorph that follows sibilants; note that + marks a morpheme boundary and # marks a word boundary.

Schwa Insertion Rule A

/z/ ➜ [əz] / sibilant + ___ #

(Schwa is inserted before a word-final /z/ that follows a morpheme ending in a sibilant.)

In order to derive the allomorph [s] from the underlying morpheme /z/ following voiceless sounds, a rule that partially assimilates the voiced /z/ to the unvoiced sound of the stem morpheme would be needed.

Assimilation Rule A

/z/ ➜ voiceless / voiceless + ___ #

(Word-final /z/ is devoiced following a morpheme that ends in a voiceless sound.)

In order to derive the correct forms of all regular plural nouns, these two rules must have considerable generality. Table 4–9 illustrates this for the nouns *coops, judges,* and *weeds.* (*DNA* means a rule does not apply because some necessary condition is missing; slanted lines / / represent underlying forms; square brackets [ ] represent forms derived by application of a phonological rule.)

Table 4-9
Derivation of English Plural Nouns

	COOPS	PIECES	WEEDS
Underlying forms	/kup+z/	/pis+z/	/wid+z/
Schwa insertion	DNA	applies ↓	DNA
Derived form	[kup+z]	[pis+əz]	[wid+z]
Assimilation	applies ↓	DNA	DNA
Surface form	[kup+s]	[pis+əz]	[wid+z]

You may be surprised to know that our rules for deriving the plural forms of regular nouns have wide applicability in English. For two other extremely common inflectional morphemes of English—namely, the possessive marker on nouns (*judge's, cat's,* and *dog's)* and the third-person singular marker on verbs (*teaches, laughs,* and *swims)*—the distribution of their allomorphs is parallel to the distribution for plurals.

Possessive Morpheme on Nouns

[s]   for: *ship, cat, Jack* . . .

[z]   for: *John, arm, dog* . . .

[əz]   for: *church, judge, fish* . . .

Third-Person Singular Morpheme on Verbs

[s]   for: *leap, eat, kick, laugh* . . .

[z]   for: *hurry, seem, lean, crave, see* . . .

[əz]   for: *preach, tease, judge, buzz, rush* . . .

If we posit /z/ as the underlying phonological form of these morphemes, the very same rules that derive the correct allomorphs of the plural morpheme will also derive the correct allomorphs of the possessive morpheme of nouns and the third-person singular morpheme of verbs. (Unlike plurals, some of which are irregular, all nouns have regular possessive morpheme allomorphs, and all verbs are regular with respect to the third-person singular morpheme except for *is, has, says,* and *does.)*

English Past-Tense Morpheme

The inflectional morpheme that marks the past tense of regular verbs in English has three allomorphs:

[t]   for: *wish, kiss, talk, strip, preach* . . .

[d]   for: *wave, bathe, play, lie, stir, tease, roam, ruin* . . .

[əd]   for: *want, wade, wait, hoot, plant, seed* . . .

If we posit /d/ as the underlying phonological form of the past-tense morpheme, we need only two simple rules to derive the past-tense forms on all regular verbs.

Schwa Insertion Rule B

/d/ ➔ [əd] / alveolar stop + ___#

(Schwa is inserted preceding a word-final /d/ that follows a morpheme ending in an alveolar stop.)

Assimilation Rule B

/d/ ➔ voiceless / voiceless + ___#

(Word-final /d/ is realized as [t] following a morpheme that ends in a voiceless sound.)

Derivations of the past-tense forms of the verbs *wish, want,* and *wave* are provided in Table 4–10 on page 132 as examples.

Table 4-10
Derivation of English Past-Tense Verbs

	WAVED	WISHED	WANTED
Underlying form	/wev+d/	/wɪʃ+d/	/wɑnt+d/
Schwa insertion	DNA	DNA	applies ↓
Derived form	[wev+d]	[wɪʃ+d]	[wɑnt+əd]
Assimilation	DNA	applies ↓	DNA
Surface form	[wev+d]	[wɪʃ+t]	[wɑnt+əd]

The last two sets of rules show striking similarities in the schwa insertion processes and in the assimilation processes required to generate the correct forms of the plural and possessive forms of nouns, the third-person singular forms of verbs, and the past-tense forms of verbs.

Underlying Phonological Form of Morphemes in the Lexicon

This section explores the phonological form of words as they are thought to exist in speakers' mental lexicons. The form of a word in the lexicon is called its *underlying form,* and the form in the lexicon may not be the same as the pronounced form.

Consonants The same kinds of phonological processes that operate between a stem and an inflectional suffix also operate between a stem and a derivational morpheme (e.g., between WISH and FUL). Think about a child who knows the words *metal* and *medal.* In North American English, the sound that occurs in the middle of both words is the alveolar flap, not [t] or [d] but [ɾ]. (An alveolar flap is the sound created when the tip of the tongue flaps quickly against the alveolar ridge: *later, ladder.)*

As an American child hearing *metal* and *medal,* you would have entered exactly what you heard into your lexicon—/mɛɾəl/ (with a flap) in both cases. But consider what happens after you hear someone say her new car is painted *metallic* [mətʰæl + ək] *red.* If you recognized that *metallic* is made up of METAL and the derivational suffix -IC (as in *atomic, Germanic),* then the two pronunciations [mɛɾəl] and [mətʰæl + ək] must be reconciled. The task of a language learner is to posit an efficient underlying form that will yield the right pronunciations when the phonological rules of English apply.

Next consider your task when you subsequently hear someone report that the car's *medallion* is missing from the hood. For *medal* and *medallion,* you hear [mɛɾəl] and [mədæljən]. What underlying form must you posit in the lexicon once the morpheme MEDAL is recognized as occurring in both words?

Assume that you recognized METAL as a common element in *metal* and *metallic* and MEDAL as a common element in *medal* and *medallion*. Here are the pronunciations you've observed:

METAL		MEDAL	
[mɛɾəl]	[məthæl + ək]	[mɛɾəl]	[mədæl + jən]
metal	metallic	medal	medallion

You could account for the different pronunciations of the morpheme METAL by positing the form /mɛtæl/ in the lexicon and applying phonological rules that change this underlying form into the occurring surface forms. Focusing on the consonants and ignoring the vowels for a moment, the underlying form /mɛtæl/ will require a process that changes /t/ into [ɾ] in the word *metal* [mɛɾəl]. (Below you'll see why we've used the æ.)

This same process will be needed to change /d/ into [ɾ] in the word *medal* [mɛɾəl]. The flapping rule changes underlying /t/ and /d/ into [ɾ] when they occur between a stressed vowel and an unstressed vowel. Using a more formal notation, the rule would be:

$$\begin{matrix} \text{alveolar} \\ \text{stop} \end{matrix} \quad \rightarrow \quad \text{flap} \quad / \quad \begin{matrix} \text{vowel} \\ \text{stressed} \end{matrix} \quad \underline{\quad} \quad \begin{matrix} \text{vowel} \\ \text{unstressed} \end{matrix}$$

It's not surprising that phonological rules postulated to account for one set of facts may also account for other facts. After all, phonological rules apply to *all* morphemes and words unless they have been blocked by a specific marking for a particular morpheme. For instance, nouns like *tooth* and *foot* that have irregular plural forms are marked in the lexicon as not taking the regular plural morpheme. If they weren't marked as irregular, you'd say *tooths* and *foots* just as children do before they learn to exempt these morphemes from these regular processes.

Thus, the relationship between the phonological representation of morphemes in the lexicon and their actual pronunciation in speech is mediated by a set of phonological processes that can be represented in rules of significant generality. Not only will *metal* and *medal* be affected by the flapping rule, but every word will be that meets the conditions specified in the rule. This includes single-morpheme words like *butter, bitter,* and *meter;* two-morpheme words like *writer, rider, raider, rooter;* and thousands more.

Vowels Consider a youngster who knows the words *photograph* and *photographer* (pronounced [forəgræf] and [fəthɑgrəfər]). At some point the youngster posits the single entry PHOTOGRAPH in the lexicon to represent the core of these two words. A moment's thought will suggest that if the underlying form were /fotɑgræf/ it would represent the baseline knowledge needed to produce the two pronunciations. Given the underlying representation /fotɑgræf/ and the surface forms [forəgræf] and [fəthɑgrəfər], a rule that changes unstressed vowels into [ə] will produce the correct vowels.

If /ə/ appeared in the underlying form, there is no rule that would produce the correct surface forms. In order to produce the [ɑ] in [fətʰɑgrəfər] from an underlying form with schwas /fətəgrəf + ər/, we would need one rule that produced [ɑ] from underlying /ə/. For the word *photograph,* we would need a rule that produced [o] from underlying /ə/ in the first syllable and [æ] from underlying /ə/ in the third syllable. This would amount to knowing which vowels exist in the surface pronunciation and encoding that knowledge in the underlying form along with the /ə/, but that is exactly what we assume does not happen. Instead, if we postulate different vowels in the underlying forms, a single rule can derive [ə] from any underlying vowel when it occurs in an unstressed syllable. We can now derive the pronunciations for these words. We formulate the rule as follows:

$$\begin{matrix} \text{vowel} \\ \text{unstressed} \end{matrix} \quad \rightarrow \quad [\text{ə}]$$

(An unstressed vowel becomes schwa.)

This rule does not affect stressed vowels; it says that unstressed vowels become schwa [ə]. Of course, a rule that relies on information about stress requires prior assignment of stress, but the rules for assigning stress in English are beyond our scope. If you want to pursue the topic further, certain references at the end of this chapter contain treatments of the stress placement rules.

Computers and Phonology

Several decades ago researchers thought it would be a matter of only a few years before computers would be able to recognize speech and synthesize it. (Think of *speech recognition* as turning speech into print, and of *speech synthesis* as turning print into speech.) The process is taking longer than researchers had anticipated, and the reasons don't lie in a lack of sophistication in computers or technology. Despite the fact that children master the phonology of their languages at very young ages, adult researchers still have not figured out the extraordinary complexity of the phonological processes that characterize human languages. We still have not sufficiently modeled exactly what we do when we produce spoken utterances and how we understand the utterances of others. As you saw in this chapter, natural speech occurs in a continuous stream and cannot be readily segmented without knowledge of the particular language involved. Just how human beings segment a continuous stream of spoken language into distinct words and recognize the sound segments in those words is not yet well understood.

The synthesis of speech by machine has also proved challenging. To understand why, focus on the string of sounds that would occur in a simple word like *sand.* It might seem relatively simple to put together a machine-generated form of /sænd/: the machine would need only to produce a voiceless alveolar fricative, then the vowel /æ/, then the alveolar nasal /n/, and finally the alveolar stop /d/. Seems simple enough. Notice, though, that when you pronounce *sand,* its vowel quality differs markedly from the "same" vowel in *hat.* If a speech synthesizer produced the vowel of *hat* in the word *sand,* it would sound artificial, just as it would if it produced the vowel of *sand* in the word *hat.* You already know that the vowel of *sand* is nasalized (because it appears before the nasal stop that follows it, as described in the rule on p. 119). As the vocal tract starts to move toward that nasal consonant, the vowel that precedes it takes on nasal characteristics. Therein lies one challenge for speech synthesis: how to blend sounds into one another the way that people do. There is no separation between words in ordinary human speech, and there is no separation between sounds.

But the situation is even more complex than this. A sound is essentially a bundle of phonetic features. You could think of the phonological form of *sand* as having not just four segments /s æ n d/ but also the features given below each segment:

/s/	/æ/	/n/	/d/
voiceless	voiced	voiced	voiced
alveolar	low front	alveolar	alveolar
fricative	unrounded	nasal	stop

The phonetic characteristics of the segments in *sand* are more complicated than we've indicated, but the representation above will do for our purposes.

Consider that the articulation of each phonetic feature in a segment does not start and end at the same time as the other features. The voicelessness of /s/ doesn't abruptly end and the voicing of /æ/ start at exactly the same point as the fricative character of the consonant stops and the vowel character of /æ/ begins. The mouth and other features of the vocal tract move continuously in the production of even simple words like *sand* (as you can feel by saying the word and concentrating on your tongue movement).

To make artificial speech sound natural, a good deal more about the nature of phonetic realizations of underlying phonological forms must be understood. (In the section on Internet resources below, you'll find addresses for Web sites at which you can hear speech synthesized from your typewritten message.)

SUMMARY

- Phonology is the study of the sound systems of languages.

- A phoneme is a unit in the sound system of a language. It is an abstract element, a set of phonological features (e.g., bilabial, stop) having several predictable manifestations (called allophones) in speech.

- Two words can differ minimally by virtue of having a single pair of different phonemes (as in *pin/bin* or *tap/tab*).

- Each phoneme comprises a set of allophones. Each allophone is the specific rule-governed and therefore predictable realization of the phoneme in a particular linguistic environment.

- The allophones of a phoneme occur in complementary distribution or in free variation; they never contrast. Allophones of a single phoneme cannot be the sole difference in a minimal pair of words with different meanings.

- Two languages can have the same sounds but structure them differently within their systems. Both Korean and English have the three sounds [p], [pʰ], and [b]. In English, unaspirated [p] and aspirated [pʰ] are allophones of one phoneme, while [b] belongs to a different phoneme. In Korean, aspirated [pʰ] and unaspirated [p] are separate phonemes (they contrast), while [b] is the allophone of the phoneme /p/ that occurs between voiced sounds.

- Each simple word in a speaker's lexicon consists of a sequence of phonemes that constitutes the underlying phonological representation of the word. Underlying forms differ from pronunciations and cannot generally be observed in speech directly.

- From the underlying form of a word, the phonological rules of a language specify the allophonic features of a phoneme in accordance with its linguistic environment.

- One task of children in acquiring a language is to uncover its phonological rules and to infer efficient, economical underlying forms for word units. Given these underlying forms, the phonological rules of a language will specify the rule-governed features of the surface form.

- Phonological rules may be ordered with respect to one another, the first applicable rule applying to the underlying form to produce a derived form, and the subsequent rules applying in turn to successive derived forms until the last applicable rule produces a surface form. The surface form is the basis of a word's pronunciation. Two dialects of a language may contain some of the same rules but apply them in a different order, thereby producing different surface forms for different pronunciations.

- Words are made up of groups of sounds called syllables, not of sounds themselves.

- Languages have sequence constraints on the structure of permissible syllable types and the occurrence of particular consonants and vowels within syllable types.

- CV is the most common syllable type in the world's languages. English has an unusually large range of syllable types, including clusters of two and three consonants. The particular consonants that can appear in each position are constrained.

- Stress is contrastive in English: "Not every white house is the White House."

- Phonological processes (for example, aspiration and flapping in English) can depend on syllable structure and stress, as well as on a sequence of sound segments.

WHAT DO YOU THINK? REVISITED

❖ *All a blur.* In ordinary speech the words of every language run together, so that listeners cannot readily distinguish one word from the next by virtue of any pause or silence between them. What enables a listener to tell where one word ends and the next begins is an understanding of the language and a knowledge of its words. This is equally true for English, German, French, and Spanish.

❖ *French cabbie.* You'd have to know French nearly as well as the cabbie to tell your cousin what features of his pronunciation gave away his English-speaking origins. Part of the answer would almost surely lie in using the distribution of English allophones instead of French ones, as in aspirating initial /p/ sounds, as English does, but not French. There are many other allophonic processes that are subtle and operate below the level of conscious awareness for native speakers and non-native speakers alike. These have to do with length of vowels and consonants, with stress patterns on words, and with intonation patterns for sentences.

❖ *Jules Biker.* One explanation is that the /p/ in Jewel Spiker's family name is neutralized in the environment following /s/. In other words, because English does not depend on the /p/ - /b/ contrast in that environment, the sounds can be pronounced more alike, and are. While initial /p/ in English is aspirated, initial /b/ is not. In the environment following /s/ as in *Spiker,* /p/ is not aspirated, and the absence of aspiration contributes to the easy confusion of /p/ and /b/ in that spot.

❖ *Techie friend.* On the Internet, you can quickly discover that while speech can be readily synthesized sound for sound, it is not nearly so easy to achieve a natural connection between sounds in a word or across words, or to create natural-sounding intonation patterns.

EXERCISES

Based on English

4-1 Consider the following words of English with respect to how the sound represented by <t> is pronounced. For each column, specify the phonetic character of the allophone (how it is pronounced). Is it aspirated? Flapped? Then, as was done in this chapter for the allophones of English /p/, describe the allophones of /t/ and specify their distribution.

A	B	C	D
tougher	standing	later	petunia
talker	still	data	potato
teller	story	petal	return

4-2 Using the monosyllabic English words below, provide a list of 15 ordered pairs whose stress pattern indicates they are compounds—that is, with stress as in the examples. It will be helpful to mark the stress pattern on the vowel of each element, using ´ for primary and ` for secondary stress.

Examples: tímezòne, shówhòrse

ball	beam	court	face	fall	free	gear	hand	hat
heart	hold	horse	house	kick	lance	land	lap	life
light	paint	port	rein	ride	road	show	style	table
throw	tide	time	top	way	weight	year	zone	

4-3 Apparently, the following words do not exist in English. Some are "sniglet" candidates (they could exist), but others violate the sequence constraints of English and could not exist. Identify the potential sniglets, and explain why the others are not permitted. For the potential sniglets, provide an appropriate spelling in the standard orthography.

pɛtribɑr	twɪntʃ	rizənənt
pʌpkəss	blɪbjulə	læktomæŋgjuleʃɛn
pæŋgəkd	spret	spwənt

4-4 **a.** Make a list of as many words as you can, each of which represents a different onset of three consonants. *Example: spr in spread*

b. Examine the initial clusters you listed in (a) and answer these questions about English:

Which consonants can occur first in an initial three-consonant cluster?
Which consonants can occur second in an initial three-consonant cluster?
Which consonants can occur third in an initial three-consonant cluster?

Examine the three lists you have made to decide whether or not they constitute natural classes, and provide the name for any that do constitute a natural class.

4-5 Although English makes a contrast between /p/ and /b/ (*pill* versus *bill*), it doesn't exploit the contrast in the environment following /s/ (as in *spell* and *spin*). Hence, there is no pair of words such as /sbɪn/ and /spɪn/. When a language exploits a distinction in some environments but not all, the potential contrast tends to be neutralized where it isn't exploited. As a consequence, the /p/ of *pill* differs more from the /b/ of *bill* than does the /p/ of *spin* (try distinguishing "spin" from "sbin"). For one thing, the /p/ of *spin* (but not the /p/ of *pill*) lacks aspiration, like the /b/ of *bill*. Thus a feature that distinguishes /p/ and /b/ elsewhere is not exploited following /s/.

Below are two sets of words. Those in column I contain a contrast that English exploits in that environment but not in the environment of column II. In other words, for the words in column II there cannot be a contrast based on the sound difference represented in the pair of words in the same line in column I.

	I	II
i.	sit seat	sing ring king
ii.	bit beat	here beer peer
iii.	hat hate	hang sang rang
iv.	tad dad	sting star study
v.	cad gad	skill score scam

a. Identify the segment that is likely to prompt different phonetic transcriptions and specify what those transcriptions would be.

b. Characterize the environment (in column II) that supports the neutralization.

c. Based on your knowledge of English phonology (such as its sequence constraints), provide reasons for preferring one of the transcriptions over the other.

4-6 On page 129, we said you could probably imagine that the English flapping rule could be reformulated in terms of syllables and their parts instead of in terms of vowel segments, as formulated on page 123. Formulate the flapping rule in terms of syllables and their parts.

4-7 For each English word below, identify each syllable's nucleus and (where appropriate) onset, rhyme, and coda. *Example:* for *past*, nucleus: *a*; onset: *p*; rhyme: *ast*; coda: *st*

twin turned e-ven love-li-est a-ny-bo-dy de-fi-ni-tion na-sa-li-za-tion

4-8 **a.** The nasalization rule (page 119) and the assimilation rules A and B (pages 130 and 131) have the effect of making nearby sounds more alike. In the nasalization rule, which feature spreads from one sound to another sound? Which feature spreads in the assimilation rules?

b. One way to characterize schwa insertion rules A and B (pages 130 and 131) is to say they make neighboring sounds dissimilar. Another way to characterize schwa insertion is to say it separates sounds that are very similar. What features do the neighboring sounds share before schwa insertion A? What about schwa insertion B?

c. In light of the rules mentioned in (a) and in (b), we can see that English has some rules that make neighboring sounds more alike and other rules that make neighboring sounds more dissimilar. Examine these rules carefully and propose an explanation of these competing tendencies. *Hint:* Think about how hard or easy it might be to pronounce these sequences without the rules; think about how hard or easy it might be to perceive these sequences without the rules.

Based on Languages Other Than English

4-9 Fijian has prenasalized stops among its inventory of phonemes. The prenasalized stop [^{n}d] consists of a nasal pronounced immediately before the stop, with which it forms a single sound unit. Consider the following Fijian words as pronounced in fast speech:

vi^{n}di	'to spring up'	dina	'true'
ke^{n}da	'we'	dalo	'taro plant'
tiko	'to stay'	vu^{n}di	'plantain banana'
tutu	'grandfather'	ma^{n}da	'first'
viti	'Fiji'	tina	'mother'

dovu	'sugarcane'	mata	'eye'
doⁿdo	'to stretch out one's hand'	mokiti	'round'
		veveⁿdu	(a type of plant)

On the basis of these data, determine whether [d], [ⁿd], and [t] are allophones of a single phoneme or constitute two or three separate phonemes. If you find that two of them (or all of them) are allophones of a single phoneme, give the rule that describes the distribution of each allophone. If you analyze all three as separate phonemes, justify your answer. (*Note:* In Fijian all syllables end in a vowel.)

4-10 Examine the following words of Tongan, a Polynesian language. (*Note:* In Tongan all syllables end in a vowel.)

tauhi	'to take care'	sino	'body'
sisi	'garland'	totonu	'correct'
motu	'island'	pasi	'to clap'
mosimosi	'to drizzle'	fata	'shelf'
motomoto	'unripe'	movete	'to come apart'
fesi	'to break'	misi	'to dream'

a. On the basis of these data, determine whether [s] and [t] are allophones of a single phoneme in Tongan or are separate phonemes. If you find that they are allophones of the same phoneme, state the rule that describes where each allophone occurs. If you conclude that they are different phonemes, justify your answer.

b. In each of the following Tongan words, one sound has been replaced by a blank. This sound is either [s] or [t]. Without more knowledge of Tongan than you could figure out from the preceding question, is it possible to make an educated guess as to which of these two sounds fits in the blank? If so, provide the sound; if not, explain why.

___ ili	'fishing net'	fe ___ e	'lump'
___ uku	'to place'	lama ___ i	'to ambush'

c. In the course of the last century, Tongan borrowed many words from English and adapted them to fit the phonological structure of its words.

kaasete	'gazette'	suu	'shoe'
tisi	'dish'	koniseti	'concert'
sosaieti	'society'	pata	'butter'
salati	'salad'	suka	'sugar'
maasolo	'marshall'	sikaa	'cigar'
sekoni	'second'	taimani	'diamond'

How does the phonemic status of [s] and [t] differ in borrowed words and in native Tongan words? In other words, is the situation the same in these borrowed words? Write an integrated statement about the status of [s] and [t] in Tongan. (*Hint:* Your statement will have to include information about which area of the Tongan vocabulary each part of the rule applies to.)

4-11 The distribution of the sounds [s] and [z] in colloquial Spanish is represented by the following examples in phonetic transcription:

izla	'island'	tʃiste	'joke'
fuersa	'force'	eski	'ski'
peskado	'fish'	riezgo	'risk'

muskulo	'muscle'	fiskal	'fiscal'
sin	'without'	rezvalar	'to slip'
rasko	'I scratch'	dezde	'since'
resto	'remainder'	razgo	'feature'
mizmo	'same'	beizbɔl	'baseball'
espalda	'back'	mas	'more'

Are [s] and [z] distinct phonemes of Spanish or allophones of a single phoneme? If they are distinct phonemes, support your answer. If they are allophones of the same phoneme, specify their distribution.

4-12 Consider the following Russian words. On the basis of this limited list, where does Russian appear to have a contrast between [t] and [d] and where does it appear not to have one? (*Note:* An apostrophe marks a palatalized consonant.)

pərʌxot	'steamboat'	t'ɛlə	'body'
gʌz'ɛtə	'newspaper'	pot	'perspiration'
zapət	'west'	dərʌgoj	'dear'
rat	'glad'	d'ɛlə	'business'
zdan'ijə	'building'	ʃtat	'state'
most	'bridge'	pot	'under'

4-13 In Samoan, words may have two forms, one called "bad speech" (used in informal oratory when addressing peers or kin) and another called "good speech" (used with chiefs or strangers in literary and religious situations). The difference between the two forms can be described by phonological rules. (*Note:* The Samoan words for "good" and "bad" do not carry the same connotations in this case as the English words.)

"bad"	**"good"**	
taatou	kaakou	'us all'
teine	keiŋe	'girl'
taŋata	kaŋaka	'man'
ŋaŋana	ŋaŋana	'language'
totoŋi	kokoŋi	'price'
nofo	ŋofo	'to stay'
ŋaalue	ŋaalue	'to work'
fono	foŋo	'meeting'

a. Describe the phonological difference between the "bad" and "good" forms. Which form is more basic—the "good" form or the "bad" form? (In other words, which one can serve as the underlying form for both forms?)

b. Wherever possible, fill in the blanks in the following table. If it is impossible to know the form of a missing word, say why.

"bad"	**"good"**	
manu	_____	'bird'
mate	_____	'dead'
_____	maŋoo	'shark'
_____	kili	'fishing net'
tonu	_____	'correct'
_____	kaŋi	'to cry'

4-14 In German, the sequence of letters <ch> can represent (among other things) either of two sounds: [ç] (a voiceless palatal fricative) or [x] (a voiceless velar fricative). On the basis of the following data, determine whether these two sounds are distinct phonemes or allophones of a single phoneme.

kɛlç	*Kelch*	'cup'
fɪçtə	*Fichte*	'fir tree'
knœçl	*Knöchel*	'knuckle'
kɔx	*Koch*	'cook'
tsurɛçt	*zurecht*	'in good order'
vʊxt	*Wucht*	'weight'
çɪrʊrk	*Chirurg*	'surgeon'
nüçtərn	*nüchtern*	'sober'
bux	*Buch*	'book'
bərajç	*Bereich*	'scope'
hɛkçən	*Häkchen*	'apostrophe'
bax	*Bach*	'brook'

If [ç] and [x] are distinct phonemes, justify your answer. If they are allophones of the same phoneme, specify their distribution.

4-15 On page 127 you learned that Japanese sequence constraints allow syllables of the forms CV, V, and (when the second C is a nasal) CVC. Using that information, divide the words given in the Japanese vowel chart (Table 3–5 on page 99) into syllables: *ima* 'now'; *aki* 'autumn'; *buji* 'safe'; *yoru* 'to approach'; *sensei* 'teacher.' Now do the same for the borrowed words *beesubooru* 'baseball' and *sutoraiku* 'strike,' where <ee> and <oo> represent long vowels, not two vowels.

4-16 In light of our discussions in this chapter and your experience with some of the preceding exercises, discuss the following quote from Halle and Clements (1983).

> The perception of intelligible speech is . . . determined only in part by the physical signal that strikes our ears. Of equal significance . . . is the contribution made by the perceiver's knowledge of the language in which the utterance is framed. Acts of perception that heavily depend on active contributions from the perceiver's mind are often described as illusions, and the perception of intelligible speech seems . . . to qualify for this description. A central problem of phonetics and phonology is . . . to provide a scientific characterization of this illusion which is at the heart of all human existence.

Especially for Educators and Future Teachers

4-17 As an exercise for a class of middle-school international students studying English, you've asked them to draw up a list of English names for games, and they offer these: *skokey, skwinty, twint, stwink, plopo, splopt, sprats, skretsht, spretched, skwickt, spwint, stwirl, tprash, stpop, frash, quirt, splast, plsats.* You recognize that a few names are not legitimate because they have sequences of *sounds* (not letters) that English doesn't permit. Which are impossible, and what explanation can you give the students about why they are impossible?

4-18 Using phonological terms from this and the previous chapter, identify two characteristic features of "foreign accent" for students represented in the schools of your community. Aim to account for the differences between the way native and non-native speakers of English pronounce certain accented words. It may help to reflect on: (a) inventory of sounds; (b) phonological rules for the distribution of allophones; (c) sequence constraints for sounds.

4-19 Recall from Chapter 3 (page 91)—and perhaps your own experience—that French speakers tend to pronounce the English word *thin* as "sin" and *this* as "zis." From this observation, what can you say about (a) the inventory of French consonants as compared to English ones; and (b) whether or not French uses voicing as a contrastive feature? Finally, what would you predict about how a French student might tend to pronounce the English words *then* and *thick?*

4-20 Focusing on high front vowels, carefully compare the Spanish vowel chart (Table 3–3 on page 98) with the English vowel chart (inside front cover and page 95). Relying on those charts and any relevant experience of yours, identify with IPA symbols which pair of distinctive vowels in English you would predict to be challenging for Spanish-speaking students learning English, and explain why. Then cite two minimal pairs of English words (words that are identical except for those vowels) that could prove challenging for those students to perceive and produce.

OTHER RESOURCES

- **Speech on the Web: http://www.tue.nl/ipo/hearing/webspeak.htm#On-line**

  If you're interested in hearing synthesized speech, several Web sites can provide examples. This site is a "jump station" providing links to speech synthesizers around the globe. Once you choose one, you can type in something you wish to hear synthesized. Then, assuming that your computer has multimedia capabilities, you can experience state-of-the-art text-to-speech synthesis.

- **Voices Demonstration Page: http://www.att.com/aspg/odemo.html**

  This demo illustrates the capabilities of the WATSON Flex Talk™ speech synthesizer. You can type in up to 50 words and receive an audio file of what you've typed that is compatible with your computer and can be played using your multimedia capabilities. You can choose from among several voices, including child, woman, man, raspy, or singer.

- **SpeechLinks: http://www.speech.cs.cmu.edu/comp.speech/SpeechLinks.html**

  This is a speech technology hyperlinks page containing hundreds of links to projects around the world. Besides the links to technical papers (most of which will be beyond the reach of beginning students), you'll also find links to sites exploring speech recognition and speech synthesis.

- **Museum of Speech Synthesis Systems: http://www.cs.bham.ac.uk/~jpi/museum.html**

  This set of links will steer you to a wide variety of speech synthesis systems, some of which will allow you to do test runs and make your own judgments as to promise and naturalness.

SUGGESTIONS FOR FURTHER READING

- **Carlos Gussenhoven & Haike Jacobs. 1998.** *Understanding Phonology* (London: Arnold). An excellent follow-up to this chapter; rich and largely accessible.
- **Francis Katamba. 1989.** *Introduction to Phonology* (New York: St. Martin's). A thorough treatment, sensitive to theoretical and descriptive concerns.

ADVANCED READING

Clark and Yallop (1990) and Carr (1993) are basic textbooks that will be largely accessible to readers who have mastered some phonetics and the phonology of this chapter. The "problem book" by Halle and Clements (1983) covers a broad range of languages and has an excellent introductory chapter going beyond what we have covered; it also has separate chapters on complementary distribution, natural classes, phonological rules, and systems of rules. Kaye (1989) is a lively, provocative, and mostly accessible follow-up to this chapter. More specialized treatments are available in Hogg and McCully (1987), Bybee (2002), and Goldsmith (1996).

REFERENCES

- Bybee, Joan. 2002. *Phonology and Language Use* (Cambridge: Cambridge University Press).
- Carr, Philip. 1993. *Phonology* (New York: St. Martin's).
- Clark, John, & Yallop, Colin. 1995. *An Introduction to Phonetics and Phonology,* 2nd ed. (Malden, MA: Blackwell).
- Goldsmith, John A., ed. 1996. *The Handbook of Phonological Theory.* (Malden, MA: Blackwell).
- Hall, Rich. 1984. *Sniglets* (New York: Collier).
- Halle, Morris, & G. N. Clements. 1983. *Problem Book in Phonology* (Cambridge, MA: MIT Press).
- Hogg, Richard, & C. B. McCully. 1987. *Metrical Phonology: A Coursebook* (Cambridge: Cambridge University Press).
- Kaye, Jonathan. 1989. *Phonology: A Cognitive View* (Hillsdale, NJ: Erlbaum).

Chapter 5

The Structure and Function of Phrases and Sentences: Syntax

WHAT DO YOU THINK?

❖ Rudy, your linguistics classmate, says he knows that we readily produce routine expressions like "What time is it?" and "Fine, thanks" because we hear them so frequently. But, he asks, how do we produce sentences we've never heard before? What's your answer?

❖ Your friend Amber reports that reading Steven Pinker's *The Language Instinct* has made her think about ambiguity. She understands how an ambiguous word like *bank* can mean 'savings bank' or 'river bank' but wonders what makes a string of unambiguous words such as *new drug combinations* ambiguous. What's your explanation?

❖ Your nerdy friend Ned expresses annoyance that the grammar checker in his word processor objects to nearly every passive sentence he writes. Instead of *The winning team was hobbled together by a hodgepodge of friends*, the checker recommended *A hodgepodge of friends hobbled together the winning team*. Ned claims the checker assumes that all passives are bad and wonders what you think. Well?

INTRODUCTION

In this chapter we explore how words and morphemes are organized in phrases and sentences and also explore the relationships between certain kinds of sentences such as declaratives and interrogatives. We investigate how a finite grammar can generate an infinite number of sentences and how the "creative" aspects of producing sentences and the ready understanding of novel sentences are normal parts of everyone's competence.

All languages have ways of referring to entities—people, places, things, ideas, events, and so on. The expressions used to refer to entities are known as noun phrases. The proper nouns *Lauren* and *Louisiana,* the common nouns *jelly* and *justice,* and the personal pronouns *he* and *she* are noun phrases. So are more complicated expressions such as *his mother, that book of magic, the star of the show,* and *a judge from Michigan.* All of these are referring expressions; all are noun phrases.

Languages also have ways of saying something about the entities referred to. All languages have ways of making affirmative and negative statements. They also permit speakers to ask questions, issue directives, and so on.

Let's illustrate with affirmative statements. In the following sentences, reference is made to an entity and then a predication is made about it.

Referring Expression	Predication
Judge Judy	has a daughter.
A poltergeist	appeared last night.
Julian	bought an answering machine.

In the first example, reference is made to "Judge Judy," and then something is predicated of her, namely, that she "has a daughter."

Try it yourself: In the second example above (*A poltergeist appeared last night.*), reference is made to "a poltergeist" and then a predication is made of it. What's the predication? In the third example, what's the referent and what predication is made of him?

Syntax is the part of grammar that governs the form of strings by which language users make statements, ask questions, give directives, and so on. The study of syntax addresses the structure of sentences and their structural and functional relationships to one another. What in functional terms we call referring expressions we call noun phrases when we use grammatical terms. From a functional perspective, expressions such as *has a daughter* and *bought an answering machine* are predicates; from a grammatical point of view, they're verb phrases. However much languages may differ from one another in other ways, they all have noun phrases and verb phrases.

A simple sentence contains a single verb (or predicate) and any other expressions the verb requires as part of its structural characteristics. In Chapter 2 we discussed subcategories of verbs and said that speakers must know the kinds of sentence structures each verb permits. We noted that verbs permit different complements: some require a noun phrase; some do not permit one. In the following examples, the verb is italicized:

Danny *fell*.

Dimas *cooked* the hot dogs.

A runner from Ohio *won* the marathon Sunday.

Britney *will buy* a new raincoat this fall.

Her uncle *had piled* the gifts in the car.

The psychiatrist *should have listened* to her patient.

Each of these sentences contains only one verb, even though the verb can consist of a single word (*fell, cooked, won*) or more than one word (*will buy, had piled, should have listened*). From a syntactic point of view, the pivotal element in a sentence is the verb. For one thing, its subcategorization determines what complements it may have. (Later in this chapter, we'll see that a simple sentence may function as part of another sentence; in that case the simple sentence may be called a clause.)

CONSTITUENCY AND TREE DIAGRAMS

In analyzing sentences, a useful tool is the notion that sentences consist *not* of words, but of **constituents.** Consider the sentence *Harry saw a ghost.* Obviously, it is made up of words, and each word contains at least one morpheme. Since these morphemes have sounds associated with them, we can say that the sentence is made up of sounds (such as /g/, /o/, /s/, /t/ in *ghost),* of morphemes (SEE and 'PAST TENSE'), or of words (*Harry* and *saw).* Such an analysis is accurate, but it misses the point. It is akin to describing a shopping mall as consisting of concrete and electrical wires. We want to say that a shopping mall has retail shops, restaurants, parking areas, movie theaters, and so on. We could then go further and describe the composition of these units and their relationship to one another. The point in any analysis is to identify *structural units* that are relevant to some purpose or level of organization. In analyzing sentences, those structural units are called constituents.

Tree Diagrams

One way of representing syntactic relationships is with tree diagrams. The tree in Figure 5–1 on page 148 represents the fact that the sentence *Harry liked Peeves* consists of two parts: the referring expression *Harry* and the predicate expression *liked Peeves.* In the tree diagram, *S* stands for sentence, *N* stands for noun or pronoun, and *V* stands for verb. This same tree can also represent other sentences, such as *Harry saw it* in Figure 5–2 on page 148. (The trees in Figures 5–1 and 5–2 are oversimplified, as we'll see later.)

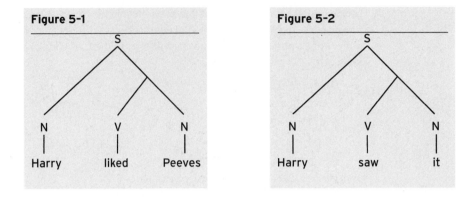

Figure 5-1

S

N — Harry
V — liked
N — Peeves

Figure 5-2

S

N — Harry
V — saw
N — it

Constituency

We can view sentences as being made up, first, of their largest constituents. These large units can be analyzed into smaller units, which can also be analyzed.

Linear Ordering of Constituents   It's obvious that the words of any sentence occur in a particular order. Necessarily, then, the constituents in a sentence also have ordered elements. To put it simply, sentences are expressed with an ordered sequence of words, as in these examples:

> A plump plumber from Pasadena skated in the park.
>
> Hillary hated the harp.
>
> Xavier comes from Xanadu.

Now we ask whether the order in which words are arranged is fixed. If it is fixed, is it equally fixed across different languages? We begin by examining the following sentences:

> The farmer saw the poltergeist.
>
> The poltergeist saw the farmer.

Both sentences are well formed and contain exactly the same words, but they mean different things. Given their identical words, the difference in meaning must be signaled by the difference in word order. Thus, word order is an essential part of English sentence structure. In this case, it is from the word order that we understand *who* is seeing and *who* is being seen.

Now consider the following:

> The farmer saw the poltergeist.
>
> *Farmer the poltergeist the saw.

While the first string is well formed, the second is not. This, too, demonstrates that word order is an essential part of English sentence structure. If we rearrange the words, we sometimes produce other well-formed sentences with a different meaning, but we may produce a string of words that is ill formed (or "ungrammatical"). Sometimes a change of word order can produce a different well-formed sentence with the same meaning, as in these pairs of examples:

1a.   Yesterday he saw a poltergeist in the castle.

 b.   He saw a poltergeist in the castle yesterday.

2a.   When he made the sauce, he forgot to put the basil in.

 b.   When he made the sauce, he forgot to put in the basil.

Word order is thus not absolutely fixed.

Not all languages exploit word order to the same extent that English does. We saw in Chapter 2 that Latin could express 'The farmer saw the wolf' by using any of several word orders; here we illustrate with a similar sentence:

Agricola vīdit umbram.
FARMER   SAW   POLTERGEIST   }   'The farmer saw the poltergeist.'

Agricola umbram vīdit.
Umbram agricola vīdit.

In these Latin sentences, *who* did what to *whom* is indicated *not* by word order but by inflectional suffixes. The same is true of sentences in many other languages, including Russian and German. Thus, keeping the same inflection on each noun, the following Latin sentences have the same meaning:

Umbra   vīdit agricolam.
POLTERGEIST SAW   FARMER   }   'The poltergeist saw the farmer.'

Umbra   agricolam vīdit.
Agricolam umbra   vīdit.

The three other possible orders for arranging these words in sequence also indicate the same meaning. Word order is thus not equally fixed across different languages.

Hierarchical Ordering of Constituents   As is apparent in the tree diagrams of Figures 5–1 and 5–2, there is more organization to a sentence than the linear order of its words. To explore the notion of internal structure further, consider the expression *current information technology,* which is ambiguous in that it can mean either 'technology for current information' or 'information technology that is current.' The internal organization of a linear string of words is called its constituent structure and can be represented in a tree diagram, as in Figure 5–3 and Figure 5–4 on page 150.

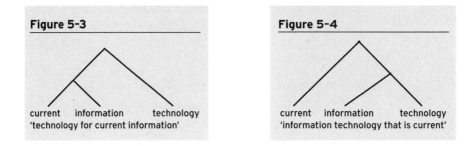

Figure 5-3

current   information   technology
'technology for current information'

Figure 5-4

current   information   technology
'information technology that is current'

As a second example, consider the expression *gullible boys and girls*. It can mean either 'gullible boys and gullible girls' or 'girls and gullible boys.' This ambiguity reflects the fact that the expression *gullible boys and girls* has two possible constituent structures, depending on whether *gullible* modifies *boys and girls* or only *boys*. In the tree diagram of Figure 5–5, you'll notice that at the highest level there are two branches—that is, two constituents—while in the tree diagram of Figure 5–6 there are three branches and therefore three constituents. Notice, too, that in Figure 5–5 *boys and girls* is a constituent (but *gullible boys* is not), whereas in Figure 5–6 *gullible boys* is a constituent (but *boys and girls* is not). The trees thus capture the two possible constituent structures (and explain the respective readings) of *gullible boys and girls*.

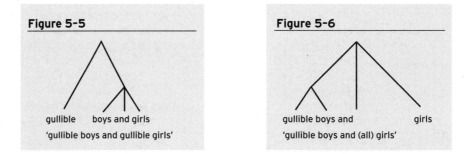

Figure 5-5

gullible   boys and girls
'gullible boys and gullible girls'

Figure 5-6

gullible boys and   girls
'gullible boys and (all) girls'

These figures show that a given word string may have more than one internal organization or internal architecture. Figures 5–5 and 5–6 represent the same four words in the same linear order, but with different constituent structures. The ambiguity in meaning in this sequence of words arises from the sequence's having two possible constituent structures.

Try it yourself: Choose one of these structurally ambiguous expressions and provide a pair of tree diagrams that capture the possible constituent structures: *excessive light and glare* or *modern novel reader.*

Structural Ambiguity   Structural ambiguity can also occur in the organization of sentences. Examine sentence 1 below.

1. He sold the car to his brother in New York.

Despite the fact that the individual words are unambiguous, this string of words has more than one possible interpretation. You may already suspect that the ambiguity arises from two possible constituent structures. Using brackets instead of a tree diagram, we can represent the ambiguity of 1 in 2 and 3 below.

2. He sold the car [to [his brother in New York]].
3. He sold the car [to his brother] [in New York].

We can paraphrase sentence 2 in 4 below, but not in 5 or 6. By contrast, we can paraphrase sentence 3 above in 5 or 6 below, but not in 4:

4. It was to his brother in New York that he sold the car.
5. It was in New York that he sold the car to his brother.
6. In New York he sold the car to his brother.

These examples illustrate that the words of a sentence have an internal organization that is not apparent from simple inspection of a word string. The linear order of words in a sentence—which is first, which second, and so on—is obvious from inspection. But only a speaker of English can recognize the constituent structure in an English sentence and know when a given string has more than one possible internal organization.

MAJOR CONSTITUENTS OF SENTENCES: NOUN PHRASES AND VERB PHRASES

To repeat what we have just said, besides their obvious linear order, the words in a sentence have a constituent structure that is not obvious but that is understood by speakers of the language. Consider the sentence in Figure 5–7, with its two constituents. More elaborate sentences, such as those in Figure 5–8, can be analyzed similarly.

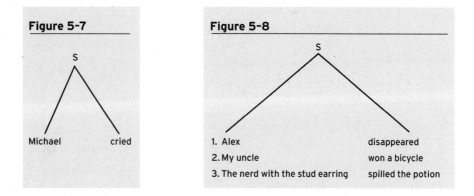

Figure 5-7

Figure 5-8

Noun Phrase and Verb Phrase

Sentences like those we've been examining consist of two principal constituents: Noun Phrase (NP) and Verb Phrase (VP). (These structures correspond roughly to the functional features of referring expression and predication discussed earlier.) In turn, each NP contains a noun (*Alex, uncle, nerd*) and each VP contains a verb (*disappeared, won, spilled*). NPs and VPs can be identified by the slots they fill in a sentence and sometimes by their functions as well. Thus in Figure 5–8, *Alex* in 1, *My uncle* in 2, and *The nerd with the stud earring* in 3 function as referring expressions about which a predication is made. Similarly, *disappeared, won a bicycle,* and *spilled the potion* function alike; they make predications about an NP.

NPs can also be identified by substitution procedures such as those implied in the list of alternatives to the two-part structure shown in Figure 5–8. Thus, for *Alex* we could substitute *My uncle* or *The nerd with the stud earring*. All three are NPs because they can occur in the slot _____ *won a bicycle* or _____ *spilled the potion* or _____ *disappeared*.

In sentence 2 below, the VP is *spilled the potion*. Unlike the VP of 1, which consists of the single word *disappeared,* the VP of 2 contains the verb *spilled* and the NP *the potion*. Thus a VP may contain an NP. Further, as 3 shows, VP may also contain a prepositional phrase (*in a contest*).

NP	VP
1. [Alex]	[disappeared]
2. [Bob]	[spilled the potion]
3. [The nerd with the stud earring]	[won the bike in a contest]

The NPs in the three sentences above include *Alex, Bob, the potion, the nerd, the stud earring, the bike,* and *a contest*. In fact, anything you could insert in the slots below would be an NP:

She enjoyed talking about _____ .

Invariably, _____ upset her.

Inserted into either slot, the following expressions would produce a well-formed English sentence and are therefore NPs; in each case, the "head noun" is italicized.

animals	his *return* to his first love
the *weather*	his *resolve* to go the distance
her youthful *instructor*	Walter's *winning* the race
the *thief* who stole her purse	an old *cyclist* from Cincinnati

Notice, too, that an NP can be a pronoun:

She enjoyed talking about *him/her/it/them/us*.

Invariably, *he/she/it/they/we* upset her.

NPs and pronouns have the same distribution in sentences; wherever an NP can occur, a pronoun can occur instead. Thus, pronouns are NPs.

VPs can be identified using similar substitution procedures. Consider the sentence *Lou cried,* where *cried* constitutes the VP. Among many others, the following strings can substitute for *cried* in the slot *Lou* _____. They thus fit the frame and are VPs (the verb in each VP is italicized):

Lou
$\begin{cases} \textit{fell} \\ \textit{lost} \text{ the race} \\ \textit{won} \text{ a prize for his efforts in the tournament} \end{cases}$

To this point, we have seen two major constituents of a sentence: NP and VP.

Active and Passive Sentences

Regardless of how many words it contains, an NP functions as a unified constituent in a sentence. Even elaborate NPs such as *the nerd with the stud earring* or *what she wanted to receive for her twenty-first birthday* are structural units, just like simple NPs such as *lions, she,* and *Robb.* To see more clearly what we mean by a structural unit, a constituent, let's focus on active and passive sentences.

Consider the sentences below, where in each pair the first sentence is active, the second passive:

1a. Zelda auctioned the famous wooden spoon. (*ACTIVE*)

  b. The famous wooden spoon was auctioned by Zelda. (*PASSIVE*)

2a. The judge fined an old plumber from Pasadena. (*ACTIVE*)

  b. An old plumber from Pasadena was fined by the judge. (*PASSIVE*)

3a. The mail truck crushed Karen's bike. (*ACTIVE*)

  b. Karen's bike was crushed by the mail truck. (*PASSIVE*)

Try it yourself: Following the pattern in the three pairs of sentences above, provide the passive version of *Dean Kamen invented the heart stent and the Segway* and the active version of *The pantry must be stocked by the husbands who stay at home and mind the kids.*

Many children who have never heard of active and passive sentences can provide the passive version of an active sentence when a few model pairs have been illustrated for them. They implicitly know how a passive sentence is related to an active one. Let's attempt to make explicit what that knowledge must be.

On the basis of sentences 1a and 1b above, we might hypothesize this rule: "To change an active sentence to a passive one, interchange the first word (*Zelda*) with the last four (*the famous wooden spoon*)." (For present purposes, we will ignore the verb *was* and the preposition *by,* but in a complete statement of the rule those features would have to be specified as well.) Our rule produces a well-formed string when applied to sentence 1a; but when applied to 2a it produces the ill-formed string given in 2c below, and when applied to 3a it produces the ill-formed string given in 3c below:

2a. The judge fined an old plumber from Pasadena.

  c. *Old plumber from Pasadena judge was fined an by the.

3a. The mail truck crushed Karen's bike.

  c. *Truck crushed Karen's bike mail was by the.

Check for yourself to see that 2c and 3c would result from interchanging the first word and the last four words of 2a and 3a (assuming the introduction of *by* and an appropriate form of the verb BE). Clearly, what even young speakers know about the relationship between active and passive sentences does *not* involve counting words. Instead, as you recognize by now, it involves constituent structure. The operation that relates active and passive sentences is a *structure dependent* operation.

Refer again to the constituents that are interchanged in the active/passive pairs of sentences 1a and b, 2a and b, and 3a and b. The strings of words in each of the following sets share a structural property in that they function similarly:

4. Zelda/The judge/The mail truck

5. the famous wooden spoon/an old plumber from Pasadena/Karen's bike

The NPs in sets 4 and 5 move *as units* in the syntactic operation of forming a passive sentence from an active one. In relating active and passive sentences, NPs function as constituents, no matter how many words they contain.

PHRASE-STRUCTURE RULES

Expanding Noun Phrase

Relying on the analysis of categories (parts of speech) in Chapter 2, we can now characterize and exemplify certain NP types:

Noun (N): *Karen, oracles, justice, swimming*

Determiner (Det) + Noun: *that amulet, a potion, some gnomes, my saucer*

Determiner + Noun + Prepositional Phrase (PP): *the book on the table, a rise in prices, the marketplace of ideas, the man behind the curtain*

Determiner + Adjective (A) + Noun: *an ancient oracle, these hellish precincts, the first omen, my flat saucer*

To represent these various NP patterns we use **phrase-structure rules** such as the following:

1. NP →   N   (NP consists of N)

2. NP → Det   N   (NP consists of Det + N)

3. NP ➜ Det   N PP   (NP consists of Det + N + PP)

4. NP ➜ Det A N   (NP consists of Det + A + N)

These four rules, or expansions, can be combined into one rule. To do that, we place parentheses around optional elements, or those that don't need to occur. Notice that N is the *only* constituent required in every NP expansion; the others are optional and must be placed in parentheses. The combined rule looks like this:

5. NP ➜ (Det) (A) N (PP)

Rule 5 can be expanded into the four separate rules (1–4) that we intended to capture. In addition, though, it has several expansions that we did not anticipate. Because Det, A, and PP are optional, we can rewrite NP not only as in 1, 2, 3, and 4, but also in other ways:

6. NP ➜ A   N

7. NP ➜ Det A N PP

Rule 5 thus suggests additional expansions that we did not set out to capture. If English in fact has well-formed NP structures consisting of A N (as in 6) and of Det A N PP (as in 7), as well as any other expansions that 5 would permit, then 5 is valid. Otherwise, we would have to revise it to exclude ill-formed structures.

Of course, some English NPs are composed of A and N (*ordinary superheroes; natural grace; great imagination),* while others consist of Det A N PP (*his sorry life on the sidelines; the white whale on the beach; those fantastic clouds in the sky).* One advantage of formalisms such as the combined rule 5 is that they often entail unanticipated claims that can be checked against other data. They thus provide a test of their own validity.

Expanding Prepositional Phrase

PP stands for prepositional phrase, of which previous examples include *in the car, from Xanadu, in New York, to his brother, with the stud earring,* and *by the judge.* PPs consist of a preposition (PREP) and, typically, a noun phrase (NP), so the phrase-structure rule for PP is:

PP ➜ **PREP** NP

If NP is taken to be optional (as in *She walked behind the wagon/She walked behind),* then the rule would place NP in parenthesis.

Expanding Sentence and Verb Phrase

To capture the fact that sentences and clauses have two basic constituent parts, we can formulate the following phrase-structure rule:

S ➜ NP VP

Every phrase-structure rule can generate a tree diagram, and this one generates the following tree:

Having already seen various expansions of NP, we can now turn to the internal structure of VP and explore its expansions. The following expansions of our frame for identifying VPs reveal that the structures on the right (those following *Lou*) are VPs; the labels under constituents of the VP indicate their categories.

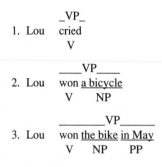

1. Lou   _VP_
      cried
       V

2. Lou   ____VP____
      won <u>a bicycle</u>
       V   NP

3. Lou   _____VP_____
      won <u>the bike</u> <u>in May</u>
       V   NP   PP

Sentences 1, 2, and 3 above indicate three ways to expand VP:

VP → V

VP → V NP

VP → V NP PP

V is the only constituent that occurs in all these rules. By contrast, NP and PP are optional. Using parentheses for optional elements, the three expansions above can be combined into a single phrase-structure rule, which represents that VP must have V and may have NP, PP, or both:

VP → V (NP) (PP)

Just as we discovered unanticipated options when we combined four expansions of NP into one, so the combined rule for VP will generate the structure V PP. Notice that V PP is not represented among sentences 1, 2, and 3, which formed the basis of the constituent structure rules for VP. We can check the validity of the expansion, and see that V PP is in fact necessary to represent the internal structure of VP in sentences such as *(Finian) played in the yard, (Dana) raced around the track,* and *(Pat) flew to Ballina,* the last of which is illustrated below.

Pat   _____VP____
        flew <u>to Ballina</u>
        V   PP

Phrase-Structure Rules and Tree Diagrams

We have formulated four phrase-structure rules:

S   → NP VP

NP → (Det) (A) **N** (PP)

VP → **V** (NP) (PP)

PP → **PREP** (NP)

These represent the fact that a sentence has an NP and a VP; that an NP has an N; that a VP has a V; and that a PP has a PREP. According to these phrase-structure rules, all other possibilities are optional.

The following tree diagram can be generated by our rules:

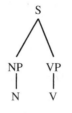

That is the simplest structure generated by our phrase-structure rules and represents sentences such as *Lou disappeared* and *That stinks*. Now consider the more complicated structure given in Figure 5–9, where we have supplied one sample sentence for the structure. It is clear that our four phrase-structure rules can represent sentences that are structurally simple or structurally elaborate.

Figure 5-9

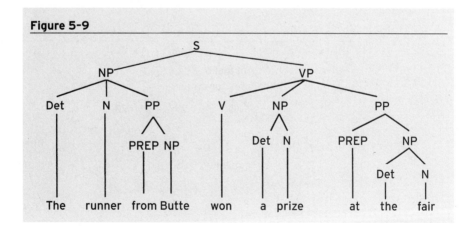

Try it yourself: Come up with a sentence whose constituent structure is the same as the one in Figure 5–9. Then, using the four phrase-structure rules that produced Figure 5–9, provide a *different* structure and two example sentences to illustrate it.

GRAMMATICAL RELATIONS: SUBJECT, DIRECT OBJECT, AND OTHERS

Using phrase-structure rules, we can precisely define subject and direct object. In defining them, these two phrase-structure rules are important:

S → NP VP

VP → V (NP) (PP)

Immediate Dominance

We can represent the relevant parts of these phrase-structure rules in a tree diagram. In Figure 5–10, the circled NP is directly under the S node, the boxed NP is directly under the VP node, and the VP node is directly under the S node. When a node is directly under another node, we say it is *immediately dominated* by that other node. Thus in Figure 5–10, V is immediately dominated by VP; the circled NP is immediately dominated by S; the boxed NP is immediately dominated by VP; and both VP and the circled NP are immediately dominated by S.

Subject and Direct Object

We can now define subject and direct object in terms of phrase-structure rules and the tree diagrams they generate. In English, **subject** is defined as the NP that is immediately dominated by S. In our diagram, the circled NP is the *subject*. **Direct object** is defined as an NP that is immediately dominated by VP. In Figure 5–10 it is the boxed NP. Because NP is an optional element in the expansion of VP, it follows that not every sentence will have an NP immediately dominated by VP, and thus not every sentence will have a direct object.

Figure 5-10

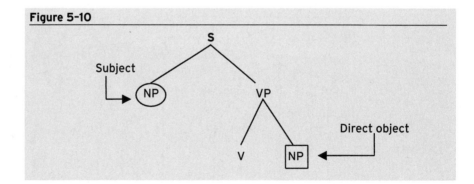

Transitive and Intransitive Recall from Chapter 2 that a sentence lacking a direct object contains an *intransitive* verb. Intransitive verbs can be exemplified by *cry, hurry, laugh,* and *disappear,* none of which can take a direct object. By contrast, verbs that take a direct object are called *transitive* verbs; examples include *make, buy,* and *find,* as in *make a potion, buy a motorbike,* and *find a penny.* While some verbs can be both transitive and intransitive, as shown in the first three pairs of sentences below, others are only transitive or only intransitive:

Intransitive	Transitive
Joshua won.	Joshua won a prize.
Taylor sings.	Taylor sings lullabies.
Suze studied at Oxford.	Suze studied economics at Oxford.
Miguel disappeared.	*Miguel disappeared the dishes.
*Michael frightened.	Michael frightened the kittens.

Try it yourself: Come up with a sentence with a verb that can only be intransitive and another with a verb that can only be transitive. Then give a pair of sentences that use the same verb but in one case is transitive and in the other intransitive.

Grammatical Relations

Certain structural properties of subjects and direct objects cannot be equated with anything else, including meaning. Subject and direct object are grammatical relations. **Grammatical relation** is the term used to capture the syntactic relationship in a clause between an NP and the predicate. In other words, grammatical relations indicate the syntactic role that an NP plays in its clause. Besides subject and direct object, sentences can have other grammatical relations, such as **indirect object, oblique,** and **possessor.** English has the grammatical relations *oblique* for NPs that are the object of a preposition (*The poltergeist pointed to **his tooth***) and *possessor* (***Josh's** car*).

Passive Sentences and Structure Dependence

Having defined subject and direct object in structural terms, we can now return to a syntactic relationship examined earlier. The notions of subject and direct object allow us to reformulate the relationship between active and passive sentences as follows:

> To convert an active sentence to a passive one, interchange the subject NP and the direct object NP.

(As before, provision must be made for the preposition *by* and a form of the verb BE.) Here's an example:

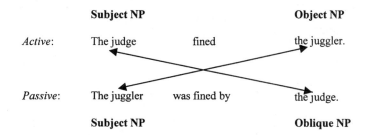

	Subject NP		**Object NP**
Active:	The judge	fined	the juggler.
Passive:	The juggler	was fined by	the judge.
	Subject NP		**Oblique NP**

You can see that in a passive sentence the direct object of the active sentence appears as subject, and the subject of the active sentence appears as an oblique (preceded by the preposition *by).*

SURFACE STRUCTURES AND UNDERLYING STRUCTURES

We have now seen that speakers understand more about the structure of a sentence than is apparent in the linear sequence of its words. Not only do speakers have implicit knowledge of constituent structure, but speakers also often understand more constituents in a sentence than are actually expressed. For example, knowledge of English syntactic rules is essential to understand the meaning of sentences such as the following:

Lisa won a prize, but Larry
1. didn't.
2. didn't care.
3. didn't tell Sarah.
4. didn't celebrate with her.
5. didn't visit Paris to buy a tie.
6. didn't train tigers.
7. didn't win a prize.

Although the list of possible sentences following this pattern is endless, the only legitimate interpretation of sentence 1 is sentence 7. Sentences 2 through 6 are not possible interpretations of 1. We understand sentence 1 as having the implicit completion *win a prize*.

To explain this, recall that in Chapter 4 we postulated underlying forms of sounds and underlying forms of morphemes. One way to accommodate implicit knowledge about sentence structure is to posit underlying syntactic structures. For instance, we can represent the meaning of sentence 1 by positing an underlying form something like *Lisa won a prize, but Larry didn't win a prize*. If we assumed such an underlying form, we would also have to postulate certain syntactic processes in order to delete the second occurrence of *win a prize* and generate the sentence *Lisa won a prize, but Larry didn't*.

Syntactic Operations

We have seen examples of syntactic operations of English, including passivization. Now we will analyze others.

Question Formation

English has two principal kinds of questions. Yes/no questions can be answered with a reply of yes or no (*Was it a frank discussion?*). Information questions include a WH-word like *who, what,* or *when* and require more than a simple yes or no reply.

Yes/No Questions   Examine the pairs of statements and yes/no questions below.

1. Suze will earn a fair wage.
   Will Suze earn a fair wage?

2. Tony was winning the race when he stumbled.
   Was Tony winning the race when he stumbled?

In each case, if you compare the *form* of the statement with the *form* of the question, you'll see that forming the yes/no question requires moving the auxiliary verb to a position before the subject NP. (Verbs such as *will* in 1 and *was* in 2—as well as *did* and *does* in 3 and 4 below—are called auxiliary verbs and are distinguished from main verbs such as *earn* and *winning*. Verbs that can be moved in front of the subject NP to form questions are called **auxiliary verbs** or helping verbs; auxiliaries are also the constituent of the VP that carries the negative element in contractions such as *can't, shouldn't,* and *wasn't.*) In fact, yes/no questions have an auxiliary even when the corresponding statements do not, as 3 and 4 show:

3. Alvin *studied* alchemy in college.
   Did Alvin *study* alchemy in college?

4. Inflation always *hurts* the poor.
   Does inflation always *hurt* the poor?

Sentence pairs such as 3 and 4 provide an argument for positing an auxiliary in the underlying structure of *every* sentence, even though not every sentence expresses an auxiliary in the surface structure. Notice, however, that in English an auxiliary must appear in the surface structure of negative sentences (*Alvin didn't study alchemy*) and questions (*Does inflation hurt the poor?*). It is also typically used to express emphasis (*But she does exercise every day!*) and certain other semantic information such as time reference (*She will win*) and aspect (*They are walking home*). (Aspect and time reference are discussed in Chapter 6.)

Given that an auxiliary often appears in the surface structure (and also for other reasons not discussed here), an auxiliary constituent is postulated in the underlying structure of sentences. Like all constituents in the underlying structure, the auxiliary is generated by a phrase-structure rule. Instead of the earlier rule that expanded S as NP VP, we can postulate the following rule:

S   →   NP   AUX   VP

We can represent the structure generated by this rule in a tree diagram:

The operation that changes the constituent structure of the statements in 1, 2, 3, and 4 above to the constituent structure of their respective yes/no questions moves AUX to a slot preceding the subject NP, as represented below:

We thus represent the underlying form of the sentences of 1 on page 160 as in the tree on the left in Figure 5–11. The tree on the right is the constituent structure that results from application of the subject-auxiliary inversion operation.

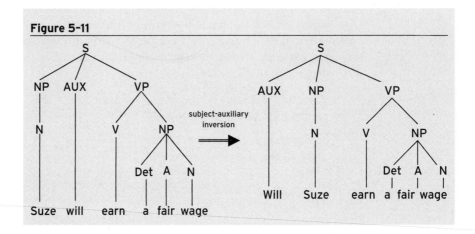

Figure 5-11

The rule could be written as follows:

NP AUX VP ⟹ AUX NP VP

Information Questions   In an information question, the information that is sought—the questioned constituent—is represented by a WH-word. Information questions contain a WH-word (*who, why, when, where, which, what, how*) and are sometimes called WH-questions. (*Note:*In the remainder of this chapter, we will sometimes ignore the distinction drawn between the use of *who* and *whom* in traditional grammar and in much careful writing and speaking.)

Information questions occur in two forms. One "echoes" the form of the statement, as in these examples:

(He's boiling horsefeathers.)   He's boiling *what?*

(She was looking for Sigmund Freud.)   She was looking for *who?*

Such echo questions are used when you have failed to hear something completely or can't believe what you've heard. Their linear form is identical to that of the statement, except that a WH-word occurs in place of the questioned constituent.

More common than echo questions are ordinary information questions. They take the form illustrated below, in which an operation called WH-movement has fronted the WH-word:

1. What is he   boiling — ? (He is boiling what?)

2. Who was she   looking for — today? (She was looking for who today?)

If you compare these ordinary information questions with the parenthesized echo questions, you can see that two alterations have occurred:

- The WH-word (the questioned constituent) appears at the front of its clause.
- The auxiliary constituent precedes the subject NP.

Notice that ordinary information questions leave a "gap" in the structure at the place vacated by the fronted WH-word (indicated here by a dash —). This isn't true of echo questions because the WH-word stays in its underlying position.

Embedded Clauses

We have already examined sentences such as *Lou cried*. We want now to examine sentences that have other sentence-like structures embedded within. In the following examples, the italicized clause is incorporated (or embedded) into another sentence.

1. Suze said *Lou cried.*
2. *That James won the marathon* surprised Sheila.

In sentence 1, the clause *Lou cried* is embedded into the clausal structure *Suze said —*. The clause *Lou cried* thus corresponds structurally to the word *something* in the sentence *Suze said something*. In 2, the clause *That James won the marathon* is embedded into the structure *— surprised Sheila*. The embedded clause in 2 (*That James won the marathon*) is structurally equivalent to *It* in *It surprised Sheila* or *The news* in *The news surprised Sheila*.

Subordinators

The embedded clause often is introduced by a word that would not occur in that position if the clause were standing as an independent sentence, such as *That* in 2. This word is called a subordinator. Subordinators serve to mark the beginning of an embedded clause and to help identify its function in the sentence. Not all embedded clauses must be introduced by a subordinator, although in English they usually can be. Compare these sentence pairs:

1. Suze said *that* Dan washed the dishes.
2. Suze said Dan washed the dishes.
3. *That* she won surprised us.
4. *She won surprised us.

Notice that 1 and 2 are well formed with or without the subordinator *that*. But while 3 is well formed, 4 is not.

In the sentences we have been examining, one clause is subordinate to another and functions as a grammatical part of the other clause. The subordinate clause is an *embedded clause* and the sentence in which it is embedded is a *matrix clause*. By definition, every subordinate clause is embedded in a matrix clause and serves a grammatical function in it. (Grammatical functions include subject and direct object, which we'll discuss further below.) For example, in sentences 1 and 3 below, where brackets set off embedded clauses, each embedded clause functions as a grammatical unit in its matrix clause. Each embedded clause has the same grammatical function in its matrix clause as the underscored word has in the sentence directly below it:

1. Harry said [he saw a ghost].
2. Harry said <u>it</u>.
3. [That Josh feared witches] upset his wife.
4. <u>It</u> upset his wife.

Tree diagrams can also illustrate the relationship among the clauses of a sentence such as *Harry said he saw a ghost.* In representing such a sentence, we can substitute the clause *he saw a ghost* for the word *it,* as in Figure 5–12. This tree diagram captures the fact that the embedded clause S_2 *(he saw a ghost)* functions structurally as part of the matrix clause S_1 *(Harry said —).* The embedded clause fills the same slot in the matrix clause as the word *it* fills in the clause *Harry said it.*

Figure 5-12

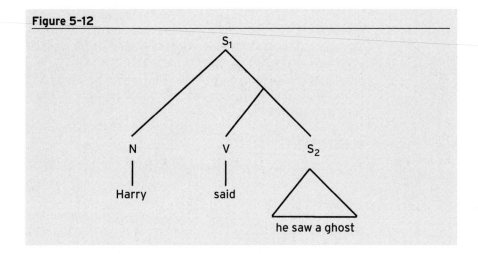

Relative Clauses

A **relative clause** is formed when one clause is embedded into an NP of another clause to produce structures such as those below (the relative clauses are italicized):

1. The principal praised [the teacher *who flunked me*].
2. [The jewels *that he borrowed*] were fakes.
3. Sally saw the new film by [the French director *that Kim raved about*].
4. Sally saw the new film by [the French director *Kim raved about*].

When NPs that have the same referent occur in two clauses, a relative clause can be formed by embedding one clause into the other, as in the example below. The identical indexes on *cousin* are used to indicate identical referents:

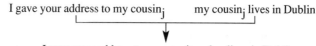

I gave your address to my cousin$_j$ who$_j$ lives in Dublin

English relative clauses are usually introduced by a relative pronoun such as *who* (or *whom* or *whose*), *which,* or *that.* As in 4 above, the pronoun may be omitted in specific circumstances. Relative clauses modify nouns, and the noun that the relative clause modifies is called the *head noun.* In English, the head noun is "repeated" in the embedded clause, where it is *relativized* (takes the form of a relative pronoun). A relative clause is part of the same noun phrase as its head noun. The structure of the resulting noun phrase can be represented as in Figure 5–13, in which the head noun *cousin* is labeled N. Notice that in this instance the relativized NP *who* functions as the subject of its clause (the NP that is immediately dominated by S).

Figure 5-13

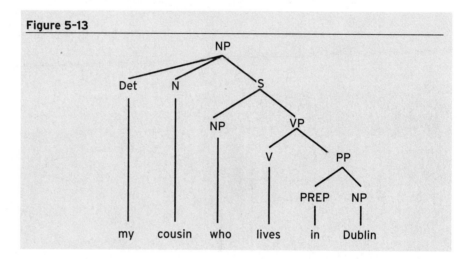

In other clauses, the relativized NP may be another grammatical relation such as a direct object, as in this illustration:

The jewels *that he borrowed* were fakes.

Here the relative clause *that he borrowed* derives from the underlying clause *he borrowed the jewels.*

A relativized NP can also be an oblique as in 1 or a possessor as in 2:

1. This is the officer *whom I told you about.* (cf. *I told you about the officer*)
2. This is the officer *whose car was vandalized.* (cf. *the officer's car was vandalized*)

In English, then, a relativized NP can have the following grammatical relations within its clause: subject, direct object, oblique, or possessor.

COMP Node

Now let's analyze the syntactic processes associated with relative clause formation in English. Examine the following sentences, noting the "gap" in the structure (indicated by a dash —):

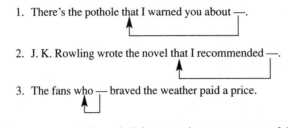

1. There's the pothole that I warned you about —.

2. J. K. Rowling wrote the novel that I recommended —.

3. The fans who — braved the weather paid a price.

We can represent the underlying constituent structure of these sentences in a tree diagram, as Figure 5–14 illustrates for sentence 2.

Figure 5-14

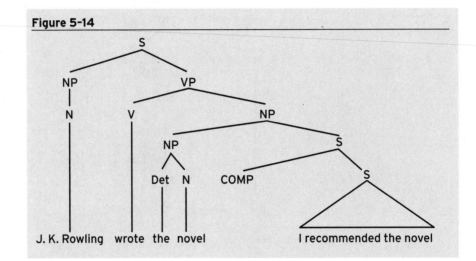

In order to produce the relative clause structure of 2, the relativized NP *the novel* is pronominalized and moved to the front of its clause by the WH-movement operation we described for information questions. In Figure 5–14 there is a node labeled COMP (for 'complementizer'), which we have not previously identified. It is possible to discuss the WH-movement operation for relative clauses without utilizing the COMP node (as we did for information questions), but there is reason to posit such a node in the underlying structure. Among other functions, it serves as a kind of "magnet" for WH-constituents, such as *that, which, who*, and other relative pronouns, as well as the WH-constituents of information questions.

Since syntactic operations change one constituent structure into another, we can represent the output of WH-movement as applied to Figure 5–14 by the tree given in

Figure 5–15. Thus, by WH-movement, a WH-constituent is extracted from S and attached to the COMP node. We have examined WH-movement with respect to relative clauses, but the same operation could move any WH-constituent to the COMP node, including question words in the formation of information questions.

Figure 5-15

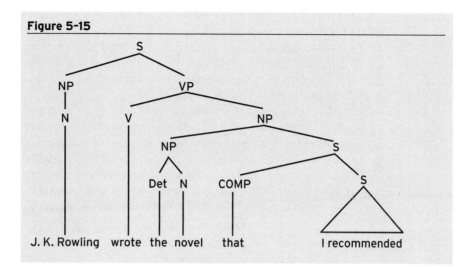

TYPES OF SYNTACTIC OPERATIONS

While it is not known how many types of syntactic processes exist in human languages, recent theories of syntax reflect evidence that these operations are considerably more general than our detailed specifications of particular ones might suggest. Movement operations are extremely common in the languages of the world, and in one theoretical model of syntax all transformations are movement rules.

FUNCTIONS OF SYNTACTIC OPERATIONS

We have now examined several syntactic operations, principally from a structural perspective. We've emphasized the fact that syntactic operations are structure dependent. For example, irrespective of the length or grammatical complexity of the subject and object, active and passive sentences are related in that the object of the active sentence (for example, *The judge fined **Jaime***) is the subject of the related passive sentence (***Jaime** was fined by the judge*), and the subject of the active sentence becomes an oblique (*by the judge*) in the passive structure. Before concluding our discussion of syntax, we want to inquire into the purpose of having syntactic operations such as those that form passives. We exemplify with English examples, but comparable analyses apply to syntactic operations in other languages.

We begin with a straightforward example. In English, as we saw, yes/no questions are formed by moving the auxiliary in certain structural patterns. Thus, from the structure underlying *She will swear to it,* a syntactic operation produces the structure *Will she swear to it?* From a functional perspective, the declarative makes a statement; the interrogative asks a question. That's no surprise, of course, because languages must have ways to make statements and ask questions. The point we want to emphasize is that, as in these English examples, the form of the question is related to the form of the statement and is achieved in this case by the syntactic operation of what we have called subject-auxiliary inversion. (English has other ways of forming questions, including assigning a special intonation pattern to a declarative structure, but we don't examine those other ways here.)

More interesting and less obvious are the *functions* served by having active and passive structures. Generally speaking, active and passive sentences mean the same thing. After all, if Jaime was fined by the judge, it must also be the case that the judge fined Jaime. Why, then, should there be two ways of saying the same thing? Why does English syntax provide both active and passive versions of a sentence? To figure out the answer, consider the passage below about a baseball player named Odalis Perez; it appeared in an article in the Sports section of the *Los Angeles Times.*

> **Perez** *gave up* an infield single to Barry Bonds before getting Andres Galarraga on another infield popup for the final out. **Perez** *re-engaged* Hernandez as **he** *was walking* off the field, triggering the ejection. **He** *was* also *ejected* June 13 against the Cleveland Indians at Jacobs Field.

Perez is the grammatical subject of the first two sentences, and *He* (that is, Perez) the grammatical subject of the third sentence. (The *he* in the embedded clause in the second sentence also refers to Perez.) Of the four italicized verbs, the first three are active, and all three have *Perez* or *he* (meaning Perez) as the subject: Perez *gave up*; Perez *re-engaged*; he *was walking*. It's clear that the writer's focus is on Perez.

Let's examine the final sentence as originally written (repeated in 1 below) and as an active sentence (number 2):

1. *He* *was* also *ejected* June 13 against the Cleveland Indians at Jacobs Field.

2. **An umpire** *ejected* him June 13 against the Cleveland Indians at Jacobs Field.

Using a passive structure in the final sentence of the published passage allows the writer to keep the focus on Perez. The reason is that in English the subject tends to be the topic of its sentence, the center of attention (a matter to which we return in Chapter 8). Introducing an umpire into the passage as the grammatical subject of the third sentence would remove the focus from Perez; it would make the umpire the topic of that sentence.

As a further point, note that in a passive sentence the subject of the corresponding active sentence can be omitted altogether. Instead of *He was ejected by an umpire*, the writer could simply say *He was ejected*. By using a passive, in particular an agentless passive, the writer keeps the focus of the entire passage on Perez.

Try it yourself: Explain why the writer in the passage below uses the underlined passive structure in sentence 3 and also why that sentence combines an active (*over-ran*) and passive verb (*was thrown*). 1. *The Dodgers scored only one run despite twice loading the bases in the sixth, and Daryle Ward's baserunning blunder in the ninth stirred more frustration for a team encountering a lot in Northern California. 2. With Jolbert Cabrera on first and one out, Ward singled through the hole on the right side, sending Cabrera to third. 3. But Ward overran the bag and <u>was thrown out</u>, quickly dampening the Dodgers' mood.*

Computers and the Study of Syntax

 We saw in Chapter 2 that computer programs can do a good job of tagging the words in sentences with their part of speech, identifying lexical categories for many English words. But even a sentence whose words have been tagged with their part of speech is very far from being syntactically analyzed. Programs that can analyze a string of lexical categories for their constituent structure are known as *parsers,* and some parsers achieve impressive success in assigning constituent structure to a string of lexical catetories. (You can judge for yourself just how good they are by going to the Web site listed in the Internet Resources section of this chapter.)

Tagging the words of a sentence for a lexical category is not the same thing as identifying constituent structure. For one thing, just as a string of words may have more than one constituent structure, so may a particular string of lexical categories. As we saw earlier, the noun phrase *gullible boys and girls* has two possible constituent structures. It follows that the string of lexical categories for that phrase could likewise have two bracketings, either

[A [N Conj N]]   or   [A N] [Conj] [N].

Some sophisticated computer programs can analyze tagged sentences and produce a labeled constituent structure or tree diagram. In the case of *gullible boys and girls,* a parser would produce two candidate constituent structures.

Researchers have faced substantial challenges constructing parsers that can analyze a wide range of natural English sentences. Many English sentences are relatively straightforward and easy to parse, but many others are not. Interestingly, made-up sentences tend to be easier to parse than sentences that occur in ordinary conversation. Let's see how a parser would operate.

First, given a sentence such as *That rancher saw the wolves,* a tagger would readily assign parts of speech to the words as follows:

That$_\text{Det}$ rancher$_\text{N}$ saw$_\text{V}$ the$_\text{Det}$ wolves$_\text{N}$

In principle, *saw* could be a noun or a verb and *that* could also have several possible tags, but even moderately sophisticated taggers will not have difficulty determining the correct tags in a sentence like this. Once part-of-speech tags have been assigned, a parser uses only a few phrase-structure rules to produce a tree diagram or a constituent-structure bracketing for the string. You can envision the process as something like working from the bottom of a tree structure to the top. For example, the phrase-structure rule NP → Det N brackets *that rancher* and *the wolves* as NPs, which yields the bracketing NP V NP. The phrase-structure rule VP → V NP allows *saw the wolves* to be bracketed as VP, giving NP VP. That in turn is recognized as a representation of S. Taken together then, the tagged string can be parsed as follows:

[s [NP [That Det] [rancher N] NP] [VP [saw V [NP [the Det] [wolves N] NP] VP] s]

This labeled bracketing is entirely equivalent to the tree diagram below:

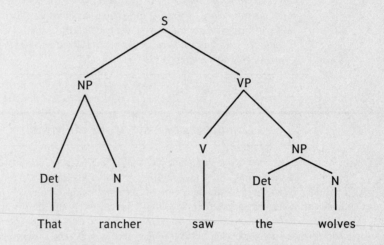

With more complicated strings (as most naturally occurring ones are), assigning the correct constituent structure may not be so straightforward.

Grammar checkers in word processors have relatively simple parsers in them. On the basis of those parsers, they sometimes suggest changes to your syntax in the interest of grammatical correctness or stylistic refinement. As you may have experienced, such grammar checkers often suggest revisions that indicate they have incorrectly parsed the sentence. Often, too, grammar checkers working on natural sentences find them too long to parse, and the most they can do is suggest that the sentence be shortened.

SUMMARY

- The rules governing the formation of sentences constitute the syntax of a language. The study of sentence structure is also called syntax.
- All languages have referring expressions and predication expressions.
- In syntactic terms, a referring expression is an NP (noun phrase) and a predication expression a VP (verb phrase).
- A sentence (and a clause) consists of a verb with the necessary set of NPs.
- Speakers of every language can generate an unlimited number of sentences from a finite number of rules for combining phrases.
- Syntactic rules are of two types—phrase-structure rules and syntactic operations. The latter may be called "transformations."
- Phrase-structure rules generate underlying constituent structures.

- Syntactic operations change one constituent structure into another constituent structure.
- Positing underlying constituent structures captures the striking regularity of certain relationships between sentences.
- Positing underlying structures helps explain some elements of meaning and certain syntactic and semantic relationships between sentences.
- In order to explain how speakers relate two structures to one another (such as *Martha doesn't believe in poltergeists* and *Doesn't Martha believe in poltergeists?*), linguists posit a rule of English that transforms the structure underlying the basic declarative sentence into the structure underlying the derived interrogative one.
- It appears that the most important and most general syntactic operations involve movement such as WH-movement.

WHAT DO YOU THINK? REVISITED

❖ *Your classmate Rudy.* We hear some expressions so frequently that it's easy to guess how we know them. But probably most of the things we say in our interactions we have neither heard nor read before. Fortunately, the structures that underlie what we say and hear are relatively few. By combining these few structures in different ways, we can generate or understand completely new sentences easily and accurately.

❖ *Amber and ambiguity.* Ambiguous words often don't call attention to themselves because particular contexts readily promote a particular reading. An utterance such as *I'm going to the bank to deposit a check* excludes the likelihood of a river bank. Another kind of ambiguity arises when a string of words has more than one possible internal organization. A phrase such as *new drug combinations* can mean 'combinations of new drugs' or 'new combinations of drugs,' depending on which words go together: does *new* go with *drug* or with *drug combinations?*

❖ *Nerdy Ned.* Ned should consider offing a grammar checker that's so unsophisticated it recommends changing every passive sentence he writes. Sometimes a passive sentence is precisely what's needed to keep the focus where a writer intends it to be. If Ned was writing about a winning team, he probably wants to keep the focus there, and one way to do that is by making *the winning team* the subject of the sentence.

EXERCISES

Based on English

5-1 **a.** List as many examples of these constituents as you can identify in sentences 1) and 2) below: NP, PP, VP.

  b. List as many examples of these lexical categories as you can identify in sentences 1) and 2) below: N, PREP, V.

   1) A concert at an arena near St. Louis ended in disaster after some fans staged a full-fledged riot.

   2) The trouble started when Axl Rose asked venue security to confiscate a camera he saw near the front of the stage.

5-2   For each of the expansions of VP given on page 156, provide an illustration.

   Example: **V NP** — *ate an apple.*

5-3   **a.** Draw a labeled tree diagram for each phrase given below.

   1) ancient inscriptions
   2) in the dark night
   3) concocted a potion
   4) borrowed the book that the teacher recommended
   5) the monstrous members of a terrible kingdom

   b. Provide a tree diagram for each sentence below (for the moment, ignore the italics).

   1) Witches *frighten him.*
   2) The skies deluged the earth *with water.*
   3) *A ghost has the spirit* of a dead person.
   4) *Do ghosts exist* in *the physical world?*
   5) *Does she* believe that ghosts exist?
   6) The teacher *that I described to you* won the race.

   c. For each italicized group of words in the sentences above, determine whether or not it is a constituent, and, if it is, provide its name.

5-4   What is the difference in the relationship between *Harry* and the verb *see* in 1) and 2) below? Draw tree diagrams of the underlying structure of the two sentences that reveal the difference in the structures.

   1) Josh advised Harry to see the doctor.
   2) Josh promised Harry to see the doctor.

5-5   English has a syntactic operation called dative movement that derives sentence 2) from the structure underlying sentence 1):

   1) I sent a letter to Hillary.
   2) I sent Hillary a letter.

The following also exemplify sentences with dative movement:

   He sold *his brother* a sailboat.
   Hal won't tell *me* Daniel's new phone number.
   I'm giving *my cousin* a new pair of pajamas.

   a. Give the three basic sentences corresponding to the three derived sentences.

   b. Dative movement applies to prepositional phrases that begin with the preposition *to* but cannot apply to prepositional phrases that begin with most other prepositions:

   *I will finish you the homework. (from *I will finish the homework with you.*)
   *My neighbor heard the radio the news. (from *My neighbor heard the news on the radio.*)

   But dative movement does not apply to all phrases that begin with the preposition to. The sentences in 3) below cannot undergo dative movement, as shown by the ungrammaticality of the corresponding sentences in 4).

   3) He's driving a truck to New Orleans.
       He'll take his complaint to the main office.

    4) *He's driving New Orleans a truck.

       *He'll take the main office his complaint.

  Describe dative movement in detail.

c. Now observe the ungrammatical sentences in 5) below, which are derived through dative movement from the sentences underlying the corresponding basic sentences in 6). How must you modify your description of dative movement so that it does not generate the ungrammatical sentences of 5)?

    5) *I gave my new neighbor it.

       *I'm taking my little sister them.

       *They will probably send him me.

    6) I gave it to my new neighbor.

       I'm taking them to my little sister.

       They will probably send me to him.

5-6 English has the grammatical relations of subject, direct object, oblique, and possessor. But it is debatable whether indirect object is a distinct grammatical relation and, if so, whether it occurs in sentences such as *The witch offered **the child** a potion* or *The witch offered a potion to **the child***. The syntactic properties of *the child* differ in the two sentences. What syntactic evidence can you offer for arguing that *the child* does not have the same grammatical relation in each of these sentences? (*Hint:* At least one syntactic operation examined in this chapter does not produce grammatical strings for both sentences.)

5-7 English has two types of relative clauses. Type 1 was described in this chapter; it leaves prepositions where they are in the original clause.

    This is the man [who I talked *to* — last night]. (original clause: *I talked to the man last night*)

In Type 2, the preposition *to* moves with the WH-word to the beginning of the clause.

    This is the man [*to* whom I talked last night].

Describe the relative-clause operation that forms Type 2 relative clauses, focusing on how it differs from the operation that forms Type 1 relative clauses. Identify which relative pronouns can occur in which type of relative clause, and in which cases the two types differ. Base your discussion on the following data:

This is the man [that left]. (Types 1 and 2)
*This is the man [left]. (Types 1 and 2)

This is the man [that I saw]. (Types 1 and 2)
This is the man [who I saw]. (Types 1 and 2)
This is the man [whom I saw]. (Types 1 and 2)
This is the man [I saw]. (Types 1 and 2)

This is the man [who I gave the book to]. (Type 1)
This is the man [whom I gave the book to]. (Type 1)
This is the man [that I gave the book to]. (Type 1)
This is the man [I gave the book to]. (Type 1)

*This is the man [to who I gave the book]. (Type 2)
This is the man [to whom I gave the book]. (Type 2)
*This is the man [to that I gave the book]. (Type 2)
*This is the man [to I gave the book]. (Type 2)

5-8 On p. 165 we noted that the relative pronoun may be omitted from certain structures. Thus, in the following sentence, Ø represents an omitted relative pronoun:

Sally saw a new film by the French director Ø Kim raved about.

  a. For each of the following sentences, identify the grammatical relation of the relativized NP within its clause, using S for subject, DO for direct object, and Obl for oblique.

   1) I lost the book [that you gave me].

   2) He rented the video [that frightened you].

   3) I bumped into the teacher [who taught me solid geometry].

   4) I met the poet [who(m) we read about last week].

   5) I found the video [that you lost].

   6) I saw the oak tree [that you slept under].

   7) The new teacher [that Lou liked] just quit.

   8) The new teacher [who liked jazz] just quit.

   9) I picked an apple from the tree [that you planted].

   10) I like the new lyrics [that you complained about].

  b. Which sentences would permit the relative pronoun to be omitted?

  c. Which would not permit the relative pronoun to be omitted?

  d. Which grammatical relations permit the relative pronoun to be omitted?

  e. Which grammatical relations do not permit the relative pronoun to be omitted?

  f. Rewrite sentences 4, 6, and 10, fronting the preposition with the relative pronoun.

  g. Can the relative pronoun be omitted from the rewritten versions of 4, 6, and 10?

  h. What generalization can you make about when a relative pronoun can be omitted from its clause?

5-9 Keeping in mind the movement rules for forming questions, analyze what has happened in the derivation of the sentences below to produce the ill-formed sentence. How would you formulate the auxiliary movement rule to avoid the ungrammatical example?

   The teacher who will give that lecture is Lily's aunt.

   *Will the teacher who give that lecture is Lily's aunt?

   Is the teacher who will give that lecture Lily's aunt?

5-10 Below are six examples of sentences that a word processor's grammar checker found objectionable, along with the comment that suggests a particular correction. In each case, the grammar checker has made an incorrect analysis and the suggested correction would yield an ill-formed sentence. For each example, identify the word or constituent structure that the grammar checker has wrongly analyzed and explain the basis for its suggested correction.

Example: "In this sentence, each embedded clause functions as a grammatical unit in its matrix clause."

Comment: The word *each* does not agree with *functions*. Consider *function* instead of *functions*. Explanation: Likely that grammar checker incorrectly analyzed *functions* as a plural noun (rather than a third-person-singular verb) and took *embedded clause functions* to be a noun phrase. If the analysis were correct, "each embedded clause function" would be well formed.

1) "It is the word order in the sentence that signals who is doing what to whom."
   Comment: Consider *are* instead of *is*.

2) "Do 'George Washington' and 'the first president of the United States' mean the same thing?"
   Comment: Consider *presidents* instead of *president* or consider *means* instead of *mean*.

3) "When a student volunteers, 'Disneyland is fun,' . . ."
   Comment: The word *a* does not agree with *volunteers*.

4) "Linguistic semantics is the study of the systematic ways in which languages structure meaning."
   Comment: Consider *language's* or *languages'* instead of *languages*.

5) "Sentence 2 is true because we know the word *dogs* describes entities that are also described by the word *animals*."
   Comment: Consider *describe* instead of *describes*.

6) "Harold, who has two doctorates, gave me a fascinating overview of Warhol's art last night."
   Comment: Consider *given* instead of *gave*.

Based on Languages Other Than English

5-11 Examine the tree diagram for this Fijian sentence:

ea-biuta	na	ŋone	vakaloloma	na	tamata	ðaa	e	na	basi
Past-abandon	the	child	poor	the	man	bad	on	the	bus

'The bad man abandoned the poor child on the bus.'

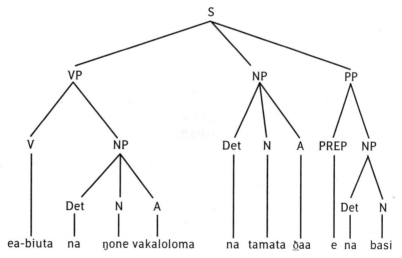

a. Provide the phrase-structure rules that will generate this constituent-structure tree.

b. Notice that the order of certain constituents in the Fijian sentence differs from that of English. With respect to constituent order, what are the major differences between Fijian and English?

c. On the basis of the tree structure, determine which of the following sequences of words are constituents and give the name of each constituent.

na basi	ea-biuta na ŋone vakaloloma
vakaloloma na tamata	e na
e na basi	na ŋone
na tamata ɗaa	na ŋone vakaloloma na tamata ɗaa
ɗaa e na basi	ŋone vakaloloma
ea-biuta	e-biuta na ŋone

Especially for Educators and Future Teachers

5-12 Although we have downplayed the difference between *who* and *whom* in the examples in this chapter, writers who regularly make a distinction between *who* and *whom* in relative clauses do so as follows:

1) That's the goblin *who* visits me each year.

2) She admired the author *whom* you talked about in class.

3) That's the wizard from *whom* I bought the potion.

4) That's the witch *whom* I stole the breadcrumbs from.

5) That's the witch *who* married the wizard.

6) Which is the demon to *whom* he lost his health?

7) That's the ghost of the man *whom* Grendel slew.

After examining these sentences, formulate a statement that will capture the facts about when such writers use *who* and use *whom* in relative clauses. (*Hint:* Bracket the relative clause and examine the grammatical relation of the relative pronoun within its clause.)

5-13 In this chapter, we discussed the use of *who* and *whom* in different ways. On page 162, we said we sometimes would ignore the distinction drawn between *who* and *whom* in traditional grammar and in much careful writing and speaking. We took a *descriptive* approach to grammar and simply relied on the forms that speakers of English use most commonly. Elsewhere (for example, in Exercise 5–12), we considered a more traditional analysis. Besides descriptive grammar, another approach called *prescriptive* grammar has been associated with editors and teachers (and some parents). Descriptive grammars *describe* language use as it is; prescriptive grammars *prescribe* it as some people think it *should be*. What position do you think a teacher should take with respect to forms of a language that are in common use but are criticized by prescriptive grammarians? What should students understand about the role of language prescription in their lives? Should that role be the same for students as writers and for students as conversationalists? Should teachers at different levels of education take different approaches to description and prescription? Justify your position.

OTHER RESOURCES

- **LTG Helpdesk: http://www.ltg.ed.ac.uk/helpdesk/faq/index.html**
  Provides answers to frequently asked questions (FAQs) and links to a variety of language technology projects, including parsers. Among the FAQs: "Can anyone help with determining authorship through textual analysis?" "Where can I find simple phrase structure grammar rules of the form S ➜ NP VP, NP ➜ Det N, VP ➜ V?" "Who has the best parser?"

SUGGESTIONS FOR FURTHER READING

- **Bernard Comrie. 1989.** *Language Universals and Linguistic Typology: Syntax and Morphology,* **2nd ed.** (Chicago: University of Chicago Press). A clear, accessible discussion of syntactic universals across a wide range of languages; as a follow-up to the present chapter, the chapters on "Word Order," "Subject," "Case Marking," and "Relative Clauses" are recommended.

- **Jim Miller. 2002.** *An Introduction to English Syntax* (Edinburgh: Edinburgh University Press). A basic introduction to the syntax of English, combining structural and functional considerations; more thorough and advanced than other books suggested here.

- **Maggie Tallerman. 1998.** *Understanding Syntax* (New York: Oxford University Press; London: Arnold). Part of the "Understanding Language Series," this book is a very clear introduction to syntax as structure.

- **Linda Thomas. 1993.** *Beginning Syntax* (Malden, MA: Blackwell). A very basic introduction to syntax, emphasizing structure but with some attention to function.

ADVANCED READING

Comprehensive and accessible treatments of syntax can be found in Aarts (1997) and Radford (1997). The volumes edited by Shopen (1985) contain a wealth of useful material. Probably accessible to interested readers who have mastered the present chapter are two excellent chapters of volume I: "Parts of Speech Systems" and "Passive in the World's Languages"; volume II contains valuable chapters discussing "Complex Phrases and Complex Sentences," "Complementation," and "Relative Clauses." More advanced than any of the readings in the list of suggested readings above is Thompson (1996).

REFERENCES

- Aarts, Bas. 1997. *English Syntax and Argumentation* (New York: St. Martin's).

- Radford, Andrew. 1997. *Syntax: A Minimalist Introduction* (Cambridge: Cambridge University Press).

- Shopen, Timothy, ed. 1985. *Language Typology and Syntactic Description* (Cambridge: Cambridge University Press).

- Thompson, Geoff. 1996. *Introducing Functional Grammar* (London: Arnold; New York: St. Martin's).

Chapter 6

The Study of Meaning: Semantics

WHAT DO YOU THINK?

❖ Your classmate Holly, a philosophy major, frequently comes up with language questions for her friends. Recently, she asked, "What do you think, do *George Washington* and *the first president of the United States* mean the same thing?" What do you tell her?

❖ Your friend Nathan claims that there are no true synonyms. You counter with *fast* and *quick* as examples of synonyms that both mean 'speedy.' Nathan one-ups you by pointing out that *a fast talker* isn't necessarily *a quick talker*, and from that he argues that since you can't always exchange *fast* and *quick,* they're not synonyms. Now what do you say?

❖ An uncle who knows you are studying linguistics this term asks you whether there's a word to capture the relationship between word pairs such as *uncle* and *nephew, student* and *teacher, doctor* and *patient.* "They're not opposites like *hot* and *cold,*" he says. "But what are they?" What do you tell him?

❖ At a family picnic you listen to your cousin tease his four-year-old daughter about a coloring book he has taken from her. The girl says, "That's *mine.*" Her father says, "That's right, it is mine." The girl repeats, "No, it's *mine.*" Her father says, "That's what I said: it's *mine.*" "No, it's not," his daughter insists. Then she grabs her coloring book and walks away. What is it about the meaning of the words *yours* and *mine* that makes it possible for your cousin to tease his daughter this way?

INTRODUCTION

Of the various parts of grammar to which people may refer, "semantics" is a more familiar term than phonology, morphology, or syntax. "That's just semantics" is a common claim in arguments. Even the proverbial man or woman in the street knows that semantics has to do with meaning. Linguistic semantics is the study of the systematic ways in which languages structure meaning, especially in words and sentences.

In defining linguistic semantics (which we'll call "semantics" from now on), we must invoke the word *meaning*. Just as we have many everyday notions of what semantics is, we use the words *meaning* and *to mean* in different contexts and for different purposes. For example:

The word *perplexity means* 'the state of being puzzled.'

Rash has two *meanings:* 'impetuous' and 'skin irritation.'

In Spanish, *espejo means* 'mirror.'

I did not *mean* that he is incompetent, just inefficient.

The *meaning* of the cross as a symbol is complex.

I *meant* to bring you my paper but left it at home.

What Is Meaning?

Linguists also attach different interpretations to the word *meaning*. Because the goal of linguistics is to explain precisely how languages are structured and used, it is important to distinguish among the different ways of interpreting the word *meaning*.

A few examples will illustrate why we need to develop a precise way of talking about meaning. Consider these sentences:

1. I went to the store this morning.
2. All dogs are animals.

The truth of sentence 1 depends on whether or not the speaker is in fact telling the truth about going to the store; nothing about the words of the sentence makes it inherently true. By contrast, sentence 2 is true because the word *dogs* describes entities that are also described by the word *animals*. The truth of 2 does not depend on whether or not the speaker is telling the truth; it depends solely on the meaning of the words *dogs* and *animals*.

Now compare the following pairs of sentences:

3. You are too young to drink.
   You are not old enough to drink.
4. Matthew spent several years in northern Tibet.
   Matthew was once in northern Tibet.

The sentences of 3 basically "say the same thing" in that the first describes exactly what the second describes. We say they are *synonymous* sentences, or that they paraphrase each other. In 4, the first sentence *implies* the second, but not vice versa.

If Matthew spent several years in northern Tibet, he must have set foot there at some point in his life. On the other hand, if Matthew was once in northern Tibet, it is not necessarily the case that he spent several years there.

Next, consider the following sentences:

5. The unmarried woman is married to a bachelor.

6. My toothbrush is pregnant.

Sentences 5 and 6 are well formed syntactically, but there is something amiss with their semantics. The meanings of the words in 5 contradict each other: an unmarried woman cannot be married, and certainly not to a bachelor. Sentence 5 thus presents a *contradiction.* Sentence 6 is not contradictory but semantically *anomalous:* toothbrushes are not capable of being pregnant. To diagnose precisely what is wrong with these sentences, we need to distinguish between contradictory and anomalous sentences.

Finally, examine sentences 7 and 8:

7. I saw her duck.

8. She ate the pie.

Sentence 7 may be interpreted in two ways: *duck* may be a verb referring to the act of bending over quickly (while walking through a low doorway, for example), or it may be a noun referring to a type of waterfowl. These word meanings give the sentence two distinct meanings. Because there are two possible readings of 7, it is said to be **ambiguous.** On the other hand, sentence 8 is not ambiguous, but has an imprecise quality at least when considered out of context. While we know that the subject of 8 is female, we cannot know who it is that *she* refers to or which particular pie was eaten, although the structure of the phrase *the pie* indicates that the speaker has a particular one in mind. Taken out of context, 8 is thus *vague* in that certain details are left unspecified; but it is not ambiguous.

These observations illustrate that meaning is a multifaceted notion. A sentence may be meaningful and true because it states a fact about the world or because the speaker is telling the truth. Two sentences may be related to each other because they mean exactly the same thing or because one implies the other. Finally, when we feel that there is something wrong with the meaning of a sentence, it may be because the sentence is contradictory, anomalous, ambiguous, or merely vague. One purpose of semantics is to distinguish among these different ways in which language "means."

LINGUISTIC, SOCIAL, AND AFFECTIVE MEANING

For our purposes we can initially distinguish three types of meaning. **Linguistic meaning** encompasses both sense and reference. **Social meaning** is what we rely on when we identify certain social characteristics of speakers and situations from the character of the language used. **Affective meaning** is the emotional connotation that is attached to words and utterances.

Linguistic Meaning

Meaning is a very complicated matter and there is no single theory about how languages mean.

Referential Meaning   One way of defining meaning is to say that the meaning of a word or sentence is the actual person, object, abstract notion, event, or state to which the word or sentence makes reference. The **referential meaning** of *Alexis Rathburton,* then, would be the person who goes by that name. The phrase *Scott's dog* refers to the particular domesticated canine belonging to Scott. That particular animal can be said to be the referential meaning of the linguistic expression *Scott's dog.* The canine described by the expression *Scott's dog* is the **referent** of that expression.

Words, of course, are not the only linguistic units to carry referential meaning. Sentences also have meaning because, like words and phrases, they refer to actions, states, and events in the world. *Rahul is sleeping on the sofa* refers to the fact that a person named Rahul is currently asleep on an elongated piece of furniture generally meant to be sat upon. The referent of the sentence is thus Rahul's state of being on the piece of furniture in question.

Sense   Referential meaning may be the easiest kind to recognize, but it is not sufficient to explain *how* some expressions mean what they mean. For one thing, not all expressions have referents. Neither *a unicorn* nor *the present king of France* has an actual referent in the real world, but both expressions have meaning. Even leaving social and affective meaning aside, if expressions had only referential meaning, then the sentences in 9 below would mean exactly the same thing, as would those in 10, but neither pair has an identical meaning.

9. George Washington was the first president of the United States.
    George Washington was George Washington.

10. Jacqueline Bouvier married John F. Kennedy in 1953.
    Jacqueline Bouvier married the thirty-fifth president of the United States in 1953.

The sentences of 10 do not mean the same thing, and the second sentence of the pair seems odd, in part because it would have been impossible to marry the thirty-fifth president in 1953 since the United States did not have its thirty-fifth president until 1960.

Proper nouns such as *George Washington, Jacqueline Bouvier,* and *John F. Kennedy* constitute a special category, and we might say that the meaning of proper nouns is the person named, the person to whom the proper noun refers. By contrast, the meaning of expressions such as *the first president of the United States* and *the thirty-fifth president of the United States* cannot be reduced to their referents. Consider the sentences of 11:

11. Al Gore nearly became the forty-third president of the United States.
    Al Gore nearly became George Bush.

Obviously, these sentences do not mean the same thing despite the fact that the expressions *George Bush* and *the forty-third president of the United States* have the same referent. This is why the sentences in 9 do not have identical meanings. In general, then, we cannot equate the meaning of an expression with the referent of the expression. We say that expressions have 'senses,' and any theory of how language means must take sense meaning into account.

Social Meaning

Linguistic meaning is not the only type of meaning that language users communicate to each other. Consider the following sentences:

1. So I says to him, "You can't do nothin' right."
2. Is it a doctor in here?
3. Y'all gonna visit over the holiday?
4. Great chow!

In addition to representing actions, states, and mental processes, these sentences convey information about the identity of the person who has uttered them or about the situation in which they have been uttered. In 1, use of the verb *says* with the first-person singular pronoun *I* indicates something about the speaker's social status. In 2, the form *it* where some other varieties use *there* indicates a speaker of an ethnically marked variety of English (African American English). In 3, the pronoun *y'all* identifies a particular regional dialect of American English (Southern). Finally, the choice of words in 4 indicates that the comment was made in an informal context. Social status, ethnicity, regional origin, and context are all social factors. In addition to linguistic meaning, therefore, every utterance also conveys social meaning, not only in the sentence as a whole but in word choice (*y'all* and *chow*) and pronunciation (*gonna* or *nothin'*).

Affective Meaning

There is a third kind of meaning besides linguistic and social meaning. Compare the following examples:

1. Tina, who always boasts about her two doctorates, lectured me all night on Warhol's art.
2. Tina, who has two doctorates, gave me a fascinating overview of Warhol's art last night.

Because these two sentences can be used to describe exactly the same event, we can say they have similar referential meaning. At another level, though, the information they convey is different. Sentence 1 gives the impression that the speaker considers Tina a pretentious bore. Sentence 2, in contrast, indicates that the speaker finds her interesting. The "stance" of the speaker in these utterances thus differs.

Word choice is not the only way to communicate feelings and attitudes toward utterances and contexts. A striking contrast is provided by sentences that differ only in terms of stress or intonation. This string of words can be interpreted in several ways depending on the intonation:

Erin is really smart.

The sentence can be uttered in a matter-of-fact way, without emphasizing any word in particular, in which case it will be interpreted literally as a remark acknowledging Erin's intelligence. But if the words *really* and *smart* are stressed in an exaggerated manner, the sentence may be interpreted sarcastically to mean exactly the opposite. Intonation (often accompanied by appropriate facial expressions) can be used as a device to communicate attitudes and feelings, and it can override the literal meaning of a sentence.

Consider a final example. Suppose that Andy Grump, father of Sara, addresses her as follows:

Sara Grump, how many times have I asked you not to channel surf?

There would be reason to look beyond the words for the "meaning" of this unusual form of address. Mr. Grump may address his daughter as *Sara Grump* to show his exasperation, as in this example. By addressing her as *Sara Grump* instead of the usual *Sara,* he conveys frustration and annoyance. His choice of name thus signals that he is exasperated. Contrast the tone of that sentence with a similar one in which he addresses her as *dear.*

The level of meaning that conveys the language user's feelings, attitudes, and opinions about a particular piece of information or about the ongoing context is called *affective* meaning. Affective meaning is not an exclusive property of sentences: Words such as *Alas!* and *Hurray!* obviously have affective meaning, and so can words such as *funny, sweet,* and *obnoxious.* Even the most common words—such as *father, democracy,* and *old*—can evoke particular emotions and feelings in us. The difference between synonymous or near-synonymous pairs of words such as *vagrant* and *homeless* is essentially a difference at the affective level. In this particular pair, *vagrant* carries a negative affect, while *homeless* is neutral. Little is known yet about how affective meaning works, but it is of great importance to all verbal communication.

From our discussion so far, you can see that meaning is not a simple notion but a complex combination of three aspects:

- Linguistic meaning, including referential meaning (the real-world object or concept described by an expression) and sense meaning.
- Social meaning: the information about the social nature of the language user or of the context of utterance
- Affective meaning: what the language user feels about the content or about the ongoing context

The linguistic meaning of a word or sentence is frequently called its *denotation,* in contrast to the *connotation,* which includes both social meaning and affective meaning.

This chapter focuses primarily on linguistic meaning, the traditional domain of semantics, but we occasionally refer to the three-way distinction. Social meaning will be investigated in detail in Chapters 10 and 11.

WORD, SENTENCE, AND UTTERANCE MEANING

Meaning of Words and Sentences

We have talked about words and sentences as the two units of language that carry meaning. **Content words**—principally nouns, verbs, prepositions, adjectives, and adverbs—have meaning in that they refer to concrete objects and abstract concepts; are marked as being characteristic of particular social, ethnic, and regional dialects and of particular contexts; and convey information about the feelings and attitudes of language users. **Function words** such as conjunctions and determiners also carry meaning, though in somewhat different ways from content words, as you will see later in this chapter. Like individual words, sentences also have social and affective connotations. The study of word meaning, however, differs from the study of sentence meaning because the units arc different in kind.

In order for a sentence to have meaning, we must rely on the meaning of the individual words it contains. How we accomplish the task of retrieving sentence meaning from word meaning is a complex question. One obvious hypothesis is that the meaning of a sentence is simply the sum of the meanings of its words. To see that this is *not* the case, consider the following sentences, in which the individual words (and therefore their *sum* meanings) are the same:

> The lion licked the trainer.
>
> The trainer licked the lion.

Obviously, the sentences refer to different events and hence have distinct linguistic meanings. This is conveyed by the fact that the words of the sentences are ordered differently. Thus we cannot simply say that all we need to do to retrieve the meaning of a sentence is add up the meanings of its parts. We must also take into consideration the *semantic role* assigned to each word. By *semantic role* we mean such things as *who did what to whom, with whom,* and *for whom.* In other words, the semantic role of a word is the role that its referent plays in the action or state of being described by the sentence. Sentence semantics is concerned with semantic roles and with the relationship between words within a sentence.

Scope of Word Meaning　While it is important to distinguish between word meaning and sentence meaning, the two interact on many levels, as the following sentence indicates:

> He may leave tomorrow if he finishes his term paper.

In this sentence, the individual words *may, tomorrow,* and *if* have meanings: *may* denotes permission or possibility; *tomorrow* indicates a future time unit that begins at midnight; and *if* indicates a condition. But the impact of these words goes beyond the phrases in which they occur and affects the meaning of the entire sentence. Indeed, if we replace *may* with *will,* the sentence takes on a completely different meaning:

He will leave tomorrow if he finishes his term paper.

The sentence with *may* denotes permission or possibility, while the sentence with *will* simply describes a future event. Thus *may* affects the meaning of the *entire* sentence. The *scope* of the meaning of the word *may* is the entire sentence. This is true also of *tomorrow* and *if.* What these examples illustrate is that word meaning and sentence meaning are intimately related.

Try it yourself: Determine the scope of *only* in the sentences below. Using 1 as a model, provide a sentence that illustrates the scope of *only* for 2 and 3. Where the scope of *only* is ambiguous, give alternative "cf." sentences, each of which is *unambiguous.*

1. He wants *only* you to be happy. (cf.: He wants only you to be happy; he doesn't care about her.)

2. *Only* she wants you to win.

3. She *only* wants to talk to her daughter.

Meaning of Utterances

In addition to words and sentences, there is a third unit that carries meaning; however, we may not notice it as clearly because we take it for granted in day-to-day interactions. Consider this utterance:

I now pronounce you husband and wife.

This sentence may be uttered in very different sets of circumstances: (1) by an officient at a ceremony, speaking to a couple getting married in the presence of their families and friends; or (2) by an actor dressed as an officient, speaking to two actors before a congregation of Hollywood extras assembled by a director filming a soap opera. In the first instance, *I now pronounce you husband and wife* creates a marriage for the couple intending to get married. But that same utterance has no effect on the marital status of any actor on the filming location. Thus the circumstances of utterance create different meanings, although the linguistic meaning of the sentence remains unchanged. It is therefore necessary to know the circumstances of utterance in order to understand the utterance's effect or force. We say that the sentence uttered in the wedding context and the sentence uttered in the film context have the same linguistic meaning but are different **utterances,** each with its own *utterance meaning.*

The difference between sentence meaning and utterance meaning can be further illustrated by the question *Can you shut the window?* There are at least two ways in which an addressee might react to this question. One would be to say *Yes* (meaning 'Yes, I am physically capable of shutting the window') and then do nothing about it.

This is the "smart-aleck" interpretation; it is of course not the way such a question is usually intended. Another way in which the addressee might react would be to get up and shut the window. Obviously, these interpretations of the same question are different: the smart-aleck interpretation treats the question as a request for information; the second interpretation treats it as a request for action. To describe the difference between these interpretations, we say that they are *distinct utterances.*

Sentence semantics is not concerned with utterance meaning. (Utterances are the subject of investigation of another branch of linguistics called *pragmatics,* which is the topic of Chapters 8 and 9.) One of the premises of sentence semantics is that sentences must be divorced from the context in which they are uttered—in other words, that sentences and utterances must be distinguished. To experienced language users, this premise may appear strange and counterintuitive because so much meaning depends on context. The point is not to discard context as unimportant but to recognize that sentences may carry meaning independently of context, while utterance meaning depends crucially on the circumstances of the utterance. **Semantics** is the branch of linguistics that examines word and sentence meaning while generally ignoring context. By contrast, **pragmatics** pays less attention to the relationship of word meaning to sentence meaning and more attention to the relationship of an utterance to its context.

LEXICAL SEMANTICS

The *lexicon* of a language can be viewed as a compendium of all its words. Words are sometimes called **lexical items,** or *lexemes* (the *-eme* ending as in *phoneme* and *morpheme).* The branch of semantics that deals with word meaning is called **lexical semantics.**

Lexical semantics examines relationships among word meanings. For example, it asks what the relationship is between the words *man* and *woman* on the one hand and *human being* on the other hand. How are the adjectives *large* and *small* in the same relationship to each other as the pair *dark* and *light?* What is the difference between the meaning of words such as *always* and *never* and the meaning of words such as *often* and *seldom?* What do language users actually mean when they say that a dog is "a type of" mammal? Lexical semantics investigates such questions. It is the study of how the lexicon is organized and how the meanings of lexical items are interrelated, and its principal goal is to build a model for the structure of the lexicon by categorizing the types of relationships between words. Lexical semantics focuses on linguistic meaning.

Semantic Fields

Consider the following sets of words:

1. cup, mug, wine glass, tumbler, plastic cup, goblet
2. hammer, cloud, tractor, eyeglasses, leaf, justice

The words of set 1 all denote concepts that can be described as 'vessels from which one drinks,' while the words of set 2 denote concepts that have nothing in common. The words of set 1 constitute a **semantic field**—a set of words with an identifiable semantic affinity. The following set is also a semantic field, all of whose words refer to emotional states:

angry, sad, happy, exuberant, depressed, afraid

Thus we see that words can be classified into sets according to their meaning.

In a semantic field, not all lexical items necessarily have the same status. Consider the following sets, which together form the semantic field of color terms (of course, there are other terms in the same field):

1. blue, red, yellow, green, black, purple
2. indigo, saffron, royal blue, aquamarine, bisque

The colors referred to by the words of set 1 are more "usual" than those described in set 2. They are said to be less **marked** members of the semantic field than those of set 2. The less marked members of a semantic field are usually easier to learn and remember than more marked members. Children learn the term *blue* before they learn the terms *indigo, royal blue,* or *aquamarine.* Often, a less marked word consists of only one morpheme, in contrast to more marked words (contrast *blue* with *royal blue* or *aquamarine*). The less marked member of a semantic field cannot be described by using the name of another member of the same field, whereas more marked members can be thus described (*indigo* is a kind of blue, but *blue* is not a kind of indigo). Less marked terms also tend to be used more frequently than more marked terms; for example, *blue* occurs considerably more frequently in conversation and writing than *indigo* or *aquamarine.* (In the million-word Brown Corpus of written American English, there are 126 examples of *blue,* but only one of *indigo* and none at all of *aquamarine.*) Less marked terms are also often broader in meaning than more marked terms; *blue* describes a broader range of colors than *indigo* or *aquamarine.* Finally, less marked words are not the result of the metaphorical usage of the name of another object or concept, whereas more marked words often are; for example, *saffron* is the color of a spice that lent its name to the color.

Try It Yourself: Rust, silver, orchid, and champagne are members of the semantic field of colors, and you can readily identify the sources that gave rise to these color terms. Fruits, flowers, gems, and other natural objects are notable sources of terms in this semantic field. Identify five additional color terms directly borrowed from the name of a real-world object of that color.

Using our understanding of semantic field and markedness, we now turn to identifying types of relationships between words. We'll see how the words of a semantic field can have different types of relationships to each other and to other words in the lexicon, and we'll classify these relationships.

Hyponymy

Consider again this set of unmarked color terms: *blue, red, yellow, green, black, purple*. What they have in common is that they refer to colors. We say that the terms *blue, red, yellow, green, black,* and *purple* are hyponyms of the term *color.* A **hyponym** is a subordinate, specific term whose referent is included in the referent of a superordinate term. Blue is a kind of color; red is a kind of color, and so on. They are specific colors, and *color* is the general term for them. We can illustrate the relationship by the following diagram, in which the lower terms are the hyponyms (*hypo-* means 'below'). The higher term—in this case, *color*—is called the superordinate term (technically, the *hypernym*).

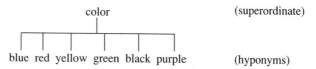

Another example is the term *mammal,* whose referent includes the referents of many other terms.

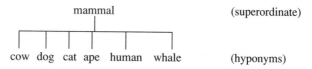

The relationship between each of the lower terms and the higher term is called *hyponymy.*

Hyponymy is not restricted to objects such as *mammal* or abstract concepts such as *color*—or even to nouns, for that matter. Hyponymy can be identified in many other areas of the lexicon. The verb *to cook,* for example, has many hyponyms.

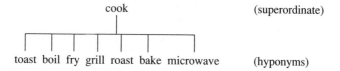

Not every set of hyponyms has a superordinate term. For example, *uncle* and *aunt* form a lexical field because we can identify a shared property in their meanings. Yet English does not have a term that refers specifically to both uncles and aunts (that is, to siblings of parents and their spouses).

| ? | (superordinate) |
| uncle   aunt | (hyponyms) |

By contrast, some other languages have a superordinate term for the equivalent field. In Spanish, the plural term *tios* can include both aunts and uncles, and the Spanish equivalents of the terms *uncle* and *aunt* are therefore hyponyms of *tios.*

While hyponymy is found in all languages, the concepts that have words in hyponymic relationships vary from one language to the next. In Tuvaluan (a Polynesian language), the higher term *ika* (roughly, 'fish') has as hyponyms not only all terms that refer to the animals that English speakers would recognize as fish but also terms for whales and dolphins (which speakers of English recognize as mammals) and for sea turtles (which are reptiles). Of course, we are dealing with folk classifications here, not scientific classifications.

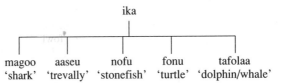

magoo	aaseu	nofu	fonu	tafolaa
'shark'	'trevally'	'stonefish'	'turtle'	'dolphin/whale'

Thus there is variability across languages as to the exact nature of particular hyponymic relationships.

In a semantic field, hyponymy may exist at more than one level. A word may have both a hyponym and a superordinate term, as *blue* has in Figure 6–1. Because they refer to different "types" or "shades" of blue, the terms *turquoise, aquamarine,* and *royal blue* are hyponyms of *blue*. *Blue* in turn is a hyponym of *color*. We thus have a hierarchy of terms related to each other through hyponymic relationships. Similar hierarchies can be established for many semantic fields, almost without limit. In the "cooking" field, *fry* has hyponyms in the terms *stir-fry, saute,* and *deep-fry* and is itself a hyponym of *cook*. The lower we get in a hierarchy of hyponyms, the more marked the terms: *cook* is relatively unmarked; *stir-fry* is considerably more marked. The intermediate term *fry* is less marked than *stir-fry* but more marked than *cook*.

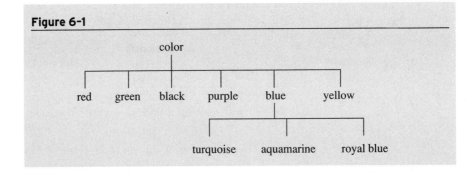

Figure 6-1

Examples of multiple layers of hyponymic relationships abound in the area of folk biological classification, as illustrated in Figure 6–2 on page 191. Note that the term *animal* appears on two levels. English speakers use *animal* for at least two different referents: (1) animals as distinct from plants and rocks, and (2) animals (generally mammals other than humans) as distinct from humans, birds, and bugs. Cases in which a word has different senses at different levels of a hyponymic hierarchy are not uncommon.

Figure 6-2

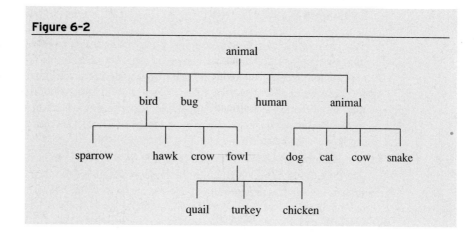

Hyponymy is one of several relationship types with which language users organize the lexicon. It is based on the notion of *inclusion:* if the referent of term *A* (for example, *color)* includes the referent of term *B* (for example, *red)*, then term *B* (*red)* is a *hyponym* of term *A* (*color)*. Hyponymy is important in everyday conversation—we use it whenever we say "B is a kind of A" (*red* is a kind of *color)*—and for such tasks as using a thesaurus, which is organized according to hyponymic relationships.

Part/Whole Relationships

A second important hierarchical relationship between words is the one found in pairs such as *hand* and *arm* or *room* and *house*. In each pair, the referent of the first term is part of the referent of the second term. A hand, however, is not "a kind of" arm, and thus the relationship between *hand* and *arm* is not hyponymic. Instead, we call it a *part/whole relationship*. Part/whole relationships are not a property of pairs of words only: *hand, elbow, forearm, wrist,* and several other words are in a part/whole relationship with *arm*. Other important examples of part/whole relationships include words such as *second* and *minute, minute* and *hour, hour* and *day, day* and *week,* none of which could be described without reference to the fact that one is a subdivision of the other. Figure 6–3 illustrates the difference between a part/whole relationship and a hyponymic relationship for the word *eye*.

Figure 6-3

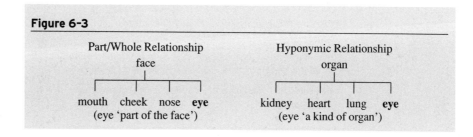

Synonymy

Two words are said to be **synonymous** if they mean the same thing. The terms *movie, film, flick,* and *motion picture* all have the same set of referents in the real world and are usually taken to be synonymous terms. To address the notion of synonymy more formally, we can say that term *A* is synonymous with term *B* if every referent of *A* is a referent of *B* and vice versa. For example, if every movie is a film and every film is a movie, the terms *movie* and *film* are synonymous. The "vice versa" is important: without it, we would be defining hyponymy.

You may wonder why speakers of a language bother to keep synonyms, given that they only add redundancy to the lexicon. English has many synonymous pairs such as *cloudy* and *nebulous, help* and *assist, skewed* and *oblique* (the result of English having borrowed the second term of each pair from French or Latin). When we assert that two terms are synonymous, we usually base that judgment on linguistic meaning only. Thus, even though *movie, film, flick,* and *motion picture* have the same linguistic meaning, they differ in social and affective meaning. *Film* may strike you as appropriate for movie classics or art movies; it is a more highbrow term. You recognize that *flick* is used chiefly in informal contexts, while *motion picture* is more traditional or industry related. Thus we can consider the terms to be synonymous if we specify that we are taking only linguistic meaning into account. At the social and affective levels, however, they are not synonymous.

In fact, there are very few true synonyms in the lexicon. More often than not, terms that appear to be synonymous have different social and affective connotations. Even if we restrict meaning to linguistic meaning, words that appear synonymous at first glance often refer to slightly different sets of concepts or are used in different situations. The adjectives *fast, quick,* and *rapid* may be used interchangeably in reference to someone's running speed, but a *fast talker* (a 'slippery or deceptive person') is different from a "quick talker"; some people live lives in the *fast lane,* not the "rapid lane"; and *quick* is the most appropriate term to describe a mind or a glance, while *rapid* is the usual term when reference is made to a person's *stride,* especially metaphorical strides, as in learning to type or do mathematics. Under the circumstances, is it accurate to say that these adjectives are synonymous?

Try It Yourself: For each of these, think of a synonym or near synonym in the same word class:

Adjective: *keen (sharp), former, juvenile, speedy, speechless, strong, fertile, bare, petite, inebriated*

Noun: *bard (poet), juvenile, ardor, appointment, tool, agony, matrimony, designation, rubbish, chief*

Verb: *enclose (fence), kidnap, stammer, seek, praise, clothe, agitate, pester, commit, inaugurate*

The fact that there are few true synonyms in the lexicon of a language reflects the general tendency of language users to make the most of what's available to them. If two terms have the same referent, the meaning of one is usually modified to express differences in linguistic, social, or affective meaning. Although true synonymy is rare, the notion is useful because it helps describe similarities between the meanings of different terms in the lexicon.

Antonymy

The word **antonymy** derives from the Greek root *anti-* ('opposite') and denotes opposition in meaning. In contrast to synonymy and hyponymy, antonymy is a *binary* relationship that can characterize a relationship between only two words at a time. Terms *A* and *B* are antonyms if, when *A* describes a referent, *B* cannot describe the same referent, and vice versa.

The prototypical antonyms are pairs of adjectives that describe opposite notions: *large* and *small, wide* and *narrow, hot* and *cold, married* and *single, alive* and *dead.* Antonymy is not restricted to adjectives, however. The nouns *man* and *woman* are also antonyms because an individual cannot be described by both terms at once. *Always* and *never* form an antonymous pair of adverbs: they have mutually exclusive referents. The verbs *love* and *hate* can also be viewed as antonyms because they refer to mutually exclusive emotions. Antonymy is thus a binary relationship between terms with complementary meanings.

Intuitively, you can see a difference between the antonymous pair *large* and *small* and the antonymous pair *single* and *married.* The first pair denote notions that are relatively subjective. You would agree that blue whales are large mammals and that mice are small mammals, but whether German shepherds are large or small dogs depends on your perspective. The owner of a Chihuahua will say that German shepherds are large, but the owner of a Great Dane may judge them to be on the small side. Furthermore, adjectives such as *large* and *small* have superlative and comparative forms: blue whales are the *largest* of all mammals; German shepherds are *larger* than Chihuahuas but *smaller* than Great Danes. Antonymous pairs that have these characteristics are called *gradable* pairs.

In contrast to *large* and *small, single* and *married* are mutually exclusive and complementary. A person cannot be single and married at the same time. With respect to marital status, a person cannot be described with a term that does not have either *single* or *married* as a hyponym; thus *single* and *married* are complementary. Furthermore, *single* and *married* generally cannot be used in a comparative or superlative sense (someone's being legally "more single" than another single person is impossible). The pair constitute an example of *nongradable* antonymy (also sometimes called *complementarity).*

There are thus two types of antonymy: gradable and nongradable. If terms *A* and *B* are *gradable* antonyms and if *A* can be used to describe a particular referent, then *B* cannot be used to describe the same referent, and vice versa. If *A* and *B* are *nongradable* antonyms, the same condition applies along with an additional condition: if *A* cannot describe a referent, then that referent must be describable by *B,* and vice versa. So *male* and *female, married* and *single, alive* and *dead* can be viewed as nongradable antonyms, while *hot* and *cold, love* and *hate, always* and *never* are gradable. Typically, for gradable antonyms, there will be words to describe intermediate stages: *sometimes, seldom, occasionally, often* are gradations between *always* and *never.*

As you recognize, the distinction between gradable and nongradable antonymy is sometimes blurred by language users. In English, for example, it is reasonable to assume that whatever is alive is not dead and that whatever is dead is not alive, and thus that the adjectives *dead* and *alive* form a nongradable pair. However, we do have expressions such as *half dead, barely alive,* and *more dead than alive.* Such expressions suggest that, in some contexts, we see *alive* and *dead* as gradable antonyms. The distinction between gradable and nongradable antonymy is nevertheless useful in that it describes an important distinction between two types of word relationships.

Try It Yourself: For each of these, think of an antonym in the same word class:

Adjective: *palatable (distasteful), open, outside, haughty, shallow, chilly, entire, fertile, rare*

Noun: *hindsight (foresight), insider, friendship, failure, freedom, benefit, chaos, certitude, fecundity*

Verb: *ignite (extinguish), reveal, remember, dishonor, ignore, appear, expand, cleanse, bend*

Finally, antonymous words often do not have equal status with respect to markedness. For example, when you inquire about the weight of an object, you ask *How heavy is it?* and not *How light is it?*—unless you already know that the object is light. Notice also that the noun *weight,* which describes both relative heaviness and relative lightness, is associated with *heavy* rather than with *light* (as in the expressions *carry a lot of weight* and *throw one's weight around).* Of the antonymous pair *heavy* and *light, heavy* is more neutral than *light* and is thus less marked. In the same fashion, *tall* is less marked than *short, hot* less marked than *cold,* and *married* less marked than *single* (we say *marital status,* not "singleness status"). Although there is some variation across languages as to which word of a pair is considered less marked, there is a surprising agreement from language to language.

Converseness

Another important relationship invokes the notion of oppositeness, although it does so in a way that differs from antonymy. Consider the relationship between *wife* and *husband.* If A is the husband of B, then B is the wife of A. Thus *wife* is the converse of *husband,* and vice versa. **Converseness** characterizes a reciprocal semantic relationship between pairs of words. Other examples of converse pairs include terms denoting many other kinship relations, such as *grandchild* and *grandparent* or *child* and *parent;* terms describing professional relationships, such as *employer* and *employee* or *doctor* and *patient;* and terms denoting relative positions in space or time, such as *above* and *below, north of* and *south of,* or *before* and *after.*

Converse pairs can combine with other types of opposition to form complex relationships. The antonymous pair *father: mother* is in a converse relationship with the antonymous pair *son: daughter.* Generally, converse pairs denote relationships between objects or between people. Some converse relationships are a little more complex. The verb *give,* for example, requires a subject and two objects (*She gave him the book).* The converse of *give* is *receive,* except that the relationship is neither a "reversal" of the subject and the direct object as it would be with *kiss* and *be kissed (Smith kissed Jones* versus *Jones was kissed by Smith)* nor a mutual subject/possessor relation such as *husband* and *wife;* rather, the relationship is between the subject and the indirect object.

> Siddharta gave Jessie a present.
>
> Jessie received a present from Siddharta.

Other pairs of words with a similar relationship include *lend* and *borrow* and *buy* and *sell.* Note that *rent* is its own converse in American English.

> Eve rents an apartment to Adam.
>
> Adam rents an apartment from Eve.

When there is a possibility of confusion, the preposition *out* can be attached to *rent* in the meaning of 'lending out for money.' In British English, this sense of *rent* is described by the verb *let (flat to let).* In some languages, a single word is used for 'buy' and 'sell.' In Samoan, for example, the word *faʔatau* carries both meanings, while the Mandarin Chinese words *mǎi* 'buy' and *mài* 'sell' are etymologically related. These facts suggest that converseness is an intuitively recognizable relationship.

Polysemy and Homonymy

Two other notions that are closely related to the basic relationship types are **polysemy** and **homonymy.** In contrast to the notions discussed above, polysemy and homonymy refer to similarities rather than differences between meanings. A word is *polysemous* (or polysemic) when it has two or more related meanings. The word *plain,* for example, can have several related meanings, including:

> (1) 'easy, clear' (*plain English)*
>
> (2) 'undecorated' (*plain white shirt)*
>
> (3) 'not good-looking' (*plain Jane)*

Homographs have the same spelling but different meanings (and pronunciations), such as *dove* 'a kind of bird' and *dove* 'past tense of *dive'* or *conduct* as a verb and *conduct* as a noun, where the verb has primary stress on the second syllable and the noun has it on the first syllable. *Homophones* have the same pronunciation but different senses: *sea* and *see, so* and *sew, two* and *too, plain* and *plane, flower* and *flour, boar* and *bore, bear* and *bare,* or *eye, I,* and *aye.* Words are *homonymic* when they have the same written *or* spoken form but different senses. A narrower definition of homonym limits the term to word sets that are both homographic *and* homophonous, as with *bank* of a river and savings *bank* ('a financial institution') or the adjective *still* 'quiet' (*still waters)* and the adverb *still* 'yet' (*still sick).* Languages exhibit polysemy and homonymy in their lexicons to varying degrees. A language such as Hawaiian, which has a restricted set of possible words because of its phonological structure, has a good deal more homonymy than English has (see "Sequence Constraints" in Chapter 4 and Fig. 7–3 on p. 231).

A difficulty arises in distinguishing between homonymy and polysemy: How do we know if we have separate lexical items rather than a single word with different senses? Consider *plain.* How would we know whether or not the three adjectival senses ('easy,' 'undecorated,' 'not good-looking') constitute different words that happen to sound the same? Using spelling as a criterion is misleading: many sets of words are distinct but have the same spelling—as, for example, the noun *sound* 'noise' and the noun *sound* 'channel of water,' or *bank* 'financial institution' and *bank* 'shore of a river.' Yet the problem is important for anyone who wants to arrange or use the entries of a dictionary (in which different senses of the same word are grouped under a single entry but each homonymous form has its own distinct entry).

There is no simple solution. If there is a clear distinction between polysemy and homonymy, it must involve several criteria, no one of which would be sufficient by itself and some of which may yield different results. We have already excluded spelling as an unreliable criterion. One modestly reliable criterion is a word's historical origin, or *etymology.* We can consider that there are two words of the form *sound* corresponding to the two meanings given above because they derive from different historical roots. Likewise, the word *bank* meaning 'financial institution' is a borrowing from French, whereas *bank* meaning 'shore of a river' has a Scandinavian origin. The various antonyms and synonyms of a word provide a different kind of criterion for distinguishing between polysemy and homonymy. *Plain* in the sense of 'easy, clear' and *plain* in the sense of 'undecorated' share a synonym in *simple* and an antonym in *complex.* This fact suggests that they are indeed two meanings of the same polysemic word. No shared synonym or antonym can be identified for the two meanings of *sound,* as shown in Figure 6–4.

Figure 6-4

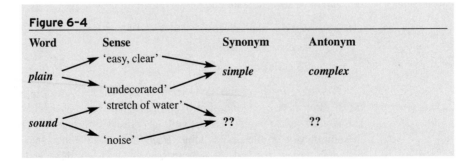

Finally, we can ask whether there is any commonality between different senses of what appears to be the same word. The two meanings of *plain* indicated above can be characterized as 'devoid of complexity,' which suggests that they are related, but no such superordinate description exists for *sound* 'stretch of water' and *sound* 'noise.' Thus *plain* in these two senses is polysemic, while the two senses of *sound* reflect homonymous lexical items. (Of course, other senses of *plain* may or may not belong to separate words.)

While these criteria help distinguish between polysemy and homonymy, they are not foolproof. It is often difficult to decide whether a particular pair of look-alike and sound-alike word forms are separate homonymous words or simply the same poly-semic word with different senses. Although homonymy and polysemy can be distin-guished as different notions, the boundary between them may not be clear-cut in particular cases.

Metaphorical Extension

The difficulties in defining the distinction between polysemy and homonymy arise partly from the fact that language users often extend the primary sense of words to form metaphors. A **metaphor** is an extension in the use of a word beyond its primary sense to describe referents that bear similarities to the word's primary referent. The word *eye,* for example, can be used to describe the hole at the dull end of a needle, the bud on a potato, or the center of a storm. The similarities between these referents and the primary referent of the word *eye* are their roundish shape and their more or less central role or position in a larger form. People frequently create new metaphors, and once a metaphor becomes accepted speakers tend to view the metaphorical meaning as separate from its primary sense, as in *booking* a flight, *tabling* a motion, *seeing* the point, *stealing* the *head*lines, *buying* time, studying a foreign *tongue*. It's thus tough to determine whether one word with two meanings exists or two words with different but metaphorically related meanings.

Metaphors occur constantly in day-to-day speaking and writing. The following examples were gleaned from the front page of a typical newspaper:

Tennis star Serena Williams <u>breezed</u> through the early matches.

The dollar is <u>falling sharply.</u>

His speech was the <u>catalyst</u> for a new popular upheaval.

In the first example, the verb *breeze* is of course not meant literally; it is used to give the impression that Williams won the matches effortlessly, as a breeze would blow over a tennis court. Similarly, the underlined words in the other two sentences are meant to be interpreted as metaphors, whose effectiveness relies on our ability to see that in some contexts words are not to be interpreted literally. (The mechanisms that we use in figuring out when a word must be interpreted metaphorically will be dis-cussed in Chapter 9.)

Metaphors aren't formed haphazardly. Observe, for example, the following metaphors that refer to the notion of time:

I look <u>forward</u> to seeing you again this weekend.

Experts do not <u>foresee</u> an increase in inflation in the near future.

He <u>drags up</u> old grudges from his youth.

Once in a while, we need to <u>look back over our shoulders</u> at the lessons that history has taught us.

A pattern is apparent in these examples: In English, we construct time metaphors as if we physically move through time in the direction of the future. Thus the future is forward in the first two examples. Metaphors that refer to the past use words that refer to what is left behind, as in the latter two examples. Metaphors that violate this pattern would sound very strange:

*I look <u>back</u> to seeing you again this weekend.

*He <u>drags down</u> old grudges from his youth.

Another principle that governs the creation of metaphors is this: "Ideas are objects that can be sensed." Thus they can be smelled, felt, and heard.

Your proposal <u>smells</u> fishy.

I failed to <u>grasp</u> what they were trying to prove.

I'd like your opinion as to whether my plan <u>sounds</u> reasonable.

Writers and critics often talk about the writing process as "cooking."

I let my manuscript <u>simmer</u> for six months.

Who knows what kind of a story he is <u>brewing</u>!

Their last book was little more than a <u>half-baked concoction</u> of earlier work.

"The heart is where emotions are experienced" is a common principle on which our metaphors for emotions are based.

It is with a <u>heavy heart</u> that I tell you of her death.

You shouldn't speak <u>lightheartedly</u> about this tragedy.

The rescuers received the survivors' <u>heartfelt</u> thanks.

The construction of metaphors thus follows preset patterns.

Most of the metaphors discussed so far are relatively conventionalized—that is, they are found commonly in speech and writing because they are preset. But language lends itself to creative activities, and language users do not hesitate to create new metaphors. Even when we create our own metaphors, however, we must follow the principles that regulate conventionalized metaphors. In English, metaphors that refer to time must obey the convention of "moving through time in the direction of the future."

There is strong evidence that some metaphorical patterns are frequent across the world's languages. For example, in many languages the word for 'eye' is used metaphorically to refer to roundish objects like protuberances on a potato and the pivotally located portion of an object like the center of a storm.

But other principles of metaphorical extension vary from language to language. For example, in many languages it is not the heart that is the seat of emotions. Polynesian languages such as Samoan and Tahitian treat the stomach as the metaphorical seat of emotions. It is likely that some of these principles reflect different cultures' views of the world. The exact workings of the link between culture and language are still poorly understood. Increased knowledge about metaphors in different languages should help us determine which principles are widely shared by languages, which are specific to some languages, and to what extent metaphors reflect cultural perspectives.

Lexical Semantics: Discovering Relationships in the Lexicon

Hyponymy, part/whole relationships, synonymy, gradable and nongradable antonymy, converseness, polysemy, homonymy, and metaphorical extension—lexical semantics is primarily concerned with discovering relationships in the lexicon of languages. The semantic relationships of a word are, in a sense, part of its meaning: the word *cold* can be defined as a gradable antonym of *hot,* as having the expression *sensation of heat* as a superordinate term, and as being more marked than *hot* but less marked than *chilly* and *freezing.* By knowing how the meaning of a word interacts with the meaning of other words, we can begin to understand its meaning.

Lexical semantics, of course, does not explain the difference in meaning between words that are as unlike as *gorilla* and *doubtful.* For lexical semantics to be useful, it must be applied to particular areas of the lexicon in which word senses have shared characteristics. Thus the notion of semantic field becomes useful. If the word *gorilla* is placed in its appropriate semantic field, its relationship to *chimpanzee* and *great ape* can be investigated. Similarly, the word *doubtful* can be contrasted with *certain, probable, likely,* and other words that express likelihood or certainty.

The different types of relationships described above are the most basic tools of lexical semantics. They are basic because one type cannot be characterized in terms of another type. For example, an antonymous relationship between two words cannot be explained in terms of hyponymy, part/whole relationships, synonymy, converseness, or metaphorical extension.

FUNCTION WORDS AND CATEGORIES OF MEANING

The lexicon is not made up exclusively of content words such as *father, pigeon, stir-fry,* and *democracy,* which refer to objects, actions, or abstract concepts. It also contains function words such as the conjunctions *if, however,* and *or;* the determiners *a, the,* and *these;* and the auxiliaries *may, should,* and *will.* The role of these categories is to signal grammatical relationships.

Tense and Modality

Many categories of meaning are associated with function words and function morphemes. Bound morphemes can denote several categories of meaning in English, including number (*toys* v. *toy*) and tense (*walked* v. *walk*). In other languages, the same categories are expressed not by means of bound morphemes but by separate words. In Tongan, the function word *ʔoku* denotes present tense, while *naʔe* denotes past tense.

> ʔoku   ʔalu e   fineʔeiki ki kolo
> Present go   the woman   to town
> 'The woman is going to town.'

> naʔe   ʔalu e   fineʔeiki ki kolo
> Past   go   the woman   to town
> 'The woman was going to town.'

Whether tense is expressed through bound morphemes or separate lexical items is not important for semantics. What is important is that there is a semantic category *tense* that affects the meaning of sentences in both Tongan and English.

Semantic categories such as tense are conveyed by function words and function morphemes, but their scope extends beyond the constituent in which they occur. The meaning of a tense morpheme affects the whole sentence because the **tense** of the verb determines the time reference of the entire clause. The category *tense* (and other semantic categories like it) thus refers to both word meaning and clause meaning.

Modality, or *mood,* is a category through which speakers can convey their attitude towards the truth or reliability of their assertions (called *epistemic modality)* or express obligation, permission, or suggestion (called *deontic modality).* The sentences in the following pairs differ as to their *epistemic* modality:

1. She has *probably* left town by now. (probability)
   She has left town by now. (assertion)
2. Harry *must've* been very tall when he was young. (conjecture)
   Harry was very tall when he was young. (assertion)
3. They *may* come to the party. (possibility)
   They are coming to the party. (assertion)

And those in the following pairs differ as to their *deontic* modality:

4. He *must* come tomorrow. (command)
   He is coming tomorrow. (statement)
5. They *may* take the dishes away. (permission)
   They are taking the dishes away. (statement)

The two types of modality are interrelated, as witnessed by the fact that the same words (*must* and *may,* for example) can denote either type, depending on the context. Modality can be expressed through auxiliary verbs such as *may, should,* or *must* (which are called *modal* auxiliaries); through *modal* verbs such as *order, assume,* and *allow;* through *modal* adverbs such as *possibly* or *certainly;* and in some languages through affixes attached to verbs or nouns. Such affixes are common in Native American languages, some of which can have extremely complex systems of modal affixes and particles.

Reference

A noun phrase in an utterance may or may not have a corresponding entity in the real world. **Reference** concerns the ability of linguistic expressions to refer to real-world entities. If someone says *I read a new biography of James Joyce last weekend,* the expressions *I* and *a new biography of James Joyce* refer to real-world entities. By contrast, if someone says *I'd like to find a short biography of James Joyce,* there is in the speaker's mind a real-world entity corresponding to *I* but not to *a short biography of James Joyce.* (A short biography of James Joyce may exist, but in this sentence the speaker does not have in mind a real-world entity to which the expression refers.)

In the examples below, note the difference in reference for different uses of a given phrase. In examples 1, 3, and 5, the underscored phrases do not have a referent; we say they are not referential or that they are nonreferential. In 2, 4, and 6, the very same expressions do have referents in the real world; they are referential.

1. Can you recommend <u>a good western</u> for kids? (nonreferential)
2. Last night I saw <u>a good western</u> on HBO. (referential)
3. She'd buy <u>a new Ford Bronco</u> if she found one on sale. (nonreferential)
4. She test-drove <u>a new Ford Bronco</u> that she liked. (referential)
5. I'm searching for <u>the best Chinese restaurant in the city.</u> (nonreferential)
6. On Tuesday I ate at <u>the best Chinese restaurant in the city.</u> (referential)

As these examples show, reference is a property, not of words or phrases as such, but of linguistic expressions as they occur in actual discourse. The same phrase can be referential in one utterance and nonreferential in another. Note, too, that reference cannot be equated with definiteness, a subject to which we return below. (Reference is investigated further in Chapter 8.)

Deixis

The word *deixis* comes from the Greek adjective *deiktikos* meaning 'pointing, indicative.' **Deixis** is the marking of the orientation or position of entities and events with respect to certain *points of reference.* Consider the following sentence addressed to a waiter by a restaurant customer while pointing to items on a menu:

> I want this dish, this dish, and this dish.

To interpret this utterance, the waiter must have information about who *I* refers to, about the time at which the utterance is produced, and about what the three noun phrases *this dish* refer to. We say that *I* is a *deictic expression,* and so are the present-tense form of the verb and the three noun phrases *this dish.* Our ability to interpret them enables us to interpret the sentence.

Deixis consists of three semantic notions, all related to the orientation or position of events or entities in the real world. *Personal deixis* is commonly conveyed through personal pronouns: *I* versus *you* versus *he* or *she*. *Spatial deixis* refers to orientation in space: *here* versus *there* and *this* versus *that*. *Temporal deixis* refers to orientation in time, as in present versus past, for example.

Personal Deixis　Many of the utterances that we produce daily are comments or questions about ourselves or our interlocutors.

> *I* really should be going now.
> Did *you* return the video *I* asked *you* to?
> In this family, *we* never smoke and seldom drink.

The pronouns *I, you,* and *we*—along with *she, he, it,* and *they* (and alternative forms)—are markers of personal deixis. When we use these pronouns, we orient our utterances with respect to ourselves, our interlocutors, and third parties.

Personal pronouns are, of course, not the only tool used to mark personal deixis. The phrase *this person* in the sentence *You may enjoy scary roller-coaster rides, but this person doesn't care for them at all* may be used to refer to the speaker if the speaker wishes to express, say, annoyance or disdain. Likewise, in court, etiquette may require you to use the noun phrase *Your Honor* in addressing a judge: *Would Your Honor permit a brief recess?* Personal deixis is thus not associated exclusively with pronouns, although pronouns are the most common way to express personal deixis. In this discussion, we concentrate primarily on pronouns as markers of personal deixis.

The most basic opposition in personal-deixis systems is that between speaker (English *I;* German *ich;* Persian *man;* Thai *chǎn*) and addressee (English *you;* German *du;* Persian *to;* Thai *thɔɔ*). This opposition in *person* is so basic that it is reflected in the pronominal systems of all languages. Pronouns that refer to the speaker (or to a group including the speaker) are called *first-person* pronouns, and pronouns that refer to the addressee (or to a group including the addressee) are called *second-person* pronouns.

Besides the contrast between first person and second person, pronoun systems often have separate forms for the *third person*—that is, any entity other than the speaker and the person spoken to. In English, *he, she, it,* and *they* denote third-person entities. But third-person pronouns are not found in all languages. Some languages simply do not have special forms to refer to third-person entities. In these languages, third-person entities are referred to with a demonstrative such as *this* or *that,* or they remain unexpressed. In Tongan, a verb without an expressed subject is understood as having a third-person subject.

> naʔe　　　aʔu
> Past　　　arrive
> '(He/She/It) arrived.'

Tongan does have a third-person pronoun form but uses it only for emphasis.

> naʔe　aʔu　　ia
> Past　arrive　he/she
> 'He/She is the one who arrived.'

That some languages lack separate third-person pronouns reflects the fact that the third person is less important than the first and second persons in personal deixis. In fact, the third person can be defined as an entity *other than* the first person and *other than* the second person. Because it can be described in terms of the other two persons, it is a less basic distinction in language in general. The singular pronoun system of English can thus be described as follows:

speaker only	I
hearer only	you
neither speaker nor hearer	he/she/it

Some languages make finer distinctions in their pronominal systems, while others make fewer distinctions (see the section on "Semantic Universals" in Chapter 7). In *all* languages, though, there are separate first-person and second-person pronouns.

Besides person, personal-deixis systems may mark distinctions in gender and number. In English, a gender distinction is made only in the third-person singular: *he* for masculine and *she* for feminine referents. In other languages, gender may be marked in other persons as well. In Hebrew, the second-person singular pronoun is *ata* for masculine referents but *at* for feminine referents. Number is marked on English pronouns in the first person (*I* versus *we)* and the third person (*he/she/it* versus *they); the second-person pronoun *you* is used for reference to both singular and plural entities. In many languages, there are separate second-person singular and plural pronouns (French *tu* and *vous;* German *du* and *ihr;* Persian *to* and *šoma).* Singular and plural are not the only number categories that can be distinguished: some languages have distinct dual forms to refer to exactly two people, and a few languages even mark a distinction between "a few" and "many" referents (see the chart of Fijian pronouns on p. 229 in Chapter 7).

Finally, personal deixis frequently reflects the social status of referents. In French the choice of a pronoun in the second person depends on the nature of the speaker's relationship to the addressee. If speaker and addressee are of roughly equal social status, the pronoun *tu* is used; to mark or create social distance or social inequality, a speaker uses the plural pronoun *vous* instead of *tu,* even when addressing one person. Considerably more complex systems are found in languages such as Japanese, Thai, and Korean. Strictly speaking, the use of deictic devices to reflect facts about the social relationship of the participants is a distinct type of deixis, commonly referred to as *social deixis.*

Thus personal deixis can mark a number of overlapping distinctions: person, gender, number, and social relations. Languages combine these distinctions in different combinations, marking some and not marking others. The basic distinction between first person and second person, however, is found in all languages and appears to be a basic semantic category in all deictic systems.

Spatial Deixis Spatial deixis is the marking of the orientation or position in space of the referent of a linguistic expression. The categories of words most commonly used to express spatial deixis are demonstratives *(this, that)* and adverbs *(here, there).* Demonstratives and adverbs of place are by no means the only categories that have spatial deictic meaning; the directional verbs *go* and *come* also carry deictic information, as do *bring* and *take*.

Languages differ in terms of the number and meaning of demonstratives and adverbs of place. The demonstrative system of English distinguishes only between *this* (proximate—close to the speaker) and *that* (remote—relatively distant from the speaker). It is one of the simplest systems found. At the other extreme are languages such as Eskimo, which has 30 demonstrative forms. In all languages, however, the demonstrative system treats the speaker as a point of reference. Thus the speaker is a basic point of reference for spatial deixis.

Many spatial-deixis systems have three terms. Three-term systems fall into two categories. In one category, the meanings of the terms are 'near the speaker,' 'a little distant from the speaker,' and 'far from the speaker.' The Spanish demonstratives *este, ese, aquel* have these three respective meanings. In another type of three-term demonstrative system, the terms have the meanings 'near the speaker,' 'near the hearer,' and 'away from both speaker and hearer.' Fijian exemplifies such a system.

na   ŋone   oⁿgo
the   child   this (near me)
'this child (near me)'

na   ŋone   oⁿgori
the   child   this (near you)
'that child (near you)'

na   ŋone   oya
the   child   that (away from you and me)
'that child (away from you and me)'

In both systems, however, the speaker is taken as either the sole point of reference or as one of two points of reference.

Spatial deixis thus represents the orientation of actions and states in space, and it is most commonly conveyed by demonstratives and by adverbs of place. Languages may have anywhere from 2 to 30 distinct demonstrative forms, but all demonstrative systems take the speaker as a basic point of reference.

Temporal Deixis   A third type of deixis is temporal deixis—the orientation or position of the referent of actions and events in time. All languages have words and phrases that are inherently marked for temporal deixis, such as the English terms *before, last year, tomorrow, now,* and *this evening.* In many languages temporal deixis can be marked through tense, encoded on the verb with affixes, or expressed in an independent morpheme. In English, you must make an obligatory choice between the past-tense and the nonpast-tense form of verbs.

I walk to school every day. (nonpast tense)
I walked to school every day. (past tense)

To express a future *time,* English has no distinct verbal inflection (it lacks a future *tense)* but uses a multiword verb in the nonpast tense.

> I will walk to school next week. (nonpast tense for future time)

Tuvaluan is like English: *e* denotes nonpast, while *ne* is a past-tense marker.

> au e   fano ki te fakaala
> I   Nonpast go   to the feast
> 'I am going/will go to the feast.'

> au ne fano ki te fakaala
> I   Past go   to the feast
> 'I went to the feast.'

In some languages, the choice is between future and nonfuture (with undifferentiated present and past).

In a number of languages, temporal deixis can be marked only with optional adverbs. This Chinese sentence can be interpreted as past, present, or future, depending on the context:

> xià   yǔ
> down   rain
> 'It was/is/will be raining.'

When there is the possibility of ambiguity, an adverb of time ('last night,' 'right now,' 'next week') is added to the sentence.

In languages that do not mark tense on verbs, another semantic category called **aspect** is frequently obligatory. Aspect is not directly related to temporal deixis but refers to the ways in which actions and states are viewed: as continuous (*I was talking),* repetitive (*I talked [every day]),* instantaneous (*I talked),* and so on.

Tense is thus not the only marker of temporal deixis, although it is very frequently exploited by languages as the primary means of marking temporal deixis.

The most basic point of reference for tense is the moment at which the sentence is uttered. Any event that occurs before that moment may be marked as past, and any event that occurs after that moment may be marked as future.

> The train arrived. (any time before the utterance moment)

> The train is arriving. (at the moment of utterance)

> The train will arrive. (any time after the utterance moment)

When the point of reference is some point in time other than the moment of utterance, we say that tense is *relative.* Relative tense is used in many languages when speakers wish to compare the time of occurrence of two different events.

> After I had bought two, they gave me another one.

> Before I saw you yesterday, I had been sick for a week.

Languages sometimes have complex rules of *tense concord* that dictate the form of verbs in relative contexts.

Deixis as a Semantic Notion   The three types of deixis illustrate how semantic categories permeate language beyond the simple meaning of words. The deictic orientation of a sentence or part of a sentence can be conveyed through bound morphemes such as tense endings, through free morphemes and function words such as pronouns and demonstratives, or through content words such as *here* and *bring*. Deictic meaning is independent of the means used to convey it.

One of the purposes of semantics is to describe which parameters are important or essential to characterize deixis (as well as other semantic categories) in language in general. We noted, for example, that distinguishing between the speaker and the addressee is an essential function of the personal deixis system of all languages. Similarly, we found that every spatial deixis system has at least one point of reference, a location near the speaker. A spatial deixis system may also have a secondary point of reference near the hearer.

There is considerable overlap between the different types of deixis. For example, personal, spatial, and temporal deixis all share a basic point of reference: the speaker's identity and location in space and time. Many linguistic devices can be used to mark more than one kind of deixis. The English demonstrative *this* can be used for personal deixis (*this person),* spatial deixis (*this thing),* and temporal deixis (*this morning).* Clearly, personal, spatial, and temporal deixis are closely related notions.

Textual Deixis   One type of deixis that we have not yet discussed is *textual deixis,* which is the orientation of an utterance with respect to other utterances in a string of utterances. Consider, for example, the following pair of sentences:

He started to swear at me and curse. *That* made me even more angry.

The demonstrative *that* at the beginning of the second sentence refers not to a direction in space or time but rather to something previously mentioned. It marks textual deixis. Textual deixis is thus a tool that enables language users to package utterances together and indicate relationships across utterances. Because textual deixis is primarily concerned with utterances and their context, it goes beyond the scope of semantics as traditionally defined, although its importance is not to be underestimated.

SEMANTIC ROLES AND SENTENCE MEANING

We have noted that although, like words, sentences must carry meaning for language speakers to understand each other at all, the meaning of sentences cannot be determined merely by adding up the meaning of each content word of the sentence. This fact was illustrated in the last section, where you saw that bound morphemes and function words may carry meaning that has implication for the meaning of the entire sentence. We also noted that sentences such as *The trainer licked the lion* and *The lion licked the trainer* have very different meanings, even though they contain exactly the same words. Clearly, adding together the meaning of each word will not produce the full meaning of a sentence. Such a process will not even distinguish between the two simple illustrative sentences in this paragraph. More than just the meaning of the individual content words must be taken into consideration when defining what the meaning of a sentence consists of.

Consider the following active/passive counterparts, which, at the level of referential meaning, describe the same situation:

1. The lion licked the trainer.
2. The trainer was licked by the lion.

These sentences differ in that 2 is a passive structure, whereas 1 is not. Since our concern here is with meaning, we ask how to account for the synonymy between 1 and 2.

Furthermore, consider the following sentences:

3. David sliced the salami with a knife.
4. David used a knife to slice the salami.

Here is a situation not unlike the active/passive counterparts of 1 and 2, in that the sentences have the same referential meaning. Nevertheless, we need to describe how sentences 3 and 4 mean "the same thing."

The situations just presented suggest that the crucial factor in the way sentence meaning is constructed is the *role* played by each noun phrase in relation to the verb. We thus need to introduce the notion **semantic role** of a noun phrase. *Semantic role* refers to the way in which the referent of the noun phrase contributes to the state, action, or situation described by the sentence. The semantic role of a noun phrase differs from its syntactic role (as subject, object, and so on), as illustrated by the contrast between sentences 1 and 2. In both 1 and 2, the way in which the lion is involved in the action is the same; and the way in which the trainer is involved is the same. By contrast, despite its having the same semantic role in both, *the trainer* has different syntatic roles, as the direct object of the verb in 1 and the grammatical subject of 2.

Semantic role is not an inherent property of a noun phrase: a given noun phrase can have different semantic roles in different sentences, as in the following:

Michael was injured by <u>a friend.</u>
Michael was injured with <u>a friend.</u>

Semantic role is a way of characterizing the meaning relationship between a noun phrase and the verb of a sentence.

Agents and Patients   The first semantic roles we need to identify are agent (the responsible initiator of an action) and patient (the entity that undergoes a certain change of state). In both sentence 1 and sentence 2, above, the agent is the lion, and the patient is the trainer. That both sentences describe the same situation (and hence have the same referential meaning) can thus be explained by the fact that in both sentences each noun phrase has the same semantic role.

Experiencers   The role of the subject noun phrases in the following sentences is not that of agent, because Courtney is not really the responsible initiator of the actions denoted by the verbs:

<u>Courtney</u> likes blueberry pancakes.
<u>Courtney</u> felt threatened by the lion.

In both sentences, Courtney experiences a physical or mental sensation. The semantic role of Courtney is *experiencer,* defined as that which receives a sensory input. In English, experiencers can be either subjects or direct objects, depending on the verb. Compare the sentences about Courtney, in which the experiencer is the subject, with the following sentence, in which the experiencer is the direct object:

Dwayne sometimes astounds <u>me</u> with his wit.

Instruments and Causes   Now consider the semantic roles of the underscored noun phrases in the following sentences:

5. Michael was injured by <u>a stone.</u>
6. Michael was injured with <u>a stone.</u>

The difference between these sentences is that 6 implies that someone used a stone to attack Michael, while 5 does not require that implication. In sentence 6, we say that *a stone* is the *instrument,* or the intermediary through which an agent performs the action; note that the definition requires that there be an agent, which is consistent with our interpretation of sentence 6. In sentence 5, *a stone* could be assigned the role of instrument only if there was an agent doing the injuring. If the stone that injured Michael were part of a rockfall, *a stone* would be assigned the semantic role of *cause,* defined as any natural force that brings about a change of state. Instruments and causes can be expressed as prepositional phrases (as in the previous examples) or subjects.

<u>The silver key</u> opened the door to the wine cellar. (INSTRUMENT)

<u>The snow</u> caved in the roof. (CAUSE)

That the noun phrase *the silver key* is indeed an instrument and not an agent is supported by the fact that it cannot be conjoined (linked by *and)* with an agent, as the following anomalous example shows:

*The silver key and John opened the door to the cellar.

However, an instrument *can* be conjoined with another instrument, and an agent with another agent.

<u>A push</u> and <u>a shove</u> opened the door to the cellar.

<u>John</u> and <u>Chelsey</u> opened the door to the cellar.

Recipients, Benefactives, Locatives, Temporals   A noun phrase can be a *recipient* (that which receives a physical object), a *benefactive* (that for which an action is performed), a *locative* (the location of an action or state), or a *temporal* (the time at which the action or state occurred).

I gave <u>Yolanda</u> a puppy. (RECIPIENT)

Stefan passed the message to me for <u>Yolanda.</u> (BENEFACTIVE)

<u>The Midwest</u> is cold in winter. (LOCATIVE)

She left home <u>the day before yesterday</u>. (TEMPORAL)

The point of this enterprise is to characterize the possible semantic roles that noun phrases can fill in a sentence. Every noun phrase in a clause is assigned a semantic role, and, aside from coordinate noun phrases, the same semantic role cannot be assigned to two different noun phrases within the same clause. Consequently, a sentence such as the following is ruled out as being semantically odd or anomalous because it contains two instrumental noun phrases, which are underlined:

*<u>This ball</u> broke the window with <u>a hammer</u>.

In addition, in most cases a single noun phrase can be assigned only one semantic role. In rare instances, a noun phrase can be assigned two different roles; in the sentence *Geoff rolled down the hill,* if Geoff rolled down the hill deliberately, he is both agent and patient, because he is at once the responsible initiator of the action and the entity that undergoes the change of state.

SEMANTIC ROLES AND GRAMMATICAL RELATIONS

It is important to understand the relationship between semantic roles and grammatical relations because they are not the same. For example, in English, the subject of a sentence can be an agent (as in the underlined noun phrase in sentence 1), a patient (as in 2), an instrument (3), a cause (4), an experiencer (5), a benefactive (or recipient) (6), a locative (7), or a temporal (8), depending on the verb.

1. <u>The janitor</u> opened the door. (AGENT)
2. <u>The door</u> opened easily. (PATIENT)
3. <u>His first record</u> greatly expanded his audience. (INSTRUMENT)
4. <u>Bad weather</u> ruined the corn crop. (CAUSE)
5. <u>Serge</u> heard his father whispering. (EXPERIENCER)
6. <u>The young artist</u> won the prize. (BENEFACTIVE OR RECIPIENT)
7. <u>Arizona</u> attracts asthmatics. (LOCATIVE)
8. <u>The next day</u> found us on the road to Alice Springs. (TEMPORAL)

Furthermore, in certain English constructions the subject does not have any semantic role; such is the case of the so-called "dummy *it*" construction, in which the pronoun *it* fills a semantically empty subject slot.

<u>It</u> became clear that the government had jailed him there.

So the notion of subject is independent of the notion of semantic role; and we could show the same thing for direct objects and other grammatical relations. Conversely, semantic roles do not appear to be constrained by grammatical relations. A locative, for example, may be expressed as a subject (as in sentence 1), a direct object (2), an indirect object (3), or an oblique (4).

1. <u>The garden</u> will look great in the spring.
2. William planted <u>the garden</u> with cucumbers and tomatoes.

3. The begonias give <u>the garden</u> a cheerful look.
4. The gate opens on <u>the garden</u>.

Nevertheless, there is a relationship between grammatical relations and semantic roles. Consider the following sentences, all of which have *open* as a verb:

Michele opened the door with this key.
The door opens easily.
This key will open the door.
The wind opened the door.

The grammatical subjects of the sentences above are an agent (*Michele),* a patient (*the door),* an instrument (*this key),* and a cause (*the wind).* Such extreme variety is not found with all verbs. The verb *soothe* can take an instrument or a cause as subject.

This ointment will soothe your sunburn.
The cold stream soothed my sore feet.

To have an experiencer as the grammatical subject of the verb *soothe,* we use a passive construction.

I was soothed by the herbal tea.

Clearly, the verb controls the range of variation allowed in each case. Language users know the semantic roles that each verb allows as subject, direct object, and so on. In the mental lexicon, there is a tag attached to the verb *soothe* indicating that only instruments and causes are allowed in subject position, whereas the tag attached to the verb *open* permits the subject to be agent, patient, instrument, or cause.

Semantic roles are universal features of the semantic structure of all languages, but how they interact with grammatical relations such as subject and direct object differs from language to language. Equivalent verbs in different languages do not carry similar tags. The tag attached to the English verb *like,* for example, permits only experiencers as subjects.

I like French fries.

But only patients can be the subjects of the equivalent Spanish verb *gustar.*

Las	papas fritas	me	gustan.
the	French-fries	to-me	like

'I like French fries.' (Literally, 'French fries to me are pleasing.')

A similar situation is found for verbs of liking and pleasing in many other languages, including Russian. In some languages, the verb 'understand' allows its subjects to be experiencers or patients, as in Samoan. The choice depends on emphasis and focus.

ʔua	maalamalama	aʔu	i		le	mataaʔupu.
Present-tense	understand	I	Object-marker		the	lesson

'I understand the lesson.'

ʔua   maalamalama   le   mataaʔupu   iate   aʔu.
Present-tense   understand   the   lesson   to   me
'I understand the lesson.' (Literally: 'The lesson understands to me.')

Some languages distinguish between agent and experiencer much more carefully than English does. For example, the verb might take a subject when the action described is intentional but take a direct object when the action is unintentional.

In addition to cross-linguistic variation with respect to specific verbs, languages vary in the degree to which different semantic roles can fit into different grammatical slots in a sentence. In English, the subject slot can be occupied by noun phrases of any semantic role—depending, of course, on the verb. Many English verbs allow different semantic roles for subject, direct object, and so on. But the situation is different in many other languages. In languages such as Russian and German, verbs do not allow nearly as much variation in semantic roles as English verbs do, and there is a much tighter bond between semantic roles and grammatical relations.

Computers, Corpora, and Semantics

Computerized corpora are useful to dictionary makers and others in establishing patterns of language that are not apparent from mere introspection. For example, patterns of collocations—which words go together—are much more readily understood with the help of a computerized corpus of natural-language texts. Such patterns can be very helpful in highlighting meanings, including parts of speech, and words that co-occur with some frequency.

Further, while it may appear that synonymous words can be used in place of one another, corpora can show that it is not in fact common for words to be readily substitutable. For example, *little* and *small*, *big* and *large*, and *fast* and *quick* are generally considered synonyms. But as a cursory examination of key word in context (KWIC) concordances for these pairs shows, they are not straightforwardly substitutable. Table 6–1 on page 212 shows a selection of KWIC entries for the word *little*, and Table 6–2 on page 213 shows a selection of KWIC entries for *small*. (The samples are taken from the British National Corpus and have been concordanced with WordSmith.)

Note in Table 6–1 that quite a few of the sentences would not tolerate the substitution of *small* for *little*—for example, 2, 3, 5, 6, 9, 10, 11, 15, 16, 17, and 21. Taking 3 as an example, English does not permit "not a small irritated." Of those instances where the substitution is possible, several would sound very odd or convey a different connotation, such as 1, 4, and 8. In 1, "poor little rich boy" and "poor small rich boy" carry different senses. As the examples in Table 6–2 show, *little* is more readily substitutable for *small*; part of the reason is that in its use as an adjective *little* does in fact carry denotations and connotations much like those of most uses of *small*. But, looking back to Table 6–1, we see that the opposite is not true. This is because *little* is not only an adjective meaning 'small' but also part of an adverb, in the expressions *a little ruffled, a little dispirited,* and *a little open* (13, 20, 24) where it modifies an adjective, and *a little longer* (12) where it modifies an adverb. Yet dictionaries cite *little* and *small* as synonyms. At the end of this chapter you will find the address for getting a sample of sentences containing any word or expression that you are interested in examining. From such a list you can learn a great deal about the semantics of any word or phrase.

Table 6-1

Concordance for little

1	ke council activities and so on. The poor	**little**	rich boy was looked after by a second
2	a few hours of stall avoidance training and	**little,**	if any, spinning. Vienna Dear Fräu
3	andt, I am deeply distressed, and also not a	**little**	irritated, by the direction events hav
4	Even without the threat to his job, he had	**little**	choice. There may be little or no
5	job, he had little choice. There may be	**little**	or no hope of finding those particular
6	cted, some as yet unrecorded. But he had	**little**	reason yet to ask for a search warrant
7	him if he so much as tried. But there is	**little**	point, for instance, in turning on an
8	and those of his friends. You noticed my	**little**	ploy. Current findings suggest a c
9	of success between classes have changed very	**little.**	Objectively, he was little more a
10	changed very little. Objectively, he was	**little**	more attractive to the Conservatives w
11	nd that it was necessary for him to retire a	**little**	from the active life in which he had p
12	d energy upon his real work. We talked a	**little**	longer, and then I bought some chocola
13	ess was still there, but the fur was maybe a	**little**	ruffled. I wish all men enjoyed th
14	joyed their whole bodies, rather than just a	**little,**	wobbly bit of it.' There is a nee
15	it.' There is a need, however, to look a	**little**	more at the role of Parliament. ON
16	role of Parliament. ON A SLOW pitch with	**little**	bounce, South Africa once again were u
17	and seven overs to spare. Addition of a	**little**	silicone lubricant (vacuum grease, DOW
18	f air and quite softly-spoken and actually a	**little**	shy-looking, and he'd made a point of
19	is ugly body quiet and still above them as a	**little**	gravestone. Once the carriage was
20	motion, she closed her eyes, tired now and a	**little**	dispirited. Then the front zip of
21	to his importuning hands and he eased away a	**little**	so that his fingers could slide inside
22	original access to land, an issue upon which	**little**	progress had been made — with the pos
23	survey, the privatization programme involved	**little**	change in management or improvement in
24	rovement in efficiency. Might leave us a	**little**	open sometimes, but with the pace we s
25	core a few goals!! we reckoned we knew a	**little**	bit more about what makes children tic
26	unge and the dining room area was probably a	**little**	bit smaller If you want to be happ
27	be happy and have a happy face and spread a	**little**	joy around then there is just one way.

Table 6-2

Concordance for small

1	ad of papers with individual readerships too	**small**	for us to analyse (the Scotsman, the G
2	into tears at the sight of the house and the	**small**	familiar crowd waiting for her outside
3	McCloy, who lives here in town, runs a very	**small**	unsuccessful sort of decorating busines
4	the Führer down to spring 1941 rested in no	**small**	measure on the lack of serious interfer
5	ws volatile session His clothes were too	**small**	now, pinching him at the neck, the wais
6	(although of course the numbers are far too	**small**	for any quantitative analysis) can be s
7	illery and mortars, and themselves down to a	**small**	amount of ammunition, the remnants of t
8	The Captain's white face had greyed, his	**small**	mouth tightening into a cruel line.
9	esult, the individual may retain only a very	**small**	percentage of the extra income earned a
10	unications products are helping both big and	**small**	businesses in more than one hundred co
11	ex longed for a pond in the garden, but with	**small**	children around the idea was shelved —
12	subsequent continuation of a large number of	**small**	unions and, as a secondary consequence,
13	le, often near remote skerries, headlands or	**small**	uninhabited islands, and this necessita
14	ime of the Russian conquest, although only a	**small**	remnant of this nationality survives to
15	d bought their house and provided her with a	**small**	income. perfect like a small velvet
16	ences for arbitrage risk were also generally	**small,**	and 88% of the cases fell within the r
17	ntract). In doing so, she knocked down a	**small**	boy and immediately went down again to
18	essible to teachers, along with a monitor (a	**small**	black and white one would do), then it
19	In the end they hauled the Gnomes into a	**small**	ante-room across the galleried landing
20	e famous Shaker pegged wall-rail for hanging	**small**	cupboards, shelves, mirrors and even ch
21	ne.' The most marked contrast between the	**small**	towns and their larger counterparts is
22	ment. Thirty years later what had been a	**small**	village was a big town and would have b
23	ves that churchyards provide a focus and are	**small**	enough for a group of local enthusiasts
24	s pursuing a policy of devaluing the yuan in	**small,**	frequent steps, in an effort to boost
25	any factors specific for countries, even for	**small**	regions within a country and for groups
26	5°F/Gas Mark 3), allowing 40 minutes for the	**small**	basins and 50 minutes for the large bow
27	and the back of the Admiralty proper runs a	**small**	unnamed side-street which I must have p
28	might reply `Yes, but these cost savings are	**small**	compared to the fuel savings you get wi

SUMMARY

- Semantics is the study of meaning in language.

- Semantics traditionally focuses on linguistic meaning, but languages also convey social meaning and affective meaning.

- Words, sentences, and utterances can all carry meaning, and sentence meaning and utterance meaning must be distinguished.

- The study of sentence meaning falls primarily within the domain of semantics.

- Within a sentence words may have *scope* over other constituents, as *only* has scope over the bracketed constituent in *He only knew [what he had read in the letter]*.

- Pragmatics is the branch of linguistics that concerns itself with utterance meaning.

- Lexical semantics is the study of meaning relationships in vocabulary. The *types* of relationships that hold among sets of words are universal, though the particular word sets to which they apply vary from language to language.

- Semantic fields are sets of words whose referents belong together on the basis of fundamental semantic characteristics.

- The words in a semantic field can be arranged in terms of these relationships: hyponymy (a kind of), part/whole (subdivision), synonymy (similar meaning), gradable and nongradable antonymy (opposite meaning), converseness (reciprocal meaning), polysemy (multiple meanings), homonymy (same written or spoken form), and metaphorical extension (derived meaning).

- Semantic notions such as deixis can be expressed by bound morphemes (-*ed* in *walked)* and function words (*that* in *that one)* as well as by content words (*tomorrow).*

- There are several types of deixis: personal (*you, me),* spatial (*here, there),* and temporal (*now, then).* All require that a point of reference be identified.

- In relation to the speaker and the moment of utterance, the here and now is highly privileged as a point of reference in all three types of deixis.

- The meaning of a sentence is not simply the sum meaning of its words.

- Sentence semantics aims to uncover the basic relationships between the noun phrases and the verb of a sentence.

- Semantic roles (e.g., agent or instrument) are not inherent properties of noun phrases but are relational notions. They are independent of the grammatical relations (e.g., subject or object) of the noun phrase. The verb determines which semantic role may be used in particular grammatical slots of a sentence.

- This chapter has described these semantic roles: agent, patient, experiencer, instrument, cause, benefactive, recipient, locative, and temporal.

- While semantic roles are universal, languages differ as to how particular roles are encoded in syntax.

WHAT DO YOU THINK? REVISITED

❖ *Holly's question. George Washington* and *the first president of the United States* usually refer to the same person, namely that man who lived from 1732 to 1799 and became president of the United States in 1789. *George Washington* is the name of that man, but *George Washington* does not mean 'the first president of the United States.' The two expressions have the same referent, but they have different *senses.* The fact that two expressions refer to the same entity does not necessarily entail that they *mean* the same thing. You should be able to think of sentences in which one of these expressions would be appropriate, but not the other, or both could appear but could not be interchanged. As an example, consider this sentence: "Some Maryland residents like to claim that John Hanson was the first president of the United States." Even though that statement is true, it would not be true to say, "Some Maryland residents like to claim that John Hanson was George Washington." The fact that one is true but not the other is a demonstration that they do not mean the same thing.

❖ *Nathan's notion.* Although synonyms might not have the same co-occurrence patterns with other words, they still mean the same thing. Nathan has identified a frame into which you could slot *fast* or *quick* but not both, and that fact seems to be an argument that the two words are not used exactly the same way, but they are synonymous.

❖ *Your uncle.* The term that characterizes the semantic relationship described by your uncle is *converse. Uncle* and *nephew* are converses; so are *student* and *teacher.* Among other meanings, *hot* means 'not cold,' but *nephew* is not the same as 'not uncle.' In addition, opposites are usually the extremes of words that can be arrayed along a continuum, for example from *hot* to *warm* to *lukewarm* to *cold,* where *hot* and *cold* are opposites.

❖ *Family picnic.* Words like *mine* and *yours* are deictic expressions, and their meaning depends, in this case, on who is saying them. *Mine* means something like 'belonging to the speaker' (or the reported speaker), so when your cousin says "It's mine," he is claiming ownership, and when his daughter uses the very same words she is claiming ownership. That is because deictic words must be interpreted in their context, as with who is speaking. Other examples are words like *yesterday* and *now,* whose meanings vary depending on the time of the utterance containing them.

EXERCISES

Based on English

6-1 In the first section of the chapter we introduced notions of *synonymy, implication, contradiction, anomaly, ambiguity,* and *vagueness* to describe various sentences and sentence pairs. Determine which of these notions applies to each of the following sentences and sentence pairs:

1) Harry's cat called me on the phone.

2) Visiting relatives can be boring.

3) His daughter is her brother's grandmother.

4) My husband just returned from the store. I am a married woman.

5) I don't like locking my car. My car's doors can be locked.

6) The basil seeds I will plant next weekend are growing well.

7) She swims.

8) I was fatally ill last year.

9) It is still too warm to start a fire. It is not cold enough to start a fire.

10) The wine I didn't taste tasted sour to me.

11) My dog wants out. The canine creature that belongs to me is experiencing a desire to proceed outdoors.

12) Pat kissed Linda, and Lou, too.

6-2 The following sentences are ambiguous. Based on the discussion in this chapter and Chapter 5, describe the ambiguity.

1) They found the peasants revolting.

2) The car I'm getting ready to drive is a Lamborghini.

3) There is nothing more alarming than developing nuclear power plants.

4) Erika does not like her husband, and neither does Natalie.

5) They said that they told her to come to them.

6) Challenging wrestlers will be avoided at all costs.

7) He met his challenger at his house.

6-3 Identify the differences in linguistic, social, and affective meaning among the words and phrases in each of the following sets:

1) hoax, trickery, swindle, rip-off, ruse, stratagem

2) delightful, pleasant, great, far-out, nice, pleasurable, bad, cool

3) man, guy, dude, jock, imp, lad, gentleman, hunk, boy

4) eat, wolf down, nourish, devour, peck, ingest, chow down, graze, fill one's tummy

5) tired, fatigued, pooped, weary, languorous, zonked out, exhausted, fordone, spent

6) stupid person, idiot, nerd, ass, jerk, turkey, wimp, punk, airhead, bastard

6-4 Some of the sets of terms below form semantic fields. For each set:

a. Identify and disregard the words that do *not* belong to the same semantic field as the others in the set.

b. Identify the superordinate term of the remaining semantic field, if there is one (it may be a word in the set).

c. Determine whether some terms are less marked than others, and justify your claim.

1) acquire, buy, collect, hoard, win, inherit, steal

2) whisper, talk, narrate, report, tell, harangue, scribble, instruct, brief

3) road, path, barn, way, street, freeway, avenue, thoroughfare, interstate, method

4) stench, smell, reek, aroma, bouquet, odoriferous, perfume, fragrance, scent, olfactory

6-5 For each semantic relationship specified below, provide one or more examples of words whose referents have that relationship to the specified word and identify the name of the semantic category that is used to cover your answer.

Example: fish is the superordinate term (hypernym)

Answer: *salmon, trout, ling cod, flounder, swordfish, tuna* are its hyponyms

1) *Irish setter, dalmatian, cocker spaniel* are the hyponyms

2) *tabby, tom, Persian, alley* are the hyponyms

3) *dog, cat, goldfish, parakeet, hamster* are the hyponyms

4) *knife, fork, spoon* are the hyponyms

5) *true* is the antonym

6) *inaccurate* is the antonym

7) *sister* is the converse

8) *teacher* is the converse

9) *partner* is the converse

10) *toe* is the part

11) *menu* is the whole

12) *friend* is the synonym

13) *teacher* is the synonym

6-6   Consider the following two sequences of dictionary entries, taken (slightly abbreviated) from *The American Heritage Dictionary of the English Language,* 3rd ed. (Boston: Houghton Mifflin, 1992):

Sequence 1

husk·y[1] adj. **-i·er, -i·est. 1.** Hoarse or rough in quality: *a voice husky with emotion.* **2.a.** Resembling a husk. **b.** Containing husks. [From HUSK]—**husk´i·ly** adv.

hus·ky[2] adj. **-i·er, -i·est. 1.** Strongly built; burly. **2.** Heavily built: *clothing sizes for husky boys.*—**husky** n., pl. **-ies.** A husky person. [Perhaps from HUSK]

hus·ky[3] n., pl. **-kies 1.** Often **Husky** or **Huskie.** A dog of a breed developed in Siberia for pulling sleds and having a dense, variously colored coat. Also called *Siberian husky.* **2.** A similar dog of Arctic origin. [Probably from shortening and alteration of ESKIMO.]

Sequence 2

jun·ior adj. **1.** Abbr. **jr., Jr., Jun., jun., jnr.** Used to distinguish a son from his father when they have the same given name. **2.** Intended for or including youthful persons: *junior fashions; a junior sports league.* **3.** Lower in rank or shorter in length of tenure: *a junior officer; the junior senator from Texas.* **4.** Of, for, or constituting students in the third year of a U.S. high school or college: *the junior class; the junior prom.* **5.** Lesser in scale than the usual. **-junior** n. Abbr. **jr., Jr., Jun., jun., jnr. 1.** A person who is younger than another: *a sister four years my junior.* **2.** A person lesser in rank or time of participation or service; subordinate. **3.** A student in the third year of a U.S. high school or college. **4.** A class of clothing sizes for girls and slender women. In this sense, also called *junior miss.*

Using the terms introduced in our discussion of lexical semantics, describe in detail how these dictionary entries are organized. Include a discussion of the criteria that are used to create different entries or subentries for homonymous words.

6-7   In the following sets of sentences one or more words are used metaphorically. Provide a general statement describing the principle that underlies each set of metaphors; then add to the set one metaphor that follows the principle.

Example:

I let my manuscript *simmer* for six months.

She *concocted* a retort that readers will appreciate.

There is no easy *recipe* for writing effective business letters.

General statement: "The writing process is viewed as cooking." Additional example: "He is the kind of writer who *whips up* another trashy novel every six months."

1) Members of the audience besieged him with counterarguments.
   His opponents tore his arguments to pieces.
   My reasoning left them with no ammunition.
   The others will never be able to destroy this argument.
   His question betrayed a defensive stance.

2) This heat is crushing.
   The sun is beating down on these poor laborers.
   The clouds seem to be lifting.
   The northern part of the state is under a heavy snowstorm.
   The fresh breeze cleared up the oppressive heat.

3) She has an eye for handsome men.
   He has a palate for good Indian curry.
   My neighbor has an ear for gossip.
   I used to have an eye for good etchings.
   The French have a nose for cheese.

6-8 Determine whether the words in each of the following sets are polysemic, homonymous, or metaphorically related. In each case, state the criteria used to arrive at your conclusion. You may use a dictionary.

1) to run down (the stairs); to run down (an enemy); to run down (a list of names)

2) the seat (of one's pants); the seat (of government); the (driver's) seat (of a car)

3) an ear (for music); an ear (of corn); an ear (as auditory organ)

4) to pitch (a baseball); pitch (black); the pitch (of one's voice)

5) to spell (a word); (under) a spell; a (dry) spell

6) vision (the ability to see); (a man of) vision; vision (as a hallucination)

7) the butt (of a rifle); the butt (of a joke); to butt (as a ram)

6-9 Identify the semantic role of each underscored noun phrase in these sentences:

1) In October, I gazed from the wooden bridge into the small river behind our college.

2) I have forgotten everything that I learned in grade school.

3) The Grand Tetons tower majestically over the valley.

4) The snow completely buried my car during the last storm.

5) Fifty kilos of cocaine were seized by the DEA.

6) Natalie was awarded one thousand dollars' worth of travel.

7) The hurricane destroyed the island.

8) Their ingenuity never ceases to amaze me.

6-10 a. Examine Table 6–1 on page 212 to determine which words frequently co-occur with *little,* either preceding or following it.

b. List and name all the immediate constituents of which *little* is an element in the examples of Table 6–1.

Example #12: a little longer—adverb phrase; #20: a little dispirited—adjective phrase

Based on English and Other Languages

6-11 A "tag" is attached to every verb in the lexicon, indicating which semantic role can be assigned to each noun argument. For example, the verb *bake* can have an agent as its subject (as in sentence 1), a patient (as in sentence 2), a cause (3), or an instrument (4). But in subject position it does not allow locatives (5) or temporals (6).

1) Matthew baked scones.

2) The cake is baking.

3) The sun baked my lilies to a crisp.

4) This oven bakes wonderful cakes.

5) *The kitchen bakes nicely.

6) *Tomorrow will bake nicely.

a. Determine which semantic roles these verbs allow as subject on the basis of the sentences provided: *feel, provide, absorb, thaw, taste.*

1) His hands felt limp and moist.
I could feel the presence of an intruder in the apartment.
This room feels damp.
They all felt under the blanket to see what was there.
This semester feels very different from last semester.

2) Gas lamps provided light for the outdoor picnic.
These fields provide enough wheat to feed a city.
Who provided these scones?
The accident provided me plenty to worry about.
Your textbooks provide many illustrations of this phenomenon.
The bylaws provide for dissolution of the board in these cases.

3) The students have absorbed so much material that they can't make sense of it anymore.
This kind of sponge does not absorb water well.
The United States absorbed the Texas Republic in 1845.
My work hours are absorbing all my free time.
The soil is absorbing the rain.

4) If Antarctica suddenly thawed, the sea level would rise dramatically.
Chicken does not thaw well in just two hours.
The crowd thawed after Kent arrived.
Kent's arrival thawed the party.
The heat of the sun will thaw the ice in the ice chest.
Ice thaws at 0 degrees Celsius.
The peace treaty will thaw relations between the United States and China.

5) This wine tastes like vinegar.
He's tasted every single hors d'oeuvre at the party.
I can taste the capers in the sauce.

b. Languages may differ with respect to the semantic roles that particular verbs may take. The following are semantically well-formed French sentences with the verb *goûter* 'taste':

Il   n'a   jamais goûté au caviar.
he not-have ever   tasted the caviar
'He's never tasted caviar.'

Je goûte un goût amer dans ce   café.
I   taste   a   taste bitter in   this coffee
'I taste a bitter taste in this coffee.'

By contrast, the following sentence is not well constructed:

*Les cuisses de grenouille goûtent bon.
the   thighs   of frog   taste   good
'Frog's legs taste good.'

What is the difference between English *taste* and French *goûter* in terms of the range of semantic roles that they permit as subject?

Especially For Educators and Future Teachers

6-12   Your high school ESL class asks you whether *bank* in the expression *river bank* and *bank* in *savings bank* are the same word or different words. You note that they're both nouns and are spelled alike and pronounced alike. By trying to identify synonyms and antonyms (as in Figure 6–4 on p. 196), you construct an argument designed to persuade your students that they are different words and not the same word with different senses. To show the contrast, identify another pair of word forms that represent different senses of the same word, again constructing the argument by identifying synonyms and antonyms.

6-13   In your first year of teaching, you tell your middle school English class that the subject of a sentence is the "doer" of the action, and give as an example, *Devon scored the most points.* When you ask for other examples, a student volunteers *Disneyland is fun,* and you immediately see a problem: *Disneyland* is the subject of the sentence but not the doer of any action. What do you say to correct your explanation about the roles that subjects play in sentences?

6-14   Draw up characterizations of one or at most two sentences each to help your students remember the difference between a grammatical relation (e.g., subject or object) and a semantic role (e.g., agent or means).

6-15   Cite three pairs of expressions, in each of which the referent for the two expressions is the same but the sense is different. Ex.: *Kofi Annan* and *the secretary-general of the U.N.*

6-16   Writing handbooks sometimes urge writers to be cautious about where in a sentence to position the word *only.* They may recommend placing *only* immediately in front of the constituent within its scope (handbooks are more likely to say in front of the words that *only* modifies). In the sentences below, bracket the constituent within the scope of *only,* and insert a caret where *only* could be placed to have it directly preceding the structure in its scope. (*Note:* These sentences are adapted from the British National Corpus.)

Ex.: That *only* leaves ∧ [one logical explanation]. (=That leaves *only* one logical explanation.)

a. It was *only* a matter of time.

b. She *only* needed to rest.

c. I *only* saw one tiny bit of it.

d. The opportunities have *only* been adopted half-heartedly.

e. Ads in newspapers usually *only* offer one product or a small range of products.

f. Cassie *only* knew of one stone like that.

OTHER RESOURCES

- **British National Corpus: http://thetis.bl.uk/lookup.html**
  Here you can obtain up to 50 example sentences, chosen at random from the 100 million word resources of the British National Corpus. You may want to go to the general information page for the BNC at http://info.ox.ac.uk:80/bnc/ and from there pursue the link to the sample search.

- **Roget's Internet Thesaurus: http://www.thesaurus.com/**
  At this Web site you will find access to an on-line thesaurus. With it you can explore the relationships among words, especially those in hyponymic relationships.

SUGGESTIONS FOR FURTHER READING

- **Stephen R. Anderson & Edward L. Keenan. 1985. "Deixis," in Timothy Shopen, ed.,** *Language Typology and Syntactic Description,* vol. 3 (Cambridge: Cambridge University Press), pp. 259–308. A relatively brief and comprehensive treatment of deixis.

- **Sandra Chung & Alan Timberlake. 1985. "Tense, Aspect, and Mood," in Timothy Shopen, ed.,** *Language Typology and Syntactic Description,* vol. 3 (Cambridge: Cambridge University Press), pp. 202–258. Provides a concise discussion of tense and related notions.

- **George A. Miller. 1996.** *The Science of Words* (Indianapolis: W. H. Freeman). An accessible and award-winning treatment of the psychology of lexical meaning.

- **Sebastian Lobner. 2002.** *Understanding Semantics* (New York: Oxford University Press). Appearing in the "Understanding Language Series," this is a thorough and wide-ranging introduction to semantics in general. It goes beyond the current chapter by treating sentence meaning more fully and by treating cognition, translation, and formal semantics.

ADVANCED READING

The major reference work for semantics is Lyons (1977), which provides a wealth of information and critical discussion. Easier and more accessible are Lyons (1996), Saeed (1997), and Leech (1981). Palmer (1981) provides a concise overview of the field. Lexical semantics is discussed in Lehrer (1974), which focuses on semantic universals (discussed in Chapter 7 of this textbook), and in Wierzbicka (1985), in which the main concern is the meaning of the notion 'kind of.' Cruse (1986) is a good overview of lexical semantics. Hurford and Heasley (1983) is a good coursebook. Several of the papers in Holland and Quinn (1987) investigate connotation and the cultural elements in the organization of semantic fields. A basic work on metaphors is Lakoff and Johnson (1980); ideas presented in that earlier work are developed further in Lakoff (1987). Deixis is discussed in detail in Chapter 2 of Levinson (1983). A thorough discussion of mood and modality can be found in Palmer (1986). Approaches to lexicography based on analyses of corpora can be found in Sinclair (1991).

REFERENCES

- Cruse, D. A. 1986. *Lexical Semantics* (Cambridge: Cambridge University Press).

- Holland, Dorothy, & Naomi Quinn, eds. 1987. *Cultural Models in Language and Thought* (Cambridge: Cambridge University Press).

- Hurford, James R., & Brendan Heasley. 1983. *Semantics: A Coursebook* (Cambridge: Cambridge University Press).

- Lakoff, George. 1987. *Women, Fire, and Dangerous Things: What Categories Reveal about the Mind* (Chicago: University of Chicago Press).

- Lakoff, George, & Mark Johnson. 1980. *Metaphors We Live By* (Chicago: University of Chicago Press).

- Leech, Geoffrey. 1981. *Semantics: The Study of Meaning*, 2nd ed. (London: Penguin).

- Lehrer, Adrienne. 1974. *Semantic Fields and Lexical Structure* (Amsterdam: North-Holland).

- Levinson, Stephen C. 1983. *Pragmatics* (Cambridge: Cambridge University Press).

- Lyons, John. 1977. *Semantics*, 2 vols. (Cambridge: Cambridge University Press).

- Lyons, John. 1996. *Linguistic Semantics: An Introduction* (Cambridge: Cambridge University Press).

- Palmer, F. R. 1981. *Semantics*, 2nd ed. (Cambridge: Cambridge University Press).

- Palmer, F. R. 1986. *Mood and Modality* (Cambridge: Cambridge University Press).

- Saeed, John I. 1997. *Semantics* (London: Blackwell).

- Sinclair, John. 1991. *Corpus, Concordance, Collocation* (Oxford: Oxford University Press).

- Wierzbicka, Anna. 1985. *Lexicography and Conceptual Analysis* (Ann Arbor, MI: Karoma).

Chapter 7

Language Universals and Language Typology

❖ Your third-grade niece returns from school one day and announces that her teacher said English has 13 vowels. She asks you whether all languages have 13 vowels. At first you want to say that English has just 5 vowels, but then you remember that's not accurate. What do you tell her?

❖ Several cousins are visiting you in Chicago for your twenty-first birthday celebration, and you notice that your cousin Laura from Texas says "y'all" when she's talking to more than one person, while your cousin Rudy from New York City sometimes says "youse" in the same circumstances. You can't help wondering whether their dialects are faulty (they don't sound "standard") or better than yours (they make a useful distinction that's not made in your Chicago English). You think about other languages you've studied and wonder whether it's typical for languages to have equivalents of *y'all* and *youse* or to have one form for both singular and plural *you*, as standard English has. What do you conclude?

❖ A classmate who is enrolled in an introductory Japanese course comments that Japanese word order is odd. He says Japanese puts verbs at the end of the sentence instead of after the subject—"where they belong." He claims that the logical order is Subject-Verb-Object, as in English. You remember that a Japanese exchange student you tutored felt exactly the opposite. She thought the Japanese order of Subject-Object-Verb was logical and the English word order was not. You're convinced that logic isn't the issue—that both orders are equally logical (or equally illogical). What's the best argument you can make to your classmate to convince him that word order is not a matter of logic and that Japanese and English are equally logical (or illogical) in this regard?

SIMILARITY AND DIVERSITY ACROSS LANGUAGES

The various languages of the world are structured according to many different patterns of phonology, morphology, syntax, and semantics. Some languages have very large inventories of phonemes; others have very few. In some languages, including French, Italian, and English, the basic structure of the clause is SVO, that is, the subject comes before the verb, and the verb comes before the direct object, as in these examples:

	Subject (S)	Verb (V)	Object (O)
French:	Haussmann	fait aménager	la place.
English:	Haussmann	redesigned	the square.
Italian:	Keplero	modificò	la teoria di Copernico.
English:	Kepler	modified	Copernicus's theory.

In languages such as Japanese and Persian, both the subject and the direct object occur before the verb, in an SOV pattern:

	Subject (S)	Object (O)	Verb (V)	
Japanese:	Sono hebi ga	inu o	korosita.	
	That snake	the dog	killed.	'That snake killed the dog.'
Persian:	Ali	ketabhara	mibæræd.	
	Ali	the books	is carrying.	'Ali is carrying the books.'

Given such variation, you might wonder whether the world's languages share any characteristics. As it happens, there are basic principles that govern the structure of *all* languages. These **language universals** determine what is possible and what is impossible in language structure. For example, while some languages have voiced and voiceless stops (*b* and *p; d* and *t*) and others have only voiceless stops (*p* and *t),* no language has yet been encountered that has voiced stops but no voiceless stops. This observation can be translated into a rule expressing what is possible in the structure of a language (that is, a language can have both voiced and voiceless stops or only voiceless stops in its phonemic inventory) and into a law that excludes a combination of phonemes that is not known to occur in any of the world's languages (that is, voiced stops without voiceless stops).

Why Uncover Universals?

Language universals are statements of what is possible and impossible in languages. Viewed from a purely practical perspective, such principles are useful in that, if we can assume them to apply to all languages, they need not be repeated in the description of each language. Thus the study of language universals underscores the unity underlying the enormous variety of languages found in the world.

Language universals are also important to our understanding of the brain and of the principles that govern interpersonal communication in all cultures. In the course of evolution, the human species alone has developed the ability to speak, thus distinguishing itself from all other animals, including other higher mammals. Humans have developed, not a single language that is spoken and understood by everybody, but more than 5000 different languages, each of which is complex and sophisticated. If basic principles govern *all* languages, they are likely to be the result of whatever cognitive and social skills enabled human beings to develop the ability to speak in the first place. By studying language universals, we begin to understand what in the human brain and the social organization of everyday life enables people to communicate through language. The study of language universals offers a glimpse of the cognitive and social foundations of human language, about which so little is known.

When postulating language universals, researchers must exercise caution because only relatively few of the world's languages have been adequately described. Further, much more is known about European languages and the major non-Western languages (such as Chinese, Japanese, Hindi, and Arabic) than about the far more numerous other languages of Africa, Asia, the Americas, and Oceania. In Papua New Guinea alone (an area about the size of the states of Washington and Oregon combined), over 700 languages are spoken, although grammatical descriptions of only a few dozen are available; very little—or in some cases nothing at all—is known about the others. Linguists proposing language universals must ensure that the proposed principles are applicable to more than the familiar European languages. Language universals must be generally valid for the languages of the world, whether those languages are spoken by only a few dozen people in a highlands village of Papua New Guinea or by millions of people in Europe, Africa, or Asia. Since little or nothing is known about the structure of hundreds of languages, universal principles can be proposed only as tentative hypotheses based on the languages for which descriptions are available. Fortunately, many linguists are now studying lesser-known languages. More often than not, first-time grammars confirm rather than disprove the language universals that have been proposed.

Caution must also be exercised in drawing inferences from language universals. These universal principles help explain why language is species specific, but there is a big step between uncovering a universal and explaining it in terms of human cognitive or social abilities. More often than not, explanations for language universals as symptoms of cognitive or social factors rely on logical arguments rather than on solid scientific proof. Of course, the fact that explanations can be only tentative does not mean they should not be proposed, but it does mean that linguists must be cautious and keep in mind that languages fulfill many roles at once.

Language Types

A prerequisite to the study of universals is a thorough understanding of the variety found among the world's languages. **Language typology** focuses on classifying languages according to their structural characteristics. (*Typology* means the study of types or the classification of objects into types.) Examples of typological classifications are "languages that have both voiced and voiceless stops in their phonemic inventories" (like English, French, and Japanese) and "languages that have only voiceless stops" (like Mandarin Chinese, Korean, and Tahitian). Since no language has voiced stops without voiceless stops, that type does not exist. Of course, the languages in each category will differ, based on the criteria of classification. For instance, if we establish a typology of languages according to whether they have nasal vowels in their phonemic inventory, English, Japanese, Mandarin Chinese, Korean, and Tahitian will fall into the category of languages that lack nasal vowels. In contrast, Standard French has four nasal vowels (some French dialects have only three): /ɛ̃/ as in *faim* /fɛ̃/ 'hunger'; /œ̃/ as in *brun* /bʁœ̃/ 'brown'; /ɑ̃/ as in *manger* /mɑ̃ʒe/ 'to eat'; and /ɔ̃/ as in *maison* /mɛzɔ̃/) 'house.' It thus falls into the category of languages that have nasal vowels, along with Hindi, Tibetan, and Yoruba (a language widely spoken in Nigeria). Of course, linguists can establish categories only according to specific criteria; the world's languages are so diverse in so many different ways that no overall typological classification of languages exists, even within a single level of linguistic structure such as phonology.

Typological categories have no necessary correspondence with groups of languages that have descended from the same parent language; in fact, typological categories cut across language families. In the example just given, English, Japanese, and Tahitian are not related languages; yet they fall into the same language type with respect to the presence or absence of nasal vowels. On the other hand, French and English *are* related, but fall into different types. Language types are independent of language families in principle, but members of the same family often do share certain typological characteristics as a result of their common heritage. Consequently, linguists include as many unrelated languages as possible in their proposed language types to ensure that the similarities between languages of any category are not the result of familial relationships.

This chapter explores both the variety found among the world's languages and the unity that underlies this variety. Uncovering language universals and classifying languages into different types are related and complementary tasks. In order to uncover universal principles, we first need to know the extent to which languages differ from one another in terms of their structure. We would not want to posit a language universal on the basis of a limited sample of languages, only to discover that the proposed universal did not work for a type of language that we had failed to consider. A universal must work for all language types and all languages.

Similarly, the way in which we go about classifying languages and describing the different types of structures is determined in large part by the search for universals. It would be possible, for example, to set up a typological category grouping all languages that have the sound /o/ in their phonemic inventory. But such a typology tells us nothing about any universal principle underlying the structure of these languages; indeed, their structures might have little in common other than the fact that /o/ is an element of their phonemic inventory. In contrast, a typology of languages based on the presence or absence of nasal vowels reveals interesting patterns. It turns out that no language in the world has only nasal vowels. All languages must have oral vowels, whether or not they also have nasal vowels. This suggests that oral vowels are in some sense more "basic" or more indispensable than nasal vowels, which could be of great interest to our understanding of language structure. Therefore, this typology is useful, in that it has helped uncover a language universal. Whether a particular typological classification is interesting or useful depends on whether it helps uncover universal principles in the structure of languages.

The next few sections present examples of language universals and language types from semantics, phonology, syntax, and morphology. For each example, observe the interaction of typologies with universals, and note how different kinds of language universals are stated. Some examples will be taken up again toward the end of the chapter, where we examine cognitive and social explanations that have been proposed to account for language universals and language types.

SEMANTIC UNIVERSALS

Semantic universals govern the composition of the vocabulary of all languages. That semantic universals should exist at all may seem surprising at first. Anyone who has studied a foreign language knows how greatly the vocabularies of two languages can differ. Some ideas that are conveniently expressed with a single word in one language may require an entire sentence in another language. The English word *privacy,* for example, does not have a simple equivalent in French. (That doesn't mean that the French lack the notion of privacy!) Similarly, English lacks an equivalent for the Hawaiian word *aloha,* which can be roughly translated as 'love,' 'compassion,' 'pity,' 'hospitality,' or 'friendliness' and is also used as a general greeting and farewell. Despite these cross-linguistic differences, however, there are some fundamental areas of the vocabulary of every language that are subject to universal rules. These areas include color terms, body part terms, animal names, and verbs of sensory perception.

Semantic universals typically deal with the less marked members of semantic fields (see Chapter 6), which are called *basic terms* in this context. As an example, consider the following terms, which all refer to shades of blue: *turquoise, royal blue,* and *blue. Blue* is a more basic term than the others: *turquoise* derives from the name of a precious stone of the same color, while *royal blue* refers to a shade of blue. The word *blue* is thus more basic than each of the other words, although for different reasons: unlike *turquoise, blue* refers primarily to a color, not an object; unlike *royal blue, blue* is a simple, unmodified term. The combination of these characteristics makes *blue* a less marked—more basic—color term than the others. *Basic terms* have three characteristics:

1. Basic terms are morphologically simple.
2. Basic terms are less specialized in meaning than other terms.
3. Basic terms are not recently borrowed from another language.

Semantic universals deal with terms like *blue* and not with terms like *turquoise* and *royal blue.*

Pronouns

Although pronoun systems can differ greatly from language to language, the pronoun system of every language follows the same set of universal principles.

First, all known languages, without exception, have pronouns for at least the speaker and the addressee: the first person (*I, me*) and the second person (*you*). But there is great variability among the world's languages in the number of distinctions that are made by pronouns. The following chart presents the English pronominal system (we limit ourselves to subject pronouns).

English Pronouns		
	SINGULAR	PLURAL
FIRST PERSON	I	we
SECOND PERSON	you	you
THIRD PERSON	he, she, it	they

In this chart, columns represent number: the first column "singular," the second column "plural." The rows list person: the first row shows first-person pronouns, the second row shows second-person pronouns, and the third row shows third-person pronouns. Standard American English uses the same form for both the singular and plural second-person pronoun (*you*).

The pronoun systems of other languages display other patterns. Spoken Castilian Spanish has separate forms for the singular and plural in each person; in the example below, the two plural forms are the masculine and feminine pronouns. (Spanish also has "polite" pronoun forms, but we have ignored them here.)

Castilian Spanish Pronouns			
	SINGULAR	PLURAL	
		M	F
FIRST PERSON	yo	nosotros	nosotras
SECOND PERSON	tú	vosotros	vosotras
THIRD PERSON	él, ella	ellos	ellas

Some languages make finer distinctions in number. Speakers of ancient Sanskrit made a distinction between two people and more than two people. The form for two people is called the *dual,* and the form for more than two is called the *plural.* (In the chart below, the three words for the third person are the masculine, feminine, and neuter forms.)

Sanskrit Pronouns			
	SINGULAR	DUAL	PLURAL
FIRST PERSON	aham	āvām	vayam
SECOND PERSON	tvam	ūvām	yāyam
THIRD PERSON	sas, tat, sā	tau, te, te	te, tāni, tās

Other languages have a single pronoun to refer simultaneously to the speaker and the addressee (and sometimes other people) and a separate pronoun to refer to the speaker along with other people but excluding the addressee. The first of these is called a first-person *inclusive* pronoun, and the second is called a first-person *exclusive* pronoun. In English, both notions are encoded in the pronoun *we*. In contrast, Tok Pisin has separate inclusive and exclusive pronouns.

Tok Pisin Pronouns		
	SINGULAR	PLURAL
FIRST PERSON EXCLUSIVE	mi	mipela
FIRST PERSON INCLUSIVE		yumi
SECOND PERSON	yu	yupela
THIRD PERSON	em	ol

Tok Pisin is an English-based creole (see Chapter 13), with most of its vocabulary coming from English. The English pronouns and other words that were taken by Tok Pisin speakers to form their pronoun system are easily recognizable: *mi* is from *me, yu* from *you, em* probably from *him, yumi* from *you-me, ol* from *all,* and the plural suffix *-pela* probably from *fellow.*

Fijian has one of the largest pronoun systems of any language. It has a singular form for each pronoun, a dual form for two people, a separate "trial" form that refers to about three people, and a plural form that refers to more than three people (in actual usage, trial pronouns refer to a few people and the plural refers to a multitude). In addition, in the first-person dual, trial, and plural, Fijian, like Tok Pisin, has separate inclusive and exclusive forms.

Fijian Pronouns				
	SINGULAR	DUAL	TRIAL	PLURAL
FIRST PERSON EXCLUSIVE	au	keirau	keitou	keimami
FIRST PERSON INCLUSIVE		kedaru	kedatou	keda
SECOND PERSON	iko	kemudrau	kemudou	kemunii
THIRD PERSON	koya	rau	iratou	ira

Between the extremes represented by English and Fijian are many variations. Some languages have separate dual pronouns, while others do not; some systems make a distinction between inclusive and exclusive pronouns, while others do not.

All the world's languages, however, have distinct first- and second-person pronouns, and most languages have third-person pronouns, inclusive first-person pronouns, and exclusive first-person pronouns. A four-person system (inclusive first- and exclusive first-person, second-person, and third-person pronouns) is by far the most common. The four-person type of pronoun system is thus somehow more basic than a two-person or three-person type. In this respect, English is atypical.

Variations in pronoun systems are governed by a set of universal rules. To discover these universals, we need to establish a typology of pronoun systems.

Some Types of Pronoun Systems in the World's Languages
Systems with singular and plural forms—e.g., English, Spanish
Systems with singular, dual, and plural forms—e.g., Sanskrit
Systems with singular, dual, trial, and plural forms—e.g., Fijian
Systems lacking inclusive/exclusive distinction in first-person plural—e.g., English, Spanish
Systems with inclusive/exclusive distinction in first-person plural—e.g., Tok Pisin, Fijian

Some Types of Pronoun Systems That Do *Not* Occur
Systems lacking first-person and second-person pronouns
Systems with singular and dual forms but no plural forms
Systems with singular, dual, and trial forms but no plural forms
Systems that make an inclusive/exclusive distinction, but not in the first person (a logical impossibility)

Based on what we do and don't find in our typology, we postulate some universal rules.

Some Universal Rules

1. All languages have at least first-person and second-person pronouns.
2. If a language has singular and dual forms, then it will also have plural forms.
3. If a language has singular, dual, and trial forms, then it will also have plural forms.
4. If a language makes an inclusive/exclusive distinction in its pronoun system, it will make it in the first person.

Note that the converse of these rules is not true. The converse of universal rule 2, for instance, would state that if a language had separate plural forms, it would have separate dual forms. But even English proves this generalization wrong: it has separate plural forms but no dual. The implications thus go in only one direction.

It is important to note that semantic typologies and universals do not represent a measure of complexity in language or culture. The most we can infer from these differences is that some categories are more salient in some cultures than in others. Comparing the two examples of semantic universals discussed in this section, we also see that the pronoun system of English is one of the most restricted in the world, despite the fact that English has very rich scientific and color lexicons, to mention only two arenas. Thus, different arenas of the lexicon exhibit different degrees of elaboration in different languages. This does not mean that some languages are "richer" or "better" or "more developed" than others.

PHONOLOGICAL UNIVERSALS

Vowel Systems

Another level of linguistic structure in which we can identify universal rules and classify languages into useful typological categories is phonology. In Chapter 3 we discussed the fact that languages can have very different inventories of sounds. Figure 7–1 on page 231 represents the vowel system of standard American English, classified according to place of articulation. Compare this with Figure 7–2 on page 231, which represents the vowel system of standard Parisian French (a conservative dialect retaining certain oppositions that have been lost in many other French dialects). The symbol /ü/ represents a high front rounded vowel as in the word /ʁü/ *rue* 'street'; /ø/ is an upper mid rounded vowel as in /fø/ *feu* 'fire'; /œ/ is a lower mid rounded vowel as in /bœʁ/ *beurre* 'butter'; and /ɛ̃/, /œ̃/, /ɔ̃/, and /ɑ̃/ are nasal vowels. Finally, Figure 7–3 compares the vowel systems of Quechua (spoken in Peru and Ecuador) and Hawaiian.

Figure 7-1

Vowels of American English

i						u
	ɪ					ʊ
		e		ə		o
			ɛ		ʌ	ɔ
			æ		a	ɑ

Figure 7-2

Oral and Nasal Vowels of Parisian French

	Oral				Nasal	
i		ü		u		
	e		ø		o	
		ɛ		œ	ɔ	ɛ̃ œ̃ ɔ̃
				a		ɑ̃

Figure 7-3

Vowels of Quechua and Hawaiian

i		u		i	u
				e	o
	a				a
	Quechua			Hawaiian	

The first thing these four examples demonstrate is that different languages may have very different sets of vowels: English has several vowels in its inventory that French does not have, and vice versa. Second, the number of vowels in a language can vary considerably. Quechua has only 3 distinct vowels; along with the vowel systems of Greenlandic Eskimo and Moroccan Arabic, the Quechua vowel system is one of the smallest in the world. Hawaiian has 5 vowels, a very common number among the world's languages. At the other end of the spectrum, English has 13 vowels and French has 15, including the four nasal vowels.

Underlying such diversity, however, we find universal patterns. If we charted the vowel inventories of all known languages, we would confirm that languages usually have vowel systems that fall between the two extremes represented by Quechua and French. Thus every language has at least 3 vowel phonemes. Some have 4 vowels, like Malagasy, the language of Madagascar (whose vowels are / i ɛ ə ʊ /), and the Native American language Kwakiutl (which has /i a ə ʊ/). Some have 5 vowels, such as Hawaiian, Mandarin Chinese, and, as shown in Tables 3–3 (page 98) and 3–5 (page 99), Spanish and Japanese. Others, such as Persian and Malay, have 6 vowels; and so on up to 15.

Comparing the charts, we find that all languages include in their vowel inventory a high front unrounded vowel (/i/ or /ɪ/), a low vowel (/a/), and a high back rounded (/u/ or /ʊ/) or unrounded (/ɯ/) vowel. These vowels have allophones in some languages, particularly in languages with few vowels. In Greenlandic Eskimo, for example, /i/ has the allophones [i], [e], [ɛ], and [ə], depending on the consonants that surround it; but there are no minimal pairs that depend on these variants. Small variations also exist, but these variations do not really contradict the universal rule, which can be stated as follows: **All languages have a high front unrounded vowel, a low vowel, and a high back rounded or unrounded vowel in their phoneme inventory.** Note that this first universal rule describes what constitutes the minimal type and what is included in all other types.

The second universal rule is stated: **Of the languages that have four or more vowels, all have vowels similar to /i a u/** (as indicated by the first universal rule) **plus either a high central vowel /ɨ/** (as in Russian *vɨ* 'you') **or a mid front unrounded vowel /e/ or /ɛ/.** The third universal rule we can uncover from our vowel charts is this: **Languages with a five-vowel system include a mid front unrounded vowel.** In the five-vowel system of Hawaiian, for example, /e/ has allophones [ɛ] and [e]. Other languages with five-vowel inventories include Japanese (whose inventory is /i ɛ a ɔ ɯ/) and Zulu (/i ɛ a ɔ u/). Most languages with five vowels have a mid back rounded vowel (either /ɔ/ or /o/) in their inventory, like Japanese, Hawaiian, and Zulu. A few languages with a five-vowel system lack a mid back rounded vowel, although a similar sound is often included, as with Mandarin Chinese, whose inventory (/i ü a ë u/) includes the lower-mid back unrounded vowel /ë/.

We can thus state that languages with five-vowel inventories *generally* (but not always) have a mid back rounded vowel. This observation is applicable to languages with more than five vowels as well. The fourth universal rule thus reads: **Languages with five or more vowels in their inventories generally have a mid back rounded vowel phoneme.** This rule is stated in a different way from the first three rules in that it is not absolute. But it is a useful observation because it describes a significant tendency across languages.

Languages with six-vowel inventories like Malayalam (spoken in southwestern India) include /ɔ/ in their inventory and either /ɨ/ or /e/. Malayalam has in its inventory the three "obligatory" vowels /i a u/; the vowels /e/ and /ɔ/, as predicted by the second and third universal rules; and /ɨ/. These universal rules can be summarized as in Figure 7–4.

Figure 7-4

Summary of Universal Vowel Rules

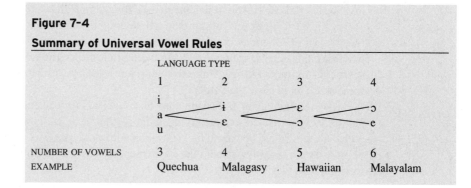

	LANGUAGE TYPE			
	1	2	3	4
NUMBER OF VOWELS	3	4	5	6
EXAMPLE	Quechua	Malagasy	Hawaiian	Malayalam

Nasal and Oral Vowels

Other universal rules that regulate the vowel inventories of the world's languages can be uncovered, but we will mention only two more. The first states: **When a language has nasal vowels, the number of nasal vowels never exceeds the number of oral vowels.** We can find examples of languages with fewer nasal vowels than oral vowels: Standard French, for example, has four nasal vowels and eleven oral vowels. We can also find examples of languages with an equal number of oral and nasal vowels: Punjabi (a language of northern India) has ten of each. But there are no languages with a greater number of nasal vowels than oral vowels.

The second universal rule of interest is not a rule in the usual sense but a description of the most common vowel system: a five-vowel system consisting of a high front unrounded vowel (/i/ or /ɪ/), a mid front unrounded vowel (/e/ or /ɛ/), a low vowel (/a/), a mid back rounded vowel (/o/ or /ɔ/), and a high back rounded vowel (/u/ or /ʊ/). Hawaiian is an example of such a system, as you can see by looking at the symmetry in the chart for Hawaiian vowels (page 231). Each vowel is maximally distant from the others, which minimizes the possibility of two vowels being confused. Such a five-vowel system thus has an ideal quality, a matter to which we return later in this chapter.

Consonants

Vowel systems are not the only area of phonology in which universal rules operate. The consonant inventories of the languages of the world also exhibit many universal properties. A few examples are presented here, although not in great detail since they do not differ in nature from universals of vowel systems.

Recall (from Chapter 3) that the sounds /p t k/ are voiceless stops. Every language has at least one of these voiceless stops as a phoneme. While some languages lack affricates or trills, voiceless stops are found in all languages. In fact, most languages have all three of these sounds, even languages with small consonant inventories. Niuean (a Polynesian language), for example, has only three stops, three nasals, three fricatives, and an approximant, totaling ten consonants (in contrast to the twenty-four of American English). Yet the three stops are /p t k/. Put in the form of a universal, this generalization reads: **Most languages have the three stops /p t k/ in their consonant inventory.** This universal suggests that these three consonants are in some sense more basic than others.

It is clear, given our discussion, that this universal is not an absolute rule. Hawaiian (a language related to Niuean) has only /p/ and /k/. (That is why English words with the sound /t/ are borrowed into Hawaiian with a /k/, like *kikiki* 'ticket'). This universal is thus a *tendency,* rather than a statement of what is and isn't found among the world's languages.

Another important universal referring to stops has already been mentioned. Recall that the difference between the two sets of stops /p t k/ and /b d g/ is that the first set is voiceless, the second voiced. All six sounds have phonemic status in English, as is true in French, Spanish, Quechua, and many other languages. In some languages, however, we find only voiceless stops, such as in Hawaiian (and all other Polynesian languages), Korean, and Mandarin Chinese. Thus far, we have identified two types of languages: languages with both voiced and voiceless stops, and languages with only voiceless stops. As noted, every language has at least one voiceless stop in its inventory; consequently, there are no languages that have voiced stops but no voiceless stops, and no languages that have neither voiced nor voiceless stops. This typology allows us to derive the following universal rule: **No language has voiced stops without voiceless stops.**

Note that of the universals of stop inventories explored thus far, only one rule (and it is only a tendency) says anything about *which* stops are included in the inventories of languages. But there are other universals that deal with this question. We give only one example here: **If a language lacks a stop, there is a strong tendency for that language to include in its inventory a fricative sound with the same place of articulation as the missing stop.** For instance, Standard Fijian, Amharic (the principal language of Ethiopia), and Standard Arabic all lack the phoneme /p/, which is a labial stop. As predicted by the universal rule, all these languages have a fricative /f/ or /v/, whose place of articulation is similar to that of /p/. The fricative thus "fills in" for the missing stop. This rule, too, is only a tendency, as there are languages that violate it. Hawaiian, which lacks a /t/, has none of the corresponding fricatives /ð/, /θ/, /z/, or /s/. But most languages do follow the rule.

SYNTACTIC AND MORPHOLOGICAL UNIVERSALS

Word Order

Speakers of English and other European languages commonly assume that the normal way of constructing a sentence is to place the subject of the sentence first, then the verb, and then the direct object (if there is one). Indeed, in English, the sentence *Mary saw John,* which follows this order, is well formed, while variations like *John Mary saw* and *saw Mary John* are not well formed.

However, normal word order in a sentence differs considerably from language to language. Consider the following Japanese sentence, in which the subject is a girl called *Akiko,* the verb is *butta* 'hit (past tense),' and the direct object is a boy named *Taro.*

```
akiko    ga         taroo  o        butta
Akiko    Subject    Taro   Object   hit
'Akiko hit Taro.'
```

In Japanese, the normal word order is thus subject first, direct object second, and verb last. If we changed this order (in an effort to make Japanese syntax conform to English syntax, for example), the result would be ungrammatical.

Now consider Tongan, in which the verb must come first, the subject second, and the direct object last. In the following sentence, the verb is *taaʔi* 'to hit,' the subject is a person named *Hina,* and the direct object is a person called *Vaka.*

```
naʔe taaʔi ʔe        hina   ʔa       vaka
Past hit   Subject    Hina   Object   Vaka
'Hina hit Vaka.'
```

Of course, not all English sentences follow the order subject-verb-direct object, or SVO. To emphasize particular noun phrases, English speakers sometimes place direct objects in clause-initial position as with *whom* in *It was John whom Mary saw;* such constructions are called cleft sentences. In questions like *Who(m) did you see?,* the direct object *who(m)* is in first position. Similar word order variants are found in most languages of the world. Cleft sentences and questions derive from more basic sentences, however, and are also less common than sentences that follow SVO order. Thus, even though some English constructions do not follow this order, we say that SVO order is "basic" in English, and that English is an SVO language. Examples of SVO languages include Romance languages (such as French, Spanish, and Italian), Thai, Vietnamese, and Indonesian. Japanese is an SOV language, as are Turkish, Persian, Burmese, Hindi, and the Native American languages Navajo, Hopi, and Luiseño. Tongan is a VSO language, as are most other Polynesian languages, some dialects of Arabic, Welsh, and a number of Native American languages such as Salish, Squamish, Chinook, Jacaltec, and Zapotec.

There are three other logical possibilities for combining verbs, subjects, and direct objects besides VSO, SVO, and SOV. Remarkably, however, very few languages have VOS, OVS, or OSV as basic word orders. Only a handful of languages are VOS, the best known being Malagasy and Fijian. Following is a basic sentence in Fijian showing that the direct object precedes the subject.

```
ea      taya   na ŋone   na yalewa
Past    hit    the child   the girl
'The girl hit the child'
```

OVS and OSV are the basic word order of only a handful of languages of the Amazon Basin, including Hixkaryana (OVS) and Nadëb (OSV). By far the most common word orders found among the world's languages are SVO, SOV, and, to a lesser extent, VSO.

Try it yourself: What characterizes the ordering of S and O in SVO, SOV, and VSO languages (the most common ones) and differentiates them from VOS, OVS, and OSV languages (the uncommon ones)?

In each of the three common configurations, S *precedes* O; in the uncommon configurations, S *follows* O. We can thus make a generalized statement: **In the basic word orders of the languages of the world there is an overwhelming tendency for the subject of a sentence to precede the direct object.**

There is a great deal more to universals of syntax. Two extreme cases are languages in which the verb comes first in the clause (called verb-initial languages and illustrated by Tongan) and languages in which the verb comes last (called verb-final languages and illustrated by Japanese). For the sake of simplicity, we exclude VOS and OSV languages from our discussion, though they follow basically the same rules as VSO and SOV languages respectively.

Possessor and Possessed Noun Phrases

If we look at the order of other syntactic constituents in verb-initial and verb-final languages, we find strikingly regular and interesting patterns. First of all, in most verb-final languages such as Japanese, possessor noun phrases precede possessed noun phrases.

taroo no imooto
Taro of sister
'Taro's sister'

In verb-initial languages the opposite order is most commonly found; in the following example from Tongan, the possessed entity is expressed first, the possessor last.

ko e tuonga?ane ?o vaka
the sister of Vaka
'Vaka's sister'

We have thus established the following rule: **There is a strong tendency for possessor noun phrases to precede possessed noun phrases in verb-final languages and to follow possessed noun phrases in verb-initial languages.**

Prepositions and Postpositions

To express position or direction, many languages use prepositions. As the word indicates, *prepositions* come *before* modified noun phrases (NP). In Tongan, for example, the prepositions *ki,* which indicates direction, and *?i,* which denotes location, both precede the NP they modify.

ki tonga ?i tonga
to Tonga in Tonga

Other languages have postpositions instead of prepositions. *Postpositions* fulfill the same functions as prepositions, but they follow the NP, as in this Japanese example.

tookyoo   ni
Tokyo   to
'to Tokyo'

Overwhelmingly, verb-initial languages have prepositions and verb-final languages have postpositions. The third rule can be stated as follows: **There is a strong tendency for verb-initial languages to have prepositions and for verb-final languages to have postpositions.**

Relative Clauses

Depending on the language, relative clauses either precede or follow head nouns. In English relative clause constructions (*the book that Judith wrote*), the relative clause (*that Judith wrote*) follows its head (*the book*). The same is true in Tongan.

ko e tohi   [naʔe faʔu ʔe   hina]
the book Past   write Subject Hina
'the book that Hina wrote'

In Japanese, however, the relative clause precedes its head.

[hiroo ga   kaita] hon
Hiro   Subject wrote book
'the book that Hiro wrote'

The great majority of verb-initial languages place relative clauses after the head noun, and the great majority of verb-final languages place relative clauses before the head noun. We can therefore note the following universal: **There is a strong tendency for verb-initial languages to place relative clauses after the head noun and for verb-final languages to place relative clauses before the head noun.**

Overall Patterns of Ordering

We have established that verb-initial languages (VSO) place possessors after possessed nouns, place relative clauses after head nouns, and have prepositions. Verb-final languages (SOV), on the other hand, place possessors before possessed nouns, place relative clauses before head nouns, and have postpositions.

In all these correlations a pattern emerges. Notice that possessors and relative clauses modify nouns; the noun is a more essential element to a noun phrase than any of the modifiers. In a similar sense, noun phrases modify prepositions or postpositions; likewise, though it is not intuitively obvious, the most important element of a prepositional phrase is the preposition itself, not the noun phrase—it is the preposition that makes it a prepositional phrase. Finally, in a verb phrase, the direct object modifies the verb. In light of these observations, we can draw a generalization about the order of constituents in different language types: **In verb-initial languages the modifying element follows the modified element, while in verb-final languages the modifying element precedes the modified element.** This pattern is illustrated in Table 7–1.

Table 7-1
Summary of Constituent Orders

VERB-INITIAL LANGUAGES (EXAMPLE: TONGAN)	VERB-FINAL LANGUAGES (EXAMPLE: JAPANESE)
Modified—Modifier	*Modifier—Modified*
verb—direct object	direct object—verb
possessed—possessor	possessor—possessed
preposition—noun phrase	noun phrase—postposition
head noun—relative clause	relative clause—head noun

This generalization is of course based on tendencies rather than absolute rules. At each level of the table some languages violate the correlations. Persian, for example, is an SOV language like Japanese and thus should have the properties listed in the right-hand column of the table. But in Persian possessors follow possessed nouns, prepositions are used, and relative clauses follow head nouns—all of which are properties of verb-initial languages. Such counterexamples to the correlations are rare, however.

Notice that our discussion has mentioned nothing about verb-medial (SVO) languages like English. These languages appear to follow no consistent pattern. English, for example, places relative clauses after head nouns and has prepositions (both properties of verb-initial languages). With respect to the order of possessors and possessed nouns, English has both patterns (*the man's arm* and *the arm of the man*). In contrast, Mandarin Chinese, another verb-medial language, has characteristics of verb-final languages.

Word order universals are an excellent illustration of the level that linguists attempt to reach in their description of the universal properties of language. Table 7–1 implies that in the structure of virtually all verb-initial and verb-final languages, the same ordering principle is at play at the levels of the noun phrase, the prepositional phrase, and the whole sentence. This is remarkable in that it applies to a great many languages whose speakers have never come in contact with each other. It is thus likely that some cognitive process shared by all human beings may underlie this ordering principle.

Relativization Hierarchy

Another area of syntactic structure in which striking universal principles are found is the structure of relative clauses. English can relativize the subject of a relative clause, the direct object, the indirect object, obliques, and possessor noun phrases (see Chapter 5). The following set of English examples illustrates these different possibilities.

the teacher [*who* talked at the meeting] (subject)
the teacher [*whom* I mentioned—to you] (direct object)
the teacher [*that* I told the story to—] (indirect object)
the teacher [*that* I heard the story from—] (oblique)
the teacher [*whose* book I read] (possessor)

Other languages do not allow all these possibilities. Some languages allow relativization on only some of these categories but not others. For example, a relative clause in Malagasy is grammatical only if the relativized noun phrase is the subject of the relative clause.

ny mpianatra   [izay nahita   ny vehivavy]
the student   who saw   the woman
'the student who saw the woman'

In Malagasy there is no way of directly translating a relative clause whose direct object has been relativized ('the student that the woman saw'), or the indirect object ('the student that the woman gave a book to'), or an oblique ('the student that the woman heard the news from'), or a possessor ('the student whose book the woman read'). If speakers of Malagasy need to convey what is represented by these English relative constructions, they must make the relative clause passive, so that the noun phrase to be relativized becomes the grammatical subject of the relative clause ('the student *who* was seen by the woman'). Alternatively, they can express their idea in two clauses—that is, instead of 'the woman saw the student who failed his exam,' they might say that 'the woman saw the student, and that same student failed his exam.'

Some languages have relative clauses in which subjects or direct objects can be relativized, but indirect objects, obliques, or possessors cannot. An example of such a language is Kinyarwanda, spoken in East Africa. Other languages, like Basque, have relative clauses in which the subject, the direct object, and the indirect object can be relativized, but not an oblique or a possessor. Yet another type of language adds obliques to the list of categories that can be relativized; such is the case in Catalan, spoken in northeastern Spain. Finally, languages like English allow all possibilities.

Table 7-2

Relativization Hierarchy: Types of Relative Clause Systems

LANGUAGE TYPE	SUBJECT	DIRECT OBJECT	INDIRECT OBJECT	OBLIQUE	POSSESSOR	EXAMPLE
1	+	–	–	–	–	Malagasy
2	+	+	–	–	–	Kinyarwanda
3	+	+	+	–	–	Basque
4	+	+	+	+	–	Catalan
5	+	+	+	+	+	English

Table 7–2 on page 239 recapitulates the types of relative clause systems found among the world's languages; the plus sign indicates a grammatical category that can be relativized, while a minus sign indicates one that cannot be relativized. Notice that a plus sign does not imply anything about the signs to the right of it—they may be plus or minus. A plus sign implies that all categories to its left can be relativized.

It is a remarkable fact that there are no languages in which, for example, an oblique can be relativized ('the man [that I heard the story from]') but not subjects, direct objects, and indirect objects as well. Indeed, relative clause formation in all languages is sensitive to a *hierarchy* of grammatical relations:

Relative Clause Hierarchy

Subject < Direct object < Indirect object < Oblique < Possessor.

The hierarchy predicts that if a language allows a particular category on the hierarchy to be relativized, then the grammar of that language will also allow all positions to the left to be relativized. For example, possessors in English can be relativized ('the woman [*whose* book I read]'). The hierarchy predicts that English would allow all positions to the left of possessor (namely, oblique, indirect object, direct object, and subject) to be relativized. The hierarchy also predicts that Basque, which permits indirect objects to be relativized, will allow direct objects and subjects to be relativized; Basque does *not* allow categories to the right of indirect object on the hierarchy (obliques or possessors) to be relativized. The hierarchy is thus a succinct description of the types of relative clause formation patterns found in the languages of the world.

TYPES OF LANGUAGE UNIVERSALS

In this section we draw on the universals treated in the previous sections in order to classify the different types of universals. It should be clear by now that language universals are not all alike. Some do not have any exceptions. Others hold for most languages but not all. It is important to distinguish between these two types of universals because the first type appears to be the result of an absolute constraint on language in general, while the other is the result of a tendency.

Absolute Universals and Universal Tendencies

The first two types of universals are distinguished by whether they can be stated as absolute rules. The typology of vowel systems established earlier indicates that the minimum number of vowels in a language is three: /i a u/. The two universal rules that are suggested by the typology read as follows:

1. All languages have at least three vowels.
2. If a language has only three vowels, these vowels will be /i a u/.

From the descriptions of all languages studied to date, it appears that these two rules have no exceptions. The two rules are thus examples of **absolute universals**—universal rules that have no exceptions. Other examples of absolute universals include: If a language has a set of dual pronouns, it must have a set of plural pronouns; if a language has voiced stops, it must have voiceless stops.

In contrast to absolute universals, a number of universal rules have some exceptions. A good example is the rule stating that if a language has a gap in its inventory of stops, it is likely to have a fricative with the same place of articulation as the missing stop. This rule holds for most languages that have gaps in their inventory, but not all. Such rules are called **universal tendencies.** (A possible explanation for universal tendencies is that they represent the coming together of partly competing universal rules.)

Naturally, researchers must be careful when deciding that a particular rule is absolute. Until a few years ago, it would have been easy to assume that no language existed with OVS or OSV as basic word order (since none had been described) and that there was an absolute universal stating that "no language has OVS or OSV for basic word order." However, we now know of a few OVS and OSV languages, all spoken in the Amazon Basin. Thus the rule that had been stated as an absolute universal seemed absolute only because no one had come across a language that violated it.

Implicational and Nonimplicational Universals

Independently of the contrast between absolute universals and tendencies, we can draw another important distinction—between implicational and nonimplicational universals. Some universal rules are in the form of a conditional implication, as in the following examples:

- If a language has five vowels, it generally has the vowel /o/ or /ɔ/.
- If a language is verb-final, then in that language possessors are likely to precede possessed noun phrases.

All rules of the form "if condition P is satisfied, then conclusion Q holds" are called **implicational universals.** Other universals can be stated without conditions: All languages have at least three vowels. Such universals are called *nonimplicational universals.*

There are thus four types of universals.

Types of Universals

Absolute implicational universal
> If a language has property X, it must have property Y.

Implicational tendency
> If a language has property X, it will probably have property Y.

Absolute nonimplicational universal
> All languages have property X.

Nonimplicational tendency
> Most languages have property X.

EXPLANATIONS FOR LANGUAGE UNIVERSALS

It is remarkable that all languages of the world fall into clearly defined types and are subject to universal rules, given the extreme structural diversity they otherwise exhibit. It is thus reasonable to ask why universal rules exist at all. The question is extremely complex, and no one has come up with a definitive explanation for any universal. But for many universals we can make hypotheses or at least educated guesses about the reasons for their existence.

Original Language Hypothesis

The first explanation for language universals that may come to mind is that all languages of the world derive historically from the same original language. This hypothesis is difficult to support, however. First of all, archaeological evidence strongly suggests that the ability to speak developed in our ancestors in several parts of the globe at about the same time, and it is difficult to imagine that different groups of speakers not in contact with one another would have developed exactly the same language. Second, even if we ignore the archaeological evidence, the existence of an original language is impossible to prove or disprove because we have no evidence for or against it. Thus the original language hypothesis is not a very good explanation; it is so hypothetical that it does not adequately fulfill the function of an explanation.

Universals and Perception

A more likely hypothesis explaining language universals is that they are symptoms of how all humans perceive the world and conduct verbal interactions. In the following sections, several such explanations will be applied to the universals established earlier in this chapter. In the discussion of vowel systems, you may have noticed that the three vowels found in all languages—/i a u/—are mutually very distant in a vowel chart. The two vowels /i/ and /u/ differ in terms of frontness and usually rounding, and /a/ differs from the other two in terms of frontness and height. From these observations, it is not difficult to hypothesize why these three vowels are the most fundamental vowels across languages: There is no other set of three vowels that differ from each other more dramatically.

Acquisition and Processing Explanations

Some language universals have psychological explanations with no physiological basis. The explanations that have been proposed for word order universals, for example, are based on the notion that the more regular the structure of a language, the easier it is for children to acquire. Thus the fact that verb-initial languages have prepositions and place adjectives after nouns, possessors after possessed nouns, and relative clauses after head nouns can be summarized by the following rule:

In verb-initial languages, the modifier follows the modified element. Languages that strictly follow this rule exhibit a great deal of regularity from one construction to the other; a single ordering principle regulates the order of verbs and direct objects, adpositions and noun phrases, nouns and adjectives, possessors and possessed nouns, and relative clauses and head nouns. It seems that such a language would be easier to acquire than a language with two or more ordering principles underlying different areas of the syntax. The fact that so many languages in the world follow one overall ordering pattern (modified-modifier) or the other (modifier-modified) with such regularity thus reflects the suggested general tendency for the structure of language to be as regular as possible so as to make it as easy as possible to acquire.

Psychological explanations have also been proposed to explain the relative clause formation hierarchy. Relative clauses in which the head functions as the subject of the relative clause ('the woman [who left]') are easier to learn and to understand than relative clauses in which the head functions as the direct object of the relative clause ('the man [that I saw]'). Small children generally acquire the first type before they begin using the second type. Furthermore, people take less time to understand the meaning of relative clauses on subjects than on direct objects. Relative clauses on direct objects, in turn, are easier to understand than those on indirect objects, and so on down the hierarchy: Subject < Direct object < Indirect object < Oblique < Possessor. There is thus a psychological explanation for the cross-linguistic patterns in the typology of relative clause formation: A language allows a "difficult" relative clause type only if all the "easier" types are also allowed in the language.

Social Explanations

Finally, recall that language is both a cognitive and a social phenomenon (see Chapter 1). While some language universals have a basis in cognition, others reflect the fact that language is a social tool.

Universals of pronoun systems can be explained in terms of the uses of language. Why, for example, do all languages have first- and second-person singular pronouns? Consider that the most basic type of verbal interaction is face-to-face conversation. Other contexts in which language is used to communicate (through writing, over the telephone, on the radio, and so on) are relatively recent inventions compared to the ability to carry on a conversation; they occur less frequently and perhaps less naturally than face-to-face interactions. In a face-to-face interaction, it is essential to be able to refer efficiently and concisely to the speaker and the addressee, the two most important entities involved in the interaction. An argument between two individuals who were unable to use *I* and *you,* or who had to refer to themselves and each other by name, would be notably less efficient. Obviously, first- and second-person singular pronouns are essential for ordinary efficiency of social interaction. It is thus not surprising that every language has first- and second-person singular pronoun forms, even though they may have a gap elsewhere in their pronoun systems. The universal that all languages have first- and second-person pronoun forms thus has a social motivation.

Furthermore, as noted earlier, the most frequent pronoun system has separate first-, second-, and third-person forms, and separate first-person inclusive ('you and me and perhaps other people') and exclusive ('other people and me, but not you') forms. Why would this system be so frequent and in some way more basic than other systems? Pronoun systems can be viewed as a matrix, with each slot of the matrix characterized by whether the speaker and the addressee are included in the reference of the pronoun, as in Table 7-3.

Table 7-3
Matrix of Pronoun Systems

	SPEAKER INCLUDED	SPEAKER EXCLUDED
ADDRESSEE INCLUDED	— first person inclusive plural	second person singular second person plural
ADDRESSEE EXCLUDED	first person singular first person exclusive plural	third person singular third person plural

In light of the fact that speaker and addressee are the more important elements of face-to-face interactions, it should come as no surprise that speaker and addressee inclusion or exclusion should be the crucial factor in defining each slot of the matrix. The most basic (and most common) type of pronoun system is thus the most balanced matrix, one in which each slot is filled with a separate form.

Language universals may thus stem from the way in which humans perceive the world around them, learn and process language, and organize their social interactions. Underlying the search for universals is the desire to learn more about these areas of cognition and social life.

Computers and the Study of Language Universals

For more than half a century researchers have been trying to craft devices that can translate between languages. Except in limited ways, however, that goal has eluded even the best attempts thus far. As everyone who has visited a foreign country knows, word-for-word translation does not do the trick. For one thing, as we've seen, languages differ in their word orders and, for another, the metaphors of one language may not translate into the relevant metaphor of another language. Countless other reasons also contribute to the failure of word-for-word trans-

lation, so even computerized bilingual dictionaries for each language being translated will be insufficient.

Consider two models of translation. In the first model, one set of rules or procedures is established for translating from language A into language B and a second set for translating in reverse—that is, from B into A. The rules would have to be completely explicit, and a set of procedures in *each* direction would be needed, because translation is not symmetrical. If a machine translation (MT) device were established for even six languages, then 6 x 5 (i.e., 30)

Transfer Translation

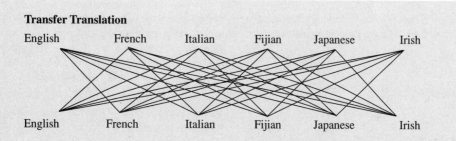

sets of procedures would be needed to translate each language into all of the other five. Such a model, referred to as a *transfer translation system,* can be represented as in the figure above.

Now consider an alternative model in which the basic semantic elements of each language can be represented abstractly and then encoded into other languages. In this model, a procedure would be needed for each language to decode it into abstract semantic elements (thus forming an abstract semantic representation), along with a second procedure for encoding abstract semantic representations into the lexicon, syntax, and (for spoken texts) phonology of each target language. Such a model is called an *interlingual translation system* and might look like the figure below.

The interlingual translation model would require twelve procedures—one *decoding* procedure and one *encoding* procedure for each of the six languages. Such a model is far simpler than the transfer translation model requiring 30 procedures. Unfortunately, it isn't clear to what extent sentences can actually be decomposed into the kinds of abstract semantic representations that would be needed for

an interlingual model, especially to make the intermediate representation language neutral.

Difficulties related to translation in either model concern what one language encodes that another may not encode. For example, as you saw in the chart of its pronouns on page 229, Fijian has four distinct second-person pronouns while English has only one. That would make it very easy to translate any second-person pronoun from Fijian into English, provided that the abstract semantic representation of the Fijian pronouns contains the element 'second person.' All such representations would be mapped onto the only second-person pronoun of English—namely, *you.* But what about translating the other way around? Would it be equally straightforward? Given an English sentence containing the pronoun *you,* no machine could determine from the form itself its underlying semantic representation, other than second person. In other words, since English does not code the potential distinction among singular, dual, trial, and plural number in the second person, an MT device could not decide which Fijian pronoun to choose if it relied solely on the form of the English pronoun *you.* We can represent the first

Interlingual Translation

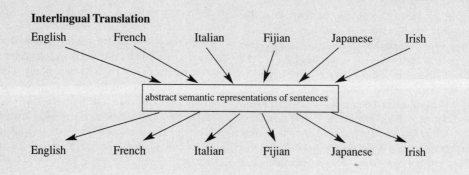

part of the problem in the following schema, where translating from Fijian to English would be easy.

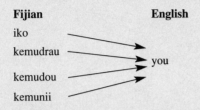

Fijian	English
iko	
kemudrau	you
kemudou	
kemunii	

But translating English *you* into Fijian would be quite a challenge. While the text or the context might make clear just how many addressees were represented by the pronoun *you,* except in rare cases (e.g., *you two, the three of you)* that information would prove difficult or impossible for an MT program to decipher.

As we have just seen, going from Fijian second-person pronouns to the single English second-person pronoun would be easy, but going from the English to the Fijian virtually impossible. Interestingly, the situation is reversed for third-person singular pronouns. In that case, Fijian does not distinguish between masculine, feminine, and neuter singular pronouns, but English does; as you saw in the chart on page 229, Fijian has only the pronoun *koya* corresponding to the three English pronouns *he, she,* and *it.*

Fijian	English
koya	? he
	? she
	? it

No device could decide from the Fijian pronoun alone which English pronoun would be the correct translation. Again, the context might make it clear, but it would be difficult at best for an MT device to decipher that information.

Having noted several ways in which automatic or machine translation would be difficult or impossible, it is also important to note that considerable progress has been made in creating MT devices. The problems that we have discussed can be minimized by limiting the translation machinery to two languages and to very specialized domains of discourse within those languages. For example, if you were translating only medical texts or only technical documents from English into another language, you would deal with a limited subset of vocabulary and structures. Analysis

of particular kinds of text may reveal that certain lexical or grammatical options rarely (or never) occur in them. When creating a list of words that appear in medical journals, for example, most informal vocabulary could be eliminated from consideration.

Similarly, to return to the pronoun problem discussed above, English-language medical journals would almost certainly not use the full range of potential semantic distinctions represented in Fijian, so for projects translating medical documents, some possible Fijian pronouns could be eliminated for practical purposes.

The need for translation has grown urgently in recent decades with the formation of the European Union, and considerable financial resources have been made available for exploring automatic translation. In pursuit of better methods of machine translation, corpora containing more than one language have been created, and analysis of them will yield findings that will be helpful in designing automatic translation devices. Some multilingual corpora contain the same *kinds* of texts but not identical texts. One such corpus is the Aarhus Corpus of Danish, French, and English law. These texts are not translations of one another but represent a reservoir of information about the language of legislation in these three languages. Other corpora contain texts that are translations of one another, as with the Canadian Hansard Corpus, which contains parliamentary proceedings in French to English and English to French translations.

When a corpus contains translations it is possible to create a "parallel aligned corpus." This is a corpus containing texts in different languages that have been aligned, sometimes automatically, so that sections correspond to one another—paragraph to paragraph or sentence to sentence. Researchers can use these corpora to explore the mathematical properties of vocabulary and syntax in languages and pairs of languages. By relying on knowledge of such properties, automatic translation may be able partly to avoid either of the models depicted above. Instead, certain mathematical properties of languages would help determine likely translations, independently of how the human mind processes languages and makes translations.

SUMMARY

- Underlying the great diversity of the world's languages, universal principles are at play at all levels of language structure—phonology, morphology, syntax, and semantics.

- The study of typology aims to catalogue languages according to types, while the study of universals aims to formulate the universal principles themselves.

- In lexical semantics, the composition of pronoun systems, in which cross-linguistic variation is found, is dictated by several universal rules that regulate distinctions in number and person.

- Vowel systems and inventories of stops are two examples of universals at play in phonology.

- In syntax and morphology, universals are found that regulate the basic order of constituents in sentences and phrases.

- In syntax, the relativization hierarchy is a striking example of a universal principle.

- The salient characteristic of all universals is that the most common patterns are the most regular and harmonious.

- Four types of universal rules can be distinguished, depending on whether they have exceptions (absolute versus tendency) and according to their logical form (implicational versus nonimplicational):

  Absolute implicational universals: Languages with property X must have property Y.
  Implicational tendencies: Languages with property X will probably have property Y.
  Absolute nonimplicational universals: All languages have property X.
  Nonimplicational tendencies: Most languages have property X.

- The ultimate goal of the study of language universals is to provide explanations for such universal principles.

- Language universals may have physiological, psychological, or social explanations.

  Physiological: Universals are often indicative of how we perceive the world around us. Thus, languages tend to highlight categories that are physiologically and perceptually salient, as with vowels.

  Psychological: Structural simplicity and consistency make languages easier to acquire and process. Thus many universals predict that the simplest and most consistent systems will be preferred.

  Social: Distinctions drawn on the expression side of language reflect important social distinctions on the content side.

WHAT DO YOU THINK? REVISITED

❖ *Your third-grade niece.* Many people tend to think about languages in terms of their written rather than their spoken form. That's why so many people will report that English has 5 vowels (*a, e, i, o,* and *u*). But Figure 7–1 (p. 231) shows your niece to be correct. Besides its 13 vowels, English has 3 diphthongs, as in the words *buy, toy,* and *cow.* Given the discussion in this chapter, you know that languages vary in the number of vowels they have. Quechua, Greenlandic Eskimo, and Moroccan Arabic have 3 vowels; Hawaiian has 5; English 13; Parisian French 15.

❖ *Cousins visiting Chicago.* You've noticed that many speakers of English say *you* whether they're addressing one person or several, but that other speakers use a distinct form for more than one addressee; they may say *y'all, youse,* or *y'uns* (Chapter 11 reports who says *y'uns*). You may have noticed that you or some of your friends say *you guys* when addressing more than one person. As shown in the pronoun charts on pages 228–229, it is not at all unusual for languages to have distinct singular and plural forms for second-person pronouns—and even sometimes to distinguish two addressees from more than two. Fijian, for example, has four distinct forms: one for addressing one person (singular), another for two persons (dual), another for three (trial), and still another for more than three (plural). It is noteworthy that English has different configurations in its various dialects, with some, but not all, varieties distinguishing between second-person singular and second-person plural pronouns. *You guys* seems increasingly to be used by speakers whose variety does not have a distinct second-person plural form.

❖ *Classmate in introductory Japanese.* It seems second nature to think one's own language natural and logical and to suspect that other languages are odd or illogical if they differ. Perhaps nowhere is this more true than with word order. Like other aspects of language, though, word order isn't a matter of logic. While some languages have an SVO order, others have SOV or some other order. German uses SVO in main clauses and SOV in subordinate clauses, whereas English uses SVO for main clauses (*I bought it*) and subordinate clauses (*because I wanted it*). Despite the fact that the basic English word order is SVO, other word orders are possible, as in sentences like *Peas I like.* The OSV order of *Peas I like* is just as logical (or illogical) as the SVO order of *I like peas.* Still, as this chapter shows, some word order patterns generally go together in a language and invite hypotheses about why they do so.

EXERCISES

Based on English and Other Languages

7-1 Make a judgment about how usual or unusual the following features of standard English are in comparison with other languages discussed in this chapter. Explain your judgment in each case.

1) a 13-vowel system

2) no (phonemically distinct) nasal vowels

3) Subject-Verb-Object word order

4) adjectives preceding head nouns

5) relative clauses following head nouns

6) no dual pronoun forms

7) no trial pronoun forms

8) no distinct second-person plural pronouns

9) no distinction between inclusive and exclusive pronouns

7-2 Determine whether each of the following is an absolute implicational universal, an absolute nonimplicational universal, an implicational universal tendency, or a nonimplicational universal tendency.

1) The consonant inventories of all languages include at least two different stops that differ in terms of place of articulation.

2) Languages always have fewer nasal consonants than oral stops.

3) In all languages, the number of front vowels of different height is greater than or equal to the number of back vowels of different height.

4) Most VSO languages have prepositions, not postpositions.

5) Diminutive particles and affixes tend to exhibit high vowels.

6) If a language has separate terms for 'foot' and 'leg,' then it must also have different terms for 'hand' and 'arm.'

7) The future tense is used to express hypothetical events in many languages, and the past tense is often used to express nonhypothetical events.

8) Languages that have a relatively free word order tend to have inflections for case.

9) Many verb-initial languages place relative clauses after the head of the relative clause.

7-3 In English, conditions can be expressed in two ways: by placing the conditioning clause first and the conditioned clause second, as in (1) below, or by placing the conditioning clause second and the conditioned clause first, as in (2). In numerous languages, however, only the first pattern is grammatical. In Mandarin Chinese, the conditioning clause must come first, as in (3); if it is placed second, as in (4), the resulting string is ungrammatical. No language allows only pattern (2)—conditioning clause second, conditioned clause first.

1) If you cry, I'll turn off the TV.

2) I'll turn off the TV if you cry.

3) rúguǒ wǒ dìdi   hē   jiǔ   wǒ jiù   hěn   shēngqì
   If   my   younger-brother drink wine   I   then   very angry
   'If my younger brother drinks wine, I'll be very angry.'

4) *wǒ hěn   shēngqì rúguǒ wǒ dìdi   hē   jiǔ
   I   very angry   if   my   younger-brother drink wine

a. From this information, formulate descriptions of an absolute implicational universal, an absolute nonimplicational universal, and a universal tendency, all of which refer to conditional clauses.

b. Propose an explanation for the universal ordering patterns that you formulated in (a). (*Hint:* Think of the order in which the actions denoted by the conditioning and the conditioned clauses must take place.)

7-4 The composition of vowel inventories of the world's languages is predicted by the hierarchy given in Figure 7–4 (p. 233). The hierarchy predicts the composition of a vowel inventory consisting of six phonemes. Complete the next step in the hierarchy by determining the composition of seven-vowel inventories. Use the following information on the composition of the seven-vowel inventories of three languages, which you should assume are representative of possible seven-vowel inventories.

Burmese	i e ɛ ɔ o u
Sundanese	i ɨ ɛ ɔ a u ə
Washkuk	i ɨ e ɛ ɔ a u

7-5   Consider the following typology of pronoun systems found among the world's languages. The first column of each set represents singular pronouns, the second column dual pronouns, and the third column plural pronouns. An example of a language also is given for each type (incl. = inclusive, excl. = exclusive).

8-pronoun Systems

1) I   we-2   we   Greenlandic Eskimo
    thou   you-2   you
    s/he   they

2) I   we   Arabic
    thou   you-2   you
    s/he   they-2   they

3) I   we-2-incl   we-incl.   Southern Paiute (North America)
    thou   you
    s/he   they

9-pronoun Systems

1) I   we-2   we   Lapp (Arctic Scandinavia)
    thou   you-2   you
    s/he   they-2   they

2) I   we-2-incl. we-incl.   Maya (Central America)
                  we-2-excl. we-excl.
    thou   you
    s/he   they

3) I   we-2-incl. we   Lower Kanauri (India)
                  we-2-excl.
    thou   you-2   you
    s/he   they

10-pronoun Systems

1) I   we-2-incl   we   Coos (North America)
                  we-2-excl.
    thou   you-2   you
    s/he   they-2   they

2) I   we-2-incl   we-incl.   Kanauri (India)
                  we-2-excl. we-excl.
    thou   you-2   you
    s/he   they-2   they

11-pronoun Systems

1) I   we-2-incl. we-incl.   Hawaiian
                  we-2-excl. we-excl.
    thou   you-2   you
    s/he   they-2   they

2)

I	we-2-incl.	we-incl.	Ewe (West Africa)
	we-2 excl.	we-excl.	
thou	you-2	you	
s/he	they-2	they	
		he and they	

a. On the basis of these data, which you may assume to be representative, formulate a set of absolute universal principles that describe the composition of 8-, 9-, 10-, and 11-pronoun systems. State your principles as generally as possible.

b. Of these systems, the most commonly found is the 11-pronoun system of type 1, exemplified by Hawaiian, followed by the 9-pronoun system of type 1, exemplified by Lapp. Formulate a set of universal tendencies that describe the preponderance of examples of these two systems.

7-6 From a logical standpoint, the possible basic ordering combinations of subject, verb, and direct object are SOV, SVO, VSO, VOS, OVS, and OSV. We have seen that there is great variation in the percentage of languages exhibiting each combination as a basic word order. Linguists have recognized this fact for several decades, but there has been little agreement on the exact distribution of these basic word order variations across the world's languages. Here are results from five researchers who conducted cross-linguistic analyses of the distribution of basic word order possibilities. (The figures are cited from Tomlin 1986.)

	LANGUAGES		PERCENTAGE					
RESEARCHER	SAMPLED	SOV	SVO	VSO	VOS	OVS	OSV	UNCLASSIFIED
Greenberg	30	37	43	20	0	0	0	0
Ultan	75	44	34.6	18.6	2.6	0	0	0
Ruhlen	427	51.5	35.6	10.5	2.1	0	0.2	0
Mallinson/Blake	100	41	35	9	2	1	1	11
Tomlin	402	44.8	41.8	9.2	3.0	1.2	0	0

a. In what ways do these researchers' data agree, and where do they disagree? Describe in detail.

b. What are the possible causes of the discrepancies in the results?

c. What lesson can typologists learn from this comparison?

7-7 Relative clauses can be formed in a variety of ways. In English, we "replace" the relativized element by a relative pronoun that links the relative clause to its head (type 3). Other languages do not have distinct relative pronouns but replace the relativized element by a personal pronoun (type 2). For example, in Gilbertese (spoken in the central Pacific), the position of the relativized element in the relative clause is marked with a personal pronoun.

Type 2						Type 2		
te	ben	[e bwaka	iaon	te	auti]	te	anene	[i nori-a]
the	coconut	it fall	on	the	house	the	coconut	I saw-it
'the coconut [that fell on the house]'						'the coconut [that I saw]'		

In other languages, such as Finnish, relative clauses are formed by simply deleting the relativized element from the relative clause; no relative pronoun or personal pronoun is added to the relative construction (type 1).

Type 1		Type 1	
[tanssinut]	poika	[näkemäni]	poika
had-danced	boy	I-had-seen	boy
'the boy [that had danced]'		'the boy [that I had seen]'	

Some languages have several types of relative clauses. Mandarin Chinese has types 1 and 2. (In Mandarin the relative clause is ordered before its head and is separated from the head by the particle *de*.)

Type 1

[mǎi píngguǒ de] rén
buy apples Particle man
'the man [who bought apples]'

Type 2

[tā jièjie zài měiguó de] rén
he sister is-in America Particle man
'the man [whose sister is in America]'

In Mandarin Chinese, type 1 is used only when relativizing a subject or direct object, while type 2 can be used when relativizing a direct object, an indirect object, an oblique, or a possessor, as indicated in the table below. Whenever two types of relative clauses are found in a language, the pattern is the same: as we go down the relativization hierarchy (from subject to direct object to indirect object to oblique to possessor), one type can end but the other type takes over. Here are the patterns for some languages:

Grammatical Relation Relativized

	SUBJECT	DIRECT OBJECT	INDIRECT OBJECT	OBLIQUE	POSSESSOR
Aoban (South Pacific)					
Type 1	+	–	–	–	–
Type 2	–	+	+	+	+
Dutch					
Type 1	+	+	–	–	–
Type 2	–	–	+	+	+
Japanese					
Type 1	+	+	+	+	+
Type 2	–	–	–	–	+
Kera (Central Africa)					
Type 1	+	–	–	–	–
Type 2	–	+	+	+	+
Mandarin Chinese					
Type 1	+	+	–	–	–
Type 2	–	+	+	+	+
Roviana (South Pacific)					
Type 1	+	+	+	–	–
Type 2	–	–	–	+	+
Tagalog (Philippines)					
Type 1	+	–	–	–	–
Type 2	+	–	–	–	–
Catalan (Spain)					
Type 1	+	+	+	–	–
Type 2	–	–	–	+	–

What cross-linguistic generalizations can you draw from these data on the distribution of relative clause types in each language? How can we expand the universal rules associated with the hierarchy to describe these patterns?

7-8 Below is a sentence from the program notes to *Officium,* produced by ECM Records. After that, in sections, the sentence is repeated with translations from the program notes in German and French. Comparable sections are marked typographically. After examining the English sentence and the three translations, answer the questions that follow.

> The oldest pieces on this record (if one can use words like "new" and "old" in this context) are the chants, the origins of which are not known to us.

The **oldest** pieces				on this record		
Die **ältesten** Stücke				dieser Aufnahme		
Les morceaux	**les**	**plus**	**anciens** figurant	*sur*	*ce*	*disque*
the pieces	the	most	old figuring	on	this	record

(if one *can use words* like "new" and "old" in this context)
—so man in diesem Zusammenhang überhaupt von „neu" und „alt" *sprechen kann*—
if one in this situation at all of new and old speak can

(si tant est que les termes «nouveau» et «ancien» conviennent à ce contexte)
if such it is that the terms new and old suit to this context

are the chants, the	origins of which	<u>are not known</u> **to us.**
sind Gesänge, deren Ursprung		**uns** nicht bekannt ist.
are chants whose origin		to-us not known is.

| sont les chants, dont | l'origine **nous** est inconnue. |
| are the chants whose origin | to-us is unknown |

a. Which of the languages have prepositions, and which have postpositions?

b. Each of the translations contains three clauses, the equivalents of
   i. the oldest pieces on this record are the chants
   ii. if one can use words like "new" and "old" in this context
   iii. the origins of which are not known to us

   Do any of the languages use a word order other than SVO in the main clause? In the subordinate clauses? If any other word orders are represented, identify them.

c. Which languages have adjectives preceding head nouns? Which have adjectives following head nouns?

d. Neither German nor French uses a prepositional phrase to express what English expresses as *to us*. What do they do instead, and how is the meaning conveyed without a preposition?

Especially for Educators and Future Teachers

7-9 This chapter has described "language universals." Do you think that everything said in this chapter about language universals applies to all varieties of every language—in other words, to all dialects of a language as well? What about nonstandard dialects? Explain your position.

7-10 At an appropriate level for the students you teach or are preparing to teach, explain what a language universal is and how there can be so much diversity in the world's languages when such universals exist.

OTHER RESOURCES

- **The I Can Eat Glass Project: http://hcs.harvard.edu/~igp/glass.html**
  Enterprising Harvard University student Ethan Mollick (who has now graduated) compiled a list of ways to say "I can eat glass, it doesn't hurt me" in over 100 languages. In Mollick's words, "The project lists the language, the location in which it is spoken, how it would be written in the language (if the tongue uses the Roman alphabet), and a transliteration if available."

SUGGESTIONS FOR FURTHER READING

- **Bernard Comrie. 1989.** *Language Universals and Linguistic Typology,* **2nd ed.** (Chicago: University of Chicago Press). This is an accessible basic book on the study of language universals and linguistic typology; it focuses principally on syntax and morphology.
- **William Croft. 2003.** *Typology and Universals,* **2nd ed.** (Cambridge: Cambridge University Press). A more advanced and wide-ranging treatment, this book is particularly good on explanations for various kinds of universals.
- **Jae Jung Song. 2001.** *Linguistic Typology* (Harlow, Essex: Pearson). This book, focused on morphological and syntactic typologies, is an accessible treatment.
- **Lindsay J. Whaley. 1997.** *Introduction to Typology: The Unity and Diversity of Language* (Thousand Oaks, CA: Sage). This accessible book is probably the most basic of the four listed.

ADVANCED READING

Mallinson and Blake (1981) is a good introduction to typology. Shopen (1985) is a collection of excellent essays by distinguished researchers on selected areas of syntactic typology, and is also useful on the range of morphological and syntactic variation found among the world's languages. The first volume treats clause structure, the second complex constructions, and the third grammatical categories and the lexicon. Some of the most influential work on language universals was conducted by Greenberg, who has edited a four-volume compendium of detailed studies of universals on specific areas of linguistic structure (1978); chapters from these volumes provided data for some of the exercises of this chapter. Brown (1984) is an interesting investigation of universals of words for plants and animals. Lehrer (1974) is a good summary of research on semantic universals. Tomlin (1986) surveys the basic word orders of the world's languages. The relativization hierarchy was uncovered by Edward L. Keenan and Bernard Comrie, and Chapter 7 of Comrie (1989) offers a clear discussion of the topic. Butterworth, Comrie, and Dahl (1984) is a collection of papers on theoretical explanations for language universals.

REFERENCES

- Brown, Cecil H. 1984. *Language and Living Things: Uniformities in Folk Classification and Naming* (New Brunswick, NJ: Rutgers University Press).

- Butterworth, Brian, Bernard Comrie, & Osten Dahl, eds. 1984. *Explanations for Language Universals* (Berlin: Mouton).

- Greenberg, Joseph H., ed. 1978. *Universals of Human Language,* 4 vols. (Stanford: Stanford University Press).

- Lehrer, Adrienne. 1974. *Semantic Fields and Lexical Structure* (Amsterdam: North-Holland).

- Mallinson, George, & Barry J. Blake. 1981. *Language Typology* (Amsterdam: North-Holland)

- Shopen, Timothy, ed. 1985. *Language Typology and Syntactic Description,* 3 vols. (Cambridge: Cambridge University Press).

- Tomlin, Russell S. 1986. *Basic Word Order: Functional Principles* (London: Croom Helm).

Part Two

Language Use

In Part One you examined the structure of words, phrases, and sentences. In Part Two you'll examine how you use those structures in ordinary social interactions. You'll see that languages provide alternative ways of saying the same thing, and you'll see what those alternative ways accomplish socially and communicatively. Language exists only to be used, and our use of language distinguishes human beings from all other animals. It is language use that makes us uniquely human. By putting language to use, we accomplish things and can achieve deep social and intellectual satisfaction.

The forms of language that you use reflect your social identity and mirror the character of the situation in which you're communicating. Part Two explores *dialects*—the patterns of linguistic variation across diverse social groups—and *registers,* the patterns of linguistic variation across communicative situations. Here you will also examine writing systems and the relationships between written and spoken expression.

Chapter 8

Information Structure and Pragmatics

❖ An international student you are tutoring asks about the function of definite and indefinite articles in English. You explain that the definite article *(the)* refers to particular persons, places, or things—*the Golden Gate Bridge, the mayor.* By contrast, you say, the indefinite article (*a* or *an*) is used to refer to any person, place, or thing—*a chef, a park, an apple.* The student says she's been paying attention to what people say, and that your answer doesn't quite match what she has heard. She reminds you that you yourself had recommended *"a movie"* you'd seen and that you meant *"Chicago,"* which is a particular movie. You recognize she's right. What better explanation can you offer for the use of definite and indefinite articles?

❖ During an ESL class discussion about active and passive sentences, a student from Taiwan asks why English has these two ways of saying exactly the same thing. As an example, he cites these sentences:

> *The Anaheim Angels won the 2002 World Series.* (active)
> *The 2002 World Series was won by the Anaheim Angels.* (passive)

Fortunately, you're saved by the bell and can think about your answer overnight. At the next class meeting, what explanation do you give?

❖ A classmate who's majoring in business wants to know when you can put objects before subjects in English. He noticed a TV commentator say about the mayor of New York City, *Him I like!* And he wants to know what you think. Well?

INTRODUCTION: ENCODING INFORMATION STRUCTURE

Syntax and semantics are not the only regulators of sentence structure. A sentence may be grammatically and semantically well formed but still exhibit problems when used in a particular context. Examine the following two versions of a local news report. (The sentences of Version 1 are numbered because we will refer to them later.)

Version 1

(1) At 3 A.M. last Sunday, the Santa Clara Fire Department evacuated two apartment buildings at the corner of Country Club Drive and Fifth Avenue. (2) Oil had been discovered leaking from a furnace in the basement of one of the buildings. (3) Firefighters sprayed chemical foam over the oil for several hours. (4) By 8 A.M., the situation was under control. (5) Any danger of explosion or fire had been averted, and the leaky furnace was sealed. (6) Residents of the two apartment buildings were given temporary shelter in the Country Club High School gymnasium. (7) They regained possession of their apartments at 5 P.M.

Version 2

As for the Santa Clara Fire Department, it evacuated two apartment buildings at the corner of Country Club Drive and Fifth Avenue at 3 A.M. last Sunday. In the basement of one of the buildings, someone had discovered a furnace from which oil was leaking. What was sprayed by firefighters over the oil for several hours was chemical foam. It was by 8 A.M. that the situation was under control. What someone had averted was any danger of explosion or fire, and as for the leaky furnace, it was sealed. What the residents of the two apartment buildings were given in the Country Club High School gymnasium was temporary shelter. Possession of their apartments was regained by them at 5 P.M.

Virtually the same words are used in the two versions, and every sentence in both versions is grammatically and semantically well formed. Still, something is fundamentally odd about Version 2. It runs counter to our expectations of how information should be presented in a text. Somehow, it emphasizes the wrong elements or emphasizes the right elements at the wrong time. Though grammatical, the structures of Version 2 seem inappropriate.

The problem with Version 2 is the way in which different pieces of information are marked for relative significance. In any sequence of sentences, it is essential to mark elements as being more or less important or necessary. Speakers and writers are responsible for bringing to the foreground certain elements and putting others in the background, just as a painter uses color, shape, and position to highlight some details and de-emphasize others.

In language texts, such highlighting and de-emphasizing is called **information structure.** Unlike syntax and semantics, which are sentence-based aspects of language, information structure requires consideration of discourse—sequences of sentences rather than isolated sentences. Out of context, there is nothing wrong with the first sentence of Version 2:

As for the Santa Clara Fire Department, it evacuated two apartment buildings at the corner of Country Club Drive and Fifth Avenue at 3 A.M. last Sunday.

However, when it opens a news report it strikes us as odd and inappropriate. When we talk about information structure we need to account for *discourse context—* that is, the environment in which a sentence is produced and especially what precedes that sentence. We can describe a **discourse** as a sequence of spoken or written utterances that "go together" in a particular situation. A conversation at dinner, a newspaper column, a personal letter, a radio interview, and a subpoena to appear in court are examples of discourse. We could even say that an utterance like *Oh, look!* (uttered to draw attention to a beautiful sunset, for example) is discourse although it is not a sequence of utterances, because it is produced within a situational context that helps determine an appropriate information structure.

In order to mark information structure in a sentence, speakers rely on the fact that syntactic operations permit alternative ways of shaping sentences. For example, the following sentences are alternative ways of saying the same thing.

1. The firefighter discovered a leak in the basement.
2. In the basement, the firefighter discovered a leak.
3. A leak in the basement was discovered by the firefighter.
4. It was the firefighter who discovered a leak in the basement.
5. What the firefighter discovered in the basement was a leak.
6. It was a leak that the firefighter discovered in the basement.
7. What was discovered by the firefighter was a leak in the basement.
8. The firefighter, he discovered a leak in the basement.

Try it yourself: To the eight sentences above, add two other sentences that say the same thing, stated differently, containing the same information as sentence 1 (and all the others), no more, no less.

It is such a choice of alternatives that we exploit to mark information structure. You might ask yourself what question each of the sentences above is an appropriate answer to. This chapter will describe how that can be discovered.

Pragmatics is the branch of linguistics that studies information structure. In Chapter 9, we'll discuss other aspects of language use that fall under the umbrella of *pragmatics.*

CATEGORIES OF INFORMATION STRUCTURE

In order to describe the differences between alternative ways of saying the same thing, we must identify the basic categories of information structure. These categories must be applicable to all languages (although how each category is used may differ). With these categories, we want to explain how discourse is constructed in any language. These explanations ultimately may suggest hypotheses about how the different components of the human mind (such as memory, attention, and logic) work and interact with each other. Thus, categories of information structure, like other aspects of linguistics, should be as independent of particular languages as possible.

There is an important difference between the types of syntactic constructions found in particular languages and the categories of information structure. The range of syntactic constructions available differs considerably from language to language. For example, some languages have a passive construction *(She was fooled by a con artist),* but others do not. Since the categories of information structure are not language-dependent, they cannot be defined in terms of particular structures. Nevertheless, there is a close kinship between pragmatics and syntax. In all languages, one principal function of syntax is to encode pragmatic information. What differs from language to language is how pragmatic structure maps onto syntax.

Given Information and New Information

One category of information structure is the distinction between given and new information. **Given information** is information currently in the forefront of the addressee's mind; **new information** is information just being introduced into the discourse. Consider the following two-turn interaction:

Alice: Who ate the pizza?
Dimas: Erin ate the pizza.

In Dimas's answer, the noun phrase *Erin* represents new information because it is being introduced into the discourse there; by contrast, *the pizza* in the reply is given information because it can be presumed to be in the mind of Alice, who has just introduced it into the discourse in the previous turn. (We'll see shortly that given information often finds expression in condensed form, for example, as *Erin ate it* or *Erin did.*)

Given information need not be introduced into a discourse by a second speaker. In the following sequence of sentences, uttered by a single speaker, the underlined element represents given information because it has just been introduced in the previous sentence and can thus be assumed to be in the addressee's mind.

A man called while you were on your break. He said he'd call back later.

As another example, look at Version 1 of the Santa Clara Fire Department newspaper piece on page 260. Notice in (1) that the noun phrase *two apartment buildings* is new information and in (2) that *Oil* and *a furnace* are new information in that they have not been mentioned earlier and cannot be presumed to exist in a reader's mind. Note, too, that in (2) *the buildings* is given information, following mention of *two apartment buildings* in (1). In (3), *the oil* is given information by virtue of *Oil* having been mentioned previously in (2). Likewise, in (5) reference is made to *the leaky furnace,* which is given information because *a furnace* was previously mentioned in (2), along with the fact that it was leaking. Below, we'll see that the difference between new information and given information is connected to the use of indefinite and definite articles in phrases like *a furnace* and *the furnace.*

A piece of information need not be explicitly mentioned in order to be given information. Information is sometimes taken as given because of its close association with something that has been introduced into the discourse. For example, when a noun phrase is introduced into a discourse, all the subparts of the referent can be treated as given information.

> Kent finally returned my car last night. The battery was charged, but the gas tank was nearly empty.
>
> My mother went on <u>a Caribbean cruise</u> last year—she loved <u>the food</u>.

In the first sentence, *my car* is new information, but because a car typically has a battery and a gas tank, mention of *my car* suffices to make *the gas tank* and *the battery* given information. Similarly, *the food* is given information in the second example; mention of *a Caribbean cruise* suffices to enable the reader or addressee to have in mind all those things customarily associated with a cruise, including the meals.

Try it yourself: Examine Version 1 of the newspaper report on page 260. In sentence (2), note the constituent *a furnace in the basement of one of the buildings*. Sentence (1) mentions two apartment buildings, but prior to (2) there has been no mention of a furnace or a basement. Assess whether *a furnace* and *the basement* in (2) represent given or new information, and explain your assessments.

Because face-to-face conversation and most other kinds of discourse have at least implicit speakers and addressees, participants always take the speaker and first-person pronouns such as *I* and the addressee and second-person pronouns such as *you* to be given information. They do not need to be introduced into the discourse as new information.

Expressing New Information   Noun phrases representing new information usually receive more stress than those carrying given information and are commonly expressed in a more elaborate fashion—for example, with a full noun phrase instead of a pronoun, and sometimes with a relative clause or other modifiers. The following is typical of how new information is introduced into a discourse.

> When I entered the office, I saw <u>a tall man wearing an old-fashioned hat</u>.

Expressing Given Information   Given information is commonly expressed in more reduced or abbreviated ways. Typical reducing devices for encoding given information include *pronouns* and *unstressed noun phrases*. Sometimes given information is simply left out of a sentence altogether. In the following interaction, the information given by Adam's question (namely, *is at the door*) is entirely omitted from Bella's answer, which expresses only new information.

> Adam: Who's at the door?
> Bella: The mail carrier.

Try it yourself: Look for abbreviating devices used for given information in Version 1 of the newspaper report on page 260. For example, in (4) instead of saying *By 8 A.M. last Sunday,* the report leaves out *last Sunday* because, having already been expressed in (1), it is given information. Identify two additional instances of given information omitted from Version 1. Next, identify a pronoun used to encode given information and specify which full noun phrase the pronoun represents.

The contrast between given and new information is important in characterizing the function of several constructions in English and other languages, as you will see in the next section.

Topics

The **topic** of a sentence is its *center of attention*—what the sentence is about, its point of departure. The notion of topic is opposed to the notion of *comment,* which is the element of the sentence that says something about the topic. Often, given information is the sentence element about which we say something; it is the topic. New information represents what we say about the topic; it is the comment. Thus, if *Erin ate the pizza* is offered in answer to the question *What did Erin do?,* the topic would be *Erin* (the given information) and the comment would be *ate the pizza* (the new information). The topic of a sentence can sometimes be phrased as in these examples:

Speaking of Erin, she ate the pizza.

As for Erin, she ate the pizza.

The topic is not always given information. In the second sentence of the sequence below, the noun phrase *her little sister* is not given information (it is new information), but it is the topic.

Erin ate the pizza. As for her little sister, she preferred the ice cream.

Note that in the phrase *her little sister,* the word *her* anchors the new information to the given information represented by *Erin.*

In conversation, we often first establish a topic with a preliminary remark or question and only then make a comment about it.

Sheila: Remember that guy I said was pestering me?

Eammon: Yeah.

Sheila: Well, he fell off his bike in front of the whole class today.

In Sheila's second turn, *he* is the topic and *fell off his bike in front of the whole class today* is the comment.

Given information can sometimes serve as comment, as in the underlined element in the following sequence:

Hal didn't believe anything the charlatan said. As for Sara, she believed it all.

So the given/new contrast differs from the topic/comment contrast.

It is difficult to define precisely what a topic is. While the topic is the element of a sentence that functions as the center of attention, a sentence like *Oh, look!,* uttered to draw attention to a stunning sunset, has an unexpressed topic (the setting sun, or the sky). Thus, topic is not necessarily a property of the sentence; it may be a property of the discourse context.

Topics are less central to the grammar of English than to the grammar of certain other languages. In fact, the only construction that unequivocally marks topics in English is the relatively uncommon *as for* construction in a sentence such as the following:

As for Colin, he'd seen enough and he went to bed.

In English, marking the topic of a sentence is far less important than marking the subject.

Marking topic is considerably more important in certain other languages. Korean has function words whose sole purpose is to mark a noun phrase as topic. The same is true of Japanese, as we'll discuss below. In Chinese and some other languages, no special function words attach to topic noun phrases, but they are marked by word order. In Korean, Japanese, and Chinese, noun phrases marked as topic occur very frequently. Thus, despite the difficulty in defining it, topic is an important notion and needs to be distinguished from other categories of information structure.

Contrast

A noun phrase is said to be **contrastive** when it occurs in opposition to another noun phrase in the discourse. Here, for example, *Sara* in Beth's answer is contrasted with *Matt* in Alan's question.

Alan: Did Matt see the ghost?

Beth: No, <u>Sara</u> did.

Contrast Beth's answer with another possible one in which the noun phrase would not be contrastive: *Yes, he did.*

Contrast is also marked in sentences that express the narrowing down of a choice from several candidates to one. In such sentences, the noun phrase that refers to the candidate thus chosen is marked contrastively.

Of everyone present, only <u>Sara</u> knew what was going on.

Compare that sentence with the following one, in which *Sara* is not contrastive.

Gerard knew what was going on, and Sara did, too.

A simple test exists for contrast: if a noun phrase can be followed by *rather than,* it is contrastive.

Speaker A: Did Matt see the ghost?

Speaker B: No, <u>Sara</u>, rather than Matt, saw the ghost.

A single sentence can have several contrastive noun phrases. In the following exchange, *Sara* contrasts with *Matt*, and *an entire cast of spirits* contrasts with *a ghost*.

> Aaron: Did Matt see a ghost?
>
> Bella: Yes, Matt saw a ghost, but <u>Sara</u> saw <u>an entire cast of spirits</u>.

The entity with which a noun phrase is contrasted may be understood from the discourse context or from the situational context. In the following example, *Sara* could be marked contrastively if the sentence were part of a conversation about how the interlocutors dislike going to Maine during the winter.

> <u>Sara</u> likes going to Maine during the winter.

Below, in an exchange between an employee and one of several managers, the noun phrase *I* in the manager's reply can be made to contrast with *other managers,* which is not expressed but is understood from the situational context.

> Employee: Can I leave early today?
>
> Manager: <u>I</u> don't mind.

With strong stress on *I,* the implication of the manager's answer is, 'It's fine with me, but I don't know about the other managers.' The employee can readily understand the implication from shared knowledge of the situational context.

In English, contrastive noun phrases can be marked in a variety of ways, most commonly by pronouncing the contrastive noun phrase with strong stress.

> You may be smart, but <u>he</u>'s popular.

Other ways of marking contrastiveness will be investigated in the next section.

Definite Expressions

Speakers mark a noun phrase as **definite** when they assume that the addressee can identify its referent. Otherwise, the noun phrase is marked as **indefinite.** In the example below, the definite noun phrase *the neighbor* in Bundy's answer presupposes that Andrea can determine which neighbor Bundy is talking about.

> Andrea: Who's at the door?
>
> Bundy: It's <u>the neighbor</u>.

Bundy's answer is appropriate if she and Andrea have only one neighbor or have reason to expect a particular neighbor. If they have several neighbors and Bundy cannot assume that Andrea will be able to identify which neighbor is at the door, the answer to Andrea's question would be indefinite: *It's <u>a neighbor</u>.*

Pronouns and proper nouns are generally definite. Pronouns such as *you* and *we* usually refer to particular individuals who are identifiable in the context of the discourse. And a speaker who refers to someone by name (say, *Laura* or *Tony Blair)* assumes that the addressee will be able to determine the referents of those proper nouns. Still, there are exceptions. Clerks in a government office may say to each other:

> I have a Susie Schmidt here who hasn't paid her taxes since 1997.

Use of the indefinite article *a* marks *Susie Schmidt* as indefinite. In other words, the clerks can do this because neither the speaker nor the addressee knows the particular individual who goes by the name of Susie Schmidt.

Definiteness in English and many other languages is marked by the choice of articles (definite *the* versus indefinite *a*) or by demonstratives (*this* and *that*, both definite). Indefinite noun phrases in English are marked by *a* or *an* (*a furnace, an apartment building*) or by the absence of any article (*oil, fire, apartment buildings*). While the definite article can be used with singular and plural nouns (*the building, the buildings*), the indefinite article can be used only with singular nouns (*a building, *a buildings*). However, even though plural nouns don't take indefinite articles, they can still be indefinite.

Try it yourself: To determine how English expresses indefiniteness with plural noun phrases, examine the first words of sentences (3) and (6) in Version 1 of the Santa Clara Fire Department newspaper report on page 260.

Article choice is not always a way to mark definiteness. Some languages have only one article. Fijian has only one article, *na,* and it is definite. To mark indefiniteness, speakers of Fijian use the expression *e dua,* which means 'there is one.'

1. na   tuuraŋa   (definite)
   Article gentleman
   'the gentleman'

2. e dua   na   tuuraŋa   (indefinite)
   there is one Article gentleman
   'a gentleman'

Hindi, in contrast, has only an indefinite article *ek,* and a noun phrase with no article is interpreted as definite.

1. maĩ kitaab ḍʰũũṛʰ rahii tʰii   (definite)
   I   book   search -ing Past-tense
   'I was looking for the book.'

2. maĩ ek kitaab ḍʰũũṛʰ rahii tʰii   (indefinite)
   I   a book   search -ing Past-tense
   'I was looking for a book.'

Many languages do not have articles and must rely on other means to mark definiteness, if it is marked at all. Mandarin Chinese relies on word order. When the subject comes before the verb, as in 1 below, it is definite; if it follows the verb, as in 2, it is indefinite.

1. huǒchē lái   le   (definite)
   train   arrive New-situation
   'The train has arrived.'

2. lái   huǒchē le   (indefinite)
   arrive train   New-situation
   'A train has arrived.'

Other systems also exist. In Rotuman, spoken in the South Pacific, most nouns have two forms, one definite and one indefinite.

DEFINITE		INDEFINITE	
futi	'the banana'	füt	'a banana'
vaka	'the canoe'	vak	'a canoe'
rito	'the young shoot'	rjot	'a young shoot'

The indefinite form can be derived from the definite form through a set of phonological rules.

Definite vs. Given   Definiteness must be distinguished from givenness because a noun phrase can be *indefinite* and *new, definite* and *new, indefinite* and *given,* or *definite* and *given,* with the first and last combinations being the most common ones. Below, *a lecture* is indefinite and new, and *the lecturer* is definite and given.

> Last night, we went to the Hayden Planetarium for a lecture, and the lecturer fainted.

A noun phrase referring to new information can also be definite. The following sequence, in which *the plumber* is definite, is acceptable whether or not the speaker has introduced a particular identifiable plumber into the previous discourse.

> The kitchen faucet is leaking; we'd better call the plumber.

In certain circumstances, a noun phrase can be both *indefinite and given,* as with the underlined noun phrase in this example:

> I ate a hamburger for lunch—a hamburger, I might add, that was the worst I've ever eaten.

Clearly, definiteness and givenness are distinct categories of information structure.

Try it yourself: In Version 1 of the newspaper report on page 260, identify at least one noun phrase in each of the following categories: (a) indefinite and new; (b) definite and new; (c) indefinite and given; (d) definite and given.

Referential Expressions

A noun phrase is **referential** when it refers to a particular entity. In the first example below, the expression *an Italian with blue eyes* does not refer to anyone in particular and is therefore nonreferential. By contrast, in the second example, the same phrase does have a referent and is referential.

> Kate wants to marry an Italian with blue eyes, but she hasn't met one yet.   (nonreferential)

> Kate wants to marry an Italian with blue eyes; his name is Mario.   (referential)

Out of context, *Kate wants to marry an Italian with blue eyes* is ambiguous because nothing in the sentence indicates whether or not a particular Italian is intended. In everyday discourse, sentences of this type are rarely ambiguous, given the power of context to clarify.

Because referentiality and definiteness are not the same thing; a noun phrase can be

referential and definite—Where's <u>the key</u> to <u>the safe</u>?

referential and indefinite—She leased <u>a new Ford Bronco</u>.

nonreferential and definite—What's <u>the most intelligent thing</u> to do now?

nonreferential and indefinite—You need to buy <u>a new car</u>.

While pronouns and proper nouns are usually referential, certain pronouns such as *you, it, they,* and *one* are often nonreferential.

In this county, if <u>you</u> own a house <u>you</u> have to pay taxes.

<u>It</u> is widely suspected that the governor had links to the insurance industry.

<u>They</u>'re predicting thunderstorms tonight.

<u>One</u> just doesn't know what to do in such circumstances.

Because none of these pronouns refers to a particular entity, they are nonreferential.

Generic and Specific Expressions

A noun phrase may be *generic* or *specific* depending on whether it refers to a category or to particular members of a category. In the first example below, *The giraffe* is generic because it refers to the set of all giraffes; but in the second, which could have been uttered during a visit to a zoo, *The giraffe* must refer to a particular animal and is thus specific.

The giraffe has a long neck.

The giraffe has a sore foot.

In the first sentence, *The giraffe* is generic and definite, while *a long neck* is generic and indefinite. In the second sentence, *The giraffe* is specific and definite, and *a sore foot* is specific and indefinite. Thus, the generic/specific contrast differs from the definite/indefinite contrast.

Try it yourself: The sentence below appears in a U.S. Supreme Court decision about trucks on interstate highways in Iowa. Identify one underscored noun phrase that is specific and another that is generic. That leaves a third noun phrase. Is it specific or generic? Which of the noun phrases are definite and which indefinite? Are all the noun phrases referential?

Indeed, <u>the State</u> points to only <u>three ways</u> in which <u>the 55-foot single</u> is even arguably superior.

Categories of Information Structure

Information structure is not marked solely on noun phrases. Other parts of speech, verbs in particular, can represent given or new information and can also be contrastive. In the following exchange, the underlined verb represents contrastively marked new information.

> Jerry visits occasionally, but Sara <u>encamps</u> every holiday.

Similarly, prepositions can sometimes be marked for information structure. It is not difficult to come up with examples of contrastively marked prepositions.

> I said the book was *on* the table, not *under* it!

In this chapter, we concentrate almost exclusively on the marking of information structure on noun phrases, in part because the role of other constituents in the structure of discourse is still not well understood.

INFORMATION STRUCTURE: INTONATION, MORPHOLOGY, SYNTAX

Languages differ in how much pragmatic information they encode and in how they encode it. In many languages intonation is used to mark contrast. While intonation is an important tool for marking information structure in English, it is less important for information structure in languages such as French and Chinese. Other languages, such as Japanese, have function words whose sole purpose is to indicate pragmatic categories. Still others, including English, depend on syntactic structures such as passives to convey pragmatic information. Thus, different languages use different strategies to encode pragmatic information. What follows is a sampling of these strategies.

New-Information Stress

In English and some other languages, intonation is an important device for marking information. Generally, noun phrases representing new information receive stronger stress than those representing given information, and they are uttered on a slightly higher pitch than the rest of the sentence. This is called *new-information stress*.

> Aaron: Whose foot marks are these on the sofa?
>
> Bianca: They're *Lou's foot marks.*

English speakers also exploit stress to mark contrast.

> 1. Aaron: Are these your foot marks on the sofa?
>   Bianca: No, they're not mine, they're *Lou's.*
> 2. They told Hal he needed two more years to graduate, but they gave *Sara full clearance.*

Phonetically, new-information stress and contrastive stress are similar, but functionally they differ. English uses stress in complex ways, much more so than such languages as French and Chinese.

Information Structure Morphemes

Some languages have grammatical morphemes whose sole function is to mark categories of information structure. In Japanese, the function word *wa,* which is placed after noun phrases, marks either givenness or contrastiveness. When a noun phrase is neither given nor contrastive, it is marked with a different function word (usually *ga* for subjects and *o* for direct objects). That *wa* is a marker of given information is illustrated by the following exchange:

Kenn: basu ga   kimasuka
       bus   Subject come-Question
       'Is the bus coming?'

Kimiko: <u>basu</u> <u>wa</u>   kimasu
        bus   Given   coming-is
        'The bus is coming.'

In Kenn's question, *basu* could not be marked with *wa* unless he and Kimiko had been talking about the bus in the previous discourse. But in Kimiko's answer, *basu* is given information and must be marked with *wa.*

Japanese *wa* also marks contrastive information, as in the following sentence:

<u>basu</u> <u>wa</u>   kimasu   demo <u>takushi</u> <u>wa</u>   kimasen
bus   Contrast coming-is but taxi   Contrast coming-isn't
'The bus is coming. But the taxi isn't (coming).'

Here, *basu wa* need not represent given information, for *wa* can simply mark the fact that the noun phrase to which it is attached is in contrast with another noun phrase also marked with *wa* (*takushi* 'taxi').

Many other languages use function words to mark categories of information structure. This is the most transparent way of marking information structure. Such grammatical morphemes as Japanese *wa* do not affect the overall shape of a sentence. Rather, in a straightforward fashion, they point out which element of a sentence is given, which is contrastive, and so on.

Fronting

Among several syntactic operations that serve to mark information structure is *fronting.* Fronting operates in many languages, although its exact function varies from language to language. In English, it creates sentence 1 from the structure underlying sentence 2, which has the same meaning.

1. Lou I cannot tolerate.
2. I cannot tolerate Lou.

In English, one function of fronting is to mark givenness, and a fronted noun phrase must represent given information.

Avi: I heard that you really like mushrooms.
Bert: <u>Mushrooms</u> I'd kill for.

A noun phrase can be fronted if its referent is part of a set that has been mentioned previously in the discourse, even though the referent itself may not have been mentioned. In the following example, *mushrooms* is a hyponym of *vegetable,* which is mentioned in the question that immediately precedes the fronted noun phrase; the result is pragmatically acceptable.

Alex: What's your favorite vegetable?
Beth: Mushrooms I'm crazy about.

Fronted noun phrases are often contrastive in English.

Ali: Do you eat cauliflower?
Basho: I hate cauliflower, but <u>broccoli</u> I'm crazy about.

Fronted noun phrases do not always have the same function in other languages as they do in English. In Mandarin Chinese, fronted noun phrases are commonly used to represent the topic of the sentence.

1. zhèi běn   shū   pízi   hěn   hǎo kàn
   this Classifier book cover very good-looking
   'This book, the cover is nice looking.'

2. zhèi ge   zhǎnlǎnhuì wǒ kàndào hěn duō   yóuhuàr
   this Classifier exhibition I   see   very many   painting
   '(At) this exhibition, I saw many paintings.'

What is interesting about Chinese fronted noun phrases is that they do not necessarily have a semantic role in the rest of the sentence. In the following sentence, for example, *mógū* 'mushrooms' cannot be a patient because the sentence already has a patient: *zhèi ge dōngxi* 'that sort of thing.' Yet the sentence is both grammatical and pragmatically acceptable.

mógū   wǒ hěn xǐhuan chī zhèi ge   dōngxi
mushroom I   very like   eat this Classifier thing
'Mushrooms, I like to eat that sort of thing.'

Furthermore, fronted noun phrases do not need to be contrastive in Chinese, though they frequently are in English. The comparison of English and Chinese fronting illustrates an important point: a grammatical process such as a movement operation may have comparable syntactic properties in two languages, but its pragmatic functions may differ considerably.

Left-Dislocation

Left-dislocation is an operation that derives sentences such as 1 from the same underlying structures as basic sentences such as 2.

1. Holly, I can't stand her.

2. I can't stand Holly.

Though left-dislocation is syntactically similar to fronting, there are several differences between the two. In particular, a fronted noun phrase does not leave a pronoun in the sentence, whereas a left-dislocated noun phrase does.

> Holly I can't stand. (fronting)
>
> Holly, I can't stand her. (left-dislocation)

Unlike fronted noun phrases, a left-dislocated noun phrase is set off from the rest of the sentence by a very short pause, represented in writing by a comma. Left-dislocation is similar in nature and function to right-dislocation, which moves the noun phrases to the right of a sentence.

> I can't stand her, Holly.

In this discussion, we will concentrate on left-dislocation.

Left-dislocation is used primarily to reintroduce given information that has not been mentioned for a while. In the following long example, the speaker lists a number of people and comments on them. Hal, mentioned early in the discourse, is reintroduced in the last sentence. Because nothing has been said about him in the previous two sentences, the speaker reintroduces *Hal* as a left-dislocated noun phrase.

> I've kept in touch with lots of classmates. I still see Hal, who was my best friend in high school. And then there's Jim, my college roommate, and Stan and Sara, who I met as a sophomore at Ohio State. I really like Jim and Stan and Sara. But *Hal*, I can't stand him now.

In addition to reintroducing given information, left-dislocation is contrastive. In this example, *Hal* clearly contrasts with *Jim, Stan,* and *Sara.* As a result of its double function, left-dislocation is typically used when speakers go through lists and make comments about each individual element in the list. Some languages exploit left-dislocation more frequently than English does. In spoken colloquial French, left-dislocated noun phrases are considerably more frequent than the equivalent basic sentences.

> <u>Mon frère,</u> il s'en va en Mongolie.
> my   brother he is-going to Mongolia
> 'My brother, he is leaving for Mongolia.'

Right-dislocation, illustrated by the following sentence, is also common.

> J'sais   pas,   <u>moi,</u> c'qu'il veut.
> I know not   me   what-he wants
> 'Me, I don't know what he wants.'

Left-dislocation in colloquial French has a different function from the equivalent operation in English. In French, a left-dislocated noun phrase represents a topic. Left-dislocated noun phrases are particularly frequent when a new topic is introduced into the discourse (as in the first of the following examples) or when the speaker wishes to shift the topic of the discourse (as in the second example).

1. [Asking directions of a stranger in the street]

   Pardon,   <u>la   gare</u>,   où   est-elle?
   excuse-me the station where is it
   'Excuse me, where is the station?'

2. Pierre: <u>Moi</u>, j'aime bien les croissants.
           me   I like a lot the croissants
           'Me, I like croissants a lot.'

   Marie: Oui, mais <u>le pain frais</u>, c'est bon   aussi.
           yes   but   the bread fresh   it-is good too
           'Yes, but fresh bread is also good.'

The pragmatic function of left-dislocation is thus considerably broader in French than in English.

It Clefts and WH Clefts

Clefting transformations are used in English and many other languages to mark information structure. In the following examples, sentence 1 is an *it*-cleft sentence, sentence 2 is a WH-cleft sentence, and sentence 3 is the basic sentence that corresponds to 1 and 2.

1. It was Nick that Stan saw at the party.   (*it*-cleft)

2. Who Stan saw at the party was Nick.   (WH-cleft)

3. Stan saw Nick at the party.

It-cleft sentences are of the form *It is/was . . . that,* in which what comes between the first part and the second part of the construction is the clefted noun phrase, prepositional phrase (*It was in March that she last visited*), or adverb (*It's only recently that she's learned to sing*). WH-cleft constructions can be of the form *WH-word . . . is/was/will be,* in which the WH-word is usually *what.* In WH-cleft constructions, the clefted noun phrase, clefted prepositional phrase, or clefted adverb is placed after the verb *be,* and the rest of the clause is placed between the two parts of the construction. Other variants of WH-cleft sentences also exist, as in these examples:

<u>The one who</u> saw Nick at the party <u>was</u> Stan.

Nick <u>is who</u> Stan saw at the party.

Besides *is* and *was,* some other forms of *be* may also occur in clefts.

Both *it*-cleft and WH-cleft constructions are used to mark givenness. In an *it*-cleft construction, the clefted phrase presents new information, and the rest of the sentence is given information. Thus, the information question in 1 below can be answered with 2, in which the answer to the question (that is, the new information) is clefted, but not with 3, because the clefted element is not the requested new information.

1. Who did Stan see at the party?

2. It was Nick that Stan saw at the party.
3. *It was Stan who saw Nick at the party.

That the part of the sentence following *that/who* in a cleft sentence presents given information is illustrated by the fact that it can refer to something just mentioned in the previous sentence. In the following example, the second sentence is a cleft construction in which the elements following *that* are simply repeated from the previous sentence in the discourse.

> Alice told me that Stan saw someone at the party that he knew from his high school days. It turns out it was Nick <u>that Stan saw at the party</u>.

Clearly, the element following *that* in a cleft sentence represents given information.

WH-cleft constructions are similar to *it*-cleft constructions. In WH-cleft sentences, the new information comes after the verb *be,* and the rest of the clause is placed between the WH-word and the *be* verb.

1. What did Stan see at the party?
2. What Stan saw was Nick salsa dancing.

Question 1 could not be answered with either of the following clefted sentences because in neither 3 nor 4 is the clefted noun phrase the new information.

3. *The one who saw Nick salsa dancing was Stan.
4. *Where Stan saw Nick was at the party.

The rest of a WH-clefted sentence marks given information, as in an *it*-clefted sentence. The following sentence pair, in which given information is underlined, illustrates this fact.

> I liked her latest novel very much. In particular, what <u>I liked about it</u> was the character development.

Both *it*-clefting and WH-clefting highlight which element is new information and which element is given information.

In addition, both constructions can mark contrast. Consider the following two sequences. In 1 (whose second sentence is an *it*-cleft construction) and 2 (whose second sentence is a WH-cleft), the new information can readily be understood as contrastive. Possible implied information is provided in square brackets after each example.

1. Alice said Stan saw someone at the party that he knew from his high school days. It turns out it was Nick that Stan saw at the party. [. . . not Larry, as you might have thought.]
2. I liked her latest novel very much. In particular, what I liked about it was the way the characters' personalities are developed. [I liked the character development more than the style of writing.]

You might wonder why English should have two constructions with the same function. Languages usually exploit different structures for different purposes—and, indeed, there is a subtle difference in the uses for these two constructions. An *it*-cleft construction can be used to mark given information that the listener or reader is not necessarily thinking about. In a WH-cleft construction, though, the listener or reader must be thinking about the given information. Thus, it is possible to begin a narrative with an *it*-cleft construction but not with a WH-cleft construction. The first sentence below is an *it*-cleft construction and would be an acceptable opening for a historical narrative; but the second sentence is a WH-cleft construction and would not normally make a good beginning.

> It was to gain their independence from Britain that the colonists started the Revolution.

> *What the colonists started the Revolution to gain was their independence from Britain.

The first sentence is an acceptable opening because it does not necessarily assume that the reader has in mind the given information (*the colonists started the Revolution*) when the narrative begins. The second sentence does assume that the given information (*[what] the colonists started the Revolution to gain*) is in the reader's mind, and thus does not make a good opening sentence.

The difference between *it*-cleft and WH-cleft constructions shows that given information is not an absolute notion. There may be different types of givenness: information that the addressee knows but is not necessarily thinking about at the moment and information that the addressee both knows and is thinking about.

Passives

As with other languages that have a passive construction, the choice between an active sentence and its passive equivalent can be exploited in English to mark information structure. Compare the following sentences:

1. Bureaucrats could easily store and retrieve data about the citizenry. (active)
2. Data about the citizenry could easily be stored and retrieved by bureaucrats. (passive)
3. Data about the citizenry could easily be stored and retrieved. (passive)

Of these three sentences, all of which can represent the same situation, sentence 1 is active, while the other two are passive structures. In 2, the agent is expressed (*bureaucrats*), and the structure is called an *agent passive* construction. But no agent is expressed in 3, and so it is called an *agentless passive*.

Agentless passives and agent passives are used for specific purposes. A sentence is expressed as an agentless passive if the agent is particularly unimportant in the action or state that the sentence represents—for example, when the agent is a generic entity whose identity is irrelevant to the point of the sentence.

> A new shopping mall is being built near the airport.

> These laws, however noxious, are rarely enforced.

In the first sentence, the agent is likely to be some real-estate developer; in the second sentence, police authorities. In each case, the exact identity of the agent either is known or is irrelevant to the situation represented by the sentence. In spoken language, agentless passives are often equivalent to active sentences with an indefinite and nonreferential pronoun *they,* as in these examples:

> They're building a new shopping mall near the airport.
> They issue new Christmas stamps every year.

An agent passive construction is used if a noun phrase other than the agent is the given information. Imagine a news report that begins as follows:

> The World Health Organization held its annual meeting last week in Geneva.

This sentence establishes the annual meeting as given information for the rest of the report. If the next sentence uses the noun phrase *the meeting,* that phrase will likely occur in subject position because it represents given information. If the noun phrase *the meeting* does not have the semantic role of agent in the next sentence, the sentence is likely to be expressed as a passive construction in order to allow *the meeting* to be the grammatical subject.

> The meeting was organized by health administrators from 50 countries.

This generalization is not absolute, and there is nothing fundamentally wrong with a sequence in which the second sentence is active rather than the passive predicted by the generalization, as shown below:

> The World Health Organization held its annual meeting last week in Geneva. Health administrators from 50 countries organized the meeting.

But the equivalent sequence with a passive second sentence seems to flow better and may be easier to understand:

> The World Health Organization held its annual meeting last week in Geneva. The meeting was organized by health administrators from 50 countries.

In English, the choice of a passive sentence over its active counterpart is regulated by information structure. Specifically, agentless passives are used when the agent is either known or not particularly significant (as in this very sentence). Agent passives (or *by* passives, as they are sometimes called) are used when a noun phrase other than the agent of the sentence is more prominent as given information than the agent itself.

Try it yourself: In the following passive sentences, identify the two agentless ones and say what the agent is likely to be. For the agent passive, specify the agent.

1. State governors were named by the president.
2. Most people would feel fear if their capital were attacked.
3. The Japanese post office has been hurt as stock markets fell.

Not all languages have a passive construction. Chinese and Samoan, for example, do not. Such languages have other ways of saying what English speakers express with the passive. In Samoan, when the agent of a sentence is not important, it is simply not expressed; the sentence remains an active structure.

ʔua   ʔoteŋia   le teiŋe
Present-tense   scold   the young-woman
'The young woman is being scolded.' (Literally: 'Is scolding the young woman.')

Word Order

Many languages use the sequential order of noun phrases to mark differences in information structure. English cannot use the full resources of word order for this purpose because it uses word order to mark subjects and direct objects (see Chapter 5). In the sentence *The cat is chasing the dog,* the word order indicates who is doing the chasing and who is being chased. If we invert the two noun phrases, the semantics of the sentence (who is agent and who is patient) changes: *The dog is chasing the cat.*

In a language like Russian, however, we can scramble the noun phrases without changing the semantics. All the following sentences mean the same thing. (Note that š is pronounced like *sh* in English *ship.*)

1. koška presleduet sobaku
   cat   is chasing dog
2. sobaku presleduet koška
3. presleduet koška sobaku   'The cat is chasing the dog.'
4. presleduet sobaku koška
5. koška sobaku presleduet
6. sobaku koška presleduet

In each of these sentences we know *who* is doing *what* to *whom* because the inflections on the noun vary. The *-u* ending of *sobaku* 'dog' marks it as the direct object (if it were the subject, it would be *sobaka),* and the *-a* ending of *koška* 'cat' marks it as the subject (as direct object, it would be *košku).*

The differences among these versions of the same sentence reside in their information structure. More precisely, in Russian, word order marks givenness. The information question *Što koška presleduet?* 'What is the cat chasing?' can only be answered as follows:

koška presleduet sobaku
cat   is-chasing dog
'The cat is chasing the dog.'

On the other hand, the question *Što presleduet sobaku?* 'What is chasing the dog?' must be answered as follows:

sobaku presleduet koška
dog   is-chasing cat
'The cat is chasing the dog.'

Thus, what comes first in the Russian sentence is not the subject but the given information, and what comes last is the new information. In answer to the question *What is the cat chasing?*, *the dog* is new information and comes at the end of the Russian sentence. By contrast, in answer to the question *What is chasing the dog?*, *the cat* is new information and comes last in the sentence. Word order in Russian, as in many other languages, is thus used to mark givenness. Similar explanations could be offered for the other variants of the Russian sentence we have cited, but we will not develop them here. (See Exercise 8–9 on page 288.)

Typically, in languages that exploit word order to encode pragmatic information, syntactic constructions such as passives, *it*-clefts, and WH-clefts do not exist (or are rare). Russian has a grammatical construction that resembles the English passive, but it is rarely used. The reason is simple: given the rich inflectional system for marking grammatical relations, word order is left free to mark information structure, and there is no need to use complex structures like passives to mark givenness. Passives are useful in languages that exploit word order for other purposes and thus cannot manipulate it to indicate pragmatic information.

THE RELATIONSHIP OF SENTENCES TO DISCOURSE: PRAGMATICS

We have outlined some of the basic notions needed to describe how information is structured in discourse and have analyzed a number of constructions in terms of information structure. From the discussion in this and previous chapters, it should be clear that the syntactic structure of any language is driven by two factors. On the one hand, syntax must encode semantic structure: the syntactic structure of a sentence must enable language users to identify who does what to whom—the agent of a sentence, the patient, and other semantic roles. On the other hand, syntax must encode information structure: which element of a noun phrase is given information, which is new information, which can be easily identified by the addressee, which cannot, and so on. Schematically, the relationship is as follows:

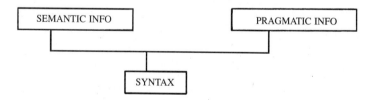

Syntax is thus used to convey two kinds of information: semantic information and pragmatic information.

Computers and Pragmatics

You've seen in this chapter that a thorough acquaintance with pragmatics is needed to understand how language works. Eventually a thorough understanding of pragmatics will prove important for speech recognition and, to a lesser extent, speech synthesis. To date, however, pragmatics has not been as well explored in computational linguistics as have morphological, lexical, phonological, grammatical, and even semantic features of texts.

One reason for the relative neglect of pragmatics is that modeling the world knowledge and the discourse knowledge that speakers rely on when producing and understanding spoken and written texts is far more challenging than creating models of structural aspects of language such as morphology and syntax. Another reason is that the kinds of linguistic features by which some pragmatic categories are realized are not always expressed in texts in ways that computers can readily track.

As we have seen in this chapter, speakers base several aspects of expression on their beliefs about what addressees know and what is in the forefront of their minds. This is true in marking noun phrases as definite or indefinite, in choosing active or passive voice, and in indicating contrast by intonation, for example. While these three features have some representation in a text, others such as given and new information have little or no textual realization and would be extremely challenging or even impossible for a computer to identify.

If you've ever used a grammar checker, you know that even rudimentary ones readily spot passive-voice verbs (by identifying forms of the verb *be* coupled with—though not necessarily adjacent to—a past participle, as in *is needed, are realized,* and *has not been explored,* all of which appear in the first two paragraphs of this section). What existing checkers cannot do is distinguish between passives that effectively serve a pragmatic function such as topicalization and passives that do not. As a result, a writer who uses a grammar checker may find that it flags every passive-voice verb, urging the writer to consider recasting them all as actives. If a writer rewrote all passives as actives, the rewritten sentences would remain grammatical, but the changes could damage the pragmatic structure of the text. (Exercise 8–7 on page 286–287 asks you to consider revising the passives in a short text.)

Computer programs can identify pragmatic categories only if they are marked in the text. Thus, the Japanese function word *wa* can be automatically identified as easily as an English passive. Likewise, most English noun phrases can automatically be identified as definite or indefinite. But other categories—for example, topic, givenness, and referentiality—cannot be identified automatically and must be identified by a speaker of the language. If researchers wanted to make use of such categories, they would have to have their texts tagged to reflect those categories. To do this, a program would tag each *potential* item—say, all referring expressions—as "given" and then present a human editor with a menu of alternatives that could be substituted for the tentative tag, much as a spell checker does. Once such categories were tagged on the referring expressions in a corpus, researchers could explore related matters, relying on the computer's capacity for speed and accuracy.

For example, suppose a corpus contained referring expressions that had been manually tagged as given or new. It would then be a simple matter to calculate the number of given and new references for any group of texts in the corpus—for example, for conversations or for news reportage in newspapers. It turns out that different kinds of texts differ significantly in the average number of given and new references they contain.

Figure 8–1 shows two sets of relations: those between given and new information in three kinds of text and those among the three kinds of text. For example, conversation has three times as many given noun phases as new ones. Academic prose, by contrast, has about half as many given noun phrases as new ones. Likewise, while conversation and news reportage have approximately the same number of noun phrases in each 200 words of text, the proportion of given and new noun phrases is reversed in these kinds of text. Conversationalists use noun phrases that are mostly given. News reportage introduces new referents about twice as often as it refers to given information. A good many noun phrases in conversation are first-person and second-person pronouns, which are of course given information. (By contrast, the use of first-person and second-person pronouns in news reportage is virtually limited to quoted speech.)

As Figure 8–1 shows, a second kind of information can be drawn from counts of given and new referring expressions (that is, noun phrases) in different kinds of text. For example, the number of new noun phrases is relatively low in conversation as compared with academic prose or news reportage. Not surprisingly, news reportage contains more than twice the number of new references and so conversation, and so does academic prose.

To take another example, if third-person pronouns in a corpus have been assigned an index that matches their referent to a preceding noun phrase, then computer programs can track the distance between them and their antecedents. For this purpose, one useful measure is the number of intervening noun phrases. By this measure, it turns out that different kinds of texts have significantly different distances intervening between third-person pronouns and their antecedents. As Figure 8–2 on page 282 shows, conversation has fewer than half the number of intervening referring expressions (that is, noun phrases) that we find in academic prose and news reportage. In part this reflects the fact that conversation is produced extemporaneously, and speakers accommodate the fact that their addressees must keep track of referents identified only by third-person pronouns (he—who? it—what?).

With suitably tagged corpora, a good deal can be learned about the character of different kinds of texts. That information will prove critical in speech recognition, machine translation, and other real-world applications of linguistics where computers and language are intertwined.

Figure 8-1

Average number of given and new referring expressions in three kinds of texts

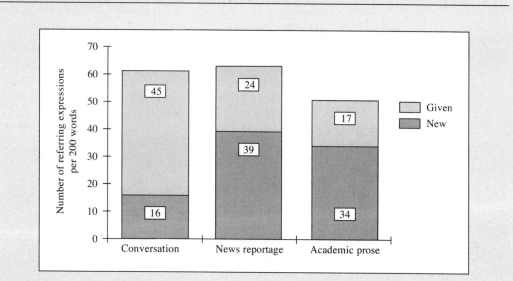

Source: D. Biber, S. Conrad, R. Reppen, *Corpus Linguistics* (Cambridge: Cambridge University Press, 1998).

Figure 8-2

Average distance between pronouns and their antecedents, measured in number of intervening referring expressions

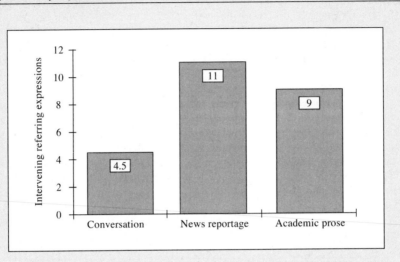

Source: D. Biber, S. Conrad, R. Reppen, *Corpus Linguistics* (Cambridge: Cambridge University Press, 1998).

SUMMARY

- Pragmatics is concerned with the encoding of information structure—the relative significance of different elements in a clause, principally noun phrases. It treats the relationship of sentences to their discourse environment.

- Relational categories include *givenness* (whether a piece of information is new or already exists in the discourse context), *topic* (the center of attention), and *contrast* (whether or not a piece of information is contrasted with another piece).

- Nonrelational notions include *definiteness* (whether or not the referent of a noun phrase is identifiable) and *referentiality* (whether or not a noun phrase has a referent).

- Some syntactic operations serve to mark certain elements of sentences for pragmatic categories. In English, fronting, left-dislocation, *it*-cleft, wh-cleft, and passivization single out particular noun phrases as sentence topics or as given information or new information.

- Contrast is marked through sentence stress and is a secondary function of certain operations such as fronting.

- Many languages exploit word order or grammatical morphemes to mark information structure.

- The functions of a particular transformation or information-structure device may differ from language to language because each language favors particular strategies over others.

- Syntax encodes two types of information: semantic information (the semantic role of a noun phrase) and pragmatic information (the relative significance of noun phrases in a discourse).

WHAT DO YOU THINK? REVISITED

❖ *The international student.* Conventional wisdom suggests that definite articles are used to refer to particular persons, places, and things, and that seems correct, as in *the Eiffel Tower* and *the movie*. But it is inaccurate to say that indefinite articles are used to refer to *any* person, place, or thing (i.e., not a particular one). Sure, that's one function of an indefinite article *(I'm looking for <u>a present</u> in the $50 range for Tony; got <u>a suggestion</u>?)*. Commonly, though, the use of an indefinite article signals that the speaker believes the addressee does not have the item referred to already in mind *(I bought <u>a present</u> for Tony after I got <u>a suggestion</u> from Barry)*. In other words, an indefinite noun phrase can signal that an item (person, place, or thing) is new to the discourse. Once the item is in the addressee's mind, speakers use definite noun phrases *(the present, the suggestion, it)* to signal that the item is given information and the speaker believes the addressee can identify it. In the course of a conversation (or newspaper article or other piece of discourse), it is routine for an initial mention of something to be indefinite and subsequent mentions to be definite.

❖ *The ESL class discussion.* In several senses, the active and passive versions of the sentence about the Anaheim Angels mean the same thing. For example, if one version is true, the other must also be true; if one is false, the other must be false. Also, they both describe the same situation in the real world. There is no more and no less information in one version or the other. Still, the two sentences would not be used in the same circumstances because they focus on different noun phrases. The active version *(The Anaheim Angels won the 2002 World Series)* says something about the Anaheim Angels. We could say the sentence is *about* the Angels. The passive version *(The 2002 World Series was won by the Anaheim Angels)* is *about* the 2002 World Series. Thus, although the two sentences mean the same thing, they present different perspectives. Consider the two requests below, and decide whether the active and passive versions above could be used equally well as answers:

  i. Tell me something good about the Anaheim Angels.
  ii. Tell me something about the recent history of the World Series.

Speakers (and writers) tend to be efficient, and while two sentences might *mean* the same thing, they can't necessarily be used interchangeably in all discourse contexts. There are different versions because there are different purposes and situations.

❖ *Your classmate.* English generally has subjects before verbs and verbs before objects *(I like him!)*, but to express contrast an object can sometimes be moved into first position before the subject.

EXERCISES

Based on English

8-1 In an article called "Ellen's 'Heart Issue': A Friend's Report," actress Kathy Najimy writes as follows about her first meeting with Ellen DeGeneres. After examining the passage (sentence numbers have been added), answer the questions that follow:

> (1) I met Ellen three or four years ago when I was a guest on her show. (2) She was funny, smart and charming, and I was moved by her vulnerability and what she was going through in regards to her sexuality. (3) We would sit in the trailer and talk about what was happening to her personally and politically. (4) It was interesting to me because I know lots of gay people, and I know lots of famous people, but I had never known anyone who was famous and gay and struggling with what to do about it. [*Los Angeles Times,* "Calendar," December 21, 1997, p. 79]

- **a.** In 1, is the pronoun *I* given or new information? Explain the basis for your answer.
- **b.** In 2, is *She* given or new information? Explain the basis for your answer.
- **c.** In 3, is *We* given or new information? Explain the basis for your answer.
- **d.** In 4, is *It* given or new information, and what constituent does *It* refer to?
- **e.** Identify the noun phrase that is the topic in sentences 2, 3, and 4.
- **f.** From your answers to b through e above, what inference can you draw about topics in this paragraph?
- **g.** From the examples you have just examined and the other pronouns in the passage, would you say that personal pronouns generally represent given information or new information?
- **h.** In 1, is *Ellen* given or new information? Definite or indefinite? Explain.
- **i.** In 1, whose show does *her show* refer to? Is *her show* definite or indefinite?
- **j.** List *all* indefinite noun phrases in the passage. (Remember that pronouns are noun phrases.)
- **k.** Prior to its mention in 3, *the trailer* has not been mentioned, so how do you explain that it is definite?

8-2 Examine the passage below and answer the questions that follow:

> (1) Beginning in 1999, the Rose Bowl will no longer have first shot at the top teams from the Big Ten and Pac-10 football conferences. (2) Instead, the "Bowl Alliance," which aims each year to match the top two teams in the country for the national title, will decide who goes where. (3) The alliance, a cooperative venture among six of the nation's strongest football conferences, has a seven-year deal with ABC Sports, which will televise the title game. (4) This agreement assures each conference champion and Notre Dame a berth in one of four bowl games—the Rose, Orange, Fiesta or Sugar—with the national championship game annually rotated among the four venues. [Adapted from an advertising supplement in the *Los Angeles Times* "Calendar," December 21, 1997, p. M]

- **a.** Identify two noun phrases that are referential and two that are not.
- **b.** Identify any contrastive noun phrases in the passage.

c. In 4, *This agreement* is given information and is marked definite. What noun phrase in 3 has the same referent as *this agreement* but is indefinite? Explain why the first of these noun phrases is indefinite and the second definite even though they have identical referents.

d. From the passage, identify a noun phrase in each of the following categories:
  (i) referential and definite
  (ii) referential and indefinite
  (iii) nonreferential and definite
  (iv) nonreferential and indefinite

8-3 Consider the following text as a complete story in a newspaper. Analyze each sentence in its context and state what is odd about it in terms of information structure.

(1) As for the Santa Clara Fire Department, it evacuated two apartment buildings at the corner of Country Club Drive and Fifth Avenue at 3 A.M. last Sunday. (2) Nancy Jenkins had discovered a furnace in the basement of a building at the corner of Country Club Drive and Fifth Avenue, and the furnace was leaking oil. (3) What the firefighters did was to spray chemical foam over the oil for several hours. (4) It was by 8 A.M. last Sunday that the situation was under control. (5) What someone had averted was any danger of the explosion or the fire, and as for a leaky furnace, it was sealed. (6) What the residents of the two apartment buildings at the corner of Country Club Drive and Fifth Avenue were given in the Country Club High School gymnasium was temporary shelter. (7) Possession of their apartments was regained by the residents of the two apartment buildings at the corner of Country Club Drive and Fifth Avenue at 5 P.M. last Sunday.

8-4 Choose a short article (approximately one newspaper column) or an excerpt of an article from the front page of a newspaper. Identify all the sentences that have undergone a syntactic operation of some kind (such as passivization or clefting). In each case, explain the most likely reason for using a transformed sentence instead of the equivalent basic sentence.

8-5 In certain dialects of English, a syntactic operation moves a noun phrase to the beginning of its clause. It derives sentence (1) from the same underlying structure as the basic sentence (2):

1) A bottle of champagne and caviar he wants.

2) He wants a bottle of champagne and caviar.

The operation is called "Yiddish movement" because it is characteristic of the English dialect spoken by native speakers of Yiddish. Yiddish movement is syntactically similar to fronting but differs in its pragmatic function. Here are three pragmatic contexts in which Yiddish movement is appropriate. On the basis of these data, describe succinctly the pragmatic function of Yiddish movement.

a) Speaker A: What does he want?
   Speaker B: A bottle of champagne and caviar he wants!

b) Speaker A: How's your daughter?
   Speaker B: So many worries she causes me to have!

c) Speaker A: Are you willing to help me?
   Speaker B: A finger I would not lift for you!

Compare in particular the following interactions. In the first, the answer can undergo Yiddish movement; in the second, it cannot.

d) Speaker A: Who is Deborah going to marry?

   Speaker B: A scoundrel Deborah is going to marry!

e) Speaker A: Who is going to marry Deborah?

   Speaker B: *Deborah a scoundrel is going to marry!

8-6   Below is an excerpt, taken and slightly adapted from a U.S. Supreme Court case (*Kassel v. Consolidated Freightways Corp.*); some noun phrases have been underscored and the sentences numbered. Read it and answer the questions that follow.

> (1) None of these findings is seriously disputed by Iowa. (2) Indeed, the State points to only three ways in which the 55-foot single is even arguably superior: singles take less time to be passed and to clear intersections; they may back up for longer distances; and they are somewhat less likely to jackknife. (3) The first two of these characteristics are of limited relevance on modern interstate highways. (4) As the District Court found, the negligible difference in the time required to pass, and to cross intersections, is insignificant on 4-lane divided highways because passing does not require crossing into oncoming traffic lanes, and interstates have few, if any, intersections. (5) The concern over backing capability also is insignificant because it seldom is necessary to back up on an interstate. (6) In any event, no evidence suggested any difference in backing capability between the 60-foot doubles that Iowa permits and the 65-foot doubles that it bans. (7) Similarly, although doubles tend to jackknife somewhat more than singles, 65-foot doubles actually are less likely to jackknife than 60-foot doubles.

a. Using notions of given and new information, explain how you know in sentence 2 that *the State* refers to Iowa.

b. Identify one underscored noun phrase in each of these categories: (i) generic and definite; (ii) specific; (iii) definite; (iv) generic and indefinite; (v) definite and referential; (vi) indefinite and referential;(vii) given and definite; (viii) given and indefinite; (ix) indefinite and new.

c. In light of the discussion of the relationship between indefinite and new, on the one hand, and definite and given, on the other, explain why these indefinite noun phrases in sentence 7 represent given information: *doubles, singles, 65-foot doubles, 60-foot singles.*

d. Identify the noun phrase that is the topic of sentences 1, 3, 4, and 5.

e. Sentence 1 uses the passive voice. The active voice equivalent is, *Iowa does not seriously dispute any of these findings.* Which noun phrase is topicalized in the passive-voice version? Given the topic that you have just identified, what is the paragraph preceding this excerpt likely to be about?

8-7   Examine the passage that follows and note the underscored passive-voice verbs. Then offer a pragmatic reason the writer may have had in using each passive. Next, for any clauses or sentences whose passive voice you cannot justify, rewrite them using an active-voice verb. Finally, consider your revised passage, and judge whether the text is more pragmatically effective than the original. Explain your answer.

One consequence of the ideological position that individuals are the basis of society is that these individuals <u>must be considered</u> to be equal to each other. As <u>will be discussed</u> below under the topic of face systems, this egalitarianism of Utilitarian discourse <u>is not applied</u> to all human beings but only to "those capable of being improved by free and equal discussion" (Mill 1990:271–2). That is to say, this egalitarianism <u>is applied</u> only to members of the Utilitarian discourse system. [Adapted from Ron Scollon and Suzanne Wong Scollon, *Intercultural Communication* (Malden, MA: Blackwell, 1995, p. 110)]

Based on Languages Other Than English

8-8   As in Russian, word order in Spanish is used to encode information structure. The constituents of a sentence may be ordered in a variety of ways, as shown by the following examples from Castilian Spanish, all of which can describe the same event. (S = subject; V = verb; O = direct object)

Consuelo envió el paquete. (SVO)
Consuelo sent   the package

Envió Consuelo el paquete. (VSO)
sent   Consuelo the package

Envió el paquete   Consuelo. (VOS)
sent   the package Consuelo

El paquete   lo envoi   Consuelo. (OVS)
the package it sent   Consuelo

'Consuelo sent the package.'

Consider the following conversational exchanges, focusing on the order of constituents in the answers.

1) Q: ¿Qué hizo Consuelo?
what did Consuelo
'What did Consuelo do?'

A: Consuelo preparó la sangria.
Consuelo prepared the sangria
'Consuelo made the sangria.'

2) Q: ¿Quién comió mi bocadillo?
who   ate   my sandwich
'Who ate my sandwich?'

A: Tu bocadillo lo comió Consuelo.
your sandwich it ate   Consuelo
'Consuelo ate your sandwich.'

3) Q: ¿A quién dió Consuelo este regalo?
to whom gave Consuelo this present
'Who did Consuelo give this present to?'

A: Este regalo lo dió   Consuelo a su madre.
this present it gave Consuelo to her mother
'Consuelo gave this present to her mother.'

4) Q: ¿Que pasó?
    what occurred
    'What happened?'

    A: Se murió Consuelo.
       died   Consuelo
       'Consuelo died.'

5) Q: ¿Recibió Consuelo el premio?
    received Consuelo the prize
    'Did Consuelo get the prize?'

    A: No, el premio lo recibió Paquita.
       no the prize it received Paquita
       'No, *Paquita* got the prize.'

6) Q: ¿Recibió Consuelo esta carta?
    received Consuelo this letter
    'Did Consuelo get this letter?'

    A: No, Consuelo recibió este paquete.
       no Consuelo received this package
       'No, Consuelo got this *package*.'

7) Q: Recibió Consuelo el premio?
    received Consuelo the prize
    'Did Consuelo get the prize?'

    A: Si, el premio lo recibió Consuelo.
       yes the prize it received Consuelo
       'Yes, Consuelo got the prize.'

a. On the basis of these data, describe how word order is used to mark information structure in Spanish statements (but not in questions). In particular, state which categories of information structure are marked through which word order possibility. Make the statement of your rules as general as possible.

b. Notice that in certain sentences the pronoun *lo* 'it' appears before the verb. What is the syntactic rule that dictates when it should and should not appear? Which rule of English does the presence of the pronoun in these sentences remind you of?

8-9 In light of the function of Russian word order, provide an information question (in English) to which sentences 5 and 6 on p. 278 would be pragmatically acceptable Russian answers.

8-10 Examine the Japanese utterances below, made while two friends are waiting at a bus stop. Explain why Yumiko uses *basu ga* to refer to the bus, while Kimiko uses *basu wa*.

Yumiko:	basu	ga	kimasu	
	bus	Subject	coming-is	'The bus is coming.'

Kimiko:	basu	wa	konde-imas	
	bus	Given	crowded-is	'The bus is crowded.'

8-11 Tongan has an operation that incorporates the direct object (Object) into the verb, forming a verb-noun compound. It generates a sentence like (a) from the underlying structure of the basic sentence (b):

a) na?a   ku inu pia   (Object incorporated)
Past-tense I drink beer
'I drank beer.' (literally: 'I beer-drank.')

b) na?a   ku inu ?a   e   pia   (Object not incorporated)
Past-tense I drink Object the beer
'I drank the/a beer.'

Below are three more examples of object-incorporated constructions (translated loosely to highlight the meaning of the Tongan sentence):

?oku   nau fie kai ika   (Object incorporated)
Present-tense they hungry-for fish
'They are fish-hungry.'

na?a   ma sio faiva   (Object incorporated)
Past-tense we see movie
'We (went) movie-watching.'

?oku   ne fa?u hiva kakala   (Object incorporated)
Present-tense she compose love-song
'She is love-song composing.'

An incorporated direct object cannot be followed by a restrictive relative clause, but a direct object that has not been incorporated can be. Compare:

*na?a   ku inu pia [na?a   nau omai]   (Object incorporated)
Past-tense I drink beer Past-tense they give-me
'I drank beer [that they gave me].'

na?a   ku inu ?a   e pia [na?a   nau omai]   (Object not incorporated)
Past-tense I drink Object the beer Past-tense they give-me
'I drank the/a beer [that they gave me].'

Assuming that restrictive relative clauses have the same function in Tongan and English, describe the pragmatic function of Tongan object incorporation.

Especially for Educators and Future Teachers

8-12 To jog your students' memories about what constitutes given and new information and how information status affects the marking of a noun phrase as definite or indefinite, you offer this short report: *Last weekend I went to <u>a</u> wedding. <u>The</u> bride and groom were friends of mine.* Then you give your students these opening lines (below) from a newspaper article about Annika Sorenstam (adapted from the *Los Angeles Times,* March 20, 2003). You instruct them to fill in the blanks with *a/an* or *the,* as appropriate. Using a level of explanation you deem appropriate for your students, tell a classmate how you would teach your students about their ability to restore definite or indefinite articles to the piece.

The best female golfer in the world is standing at ___ grill, on ___ black rubber mat, ___ squadron of pots and pans flying in formation on hooks above her head. Annika Sorenstam feels very much at home as she conducts ___ tour of ___ kitchen at the Lake Nona resort, where her thoughts are far removed from her world of professional golf.

In ___ kitchen, it's not Pak or Webb or Inkster on her mind. It's crab cakes, stuffed mushrooms and tiramisu. That's why chef Gary Hoffman handed her 60 fillets to sear for ___ recent evening meal in ___ club's dining room. Sorenstam also knows how to carve ___ flower out of ___ wedge of melon, the easiest way to peel potatoes, and how to whip up rice pilaf.

Here's ___ story she enjoys telling. One evening at dinner, ___ club member enjoyed his meal. "He said, 'Bring out the chef,'" Sorenstam said. "So Gary came out and ___ member said, 'No, not that chef, the other one.' So I came out."

8-13 In a dictionary appropriate to your current or prospective students (or a desk dictionary you use yourself), examine the entries for *a* and *the* to identify which definition among the several listed for each word best matches your understanding as discussed in this chapter. Then assess whether those definitions adequately represent the facts about indefinite and definite articles as you understand them. If they don't, write an amended definition at a level appropriate for your students.

OTHER RESOURCES

- **Voices Demonstration Page: http://www.att.com/aspg/odemo.html**

  In an earlier chapter, you may have tried this Web site to hear a demonstration of speech synthesis, and you may have been impressed with the synthesizer's ability to produce the consonantal and vocalic sounds of the sentence you submitted. It's worth returning to the site to submit sentences that illustrate some information structure devices from this chapter, for example, left-dislocation or contrast. Judge for yourself to what extent this speech synthesis engine (the WATSON Flex Talk™) captures the intonation that conveys the pragmatic information in the sentences you submit.

SUGGESTIONS FOR FURTHER READING

- **Geoffrey N. Leech. 1983.** *Principles of Pragmatics* (London: Longman). An accessible introduction to pragmatics.
- **Kenneth R. Rose & Gabriele Kasper, eds. 2001.** *Pragmatics in Language Teaching* (Cambridge: Cambridge University Press). Especially for language teachers and those learning a second language, this multi-authored set of essays is useful in emphasizing matters often overlooked in language learning and language teaching.
- **George Yule. 1996.** *Pragmatics* (Oxford: Oxford University Press). A brief and accessible introduction to pragmatics, appearing in a series designed to introduce students to various linguistic subfields. Besides the material covered in the current chapter of this text, Yule's book also treats material covered in chapters 6 and 9.

ADVANCED READING

Overviews of the issues addressed in this chapter can be found in Brown and Yule (1983), Lambrecht (1994), Foley and Van Valin (1985), Givón (1979a), and Chafe (1976). A very thoughtful discussion of topics discussed in this chapter can be found in Chafe (1994). The papers in Givón (1979b) and Li (1976) investigate the interaction of syntax and pragmatics in various languages, while Chafe (1970) examines this interaction in English. Givenness and related topics are discussed in Prince (1979), definiteness in Lyons (1999). The discussion of *it*-cleft and WH-cleft constructions in this chapter relies on Prince (1978), and the discussion of fronting and Yiddish movement on Prince (1981). Lambrecht (1981) analyzes left- and right-dislocation in spoken French. English passive constructions are investigated in Thompson (1987). A concise discussion of the function of Russian word order can be found in Comrie (1979), with which Thompson's (1978) study of English word order can be usefully contrasted. For an overview of research on intonation and sentence stress and their pragmatic functions, see Bolinger (1986). Other means of marking pragmatic structure in English are discussed in Halliday and Hasan (1976).

REFERENCES

- Bolinger, Dwight L. 1986. *Intonation and Its Parts: Melody in Spoken English* (Stanford: Stanford University Press).
- Brown, Gillian, & George Yule. 1983. *Discourse Analysis* (Cambridge: Cambridge University Press).
- Chafe, Wallace L. 1970. *Meaning and the Structure of Language* (Chicago: University of Chicago Press).
- Chafe, Wallace L. 1976. "Givenness, Contrastiveness, Definiteness, Subjects, Topics, and Point of View," in Li (1976), pp. 25–55.
- Chafe, Wallace L. 1994. *Discourse, Consciousness, and Time: The Flow and Displacement of Conscious Experience in Speaking and Writing* (Chicago: University of Chicago Press).
- Comrie, Bernard. 1979. "Russian," in Timothy Shopen, ed., *Languages and Their Status* (Cambridge, MA: Winthrop), pp. 91–151.
- Foley, William, & Robert Van Valin, Jr. 1985. "Information Packaging in the Clause," in Timothy Shopen, ed., *Language Typology and Syntactic Description* (Cambridge: Cambridge University Press), 3, pp. 282–384.
- Givón, Talmy. 1979a. *On Understanding Grammar* (New York: Academic).
- Givón, Talmy, ed. 1979b. *Syntax and Semantics 12: Discourse and Syntax* (New York: Academic).
- Halliday, M. A. K., & Ruqaiya Hasan. 1976. *Cohesion in English* (London: Longman).
- Lambrecht, Knud. 1981. *Topic, Antitopic, and Verb Agreement in Non-standard French* (Amsterdam: Benjamins).
- Lambrecht, Knud. 1994. *Information Structure and Sentence Form: Topic, Focus, and the Mental Representation of Discourse Referents* (Cambridge: Cambridge University Press).
- Li, Charles N., ed. 1976. *Subject and Topic* (New York: Academic).
- Lyons, Christopher. 1999. *Definiteness* (Cambridge: Cambridge University Press).
- Prince, Ellen F. 1978. "A Comparison of WH-clefts and *It*-clefts in Discourse," *Language* 54:883–906.

- Prince, Ellen F. 1979. "On the Given/New Distinction," *Papers from the Fifteenth Regional Meeting of the Chicago Linguistics Society* (Chicago: Chicago Linguistics Society), pp. 267–78.
- Prince, Ellen F. 1981. "Topicalization, Focus Movement, and Yiddish Movement: A Pragmatic Differentiation," *Proceedings of the Seventh Annual Meeting of the Berkeley Linguistics Society* (Berkeley: Berkeley Linguistics Society), pp. 249–64.
- Thompson, Sandra A. 1987. "The Passive in English: A Discourse Perspective," in Robert Channon & Linda Shockey, eds., *In Honor of Ilse Lehiste* (Dordrecht: Foris), pp. 497–511.

Chapter 9

Speech Acts and Conversation

WHAT DO YOU THINK?

❖ Your friend Todd wonders aloud one day why the words, "I now pronounce you husband and wife," will create a legal marriage between two people at a wedding but not when uttered in a play on stage. At first you dismiss his question as silly. "No, really," he says. "What's the difference?" You think the answer obvious, but when you try to explain it, it's tough. What's the best explanation you can give?

❖ A classmate complains to you that just last week her boyfriend promised to take her along the next time he went skiing. Then this weekend he went skiing but didn't invite her. Asked what her boyfriend said when he made his promise, your friend reports that he said "I will. I will. Honestly." You ask her whether he said "I promise." When she says "No," you tell her you think he's a lout (and worse) but also gently indicate that you're not sure he made a promise because he didn't use that word. "C'mon," she says, "a promise is a promise." How do you explain your interpretation to her?

❖ Your younger brother complains that when Robb, your French friend from college, phones to speak with you, he takes forever to get to the point and apologizes profusely for nothing! He wonders what's wrong with him and why he can't get to the point. You're aware that people from different cultures behave differently on the telephone. What explanation do you offer your brother for Robb's telephone behavior?

❖ Your grandmother is very polite when telemarketers call, though she expresses some disappointment and unhappiness when she discovers that the "caller" is actually a tape-recorded message. You, on the other hand, get impatient and hang up on even live telemarketers. Your grandmother thinks some telemarketers might regard your behavior as rude, but you don't care. What's your explanation to her?

LANGUAGE IN USE

People use language principally as a tool to *do* things: request a favor, make a promise, report a piece of news, give directions, offer a greeting, seek information, invite someone to dinner, and perform hundreds of other ordinary verbal actions of everyday life. Sometimes the things we do with language have serious consequences: propose marriage, declare a mistrial, swear to tell the truth, fire an employee, and so on. These *speech acts* are part of *speech events* such as conversations, lectures, student-teacher conferences, news broadcasts, marriage ceremonies, and courtroom trials. In addition to births, deaths, fires, robberies, hurricanes, automobile accidents, and the like, which are not speech acts, much of what is reported in the pages of newspapers are speech acts: arrests, predictions, denials, promises, accusations, announcements, warnings, and so forth. Earlier chapters in this book examined the structure of words and sentences. Now we examine what we do with these structures and how our utterances accomplish their work.

Knowing a language is not simply a matter of knowing how to encode a message and transmit it to a second party who then decodes it in order to understand what we intended to say. If language use were a matter simply of encoding and decoding messages—in other words, of *grammatical competence*—every sentence would have a fixed interpretation irrespective of its context of use. But that's not the case, as the following scenarios illustrate.

1. You're stopped by a police officer, who surprises you by informing you that you've just driven through a stop sign. "I didn't see the stop sign," you say.

2. A friend has given you directions to her apartment, including instructions to turn left at the first stop sign after the intersection of Oak and Broad. You arrive about 30 minutes late and say, "I didn't see the stop sign."

3. You're driving with an aunt, who's in a hurry to get to church. You slow down and glide through a stop sign, knowing that on Sunday mornings there is seldom traffic at that intersection. As you enter the intersection, you see a car approaching and jam on the brakes, startling your aunt. "I didn't see the stop sign," you say.

To the police officer, your statement ("I didn't see the stop sign") is an *explanation* for failing to stop and a subtle *plea* not to be cited for the violation. To the friend, your utterance is an *excuse* for your tardiness and an *explanation* that it was neither intended nor entirely your fault. To your aunt, the same sentence (an untruthful one in this case) is uttered as an *apology* for having frightened her. She recognizes your intention to apologize and says, "It's all right. But *please* be careful." The linguistic meaning of the sentence *I didn't see the stop sign* is the same in all three cases, but uttering it in these different contexts serves different purposes and conveys distinct messages.

SENTENCE STRUCTURE AND THE FUNCTION OF UTTERANCES

Traditional grammar books say that declarative sentences make statements (*It's raining*), imperative sentences issue directives (*Close the door*), and interrogative sentences ask questions (*What time is it?*). That analysis is oversimplified, even misleading. Consider the sentence, *Can you shut the window?* Taken literally, its interrogative structure asks a question about the addressee's *ability* to shut some particular window. If asked this question by a roommate trying to study while a university marching band practiced nearby, you would probably interpret it not as a question about your abilities (and therefore requiring a verbal response), but as a request to close the window. (A request in question form is marked in speech by the absence of voice raising and sometimes in writing by the absence of a question mark: *Would you please respond promptly.*) Conversely, the imperative structure *Tell me your name again* would normally be taken not as a directive to do something but as a request for information.

Take another case: Suppose a knock is heard at the door, and Megan says to Alex *I wonder who's at the door*. If Megan believed Alex knew the answer, this declarative sentence might be uttered as a request for information. Often, though, it would actually be a polite request for Alex to open the door.

Finally, interrogative sentences can sometimes be used to make statements, as in Suze's reply to Eric's question.

Eric: Is Amy pretty easy to get along with?

Suze: Do hens have teeth?

Suze's *question* communicates an emphatically negative *answer* to Eric's inquiry.

Two things are clear, then: (1) People often employ declarative, interrogative, and imperative sentences for purposes other than making statements, asking questions, and issuing commands, respectively; and (2) a pivotal element in the interpretation of an utterance is the context in which it is uttered. Recall the three faces of language use depicted in Chapter 1 (page 8), showing *context* as the base of a triangle linking *meaning* and *expression*.

You recognize that a sentence is a structured string of words carrying a certain meaning. By contrast, an *utterance* is a sentence that is said, written, or signed *in a particular context* by someone *with a particular intention,* by means of which the "speaker" intends *to create an effect* on the addressee. Thus, as an interrogative sentence, *Can you close the window?* has the meaning of a request for *information* ('Are you able to close the window?'), but as a contextualized *utterance* it would more often than not be a request for *action* ('Please shut the window'). Drawing the appropriate inferences from conversation is an essential ingredient for interpreting utterances. To understand utterances, one must be skilled at "reading between the lines," and the skills one employs in using and interpreting the sentences shaped by *grammatical competence* are part of one's *communicative competence.*

SPEECH ACTS

Besides what we accomplish through physical acts such as cooking, eating, bicycling, gardening, or getting on a bus, we accomplish a great deal each day by verbal acts. In face-to-face conversation, telephone calls, job application letters, notes scribbled to a roommate, and a multitude of other speech events, we perform verbal actions of different types. In fact, language is the principal means we have to greet, compliment, and insult one another, to plead or flirt, to seek and supply information, and to accomplish hundreds of other tasks in a typical day. Actions that are carried out through language are called **speech acts,** and a surprisingly large number of reports in newspapers are reports of speech acts.

Try it yourself: Decide which of these headlines report speech acts and which report physical acts:

Sony Unveils Ambitious Plan for Music	CSC Awarded Contract
Fight Brews at FCC	Gap Hires Founder of Etoys
Judge Limits Skid Row Sweeps	Winds Wreak Havoc
Smuggling Suspects Acquitted	POW Rescued from Captors

Types of Speech Acts

Among the various kinds of speech acts, six have received particular attention:

1. *Representatives* represent a state of affairs: assertions, statements, claims, hypotheses, descriptions, suggestions. Representatives can generally be characterized as true or false.

2. *Commissives* commit a speaker to a course of action: promises, pledges, threats, vows.

3. *Directives* are intended to get the addressee to carry out an action: commands, requests, challenges, invitations, entreaties, dares.

4. *Declarations* bring about the state of affairs they name: blessings, hirings, firings, baptisms, arrests, marryings, declaring mistrials.

5. *Expressives* indicate the speaker's psychological state or attitude: greetings, apologies, congratulations, condolences, thanksgivings.

6. *Verdictives* make assessments or judgments: ranking, assessing, appraising, condoning. Because some verdictives (such as calling a baseball player "out") combine the characteristics of declarations and representatives, these are sometimes called *representational declarations.*

Locutions and Illocutions

Every speech act has several principal components, two of which directly concern us here: the *utterance itself* and the *intention of the speaker* in making it. First, every utterance is represented by a sentence with a grammatical structure and a linguistic meaning; this is called the **locution.** Second, speakers have some intention in making an utterance, and what they intend to accomplish is called an **illocution.** (A third component of a speech act—one we will not discuss at length—is the effect of the act on the hearer; this is called the *perlocution,* or the "uptake.")

Consider the utterance, *Can you shut the window?* Like all utterances, it can be viewed as comprising a locution and an illocution. The locution is a *yes/no* question about the addressee's ability to close a particular window; as such, convention would require an answer of *yes* or *no.* Let's assume that the speaker's intention (the illocution) is to request the addressee to shut the window; as such, convention would enable the addressee to recognize the structural question as a request for action and to comply or not. In discussions of speech acts, it is common for the illocutionary act itself to be called the speech act; thus promises, assertions, threats, invitations, and so on are all speech acts.

Distinguishing Among Speech Acts

How do people distinguish among different types of speech acts? How do we know whether a locution such as *Do you have the time?* is a *yes/no* question (*Do you have the time* [to help me]?) or a request for information about the time of day? To put the matter in more technical terms, given that a locution can serve many functions, how do addressees know the illocutionary force of a speaker's utterance? The answer of course is "context." But how do people interpret context accurately?

We begin our analysis by distinguishing between two broad types of speech acts. Compare the following two utterances:

1. I now pronounce you husband and wife.
2. It is going to be a very windy day.

In the appropriate context, the first utterance creates a new relationship between two individuals; it is a declaration that effectuates a marriage. The second utterance is a simple statement or representation of a state of affairs. As any weather predictor will attest, it will have no effect on the weather. As you saw earlier, utterances such as sentence 2 make assertions or state opinions and are called *representatives.* Utterances such as sentence 1 change the state of things and are called *declarations;* they provide a striking illustration of how language in use is a form of action. Children exposed to fantastical declarations such as "Abracadabra, I change you into a frog!" eventually learn that real-life objects are more recalcitrant than fairy-tale objects, but all speakers come to recognize a verbal power over certain aspects of life, especially with respect to social relationships.

With the utterance *I now pronounce you husband and wife,* the nature of the social relationship between two people can be profoundly altered. Similarly, the utterance *You're under arrest!* can have consequences for one's social freedom, as can *Case dismissed.* An umpire can change a baseball game with so simple a declaration as *Safe!* or *Strike three!* Typically, to be effective, declarations of this type must be uttered by a specially designated person. If called by a nondesignated individual—a fan in the stands, for example—*Out!* would be a verdictive, not a declaration. Indeed, a declaration by one designated umpire will override the opposite call by an entire stadium of fans.

Appropriateness Conditions and Successful Declarations

The efficacy of any declaration depends on well-established conventions. *I now pronounce you husband and wife* can bind two individuals in marriage, but only if several conditions are satisfied: the setting must be a wedding ceremony and the utterance made at the appropriate moment; the speaker must be designated to marry others (a minister, rabbi, justice of the peace) and must intend to marry them; the two individuals must be legally eligible to marry each other; and they must intend to become spouses. Finally, of course, the words themselves must be uttered. If any condition is not satisfied, the utterance of the words will be ineffectual as a *performative* speech act—one whose words effectuate the act. Made on a Hollywood movie set by an actor in the role of a pastor and addressed to two actors playing characters about to marry, the utterance may help secure an Academy Award, but it will be vacuous as to effectuating a marriage.

The conventions that regulate the conditions under which an utterance serves as a particular speech act—as a question, marriage, promise, arrest, invitation—have been called **appropriateness conditions** by philosopher John Searle, and they can be classified into four categories.

1. *Propositional content condition* requires merely that the words of the sentence be conventionally associated with the intended speech act and convey the content of the act. The locution must exhibit conventionally acceptable words for effecting the particular speech act: *Is it raining out?, I now pronounce you husband and wife, You're under arrest, I promise to . . . , I swear . . . .*

2. *Preparatory condition* requires a conventionally recognized context in which the speech act is embedded. In a marriage, the situation must be a genuine wedding ceremony (however informal) at which two people intend to exchange vows in the presence of a witness.

3. *Sincerity condition* requires the speaker to be sincere in uttering the declaration. At a wedding, the speaker must intend that the marriage words should effectuate a marriage; otherwise, the *sincerity condition* will be violated and the speech act will not be successful.

4. *Essential condition* requires that the involved parties all intend the result; for example, in a wedding ceremony, the participants must intend by the utterance of the words *I now pronounce you husband and wife* to create a marriage bond.

Successful Promises   Now consider the commissive, *I promise to help you with your math tonight.* In order for such an utterance to be successful, it must be recognizable as a promise; in addition, the preparatory, sincerity, and essential conditions must be met. In the propositional content condition, the speaker must use the conventional term *promise* to state the intention of helping the addressee. The preparatory condition requires that speaker and hearer are sane and responsible, that the speaker believes she is able to help with the math, and that the addressee wishes to have help. The preparatory condition would be violated if, for example, the speaker knew that she could not be there or that she was incapable of doing the math herself, or if the participants were reading the script of a movie in which the utterance appears. If the speaker knew that the hearer did not *want* help, the promise would not succeed. For the sincerity condition to hold, the speaker must sincerely intend to help the addressee. This condition would be violated (and the promise formula abused) if the speaker had no such intention. Finally, the essential condition of a promise is that the speaker intends by the utterance to place herself under an obligation to provide some help to the hearer. These four appropriateness conditions define a successful promise.

Successful Requests and Other Speech Acts   Appropriateness conditions are useful in describing not only declarations and commissives but all other types of speech acts. In a typical request (*Please pass me the salt),* the content of the utterance must identify the act requested of the hearer (passing the salt), and its form must be a conventionally recognized one for making requests. The preparatory condition includes the speaker's beliefs that the addressee is capable of passing the salt and that, had he not asked her to pass the salt, she would not have ventured to do so. The sincerity condition requires that the speaker genuinely desires the hearer to pass the salt. Finally the essential condition is that the speaker intends by the utterance to get the hearer to pass the salt to him.

THE COOPERATIVE PRINCIPLE

The principles that govern the interpretation of utterances are diverse and complex, and they differ somewhat from culture to culture. Even within a single culture, they are so complex that we may wonder how language succeeds at communication as well as it does. The principles that we examine in this section, however commonsensical they may seem to Western readers, are by no means universal; as you will see later, what seems common sense to one group is not necessarily common sense to all groups.

Despite occasional misinterpretations, people in most situations manage to understand utterances essentially as they were intended. The reason is that, without cause to expect otherwise, interlocutors normally trust that they and their conversational partners are honoring the same interpretive conventions. *Hearers* assume simply that speakers have honored the conventions of interpretation in constructing their utterances. *Speakers,* on the other hand, must make a twofold assumption: not only that hearers will themselves be guided by the conventions, but also that hearers will trust speakers to have honored those conventions in constructing their utterances.

There is an unspoken pact that people will *cooperate* in communicating with each other, and speakers rely on this cooperation to make conversation efficient.

The **cooperative principle,** as enunciated by philosopher H. Paul Grice, is as follows:

> Make your conversational contribution such as is required, at the stage at which it occurs, by the accepted purpose or direction of the talk exchange in which you are engaged.

This pact of cooperation touches on four areas of communication, each of which can be described as a *maxim,* or general principle.

Maxim of Quantity

First, speakers are expected to give as much information as is necessary for their interlocutors to understand their utterances, but to give no more information than is necessary. If you ask an acquaintance whether she has any pets and she answers, *I have two cats,* it is the *maxim of quantity* that permits you to assume that she has no other pets. The conversational implication of such a reply is 'I have two (and only two) cats (and no other pets).' Notice that *I have two cats* would be true even if the speaker has six cats or six cats, two dogs, and a llama. But if she had such other pets, you would have reason to feel deceived. While her reply was not false as far as it went, your culturally defined expectation that relevant information will not be concealed would have been violated. In most Western cultures (but not in all cultures), listeners expect speakers to abide by this maxim, and—equally important—speakers know that hearers believe them to be abiding by it. It is this unspoken cooperation that creates conversational implicatures.

To take another example, suppose you asked a man painting his house what color he had chosen for the living room, and he replied:

> The walls are going to be off-white to contrast with the black sofa and the Regency armchairs that I inherited from my great-aunt. (Bless her soul, she passed away last year after a long but distressing marriage to a man who really wasn't able to appreciate her extraordinary love of the visual and performing arts.) Then the trim will be peach except near the door, which Alice said should be salmon because otherwise it will clash with the yellow, black, and red Picasso print that I brought back from Spain—I vacationed in Spain in August of, let's see, 2002, and I bought it then. Or was it July? I forget, actually. Gosh! time goes fast, don't you think? Oh, never mind. And the stairway leading to the bedrooms will be a pale yellow.

In providing too much information, far more than was sought or expected, the man is as uncooperative as the woman who withheld information about her pets. The maxim of quantity provides that, in normal circumstances, speakers say just enough, that they supply no less information—and no more—than is necessary for the purpose of the communication: *Be appropriately informative.*

Society stigmatizes individuals who habitually violate the maxim of quantity; those who give too much information are described as "never shutting up" or "always telling everyone their life story," while those who habitually fail to provide enough information are branded sullen, secretive, or untrustworthy.

Maxim of Relevance

The second maxim directs speakers to organize their utterances in such a way that they are relevant to the ongoing context: *Be relevant at the time of the utterance.* The following interaction illustrates a violation of this maxim.

> Zane: How's the weather outside?
>
> Zora: There's a great movie on HBO Thursday night.

Taken literally, Zora's utterance seems unrelated to what Zane has just said; if so, it would violate the *maxim of relevance.* Owing to the maxim of relevance, when someone produces an apparently irrelevant utterance, hearers typically strive to understand how it might be relevant (as a joke, perhaps, or an indication of displeasure with the direction of the conversation). Chronic violations of this maxim are characteristic of schizophrenics, whose sense of "context" differs radically from that of other people.

Maxim of Manner

Third, people follow a set of miscellaneous rules that are grouped under the *maxim of manner.* Summarized by the directive *Be orderly and clear,* this maxim dictates that speakers and writers avoid ambiguity and obscurity and be orderly in their utterances. In the following example, the maxim of manner is violated with respect to orderliness.

> A birthday cake should have icing; use unbleached flour and sugar in the cake; bake it for one hour; preheat the oven to 325 degrees; and beat in three fresh eggs.

This recipe is odd for the simple reason that English speakers normally follow a chronological order of events in describing a process such as baking.

Orderliness is not only dictated by the order of events: in any language there are rules that dictate a "natural" order of details in a description. Because in American English more general details usually precede more specific details, when a speaker violates this rule the result appears odd.

> My hometown has five shopping malls. It is the county seat. My father and my mother were both born there. My hometown is a midwestern town of 105,000 inhabitants situated at the center of the Corn Belt. I was brought up there until I was 13 years old.

As a third example, consider the utterance *Ted died and was hit by lightning.* If it was the lightning that killed Ted, the maxim of manner has been violated here. Although in logic *and* joins clauses whose time reference is not relevant (thus, *She studied chemistry, and she studied biology* is logically equivalent to *She studied biology, and she studied chemistry),* the maxim of manner dictates that an utterance such as *They had a baby and got married* has different conversational implications from those such as *They got married and had a baby.* The maxim of manner in this instance suggests that the sequence of expressions reflects the sequence of events or is irrelevant to an appropriate interpretation. Of course English and other languages provide ways around misinterpretation: *They had a baby before they got married; first they had a baby, and then they got married; they got married after they had a baby;* and so on.

Maxim of Quality

The fourth general principle governing norms of language interpretation is the maxim of quality: *Be truthful.* Speakers and writers are expected to say only what they believe to be true and to have evidence for what they say. Again, the other side of the coin is that speakers are aware of this expectation; they know that hearers expect them to honor the *maxim of quality.* Without the maxim of quality, the other maxims are of little value or interest. Whether brief or lengthy, relevant or irrelevant, orderly or disorderly, all lies are false. Still, it should be noted that the maxim of quality applies principally to assertions and certain other representative speech acts. Expressives and directives can hardly be judged true or false in the same sense.

It is useful to reflect further on the maxim of quality. On the one hand, it is this maxim that constrains interlocutors to tell the truth and to have evidence for their statements. Ironically, however, it is this maxim that also makes lying possible. Without the maxim of quality, speakers would have no reason to expect hearers to take their utterances as true, and without the assumption that one's interlocutors assume one to be telling the truth, it would be impossible to tell a lie. Lying requires that speakers are expected to be telling the truth.

VIOLATIONS OF THE COOPERATIVE PRINCIPLE

It is no secret that people sometimes violate the maxims of the cooperative principle. Certainly not all speakers are completely truthful on all occasions; others, although truthful, have not observed that efficiency is the desired Western norm in conversational interaction. More interestingly, speakers are sometimes forced by cultural norms or other external factors to violate a maxim. For example, irrespective of your aesthetic judgment, you may feel constrained to say *What a lovely painting!* to a host who is manifestly proud of some newly finished artwork. The need to adhere to social conventions of politeness sometimes invites people to violate maxims of the cooperative principle.

Indirect Speech Acts

As mentioned earlier, interrogative structures can be used to make polite requests for action, imperative structures can be used to ask for information, and so on. Such uses of a structure with one meaning to accomplish a different task play a frequent role in ordinary interaction, as in this exchange between colleagues who have stayed at the office after dark.

> Sue: Is the boss in?
>
> Alan: The light's on in her office.
>
> Sue: Oh, thanks.

Alan's answer makes no apparent reference to the information Sue is seeking. Thus in theory it would appear to violate the maxim of relevance. Yet Sue is satisfied with the answer. Recognizing that the *literal* interpretation of Alan's reply violates the maxim of relevance but assuming that as a cooperative interlocutor Alan is being relevant, Sue seeks an *indirect* interpretation. To help her, she knows certain facts about their boss's habits: that she works in her own office, that she does not work in the dark, and that she is not in the habit of leaving the light on when gone for the day. Relying on this information, Sue infers an interpretation from Alan's utterance: Alan believes the boss is in.

Alan's reply is an example of an **indirect speech act**—one that involves an apparent violation of the cooperative principle but is in fact indirectly cooperative. For example, an indirect speech act can be based on an apparent violation of the maxim of quality. When we describe a friend as *someone who never parts with a dime,* we don't mean it literally; we are exaggerating. By exaggerating the information, we may seem to be flouting the maxim of quality. But listeners will usually appreciate that the statement should not be interpreted literally and will make an appropriate adjustment in their interpretation. Similarly, we may exclaim in front of the Sears Tower in Chicago, *That's an awfully small building!* This utterance too appears to violate the maxim of quality in that we are expressing an evaluation that is manifestly false. But speakers readily spot the irony of utterances such as this and take them to be indirect speech acts intended to convey an opposite meaning.

Characteristics of Indirect Speech Acts   From these examples, we can identify four characteristics of indirect speech acts:

1. Indirect speech acts violate at least one maxim of the cooperative principle.

2. The literal meaning of the locution of an indirect speech act differs from its intended meaning.

3. Hearers and readers identify indirect speech acts by noticing that an utterance has characteristic 1 (it violates a maxim) and by assuming that the interlocutor is following the cooperative principle.

4. As soon as hearers and readers have identified an indirect speech act, they identify its intended meaning with the help of knowledge of the context and of the world around them.

Thus, to interpret indirect speech acts, hearers use the maxims to sort out the discrepancy between the literal meaning of the utterance and an appropriate interpretation for the context in which it is uttered.

Try it yourself: In this brief exchange, what name would you give to the speech act in A? In B? Does D represent a direct speech act or an indirect one? What about A?

    A. Anna: Who finished the bread I made yesterday?
    B. Juan: With the raisins?
    C. Anna: Yeah.
    D. Juan: Did you ask Raul?

Indirect Speech Acts and Shared Knowledge   One prerequisite for a successful indirect speech act is that interactors share sufficient background about the context of the interaction, about each other and their society, and about the world in general. If Ed asks Ellen *Are you done with your sociology paper?* and she replies *Is Rome in Spain?*, Ed will certainly recognize the answer as an indirect speech act. But whether or not he can interpret it will depend on his knowledge of geography.

Using and understanding indirect speech acts requires familiarity with both language and society. To cite an example from another culture, when speakers of the Polynesian language Tuvaluan want to comment on the fact that a particular person is in the habit of talking about himself, they may say *koo tagi te tuli ki tena igoa* 'The plover bird is singing its own name.' The expression derives from the fact that the plover bird's cry sounds like a very sharp "tuuuuuliiiii," from which speakers of Tuvaluan have created the word *tuli* to refer to the bird itself. Thus the expression has become an indirect way of criticizing the trait of singing one's own praises. In order to interpret the utterance as an indirect speech act, one must be familiar not only with the plover bird's cry and the fact that it resembles the bird's name but also with the fact that Tuvaluans view people who talk about themselves as being similar to a bird "singing its own name." Clearly, the amount of background information about language, culture, and environment needed to interpret indirect speech acts is considerable.

POLITENESS

Indirect speech acts appear to be a complicated way of communicating. Not only must you spot them, but you must then go through a complex reasoning process to interpret them. One might think it would be more efficient to communicate directly. The fact is, though, that indirect speech acts have uses besides asking and answering questions, criticizing others, and so on. They sometimes add humor and sometimes show politeness. Ellen's indirect reply (*Is Rome in Spain?*) to Ed's question suggests 'Don't be ridiculous; of course I'm not done.' Questions such as *Can you shut the window?* are perceived as more polite and less intrusive and abrasive than a command such as *Shut the window!* One message that indirect speech acts convey is 'I am being polite towards you.' Indirect speech acts are thus an efficient tool of communication: they can convey two or more messages simultaneously.

Respecting Independence and Showing Involvement

There are two basic aspects to being polite. The first rests on the fact that human beings respect one another's privacy, independence, and physical space. We *avoid* intruding on other people's lives, try *not* to be overly inquisitive about their activities, and take care *not* to impose our presence on them. We respect their independence and do not intrude (some call this *negative politeness*). On the other hand, when we let people know we enjoy their company, feel comfortable with them, like something in their personality, or are interested in their well-being, we show involvement (what some call *positive politeness*). While everyone expects both independence and involvement, the first requires us to leave people alone, while the second requires us to do the opposite. Fortunately, these competing needs usually arise in different contexts. When we shut ourselves in a room or take a solitary walk on the beach, we affirm our right to independence. When we attend a party, invite someone to dinner, or call friends on the telephone to check up on them, we show involvement. Both are forms of politeness.

In conversation, interlocutors give one another messages about their needs for independence and their wishes for involvement and acknowledge one another's needs for both types of politeness as well. The expectation that others won't ask embarrassing questions about our personal lives stems from the need for independence. By contrast, when you tell a friend about a personal problem and expect sympathy, you are seeking involvement. Excusing oneself before asking a stranger for the time acknowledges the stranger's right to freedom from intrusion. When we express the hope of meeting an interlocutor at a later date (*Let's get together soon!*), we acknowledge interlocutor's need for involvement and sociability.

SPEECH EVENTS

Political rallies, policy debates, public speeches, classroom lectures, religious sermons, and a disk jockey's "Top 40 countdown" are all speech events—social activities in which language plays a particularly important role. "Speech" events need not involve *speaking:* personal letters, short stories, shopping lists, office memos, and birthday cards are also speech events.

Conversation provides the matrix in which native languages are acquired, and it stands out as the most frequent, most natural, and most representative of verbal interactions. A person can spend a lifetime without writing a letter, composing a poem, or debating public policy, but only in rare circumstances does someone not have frequent conversation with friends and companions. Conversation is an everyday speech event. We engage in it for entertainment (gossiping, passing the time, affirming social bonds) and for accomplishing work (getting help with studies, renting an apartment, ordering a meal at a restaurant). Whatever its purpose, conversation is our most basic verbal interaction.

Although lovers in the movies can conduct heart-to-heart conversations with their backs to each other, conversation usually involves individuals facing each other and taking turns at speaking. They neither talk simultaneously nor let the conversation lag. In some societies, even with several conversationalists in a single conversation, there are only tenths of a second between turns and extremely little overlap in speaking. At the beginning of a conversation, people go through certain rituals, greeting one another or commenting about the weather. Likewise, at the end of a conversation, people don't simply turn their backs and walk away; they take care that all participants have finished what they wanted to say and only then utter something like "I have to run" or "Take care." Throughout the entire interaction, conversationalists maintain a certain level of orderliness—taking turns, not interrupting one another too often, and following certain other highly structured but implicit guidelines for conversation.

These guidelines can be considered norms of conduct that govern how conversationalists comport themselves. Though it is tempting to think of relaxed conversation as essentially free of rules or constraints, the fact is that many rules are operating, and the unconscious recognition of these rules helps identify particular interactions as conversations.

THE ORGANIZATION OF CONVERSATION

If it seems surprising that casual conversation should be organized by rules, the reason is that, as in most speech events, more attention is paid to content than to organization; we take the organization of conversations for granted. A conversation can be viewed as a series of speech acts—greetings, inquiries, congratulations, comments, invitations, requests, refusals, accusations, denials, promises, farewells. To accomplish the work of these speech acts, some organization is essential: we take turns at speaking, answer questions, mark the beginning and end of a conversation, and make corrections when they are needed. To accomplish such work expeditiously, interlocutors could give one another traffic directions.

Okay, now it's your turn to speak.

I just asked you a question; now you should answer it, and you should do so right away.

If you have anything else to add before we close this conversation, do it now because I am leaving in a minute.

Such instructions would be inefficient, however, and would deflect attention from the content. In unusual circumstances, conversationalists do invoke the rules (*Would you please stop interrupting?* or *Well, say something!*), but invoking the rules underscores the fact that they have been violated and can itself seem impolite. Conversations are usually organized covertly, and the organizational principles provide a discreet interactional framework.

The covert architecture of conversation must achieve the following: organize turns so that more than one person has a chance to speak and the turn taking is orderly; allow interlocutors to anticipate what will happen next and, where there is a choice, how the selection is to be decided; provide a way to repair glitches and errors when they occur.

Turn Taking and Pausing

Participants must tacitly agree on who should speak when. Normally we take turns at holding the floor and do so without overt negotiation. A useful way to uncover the conventions of turn taking is to observe what happens when they break down. When a participant fails to take the floor despite indications that it is his turn, other speakers usually pause, and then someone else begins speaking. In this example, Alan repeats his question, assuming that Bill either did not hear or did not understand it the first time.

Alan: Is there something you're worried about?
[pause]
Alan: Is there something you're worried about?
Bill: No, but maybe you could help me with a problem I'm having with my brother.

Turn-taking conventions are also violated when two people attempt to speak simultaneously. In the next example, the beginning and end of the overlap are marked with brackets.

Speaker 1:   After John's party we went to Ed's house.
Speaker 2:   So you—   so you—you—
                         [   ]
Speaker 3:   What—what—time did you get there?

When such competition arises in casual conversation, a speaker may either quickly relinquish the floor or turn up the volume and continue speaking. Both silence and simultaneous speaking are serious problems in conversation, and the turn-taking norms are designed to minimize them.

Different cultures have different degrees of tolerance for silence between turns, overlaps in speaking, and competition among speakers. In the Inuit and some other Native American cultures, for example, people sit comfortably together in silence. At the other extreme, in French and Argentinian cultures several conversationalists often talk simultaneously and interrupt each other more frequently than Americans typically feel comfortable doing.

However much tolerance they may have for silences and overlaps, people from all cultures appear to regulate turn taking in conversation in essentially similar ways: Speakers signal when they wish to end their turn, either selecting the next speaker or leaving the choice open; the next speaker takes the floor by beginning to talk. These simple principles, which seem second nature to us, regulate conversational turn taking very efficiently.

Turn-Taking Signals   Speakers signal that their turn is about to end with verbal and nonverbal cues. As turns commonly end in a complete sentence, the completion of a sentence may signal the end of a turn. A sentence ending in a tag question (*isn't it?*, *are you?*) explicitly invites an interlocutor to take the floor.

Speaker A: Pretty windy out today, isn't it?
Speaker B: Sure is!

The end of a turn may also be signaled by sharply raising or lowering the pitch of your voice, or by drawling the last syllable of the final word of the turn. In very informal conversations, one common cue is the phrase *or something*.

Speaker 1   So he was behaving as if he'd been hit by a truck, or something.
Speaker 2:   Really?

Other expressions that can signal the completion of a turn are *y'know, kinda, I don't know* (or *I dunno),* and a trailing *uhm.* As with *y'know,* some of these can also function within a turn for the speaker to keep the floor while thinking about what to say next. Another way to signal the completion of a turn is to pause and make no attempt to speak again.

> Daniel: I really don't think he should've said that at the meeting, particularly in front of the whole committee. It really was pretty insensitive.
>
> [pause]
>
> David: Yeah, I agree.

Of course, speakers often have to pause in the middle of a turn to think about what to say next, to emphasize a point, or to catch a breath. To signal that a speaker has finished a turn, the pause must be long enough, but "long enough" differs from culture to culture.

Nonverbal as well as verbal signals can indicate the end of a turn. Although in speaking the principal role of gestures is to support and stress what we say, continuing our hand gestures lets our interlocutors know that we have more to say. Once we put our hands to rest, our fellow conversationalists may infer that we are yielding the floor.

In a more subtle vein, eye gaze can help control floor holding and turn taking. In mainstream American society, speakers do not ordinarily stare at their interlocutors; instead, their gaze goes back and forth between their listener and another point in space, alternating quickly and almost imperceptibly. But because listeners, on the other hand, usually fix their gaze on the speaker, a speaker reaching the end of a turn can simply return her gaze to an interlocutor and thereby signal her own turn to listen and the interlocutor's to speak. In cultures in which listeners look away while speakers stare, a speaker who wishes to stop talking simply looks away. While eye gaze plays a supportive role in allocating turns, the success of telephone conversations makes it clear that eye gaze is not essential in the allocation of turns.

Getting the Floor In multiparty conversations, the speaker holding the floor can select who will speak next, or the next speaker can select himself. In the first instance, the floor holder may signal the choice by addressing the next speaker by name (*What've you been up to these days, Helen?)* or by turning toward the selected next speaker. If the floor holder does not select the next speaker, anyone may take the floor, often by beginning the turn at an accelerated pace so as to block other potential claims for the floor.

When the floor holder does not select the next speaker, competition can arise, as in the following example, in which overlaps are indicated with square brackets.

> Speaker 1: Who's gonna be at Jake's party Saturday night?
>
> [pause]
>
> Speaker 2: Todd to—
>
> [   ]
>
> Speaker 3: I don't kn—
>
> [pause]

Speaker 2: Todd told me—
          [   ]
Speaker 3: I don't know who's—
          [short pause]
Speaker 2: [to speaker 3] Go ahead!
Speaker 3: I don't know who's gonna be there, but I know it'll be pretty crowded.
Speaker 2: Yeah, that's what I was gonna say.
          Todd told me a lotta people would be there.

Friendly participants strive to resolve such competition quickly and smoothly.

Social inequality between conversationalists (boss and employee, parent and child, doctor and patient) is often reflected in how often and when participants claim the floor. In American work settings, superiors commonly initiate conversations by asking a question and letting subordinates report. Thus subordinates hold the floor for longer periods of time than superiors; subordinates perform while superiors act as spectators. In some cultures, superiors talk while subordinates listen.

Adjacency Pairs

One useful mechanism in the covert organization of conversation is that certain turns have specific follow-up turns associated with them. Questions that request information take answers. The reply to a greeting is usually also a greeting, to an invitation an acceptance or refusal, and so on. Certain sequences of turns go together, as in these *adjacency pairs*.

Request for Information and Providing Information
Adam: Where's the milk I bought this morning?
Betty: On the counter.

Invitation and Acceptance
Alex: I'm having friends to dinner Saturday, and I'd really like you to come.
Bert: Sure!

Assessment and Disagreement
Angel: I don't think Nick would play such a dirty trick on you.
Brit: Well, you obviously don't know Nick very well.

Such **adjacency pairs** comprise two turns, one of which directly follows the other. In a question/answer adjacency pair, the question is the first part, the answer the second part. Here are other examples of adjacency pairs.

Request for a Favor and Granting
Guest: Can I use your phone?
Host: Sure.

Apology and Acceptance
Eli: Sorry to bother you this late at night.
Dave: No, that's all right. What can I do for you?

Summons and Acknowledgment

Mark: Bill!

Bill: Yeah?

Structural Characteristics of Adjacency Pairs   Three characteristics of adjacency pairs can be noted.

1. **They are contiguous.** The two parts of an adjacency pair are contiguous and are uttered by different speakers. A speaker who makes a statement before responding to a question that has been asked sounds strange (and can provoke frustration) because adjacency pairs are structured to be consecutive:

   Adam: Where's the milk I bought this morning?

   Betty: They said on the radio the weather would clear up by noon.
             It's on the counter.

2. **They are ordered.** The two parts of an adjacency pair are ordered. Except on TV game shows like "Jeopardy," the answer to a question cannot precede the question. Ordinarily, one cannot accept an invitation before it has been offered, and an apology cannot be accepted before it is uttered (except sarcastically).

3. **They are matched.** The first and second parts of an adjacency pair must be appropriately matched. Appropriate matching avoids odd exchanges such as the following:

   Kimi: Do you want more coffee?

   Sasa: That's all right, you're not bothering me in the least!

Insertion Sequences   Sometimes, the requirement that the two parts of an adjacency pair be contiguous is violated in a socially recognized way.

Adam: Where's the milk I bought this morning?

Betty: The skim milk?

Adam: Yeah.

Betty: On the counter.

In this example, in order to provide an accurate answer to Adam's question, Betty must first know the answer to another question and thus initiates an *insertion sequence*—an adjacency pair that interrupts the original one and puts it "on hold." The interaction thus consists of one adjacency pair embedded in another one, as in the following telephone conversation.

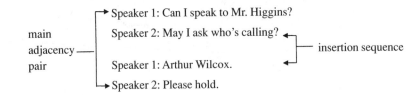

Preferred and Dispreferred Responses   Certain kinds of adjacency pairs are marked by a preference for a particular type of second part. For example, requests, questions, and invitations have preferred and dispreferred answers. Compare the following interactions, in which the first exchange has a preferred second part and the second exchange has a dispreferred one.

Fran: I really enjoyed that movie last night. Did you?
Frank: Yeah, it was pretty good.

Fran: I really enjoyed the movie last night. Did you?
Frank: No, I thought it was crummy, but I can see how you could've liked parts of it.

The preferred second part is agreement to an assessment as well.

Fiona: I think Ralph's a pretty good writer.
Kieran: I think so, too.

Fiona: I think Ralph's a pretty good writer.
Kieran: Well, his imagery's interesting, but apart from that I don't think he writes well at all.

Dispreferred second parts tend to be preceded by a pause and to begin with a hesitation particle such as *well* or *uh*. Preferred second parts tend to follow the first part without a pause and to consist of structurally simple utterances.

Michelle: Wanna meet for lunch tomorrow?
Michael: Sure!

Michelle: Would you like to meet for lunch tomorrow?
Michael: Well, um . . . tomorrow's the 24th, right? I told Lori I'd have lunch with her tomorrow. And it's her birthday, so I can't cancel. How 'bout Wednesday?

In addition, even dispreferred second parts often begin with a token agreement or acceptance, or with an expression of appreciation or apology, and characteristically include an explanation.

Wade: Can I use your phone?
Frank: Oh, I'm sorry, but I'm expecting an important long-distance call. Could you wait a bit?

Try it yourself: To an apology, a preferred second part is an acceptance, while a dispreferred second part is a refusal to accept it. For each of these speech acts, name one preferred second part and one dispreferred: request for information; invitation to a party; greeting; accusation; offer of congratulations; assessment.

Opening Sequences

Conversations are opened in socially recognized ways. Before beginning their first conversation of the day, conversationalists normally greet each other, as when two office workers meet in the morning.

Jeff:　Mornin', Stan!

Stan:　Hi. How's it goin'?

Jeff:　Oh, can't complain, I guess. Ready for the meeting this afternoon?

Stan:　Well, I don't have much choice!

Greetings exemplify opening sequences, utterances that ease people into a conversation. They convey the message "I want to talk to you."

Greetings are usually reserved for acquaintances who have not seen each other for a while, or as opening sequences for longer conversations between strangers. Some situations do not require a greeting, as with a stranger approaching in the street to ask for the time: *Excuse me, sir, do you know what time it is?* The expression *Excuse me, sir* serves as an opening sequence appropriate to the context. Thus, greetings are not the only type of opening sequences.

Very few conversations do not begin with some type of opening sequence, even as commonplace as the following:

Eric:　Guess what.

Jo:　What?

Eric:　I broke a tooth.

Conversationalists also use opening sequences to announce that they are about to invade the personal space of their interlocutors. Here, two friends are talking on a park bench next to a stranger; at a pause in their conversation, the stranger interjects:

Stranger:　Excuse me, I didn't mean to eavesdrop, but I couldn't help hearing that
　　　　　　you were talking about Dayton, Ohio. I'm from Dayton.

　　　　　　[Conversation then goes on among the three people.]

It's not surprising that opening sequences take the form of an apology in such situations.

Finally, opening sequences may serve as a display of one's voice to enable the interlocutor to recognize who is speaking, especially at the beginning of telephone conversations. Here, the phone has just rung in Alfred's apartment.

Alfred:　Hello?

Helen:　Hello!

Alfred:　Oh, hi, Helen! How you doin'?

In the second turn, Helen displays her voice to enable Alfred to recognize her. In the third turn, Alfred indicates his recognition and simultaneously provides the second part of the greeting adjacency pair initiated in the previous turn.

Opening Sequences in Other Cultures   In many cultures, the opening sequence appropriate to a situation in which two people meet after not having met for a while is an inquiry about the person's health, as in the American greeting *How are you?* Such inquiries are essentially formulaic and not meant literally. Indeed, most speakers respond with a conventional upbeat formula (*I'm fine* or *Fine, thanks*) even when feeling terrible. In other cultures, the conventional greeting may take a different form. Traditionally, Mandarin Chinese conversationalists ask *Nǐ chī guo fàn le ma?* 'Have you eaten rice yet?' When two people meet on a road in Tonga, they ask *Ko ho?o ?alu ki fe?* 'Where is your going directed to?' These greetings are as formulaic as *How are you?*

In formal contexts, or when differences of social status exist between participants, many cultures require a lengthy and formulaic opening sequence. In Fiji, when an individual visits a village, a highly ceremonial introduction is conducted before any other interaction takes place. This event involves speeches that are regulated by a complex set of rules governing what must be said, and when, and by whom. This ceremony serves the same purpose as opening sequences in other cultures.

Functions of Opening Sequences   A final aspect of opening sequences in which cultural differences are found is the relative importance of their various functions. In telephone conversations in the United States, opening sequences serve primarily to identify speakers and solicit the interlocutor's attention. In France, opening sequences for telephone conversations normally include an apology for invading someone's privacy.

> Person called: Allô?
>
> Person calling: Allô? Je suis désolé de vous déranger. Est-ce que j'peux parler à Marie-France?
>
> ('Hello? I'm terribly sorry for disturbing you. Can I speak to Marie-France?')

In an American telephone conversation, such an opening sequence is not customary. Thus, in two relatively similar cultures, the role played by the opening sequence in a telephone call is different. As a result, the French can find Americans intrusive and impolite on the telephone, while Americans are puzzled by French apologetic formulas, which they find pointless and exceedingly ceremonious.

Closing Sequences

Conversations must also be closed appropriately. A conversation can be closed only when the participants have said everything they wanted to say. Furthermore, a conversation must be closed before participants begin to feel uncomfortable about having nothing more to say. As a result, conversationalists carefully negotiate the timing of closings, seeking to give the impression of wanting neither to rush away nor to linger on. These objectives are reflected in the characteristics of the closing sequence. First of all, a closing sequence includes a conclusion to the last topic covered in the conversation. In conclusions, conversationalists often make arrangements to meet at a later time or express the hope of so meeting. These arrangements may be genuine, as in the first example here, or formulaic, as in the second.

> Carl: Okay, it's nice to see you again. I guess you'll be at Kathy's party tonight.
>
> Dana: Yeah, I'll see you there.
>
> Elizabeth: See you later!
> Farouk: See ya!

The first step of a closing sequence helps ensure that no one has anything further to say. This is accomplished by a simple exchange of short turns such as *okay* or *well*. Typically, such preclosing sequences are accompanied by a series of pauses between and within turns that decelerate the exchange and prepare for closing down the interaction. In the following example, Dana takes the opportunity to bring up one last topic, after which Carl initiates another closing sequence.

> Carl: Okay, it's nice to see you again. I guess you'll be at Kathy's party tonight.
> Dana: Yeah, I'll see you there.
> Carl: Okay.
> Dana: I hear there's gonna be lots of people there.
> Carl: Apparently she invited half the town.
> Dana: Should be fun.
> Carl: Yeah.
> Dana: Okay.
> Carl: Okay. See you there.
> Dana: Later!

Sometimes, after a preclosing exchange, speakers refer to the original motivation for the conversation. In a courtesy call to inquire about someone's health, the caller sometimes refers to this fact after the preclosing exchange.

> Person calling: Well, I just wanted to see how you were doing after your surgery.
> Person called: Well, that was really nice of you.

If the purpose of a conversation was to seek a favor, this short exchange might take place:

> Alex: Well, listen, I really appreciate your doing this for me.
> Beth: Forget it. I'm glad to be of help.

Finally, conversations close with a parting expression: *bye, goodbye, see you, catch you later.*

A striking thing about closings is their deceptive simplicity. In fact, they are complex. Participants exercise great care not to give the impression that they are rushing away or that they want to linger, and they try to ensure that everything on the unwritten agenda of any participant has been touched on. However informal and abbreviated they may be, closing sequences are characterized by a great deal of negotiated activity.

Conversational Routines

Both openings and closings are more routinized than the core parts of conversations. Core parts are relatively less predictable; while people are trained from childhood not to ask certain kinds of questions, they are also drilled on the proper way to open and close conversations. Because of the routinized nature of openings and closings, conversations can be begun and, equally important, ended expeditiously.

Repairs

A **repair** takes place in conversation when a participant feels the need to correct herself or another speaker, to edit a previous utterance, or simply to restate something, as in the following examples, in which a dash indicates an abrupt cutoff.

1. Speaker: I was going to Mary's—uh, Sue's house.
2. Speaker: And I went to the doctor's to get a new—uh—a new whatchamacallit, a new prescription, because my old one ran out.
3. Alex: Aren't those daffodils pretty?
   Kate: They're pretty, but they're narcissus.
4. Winston: Todd came to visit us over the spring break.
   David: What?
   Winston: I said Todd was here over the spring break.

In 2, the *trouble source* is the fact that the speaker cannot find a word. In 4, David initiates a repair because he has not heard or has not understood Winston's utterance. Conversationalists thus make repairs for a variety of reasons.

To initiate a repair is to signal that one has not understood or has misheard an utterance, that a piece of information is incorrect, or that one is having trouble finding a word. To resolve a repair, someone must repeat the misunderstood or misheard utterance, correct the inaccurate information, or supply the word. To initiate a repair, we may ask a question, as in 4; repeat part of the utterance to be repaired, as in example 5 below; abruptly stop speaking, as in example 6; or use particles and expressions like *uh, I mean,* or *that is,* as in example 1.

5. Speaker: I am sure—I am *absolutely* sure it was him that I saw last night prowling around.
6. Nelson: And here you have what's called the—
   [pause]
   Juan: The carburetor?
   Nelson: Yeah, that's right, the carburetor.

Repairs can be initiated and resolved by the person who uttered the words that need to be repaired or by another conversationalist. There are thus four possibilities: repairs that are self-initiated and self-repaired; repairs that are other-initiated and self-repaired; repairs that are self-initiated and other-repaired; and repairs that are other-initiated and other-repaired. Of these possibilities, conversationalists show a strong preference for self-initiated self-repairs, which are least disruptive to the conversation and to the social relationship between the conversationalists. In general, conversationalists wait for clear signals of communicative distress before repairing an utterance made by someone else. The least preferred pattern is for repairs that are other-initiated and other-repaired. Individuals in the habit of both initiating and repairing utterances for others get branded as poor conversationalists or know-it-alls.

Found in many cultures, these preference patterns reflect a widespread but unspoken rule that all participants in a conversation among equals be given a chance to say what they want to say by themselves. Conversationalists provide assistance to others in initiating and resolving repairs only if no other option is available.

Politeness: An Organizational Force in Conversation

Violating the turn-taking principles by interrupting or by failing to take turns is considered impolite. Turning one's back on interlocutors at the end of a conversation without going through a closing sequence is also stigmatized in the conventions of politeness. Other aspects of politeness are more subtle but nevertheless play an important role in structuring conversation.

There are covert ways in which we communicate respect for independence and involvement. When we expect interlocutors to allow us to both initiate and resolve a repair ourselves, we are expecting them to respect our right to make a contribution to the conversation without intrusion from others; that is, we are asking them to respect our independence. Similarly, we recognize another person's need for independence when, instead of ending a conversation abruptly, we initiate a preclosing exchange, affording our interlocutors a chance to say something further before closing. In contrast, when we initiate a conversation with a greeting, we convey concern about our addressee's health and well-being, thereby acknowledging the other's need for involvement. Many of the principles of conversational architecture can be explained in terms of politeness and the recognition of the politeness needs of others.

CROSS-CULTURAL COMMUNICATION

When people of different cultures have different norms about what type of politeness is required in a particular context, trouble can easily arise. We have described how callers in France begin telephone conversations with an apology; such apologies seldom form part of the opening sequence of an American telephone conversation. Obviously, members of the two cultures view telephone conversations differently: Americans generally see the act of calling as a sign of involvement politeness, while the French tend to view it as a potential intrusion.

As a consequence of such variability, people from different cultures often misinterpret each other's signals. In the conversations of Athabaskan Indians, a pause of up to about one and a half seconds does not necessarily indicate the end of a turn, and Athabaskans often pause that long within a turn. In contrast, most European Americans consider a pause of more than one second sufficient to signal the end of a turn (although there may be social variation). When Athabaskan Indians and European Americans interact with each other, the latter often misinterpret the Athabaskans' midturn pauses as end-of-turn signals and feel free to claim the floor. From the Athabaskans' perspective, the European Americans' claim of the floor at this point constitutes an interruption. With the same situation occurring time and again in interactions between the two groups, negative stereotypes arise. Athabaskans find European Americans rude, pushy, and uncontrollably talkative, while European Americans find Athabaskans conversationally uncooperative, sullen, and incapable of carrying on a coherent conversation. Unwittingly carrying those stereotypes into a classroom, European-American teachers may judge Athabaskan students to be unresponsive or unintelligent, because the teachers' unspoken cultural expectations are for students to speak up, interact, and be quick in their responses. While these tend to be the actions of children in mainstream European-American culture, Athabaskan children, honoring the norms of their own culture, tend not to behave in that manner. Though most people are unaware of such subtle cross-cultural differences, they can have profound social consequences.

Computers, Speech Acts, and Conversation

 As we saw in the previous chapter in this section, pragmatics has not yet been thoroughly explored in computational linguistics and corpus studies. It remains necessary to create models of politeness, turn taking, and the other phenomena discussed in this chapter before many of the applications of computer technology to speech will be mastered.

The building of corpora of written language has proceeded more quickly than the compilation of spoken corpora, and the reasons are obvious. Especially in recent years, machine-readable texts initially published as books, magazines, and newspapers have been widely available. In addition, scanners can effectively transform many printed materials of earlier ages into machine-readable text. Creating electronic representations of transcribed spoken language is quite a different matter. First of all, it must be captured, on audio or video, for example. Then it must be transcribed—a challenging and expensive task, and one partly dependent on the quality of the recording and the degree of ambient noise in the original environment.

Still, one of the earliest machine-readable corpora was a transcribed version of spoken English. Called the London/Lund Corpus, it has provided a basis for considerable investigation. A substantial part of the British National Corpus was more recently based on speech. About 100 volunteers were employed throughout Britain to carry tape recorders in the course of several days' ordinary activities, observing in a notebook the conditions surrounding the conversations and other exchanges recorded, such as the participants and their relationships to one another, the physical setting of the recorded speech, and so on. The recordings were then transcribed in ordinary English spelling. At present, the transcriptions are being used for research into the character of conversation. We have reported findings from the British National Corpus in earlier chapters of this book (for example, see the "conversation" category in Figures 8–1 and 8–2 on pages 281–282), and we will report other findings in later chapters.

SUMMARY

- Utterances accomplish things such as asserting, promising, pleading, and greeting. Actions accomplished through language are called speech acts.

- That language is commonly used to perform actions is most clearly illustrated by declarations such as *You're fired* or *Case dismissed!* Whether declarations or not, all speech acts can be described with four appropriateness conditions that identify aspects of or prerequisites for a successful speech act: the content, the preparatory condition, the sincerity condition, and the essential condition.

- In most normal circumstances, language users are bound by an unspoken pact that they adhere to and expect others to adhere to. This "cooperative principle" consists of four maxims—quantity, quality, relevance, and manner.

- On occasion, a speaker may flout a maxim to signal that the literal interpretation of the utterance is not the intended one.

- To encode and decode the intended meaning of indirect speech acts, people use patterns of conversational implicature based on knowledge of their language, their society, and the world around them.

- Indirect speech acts convey more than one message and are commonly used for politeness or humor.

- Respecting other people's needs for privacy demonstrates independence politeness, while showing interest and displaying sympathy expresses involvement politeness.

- A speech event is a social activity in which language plays an important role.

- Speech events are structured, and appropriate verbal and nonverbal behavior characteristics of particular speech events can be described systematically.

- Conversations are organized according to certain regulatory principles.

- Turn taking is regulated by one set of norms.

- Adjacency pairs are structured by a local set of organizational principles, and many have preferred and dispreferred second parts.

- Organizational principles shape conversational openings and closings.

- The organization of repairs can be described with a set of rules that rank different repair patterns in terms of preference. Repairs that are self-initiated and self-made are favored.

- At the root of many organizational principles in conversation is the need to display independence politeness and involvement politeness to other people.

- Culture-specific norms determine when and where independence politeness and involvement politeness behaviors are appropriate.

- Because the organization of polite conversational behavior differs from culture to culture, miscommunication of intent across cultures is common.

WHAT DO YOU THINK? REVISITED

❖ *Todd's question.* Every speech act has appropriateness conditions surrounding it. Among those associated with the act of pronouncing two people as married by saying certain words is the intention of the two people to get married to one another at that time. In the case of a play, the actors do not intend to get married but merely to depict a wedding ceremony. As a consequence, an essential condition of a marriage pronouncement is lacking, and the utterance is ineffectual as a marriage pronouncement.

❖ *Your classmate's complaint.* Making a promise requires using the word *promise,* as in, "I promise to do the dishes if you'll cook dinner." Without the word, there's no promise. (Of course, if someone asks, "Do you promise?" and the reply is "Yes," the reply would constitute a promise.) Pledges and expressed intentions don't require the word *promise,* so your classmate's boyfriend may have had good intentions (or may not have), but he did not make a promise.

❖ *Your brother's complaint.* Your brother's observation probably has less to do with Robb as an individual than with his French social practices. The French view telephoning someone as an intrusion and, consequently, may apologize for phoning and take longer to get to the point than Americans deem necessary. By contrast, Americans regard calling a friend as showing involvement and being generally positive, not requiring apology.

❖ *Your grandmother's polite response.* Your grandmother may regard being phoned by someone as an expression of involvement, and she may extend that view even to telemarketers whom she doesn't know. You view telemarketers not as expressing involvement but as intruding on your time and privacy. You are impatient with their impoliteness and feel free to hang up on them. You try to explain to your grandmother that since telemarketers violate politeness conventions, you feel free to do the same.

EXERCISES

Based on English

9-1 Make a list of the headlines on the first two pages of a daily newspaper. Indicate which of the headlines report physical actions and which report speech acts.

9-2 Observe a typical lecture meeting of one of your courses and identify the characteristics that define it as a lecture (as distinct from an informal conversation, workshop, seminar, or lab meeting). Identify characterizing features of the areas listed below. To what extent is there room for variability in how a lecture is conducted (depending, for example, on the personality of the participants)? When does a lecture stop being a lecture?

a) Setting (physical setting, clothing, social identity of the participants, and so on)

b) Nonverbal behavior of the participants (body movement, stance and position with respect to each other, and so on)

c) Verbal behavior of the participants (turn taking, openings, closings, assignment of pair parts among participants, and so on)

d) Topic (what is appropriate to talk about? to what extent can this be deviated from? and so on)

9-3 Make a tape recording of the first minute of a radio interview. Transcribe what is said during that first minute in as much detail as possible (indicating, for example, who talks, when pauses occur, and what hesitations occur). Label each turn as to its illocutionary force (greeting, inquiry, compliment, and so on). Then describe in detail the strategies used in opening the radio interview. Illustrate your description with specific examples taken from your transcript.

9-4 Make a tape recording of the first minute of a broadcast of the evening news on radio or television. Transcribe what is said during that minute in as much detail as possible. Then answer the following questions, citing specific illustrations from your transcript.

    a. What effect do radio or television newscasters try to achieve initially?

    b. How is this accomplished? Describe at least two strategies, using specific illustrations.

    c. Suppose you played your tape recording to friends without identifying what was taped. Exactly what features would help them recognize it as a recording of the evening news? Cite three specific telltale characteristics other than content.

    d. Which of the news items are reports of physical actions and which are reports of speech acts?

9-5 Observe the following interaction between two people who are working at nearby desks.

Anne: Ed?
Ed: Yeah?
Anne: Do you have a ruler?

Anne's first turn is an opening sequence. What does it signal, and what does Ed's response indicate? Why did Anne not open merely with *Do you have a ruler?*

9-6 The next time you talk on the telephone to a friend, observe the distinctive characteristics of talk over the telephone, and take notes immediately after you hang up. Identify several ways in which a telephone conversation differs from a face-to-face conversation. Try to recreate specific linguistic examples from your telephone conversation to illustrate your points.

9-7 Consider the following excerpts, each of which contains a repair. For each excerpt, determine whether the repair is: (a) self-initiated and self-repaired; (b) self-initiated and other-repaired; (c) other-initiated and self-repaired; or (d) other-initiated and other-repaired.

    a. Jan: What's sales tax in this state?
         James: Five cents on the dollar.
         Patricia: Five cents on the dollar? You mean six cents on the dollar.
         James: Oh, yeah, six cents on the dollar.

    b. Anne: There's a party at Rod's tonight. Wanna go?
         Sam: At Rod's? Rod's outta town!
         Anne: I mean Rick's.

    c. Peter: And then he comes along an' tells me that he's dropping his accounting—uh, his economics class.
         Frank: Yeah, he told me the same thing the next mornin'.

    d. Rick: His dog's been sick since last month an' he won't be able to go to the wedding because he's gotta take care of him.
         Alice: Well, actually, his dog's been sick for at least two months now. So it's nothin' new.

    e. Sam: Do you remember the names of all their kids? The oldest one is Daniel, the girl's Priscilla, then there's another girl—What's her name again?
         Regie: Susie, I think.
         Sam: Yeah, Susie, that's it.

    f. Ellie: What do they charge you for car insurance?
         Ted: Two thousand bucks a year, but then there's a three-hundred-dollar deductible. Three hundred or one hundred—I can't remember.

Ellie: Probably's one hundred, right?

Ted: Yeah, I think you're right. One hundred sounds right.

g. Sarah: He's been cookin' all day for that dinner party.

Anne: Actually he's been cooking for three days now.

h. Will: There wasn't much I could do for her. She needed five thousand bucks to pay for tuition and I jus' didn't have it.

David: I thought it was four thousand.

Will: Yeah, four thousand, but still I didn't have that much.

9-8 Consider the following excerpts, all of which are prestructures initiating conversation. Describe in detail the structure and the function of each prestructure using the terms *turn* (or *turn taking*), *signal, adjacency pair, first part, second part,* and *claiming the floor.*

a. Larry: Guess what.

Lauren: What?

Larry: Pat's coming tomorrow.

b. Tom: [reading the newspaper] I can't believe this!

Fred: What?

Tom: Congress passed another new immigration law.

c. Ruth: [chuckles while reading a book]

Anne: What're you chuckling about?

Ruth: This story, it's so off the wall!

9-9 Consider the following excerpt from a conversation among three friends.

1) Cindy: Heard from Jill recently? She hasn't written or called in ages.

2) Larry: Yeah, she sent me a postcard from England.

3) Barb: From England?

4) Larry: Oh, maybe it was from France, I can't remember.

5) Cindy: What's she doin—

6) Barb: No, I know it must've been from France 'cause she was gonna stay there all year.

7) Cindy: What's she doin' in France?

8) Larry: Why are you asking about her?

9) Cindy: I don't know, I've just been thinkin' about her.

10) Larry: She's on some sort of exchange program. Studyin' French or somethin'.

11) Cindy: Sounds pretty nice to me.

12) Larry: Yeah. Well, I don't know. She said she was tired of Europe and wants to come home.

a. In the conversation above, how many turns does each interlocutor have?

b. Identify an example of each of the following in the conversation above: *turn-taking signal, claiming the floor, preferred response, dispreferred response, repair, trouble source, initiation,* and *resolution.*

c. Identify an *adjacency pair* in the conversation, giving the name of the *first part* and *second part.*

9-10 Conversations in fiction and drama and those re-created in movies or on stage often differ from ordinary everyday conversations. The following is an excerpt from a conversation in Isak Dinesen's autobiographical novel *Out of Africa* (New York: Random House, 1937).

> "Do you know anything of book-keeping?" I asked him.
>
> "No. Nothing at all," he said, "I have always found it very difficult to add two figures together."
>
> "Do you know about cattle at all?" I went on. "Cows?" he asked. "No, no. I am afraid of cows."
>
> "Can you drive a tractor, then?" I asked. Here a faint ray of hope appeared on his face. "No," he said, "but I think I could learn that."
>
> "Not on my tractor though," I said, "but then tell me, Emmanuelson, what have you even been doing? What are you in life?"
>
> Emmanuelson drew himself up straight. "What am I?" he exclaimed. "Why, I am an actor."
>
> I thought: Thank God, it is altogether outside my capacity to assist this lost man in any practical way; the time has come for a general human conversation. "You are an actor?" I said, "that is a fine thing to be. And which were your favourite parts when you were on the stage?"
>
> "Oh I am a tragic actor," said Emmanuelson, "my favourite parts were that of Armand in 'La Dame aux Camelias' and of Oswald in 'Ghosts'."

On the basis of this example, analyze the differences between the organization of conversations represented in writing and the organization of actual conversations. Why do these differences exist?

9-11 The transcribed conversational excerpt below includes two adjacency pairs. Provide the letter or letters of the turn(s) for each of these categories: (1) insertion sequence; (2) first pair-part of first adjacency pair; (3) second pair-part of first adjacency pair; (4) first pair-part of second adjacency pair; (5) second pair-part of second adjacency pair. Next, match each of these speech acts to a turn that exemplifies it: (6) clarification; (7) rejection; (8) proposal; (9) request for clarification.

A. Eric: Wanna watch "Civil War" tonight?

B. Nan: The Ken Burns series?

C. Eric: He made it with his brother.

D. Nan: Sorry. I got an econ quiz tomorrow.

Especially for Teachers and Future Teachers

9-12 Below are two sets of turns from conversations among college students, most spoken within a few months after graduating from high school. In utterances (1) to (4), the highlighted word **like** is used in at least two distinct ways. Analyze (1)–(4) and characterize the two ways. In utterances (5) to (7), the word **all** is highlighted. Characterize its function in these turns. Then imagine yourself leading a discussion with your students in which you and they are analyzing a transcription. One student reports that another one of his teachers pokes fun at the use of *like,* and another student chimes in that her father ridicules it, too. What points would you make in your discussion with them to indicate that these relatively new uses for *like* and *all* function in conversation in ways that are similar to other, more traditional expressions? With what words can *like* and *all* be compared? Discuss why it may be that these newer usages are sometimes ridiculed.

1) Adam: I don't want to break up with her **like** . . . this time.
       Brent: Yeah don't break up this time.
            Break up, **like** Thanksgiving or something.

2) Ben: So she called and was **like,**
          I can't believe you did this,
          I can't believe you did this.
          I'm **like**—,

3) Ali: I was like,
         I was **like** why,
         why,
         you know . . .

4) Rod: I was **like** all happy and stuff.

5) Jose: Wait why is she **all** bitchin' at you first of all?

6) Jaime: I am **all** sitting here trying to read.

7) Danny: I was like **all** happy and stuff.

9-13 Your students are probably familiar with a version of the wise old saying that claims, "Sticks and stones may break my bones, but words will never hurt me." At a level appropriate for your students, draw up a lesson plan that analyzes this saying in terms of the power of speech acts. You might consider beginning the lesson by inquiring whether any of your students have ever been hurt by what others have said to them or about them.

9-14 Call upon students of various cultural backgrounds to discuss their experience calling and being called on the phone by members of other cultural groups. Also discuss their attitudes toward telemarketing calls and how their attitudes might reflect cultural values.

OTHER RESOURCES

- **John J. Gumperz, T. C. Jupp, and C. Roberts. 1979.** *Crosstalk: A Study of Cross-Cultural Communication* (London: National Centre for Industrial Language Training and BBC)

  A one-hour video illustrating and discussing miscommunication between East Indian immigrants and bank clerks, librarians, and other institutional figures in London; a moving demonstration of the painful difficulties that can arise from differing conversational norms across cultural boundaries.

SUGGESTIONS FOR FURTHER READING

- **Diane Blakemore. 1992.** *Understanding Utterances: An Introduction to Pragmatics* (Oxford: Blackwell). A basic introduction; a natural follow-up to the contents of this chapter.

- **Peter Grundy. 2000.** *Doing Pragmatics,* 2nd ed. (New York: Oxford University Press/ London: Arnold). A basic and clear introduction, with an effective conversational and interactive style, containing a chapter on doing project work in pragmatics and others on politeness, speech acts, and deixis (the last of which we treated in an earlier chapter); examples mostly British.

- **Jacob L. Mey. 2001.** *Pragmatics: An Introduction,* 2nd ed. (Oxford: Blackwell). A thorough and more advanced treatment, containing chapters on speech acts, pragmatics across cultures, and conversation analysis, as well as literary pragmatics.

- **Deborah Tannen. 1990.** *You Just Don't Understand: Women and Men in Conversation* (New York: Ballantine). Accessible and highly popular best-seller discusses misunderstanding between the sexes; also treats Gricean maxims very simply.

- **Deborah Tannen. 1994.** *Gender and Discourse* (New York: Oxford University Press). An accessible treatment of the background to Tannen's *You Just Don't Understand.*

- **Ronald Wardhaugh. 1985.** *How Conversation Works* (New York: Blackwell). A well-focused, basic, and accessible textbook.

ADVANCED READING

The analysis of speech acts has been an enterprise chiefly of philosophers. Austin (1975) is a set of 12 readable lectures laying out the nature of locutionary and illocutionary acts (as well as perlocutionary acts). Grice (1975, 1989) formulates the cooperative principle and enumerates the conversational maxims we've discussed. Searle (1976) discusses the classification of speech acts and their syntax, while Searle (1975) lays out the structure of indirect speech acts. Besides these primary sources, you can find good discussions in Levinson (1983) and Wardhaugh (1998).

Profoundly differing from the philosophical traditions in their methodological approach, the inductive studies of the conversation analysts are challenging to read: turn taking was first analyzed systematically by Sacks et al. (1974), closings by Schegloff and Sacks (1973), and repairs by Schegloff et al. (1977). More accessible, especially for student readers, are these textbooks on conversation analysis and language use in informal contexts: Levinson (1983) and chapters 10 and 12 of Wardhaugh (1998).

The theoretical background to the study of speech events is presented in Goffman (1986; original edition 1974) and Hymes (1974). Goffman (1981) presents interesting and entertaining analyses of various speech events, including lectures and radio talk. Goodwin (1981) describes how talk and gestures are integrated in conversation. The organization of conversation in the workplace is investigated in Boden (1988). The characterization of communication between subordinates and superordinates as spectator/performer or performer/spectator was proposed by Bateson (2000), a new edition of a classic text, laying out the philosophical foundation for the study of human communication. Cross-social and cross-cultural differences in the organization of conversation are analyzed in Gumperz (1982a, 1982b), Kochman (1981), Blum-Kulka et al. (1989), Trosborg (1995), and Scollon and Scollon (1981, 1995), from the last of which a few examples appear in this chapter. Godard (1977) is an interesting study of Franco-American differences in behavior on the telephone, and this and other aspects of French interaction are discussed in chapter 10 of Ager (1990). Brown and Levinson (1987) and various chapters of Levinson (1983) and Wardhaugh (1998) discuss politeness. Drew and Heritage (1993) is a collection of essays discussing interaction in institutional settings.

REFERENCES

- Ager, Dennis E. 1990. *Sociolinguistics and Contemporary French* (Cambridge: Cambridge University Press).

- Austin, John. 1975. *How to Do Things with Words,* 2nd ed. (Cambridge: Harvard University Press).

- Bateson, Gregory. 2000. *Steps to an Ecology of Mind: Collected Essays in Anthropology, Psychiatry, Evolution, and Epistemology* (Chicago: University of Chicago Press).

- Blum-Kulka, Shoshana, Juliane House, & Gabriele Kasper, eds. 1989. *Cross-cultural Pragmatics: Requests and Apologies* (Norwood, NJ: Ablex).

- Boden, Deirdre. 1988. *The Business of Talk: Organizations in Action* (Cambridge: Polity).

- Brown, Penelope, & Stephen C. Levinson. 1987. *Politeness: Some Universals in Language Usage* (Cambridge: Cambridge University Press).

- Drew, Paul, & John Heritage, eds. 1993. *Talk at Work* (Cambridge: Cambridge University Press).

- Godard, Daniele. 1977. "Same Setting, Different Norms: Phone Call Beginnings in France and the United States," *Language in Society* 6:209–19.

- Goffman, Erving. 1986. *Frame Analysis: An Essay on the Organization of Experience* [Repr. ed., with a foreword by Bennett Berger] (Boston: Northeastern University Press).

- Goffman, Erving. 1981. *Forms of Talk* (Philadelphia: University of Pennsylvania Press).

- Goodwin, Charles. 1981. *Conversational Organization: Interaction between Speakers and Hearers* (New York: Academic).

- Grice, H. Paul. 1975. "Logic and Conversation," in Peter Cole & Jerry L. Morgan, eds., *Syntax and Semantics 3: Speech Acts* (New York: Academic), pp. 41–58.

- Gumperz, John J. 1982a. *Discourse Strategies* (Cambridge: Cambridge University Press).

- Gumperz, John J., ed. 1982b. *Language and Social Identity* (Cambridge: Cambridge University Press).

- Hymes, Dell. 1974. *Foundations in Sociolinguistics* (Philadelphia: University of Pennsylvania Press).

- Kochman, Thomas. 1981. *Black and White Styles in Conflict* (Chicago: University of Chicago Press).

- Levinson, Stephen C. 1983. *Pragmatics* (Cambridge: Cambridge University Press).

- Sacks, Harvey, Emanuel A. Schegloff, & Gail Jefferson. 1974. "A Simplest Systematics for the Organization of Turn-Taking in Conversation," *Language* 50:696–735.

- Schegloff, Emanuel A., Gail Jefferson, & Harvey Sacks. 1977. "The Preference for Self-Correction in the Organization of Repair in Conversation," *Language* 53:361–82.

- Schegloff, Emanuel A., & Harvey Sacks. 1973. "Opening Up Closings," *Semiotica* 7:289–327.

- Scollon, Ron, & Suzanne B. K. Scollon. 1981. *Narrative, Literacy and Face in Interethnic Communication* (Norwood, NJ: Ablex).

- Scollon, Ron, & Suzanne Wong Scollon. 1995. *Intercultural Communication* (Oxford: Blackwell).

- Searle, John R. 1975. "Indirect Speech Acts," in Peter Cole & Jerry L. Morgan, eds. *Syntax and Semantics 3: Speech Acts* (New York: Academic), pp. 59–82.

- Searle, John R. 1976. "A Classification of Illocutionary Acts," *Language in Society* 5:1–23.

- Trosborg, Anna. 1995. *Interlanguage Pragmatics: Requests, Complaints and Apologies* (Berlin: Mouton de Gruyter).

- Wardhaugh, Ronald. 1998. *An Introduction to Sociolinguistics,* 3rd ed. (New York: Blackwell).

Chapter 10

Registers and Styles: Language Variation across Situations of Use

WHAT DO YOU THINK?

❖ Your neighbor's daughter Stefanie, a junior high school student, asks you why her teachers dislike slang and colloquialisms. She also wonders what's the difference between them. What can you tell her?

❖ Michael, a classmate in your linguistics course, comments that he is surprised to see contractions used in this textbook and asks whether you think contractions like *it's* and *don't* and *you've* should be avoided in textbooks. You've noticed them too but think they create an informal, relaxed tone and are appropriate in this textbook. What justification can you offer for your preference?

❖ Your friend Davin, an English major, comments that the dialogue in a P. D. James novel he's reading is awesome: it's totally natural, he says. You scoff because you've recently corrected the transcription of a deposition you'd given in connection with an automobile accident, and your answers to questions seemed convoluted and peppered with false starts and *uhms* and *uhs.* Your transcribed answers didn't look anything like fictional dialogue. And neither did the attorney's! What do you tell Davin about what's totally natural—and what's not—in fictional dialogue?

❖ Your uncle James, a recently retired attorney, has just taken up cooking. Poring over a cookbook one day, he laments, "What kind of English is this! 'Toast pine nuts in medium skillet. Remove and add 1 tbsp. oil and garlic. Cook 4 minutes and drain remaining liquid. Sprinkle salt and pepper inside trout cavity and stuff with spinach mixture. Brush trout with remaining oil.' What ever happened to words like *of* and *for* and *them* and *the* and all the other Anglo-Saxon glue of the language?" Given your belief that legalese originated on Mars and recipe language is simple, what do you say?

INTRODUCTION

You're familiar with the term *dialects* and know that it refers to language varieties spoken by different social groups. In the United States, people recognize dialects named *Brooklynese* and *Bostonese* and sometimes talk about a *southern drawl* or a *Minnesota accent. Cockney* is another well-known dialect. Dialects are the subject of the chapter following this one. In this chapter, we address language varieties characteristic of *social situations* rather than of *social groups.* We'll talk about *slang* and *legalese* and other language varieties characteristic of particular situations. Language varieties characteristic of particular social situations are called **styles** or **registers.**

Ordinarily, we don't talk to our close friends the same way we talk to our teachers, and we don't write to our parents the same way we would write to an attorney or a cleric. Across different circumstances, everyone varies language forms. For example, we may call some people *Michelle* or *Michael;* others *Dr. Lavandera* or *Mr. Olson;* still others *Your Honor* or *Mr. President;* to some we say *Sir,* to others *Madam* or *Miss.* If you use the term *dude,* you certainly don't use it indiscriminately for anyone you're in contact with. In some communities, different social situations call for altogether different languages; in other communities, different social situations call for alternative varieties of a single language. These varieties are not dialects but registers.

LANGUAGE VARIES WITHIN A SPEECH COMMUNITY

Language Choice in Multilingual Societies

You might assume that in multilingual countries such as Switzerland, Belgium, and India different languages are spoken by different groups of people. Typically, though, each language is also systematically allocated to specific social situations. In speech communities employing several languages, language choice is not arbitrary. Instead, a particular setting such as school or government may favor one language, while other languages will be appropriate in other speech situations. Although there may be roughly equivalent expressions in two languages, the social meaning that attaches to use of one generally differs from that attached to use of the other. As a result, speakers must attend to the social import of language choice, however unconsciously that choice may be made.

Linguistic Repertoires in Brussels, Tehran, and Los Angeles

The use of selected varieties from two languages among government workers in the capital of Belgium illustrates the nature of language choice in one European community.

> Government functionaries in Brussels who are of Flemish origin do not always speak Dutch to *each other,* even when they all know Dutch *very* well and *equally* well. Not only are there occasions when they speak French to *each other* instead of Dutch, but there are some occasions when they speak standard Dutch and others when they use one or another regional variety of Dutch with each other. Indeed, some of them also use different varieties of French with each other as well, one variety being particularly loaded with governmental officialese, another corresponding to the non-technical conversational French of highly educated and refined circles in Belgium and still another being not only a "more colloquial French" but the colloquial French of those who are Flemings. All in all, these several varieties of Dutch and of French constitute the *linguistic repertoire* of certain social networks in Brussels. (Fishman [1972], pp. 47–48.)

The language variety that Brussels residents use is occasioned by the setting in which the talk takes place, by the topic, by the social relations among the participants, and by certain other features of the situation. In general, the use of Dutch is associated with interaction that is informal and intimate, whereas French has more official or "highbrow" connotations. Given these associations, the choice of French or Dutch carries an associated social meaning in addition to its referential meaning.

We use the term **linguistic repertoire** for the set of language varieties exhibited in the speaking and writing patterns of a speech community. As in Brussels, the linguistic repertoire of any speech community may consist of several languages and may include several varieties of each language. Here are two cases.

In the mid-1970s, there was considerable multilingualism in Tehran, the capital of Iran. Christian families spoke Armenian or Syriac at home and in church, Persian at school, all three in different situations while playing or shopping, and Azerbaijani Turkish at shops in the bazaar. Muslim men from northwest Iran, who were working as laborers in the booming capital, spoke a variety of Persian with their supervisors at construction sites but switched to a variety of Turkish with their fellow workers and to a local Iranian dialect when they visited their home villages on holidays; in addition, they listened daily to radio broadcasts in standard Persian and heard passages from the Koran recited in Arabic. It was not uncommon for individuals of any social standing to command as many as four or five languages and to deploy them in different situations.

In a different example, the Korean-speaking community in Los Angeles supports bilingual institutions of various sorts: banks, churches, stores, and a wide range of services from pool halls and video rental shops to hotels, construction companies, and law firms. At some banks all the tellers are bilingual, and in the course of a day's work they switch often between Korean and English. As the tellers alternate between patrons, they naturally switch between Korean and English as appropriate.

Try it yourself: Think of situations in your community where people switch between one language and another in the course of a conversation, depending perhaps on the person they're speaking with or the topic or some other aspect of the social situation.

Switching Varieties within a Language

If we examine the situation in Europe, besides switching between languages we see examples of language-internal switching. Brussels residents switch not only between French and Dutch but also among varieties of French and among varieties of Dutch. In Hemnes, a village in northern Norway, residents speak two quite distinct varieties of Norwegian. Ranamål is a local dialect and serves to identify speakers of that region. Bokmål, one of two forms of standard Norwegian (the other being Nynorsk), is in use in Hemnes for education, religion, government transactions, and the mass media. All members of the community control these two varieties and regard themselves at any given time as speaking one or the other. There are differences of pronunciation, morphology, vocabulary, and syntax, and speakers do not perceive themselves as mixing the two varieties in their speech. Here's an illustration with a simple sentence meaning 'Where are you from?'

        ke du e ifrå   (Ranamål)
        vor ær du fra   (Bokmål)

While Bokmål is the expected variety in certain well-defined situations, residents of Hemnes do not accept its use among themselves outside those situations. In situations in which Ranamål is customarily used, using Bokmål would signal social distance and even contempt for community spirit. In Hemnes, to use Bokmål with fellow locals is to *snakkfint* or *snakk jalat* 'put on airs.' As the researchers who reported these findings note, "Although locals show an overt preference for the dialect, they tolerate and use the standard in situations where it conveys meanings of officiality, expertise, and politeness toward strangers who are clearly segregated from their personal life" (Blom and Gumperz [1972], pp. 433–34). Regard for the social situation is thus important even in choosing varieties of the same language.

SPEECH SITUATIONS

As we have seen in Hemnes, Los Angeles, Brussels, and Tehran, language switching can be triggered by a change in any one of several situational factors, including the setting and purpose of the communication, the person being addressed, the social relations between the interlocutors, and the topic.

Elements of a Speech Situation

If we define a **speech situation** as the coming together of significant situational factors such as purpose, topic, and social relations, then each speech situation in a bilingual community will generally allow for only one of the two languages to be used. Table 10–1 illustrates this concept for a bilingual community in Los Angeles.

Table 10-1
Linguistic Repertoire

SITUATION	RELATION OF SPEAKERS	PLACE	TOPIC TYPE	SPANISH	ENGLISH
A	intimate	school	not academic	X	
B	intimate	home	not academic	X	
C	not intimate	school	not academic		X
D	not intimate	home	academic		X
E	intimate	school	academic	X	X

As you see from Table 10–1, in situation A a variety of Spanish is appropriate; in situation C a variety of English. Only in the relatively rare case of situation E might an individual have a genuine choice between Spanish and English without calling attention to the language chosen. In situation E, a choice is allowed because of the conflict between intimacy (which usually requires Spanish, as in situations A or B) and an academic topic (for which English is usually preferred).

Table 10–2 charts certain aspects of a speech situation that may require a change in language variety.

Table 10-2
Elements of a Speech Situation

PURPOSE	SETTING	PARTICIPANTS
Activity	Topic	Speaker
Goal	Location	Addressee
	Mode	Social roles of speaker and addressee
		Character of audience

In terms of *purpose,* the kind of activity is crucial and so is your goal. Are you making a purchase, giving a sermon, telling a story? Are you entertaining, reporting information, affirming a social relationship? Greeting a friend or inviting an aunt to dinner? The activity may have an influence on your selection of language.

As to *setting*, you may switch from one language to another as the *topic* switches from a topic of local interest, say, to one of national concern, or from a personal topic to one about your studies. *Location*, too, can influence language choice in that you might well use one language in a university setting but a different one in church or at home for otherwise equivalent situations. The *mode*—that is, whether you are speaking or writing—can also influence the forms of language you select.

As to *participants*, the identity of the speaker will influence language choice, as will the identity of the person being addressed. Speakers typically adapt their utterances to the age of an addressee. In some societies, the older the person, the higher his or her social standing; younger people must address older people more respectfully than they address their peers. In French the second-person singular pronoun 'you' has two forms: *tu* is used when addressing a social equal or as an expression of intimacy, while *vous* is reserved for a person of higher social status or to mark social distance (as well as for addressing more than one person, irrespective of status). A younger person addressing an older person may be expected to use *vous*, not *tu*, unless the older person is a close relative. Given that *tu* is the grammatically singular form and *vous* the plural, French illustrates one way in which morphology may vary according to the age of the addressee. Persian also shows many of the same patterns, as do several other European tongues.

It is not just the social identity of speaker and addressee that is relevant, but also their *roles* in the particular speech situation. A judge, for example, typically speaks one variety at home—where she is mother, wife, neighbor—and another as judge in her courtroom. A parent who works as a teacher and has his child for a student may speak different varieties at home and at school, even when the topic and the addressee are the same.

The various aspects of the speech situation come together in a particular choice of language variety. In each situation—whether a general one such as home or church or a specific one such as discussing politics in a cafe with a close friend—only one variety is usually appropriate. In fact, people get so accustomed to speaking a particular language in a given setting that they may have difficulty communicating in another language in that setting, no matter how familiar the other language may be in other settings. (Exceptions to this generalization include professional translators, bilingual educators, and certain businesspeople who are regularly engaged in negotiations with members of their own and another culture.) As a result, switching between language varieties is very common throughout the world.

REGISTERS IN MONOLINGUAL SOCIETIES

The recognition that there are settings and speech situations in multilingual societies in which one language or another is appropriate has a direct parallel in monolingual speech communities, in which varieties of a single language constitute the entire linguistic repertoire. Consider the difference between the full forms of careful speech and the abbreviations and reductions characteristic of fast speech that occur in relaxed face-to-face communication: not only workaday contractions like *won't* and *I'll* but reduced sentences like *Jeetyet?* [dʒitjɛt] and *Wajjasay?* [wɑdʒəse] for 'Did you eat yet?' and 'What did you say?'

To take another example, you know that you don't typically use the same terms for certain body parts when you speak to friends and when you speak to a physician. You might use *collarbone* at home and *clavicle* with a physician, while either one could be used with friends, depending on other aspects of the speech situation. Choices made for certain other body parts would be more strikingly different.

The distribution of alternative terms for the same referent may seem arbitrary and without communicative benefit. With body parts, for example, all terms may be known (and used) by all parties in equivalent situations. A physician speaking with her own physician may use *clavicle,* but with her family and friends *collarbone.* When nonmedical people address a physician, they may use the terms appropriate to discussion of a medical situation.

Since all the terms would be equally well understood and could communicate referential meaning equally well, the choice of a socially appropriate variant is *cognitively* unhelpful. You may ask, then, why linguistic expression differs in different speech situations. The answer is that different forms for the same content can indicate your affective relationship to salient aspects of the situation (setting, addressee, topic, and so on). Such variation as has lasted for centuries in a language can be assumed to serve a fundamental need of human communication.

Try it yourself: Name a speech situation (for example, a conference with a professor, dinner with your grandparents, or a job interview) and provide a list of eight words for things you would likely talk about in that situation, but for which the expression you would use with a close friend would differ from the one you deem appropriate in the speech situation. Next to each term appropriate to the speech situation, provide the term you'd use for the same referent in speaking with a close friend.

Just as a multilingual linguistic repertoire allocates different language varieties to different speech situations, so does a monolingual repertoire. For all speakers—monolingual and multilingual—there is marked variation in the forms of language used for different activities, addressees, topics, and settings. These forms constitute the styles or registers of a linguistic repertoire. By choosing among the varieties, situational variation is both created and mirrored.

From a young age, everyone learns to control several language varieties for use in different speech situations. No one is limited to a single variety in a single language. These language varieties may belong to one language or more than one. Just which speech situations—which purposes, settings, participants—prompt a different variety depends on the norms in particular cultures. In one society, the presence of in-laws may call for a different variety (as it does in Dyirbal and several other aboriginal

Australian societies). In other societies, the presence of children or members of the opposite sex may be crucial. In Western societies, adults have a whole slew of words they avoid saying in the presence of children (and children try to avoid saying in the presence of adults). There are also differences associated with mode—with whether language is written or spoken. You are familiar with the term "colloquial" as a label for informal speech.

MARKERS OF STYLE

As languages differ from one another in vocabulary, phonology, grammar, and semantics, so styles or registers can differ at every level. There may be different interactional patterns in different speech situations as well—for example, the allocation of turns in conversation differs from the allocation of turns in a courtroom or a classroom. In addition, there are rules governing nonlinguistic behavior such as physical proximity, face-to-face positioning, standing, and sitting that also accompany register variation; both interactional patterns and body language are beyond the scope of this book, however, and we mention them only incidentally.

When you find characteristic features of a style at one level of the grammar, you can expect to find corresponding features at other levels as well. For example, to describe legalese requires attention to its characteristic vocabulary, sentence structure, semantics, and even phonology.

Lexical Markers of Style and Register

Registers vary along certain social dimensions. For example, people generally speak (and write) in markedly different ways in formal and informal situations. Formality and informality can be seen as opposite poles of a situational continuum along which forms of expression may be arranged.

The four words *pickled, high, drunk,* and *intoxicated* may mean the same thing, but you can rank them according to their formality, and you would probably agree that they could be ranked from least to most formal in the order given. In one context, to suggest inebriation may require the word *intoxicated,* while in another a more appropriate expression may be *drunk* or *under the influence. Bombed* and *pissed* are other terms used, especially by younger people in situations of considerable informality. One thesaurus lists more than 125 expressions for 'intoxicated.' Needless to say, they are not situationally equivalent.

Not every word that can be glossed as 'inebriated' is suitable for use on all occasions when reference to intoxication is intended. Word choice can indicate quite different attitudes toward the state, the addressees, the person being described, and so on. It can also index the speech situation in which the term is being used as intimate or distant, formal or informal, serious or jocular. Different expressions for 'intoxication' have different connotations, depending on the situations of use with which they are associated. These associated situations of use add a dimension of meaning that is distinct from the referential meaning.

Imagine the following dialogue between a judge and a defendant at an arraignment in a courtroom:

Judge: I see the cops say you were wasted last night and drove an old jalopy down the middle of the road. That right?

Defendant: Your honor, if I might be permitted to address this baseless allegation, I should like to report that I was neither inebriated nor under the influence of an alcoholic beverage of any kind; for the record, I imbibed no booze last evening.

In the first place, the judge's language seems out of place: words like *cops, wasted,* and *jalopy* seem inappropriate for a judge in a courtroom, even bizarre. As for the defendant's response, it too seems out of place, especially following the extremely informal speech of the judge. Even had the judge used more elevated language, the defendant's language might seem overly formal. It also seems odd for the defendant to use the informal word *booze* in an utterance in which the formal words *imbibed, inebriated, beverage,* and *allegation* occur.

Compare the judge's language above with the following, which is more appropriate to the speech situation.

Judge: You are charged with driving a 1992 blue Ford while under the influence of alcohol. How do you plead?

You can see that, even within a single language, registers or styles are chosen for specific situations of use.

Terms of Address   Appropriate forms of address for the same person may differ from situation to situation. The Queen of England is addressed as *Your Majesty* (or *Ma'am),* though her husband presumably uses a more intimate address term when speaking to her in private. In court, judges are addressed as *Your Honor,* though their friends and neighbors may call them *Ruth* or *Byron.* Each of us is addressed in multiple ways, depending on the situation: by first name *(Pat);* family name *(Smith);* family name preceded by a title *(Doctor Smith, Ms. Jones);* the second-person pronoun *(you);* terms showing respect *(Sir, Madam);* and various informal generic terms *(guy, dude).* At the opposite end of the scale are terms of disrespect such as *buster* or *you bastard.*

Slang   Probably the most famous register of all is slang. **Slang** is the register used in situations of extreme informality, and it may signal rebellious undertones or an intentional distancing of its users from certain mainstream values. As a result, slang is particularly popular among teenagers and college students. But by no means is its use limited to such groups, for slang has its wellsprings in specialized groups of all sorts, from physicians and computer "hackers" to police officers and stockbrokers.

Some slang changes as quickly as clothing fashions. Still, there are slang dictionaries, and their existence suggests that some slang expressions lead longer lives.

College Slang: The Top 20

In *Slang and Sociability,* Connie Eble reports the top slang expressions used by students at the University of North Carolina between 1972 and 1993. Which of them have you used or heard?

sweet	'excellent, superb'	wasted	'drunk'
chill/chill out	'relax'	clueless	'unaware'
slide	'easy course'	diss	'belittle, criticize'
blow off	'neglect, not attend'	pig out	'eat voraciously'
bag	'neglect, not attend'	bad	'good, excellent'
killer	'excellent, exciting'	crash	'go to sleep'
jam	'play music, dance, party'	cheesy	'unattractive, out of favor'
scope	'look for partner for sex or romance'	hook (up)	'locate a partner for sex or romance'
		trip (out)	'have a bizarre experience'
		dweeb	'socially inept person'
		buzz/catch a buzz	'experience slight intoxication'
		tool	'completely acceptable'

At the risk of seeming passé, these examples from the dust jacket of a slang dictionary may be illustrative: *awesome, bells and whistles, cover your ass, designer drug, dork, emoticon, kick ass, mallie, netiquette, pocket pool, puzzle palace, spam, tits and zits,* and *whatever!* If you're personally unacquainted with any of these terms, a classmate may be able to provide a gloss.

Slang has a legitimate place in the linguistic repertoire of speech communities. Like all registers, though, its effectiveness depends crucially on the circumstances of its use. In an appropriate situation, anyone of any age and any socioeconomic or educational status can legitimately use slang.

Just as informal clothing can extend its welcome from informal circumstances into somewhat more formal circumstances, so slang expressions often climb up the social ladder, becoming acceptable in more formal circumstances. The words *mob* and *pants* are among many that were slang at an earlier period of their history but can now be used in other than extremely informal circumstances. As words become established in more formal circumstances, they lose their status as slang, and newer slang terms replace them. (Though this rise up the social ladder is common, some slang expressions seem destined to remain forever consigned to the most informal circumstances. *Bones* meaning 'dice' was used by Chaucer in the fourteenth century, and *beat it* meaning 'scram' by Shakespeare in the seventeenth century. In these senses both words remain slang today.)

Jargon Many specialist terms, especially those used by occupational groups, are *jargon,* not slang. Jargon is the specialized vocabulary of various groups, often occupational or recreational groups. Unlike slang, jargon is not limited to situations of extreme informality and generally lacks rebellious undertones. *Argot* is another term associated with "professions," but it tends to be associated with underground or criminal activities.

Try it yourself: For a work situation or recreational situation you are familiar with, make a list of terms used by those engaged in the work or recreation but generally not known by outsiders. Share your list of words with some of your classmates to check your impression that the terms are unknown to outsiders.

Phonological Markers of Style and Register

Registers are marked not only by word choice but also by grammatical features, morphology and other levels of grammar. For spoken registers this includes phonology. In a study of New York City speechways that we will discuss in detail in the following chapter, considerable phonological variation was uncovered among all groups of speakers in different situations of use.

Figure 10–1 presents frequencies for the pronunciation of -*ing* as /ɪŋ/ in three speech situations. We use -*ing* to represent the pronunciation of the suffix in words like *talking, running, eating,* and *watching.* The speech situations in this case consist of three kinds of interaction in the course of a sociolinguistic interview in the homes of four groups of respondents (labeled LC, WC, LMC, and UMC). The style of the interview, with its interlaced questions and answers, can be regarded as "careful" speech. Respondents read a set passage aloud, and "reading" style was taken to represent more careful speech than that interview style. At the end of the interview, in order to prompt relaxed speech, the interviewer asked respondents whether they'd ever had a close call with death, and this gambit usually elicited a relaxed, unguarded variety, here called "casual" speech.

Figure 10-1

Percentage of Pronunciation of -ing as /ɪŋ/ in Three Speech Situations among Four Social Groups in New York City

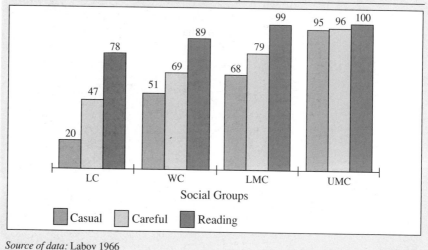

Source of data: Labov 1966

In their casual speech, LC respondents (LC is an abbreviation for lower class, a socioeconomic ranking based on a combination of income, education, and employment type) pronounced the *-ing* suffix as /ɪŋ/ 20% of the time (the other 80% as /ɪn/). In their careful speech, the occurrence of /ɪŋ/ increased to 47% (while /ɪn/ decreased to 53%). When reading a passage aloud, the LC respondents pronounced /ɪŋ/ 78% of the time (and /ɪn/ only 22%). This represents a dramatic increase of /ɪŋ/ pronunciations as the speech situation becomes more formal. Exactly the same overall pattern holds for the three other social groups. Each of them uses more /ɪŋ/ pronunciations in careful speech than in casual speech and more in reading style than in careful speech. We can generalize this finding by saying that in this speech community /ɪŋ/ indexes formality, and more frequent /ɪŋ/ pronunciations signal increased formality.

In another study, college students in Los Angeles gathered data showing that both males and females used more /ɪŋ/ pronunciations in arguments than in joking. Again, we can think of arguing as a less relaxed or more careful register than joking. The frequencies are given in Figure 10–2. Although men and women differ in their use of this phonological variable (a topic we return to in Chapter 11), both sexes exploit it in the same way to index different situations of use.

Figure 10-2

Percentage of -ing Pronounced as /ɪŋ/ in Two Speech Situations by Males and Females in Los Angeles

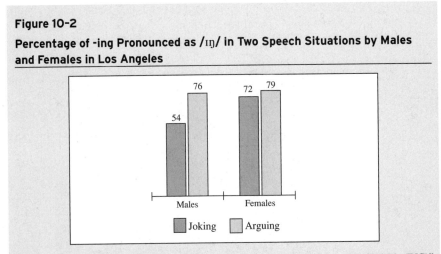

Source of data: B. Wald and T. Shopen, "A Researcher's Guide to the Sociolinguistic Variable (ING)" in Shopen and Williams (1981), p. 247.

A study in Norwich, England uncovered similar patterns of variation across registers. Among five different social groups, the middle middle class (the highest ranking group in the study) *always* used /ɪŋ/ in the formal register of reading style, while lower working class residents *never* used it in their most casual speech. Thus, while all five social groups used both pronunciations in their speech, at the extremes of socioeconomic status and situational formality, the range of difference was 100%.

As the frequencies in Figure 10–3 show, the pattern in Norwich is the same as in New York City: each social group uses the most /ɪŋ/ in reading style and the least in its casual speech, with an intermediate percentage for careful speech. It is clear that on this variable three widely separated English-speaking communities use /ɪŋ/ to index situations of greater and lesser formality. Note that it is not the absolute percentage that indexes situations, but the *relative* percentage with respect to other situations. The data indicate that this linguistic marker of situation is a continuous variable, able to indicate fine distinctions in degrees of formality across a range of speech situations.

Figure 10-3

Percentage of Pronunciation of -ing Pronounced as /ɪŋ/ in Three Speech Situations among Five Social Groups in Norwich, England

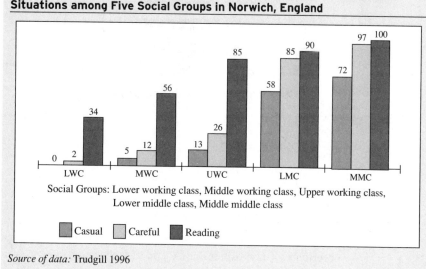

Social Groups: Lower working class, Middle working class, Upper working class, Lower middle class, Middle middle class

Casual Careful Reading

Source of data: Trudgill 1996

As another example of phonological variation (or its equivalent spelling variation), we examine the distribution of ordinary contractions like *can't, won't,* and *I'll* in different situations of use, from telephone conversations between personal friends and between people who do not know one another to writing in newspapers (Press) and academic journals. Even in so straightforward a feature as contractions, speakers exhibit differential use of forms in different speech situations. The counts in Figure 10–4 are based on a corpus of written and spoken British English and represent the average number of contractions per 1000 words. Notice that in going from telephone conversation with friends to telephone conversation with strangers to interviews to broadcasts and so on up the list, there is a graded increase in formality. The increasing formality is accompanied by a decrease in the frequency of contractions.

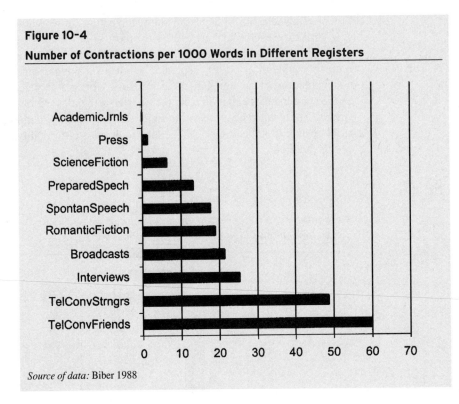

Figure 10-4

Number of Contractions per 1OOO Words in Different Registers

Source of data: Biber 1988

Grammatical Markers of Register

Situations of use are also marked by syntactic variables. As an example, consider the occurrence of prepositions at the end of a clause or sentence. You may recall from your school days that some teachers frowned on sentence-final prepositions. Instead of *That's the teacher I was telling you about,* they recommended *That's the teacher about whom I was telling you.* Well, it's no secret that, despite the admonition to avoid them, sentence-final prepositions abound in English. What's less well-known is that they don't occur with equal frequency in all speech situations. Using the same corpus of texts as was used for contractions, Figure 10–5 presents the number of sentence-final prepositions per 1000 prepositions for nearly a dozen spoken and written registers. This figure does not show the same continuous incline from least formal to most formal that we saw with contractions. Instead, there is a major distinction between speech and nonfiction writing, with fiction writing (which includes fictional dialogue) having intermediate values. In the spoken registers, average counts of between 33 and 56 prepositions per 1000 appear in sentence-final position. In the registers of nonfiction writing, though, final prepositions are fewer than in any of the spoken registers. Thus, there is a notable difference between speech and writing with respect to sentence-final prepositions.

Figure 10-5

Number of Sentence-Final Prepositions per 1000 Prepositions in Different Registers

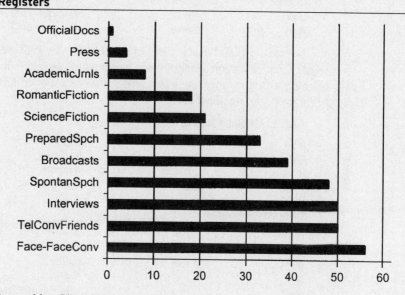

Source of data: Biber 1988

As a second example of grammatical variation across different situations of use, examine this brief passage of *legalese,* a register that is identified by name.

> Upon request of Borrower, Lender, at Lender's option prior to full reconveyance of the Property by Trustee to Borrower, may make Future Advances to Borrower. Such Future Advances, with interest thereon, shall be secured by this Deed of Trust when evidenced by promissory notes stating that said notes are secured hereby.

This passage illustrates several syntactic features characteristic of legalese:

1. Frequent use of passive structures: *shall be secured, are secured*
2. Preference for repetition of nouns in lieu of pronouns: *Lender/at Lender's option, promissory notes/said notes, Future Advances/Such Future Advances*
3. Omission of some indefinite and definite articles: *Upon request, of Borrower, to Borrower, Lender, at Lender's, by Trustee*

Semantic Markers of Register

A given word often carries different meanings in different registers. Consider the word *notes.* As used in the legalese passage above, *notes* means promissory notes, or IOUs. In its everyday meaning, though, *notes* refers to brief, informal written messages on any topic. Among words with one meaning in common everyday use but with a different meaning in legal register are the ones given below.

Expressions Carrying a Distinctive Sense in Legalese

to continue	hearing	sentence
to alienate	action	rider
to serve	executed	motion
save	suit	reasonable man
party	notes	consideration

Not only lawyers but also some of their clients may give specialized meanings to words. Criminal jargon contains many words and expressions that are in common use but carry a different meaning when used in the context of criminal behavior. The following two lists are illustrative.

General Criminal Jargon

mob	sing	bug
hot	rat	bird cage
fence	racket	slammer
sting	a mark	joint ('prison')

Drug World Jargon

crack	pot	downer
coke	grass	speed
snow	toot	pusher
rock	high	dealer
dime	down	joint ('marijuana cigarette')

Each of these expressions bears one meaning in everyday situations but a quite different meaning in the underworld.

Try it yourself: While some of the following expressions carry a sense that is not slang, each also carries a slang sense in extremely informal social situations. Provide a slang sense for each term: the nouns *skinny, main squeeze, hunk, dork, nerd, wuss, spaz,* and *tube;* the verbs *veg out, party, wig out,* and *nuke;* the adjectives *awesome, cool,* and *clueless;* the directives *get a life* and *get a clue.*

SIMILARITIES AND DIFFERENCES BETWEEN SPOKEN AND WRITTEN REGISTERS

Although it is sometimes said that writing is simply speech written down—visual language as distinct from audible language—writing and speaking ordinarily serve different purposes and have distinct linguistic characteristics. Conversation is not a written register, of course, but it can be represented in novels and screenplays. Nor are legal contracts ordinarily spoken. Imagine how the words and the syntax of a handwritten last testament or will would differ from one made by a testator speaking on a videotape. Or consider the linguistic differences between a note stuck on a refrigerator door and the same basic message spoken to someone face-to-face. You'll quickly recognize that speaking and writing are not mirror images of one another.

1. **Oral communication can exploit intonation and voice pitch to convey information.** Face-to-face communication can also utilize gestures, posture, and physical proximity between participants. In writing, the only channels available are words and syntax, supplemented by typography and punctuation. In speaking, communication is possible on multiple channels simultaneously. We can criticize someone's personality in a seemingly objective manner while expressing with intonation or body language how much we greatly admire the person, or vice versa. In writing, much more must be communicated lexically and syntactically, although there are ways of achieving ironic and sarcastic tones that enable addressees to read "between the lines."

2. **Speech and writing differ in the amount of planning that is possible.** For most written registers, you have time for composing and revising. During a conversation, on the other hand, pausing to find just the right word can test your interlocutor's patience and risk your losing the floor. The difference in the available time for planning and editing in written registers produces characteristic syntactic patterns that are difficult to achieve under the immediate processing constraints imposed in spontaneous speech. Written registers typically show a more specific and varied vocabulary, in part because writers have time to choose their words carefully and even consult a thesaurus. Of course, not all written registers are more planned than all spoken registers. Academic lectures and job interviews reflect some of the characteristics of planned writing. On the other hand, some types of writing are produced with relatively little planning, and the language of a letter scribbled a few minutes before the mail pickup is likely to be quite speechlike.

3. **Speakers and addressees often stand face-to-face, whereas writers and readers do not.** In face-to-face interactions, the immediacy of the interlocutors and the contexts of interaction allow them to refer to themselves (*I think, you see*) and their own opinions and to be more personal in their interaction. By contrast, the contexts of writing limit the degree to which written expression can be personal. But be careful not to overgeneralize. Consider, for example, a personal letter and a face-to-face friendly conversation. People may feel they have a right to be equally personal in both contexts. An impersonal stance is thus a feature of only some written registers, as a personal stance is a feature of only some spoken registers.

4. **Written registers tend to rely less on the context of interaction than spoken registers do.** Writing is more independent of context. In spoken registers, expressions of spatial deixis (such as the demonstrative pronouns *this* and *that*) and temporal deixis (like *today* and *next Tuesday)* can be understood with reference to the here and now of the utterance. By contrast, in writing, the lack of a shared environment tends to make such expressions opaque or confusing. To which day would *today* refer in an undated written text? And to what would *this* refer when found in a printed document? Like other distinctions among registers, reliance on deictic expressions does not constitute an absolute difference between speech and writing. In telephone conversations, for example, you cannot say *this thing* (referring to something in the speaker's environment) without risking opaqueness. In contrast, you can leave a written note on the kitchen table that reads *Please don't eat this!* as long as the referent of *this* is obvious from what is near the note; an author of a textbook can reliably refer to *this page* or *this sentence*.

There are many ways in which spoken and written registers differ. But when we examine the differences, we find no absolute dichotomy between them. For example, not many words could occur only in speech or only in writing, even though certain words may occur more frequently in one mode or the other. Written registers tend to be more formal, more informational, and less personal. Along a "personal/impersonal" continuum, the type of writing found in legal documents is at the impersonal end, while informal conversation tends toward the personal end. But personal letters may be close to conversation in their linguistic character. Writing and speaking thus do not form a simple dichotomy, and to describe their differences we must observe which written register and which spoken register is being considered. With all language, the situation of use is the *most* influential factor in determining linguistic form.

TWO REGISTERS COMPARED

By way of illustrating the nature of register variation, let's examine two brief passages of English-language text. The first passage will be immediately recognizable as legalese. While critics have remarked that legalese could be considered a foreign language because it is so different from ordinary writing and speaking, it is simply one of the many registers of English. For people not accustomed to using it, it may be more opaque than other registers, but it is not a foreign tongue. This passage comes from a rider to a deed of trust. A deed of trust is a written agreement that places the title to real estate in the hands of a trustee to ensure that money borrowed with the property as collateral will be repaid; a rider is simply an addition to the basic document.

A Rider to a Deed of Trust	**Line**	**Sentence**
Notwithstanding anything in the Deed of Trust to the contrary, it is	1	1
agreed that the loan secured by this Deed of Trust is made pursuant	2	
to, and shall be construed and governed by the laws of the United	3	
States and the rules and regulations promulgated thereunder,	4	
including the federal laws, rules and regulations for federal savings	5	
and loan associations. If any paragraph, clause or provision of this	6	2
Deed of Trust or the Note or other obligations secured by this Deed	7	
of Trust is construed or interpreted by a court of competent	8	
jurisdiction to be invalid or unenforceable, such decision shall	9	
affect only those paragraphs, clauses or provisions so construed	10	
or interpreted and shall not affect the remaining paragraphs,	11	
clauses and provisions of this Deed of Trust or the Note or	12	
other obligations secured by this Deed of Trust.	13	

The second passage is from a face-to-face interview of former president Harry Truman by biographer Merle Miller (*Plain Speaking* [New York: Berkley Books, 1974], p. 242).

An Interview with Harry Truman	Line	Sentence
Q. What do you consider the biggest mistake you made as President?	1	1
A. That damn fool from Texas that I first made Attorney General	2	2
and then put on the Supreme Court.	3	
I don't know what got into me.	4	3
He was no damn good as Attorney General, and on the Supreme	5	4
Court . . . it doesn't seem possible, but he's been even worse.	6	
He hasn't made one right decision that I can think of.	7	5
And so when you ask me what was my biggest mistake, that's it.	8	6a
Putting Tom Clark on the Supreme Court of the United States.	9	6b
I thought maybe when he got on the Court he'd improve,	10	7
but of course, that isn't what happened.	11	
I told you when we were discussing that other fellow.	12	8a
After a certain age it's hopeless to think people are going to	13	8b
change much.	14	

It's apparent at a glance how strikingly different these passages are. The trust deed is 138 words long and comprises only two sentences. By contrast, the 135 words of the Truman interview occur in eight sentences. The average sentence length is 69 words for the trust deed, 17 for the interview. (In transcribing Truman's words, the interviewer made nine sentences; in numbering them here, we have used the letters *a* and *b* to indicate a combining of two interviewer's sentences into single sentences so as not to exaggerate the number of separate sentences.)

You will find it instructive to examine the passages carefully to identify other linguistic features that contribute to making the registers different.

Try it yourself: Before you read the analysis that follows, jot down as many observations about differences in vocabulary and grammar as you can note in the trust deed and the Truman interview.

Lexicon and Grammar

One easily observed difference between the passages is in vocabulary. The deed of trust contains certain words and phrases that might seem odd if they appeared in the interview. Likewise, Truman's language contains certain earthy words that might strike you as inappropriate in a legal document.

You will also see that in the collocation of words with other words, as well as in preferred lexical categories and in syntax, there are striking differences between the passages. Such features—not in isolation, but taken together—help mark passages as being particular *kinds* of text, particular language varieties suitable in particular speech situations, particular *registers*.

Vocabulary   In contrast to the short everyday words of the interview, the deed of trust uses more uncommon words, as is notoriously characteristic of legalese. Its vocabulary is more "Latinate," the words longer: *promulgated, construed, governed, regulations, obligations, decision, jurisdiction, provisions, invalid, unenforceable, pursuant, secured.* Note also the markedly legal collocation *competent jurisdiction,* in which *competent* does not carry its ordinary meaning of 'capable' but the legal meaning 'having proper authority over the matter to be decided.' Many words that are used in other registers with one meaning carry a different sense in legalese. Besides *competent,* other words in the passage have specific legal senses: *deed, trust, obligation, decision, provisions,* and *note* (as well as *rider,* which doesn't appear in the passage itself).

Nouns and Pronouns   In comparable amounts of text, the trust deed has a total of 40 nouns, the interview only 17. On the other hand, the interview has many more pronouns than the trust deed. It uses first- and second-person pronouns frequently (a total of twelve times): *I, me,* and *we* eight times and *you* four times. (The possessive determiner *my* also occurs once.) By contrast, the trust deed has no occurrences of first- or second-person pronouns.

The interview also exhibits frequent third-person pronouns: Truman uses *he* five times in reference to Tom Clark. By contrast is the repetition of full noun phrases in the trust deed: *Deed of Trust* occurs six times, the coordinate noun phrase *rules and regulations* twice, and the triple coordinate *paragraph, clause or provision* three times (once in the singular and twice in the plural). One exceptionally long noun phrase constituent is repeated, and it contains a repetition of *Deed of Trust* within it: *this Deed of Trust or the Note or other obligations secured by this Deed of Trust.*

There are other differences in pronominal use as well. Truman uses the demonstrative pronoun *that* as a "sentence" pronoun, referring not to a noun phrase but to an entire clause, as in *that isn't what happened* (line 11). In *that's it* (line 8) *that* may refer back to *my biggest mistake* or ahead to *Putting Tom Clark on the Supreme Court of the United States.*

Prepositions and Prepositional Phrases   The trust deed has 19 prepositions, compared to only 12 in the interview. Given the need for a trust deed to be quite specific and the fact that the function of prepositional phrases is to express specific semantic roles—for example, agent (*by a court*), instrument (*by this Deed*), location (*in the Deed*)—the frequency of prepositions in the trust deed is not surprising. Registers whose purpose is in large part informational generally show a much higher proportion of prepositions than other kinds of registers, precisely because prepositions provide frames for semantic information.

Note that the interview has only one instance of prepositional phrases used consecutively (*on the Supreme Court of the United States),* but the trust deed has seven, including this sequence of three: *in the deed of Trust to the contrary.* Further, the interview has an example of a sentence-final preposition (*He hasn't made one right decision that I can think of*), a feature that does not occur in the passage of legalese and occurs very rarely in formal writing of any kind (as Figure 10–5 on page 341 shows).

Verbs If we regard the phrase *shall be construed and governed* as including two verbs, the number of verb groups in the trust deed is nine, about one-third the number in the Truman interview. Thus the interview is highly *verbal.* As to particular verbs, Truman uses *think, know,* and *seem,* and his interviewer uses *consider.* Such "private" verbs represent the internal states of a speaker or writer. They are appropriate in an interview and appear very frequently in conversation, though they would be out of place in the trust deed. Truman also employs pro-verbs of various sorts (pro-verbs take the place of other verbs, much as pronouns take the place of nouns): *do* and *happen,* which can be substituted for many verbs; *put* and *get,* which are more limited but still have far-ranging uses. In conversation, where there is pressure to find your words speedily, pro-verbs tend to occur frequently, in part because they save the time that would be needed to find a more explicit verb. In this short passage *got* appears twice, and Truman uses *put on* and *putting on* (the Supreme Court) instead of, say, *appointed to.* The verb *to be*—the most common verb in English—occurs as a main verb seven times, whereas in the trust deed it occurs four times as an auxiliary (*is agreed, is made, be construed,* and *is construed*) but just once as a main verb (*to be void*).

Some verbs in the trust deed are related to the topic of discussion and therefore to the register of the passage: *agree, construe, govern, promulgate, interpret,* and *affect.* Not related to topic but characteristic of legalese is the use of *shall* as an auxiliary verb. While *shall* occurs in other registers, its use is exceptionally common in legalese. *Shall* occurs as an auxiliary in both sentences of the trust deed.

The interview concerns the years of Truman's presidency, as the preponderance of past-tense verbs reflects. Among its 25 verb groups, 14 are in the past tense, while the 8 present-tense verbs generally make reference to the ongoing interaction between Truman and the interviewer or to Truman's own thought processes in the course of the interview: *what do you consider, when you ask, I don't know, I can think.* The one verb that refers to future time uses the construction *are going to* instead of *shall* or *will.*

Negation In the interview, four out of five negative morphemes occur as the negative adverb *not* (attached to the verb as a contraction). The fifth is the adverb *no* modifying *(damn) good.* In contrast, the trust deed incorporates elements of negation into adjectives or prepositions by the processes of derivational morphology (*invalid,* *unenforceable*) or compounding (*notwithstanding*); there is one isolated *not* (which occurs with reference to future time *shall not*, in contrast to a future positive *shall*). One characteristic difference between speech and writing is the much higher frequency of negation in spoken registers, where the vast majority of negative elements are separate like *not* (which is often realized as *-n't*) rather than incorporated into words like *invalid*.

Adverbs   Legalese is famous for its use of compound adverbs such as *thereto* and *hereinunder*. Our passage contains only one example of *thereunder*. In fact, besides a single instance of *not*, the legal passage contains only the two adverbs *only* and *so*. Truman's adverbs are different. He uses them to make reference to time (*first, then*) and as hedges to indicate his stance toward what he is saying, as with *of course* and *maybe*.

Passive Voice   One striking feature of the deed of trust is its frequent use of passive voice verbs (*is agreed, is made, shall be construed and governed, is construed or interpreted*). Passive constructions demote an agent subject to object of a preposition, thereby permitting omission of the agent (*Lightning struck the house/The house was struck by lightning/The house was struck*). In legalese, both agentless passives (those lacking the *by* phrase) and passives with *by* are common. In marked contrast to the deed of trust, Truman and his interviewer use *only* active voice verbs.

Questions   In using the form of a direct question (*When you ask me <u>what was my biggest mistake</u>*) instead of an indirect question (*When you ask me <u>what my biggest mistake was</u>*), Truman contributes to an impression of informality. And, although it may seem too obvious to mention, the interview contains a question (as interviews naturally do), which is not only a syntactic structure that does not appear in this trust deed but also would be unusual in such legal documents.

Reduced Relative Clauses   Another characteristic feature of legalese is the frequency of reduced relative clauses, in which the relative pronoun and a form of the verb *be* do not appear where they might. These examples show the omitted words in parentheses.

> loan (that is) secured
>
> rules and regulations (that are) promulgated thereunder
>
> paragraphs, clauses or provisions (that are) so construed or interpreted

Conjoining   The Truman interview shows frequent coordinating conjunctions, such as *and, but, and then, and so,* which serve chiefly to link clauses, as in lines 5, 6, and 8. These conjunctions are lacking in the legalese passage except for *and*, which is not used to link clauses but to link verbs, nouns, or adjectives.

Another feature typical of legalese is triple phrasal conjoining "X, Y and Z" or "X and Y and Z." In legal registers, X, Y, Z can be members of almost any category, but are most commonly noun phrases, adjectives, or verbs; they are ordinarily members of the same lexical or phrasal category. Here are some examples of this pattern:

laws, rules and regulations (nouns)

paragraph, clause or provision (nouns)

deed of trust or the note or other obligation (noun phrases)

void, invalid or unenforceable (adjectives)

Sometimes variation within the X, Y, and Z constituents produces similar but not completely parallel structures, as in these examples:

1. is made pursuant to, and shall be construed and governed by
2. the laws of the United States and the rules and regulations

In 1, there are two verb-phrase structures conjoined by *and,* but the second verb phrase itself contains two conjoined verbs (*construed and governed).* In 2, we might more accurately describe the structure not as "X, Y, and Z" but as "X and Y," with Y being a compound M and N; thus, "X and (M and N)."

Phonology

Since only one of the two passages originated in speech, we cannot make straightforward phonological comparisons. We do not have a phonetic transcription, but we can infer from the transcribed text that Truman exhibited frequent phonological abbreviation. Instead of full forms like *do not,* eight contractions occur even in this small sample: *don't, doesn't, isn't, hasn't, he's, he'd, that's,* and *it's.* In line 1, the one place in the deed of trust where a comparable form might appear, *it is* occurs, not *it's.* If we were comparing two forms of spoken English and had suitable transcriptions, we could say more about phonological similarities and differences.

Comparing Registers

In comparing and contrasting the two passages, no single feature identifies which registers they exemplify. Rather, various features occurring in combination characterize the first passage as legalese and the second as an interview. Truman's style is so informal that it suggests conversation rather than a formal interview; this may be partly the result of the interviewer's having spent several months with Truman, morning and afternoon. No doubt as the days passed, the interview came increasingly to resemble conversation between friends.

You have now seen that language features differ from one speech situation to another. Sometimes there is more of one feature in a given register than in another, and occasionally a feature occurs in one register exclusively, or almost exclusively. Sometimes the same form occurs in more than one register but with different meanings or different uses.

Computers and the Study of Register Variation

In the field of artificial intelligence, in expert systems, and in a number of critically important high-tech fields today, the role of registers is crucial. The reasons are complex, but you can get a feel for some of them simply by considering the different patterns of syntax and vocabulary across registers that any system would need to master, such as information given in the form of headlines or medicalese or legalese or conversation. Think of it this way: if your corpus contained nothing but writings from newspapers but failed to distinguish among the distinctly different kinds of newspaper texts (reportage, personal ads, editorials and editorial letters, advertising, cartoons, sports commentary, business analysis, stock market and weather reports, and so on), it would have to be immeasurably more complicated than would a set of individual systems designed to handle various registers one by one.

It would be difficult to overestimate the importance of computers to the study of register and register variation. Compilers of corpora have always been mindful of the importance of sorting texts into registers. (In effect, this means designating each text as belonging to a particular register.) Since so much study of registers has been quantitative, large-scale corpora help ensure reliability and validity, although the design of a corpus is critically important in establishing validity. Earlier we saw that the Brown and LOB corpora of English ran to about 1,000,000 words each. By today's standards, those are not big corpora. Although even the British National Corpus is not the biggest corpus in the world, it has 100,106,008 words. According to information provided at the BNC Web site,

> The Corpus occupies about 1.5 gigabytes of disk space—the equivalent of more than a thousand high capacity floppy diskettes.

To put these numbers into perspective, the average paperback book has about 250 pages per centimetre of thickness; assuming 400 words a page, we calculate that the whole corpus printed in small type on thin paper would take up about ten metres of shelf space. Reading the whole corpus aloud at a fairly rapid 150 words a minute, eight hours a day, 365 days a year, would take just over four years.

Some of the research findings reported in this chapter, with its emphasis on quantitative assessments of corpora, have relied on computers. Leaving aside the tasks of their physical creation on paper, the data in several tables and figures were generated without computers, such as Figure 10–2 on page 338, which reports the frequency of -*ing* pronounced as /ɪŋ/ among males and females in Los Angeles. But for other data, computers were needed, at least in a practical sense. Identifying some features would be utterly straightforward, given a tagged corpus. In the straightforward category we can include nouns, prepositions, demonstrative pronouns, private verbs, and so on. Depending on the extent of the tagging, other categories could be identified, such as past-tense verbs, but if the corpus wasn't tagged for tense, an algorithm would have to be specified to instruct the computer what to look for. Algorithms would also be necessary to identify such structures as sentence pronouns and sentence-final prepositions. Some algorithms would prove particularly tricky to design. In this regard, you might want to think about the nature of the algorithm that would instruct a computer how to identify *that* omissions, as in *She said he tried* rather than *She said that he tried*. After all, it's one thing to write an algorithm that identifies a feature that is present, but identifying a feature that is not present is much more challenging.

SUMMARY

- Three principal elements determine each *speech situation:* setting, purpose, and participants.

- Topic and location are part of *setting.*

- Activity type and goals are part of *purpose.*

- With respect to *participants,* it is not only the people themselves who influence language form but also the roles they are playing in that speech situation.

- As we wear different clothing for different occasions and different activities, so we generally do not speak the same way in court, at dinner, and on the soccer field.

- In multilingual communities, different speech situations call sometimes for different languages and sometimes for different varieties of the same language.

- *Registers* are language varieties characteristic of particular speech situations. Registers are sometimes also called *styles.*

- The set of varieties used in a speech community in various speech situations is called its *linguistic repertoire* or its *verbal repertoire.*

- The linguistic repertoire of a monolingual community contains many registers, which differ from one another in their linguistic features either in an absolute sense or, usually, in a relative sense.

- Each register is characterized by a set of linguistic features, not by a single feature.

- The sum total of such features (lexical, phonological, grammatical, and semantic), together with the characteristic patterns for the use of language in a particular situation, determines a register.

- Because all register or style varieties within a language draw on the same grammatical system, the differential exploitation of that system to mark different registers occurs in relative terms.

- Writing differs from speaking in a number of fundamental ways, but the linguistic differences between the two *modes* are not absolute.

WHAT DO YOU THINK? REVISITED

❖ *Stefanie and slang.* Probably not all Stefanie's teachers dislike slang and colloquialisms, and certainly not all of them dislike them in all situations. But teachers understand that slang is characteristic of extremely informal situations, and they may regard classrooms or written essays as relatively formal situations. By definition, colloquial expressions characterize spoken language. Given that language-related school tasks chiefly focus on reading and writing, teachers may mark certain expressions "colloquial" when they find them written in student essays. Teachers may also think students are already familiar with slang and colloquialisms and need to achieve mastery over more formal registers in school. Language that is appropriate in a conversation may not be appropriate in a written essay.

❖ *Michael and contractions.* Contractions are a shortcut, usually for representing words in writing as they are commonly spoken in informal situations. Written contractions thus mimic the relaxed tone of conversation. When they're used, say, in friendly letters, they reflect the informality of conversation. By extension, textbooks can achieve a more relaxed and conversational tone by using contractions, because contractions not only reflect a conversational tone but also help create one. In this textbook, an interactive tone is established partly by asking readers to answer questions ("What do you think?") and to figure things out ("Try it yourself"). Contractions attempt to create a more interactive style, engaging the reader with the content of the text. Contractions aren't right or wrong in themselves; they're appropriate in some circumstances, less appropriate in others: depends on the situation.

❖ *Davin and fictional dialogue.* Few people have read a transcript of actual speech, and far fewer have transcribed an ordinary conversation. Given the spontaneous and unscripted character of conversation, speakers often need to search for words and sort out their syntax to convey what they intend. They sometimes go down what quickly appear to be syntactic dead ends and have to backtrack. For Davin, "natural" may simply mean dialogue that doesn't appear stiff or dialogue that contains colloquialisms or slang. If he had to read an actual conversation (with the kinds of hesitations and re-starts and *uhms* and *uhs* in your deposition), he would certainly grow impatient. So novelists deliberately avoid making their dialogue entirely natural.

❖ *Uncle James's recipe.* Uncle James has spotted several characteristic telegraphic features of some recipes. Because recipes were often passed on from cook to cook and written speedily on index cards or used envelopes, for example, family cooks probably omitted unnecessary words, using a kind of telegraph language. It's not surprising, then, that omitted words are ones that can be easily supplied. "Let's see," you say to Uncle James. "If we fill in the missing words here's what we'd get: 'Toast **the** pine nuts in **a** medium skillet. Remove **them** and add 1 tbsp. **of** oil and garlic. Cook **them** for 4 minutes and drain **the** remaining liquid. Sprinkle **some** salt and pepper inside **the** trout cavity and stuff **it** with **the** spinach mixture. Brush **the** trout with **the** remaining oil.' It's old-fashioned recipe style. And it should be no challenge to someone well versed in the intricacies of legalese! Now let's see how good the trout is!"

EXERCISES

Based on English

10-1   Consider the following expressions.

> Kindly extinguish the illumination upon exiting.
> Please turn off the lights on your way out.

The content of the directive is basically the same in both expressions, but the social meanings differ markedly. Identify features that highlight the differences between the two directives; then discuss the impression that each is likely to make and under which circumstances each might be appropriate.

10-2   **a.** List five pairs of body part or bodily function terms like *clavicle/collarbone* that would distinguish a conversation you were having with a physician from one with a friend on the same topic.

   b. Rank the words in each set below in order of formality:

   1) prof, teacher, instructor, mentor, educator

   2) guru, mullah, maestro, trainer, coach, don

   c. Are any of the words in (1) or (2) above so informal as to be slang? Explain.

10-3   In *Slang and Sociability,* Connie Eble reports the top 40 slang expressions used by students at the University of North Carolina between 1972 and 1993. The top 20 are given in the box on page 336. Below, the next 20 are listed, some with succinct definitions. Provide succinct definitions for the others if you are familiar with them; if you are not, what would you guess them to mean?

grub (verb)	*hot*
geek	*slack* 'below standard, lazy'
granola	*trashed*
homeboy/~girl/homey	*veg (out)*
not!	*word (up)* 'I agree'
ace (verb)	*awesome*
dude	*book* 'leave, hurry'
the pits	*turkey*
bagger 'fraternity member'	*fox/foxy*
flag 'fail'	*Sorority Sue/Sue/Suzi*

10-4   Taperecord about 30–45 seconds of a radio news report and a television news report (if possible, use the same news item). After transcribing the passages, compare them to see what effect the medium has on the choice of linguistic forms.

10-5   Here's the immediate sequel to the Truman passage quoted in this chapter; the sentences have been numbered for reference only.

   Q.   (1)   How do you explain the fact that he's been such a bad Justice?

   A.   (2)   The main thing is . . . well, it isn't so much that he's a *bad* man. (3) It's just that he's such a dumb son of a bitch. (4) He's about the dumbest man I think I've ever run across. (5) And lots of times that's the case. (6) Being dumb's just about the worst thing there is when it comes to holding high office, and that's especially true when it's on the Supreme Court of the United States. (7) As I say, I never will know what got into me when I made that appointment, and I'm as sorry as I can be for doing it. [*Plain Speaking*, p. 242].

   a. Is it clear what *that* refers to in *that's the case* (sentence 5) and *that's especially true* (sentence 6)? If so, what type of constituent does *that* refer to in these instances?

   b. What is the name of the linguistic feature that you examined in question a above?

   c. Identify all instances of *be* as a main verb. How many are there?

   d. What is the function of *well* in sentence 2?

   e. Wherever possible, supply a noun phrase that would have the same referent as the pronoun *it* in sentences 2, 3, 6 (two instances), and 7. Explain those cases where a noun phrase could not be identified as having the same referent as *it*.

10-6 **a.** Look up the definition of *slang* in a good desk dictionary and, using it as a guideline, list as many slang words and expressions as you can for two notions each in (1) and (2) below.
  1) drunk, sexually carefree person, ungenerous with money, sloppy in appearance
  2) sober, chaste person, generous with money, neat and tidy

  b. What is it about the notions represented in (1) that makes them more susceptible to slang words and expressions than those in (2)?

  c. To the extent that you could cite slang terms for the items in (2), do they have negative or positive connotations?

  d. Does the dictionary definition of slang help explain the differential distribution of slang terms in (1) and (2) and the connotations associated with the slang terms in (2)? If so, explain how. If not, revise the dictionary definition to accommodate what you have discovered about the connotations of slang terms.

10-7 Some of the most common words of English (*the, of, and, a, to, it, is, that*) appear in both the trust deed and the interview, as well as in nearly all registers of English. But one register in which these words are relatively infrequent is "headlinese."

  a. Identify two other registers in which you can observe a relatively infrequent use of these words.

  b. Choose a sample from one of the two registers you've identified or from newspaper headlines, and identify the lexical categories that strike you as occurring with higher frequency than in conversation. Note which lexical categories, if any, occur relatively infrequently.

  c. Offer a hypothesis as to why the distribution is as you found it.

  d. Examine *of course* in line 11 of the Truman interview on p. 345. On one level it could be analyzed as a prepositional phrase consisting of the preposition *of* and the noun *course*. If you think of it as a compound, what lexical category would it belong to? (*Hint:* Substitute single words for the compound, and decide which category the substitutes belong to.)

  e. In terms of its distribution with respect to other word classes, decide which lexical category *such* belongs to in line 9 of the trust deed. Using the same criterion, what is the lexical category of *so* in line 10? What about *so* in line 8 of the Truman interview?

  f. Make a list of the determiners in the deed of trust and a list of those in the Truman interview. Specify the particular word class for each determiner in your list (for example, article, demonstrative).

  g. The trust deed has one instance of *that* (line 2) and the Truman interview has six: lines 2 (twice), 7, 8, 11, and 12. Identify the word class for each of these seven instances.

  h. Give two arguments for categorizing *notwithstanding* (trust deed, line 1) as a preposition.

  i. Bearing in mind that compounds are not always written as a single word (*notwithstanding*), identify another example of a compound preposition in the trust deed.

  j. The trust deed contains several compounds (for example, the preposition *notwithstanding* and the pronoun *anything* in line 1 and the compound noun *United States* [made up of an adjective and a noun] in lines 3–4). Identify all the compounds in the Truman interview, and note their lexical categories. What similarities and differences exist between the categories of compounds in the trust deed and the interview?

  k. Examine the occurrences of *to* in the trust deed (lines 1, 3, and 9) and the Truman interview (line 13). Which, if any, of these is a preposition? What are the others?

  l. Assuming that the passages are typical of their registers, what generalizations can you make about the registers in terms of their exploitation of particular word classes?

10-8 Examine the three letters below. The first is a letter of recommendation for a student seeking admission to a master's degree program in linguistics, the second a letter to a magazine, and the third a personal letter from a woman to a female friend in another state. Identify the particular characteristics of each type of letter.

Letter of Recommendation (182 words)

I have known Mr. John Smith as a student in three of my courses at State, and on the basis of that acquaintance with him, it is my recommendation that he should certainly be admitted to graduate school.

John was a student of mine in Linguistics 100, where he did exceptionally well, writing a very good paper indeed. On the basis of that paper, I encouraged him to become a linguistics major and subsequently had the good fortune to have him in two more of my classes. In one of these (historical linguistics) he led the class, obviously working more insightfully than the other seventeen students enrolled. In the other course (introduction to phonology), he did less well, perhaps because he was under some financial pressure and was forced to work twenty hours a week while carrying a full academic load. In all three courses, John worked very hard, doing much more than was required.

I recommend John Smith to you without reservation of any kind. He knows what he wants to achieve and is clearly motivated to succeed in graduate school.

Editorial Letter (91 words)

Your story on Afghanistan was in error when it stated that the Russian-backed coup of 1973 was bloodless. As a Peace Corps volunteer in Afghanistan at the time, I saw the bodies and blood and ducked the bullets. It was estimated that between 1,000 and 1,500 died, but it is hard to get an accurate count when a tank pulls up to the house of the shah's supporters and fires repeatedly into it from 30 feet away, or when whole households of people disappear in the middle of the night.

Personal Letter (142 words)

So, what's up? Not too much going on here. I'm at work now, and it's been so slow this week. We haven't done anything. I hate it when it's so slow. The week seems like it's never going to end.

Well how have you all been? Did you get the pictures and letter I sent you? We haven't heard from you in a while. Mother has your B'day present ready to send to you and Dan's too, but no tellin' when she will get around to sending it. How are the kids? Does Dan like kindergarten? Well, Al has gone off to school. I miss him so much. He left Monday to go to LLTI. It's a trade school upstate. You only have to go for two years, and he's taking air conditioning and refrigeration and then he's going to take heating.

10-9 **a.** Review what was said about *competent* (as in *competent jurisdiction*) in the discussion on p. 346. Then try to specify the legal senses of the following words, which are also used with specialized meanings in the trust deed: *deed, trust, obligation, decision, provisions,* and *note.* List any words used with specialized senses in the Truman interview, and specify the sense.

b. List another example of a reduced relative clause in the trust deed besides the three identified on p. 348.

c. List any examples of a reduced relative clause in the Truman passages on p. 345 and in the sequel given in Exercise 10–5 above.

10-10 Below are personal ads (slightly adapted) from a weekly newspaper published in Los Angeles. Examine their linguistic characteristics and answer the questions that follow.

1) Aquarius SWM, 33, strong build, blue eyes. You: marriage-minded, bilingual Latin Female 23–30, children ok.

2) Busty, brilliant, stunning entrepreneur, 40s (looks 30). Seeks possibly younger, tall, handsome, caring SWM, who respects individuality. Someone who lives the impossible dream, financially secure, good conversation, for relationship, n/s.

3) SWM, 28, attractive college student, works for major US airlines, enjoys traveling. Seeks Female, 23–32, humorous and intelligent for world-class romance and possibly marriage.

4) English vegetarian. SWM, 31. Sincere, sensitive, original, thinking, untypical, amusing, shy, playful, affectionate professional. Seeking warm, witty, open-minded WF, under 29, to share my life with.

5) Slim, young, GWM, very straight appearance, masculine, athletic, healthy, clean-shaven, discreet. Seeks similar good-looking WM, under 25, for monogamous relationship.

6) Very romantic SBM, 24, college educated. Seeks wealthy, healthy and beautiful Lady for friendship and maybe romance. Phonies and pranksters need not apply.

7) Hispanic DF, petite but full of life, likes sports, dancing, traveling, looking for someone with same interests, 30+, race unimportant.

8) Evolved, positive thinking, spiritual, affectionate, honest, handsome, healthy, secure, 36, 6', 160#, blue-eyed, unpretentious, unencumbered, professional. Seeking counterpart, soul mate, marriage, family.

a. Compared to conversation, which lexical categories are very frequent in the ads? Which ones are particularly rare?

b. Identify eight characteristic linguistic features of personal ads. They may be features of syntax, morphology, vocabulary, abbreviation conventions, and so on.

c. List the verbs in all the ads, and identify their grammatical person (first, second, third) and number (singular, plural) where possible. (*Hint:* Supply the pronoun that would serve as subject of each verb in order to determine person and number.)

d. Choose one of the ads and attempt to write it out fully in conversational English solely by supplying additional words; keep the word order and word forms of the original ad.

e. On the basis of your attempt, what indication is there that the ads represent a reduced or abbreviated form of conversational English? If you judge the ads not to be reductions of the sentences of conversational English, what explanation can you offer for the form of their sentences?

f. Which linguistic features of personal ads strike you as conventionalized to the point of requiring previous knowledge of the register in order to understand it?

10-11 Examine a current issue of your campus newspaper and identify as many different registers as you can find in it (for example, editorials and movie reviews). Choose a passage from one register and list eight linguistic features that contribute by their high frequency to the characterization of that register; provide an example of each feature from your passage.

10-12 Recipes, obituaries, classified ads, display ads, telegrams, birthday cards, credit applications, course descriptions in college catalogs, directions for using medicines, and essay questions are just a few of the distinctive registers you may have occasion to use regularly. Choose a small textual sample from one of these registers, and provide a list of its characteristic features, with an example of each feature from your sample.

Based on English and Other Languages

10-13 Identify several instances of linguistic features that vary across registers in a foreign language you have studied. (Some features may be alluded to in your foreign language textbook, while others may have been mentioned by your instructor.) Identify at least one phonological feature, one grammatical feature, and several vocabulary items that vary across situations of use. For each feature, specify the situation in which it is appropriate and another in which it would not be. (*Hint:* Consider gross differences of situation, such as writing versus speaking, formal versus informal, fast speech versus careful speech, interaction between you and a superior versus you and someone of equal status.)

Especially for Educators and Future Teachers

10-14 Examine a foreign language textbook you have studied from or are teaching, and identify any evidence the author has provided that the particular language varies from situation to situation. That evidence may focus on formality versus informality, on differences between speech and writing, in forms of address for addressees of different social status, for slang terms or jargon, or any other linguistic variation that depends on situation of use. What's your assessment about how clear the author is as to the importance of such differences in sounding like a native or writing like one?

10-15 Examine the front matter of your dictionary (or the dictionary you recommend to your students) and locate the discussion of how it treats slang. (You may have to look under "usage" or "labels" for the discussion.) Compare what the dictionary says about slang in the front matter with the definition it gives in the main body of the dictionary's list of entries. Finally, write down six of the most common slang words your students (or classmates) use and look them up to see whether that dictionary notes the slang sense you have in mind and whether it labels it as slang. On the basis of this exercise, would you judge that particular dictionary to be a useful source of information about slang for you? For your students? Would students ordinarily use a dictionary to gather information about slang? Who would ordinarily use a dictionary to determine slang meanings? To what extent should a dictionary attempt to include slang terms and slang senses?

OTHER RESOURCES

- **British National Corpus: http://info.ox.ac.uk/bnc/**
  The home page for the British National Corpus, this one-stop supermarket provides information about and links to a myriad of other corpus pages. One link permits you to submit queries to the BNC itself and receive sample sentences containing the expression you queried. The link to "Corpora Page" leads to a host of links to other Web sites, some for corpora, some for corpus analysis tools. Well worth a visit if you are seriously interested in registers or corpora.

SUGGESTIONS FOR FURTHER READING

- **Allan Bell. 1991.** *The Language of News Media* (Cambridge, MA: Blackwell). The most accessible in-depth analysis of a single register, one that plays a prominent role in everyone's life.
- **Vijay K. Bhatia. 1993.** *Analysing Genre: Language Use in Professional Settings* (London: Longman). A qualitative approach to registers, accessible to students as a next step beyond this textbook.
- **Robert L. Chapman, ed. 1995.** *Dictionary of American Slang,* 3rd ed. (New York: HarperCollins). A handsome dictionary of slang; also discusses the nature and sources of slang. We have taken examples of slang for illustration in this chapter from the dust jacket of this volume in its current and a previous edition.
- **David Crystal & Derek Davy. 1969.** *Investigating English Style* (London: Longman). Contains accessible chapters on the language of conversation, religion, newspaper reporting, and legal documents.
- **Connie Eble. 1996.** *Slang and Sociability: In-group Language among College Students* (Chapel Hill: University of North Carolina Press). Highly informative read. Contains a glossary of over 1000 slang terms.
- **Martin Joos. 1962.** *The Five Clocks* (New York: Harcourt). A popular, entertaining treatment of the notion of style.
- **Timothy Shopen & Joseph M. Williams, eds. 1981.** *Style and Variables in English* (Cambridge, MA: Winthrop). This collection of essays for a general audience treats discourse and literary and other styles.

ADVANCED READING

Brown and Fraser (1979) surveys the elements of speech situations that can influence language. The description of switching in Brussels comes from Fishman (1972), while Blom and Gumperz (1972) describes switching between Bokmål and Ranamål. Biber (1988) is a quantitative study of variation in a corpus of spoken and written English, while Biber (1995) discusses textual variation in English, Korean, and Somali. O'Donnell and Todd (1991) treats English in the media, advertising, literature, and the classroom. Discussions of still other written registers can be found in Ghadessy (1988). Chapters in Biber and Finegan (1994) describe sports-coaching registers, personal ads, and dinner table conversations, as well as register variation in Somali and Korean. Andersen (1990) describes register use among children. Finegan (1992) discusses the evolution of fiction, essays, and letters over the course of several centuries, along with the attitudes toward standardization during that formative period. Lambert and Tucker (1976) reports several social-psychological studies of address forms, principally in Canadian French, Puerto Rican Spanish, and Colombian Spanish. Useful and insightful discussions of French registers can be found in Sanders (1993) and George (1993), while French slang and colloquial usage is abundantly illustrated in Burke (1988). Barbour and Stevenson (1990) contains two chapters that discuss aspects of situational variation in German, and Clyne (1999) touches on situational variation as well. More advanced discussions of register can be found in Leckie-Tarry (1995). Also advanced, Duranti and Goodwin (1992) provides descriptive and theoretical perspectives on the importance of context. Eckert and Rickford (2001) reflects anthropological approaches to style, the traditional sociolinguistics notion of style as attention paid to speech, the important matter of audience design, and functionally motivated situational variation. Accessible chapters on American slang (by Connie Eble), rap and hip hop (by H. Samy Alim), the language of cyberspace (by Denise E. Murray), and the language used between doctors and patients (by Cynthia Hagstrom) can be found in Finegan and Rickford (2004).

REFERENCES

- Andersen, Elaine S. 1990. *Speaking with Style* (London: Routledge).

- Barbour, Steven, & Patrick Stevenson. 1990. *Variation in German: A Critical Approach to German Sociolinguistics* (Cambridge: Cambridge University Press).

- Biber, Douglas. 1988. *Variation across Speech and Writing* (Cambridge: Cambridge University Press).

- Biber, Douglas. 1995. *Dimensions of Register Variation: A Cross-Linguistic Comparison* (Cambridge: Cambridge University Press).

- Biber, Douglas, & Edward Finegan, eds. 1994. *Sociolinguistic Perspectives on Register* (New York: Oxford University Press).

- Blom, Jan-Petter, & John J. Gumperz. 1972. "Social Meaning in Linguistic Structure," in John J. Gumperz & Dell Hymes, eds., *Directions in Sociolinguistics* (New York: Holt), pp. 407–34.

- Brown, Penelope, & Colin Fraser. 1979. "Speech as a Marker of Situation," in Klaus Scherer & Howard Giles, eds., *Social Markers in Speech* (Cambridge: Cambridge University Press), pp. 33–62.

- Burke, David. 1988. *Street French: How to Speak and Understand French Slang* (New York: John Wiley).

- Clyne, Michael G. 1999. *The German Language in a Changing Europe* (Cambridge: Cambridge University Press).

- Duranti, Alessandro, & Charles Goodwin, eds. 1992. *Rethinking Context: Language as an Interactive Phenomenon* (Cambridge: Cambridge University Press).

- Eckert, Penelope, & John R. Rickford, eds. 2001. *Style and Sociolinguistic Variation* (Cambridge: Cambridge University Press).

- Finegan, Edward. 1992. "Style and Standardization in England: 1700–1900," in Tim William Machan & Charles T. Scott, eds., *English in its Social Contexts: Essays in Historical Sociolinguistics* (New York: Oxford University Press), pp. 102–30.

- Finegan, Edward, & John R. Rickford, eds. 2004. *Language in the USA: Perspectives for the 21st Century* (Cambridge: Cambridge University Press).

- George, Ken. 1993. "Alternative French," in Carol Sanders, ed., *French Today: Language in its Social Context* (Cambridge: Cambridge University Press), pp. 155–70.

- Ghadessy, Mohsen, ed. 1988. *Registers of Written English: Situational Factors and Linguistic Features* (London: Pinter).

- Labov, William. 1966. *The Social Stratification of English in New York City* (Washington, DC: Center for Applied Linguistics).

- Lambert, Wallace E., & G. Richard Tucker. 1976. *Tu, Vous, Usted: A Social-Psychological Study of Address Patterns* (Rowley, MA: Newbury House).

- Leckie-Tarry, Helen. 1995. *Language and Context: A Functional Linguistic Theory of Register* (London: Pintner).
- O'Donnell, W. R., & Loreto Todd. 1991. *Variety in Contemporary English,* 2nd ed. (London: HarperCollins).
- Sanders, Carol. 1993. "Sociosituational Variation," in Carol Sanders, ed., *French Today: Language in its Social Context* (Cambridge: Cambridge University Press), pp. 27–54.
- Trudgill, Peter. 1996. *Sociolinguistics: An Introduction to Language and Society,* rev. ed. (New York: Penguin).

Chapter 11

Language Variation Among Social Groups: Dialects

WHAT DO YOU THINK?

❖ Returning from summer camp, your nine-year-old niece, Nina, reports that one of the counselors "talked real funny": he called the TV a *telly*, trucks *lorries,* and cookies *biscuits.* What do you tell Nina about who "talks funny" and who doesn't?

❖ Daniel, a friend of yours who teaches in Chicago, tells you that after a substitute teacher who grew up in Alabama substituted for him one day, his students said the sub spoke with a distinct Southern accent. But the sub claimed he had no accent at all. The students wondered how on earth the dude could possibly imagine he spoke without an accent. What explanation would you give them if they were your students?

❖ At a party in Cleveland, Alice from Atlanta tells you, "You don't have as strong an accent as your friends." It had never crossed your mind that you or your friends had an accent (although you thought Alice had one). Her comment makes you realize that, at least from her perspective, you carry an accent, and so do all your friends. What explanation can you offer for why you never realized that fact before?

❖ Imagine you represent your college at a county fair competition and have been challenged to think of a place you've visited where the language was the same as yours but the dialect differed. After naming the place, your challenge is to name four everyday items (such as frying pan, soda, washcloth, pancakes, baby carriage) for which the customary word in your locality differs from the customary name of the same object there. Your answer?

❖ In a discussion about whether teachers in the United States should know something about Ebonics, your classmate Justin claims that Ebonics is "just broken English" and that teachers shouldn't have to study it. What arguments can you make that, if Ebonics is "broken," then every variety of English is "broken" when viewed from the perspective of every other variety?

❖ In the cafeteria, you and your classmates are discussing to what degree male and female college students talk differently from each other. Sammy says they speak the same. What do you tell her?

LANGUAGE OR DIALECT: WHICH DO YOU SPEAK?

It is an obvious fact that people of different nations tend to use different languages: Spanish in Spain, Portuguese in Portugal, Japanese in Japan, Somali in Somalia, and so on. Along with physical appearance and cultural characteristics, language is part of what distinguishes one nation from another. Of course, it isn't only across national boundaries that people speak different languages. In the Canadian province of Quebec, ethnic French-Canadians maintain a strong allegiance to the French language, while ethnic Anglos maintain a loyalty to English. In India, scores of languages are spoken, some confined to small areas, others spoken regionally or nationally.

Among speakers of any widely spoken language there is considerable international variation, as with Australian, American, British, Indian, and Irish English, among others. Striking differences can be noted between the varieties of French spoken in Montreal and Paris and among the varieties of Spanish in Spain, Mexico, and various Central and South American countries. In addition, even casual observers know that residents of different parts of a country speak regional varieties of the same language. When Americans speak of a "Boston accent," a "Southern drawl," or "Brooklynese," they reveal their perception of American English as varying from place to place. These linguistic markers of region identify people as belonging to a particular social group, even when that group is as loosely bound together as are most American regional groups. In countries where regional affiliation may have social correlates of ethnicity, religion, or clan, regional varieties may be important markers of social affiliation. Like the existence of different languages, the existence of regional varieties of a language suggests that people who speak *with* one another tend to speak *like* one another. It's also reasonable to think that people who view themselves as distinct from other groups may tend to mark that distinction in their speech.

A language can be thought of as a collection of dialects that are historically related to one another and similar in vocabulary and structure. Dialects of a single language characterize social groups whose members choose to say they are speakers of the same language.

Social Boundaries and Dialects

Language varies from region to region and also across ethnic, socioeconomic, and gender boundaries. Speakers of American English know that white Americans and black Americans tend to speak differently, even when they live in the same city. Similarly, middle-class speakers can often be distinguished from working-class speakers. Women and men also differ from one another in their language use. Throughout the world, in addition to regional dialects, there are ethnic varieties, social class varieties, and gender varieties. These constitute what some call social dialects, although the word *dialects* is commonly limited to regional varieties.

Distinguishing among Dialect, Register, and Accent

Dialect and Register   The term **dialect** refers to the language variety characteristic of a particular regional or social group. Partly through his or her dialect we recognize a person's regional, ethnic, social, and gender affiliation. Thus the term *dialect* has to do with language *users,* with groups of speakers. In addition, as we saw in the preceding chapter, all dialects vary according to the situation in which they are used, creating what we called *registers:* language varieties characteristic of *situations of use.* In this chapter we deal with dialects—language varieties characteristic of particular social groups. Languages, dialects, and registers are all language **varieties.** What this means is that there is no linguistic distinction between a language and a dialect. Every dialect is a language, and every language is realized in its dialects. From a linguistic point of view, what is called a language and what is called a dialect are indistinguishable.

Dialect and Accent   When we say that dialect refers to a language variety, we mean a language variety in its totality—including vocabulary, grammar, pronunciation, pragmatics, and any other aspect of the linguistic system. We mean the same thing when we use the terms *language* and *variety.* Those terms refer to an entire linguistic system. When people use the word **accent,** it refers to pronunciation only, and that's how we use it in this book. When we discuss a "Southern accent" or a "Boston accent," we mean the *pronunciation* that is characteristic of the Southern dialect or the Boston dialect.

HOW DO LANGUAGES DIVERGE AND MERGE?

How is it that over time certain language varieties, once similar to one another, come to differ while other varieties remain very much alike? There is no simple answer to that question, but it seems clear that the more people interact with one another, the more alike their language remains or becomes. The less the contact between social groups, the more likely it is that their language varieties will develop distinctive characteristics.

Geographical separation and social distance promote differences in speechways. From the Proto-Indo-European language spoken about 6000 years ago have come most of today's European languages and many languages of Central Asia and the Indian subcontinent. Not only the Romance languages but the Celtic, Greek, Baltic, Slavic, and Indo-Iranian languages have developed from Proto-Indo-European, as have the Germanic languages, including English, Norwegian, Swedish, Danish, Dutch, and German. When you consider that only about 200 generations have lived and died during that 6000-year period, you can appreciate how quickly a multitude of different languages can develop from a single parent language.

Clearly, physical distance can promote dialect distinctions. Similarly, social distance can help create and maintain distinct dialects. In part, middle-class dialects differ from working-class dialects because of a relative lack of sustained interactional contacts across class boundaries in American society. African-American English remains distinct from other varieties of American English partly because of the social distance between whites and African Americans in the United States. A dialect links its users through recognition of shared linguistic characteristics, and speakers' abilities to use and understand a dialect mark them as "insiders" and allow them to identify (and exclude) "outsiders." But as we will see below, it is not necessarily the case that varieties differ from one another in a tidy fashion. It may be that two varieties share vocabulary but differ in pronunciation, or it may be that two varieties share a good deal of their phonology but differ in some other respects. All language varieties change and develop continuously, and it is not known how particular patterns develop such that residents even of a single large city share certain linguistic features but differ in their use of other features.

Language Merger in an Indian Village

Just as physical and social distance enable speakers of particular varieties to distinguish themselves from speakers of other varieties, so do close contact and frequent communication foster linguistic similarity. As varieties of the same language spoken by people in close social contact tend to become alike, different languages spoken in a community also can become similar and even tend to merge. The kind and degree of merger are determined by the kind and degree of social integration and shared values.

Kupwar is a village in India on the border between two major language families: the Indo-European family (which includes the languages of North India) and the unrelated Dravidian family (which comprises the languages of South India). Kupwar's 3000 inhabitants fall into three groups and regularly use three languages in their daily activities. The Jains speak Kannada (a Dravidian language); the Muslims speak Urdu (an Indo-European language closely related to Hindi); and the Untouchables speak Marathi (the regional Indo-European language surrounding Kupwar and the principal literary language of the area). These groups have lived in the village for centuries, and most men are bilingual or multilingual. Over the course of time, with individuals switching back and forth among at least two of these languages, the varieties used in Kupwar have come to be more and more alike. In fact, the grammatical structures of the village varieties are now so similar that a word-for-word translation is possible among the languages. This means that the word order and other structural characteristics of the three languages are now virtually identical. This merging is all the more remarkable because the varieties of these same languages that are used elsewhere are very different from one another.

Even in Kupwar, though, where the three grammars have been merging, the vocabulary of each language has remained largely distinct. On the one hand, the need for communication among the different groups has encouraged grammatical convergence. On the other hand, the social separation needed to maintain religious and caste differences has supported the continuation of separate vocabularies. As things now stand, communication is relatively easy across groups, while affiliation and group identity remain clear. This is the linguistic equivalent of having your cake and eating it, too.

In the following example sentence, the word order and morphology are relatively uniform across the three Kupwar varieties, but the vocabulary identifies which language is being spoken.

Language Merger in Kupwar

URDU	pala	jəra	kaat	ke	le	ke	a		ya
MARATHI	pala	jəra	kap	un	gʰe	un	a	l	o
KANNADA	tapla	jəra	kʰod	i	təgond	i	bə		yn
	greens	a little	cut	having	taken	having	come	Past	I

'I cut some greens and brought them.'

To a remarkable extent the three grammars have merged by combining grammatical elements from each language, while social distinctions have been preserved (and are partly maintained) by differences in vocabulary.

Language/Dialect Continua

In contrast to the situation in Kupwar, the Romance languages, which include Spanish, French, Italian, and Portuguese, have evolved distinct national varieties from the colloquial Latin spoken in their regions in Roman times. Whereas the varieties of language spoken in Kupwar have converged, the language varieties arising from Latin have diverged over the centuries. The reasons in both cases are the same. First, people use language to mark their social identity. Second, people who talk with one another tend to talk *like* one another. A corollary of the second principle is that people not talking with one another tend to become linguistically differentiated.

Today the languages of Europe, in the Romance-speaking area and elsewhere, look separate and tidily compartmentalized on a map. In reality they are not so neatly distinguishable. Instead, there is a continuum of variation, and languages "blend" into one another. Near language-area borders the change is slightly more abrupt. The national border between France and Italy also serves as a dividing line between French-speaking and Italian-speaking areas. But the French spoken just inside the French border shares features with the Italian spoken just outside it. From Paris to the Italian border lies a continuum along which local French varieties become more and more "Italianlike." Likewise, from Rome to the French border, Italian varieties become more "Frenchlike."

Similar situations exist throughout Europe. For example, Swedes of the far south can communicate better with Danish speakers in nearby Denmark using their local dialects than with their fellow Swedes in distant northern Sweden. The same situation exists with residents along the border between Germany and Holland. Using their own local varieties, speakers of German can communicate better with speakers of

Dutch living near them than with speakers of southern German dialects. Examples of geographical dialect continua are found throughout Europe. In fact, while the standard varieties of Italian, French, Spanish, Catalan, and Portuguese are not mutually intelligible, the local varieties form a continuum from Portugal through Spain, halfway through Belgium, then through France down to the southern tip of Italy. There are also a Scandinavian dialect continuum, a West Germanic dialect continuum, and South Slavonic and North Slavonic dialect continua.

Just as different languages may form a dialect continuum, so may different dialects of a single language. This is the case in China, where several mutually unintelligible varieties constitute a single language. In the case of Kupwar, if there were no outside reference varieties against which to compare the varieties spoken in the village, we might be inclined to say that the varieties spoken there were dialects of one language. The residents of Kupwar, however, have found it socially valuable to continue speaking "different" languages, despite increasing grammatical similarity. What counts most in deciding on designations for language varieties and on whether these represent dialects of a single language or separate languages are the views of their speakers.

NATIONAL VARIETIES OF ENGLISH

In this section we briefly examine some national varieties of English, with emphasis on American English and British English.

American and British National Varieties

The principal varieties of English throughout the world are customarily divided into British and American types. British English is the basis for the varieties spoken in England, Ireland, Wales, Scotland, Australia, New Zealand, India, Pakistan, Malaysia, Singapore, and South Africa. American (or North American) includes chiefly the English of Canada and the United States.

Despite the groupings just suggested, certain characteristics of Canadian English are closer to British English, while certain characteristics of Irish English are closer to North American English. And there are many differences between, say, standard British English and standard Indian English. But we can still make a number of generalizations about British-based varieties and American-based varieties, provided we recognize that neither group is completely homogeneous.

Spelling   There are well-known spelling differences between British and American English. Some are systematic, others limited to a particular word. American red, white, and blue *colors* are *colours* in Britain, and many other words ending in *–or* in American English end in *–our* in British English. Among idiosyncratic spellings are British *tyres* versus American *tires* and British *kerb* versus American *curb*. Interestingly, Canadians often use British rather than American spelling practices, a reflection of their close historical association with Britain. For the most part, these spelling differences do not reflect spoken differences. Below are listed some common American ~ British spelling correspondences.

American	British	American	British
labor, favor	labour, favour	tire	tyre
license, defense	licence, defence	curb	kerb
spelled, burned, spilled	spelt, burnt, spilt	program	programme
analyze, organize	analyse, organise	pajamas	pyjamas
center, theater	centre, theatre	check	cheque
judgment, abridgment	judgement, abridgement	ton	tonne
dialed, canceled	dialled, cancelled	catalog	catalogue
installment, skillful	instalment, skilful	czar	tsar

Pronunciation   There are differences in vowel and consonant pronunciation between American and British varieties, as well as in word stress and intonation. Combined, these contribute to creating American and British accents. Speakers of both varieties pronounce the vowel of words in the *cat, fat, mat* class with /æ/. For similar words ending in a fricative such as *fast, path,* and *half,* American English has /æ/, while some British varieties have /ɑː/, the stressed vowel of *father.* Americans pronounce the vowel in the *new, tune* and *duty* class with /u/, as though they were spelled "noo," "toon," and "dooty." Varieties of British English often pronounce them with /ju/, as though spelled "nyew," "tyune," and "dyuty," a pronunciation also heard among some older Americans.

As to consonants, perhaps the most noticeable difference has to do with intervocalic /t/. When /t/ occurs between a stressed and an unstressed vowel, Americans and Canadians usually pronounce it as a flap [ɾ]. As a result, the word *sitter* is pronounced [sɪɾər], and *latter* and *ladder* are pronounced the same. By contrast, speakers of some British varieties pronounce intervocalic /t/ as [t]. As another example, most American varieties have a retroflex /r/ in word-final position in words such as *car* and *near* and also preceding a consonant as in *cart* and *beard,* whereas many British varieties, including standard British English, do not. With respect to this post-vocalic /r/, speakers of Irish and Scottish English follow the American pattern, while speakers of dialects in New York City, Boston, and parts of the coastal South follow the British pattern.

Among differences of word stress, British English tends to stress the first syllable of *garage, fillet,* and *ballet,* while American English places stress on the second syllable. The same is true for *patois, massage, debris, beret,* and other borrowings from French. Certain polysyllabic words such as *laboratory, secretary,* and *lavatory* may have four syllables in both varieties, but the stress patterns differ, with American English preserving a secondary stress on the next-to-last syllable.

Try it yourself: Use the IPA symbols given on the inside front and back covers of this text to transcribe the words *laboratory* and *secretary* to represent both British and American pronunciations with four syllables.

Syntax and Grammar Some noun phrases that denote locations in time or space take an article in American English but not in British English.

American	British
in the hospital	in hospital
to the university	to university
the next day	next day

Some collective nouns (those that refer to groups of people or to institutions) are treated as plural in British English but usually as singular in American varieties. An American watching a soccer game might say *Cornell is ahead by two,* whereas a British observer might say *Manchester are ahead by two.* Americans rely more on form than on sense. Thus, speaking of the Anaheim Angels baseball team, a writer or sportscaster might say *Anaheim has won again* or *The Angels have won again.* In both British and American English, a noun such as *police* takes a plural verb, as in *The police are attempting to assist the neighbors.*

A further illustration of the grammatical differences between the two varieties is the use of the verb *do* with auxiliaries. If asked *Have you finished the assignment?,* American English permits *Yes, I have,* while British English allows that and *Yes, I have done.* Asked whether flying time to Los Angeles varies, a British Airways flight attendant might reply, *It can do.*

Vocabulary There are also vocabulary differences between American and British English, such as those below.

American	British	American	British
elevator	lift	second floor	first floor
TV	telly	flashlight	torch
hood (of a car)	bonnet	trunk (of a car)	boot
cookies	biscuits	dessert	pudding
gas/gasoline	petrol	truck	lorry
can	tin	intermission	interval
line	queue	exit	way out
washcloth/facecloth	flannel	traffic circle/rotary	roundabout

Try it yourself: In some cases, a word used in Britain is hardly known in the United States. In other cases, the most common British term is not the most common American term. For each of the following, give the ordinary American English equivalent: *fortnight, holiday, motorway, diversion, roadworks, joining points, tailback, hire car, car park, windscreen, spanner.*

Differences between British and American varieties are sufficient to make speakers of English everywhere view the Atlantic Ocean as a dialect boundary.

REGIONAL VARIETIES OF AMERICAN ENGLISH

Although regional differences are greater in Britain than in the United States, differences in American dialects appear to be increasing rather than, as many suppose, disappearing. Starting in the late 1940s, investigation of vocabulary patterns in the eastern United States suggested distinguishing among Northern, Midland, and Southern dialects, each with subdivisions. Midland was divided into North Midland and South Midland varieties. Boston and metropolitan New York were seen as distinct varieties of the Northern dialect. Midwestern states such as Illinois, Indiana, and Ohio, which had been formerly thought of as representing "General American," were seen as situated principally in the North Midland dialect, with a narrow strip of Northern dialect across their northernmost counties and a small strip belonging to the South Midland variety across their southern counties. More recent investigations suggest refinements of that scheme, such as those represented in the geographical patterns of Figure 11–1 on page 370.

Mapping Dialects

In order to propose a map such as the one in Figure 11–1, dialectologists investigate patterns of usage. Depending on their resources, investigators may rely on vocabulary, pronunciation, or grammar. Typically, a researcher with a lengthy questionnaire visits a town and inquires of residents what they call certain things or how they express certain meanings. Figure 11–1 is based on regional vocabulary. Note that this interpretation of the data divides the United States into two main dialects (North and South), each of which is divided in turn into Upper and Lower sections. In this mapping of vocabulary features, the West is viewed as an extension of the North dialect. The map in Figure 11–1 relies on fieldwork undertaken in the 1960s and 1970s for the *Dictionary of American Regional English,* or *DARE*. Later we'll examine that project a bit more.

Prior to *DARE,* several linguistic atlas projects were undertaken, part of a project called the Linguistic Atlas of the United States and Canada. Data collection in several regions was completed and the results published, but parts of the project remain incomplete. Still, the data collected provide a useful view of regional variation. To take an example, when Atlas investigators asked respondents for the commonly used term for the large insect with transparent wings often seen hovering over water, local terms came to light. Figure 11–2 on page 371 shows *darning needle* as the most common term in New England, upstate New York, metropolitan New York (including northern and eastern New Jersey and Long Island), and northern Pennsylvania. Elsewhere, other terms predominated: *mosquito hawk* in coastal North Carolina and Virginia, *snake doctor* in inland Virginia, and *snake feeder* along the northern Ohio River in West Virginia, Ohio, western Pennsylvania, and the upper Ohio Valley toward Pittsburgh.

You can see in Figure 11–2 that not all the terms for 'dragonfly' are tidily distributed. In some areas, only a single form occurred, but in others more than one. The O's on the map in New England and New York indicate that *darning needle* was the only

Figure 11-1

Major Dialect Regions of the USA, Based on Vocabulary

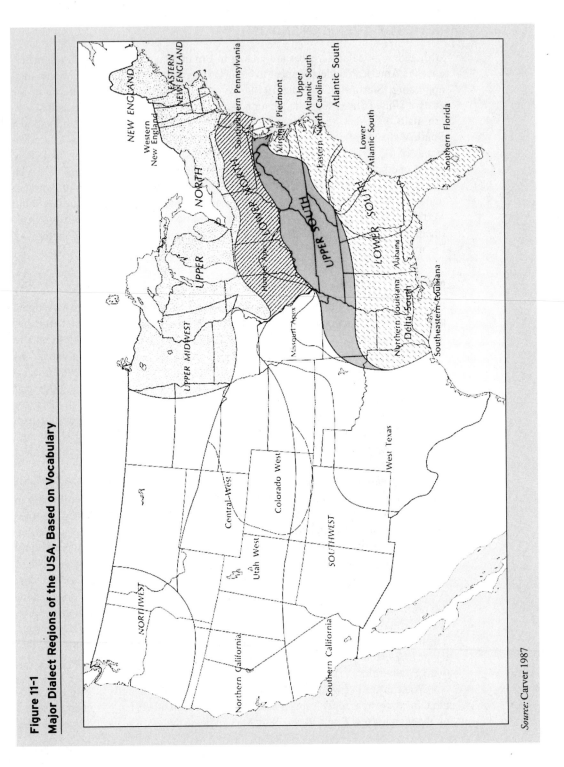

Source: Carver 1987

Figure 11-2

Words for 'Dragonfly' in the Eastern States

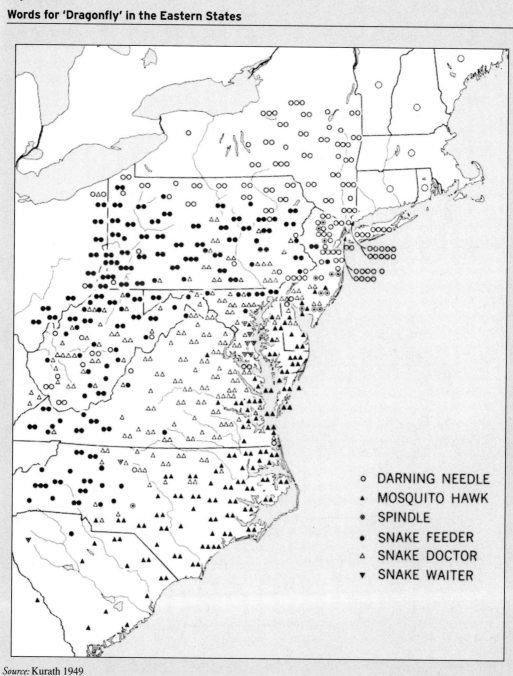

○ DARNING NEEDLE
▲ MOSQUITO HAWK
◉ SPINDLE
● SNAKE FEEDER
△ SNAKE DOCTOR
▼ SNAKE WAITER

Source: Kurath 1949

regional term found there. You can see in Figures 11–3 and 11–4 that *mosquito hawk* was virtually the only regional response given in parts of southeast Texas and portions of central Texas, as well as all of Louisiana and Florida, and much of southern Alabama, Mississippi, and Georgia. But *snake doctor* was the favored form in west, north, and northwest Texas, the western half of Tennessee, the northern parts of Alabama and Mississippi, and part of northwestern Georgia. *Snake feeder* occurred occasionally in Oklahoma along the Canadian and Arkansas rivers (which aren't labeled in our figure but can be identified within Oklahoma near the solid triangles of Fig. 11–3) and throughout eastern Tennessee (the open circles within Tennessee in Fig. 11–4). Both *mosquito hawk* and *snake doctor* were used in the southern half of Arkansas (in Fig. 11–3 and 11–4). *Darning needle,* so popular in New York and New England, occurred too infrequently even to be recorded on these maps of the South. Some respondents were unacquainted with local terms and reported using only *dragonfly.* (*Note:* If you live in or come from an area represented on the maps but find the terms indicated there unfamiliar, bear in mind that the data were often gathered in rural areas and represent "folk" speech as well as "cultivated" speech. Moreover, some of the interviews took place decades ago, and word usage may have changed in the meanwhile.)

Figure 11-3

Words for 'Dragonfly' in Texas, Arkansas, Louisiana, Oklahoma

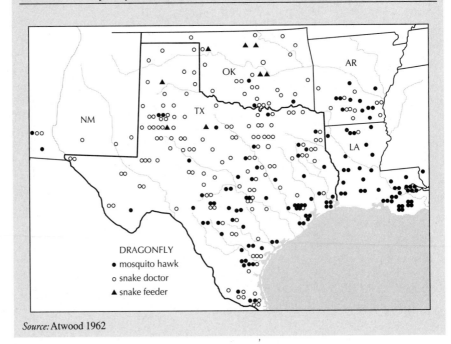

Source: Atwood 1962

Figure 11-4

Words for 'Dragonfly' in the Gulf States

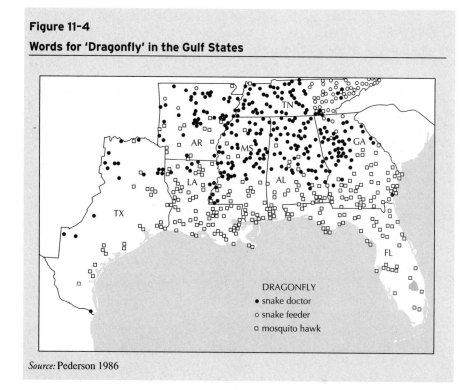

DRAGONFLY
• snake doctor
○ snake feeder
□ mosquito hawk

Source: Pederson 1986

Determining Isoglosses   Once a map has been marked with symbols for various features, lines called isoglosses can often be drawn at the boundary for the different forms. For example, in Figure 11–5 on page 374 the four isoglosses traversing the North-Central states of Ohio, Indiana, and Illinois represent the northernmost limits of *greasy* pronounced /grizi/ with a /z/, of *snake feeder* as the term for 'dragonfly,' and of two other features.

Figure 11–6 on page 375 represents seven isoglosses in the Upper Midwest. Three of them mark the southernmost boundaries of Northern features: *humor* pronounced [hjumər] (/hj/ is represented in the map's legend as /hy/); *boulevard* referring to the grass strip between the curb and sidewalk; and *come in (fresh),* meaning 'to give birth' and usually said of a cow. The four other isoglosses mark the northernmost boundaries of Midland features: the word *on* pronounced with a rounded vowel (/ɔ/ or /ɒ/, where /ɒ/ is like /ɑ/ but pronounced with lip rounding) instead of an unrounded /ɑ/; the term *caterwampus,* meaning 'askew' or 'awry'; the term *roasting ears* for 'corn on the cob'; and *lightbread* for 'white bread.'

Dialect Boundaries

Imagine each isogloss map stacked on top of one another on a transparency. The result would be a map similar to the one in Figure 11–6 and would show the extent to which the isoglosses from different maps "bundle" together. The geographical limit for the

Figure 11-5

Four Isoglosses in the North-Central States (Northern limits)

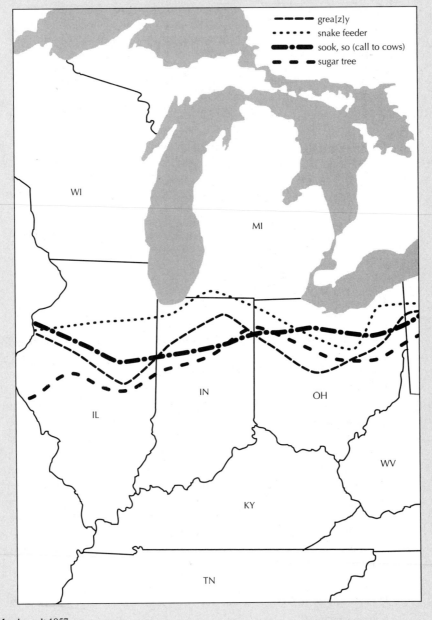

Source: Marckwardt 1957

use of a particular word (say, *caterwampus*) often corresponds roughly to the limit for other terms or pronunciations. Where isoglosses bundle, dialectologists draw dialect boundaries. Thus, a *dialect boundary* is simply the location of a bundle of isoglosses. The map in Figure 11–1 on page 370 is a distillation of dozens of maps similar to those in Figures 11–5 and 11–6.

Speech patterns in the United States, like others elsewhere in the world, are influenced partly by the geographical and physical boundaries that facilitate or inhibit communication and partly by the migration routes followed in settling a place. Among the isoglosses of Figure 11–5, the one for /grisi/ versus /grizi/ essentially follows a line (now approximated by Interstate 70) that was the principal road for the migration of pioneers during the postcolonial settlement period.

Figure 11-6

Seven Isoglosses in the Upper Midwest

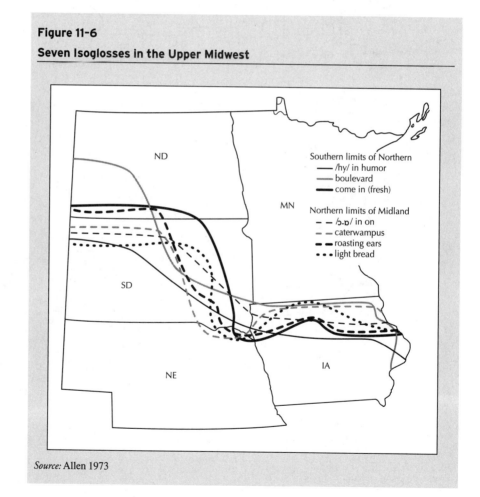

Source: Allen 1973

Figure 11-7

Comparison of *DARE* Map and Conventional Map, with State Names

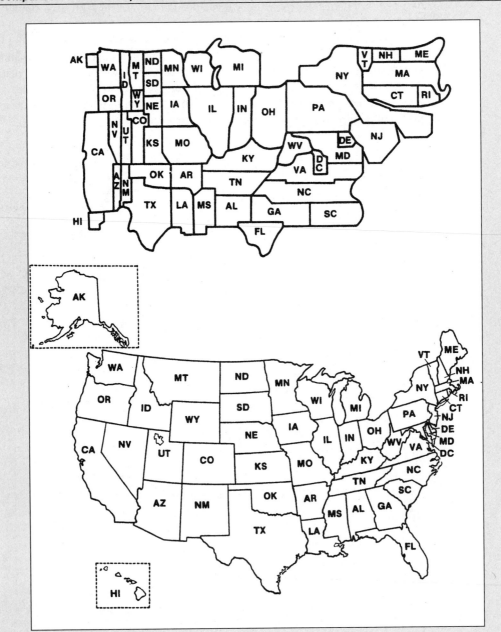

Source: Dictionary of American Regional English, I, 1985

In the western United States, the dialect situation is more complex than in the longer established areas of the East, South, and Midwest. The West drew settlers who spoke a range of dialects from various parts of the country. California continues to welcome immigrants from other parts of the country and the world. It is a magnet for races and cultures, for dialects and languages. Such flux is not conducive to the establishment of a distinctive regional variety of English and does not lend itself readily to the tidiness suggested by isoglosses. Still, there are a few dialect features characteristic of the West.

The *Dictionary of American Regional English*

The *Dictionary of American Regional English* makes available more information about regional words and expressions throughout the United States than has ever been known before. It represents the most current knowledge of American regional vocabulary, and the four volumes published to date cover regional terms in alphabetical order up through *sky writer.*

Based on answers to more than 1800 questions asked by field workers who traveled to 1002 communities across the country, the maps used for exhibiting *DARE*'s findings do not represent geographical space, as most maps do, but population density. Thus the largest states on a *DARE* map are those with the largest populations. As a result, *DARE* maps represent states in somewhat unfamiliar shapes, as the comparison in Figure 11–7 shows.

Figure 11–8 on page 378 shows the distribution of the terms *mosquito hawk* and *skeeter hawk* on a *DARE* map and a conventional map. Along with an occasional occurrence in California and New Mexico, you can see the distribution of these terms through the Gulf states and up the eastern seaboard and occasionally appearing in Minnesota, Wisconsin, Michigan, and a few other states. The word *cruller,* used to name 'a twisted doughnut,' has a very different distribution, as shown in Figure 11–9 on page 379. *Cruller* is used in the northeast, in New England, New York, New Jersey, Pennsylvania, and so on, as well as in some Great Lakes states and California, but does not occur in Alaska, Washington, Oregon, Nevada, New Mexico, and Hawaii.

As the result of various regional dialect projects, especially *DARE,* a complex picture of American English dialects emerges, as Figure 11–1 (page 370) shows. In that figure, the darker the shading of a dialect area, the greater the number of vocabulary items that distinguish it from other dialect areas. As you can see, the farther west you go, the fewer the special vocabulary characteristics that appear. To judge by vocabulary, boundaries for American dialects are better established in the eastern states than in the more recently settled western ones.

Based on the vocabulary findings of *DARE,* the United States appears to have basically North and South dialects, each divided into upper and lower regions as shown in Figure 11–1. The Upper North contains the dialects of New England, the Upper Midwest, and the Northwest, with some lesser-marked dialect boundaries in the Central West and Northern California. The Southwest is also a dialect area, with Southern California having some distinct characteristics. The South is divided into Upper South and Lower South, and each of those has subdiaries.

Figure 11-8

Distribution of *Mosquito Hawk* **and** *Skeeter Hawk* **on** *DARE* **Map and Conventional Map**

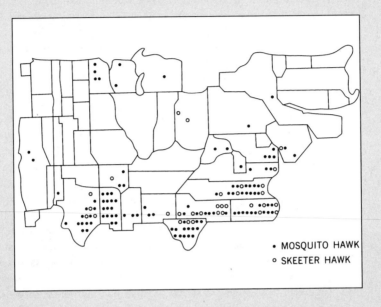

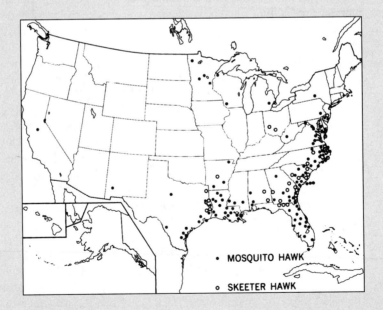

Source: Dictionary of American Regional English, I, 1985

Figure 11-9

Distribution of *Cruller* on a *DARE* Map

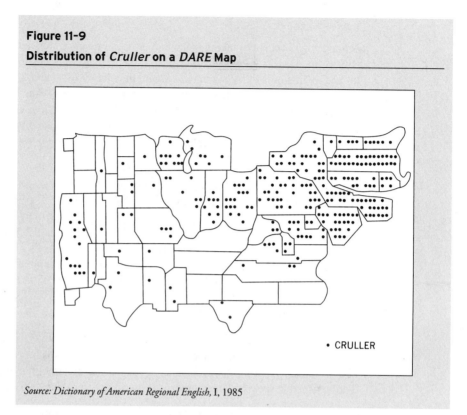

• CRULLER

Source: Dictionary of American Regional English, I, 1985

THE ATLAS OF NORTH AMERICAN ENGLISH

So far, we have focused on dialects as marked principally by vocabulary. The Linguistic Atlas of the United States and Canada also focused on pronunciation; we have examined a few pronunciation features of American dialects, as in *greasy* and *humor.* Because of the considerable time span over which data for the Linguistic Atlas projects was collected, using it for reliable comparisons of pronunciation from region to region is difficult at best.

Fortunately, a major investigation of pronunciation in U.S. and Canadian urban areas took place in the 1990s. The Atlas of North American English, or ANAE, is *not* related to the Linguistic Atlas of North America and Canada or to *DARE.* It is an independent project in its aims, methods, and findings. ANAE was created with data from a telephone survey of North American urban centers in a project called Telsur that is based at the University of Pennsylvania.

On the basis of telephone discussions with respondents who identified themselves as born or raised in the speech community in which they were reached, Telsur combined impressionistic judgments of pronunciation with rigorous acoustic analysis of tape-recorded conversations. Telsur and ANAE focused on vowel sounds, in particular several vowel pronunciations known to be in flux.

Vowel Mergers

Among notable changes taking place in North American pronunciation are mergers of vowels that were formerly separate. Two in particular are well known: the merger of /ɑ/ and /ɔ/ in words like *cot* and *caught* and the merger of /ɪ/ and /ɛ/ in words like *pin* and *pen*. If you have any familiarity with North American English, you have doubtless noted that many, but not all, speakers pronounce *cot* and *caught* alike, and you may also have noted that some speakers pronounce *pin* and *pen* alike. In fact, to distinguish these last two items, many speakers call the first a *straight pin* or *safety pin* and the second an *ink pen*.

Cot ~ Caught Merger   The traditional pronunciations of *cot* and *caught* have been distinct by virtue of the first having the nucleus /ɑ/ and the second having /ɔ/. Because /ɑ/ is a low back vowel and /ɔ/ is a lower-mid back vowel, the merger is often referred to as the **low back merger.** It involves word pairs like *Don* and *Dawn, wok* and *walk,* and *hock* and *hawk.* For the many speakers of American English who do not merge these vowels, /ɑ/ and /ɔ/ are distinct phonemes, and for those speakers all such word pairs are *minimal pairs* (which we discussed in Chapter 4). With the merger of these two phonemes, the number of vowels in the English inventory is reduced, and a good many homophonous words may result.

Pin ~ Pen Merger   Another merger involves the vowels in word pairs such as *pin ~ pen, him ~ hem, lint ~ lent,* and *cinder ~ sender.* For many speakers, these vowels are kept distinct as [ɪ] and [ɛ], but for many others they are homophonous and cannot be distinguished in speech. This merger is sometimes referred to as the IN ~ EN merger.

Conditioned and Unconditioned Mergers   The merger of /ɑ/ and /ɔ/ isn't limited to specific phonological environments within a word but occurs everywhere. Such a merger is said to be *unconditioned.* An unconditioned merger affects all words that contain the sounds, with the result that a vowel contrast is lost. By contrast, the vowels /ɪ/ and /ɛ/ merge only when they precede the nasals /n/ or /m/, but not elsewhere. Thus, speakers who pronounce *pin* and *pen* identically don't merge *pit* and *pet* ([pɪt] vs. [pɛt]), *lit* and *let, whipped* and *wept,* and so on, because these words do not match the specified phonological environment required for the merger.

We can summarize the discussion of mergers as in the chart below.

Name	Vowels	Condition	Examples
cot ~ caught merger	/ɑ/ ~ /ɔ/	unconditioned	*cot ~ caught, hock ~ hawk*
pin ~ pen merger	/ɪ/ ~ /ɛ/	preceding /n/ or /m/	*pin ~ pen, cinder ~ sender*

Vowel Shifts

Besides the mergers, other major changes in North American English involve shifting the pronunciation of vowels from one location in the mouth to another. The effect is that a word pronounced with a given vowel is heard by outsiders as having a different vowel. As an example, the word spelled *cod* may be heard as *cad.* You know that vowels can be represented in a chart such as the one in Figure 11–10. In addition to the simple vowels in the figure, English has three diphthongs: /aj/ (*my, line*), /ɔj/ (*toy, coin*), and /aw/ (*cow, town*). (In this book, we generally represent other English vowels as simple vowels, or *monophthongs*. Thus, we represent the underlying vowel of *made* as /e/, of *flowed* as /o/, and of *food* as /u/. These vowels are often pronounced as diphthongs and are represented as diphthongs in some other books, which give their underlying forms as, for example, /ey/, /ow/, and /uw/.)

Figure 11-10

The Vowels of English

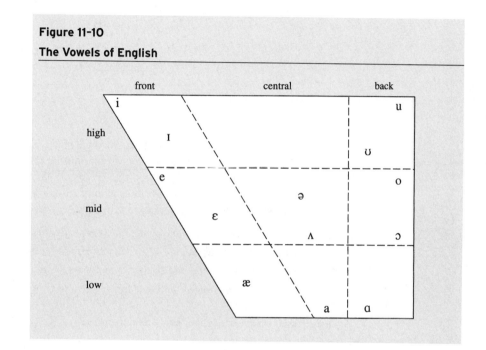

Northern Cities Shift   Across the major cities of the North—including Syracuse, Rochester, and Buffalo in New York, Cleveland and Akron in Ohio, Detroit in Michigan, Chicago and Rockford in Illinois, and Milwaukee and Madison in Wisconsin—a set of vowel shifts is occurring that is remarkable in its scope. They constitute the Northern Cities Shift and can be represented as in Figure 11–11 on page 382. This shift includes Canadian as well as U.S. cities. It has several aspects to it, including those given below. (The numbers in parentheses refer to the numbered shifts in Figure 11–11; for simplicity, we do not include shift number 6 in our list.)

1. /æ/ is raised and fronted to [iᵊ]—*man* and *bad* can even sound like the underscored vowel in *id**ea**:*[miᵊn], [biᵊd] (1 in figure)
2. /ɑ/ is fronted to [æ]—*cod* sounds like *cad* (2 in figure)
3. /ɔ/ is lowered and fronted to [ɑ]—*cawed* sounds like *cod* (3 in figure)
4. /ɛ/ is lowered and centered to [ʌ]—*Ked* sounds like *cud* (4 in figure)
5. /ʌ/ is backed to [ɔ]—*cud* sounds like *cawed* (5 in figure)

Figure 11-11
Northern Cities Shift

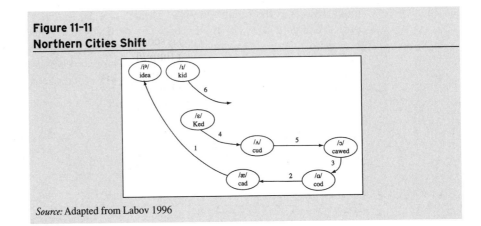

Source: Adapted from Labov 1996

Southern Shift   In the South, a different set of vowel shifts is occurring. They constitute the Southern Shift and can be represented as in Figure 11–12. The Southern Shift has several aspects, including the five listed below in which italicized words serve as examples. (The parentheses refer to the numbered shifts in Figure 11–12; for simplicity, we don't include shifts 3, 7, or 8 in our list.)

1. /aj/ is monophthongized to [a]—*hide* sounds like [had] or [haːd] (1 in figure)
2. /e/ is lowered and centralized to [aj]—*slade* sounds like *slide* (2 in figure)
3. /o/ is fronted—*code* and *boat* sound like [kɛᵒd] and [bɛᵒt] (6 in figure)
4. /ɪ/, /ɛ/, /æ/ are raised and fronted—*kid* sounds like *keyed*, *Ted* like *tid*, *pat* like *pet* (4 in figure)
5. /u/ is fronted—*cool* sounds like "kewl" (5 in figure)

Figure 11-12
Southern Shift

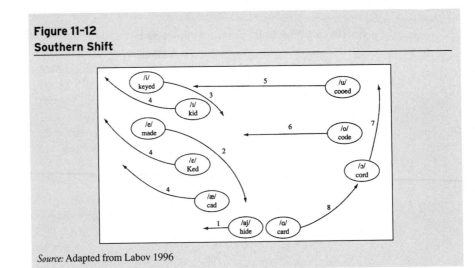

Source: Adapted from Labov 1996

ANAE Findings

The Atlas of North American English is soon to be published, but some of the principal findings are available on the internet (http://ling.upenn.edu/phono_atlas/home.html). Relying on 439 telephone respondents for whom acoustic analyses have been completed, ANAE provides a map of the United States and Canada in which new dialect boundaries are proposed. You can get a clear picture of these results at the ANAE Web site. Meanwhile, the map in Figure 11–13 on page 384 suggests the major North American dialect regions, as based on Telsur pronunciation data. In the map you can see that, besides Canada, there are four main U.S. pronunciation regions: West, North, Midland, and South. Within the North are Inland North and Western New England dialects and within the South are Texas South and Inland South dialects. You'll also note designations for dialects named Mid-Atlantic, New York City (NYC), Eastern New England (ENE), Western Pennsylvania, and others.

Below is a table adapted from the ANAE Web site that indicates some salient characteristics of the pronunciation of some dialects. In keeping with the representation of Figure 11–13, we indicate characteristics of each region as a whole and sometimes of dialects within the region.

NORTH	Less fronting of /o/ than in other areas
Inland North	Northern Cities Shift
Western New England	Less advanced Northern Cities Shift
SOUTH	Monophthongization of /aj/
Inland South	Southern Shift
Texas South	Southern Shift
MIDLAND	Transitional low back merger
	Fronting of /o/
WEST	Low back (*cot ~ caught*) merger
	Stronger fronting of /u/ than of /o/
CANADA	Low back (*cot ~ caught*) merger
Atlantic Provinces	No low back merger

Additional data appear on the map, but they are not sufficiently accessible in this black and white image to discuss further. Among the information you can glean from the color maps at the Web site are the fact that the St. Louis Corridor falls within the Midland region but nevertheless displays the Northern Cities Shift. You can also note that nearly all of Florida lies outside the South region. This is because Florida does not participate in the Southern Shift, although it does display the fronting of /u/ (step 5 in Fig. 11–12), but not of /o/ (step 6 in Fig. 11–12). In Canada, the Atlantic Provinces are conservative in pronunciation and do not (at least yet) participate in the changes characteristic of other parts of Canada such as the low back (*cot ~ caught*) merger.

Figure 11-13

Urban Dialect Areas of the United States, Based on Pronunciation

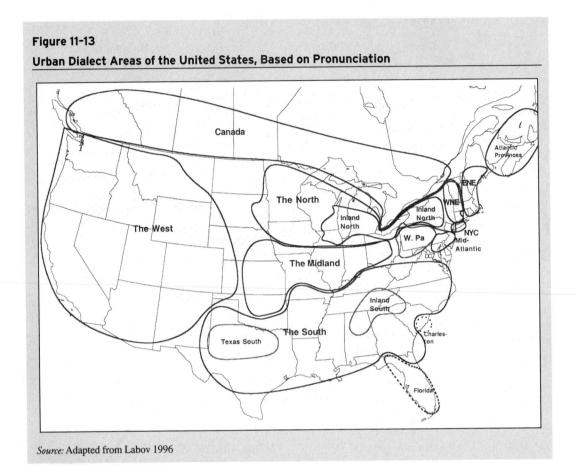

Source: Adapted from Labov 1996

ETHNIC VARIETIES OF AMERICAN ENGLISH

Just as oceans and mountains separate people and may eventually lead to distinct speech patterns, so social boundaries also promote distinct speechways. The automobile, jet plane, telephone, radio, television, and Internet have reduced the effect of physical boundaries and distances between communities, but social barriers continue to promote and maintain characteristic speech patterns that distinguish one group from another.

Society can be subdivided in many ways: by religion, ethnic background, social-class affiliation, and gender, to name a few. Groups of people claiming particular social varieties as their own may identify themselves as separate classes, separate ethnic groups, or separate religions. In addition, cutting across all other social boundaries may be differences in the ways women and men speak.

Perhaps the most notable social varieties of American English are *ethnic varieties*. Ethnicity is sometimes racial and sometimes not. For example, differences in the speech of Jewish and Italian New Yorkers have been noted, and the variety of English influenced by Yiddish speakers who settled in America is sometimes called "Yinglish." But the social separation that leads to ethnic varieties of language is particularly noticeable in the characteristic speech patterns of urban African Americans. In Philadelphia and other cities, the speech of African American residents is becoming increasingly distinct from the speech of white residents.

Such a distinction between social groups is also noticeable in the characteristic speech patterns of other ethnic groups. Spanish-speaking immigrants in Los Angeles, New York, Chicago, Miami, and elsewhere have learned English as a second language, and their English is marked by a foreign accent. The children and grandchildren of these immigrants acquire English as a native language (and many are bilingual), but the native variety of English that many Hispanic Americans speak identifies them as being of Hispanic ancestry or growing up in neighborhoods with children of Hispanic ancestry.

The discussion that follows identifies certain characteristics of African-American English and Chicano English. Both are bona fide varieties of American English like any other regional or social variety. Both have complete grammatical systems overlapping to a great degree with other varieties of English. And, like standard American English, both have a spectrum of registers. That is, speakers of African-American English and Chicano English do not speak the same way in all circumstances. While both varieties share many characteristics with other varieties of American English, they also exhibit certain distinctive features and a set of shared features that taken together distinguish each of them from all others.

It should go without saying that thinking of African-American English or Chicano English as unusual varieties or as ill formed would be erroneous. Like all other social varieties, these two have rules that determine what is well formed and what is ill formed. As in standard English, a construction can be ungrammatical in African-American English or in Chicano English. Rules govern the structures and use of all dialects throughout the world, and no dialect exists without phonological, morphological, and syntactic rules, among others. All the language universals described in Chapter 7 apply to African-American English and Chicano English as well.

African-American English

The most widespread and most familiar ethnic variety of American English is African-American English (formerly called Black English or Black English Vernacular or African-American Vernacular English and now often called Ebonics). Not all African Americans are fluent speakers of African-American English, and not all speakers of African-American English are African Americans. After all, people grow up speaking the language variety around them. In an ethnically diverse city such as Los Angeles, you can meet teenage speakers of African-American English whose foreign-born parents speak Chinese or Vietnamese. The variety of English spoken by these Asian-American teenagers reflects the characteristic speechways of their friends and of the neighborhoods in which they acquired English. To underscore an obvious but often misunderstood fact, the acquisition of a particular language or dialect is as independent of skin color as it is of height or weight.

The history of African-American English is not completely understood, and there are competing theories about its origins and subsequent development. But there is no disagreement concerning its structure and functioning. It has characteristic phonological, morphological, and syntactic features, as well as vocabulary of its own. Like all other social groups, speakers of African-American English also share characteristic ways of interacting. In this section we examine some phonological and syntactic features of African-American English, but not lexical or interactional characteristics.

Phonological Features   We examine four characteristic pronunciation features of African-American English (AAE).

1. **Consonant cluster simplification**   In AAE, consonant clusters are frequently simplified. Typical examples occur in the words *desk,* pronounced as "des" [dɛs], *passed* pronounced as "pass" [pæs], and *wild* pronounced as "wile" [wajl]. Consonant cluster simplification also occurs in all other varieties of American English. Among speakers of standard English, the consonant clusters <sk> in *desk* and <ld> in *wild* are also commonly simplified, as in "asthem" [æsðəm] for *ask them* and "tole" [tol] for *told.* But consonant cluster simplification occurs more frequently and to a greater extent in African-American English than in other varieties.

2. **Deletion of final stop consonants**   In AAE, final stop consonants, such as /d/, may be deleted in words like *side* and *borrowed.* Speakers of AAE frequently delete some word-final stops, pronouncing *side* like *sigh* and *borrowed* like *borrow.* This deletion rule is systematically influenced by the phonological and grammatical environment:

   a. Whether a word-final stop consonant represents a separate morpheme (as in the past tense marking of *followed* and *tried)* or doesn't represent a separate morpheme but is part of the word stem (as in *side* and *rapid).* Final [d] is preserved much more frequently when it is a separate morpheme.

   b. Whether word-final stops occur in a strongly stressed syllable (*tried)* or a weakly stressed syllable (*rapid)*—note that the second syllable of *rapid* is not as strongly stressed as the first syllable. Strongly stressed syllables tend to preserve final stops more than weakly stressed syllables do.

   c. Whether a vowel follows the stop (as in *side angle* and *tried it)* or a consonant follows it (as in *tried hard* and *side street).* A following vowel helps preserve the stop; in fact, it appears to be the most significant factor in determining whether a final stop is deleted.

3. **Interdental ~ labiodental substitution**   Other phonological features are less widespread. For some speakers of AAE, the *th* of words like *both, with,* and *Bethlehem* may be realized not as the voiceless interdental fricative /θ/ but the voiceless labiodental fricative /f/, yielding [bof] or [wɪf], for example. Likewise the voiced interdental fricative /ð/ in words like *smooth* or *bathe* and *brother* or *mother* may be realized with the voiced labiodental fricative /v/, yielding [smuv], [bev], [brʌvə], and [mʌvə]. Note too in *brother* and *mother* the absence of word-final /r/, a feature that AAE shares with the English of New York City, eastern New England, and parts of the coastal South.

4. ***Aunt*** **and** ***ask*** Two other AAE pronunciations are often commented upon. They do not represent systematic features but are limited to individual words. The first is that the initial vowel of *aunt* and *auntie* is pronounced as /ɑ/, a pronunciation also characteristic of eastern New England, but not of most other U.S. dialects, which have /æ/. The second is the pronunciation of *ask* as [æks] instead of [æsk]. By no means is this pronunciation unique to AAE, but it is a feature that has been stereotyped and stigmatized.

In investigations of ongoing changes in the pronunciation of American English, researchers have been surprised to discover that African Americans living in those cities affected by the Northern Cities Shift do not seem to participate in it. This is one indication that leads some observers to conclude that AAE and standard American English are diverging rather than becoming more alike.

Grammatical Features We examine four grammatical features of African-American English.

1. **Copula deletion** Compare the uses of the copula—the verb BE—in African-American English and standard American English below. Sentences 1 and 2 illustrate that AAE permits deletion of *be* in the present tense precisely where standard English permits a contracted form of the copula.

AFRICAN-AMERICAN	STANDARD AMERICAN
1. That my bike.	That's my bike.
2. The coffee cold.	The coffee's cold.
3. The coffee be cold there.	The coffee's (always) cold there.

2. **Habitual *be*** As example 3 above indicates, speakers of AAE express recurring or habitual action by using the form *be*. It may seem to speakers of other varieties that AAE *be* is equivalent to standard American English *is*. In fact, though, in sentences such as 3 *be* is equivalent to a verb expressing a habitual or continuous state of affairs. As African American linguist Geneva Smitherman wrote about sentences such as 2 and 3, "If you the cook and *the coffee cold,* you might only just get talked about that day, but if *The coffee bees cold,* pretty soon you ain't gon have no job!" Thus, the verb *be* (or its inflected variant *bees*) is used to indicate continuous, repeated, or habitual action. The following examples further illustrate this function.

AFRICAN-AMERICAN	STANDARD AMERICAN
Do they be playing all day?	Do they play all day?
Yeah, the boys do be messin' around a lot.	Yeah, the boys do mess around a lot.
I see her when I bees on my way to school.	I see her when I'm on my way to school.

3. **Existential *it*** Another feature of African-American English is the use of the expression *it is* where standard American English uses *there is*. Below are two examples of this "existential *it*":

AFRICAN-AMERICAN	STANDARD AMERICAN
Is it a Miss Jones in this office?	Is there a Miss Jones in this office?
She's been a wonderful wife and it's nothin' too good for her.	She's been a wonderful wife and there's nothing too good for her.

4. **Negative concord**   A final illustration of the distinctiveness of this ethnic variety is provided by the following examples of what is technically called *negative concord* but is better known as double negation or multiple negation:

AFRICAN-AMERICAN	STANDARD AMERICAN
Don't nobody never help me do my work.	Nobody ever helps me do my work.
He *don't never* go *nowhere.*	He *never* goes anywhere.

The African-American English sentences contain more than one word marked for negation. In AAE, multiple-negative constructions are well formed, as they are in many other varieties of American English and as they were more generally in earlier periods of English. The fact that these constructions are not well formed in standard English today has no bearing on their grammaticality or appropriateness in other varieties.

Chicano English

Another important set of ethnic dialects of American English are those called Latino English or Hispanic English. They appear in several closely related varieties in the United States. The best known is Chicano English, spoken by many people of Mexican descent in major U.S. urban centers and in rural areas of the Southwest.

Varieties of Hispanic English have not been studied as thoroughly as African-American English, so our knowledge of them is considerably more tentative. As with African-American English and all other varieties of English, certain features of Chicano English are shared with other varieties, including other varieties of Hispanic English, such as those spoken in the Cuban community of Miami and the Puerto Rican community of New York City. Chicano English comprises many registers for use in different situations. Some characteristic features doubtless result from the persistence of Spanish as one of the language varieties of the Hispanic-American community, but Chicano English has become a distinct variety of American English and cannot be regarded as English spoken with a foreign accent. It is acquired as a first language by many children and is the native language of hundreds of thousands of adults. It is thus a stable variety of American English, with characteristic patterns of grammar and pronunciation.

Phonological Features   One well-known phonological feature of Chicano English is the substitution of "ch" [tʃ] for "sh" [ʃ], as in pronouncing *she* as [tʃi] instead of [ʃi], and *shoes* as [tʃuz] (homophonous with *choose)* instead of [ʃuz], and *especially* as [ɛspɛtʃəli]. This feature is so distinctive that it has become a stereotype. There is also substitution of "sh" for "ch," as in "preash" [priʃ] for *preach* and "shek" [ʃɛk] for *check* [tʃɛk], though this feature seems not to be stereotyped. Other phonological features of Chicano English are consonant cluster simplification, as in [ɪs] for *it's,* "kine" for *kind,* "ole" for *old,* "bes" for *best,* "un-erstan" [ʌnərstæn] for *understand.* Much of this can be represented in the phrase, *It's kind of hard,* which is pronounced [ɪs kɑnə hɑr]. Another major characteristic of the phonological system of Chicano English is the devoicing of /z/, especially in word-final position. Because of the widespread occurrence of /z/ in the inflectional morphology of English (in plural nouns, posses-sive nouns, and third-person-singular present-tense verbs such as *goes),* this salient characteristic is also stereotypical. Chicano English pronunciation is also character-ized by the substitution of stops for the standard fricatives represented in spelling by *th:*[t] for [θ] and [d] for [ð], as in [tʰɪk] for *thick* and [dɛn] for *then.* Still another no-table characteristic is the pronunciation of verbal *-ing* as "een" [in] rather than /ɪn/ ([ən]) or /ɪŋ/. Other *-ng* words such as *sing* and *long* end with a combined velar nasal /ŋ/ and a velar stop /g/; thus *sing* is pronounced [sɪŋg], not [sɪŋ], and *long* is [lɔŋg] rather than [lɔŋ]. A further prominent feature of Chicano English is its use of certain intonation patterns that may strike speakers of other dialects of American English as uncertain or hesitant.

As with speakers of AAE, as we mentioned above, speakers of Hispanic varieties of English who live in cities affected by the Northern Cities Shift do not appear to be participating in these shifts, at least to the same extent as other groups.

Grammatical Features   Chicano English also has characteristic syntactic patterns, although analysis of these is not abundant. It often omits the past-tense marker on verbs that end with the alveolars /t/, /d/, or /n/, yielding "wan" for *wanted* and "wait" for *waited.* At least in Los Angeles, *either . . . or either* is sometimes heard instead of *either . . . or,* as in *Either I will go buy one, or either Terry will.* Another feature is the use of dialect-specific prepositions such as *out from* for *away from,* as in *They party to get out from their problems.* As with many other varieties, Chicano English permits multiple negation, as in *You don't owe me nothing* and *Us little people don't get nothin'.*

Ethnic Varieties and Social Identification

It's important to reemphasize that some of the customary features of Chicano English and African-American English are characteristic of other varieties of American Eng-lish. In some cases, as with consonant cluster simplification, these features are wide-spread in mainstream varieties, including standard English. In other cases, as with negative concord, they are not characteristic of standard American English but are shared with other nonstandard varieties. What makes any variety salient, what makes it seem distinct, is *not* a single feature but a cluster of features, some of which may also occur in other varieties.

Ethnic dialects are an important ingredient in social identity, and features that are recognized as characteristic of specific social groups can be used to promote or rein-force affiliation with that identity. When speaking, an African-American man or woman who wants to stress his or her social identity as an African American may choose to emphasize or exaggerate features of African-American English. The same is true for speakers of Hispanic English varieties who wish to emphasize their Hispanic identity. News correspondents on English-language radio and television broadcasts generally speak without marked social group accents. To emphasize their ethnic identity, however, some correspondents use a marked ethnic pronunciation of their own names at the conclusion of a report. A reporter named Maria Hinojosa identifies herself as mah-REE-ah ee-noh-HOH-sah, with a trill /r̄/ in REE. Geraldo Rivera pronounces his first name heh-RAHL-doh. Such ethnically marked pronunciations highlight a reporter's pride in his or her ethnic identity. Students also sometimes emphasize their ethnic identity in certain situations. They can do so in many ways, including linguistically.

Try it yourself: Consider these pronunciations of Hispanic names: "deh-lah-CROOS" for *de la Cruz;* "FWEHN-tehs" for *Fuentes;* "GAHR-sah" for *Garza,* and "ehr-NAHN-dehs" for *Hernandez.* Say these names aloud as you think they would be said without an ethnic pronunciation. Compare those pronunciations with the ones in quotation marks, and identify two features in the Hispanic pronunciations that are characteristic of Chicano English as described above. Then identify two other features that we did not discuss but that you think may reflect characteristics of Hispanic English.

SOCIOECONOMIC STATUS VARIETIES: ENGLISH, FRENCH, AND SPANISH

Less striking than regional and ethnic varieties, but equally significant, are the remarkable patterns of speech that characterize different socioeconomic status groups. Here we describe some speech patterns of the English spoken in New York City and in Norwich, England, as well as of the French of Montreal and the Spanish of Argentina.

New York City

New Yorkers sometimes pronounce /r/ and sometimes drop it in words like *car* and *beer, cart* and *fourth* (where /r/ follows a vowel in the same syllable and appears either word finally or preceding another consonant). The presence or absence of this /r/ does not change a word's referential meaning. The price of a *beer* and of a "beeah" in a given tavern is the same. A "cah pahked" in a red zone is ticketed as surely as a similarly *parked car.* And whether you live in New York or "New Yoahk," you have the same mayor (or "maya").

Still, the occurrence of /r/ in these words is anything but random and anything but meaningless. When he was a graduate student, linguist William Labov hypothesized that /r/ pronunciations in New York depended on social-class affiliation and that any two socially ranked groups of New Yorkers would differ in their pronunciation of /r/. On the basis of some preliminary observations, he predicted that members of higher socioeconomic status groups would pronounce /r/ more frequently than would speakers in lower socioeconomic class groups.

To test his hypothesis, Labov investigated the speech of employees in three Manhattan department stores of different social rank: Saks Fifth Avenue, an expensive, upper-middle-class store; Macy's, a medium-priced, middle-class store; and S. Klein, a discount store patronized principally by working-class New Yorkers. He asked supervisors, sales clerks, and stock boys the whereabouts of merchandise he knew to be displayed on the fourth floor of their store. In answer to a question such as "Where can I find the lamps?" he elicited a response of *fourth floor.* Then, pretending not to have caught the answer, he said, "Excuse me?" and elicited a repeated—and more careful—utterance of *fourth floor.* Each employee thus had an opportunity to pronounce postvocalic /r/ four times (twice each in *fourth* and *floor)* in a natural and realistic setting in which language itself was *not* the focus of attention.

Employees at Saks, the highest-ranked store, pronounced /r/ more often than those at S. Klein, the lowest-ranked store. At Macy's, the middle-ranked store, employees pronounced an intermediate number. Figure 11–14 presents the results of Labov's survey. The darker sections represent the percentage of employees who pronounced /r/ four times; the lighter sections above the darker areas represent the percentage who pronounced it one, two, or three times (but not four). Employees who did not pronounce /r/ at all are not directly represented in the bar graph. As can be seen, 30% of the Saks employees pronounced all /r/, and an additional 32% pronounced some /r/. At Macy's, 20% pronounced /r/ four times, and an additional 31% pronounced some /r/. At S. Klein, only 4% of the employees pronounced all /r/, with an additional 17% pronouncing one, two, or three /r/s. Labov's hypothesis about the social stratification of postvocalic /r/ seemed strikingly confirmed.

If you think about it, you may be able to propose other possible explanations for these findings because factors other than socioeconomic status might have influenced the results, as Labov recognized. For example, if he spoke to more men than women

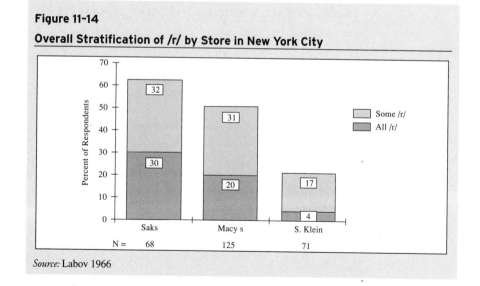

Figure 11-14

Overall Stratification of /r/ by Store in New York City

Source: Labov 1966

in one store or to more stock boys than sales clerks, or more African Americans than whites, the difference in pronunciation of /r/ could have been the result of gender, job, or ethnic differences. As it happened, there were more white female sales clerks than any other single group, and looking at their pronunciations separately from those of everyone else would eliminate the possibility of findings skewed by gender, job, or ethnicity. Figure 11–15 reveals an overall pattern of distribution similar to that for the whole sample of respondents. The white female sales clerks at Saks pronounced more /r/ than those at Macy's, who in turn pronounced more than those at S. Klein. Thus Labov ruled out the possibility that his findings reflected ethnic, gender, or in-store job differences.

In a third shuffling of the same data, Labov sought to determine whether his hypothesis would hold in an even narrower range of social ranking than the ranking of the department stores themselves. This time he examined the pronunciation of /r/ across the three occupational groups working in a single store, choosing Macy's because it provided the largest sample. Using the same hypothesis that predicted the ranking across the department stores, he predicted that he would find the highest percentage of /r/ pronunciation among the floorwalkers (supervisors) and the least among the stock boys, with the sales clerks falling between those two groups. As Figure 11–16 shows, that's exactly what he found, and he concluded that postvocalic /r/ pronunciation is indeed socially stratified in New York City—that higher-ranking social groups pronounce more postvocalic /r/ than lower-ranking groups.

Figure 11-15

Stratification of /r/ by Store in New York City White Female Sales Clerks

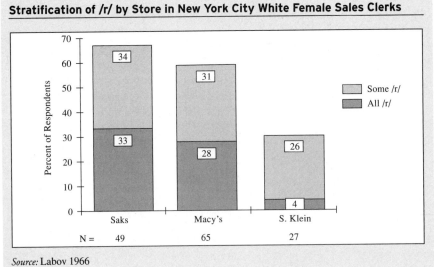

Source: Labov 1966

Figure 11-16

Stratification of /r/ by Occupational Groups in New York City

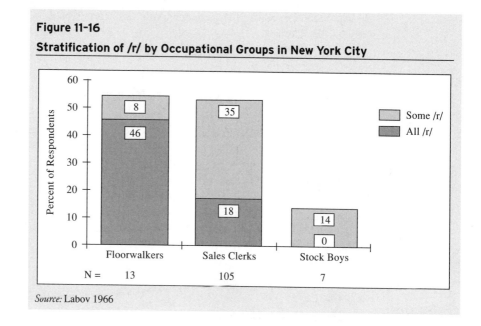

Source: Labov 1966

Labov then undertook a different kind of investigation. Equipped this time with detailed sociological descriptions of individual residents of Manhattan's Lower East Side, he spent several hours with each of about a hundred respondents there. As these New Yorkers discussed various topics, he tape-recorded the conversations. His interviewing techniques prompted the respondents to use speech samples characteristic of different speech situations, a topic we addressed in Chapter 10. Here are six variables examined:

- postvocalic /r/
- *th* in words such as *thirty, through,* and *with* (New Yorkers say *thirty* sometimes with /θ/ and sometimes with /t/)
- *th* in words such as *this, them,* and *breathe* (the infamous "dis," "dat," "dem," and "dose" words, with variants /d/ and /ð/)
- alternate pronunciation of -ING words like *running* and *talking,* with /ɪŋ/ and /ɪn/ variants (Often referred to as "dropping the g," but you know from Chapter 3 that the alternation is between velar /ŋ/ and alveolar /n/; only in the spelling is there a "g" to drop.)
- pronunciation of the vowel in the word class *coffee, soft, caught*
- pronunciation of the vowel in the word class *bad, care, sag*

In the interviews, Labov spoke with women and men, parents and children, African Americans and whites, Jews and Italians—a representative sample of Lower East Side residents. On the basis of extensive information about their background, he assigned each respondent to a socioeconomic status group based on a combination of these three factors:

- the *education* of the respondent
- the *income* of the respondent's household
- the *occupation* of the principal breadwinner in the household

Using these criteria, he placed individuals into one of four socioeconomic status categories, which he called lower class, working class, lower middle class, and upper middle class. As expected, and as Figure 11–17 shows, upper-middle-class respondents exhibited more /ɪŋ/ than lower-middle-class respondents, who in turn exhibited more than working-class respondents, who used more than lower-class respondents. Each group also pronounced more /ɪŋ/ as attention paid to speech was increased in various styles. Through several graded speech registers—casual style, interview style, and reading style—respondents in all socioeconomic groups increased the percentage of /ɪŋ/ pronounced.

Figure 11-17

Percent of *-ing* Suffix Pronounced as /ɪŋ/ by Four Socioeconomic Groups in New York City

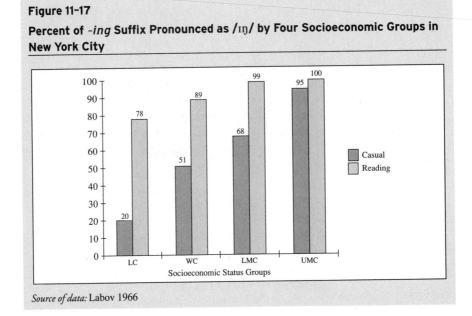

Source of data: Labov 1966

Labov found that all six variables were socially stratified. Each socioeconomic status group had characteristic patterns of pronunciation, and the percentage of pronunciation of the variants was ranked in the same way as the groups themselves. The upper middle class pronounced most /θ/ for *th* (as in *thing*), most /ð/ for *th* (as in *then*), most /ɪŋ/ (as in *running*), and most /r/ (as in *car*). The lower-class respondents pronounced fewest of these variants, while the lower middle class and working class fell in between, with the lower middle class pronouncing more than the working class. Such regular patterns of variation suggest that even subtle differences in social stratification may be reflected in language use.

The vowels were stratified in a similar way. New Yorkers have several pronunciations of the first vowel in *coffee:* it ranges from the high back tense vowel [u] through the mid back vowel [ɔ] down to the low back vowel [ɑ]. (The last pronunciation is more characteristic of the speech of much of the West and Midland United States, as we saw above in our discussion of the *cot ~ caught* merger.) The vowel of words in the *bad* class also varies—from low front lax [æ] to high front tense [iə] with an **offglide,** as we saw earlier in our discussion of the Northern Cities Shift. In New York City, higher socioeconomic status groups favored lower vowels in both cases.

Norwich, England

To see how widespread the kind of linguistic differentiation found in New York City might be elsewhere, British linguist Peter Trudgill investigated the speech patterns of residents of Norwich, England and found strikingly similar results. In Norwich, variation in syntactic as well as phonological expression was correlated with the socioeconomic status of speakers. Trudgill divided the respondents into five groups: middle middle class (MMC), lower middle class (LMC), upper working class (UWC), middle working class (MWC), and lower working class (LWC). Figure 11–18 illustrates the distribution of one phonological feature, the alternation between final /n/ and /ŋ/ in the suffix *-ing.*

Figure 11-18

Percent of *-ing* Suffix Pronounced as /ɪŋ/ by Five Socioeconomic Groups in Norwich, England

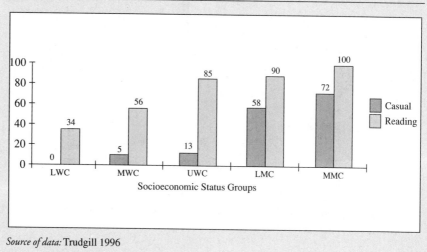

Source of data: Trudgill 1996

Comparing data from New York City (Figure 11–17 on page 394) and Norwich (Figure 11–18 on page 395) shows that the patterns of distribution for socioeconomic status are similar in the two cities. Each successively higher socioeconomic status group pronounces more /ɪŋ/ than the group immediately below it.

Montreal, Canada

In Montreal, French speakers vary the pronunciation of pronouns and definite articles. Except in the word *le,* /l/ is sometimes pronounced and sometimes omitted in personal pronouns such as *il* 'he' and *elle* 'she' and articles (and pronouns) such as *les* 'the (plural)' and *la* 'the (feminine).' (See Table 2–11, page 66.) In the usage of two occupational groups, professionals and laborers, the laborers consistently omitted /l/ more frequently than the professionals did, as shown for four such words in Figure 11–19.

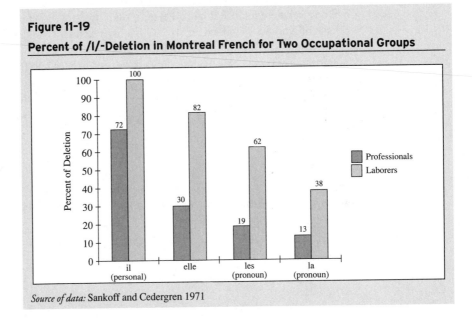

Figure 11-19
Percent of /l/-Deletion in Montreal French for Two Occupational Groups

Source of data: Sankoff and Cedergren 1971

Argentina

Spanish speakers show similar patterns of phonological variation. To cite one example in Argentina, speakers sometimes delete /s/ before pauses (as in English, /s/ is a common word-final sound in Spanish, occurring on plural nouns and on several verb forms). In a study of six Argentinian occupational groups, the percentage of /s/-deletion was greatest in the lowest-status occupations and least in the higher-status occupations, as shown in Figure 11–20.

Figure 11-20

Percent of Prepausal /s/-Deletion in Argentine Spanish for Six Occupational Groups

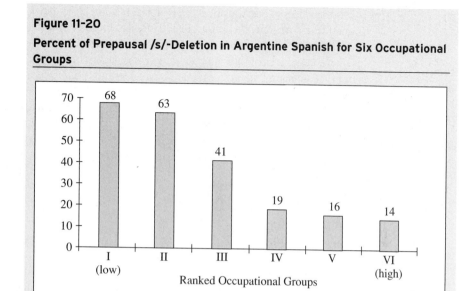

Source of data: Terrell 1981

General Comments

On the basis of evidence from these and other studies, parallel patterns of distribution may be expected for phonological variables wherever comparable social structures are found. Morphological and syntactic variation also exists, though evidence about variation at these levels of the grammar is scanty. What holds true of variation in English, French, and Spanish presumably holds true of similarly structured communities speaking other languages, although here, too, evidence is scanty.

THE LANGUAGE VARIETIES OF WOMEN AND MEN

You know that in many speech communities women and men don't speak identically. In the United States, certain words are closely associated with women and may "sound" feminine as a result. Adjectives such as *lovely, darling,* and *cute* may carry feminine associations, as do words that describe precise shades of color, such as *mauve* and *chartreuse*. Likewise (though decreasingly so), certain four-letter words may surprise some people when uttered by a woman. Margaret Cho and Mo'Nique are two comedians who capitalize on some of these gender differences, shocking audiences by their use of taboo words generally associated with male rather than female speakers.

In some languages, the differences between women's and men's speech are more dramatic than in English. In informal situations in Japanese, even the first-person pronoun 'I' differs: women use *atasi*, men *boku*. In French, *je* is the first-person pronoun for men and women, but because adjectives are marked for gender agreement, *Je suis heureux* 'I am happy' identifies a male speaker, while *Je suis heureuse* identifies a female speaker.

Among the Koasati Indians of Louisiana, women and men use different forms of certain indicative and imperative verbs. For example, men use /s/ instead of the nasalization characteristic of women in some verbs, as in (1) and (2) below; and men sometimes add /s/ where the women's form ends in a vowel plus consonant, as in (3) and (4).

Gender Differences in Koasati

	WOMEN	MEN	
1	lakawwã	lakawwás	'he will lift it'
2	kã	kás	'he is saying'
3	lakáw	lakáws	'he is lifting it'
4	íp	īps	'he is eating it'
5	ót	ótʃ	'he is building a fire'

In some cases, the forms used by women are more conservative than those used by men, reflecting older forms of Koasati usage. When the research reported here was conducted, 60 years ago, only middle-aged and elderly women used women's forms. A more recent study of Koasati suggests that socially prominent women also use "male" speech forms, and that younger women were using forms identical to those of men. In Koasati culture, men and women are familiar with both sets of forms and when stories are told, the characters speak the forms characteristic of men or women as appropriate, no matter who is telling the story. Also, when Koasati parents correct the speech of their children, fathers may correct daughters and mothers may correct sons. There is no taboo on men using women's forms or women using men's forms. Similar striking differences between the language of men and women occur in Creek and Hitchiti (other languages of the Muskogean family), Yana (a California Indian language), Siouan, and certain Eskimo languages, as well as in Carib and other South American Indian languages.

Outside the Americas, reports of striking differences between gender varieties have been reported for Chukchee (spoken in Siberia) and for Thai. In polite Thai conversation between men and women of equal rank, women say *dičʰàn* while men say *pʰŏm* for the first-person singular pronoun 'I.' Thai also has a set of particles used differently by men and women, especially in formulaic questions and responses such as 'thank you' and 'excuse me.' The polite particle used by men is *kʰráp*, while women use *kʰá* or *kʰâ*. Because these politeness particles occur frequently in daily interaction, speech differences between men and women can be quite marked in Thai, despite the fact that very few words are so differentiated.

There are also more subtle differences between men's and women's speech, the kinds of quantitative differences that we saw between other social groups. For example, in Montreal, where professionals delete /l/ from articles and pronouns less frequently than laborers do, men and women also differ in pronouncing these same words. Figure 11–21 shows that men delete /l/ more frequently than women for *il* (personal, as in *il chante* 'he sings'), for *elle,* and for the pronouns *les* and *la.*

Figure 11-21

Percent of /l/-Deletion in Montreal French for Women and Men

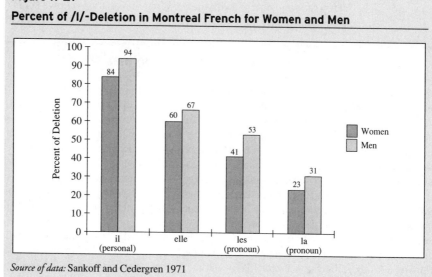

Source of data: Sankoff and Cedergren 1971

Patterns in which women delete sounds less frequently than men also appear in New York City and Norwich. In these cities, when higher social classes behave linguistically in one way to a greater extent than lower social classes, women tend to behave like the higher social classes to a greater extent than men do.

In English, besides vocabulary differences between the sexes, more subtle differences can go largely unnoticed. One study examined the pronunciation of the *-ing* suffix in words like *running* and *talking.* In a semirural New England village, the speech patterns of a dozen boys and a dozen girls between the ages of 3 and 10 showed that, even in such young children, all but three used both alveolar [n] and velar [ŋ] pronunciations for verbal *-ing.* Interestingly, twice as many girls as boys showed a preference for the /ɪŋ/ forms, as shown below.

Pronunciation of *-ing* by 12 Boys and 12 Girls in a New England Village

	PREFERENCE FOR /ɪŋ/	NO PREFERENCE FOR /ɪŋ/
GIRLS	10	2
BOYS	5	7

The finding that girls and boys differ in this way may seem surprising, since girls and boys in this New England village (as generally in Western societies) are in frequent face-to-face contact with each other. A separation in the communication channels, suggested earlier as a motivating factor in the differentiation of dialect speech patterns, does not appear to explain this case. What, then, is the explanation? One hypothesis is the "toughness" characteristic associated with working-class lifestyles combined with the "masculinity" characteristic associated with the *-in'* forms. In other words, an association between masculinity and "dropping the *g*" may outweigh the associations with prestige and higher socioeconomic status that otherwise accompany the *-ing* variant (with the *g).* What this analysis shows is that gender differences in language have little to do with biological sex and a lot to do with social roles.

Masculinity and the Toughness Factor

There's evidence for the prestige of *running* and *talking* pronunciations over pronunciations that "drop the *g*." Here are two facts. (1.) English speakers who use both variants (that's virtually all of us) "pronounce the *g*" more often when we're in situations of greater formality. (2.) Social groups with higher socioeconomic status pronounce it more than lower status groups. Interestingly, girls and women use the *-ing* pronunciation more than boys and men do. One explanation may be that women are more status conscious than men—sociologists have found that to be the case in other arenas, so it wouldn't be surprising. But linguists suggest an additional reason. Think of it as the "Toughness Factor." Boys and men may associate pronunciations like *runnin'* and *talkin'* with working-class "toughness"—and that connection apparently outweighs any link to prestige. You could say that preferring the less prestigious pronunciation marks "masculinity." Now, you might object that using the term "masculinity" to explain the linguistic behavior of boys and men seems to beg the question. After all, what's gained by calling a pronunciation "masculine" just because men use it more than women? Well, masculinity and femininity are not the same thing as male and female. Sex differences (male and female) are biological, and language differences don't reflect biology. Instead, they reflect the sociocultural phenomena of *gender*—what it *means* to be male or female. You're aware of gender differences marked by clothing, hair length, body decoration, and jewelry use. ("Wear some earrings, for God's sake," the mother of Emma Thompson's character in the movie "The Winter Guest" tells her after she's cut her hair short. "Let folks know you're a woman!") So you shouldn't be surprised that language also reflects the important social identity of gender roles. It will be interesting to track how much the ongoing efforts to equalize gender roles in Western societies also mute differences between masculine and feminine pronunciations and other patterns of speech!

WHY DO STIGMATIZED VARIETIES PERSIST?

It's no secret that some language varieties carry prestige while others are stigmatized. Whereas the degree of stigma depends on the group making the judgment, norms of evaluation are often shared throughout a speech community. You may wonder why stigmatized varieties don't die out. Why don't speakers give up their stigmatized varieties for more prestigious ones?

The explanation seems to lie in the fact that a person's identity—as a woman or man, as an American or Australian, as a member of a particular ethnic or socioeconomic group—is tied into the speech patterns of the group to which he or she belongs. Americans talk like other Americans; Australians like other Australians; men like men; women like women. While one's sex is not a matter of choice, one's gender is, at least to some extent. What is considered masculine and feminine is a cultural, not a biological, matter, and one can behave in more or less masculine or feminine ways irrespective of one's sex. To change the way you speak is to signal changes in who you are or how you want to be perceived. For a New Yorker transplanted to California, speaking like a Californian is to relinquish some identity as a New Yorker. To give up speaking African-American English is to relinquish some identity as an African American. To give up working-class speech patterns acquired in childhood is to take on a new identity. In short, to take on new speech patterns is to reform oneself and present oneself anew.

Language is not set apart from social identity and social alliances. It is a major symbol of our social identity, and we have seen how remarkably fine-tuned to that identity it can be. If you wish to identify with "nonnative" regional, socioeconomic, or ethnic groups and have sufficient contact with them, your speech will come to resemble theirs. In fact, socially mobile individuals exhibit pronunciation patterns more like the group toward which they are heading than like their group of current affiliation; this is true not only of individuals moving up the socioeconomic scale but also of those whose paths are pointing lower.

We can illustrate with a telling investigation of linguistic and social identity on Martha's Vineyard, an island off the coast of Massachusetts. There the vowels /aj/ and /aw/ have two principal variants, with the first element of each diphthong alternating between [a] and the more centralized vowel [ə]. Words like *night* and *why* may be pronounced [aj] or [əj]; words like *shout* and *how* may be pronounced with [aw] or the more centralized diphthong [əw]. These variants are not typical dialect features; they don't reflect gender, ethnicity, or socioeconomic status. Instead, on Martha's Vineyard, vowel centralization represents identity with traditional values of the island and its life. The up-island residents have more vowel centralization than do the residents in sections catering to summer visitors. Young men intending to leave the island and lead their lives on the mainland showed the least vowel centralization, while the greatest vowel centralization was shown by a young man who had moved to the mainland but returned to Martha's Vineyard. Thus the centralized diphthongs may be viewed as representing rejection of mainland values and a positive view of the values of island life.

The symbolic value of a person's language variety cannot be overestimated. In evaluating oral arguments in Britain, speakers of regional varieties rated the quality of an argument higher when presented in a standard accent, but found the same argument more persuasive when it was made using a regional accent.

It's easy for speakers higher on the socioeconomic ladder to ask about speakers lower on the ladder, "Why don't they start talking like us?" The answer may be simple: their social identity is different, and they do not necessarily share the values of the higher socioeconomic group. For some insight into the matter, think about gender dialects. Although there have been stirrings of neutrality recently, it is perfectly acceptable for women to speak like women and men to speak like men. Imagine men asking women to speak like them in order to get ahead in "a man's world." Or imagine a female head of a company asking her male truck drivers to speak more like women to get ahead in "a woman's world." These are patently unacceptable scenarios. Likewise, rough equality of status is granted to most regional varieties. Imagine a Bostonian moving to Atlanta and being told by the boss to "lose" the New England accent in order to succeed. The employee might infer that the Boston origin, not the accent, was at issue.

When it comes to ethnic and social-class varieties, perceptions are quite different. The widely held view is that African-American English, Chicano English, and the dialects of lower socioeconomic status groups cannot be employed at schools or in the professional workplace. These views reflect language attitudes. As such, they are social biases, not linguistic biases, and they are based at least in part on attitudes toward speakers, not speech.

In study after study, language has been shown to be a central factor in a person's identity. Asking people, asking *you,* to change *your* customary language patterns is not like asking you to try on different styles or colors of sweaters. It is asking you to take on a new identity and to espouse the identity and values associated with speakers of a different dialect. One reason that nonstandard varieties are so robustly resistant to the urgings of education is that all vernacular language varieties are deeply entwined with the social identities and values of their speakers.

Computers and the Study of Dialect

Given the mass of both quantitative and qualitative data represented in our discussion of dialects, it should be no surprise that computers are being used by dialectologists to accomplish their goals. Researchers are digitizing the kinds of data that in the past have been manually represented, as on some maps in this chapter. For example, researchers for the Linguistic Atlas of the Middle and South Atlantic States (LAMSAS) have used a program called MapInfo to plot longitude and latitude coordinates for the residences of all 1162 LAMSAS informants, which will enable maps of various sizes and degrees of detail to represent features that were elicited from the informants. You have also seen in Figures 11–7 on page 376 and 11–8 on page 378 the use of computers in generating nontraditional maps for dialectology. In a different vein, the work represented in the Telsur project and the Atlas of North American English depends crucially on using computers to perform acoustic analyses of vowel sounds.

In addition to a wide variety of tasks that have used computers for map-related activities, the kinds of resources that corpora make available to researchers interested in language variation are beginning to revolutionize the study of dialects. A huge project called the International Corpus of English aims to provide texts totaling about one million words of written and spoken English of the 1990s from each of 20 centers around the world, representing the English spoken in the Caribbean, Fiji, Ghana, Hong Kong, India, Kenya, Nigeria, the Philippines, and Singapore, to mention only some regions. The texts of these corpora will be tagged and annotated, making their use in dialect comparisons extremely valuable.

In our discussions of variation across dialects, we have seen that vocabulary and pronunciation vary. In the real world, an understanding of vowel variation has proven useful in keeping an innocent person out of jail. Computers have been used to help analyze the vowel characteristics in tape recordings that contained illegal speech acts—in this case, acts of threatening. Someone had telephoned a major airline with a serious threat of violence, and workers who heard the call thought they recognized the voice as belonging to a disgruntled former employee. A computer analysis of the vowel quality of the caller showed that his dialect was not the same as that of the former employee.

SUMMARY

- When separated physically or socially, people who otherwise would share speechways come to speak differently. Given sufficient time and separation, distinct languages can arise.

- Conversely, the speech of people talking as members of the same community can develop in unison, even tending to merge in some situations.

- There is no linguistic basis upon which to distinguish between a dialect and a language. Every language is made up of dialects, and in terms of linguistic principles and linguistic universals every dialect is a language.

- There are important linguistic differences among social groups within every speech community.

- Linguistic forms can vary greatly from one social group to the next, and social groups may be defined in a number of ways besides regionally.

- A social group may have ethnicity or socioeconomic status as the basis for affiliation.

- Female speakers and male speakers may also be thought of as belonging to different social groups, called gender groups.

- Combining these different group distinctions, we obtain a complex picture of the composition of society. Within a particular ethnic group, we find socioeconomic classes whose members are male or female. Differences in speechways support such social identities.

- Whatever the social group, its language variety will typically exhibit characteristics that distinguish it from the language varieties of other social groups.

- The linguistic features that characterize social varieties may also serve as markers (or symbols) of social identity.

- When anyone wishes to stress membership in his or her ethnic group, one way to do so is to emphasize or even exaggerate the characteristic features of his or her ethnic language variety.

- If a woman wants to appear particularly feminine, she may choose to exhibit features associated with women's speech and avoid "masculine-sounding" expressions.

- Individuals can take advantage of socially marked language characteristics for their own purposes.

- Everyone speaks with a pronunciation that is characteristic of social identity. No one can speak without an accent, though we tend to be acutely aware of the accents of others and to think members of our own social groups do not carry accents.

WHAT DO YOU THINK? REVISITED

❖ *Nina talks funny, too.* Nina's camp counselor appears to be a speaker of British English. As funny as the counselor's dialect may have struck Nina, her dialect might have sounded just as "funny" to the counselor. Every group's language variety differs—more or less—from those of other groups. Of course, there is nothing "funny" about anyone's speech, except possibly that it's different, and patterns that differ from our own may seem odd simply because they differ from what we're accustomed to.

❖ *Daniel's Alabama sub.* There's probably no one on earth who doesn't carry an accent, no one who doesn't speak a language variety whose pronunciation reflects his or her social identity. Even if you rid yourself of your native accent, you must replace it with another one because you can't speak without any accent at all. (See Alice below and Ex. 11–10b.)

❖ *Alice and your accent.* When the people we speak with are consistently from our own social circles, everyone we hear speaks pretty much the same as we do. It takes an outsider—someone from another speech community—to recognize that the way *we* speak shows characteristic indications of its uniqueness. It's easy to hear someone else's accent, but not easy to hear our own.

❖ *County fair competition.* There are many different answers to this question. The *Dictionary of American Regional English* will provide an abundance of examples from American English for anyone who had difficulty coming up with suitable terms.

❖ *Justin and Ebonics.* In 1997, at the height of the Ebonics controversy, much of the comment in newspapers and on radio indicated a widespread perception that a dialect can be judged as good or bad by how closely it resembles the standard variety of the same language. All language varieties differ from one another to greater or lesser degrees. This is as true of dialects of the same language as it is of different languages. French is ungrammatical if judged by the rules of Spanish or Japanese. American English is ungrammatical if judged by the rules of British English. Ebonics is ungrammatical if judged by the rules of standard English. And standard English is ungrammatical if judged by the rules of Ebonics or standard French.

❖ *Women talk, men talk.* The degree to which the talk of men and women differs isn't the same from one cultural group to the next. This is also true for variation across social groups within a given culture. Most research that has investigated differences between men's and women's speech has found some differences, such as different words for the same item or some forms used more frequently by men or women. If Sammy recalls the many ways in which boys and girls are brought up differently, she shouldn't be surprised that men and women also *speak* differently. It remains to be seen to what extent men and women will continue to speak differently as greater parity is pursued in raising boys and girls.

EXERCISES

Based on English

11-1 Distinguish between an accent and a dialect. Distinguish between a dialect and a language. What is meant by a "language variety"? Does it make any sense to say of a language variety that "it isn't a language, it's *only* a dialect"?

11-2 Examine a copy of a newspaper or magazine published in Britain (one or more of the following should be available in your library's periodicals room: *The Times, The Economist, Punch, The Spectator, The Listener*) and list as many examples of differences between American and British English as you can notice on one or two pages. Include examples of vocabulary, syntax, spelling, and punctuation. Can you identify any examples of discourse differences?

11-3 Which of the following words are you familiar with? Make two lists, one consisting of those words you normally use and the other consisting of words you don't use but have heard others use. With what regional or national group do you associate the words you have heard others use but don't use yourself? Compare your judgments with those of your classmates.

dragonfly	darning needle, mosquito hawk, spindle, snake feeder, snake doctor
pancake	fritter, hotcake, flannel cake, batter cake
cottage cheese	curds, curd cheese, clabber cheese, dutch cheese, pot cheese
string beans	green beans, snap beans
earthworm	night crawler, fishing worm, angle worm, rain worm, red worm, mud worm
lightning bug	firefly, fire bug
baby carriage	baby buggy, baby coach, baby cab, pram

11-4 The following questions (some slightly adapted) are from the questionnaire used to gather data for *DARE*. Answer each question yourself, and then compare your answers with those of your classmates. Do you and your classmates agree on the regions in which the particular variants are used? (*DARE* provides maps for answers to these questions.)

a. How do you speak of roads that have numbers or letters? For example, if someone asks directions to get to (Supply local city name), you might say, "Take ___."

b. What names are used around here for:

1) the part of the house below the ground floor?

2) the kind of sandwich in a large, long bun, that's a meal in itself?

3) a small stream of water not big enough to be a river?

4) a round cake of dough, cooked in deep fat, with a hole in the center?

5) a piece of cloth that a woman folds over her head and ties under her chin?

6) the common worm used as bait?

7) vehicles for a baby or small child, the kind it can lie down in?

8) a mark on the skin where somebody has sucked it hard and brought the blood to the surface?

9) a bone from the breast of a chicken, shaped like a horseshoe?

10) the place in the elbow that gives you a strange feeling if you hit it against something?

11) very young frogs, when they still have tails but no legs?

How do the answers of your classmates to questions (2) and (8) compare with Figures 11–22 to 11–25, the *DARE* maps for *grinder, hero, hoagie,* and *hickey?*

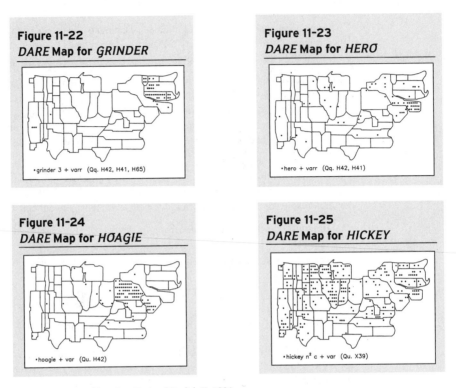

Figure 11-22
DARE Map for *GRINDER*

•grinder 3 + varr (Qq. H42, H41, H65)

Figure 11-23
DARE Map for *HERO*

•hero + varr (Qq. H42, H41)

Figure 11-24
DARE Map for *HOAGIE*

•hoagie + var (Qu. H42)

Figure 11-25
DARE Map for *HICKEY*

•hickey n^2 c + var (Qu. X39)

Source: Dictionary of American Regional English, II, 1991

11-5 What was Labov's hypothesis about the distribution of /r/ in New York City department stores? In your city or town, are there three socially ranked stores that could be similarly investigated? Which two or three phonological features do you expect to be socially differentiated in your stores? Design a question for each feature that would uncover the data needed to test your hypothesis. (Make the question a natural one for the kind of store you have in mind.) Would you ask your respondents to repeat their answers as Labov did? Explain why or why not.

11-6 "William Labov . . . once said about the use of black English, 'It is the goal of most black Americans to acquire full control of the standard language without giving up their own culture.' . . . I wonder if the good doctor might also consider the goals of those black Americans who have full control of standard English but who are every now and then troubled by that colorful, grammar-to-the-winds patois that is black English. Case in point—me."

So wrote a twenty-one-year-old African-American college sophomore in *Newsweek* (Dec. 27, 1982, p. 7). The student cites several features of African-American English such as those described in this chapter.

a. Look up the meaning of *patois* in your desk dictionary and note its connotations in referring to particular language varieties. Are those connotations positive or negative? What does the phrase "grammar-to-the-winds" suggest about the writer's attitude toward the grammaticality of African-American English?

b. What features of African-American English do you think the writer means in calling it a "grammar-to-the-winds patois"?

c. What would be the implications for communication if any speech variety were indeed "grammarless"? Give two reasons why African-American English cannot accurately be called a "grammar-to-the-winds" dialect.

d. What would you assume to be the reason for the writer's attitudes toward African-American English? What might you explain to the student about patterns of language in every variety and about the status of particular varieties *in terms of their linguistic features?*

11-7 Comment on the validity of the quotation that follows, and explain your view: "If there were as many oil barons coming up from Mexico as there are farm laborers, the accents of Pancho Villa might sound more musical to American ears." (William F. Mackey in Cobarrubias and Fishman [1983], p. 186)

11-8 Describe two ways in which the speech of women and men differs in greetings, threats, swearing, and promises. What do you think accounts for these differences? Do you think such differences are increasing or decreasing? Explain the bases for your answers.

11-9 Among many functions of the word *like* in English, it is used by certain speakers to mark the beginning of a direct quotation. Here are two examples of this quotative *like:*

"And then she's like, 'I don't want to go.' "

"So he's like, 'But you promised!' "

To complete this exercise, you will need natural data from the speech of your acquaintances. Collect 20 naturally occurring examples of quotative *like* from the speech of at least five people (including some people younger and others older than you). Write down the examples exactly as they were spoken, taking care not to call attention to the speech of your acquaintances or the fact that you are observing their language. Relying on five-year ranges (15–19, 20–24, and so on), note the approximate age of every speaker you set out to observe (whether or not they actually use quotative *like*).

a. Some researchers call this feature "quotative *be like*" because their data indicate that this use of *like* generally occurs with the verb *be,* as in the examples above. Explain whether or not your data lend support to using the alternative name.

b. Identify the tense (past or nonpast) of the verbs that precede quotative *like* in your data. Identify the time (present, past, or future) that the verbs refer to. Keep in mind that tense and time are not the same phenomena.

c. In both the examples above, the verb form has been contracted to *'s.* What percentage of your examples show a similar contraction?

d. In both the examples above, the subject of *be* in the quotative *like* clauses is a pronoun (*he, she*). What lexical categories are the subjects in your examples?

e. Grouping your speakers into five-year age ranges, identify which age groups use this feature and which do not. On the basis of your admittedly limited evidence, make a hypothesis about whether use of this feature is age related.

f. Compare your findings about use and age with the findings of some classmates, and reconsider your hypothesis in light of the pooled data.

g. Do you think that younger users will continue using quotative *like* as they get older (which would make it an example of language change in progress) or that they will not continue using it beyond a certain age (which would make it an age-graded feature)? Explain your view.

h. In your data, do you note any examples that represent uses of *like* other than the quotative, leaving aside its use as a preposition (*He looks like his dad*), subordinating conjunction (*Winstons taste good like a cigarette should*), or verb (*She likes asparagus*)? If so, analyze those uses and try characterizing them; what name(s) might suit them?

i. What other expressions have you heard that function like quotative *like*?

Especially for Educators and Future Teachers

11-10 a. Below are the opening words of a presentation by a college teacher to a group of Southern teachers at a professional meeting. (Imagine it spoken with marked Southern pronunciations: the college teacher was born in the South and clearly wished to play upon those affiliations.)

"Years ago, during my first week in Wisconsin, I was asked by a fellow teacher, 'Do you mean they let *you* teach English?' The speaker was a Canadian with what I thought a very peculiar accent. Soon after that, a woman working on a degree in speech asked me with all the kindness and gentleness of which she was capable whether I would let her teach me how to talk right. If I had had her zeal and patience and kindness, I might very well have made the offer first, for I thought her speech highly unsatisfactory."

Provide answers to these questions, most of which the teacher posed to her audience:

1) Who should teach whom?

2) Is there a standard pronunciation in American English and, if so, what is it?

3) Should education aim to make everyone sound like everyone else?

4) Is it possible that training could make everyone sound like everyone else?

5) If the training succeeded, how would everyone sound?

6) Assuming uniformity could be achieved, how long could it last?

b. The same college teacher reported these comments from a Southern teacher and a Southern physician:

Teacher: [aː hæv dɪlɪbərɪtlɪ wəkt tu gɛt rɪd av ɪnɪ tresɪz av æksɪnt æz aː θɪŋk ɔwl ɛdʒəketɪd pipəl ʃud du aː prad masɛf ðæt aː hæv nat wən ʌɪt av ɪnɪ tresəbəl æksɪnt ɪn ma spitʃ]

Physician: [mɪnɪ av ma pəjʃəns θɪŋk aː æm fram ðə nɔəθ bɪkɔwz æz ən ɛdʒəketɪd pəsən aː don av kɔəs hæv ə səðən æksɪnt]

1) After reading the comments aloud, write them out in standard orthography.

2) Give the standard orthography for these words as pronounced in the same dialect:

i) [mɔwnɪn] ii) [kaəd] iii) [kent] iv) [hɛp] v) [spikɪn] vi) [həjd] vii) [mɪnɪ] viii) [bɪnɪfɪt]

c. Compare Figure 11–12 and the description of the Southern Shift (p. 382) with the transcriptions of comments by the Southern teacher and physician. For each of the following features of the Southern Shift, cite two words from the comments or the list of words in (2) that exemplify it: (i) monophthongization of /aj/; (ii) /ɛ/ pronounced higher and fronter; (iii)

/æ/ pronounced higher and fronter. (For all examples, provide the words in standard orthography and the transcribed version.)

d. Cite a pair of words in the transcriptions that indicate whether the *pin ~ pen* merger is characteristic of this dialect. Cite a pair of words with /r/-omission after vowels. Cite a pair with /l/-omission after vowels.

(Adapted from Jane Appleby, "Is Southern English Good English?" In David L. Shores and Carol P. Hines, eds., *Papers in Language Variation* [Tuscaloosa: University of Alabama Press, 1977], p. 225.)

11-11 Looking at the content of what the physician and teacher reported in Exercise 11–10, think about and answer these questions:

a. Does the physician believe that Northerners have accents?

b. Does he or she believe that education removes or should remove a regional accent?

c. Do you think the physician is pleased that the patients believe their physician is from the North?

d. The teacher twice uses the term "traces" in reference to accent. Does "traces" suggest whether the teacher regards regional accents positively or negatively? Had this teacher grown up speaking a Northern accent, do you think he or she would have reported trying to get rid of any *traces* of accent? What do you think of this teacher's view of the relationship between education and accent?

e. Do you like it when people recognize where you're from? Do you have an accent that outsiders admire? Has anyone ever said anything unfavorable about your accent to you? Have you ever tried to get rid of any traces of accent in your speech? All things considered, what do you think about your own accent?

f. Putting yourself into the frame of mind of the Southern teacher, why might he or she believe that educated people should rid themselves of any traces of accent in their speech?

g. To judge from the transcribed comments of the teacher and the physician, how easy is it for a person to get rid of all traces of accent?

11-12 a. What would it mean to speak without an accent? (Think globally as well as regionally: what would it mean to speak English without an American, British, Canadian, Australian, or some other national accent? What would it mean to speak French without a North American, European, or other accent?) Why do you imagine some people appear to think it's better to be from nowhere than somewhere?

b. Provide a list of four regional features of *your own* pronunciation that others have called to your attention or that you are otherwise aware of.

c. Make a list of features that you admire in the speech of others. What's admirable about those features?

d. Make a list of features that you dislike or think ill of in the speech of others. Can you specify what it is about those features that you dislike?

e. What explanation can you offer for the fact that many people believe they speak *without* an accent?

11–13 Cockney is a well-known British dialect. It is spoken by working-class Londoners, and the number of speakers doubtless exceeds the estimated 1.5 million speakers of the standard variety of English known as RP or BBC English that is taught in England's private schools. Among the features of Cockney is /h/-dropping, especially in words that are not stressed, such as the pronouns *he, him,* and *her,* the verbs *has, have,* and *had,* and in all other word classes as well: nouns such as *hospital, heaven,* and *hell,* adjectives such as *hot* and *heavy,* verbs such as *help* and *hiss.* Cockney speakers pronounce a glottal stop not only for the medial /t/ as in words like *bitter* and *later* but also accompanying medial /p/ as in *paper.* Also characteristic is the pronunciation of /f/ for the initial consonant of words like *thin* and the final consonant of words like *with* and *mouth,* as well as the medial consonant in words like *pithy* and *Cathy.* Instead of [θɪn] for *thin,* Cockney speakers say "fin," and "wif" for *with,* and "Caffee" [kæfi] for *Cathy.* They merge /ð/ and /v/ in specific phonological environments: word-finally, as in "breave" and "bave" for *breathe* and *bathe,* and in medial position, yielding "bruvver" for *brother* and "muvver" for *mother.* Comment on the phonological similarity and differences between African-American English and Cockney. What do the similarities suggest about the systematic nature of phonological variants within dialects?

OTHER RESOURCES

Internet

- **American Dialect Society: http://www.et.byu.edu/~lilliek/ads/index.htm**
  This Web site contains information about the American Dialect Society (ADS), including a special page for student members. It also provides links to pages for *DARE*—the *Dictionary of American Regional English*—and for the various Linguistic Atlas projects sponsored by the ADS. There is plenty to keep a student of American dialects engaged for hours.

- **The Empirical Linguistics and Linguistic Atlas Page: http://hyde.park.uga.edu/**
  An ambitious Web site that provides information about the nine Linguistic Atlas projects in the United States. The best represented Atlas project is LAMSAS—the Linguistic Atlas of the Middle and South Atlantic States (ranging from New York to northern Florida and including West Virginia and Pennsylvania), but there is useful information about all the Atlas projects.

- **Linguist List's Topic Page on Ebonics: http://linguist.emich.edu/topics/ebonics/**
  The Linguist List is the major discussion list among linguists for issues of general interest. Ebonics was such a popular topic in 1996 and 1997 that the list managers decided to collect all the information the Linguist List has on it at one site.

- **Atlas of North American English: http://www.ling.upenn.edu/phono_atlas/home.html**
  The Atlas of North American English is based on a thorough and systematic telephone survey of the major urban areas of the United States and Canada in a project called Telsur, based at the University of Pennsylvania. The Web site presents the latest research, with plenty of colorful maps showing vowel pronunciation. When you visit the site, keep in mind that in this book we represented only three English vowels as diphthongs, but this site uses a different set of representations, which are provided here for convenience:

LISU	ANAE	WORDS	LISU	ANAE	WORDS
/aw/	/aw/	pout, plowed	/u/	/uw/	food, cooed
/aj/	/ay/	my, mine	/ɔ/	/oh/	talk, dawn, caught
/ɔj/	/oy/	boy, soy	/ɛ/	/e/	pet, Seth, wedge
/e/	/ey/	made, frayed	/ʊ/	/u/	wood, could
/o/	/ow/	flowed, code			

- **Ebonics Information Page: http://www.cal.org/ebonics/**
  Maintained by the Center for Applied Linguistics, this is a rich page, full of valuable discussion and analysis of African-American English and issues related to Ebonics.

- **Survey of English Usage: http://www.ucl.ac.uk/english-usage/**
  At this site you can find information about the International Corpus of English, especially the million-word British contribution.

Video and Audio

The videos listed below are informative and well worth viewing. Some are readily available in libraries and video rental outlets. All of them can be purchased through one of several educational video suppliers, such as Insight Media (http://www.insight-media.com). Though now dated, Linn and Zuber (1984) offers a discography of language recordings.

- **American Tongues**   This award-winning video treats regional accents from Boston to Texas, with a focus on the speech of some very engaging teenagers. Entertaining and informative.

- **Black on White**   From the BBC's *Story of English* series narrated by Robert MacNeil, this video explores the origins and spread of African-American English.

- **Communities of Speech**   In this video Walt Wolfram and Deborah Tannen debate issues as they examine the concept of standard American English and other American dialects.

- **Nu-Shu: A Hidden Language of Women in China**   This 1999 video, by Yue-Qing Yang, documents Nu Shu, a secret language of women in Hunan province. This documentary focuses on one modern-day woman still able to read and write the language. For information: Women Make Movies, 462 Broadway, New York, NY 10013; (212) 925–0606; cinema@wmm.com

SUGGESTIONS FOR FURTHER READING

- **John Baugh. 1985.** *Black Street Speech: Its History, Structure, and Survival* (Austin: University of Texas Press). Including chapters on phonology, morphology, and syntax, this is an excellent treatment of African-American English.

- **John Baugh. 2000.** *Beyond Ebonics: Linguistic Pride and Racial Prejudice* (New York: Oxford University Press). A sensible and wide-ranging analysis of the Ebonics controversy of 1996 and 1997.

- **Craig M. Carver. 1987.** *American Regional Dialects: A Word Geography* (Ann Arbor: University of Michigan Press). An overview of American English dialects based upon vocabulary findings in the *Dictionary of American Regional English.* The treatment emphasizes cultural and historical origins and has good maps and discussion.

- **Frederick Cassidy, Joan Houston Hall, eds. 1985–.** *Dictionary of American Regional English* (Cambridge, MA: Belknap Press). The most comprehensive treatment of American regional vocabulary. Four volumes have been published to date, up to and including the word *sky writer.*

- **Edward Finegan & John R. Rickford, eds. 2004.** *Language in the USA* (Cambridge: Cambridge University Press). A collection of 26 chapters treating a wide range of topics related to dialects, including American regional dialects and social varieties.

- **W. Nelson Francis. 1983.** *Dialectology: An Introduction* (New York: Longman). An excellent introductory treatment. Contains maps of the United States and United Kingdom and relates American dialect features to their British origins.

- **Arthur Hughes & Peter Trudgill. 1996.** *English Accents and Dialects: An Introduction to Social and Regional Varieties of English in the British Isles,* 3rd ed. (London: Arnold). Particularly good on pronunciation, with little attention to vocabulary or grammar. Includes discussion of Belfast, Dublin, and Edinburgh. A cassette containing edited interviews with speakers from 12 regions of Britain is available, and the edited interviews are transcribed in the book.

- **Rosina Lippi-Green. 1997.** *English with an Accent: Language, Ideology, and Discrimination in the United States* (New York: Routledge). An excellent introduction to the facts and myths surrounding the discussion of accent and other aspects of dialect in the United States.

- **Salikoko S. Mufwene, John R. Rickford, Guy Bailey, & John Baugh, eds. 1998.** *African-American English: Structure, History and Use* (New York: Routledge). Ten excellent chapters by distinguished researchers analyze the structure and use of African-American English. Chapters treat phonology, lexicon, grammar, and discourse, as well as the history and use of African-American English. Here you can find out what linguists and anthropologists think of Ebonics, the Oakland school district resolution, obscenity, hip-hop and Ice-T.

- **Joyce Penfield & Jacob L. Ornstein-Galicia. 1985.** *Chicano English: An Ethnic Contact Dialect* (Amsterdam: Benjamins). One of a very few treatments of Chicano English, this book is reasonably accessible to interested beginners.

- **Peter Stockwell. 2002.** *Sociolinguistics: A Resource Book for Students* (London: Routledge). A wide ranging and highly interactive book, with plenty for readers not only to think about but also to do.

- **Deborah Tannen. 1994.** *Gender and Discourse* (New York: Oxford University Press). Discusses differences between the sexes in conversational practices and includes a chapter on ethnic style in male-female conversation.

- **Peter Trudgill. 1990.** *The Dialects of England* (Cambridge, MA: Blackwell). A reliable treatment of traditional and modern dialects in England; contains 34 maps.

- **Peter Trudgill. 1996.** *Sociolinguistics: An Introduction to Language and Society,* rev. ed. (New York: Penguin). A very basic, accessible, and relatively brief treatment.

- **Peter Trudgill & J. K. Chambers, eds. 1991.** *Dialects of English: Studies in Grammatical Variation* (New York: Longman). Contains 22 treatments of grammar in various dialects of America, Australia, Canada, Scotland, and especially England.

ADVANCED READING

Chambers and Trudgill (1998), Hudson (1996), Wardhaugh (1998), and Fasold (1984, 1990) discuss dialects generally. Petyt (1980) has an emphasis on British dialects and other dialects of Europe. Milroy and Gordon (2003) is excellent on sociolinguistic methodology. The discussion of convergence in Kupwar reported in this chapter is based on Gumperz and Wilson (1971). Green (2002) is a thorough and accessible treatment of African-American English. Highly recommended are the more popular and less technical treatments in Rickford and Rickford (2000) and Smitherman (1977); from the latter come some examples in this chapter. On the sociolinguistics of French, see Ager (1990) and Sanders (1993); on German, see Barbour and Stevenson (1990). Routledge publishes a series of accessible "practical introductions to the sociolinguistics" of various languages: see Ball (1997) for French; Mar-Molinero (1997) for Spanish; Stevenson (1997) for German.

Ferguson and Heath (1981) is a collection of essays describing language use among Native Americans, Filipinos, Puerto Ricans, Jews, Italian Americans, French Americans, German Americans, African Americans, and other Americans. Kurath (1972) is a thorough analysis of the methods and some of the findings of dialect geography, with emphasis on American English (and its roots in England) but attention to Romance and Germanic languages as well. A brief introduction to American English dialects can be found in Reed (1977), with a number of maps, mostly of the Great Lakes states and the Northwest. The principal findings for the Linguistic Atlas of the United States for the East Coast can be found in Kurath (1949), Atwood (1953), and Kurath and McDavid (1961). See Allen (1973–1976) for the Upper Midwest, Pederson (1986–1991) for the Gulf states, Bright (1971) for California and Nevada, Atwood (1962) for Texas. Recent work taking advantage of computers is illustrated in Kretzschmar et al. (1993) for the Middle and South Atlantic states and more generally in Kretzschmar and Schneider (1996).

The relationship between language and the sexes is treated in Smith (1985). The data in the present chapter on gender differences in Koasati and Thai come from Haas (1940), who also discusses Chukchee. The more recent study of Koasati referred to in the chapter is Kimball (1987). Fischer (1958) reports the New England -ing data cited here. Philips et al. (1987) is a collection of essays examining women's and men's speech through a cross-cultural perspective and looking at gender differences in the language of children. Coates and Cameron (1988) is a collection of provocative perspectives on language and gender; Johnson and Meinhof (1997) is a collection of thoughtful essays on masculine sociolinguistics that address power, conversation, gossip, expletives, and other topics. Holmes (1995) asks whether women are more polite than men and answers the question thoroughly and interestingly. Ochs (1992) relates language and gender through social activities, social stances, and social acts. The relationship between language and social identity is treated in Edwards (1985).

REFERENCES

- Ager, Dennis. 1990. *Sociolinguistics and Contemporary French* (Cambridge: Cambridge University Press).
- Allen, Harold B. 1973–1976. *The Linguistic Atlas of the Upper Midwest,* 3 vols. (Minneapolis: University of Minnesota Press).

- Atwood, E. Bagby. 1953. *A Survey of Verb Forms in the Eastern United States* (Ann Arbor: University of Michigan Press).

- ———. 1962. *The Regional Vocabulary of Texas* (Austin: University of Texas Press).

- Ball, Rodney. 1997. *The French-Speaking World: A Practical Introduction to Sociolinguistic Issues* (New York: Routledge).

- Barbour, Stephen, & Patrick Stevenson. 1990. *Variation in German* (Cambridge: Cambridge University Press).

- Bright, Elizabeth S. 1971. *A Word Geography of California and Nevada* (Berkeley: University of California Press).

- Chambers, J. K., & Peter Trudgill. 1998. *Dialectology,* 2nd ed. (Cambridge: Cambridge University Press).

- Coates, Jennifer, & Deborah Cameron, eds. 1988. *Women in Their Speech Communities* (London: Longman).

- Cobarrubias, Juan, & Joshua A. Fishman, eds. 1983. *Progress in Language Planning: International Perspectives* (Berlin: Mouton).

- Edwards, John. 1985. *Language, Society and Identity* (New York: Blackwell).

- Fasold, Ralph W. 1984. *The Sociolinguistics of Society* (New York: Blackwell).

- ———. 1990. *The Sociolinguistics of Language* (Cambridge, MA: Blackwell).

- Ferguson, Charles A., & Shirley Brice Heath, eds. 1981. *Language in the USA* (Cambridge: Cambridge University Press).

- Fischer, John L. 1958. "Social Influences on the Choice of a Linguistic Variable," *Word* 14:47–56; repr. in Hymes 1964, pp. 483–488.

- Green, Lisa. 2002. *African American English: Character and Contexts* (Cambridge: Cambridge University Press).

- Gumperz, John J., & Robert Wilson. 1971. "Convergence and Creolization: A Case from the Indo-Aryan/Dravidian Border in India," in Dell Hymes, ed., *Pidginization and Creolization of Languages* (Cambridge: Cambridge University Press), pp. 151–167.

- Haas, Mary R. 1940. "Men's and Women's Speech in Koasati," *Language* 20:142–149; repr. in Hymes 1964, pp. 228–233.

- Holmes, Janet. 1995. *Women, Men and Politeness* (London: Longman).

- Hudson, R. A. 1996. *Sociolinguistics,* 2nd ed. (Cambridge: Cambridge University Press).

- Hymes, Dell, ed. 1964. *Language in Culture and Society* (New York: Harper & Row).

- Johnson, Sally, & Ulrike Hanna Meinhof, eds. 1997. *Language and Masculinity* (Oxford: Blackwell).

- Kimball, Geoffrey. 1987. "Men's and Women's Speech in Koasati: A Reappraisal," *International Journal of American Linguistics* 53:30–38.

- Kretzschmar, William A., Jr., Virginia G. McDavid, Theodore K. Lerud, & Ellen Johnson, eds. 1993. *Handbook of the Linguistic Atlas of the Middle and South Atlantic States* (Chicago: University of Chicago Press).

- Kretzschmar, William A., Jr., & Edgar W. Schneider. 1996. *Introduction to Quantitative Analysis of Linguistic Survey Data: An Atlas by the Numbers* (Thousand Oaks, CA: Sage).

- Kurath, Hans. 1949. *A Word Geography of the Eastern United States* (Ann Arbor: University of Michigan Press).

- ———. 1972. *Studies in Area Linguistics* (Bloomington: Indiana University Press).

- Kurath, Hans, & Raven I. McDavid, Jr. 1961. *The Pronunciation of English in the Atlantic States* (Ann Arbor: University of Michigan Press).

- Labov, William. 1966. *The Social Stratification of English in New York City* (Washington, DC: Center for Applied Linguistics).

- ———. 1972. *Sociolinguistic Patterns* (Philadelphia: University of Pennsylvania Press).

- ———. 1996. "The Organization of Dialect Diversity in America." Available at http://www.ling.upenn.edu/phono_atlas/ICSLP4.html

- Linn, Michael D., & Maarit-Hannele Zuber. 1984. *The Sound of English* (Urbana, IL: National Council of Teachers of English).

- Marckwardt, Albert H. 1957. "Principal and Subsidiary Dialect Areas in the North-Central States." Publications of the American Dialect Society 27.

- Mar-Molinero, Clare. 1997. *The Spanish-Speaking World: A Practical Introduction to Sociolinguistic Issues* (New York: Routledge).

- Milroy, Leslie, & Matthew Gordon. 2003. *Sociolinguistics: Method and Interpretation* (Maldon, MA: Blackwell).

- Ochs, Elinor. 1992. "Indexing Gender," in Alessandro Duranti and Charles Goodwin, eds., *Rethinking Context* (Cambridge: Cambridge University Press), pp. 335–358.

- Pederson, Lee. 1986–1991. *Linguistic Atlas of the Gulf States,* 7 vols. (Athens: University of Georgia Press).

- Petyt, K. M. 1980. *The Study of Dialect: An Introduction to Dialectology* (London: Andre Deutsch).

- Philips, Susan U., Susan Steele, & Christine Tanz, eds. 1987. *Language, Gender, and Sex in Comparative Perspective* (Cambridge: Cambridge University Press).

- Reed, Carroll E. 1977. *Dialects of American English,* rev. ed. (Amherst: University of Massachusetts Press).

- Rickford, John R., & Russell J. Rickford. 2000. *Spoken Soul* (New York: John Wiley & Sons).

- Sanders, Carol, ed. 1993. *French Today: Language in its Social Context* (Cambridge: Cambridge University Press).

- Sankoff, Gillian, & Henrietta Cedergren. 1971. "Some Results of a Sociolinguistic Study of Montreal French," in R. Darnell, ed., *Linguistic Diversity in Canadian Society* (Edmonton: Linguistic Research), pp. 61–87.

- Smith, Philip M. 1985. *Language, the Sexes and Society* (Oxford: Blackwell).

- Smitherman, Geneva. 1977. *Talkin and Testifyin: The Language of Black America* (Boston: Houghton Mifflin).

- Stevenson, Patrick. 1997. *The German-Speaking World: A Practical Introduction to Sociolinguistic Issues* (New York: Routledge).

- Terrell, Tracy D. 1981. "Diachronic Reconstruction by Dialect Comparison of Variable Constraints," in David Sankoff and Henrietta Cedergren, eds., *Variation Omnibus* (Edmonton: Linguistic Research), pp. 115–124.

- Wardhaugh, Ronald. 1998. *An Introduction to Sociolinguistics,* 3rd ed. (New York: Blackwell).

Chapter 12

Writing

❖ Walking with you along a Los Angeles street whose shops cater to Iranian-American customers, your friend Ira comments that the writing on the shop appears to be Arabic script. He knows Persian is an Indo-European language that's not related to Arabic, and he wonders whether the same script is used for the two languages. How do you answer Ira's question?

❖ At lunch in a Japanese restaurant, your cousin Jan asks you whether the Japanese symbols in the menu are "characters" like the ones used for writing Chinese or are letters that represent sounds, as in English. What's your answer to Jan's question?

❖ Returning from London and a visit to the British Museum, your co-worker Rose reports that the Rosetta Stone is much bigger than she'd imagined. But she still isn't sure what makes it famous. What do you tell her?

❖ After a visit to Sequoia National Park in California, Nate reports that it's named after Sequoya, a Native American who invented a writing system for the Cherokee language and that a Park Service guide claimed that each of Sequoya's symbols stood for a syllable. Nate wants to know whether that could be true and how well such a system would work. What do you tell him?

❖ In a social studies class you're teaching, Caitlin is curious about why some related languages such as Hebrew and Arabic or English and Russian have different writing systems, while some unrelated languages such as French and Vietnamese or Italian and Turkish or Arabic and Persian have similar writing systems. What's your response?

❖ In a discussion in the cafeteria, nerdy Nan says she sees how Spanish writing better represents Spanish pronunciation than English writing represents English pronunciation, but that she has no trouble speeding through English language textbooks and newspapers. She wants to know whether people's complaints about English spelling are justified. Are they?

INTRODUCTION

The ability to speak arose hundreds of thousands of years ago as part of our intellectual development during evolution, but writing was invented quite recently. Humans have been able to represent language in written form for a mere 5000 or 6000 years. Although language underlies both spoken and written communication, the two modes are fundamentally different in nature. For one thing, speaking developed in human beings naturally, but writing had to be invented. For another, speaking has been with us for hundreds of millennia, writing for only a few. In every society, every typically healthy human being knows how to speak. By contrast, writing is an advanced technology, even a luxury, and it's not possessed by everyone.

Writing may be so much a part of literate societies that it colors our thinking about language itself. Asked how many vowels there are, an English-speaking schoolboy or schoolgirl is likely to answer "five: *a, e, i, o,* and *u*" (a few may add "*y*"). In terms of speech sounds, this answer misses the mark, but it demonstrates that when we talk of *vowels* it is almost second nature to think of *letters* of the alphabet rather than speech sounds. Commonly, in literate societies people ostensibly speaking of "language" say things that are appropriate to writing but not to speech. This is perhaps not surprising in most Western societies, where language is first discussed objectively in schools whose primary linguistic goal is to teach children literacy—mastery over the *written* word. Because the spoken word typically plays only an incidental role in schooling, from an early age it is writing that comes to be the salient focus of our linguistic analysis.

In this chapter we examine the history of writing and the development of different types of writing. As will become apparent, our knowledge about the history of writing is uneven. We have a reasonably good understanding of how writing evolved over the centuries, but just how it was invented and how many times it was invented remain unclear. While we understand how spoken language and written language differ, how such differences arise is open to discussion. Such unanswered questions, however, do not prevent us from marveling at the extraordinary human achievement that writing represents. Some even claim that writing is the single most important invention in human history.

THE HISTORICAL EVOLUTION OF WRITING

Long before we developed writing, humans produced graphic representations of the objects surrounding us. The prehistoric records in the cave paintings of Spain, France, and the Sahara Desert, which are between 12,000 and 40,000 years old, bear witness to an age-old fascination with animals, hunters, and deities. In that they represent concepts rather than words, these paintings differ from writing. They are representations of real-life objects, not of the *words* that represent those objects. Writing, by contrast, is a system of *visual symbols* representing *audible symbols.*

Of course, the drawings and paintings produced by prehistoric people contained the seeds of writing. People would at first have communicated by using drawings. In time, certain stylized representations of objects such as the sun would have come to be associated with the words for those objects. To imagine an example, the drawing ☼, representing the sun as an object or concept, would have come to be associated with the sound of the word *sun*—with [sʌn]. This association—between the visual symbol ☼ and the sound [sʌn]—was the first symptom of the birth of a writing system, in which a visual representation did not directly evoke a concept but evoked the spoken word for the concept. The stage was set for using such a visual symbol to represent other words that sounded the same. If we think of English, the symbol ☼ as a representation of the sun could be extended to represent the word *son* or part of *Sunday* or *asunder.* From a picture of an object, a written symbol of speech sounds is born.

The Leap from Pictures to Writing

To use a *written* symbol to represent a sound is an extraordinary achievement. It is comparable to using a spoken symbol to represent a concept. To use a *symbol* to represent another *symbol* required a stunning leap of the imagination.

For all that, writing appears to have been invented several times in the course of human history. Still, it is not surprising that not all the world's great civilizations made the leap. The Aztecs, for example, technological geniuses of pre-Columbian Central America, developed intricate systems of drawings and symbols for calendars, genealogies, and history. An illustration of their **pictograms** is provided in Figure 12–1 on page 420. (*Pictogram* comes from the Latin root *pictus* 'painted' and the Greek root *graphein* 'to write.') But the Aztecs may not have thought of using these pictograms to represent the sounds of spoken language. In any case, Aztec pictograms did not evolve into writing.

The same impetus that gave rise to the first writing systems recurs so commonly today that it is difficult to appreciate the breathtaking magnitude of the original imaginative stroke that used a visual mark—a written symbol—not to represent an *object* but to represent a *symbol of the object.* Writing thus involved a leap from primary to secondary symbolization.

Figure 12-1

Aztec Inscription

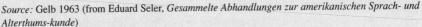

Source: Gelb 1963 (from Eduard Seler, *Gesammelte Abhandlungen zur amerikanischen Sprach- und Alterthums-kunde*)

A modest modern example of creative secondary symbolization occurs when automobile owners design their license plates. The space limitation of license plates invites such secondary symbolization as "GR8" and "GR8FUL" and "SK8ING" and "4GET IT," along with such inventive items as "C-SIDE," "7T YRS," and "PLEN-T," some of which have arisen because the traditional spellings of the words are too long or have been preempted by other license plates. A similar ingenuity originally sparked what is arguably humanity's greatest invention, for once a visual symbol such as 8 came to stand for an auditory symbol (the sound [et]), and not for the notion 'eight,' an alphabetic writing system had germinated.

Try it yourself: With a maximum of seven letters or spaces each, make up three license plates that utilize at least one symbol (a numeral or a letter) as a secondary symbolization, as in "GR8".

In what may have been the first instance, the leap of imagination that gave rise to writing took place around 3500 B.C. in Mesopotamia between the Tigris and Euphrates rivers in what is modern-day Iraq. Sometimes referred to as "the cradle of Western civilization," Mesopotamia (meaning 'between the rivers') was inhabited at the time by the Sumerians and the Akkadians, city dwellers with a sophisticated economic system based on cattle, commerce, and agriculture. How the Sumerians and Akkadians invented writing will never be known, but we can surmise that the potential for secondary symbolization was discovered fortuitously as someone struggled to formulate a visible message for which no agreed-upon visual symbols existed.

As early as 3000 B.C. the Egyptians had developed a writing system of their own, and writing also appeared in the valley of the Indus (now in Pakistan and India) around 2500 B.C. Around 2000 B.C., the Chinese began using pictograms as symbols for words rather than concepts. By 1500 B.C. several of the world's most technologically complex civilizations had developed systems to commit spoken language to visual representation.

Our most ancient inscribed stone tablets talk of cattle, sales, and exchanges. Thus the most extraordinary invention in human history may have arisen in response to the mundane task of recording commercial transactions. Gradually, our ancestors began exploring the world of possibilities opened by the invention of writing. Writing could be used to record important events in a way that was less likely to be forgotten or distorted than oral accounts. Dwellers of the ancient world also found that writing could communicate across distances: you could draft a letter and entrust it to a messenger who would deliver it to its addressee. Letters were more confidential and secure than oral messages sent by messenger because they often could not be read by the messenger and they could be sealed. The use of literacy as a recording tool and as a means to communicate at a distance could also be combined to build and maintain large states ruled by a central government, as the Mesopotamians and the ancient Chinese discovered. Laws could be recorded by those in command; orders could be transmitted to lower-echelon executives in faraway provinces; data on the citizenry could be stored and retrieved whenever needed. In short, a literate bureaucracy could function with an efficiency that could never be attained in a preliterate culture.

Of course, it took centuries for early societies to explore the avenues opened by the invention of writing. The ability to read and write does not automatically make a society more technologically developed, better equipped to become a bureaucratic state, or otherwise superior to a preliterate society. As recently as the Middle Ages, for example, the English had a basic suspicion of written land-sale contracts (because they could be tampered with), and the courts gave more credence to oral testimony in land disputes. It took centuries for Europeans to discover that sentence boundaries could be marked with punctuation to ease reading and that book pages could be numbered to ease the task of retrieving information. A literate society does not necessarily exploit all the possibilities literacy offers. Sometimes strong social pressures prohibit writing down certain materials. For example, the Warm Springs Indians of Oregon regard any attempt to make written records of their traditional religious songs and prayers as offensive. For them, writing down these texts would violate their sacredness. Literacy opens novel ways of communicating and recording language, but whether or not those possibilities are exploited depends in large part on a society's norms.

WRITING SYSTEMS

The writing systems that developed in ancient Mesopotamia, India, and China were fundamentally different from the system now used in Western societies. Ours is an *alphabetic* system based on the premise that one graphic symbol (a letter) should correspond to one significant sound in the language (a phoneme). The writing systems originally developed in the Middle East and Asia were based on a relationship, not between graphs and individual sounds, but between graphs and words or graphs and syllables. All three types of writing—alphabetic, syllabic, and word writing—are still in use today.

Syllabic Writing

When the dwellers of the ancient Middle East and Asia began developing their writing systems, they had at their disposal the earlier pictograms, which were symbols for objects and concepts. Rather than create an entirely new system of symbols, the inventors of writing modified these pictograms and used them to develop writing systems. Their shapes gradually became more and more stylized in the process of becoming written symbols. Figure 12–2 illustrates the evolution of a number of symbols over time. Its left-hand column shows the original pictograms, which become more like writing as we proceed to the right. After many centuries of evolution, the symbols illustrated in the Neo-Babylonian column had become so stylized that they no longer bore any resemblance to the pictograms from which they originated.

Figure 12-2
Evolution of Cuneiform Writing From Pictograms

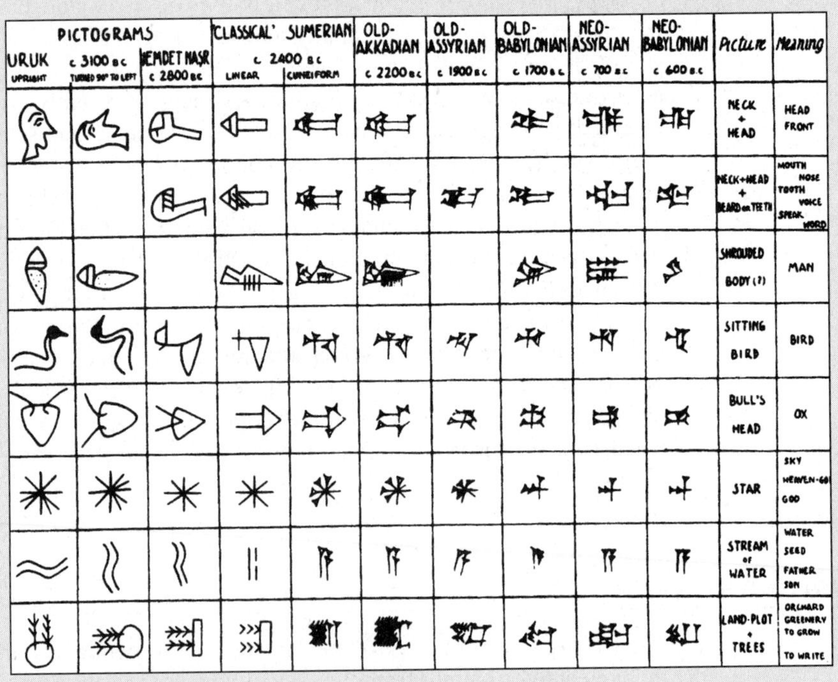

Source: Gaur 1984

The written symbols that the Sumerians and Akkadians had developed at that stage are called **cuneiform** symbols. *Cuneiform* means 'in the shape of a wedge' and refers to the peculiar form the symbols took. The ancient Mesopotamians were not familiar with paper, but clay from the Tigris-Euphrates river basin was readily available. From the beginning, writing consisted of engraving marks pressed into soft clay tablets with a hard, sharp, pointed object called a *stylus,* typically a cut reed. Since it is difficult to draw curved strokes on clay with a stylus, the first written symbols consisted of various combinations of straight strokes.

Not only the shape but also the meaning of cuneiforms evolved from early pictograms. The pictogram that represented an arrow evolved into this cuneiform symbol for the Sumerian word /ʃi/ 'arrow.'

Sumerian scribes had difficulty finding appropriate symbols for more abstract notions. There was no modified pictogram for the word 'life,' for example. But the word for 'life' happened to be homophonous with the word for 'arrow,' much as the *bank* of a river and a financial *bank* are homophonous in English. Since finding a symbol for the concept 'life' was not an easy task, why not use the symbol for 'arrow'—seeing that 'arrow' and 'life' are both pronounced /ʃi/? It was through this extension of a symbol's representing a *thing* to its representing a *sound* that writing as we know it was invented.

Having solved that problem, the Sumerians recognized that the same symbol could also be used to represent the *syllable* /ʃi/ whenever it occurred in a word. For example, they started using it to represent the first syllable of the word /ʃibira/ 'blacksmith.' In due course, the cuneiform symbol lost its original association with the concept 'arrow' and became a symbol for the syllable /ʃi/ wherever that syllable occurred. Cuneiform writing is thus a **syllabic writing** system, in which graphic symbols represent whole syllables, not individual sounds as in an alphabet. It is akin to using "4" in "4GET IT."

The process through which early pictograms evolved from being graphic symbols for concepts to being graphic symbols for syllables was a long and arduous one. Archaeological remains found in Mesopotamia indicate that for many centuries the Sumerians and the Akkadians used an extremely complex system in which some symbols were "ideograms," representing objects and concepts, while others were true writing, representing syllables. Even when all graphic symbols had come to represent syllables, the system was imperfect, because some graphs could represent different syllables depending on the word in which they were used, and several different graphs might represent the same syllable. Despite its imperfections, this system appears to have been used for centuries.

Figure 12-3

Egyptian Hieroglyphics

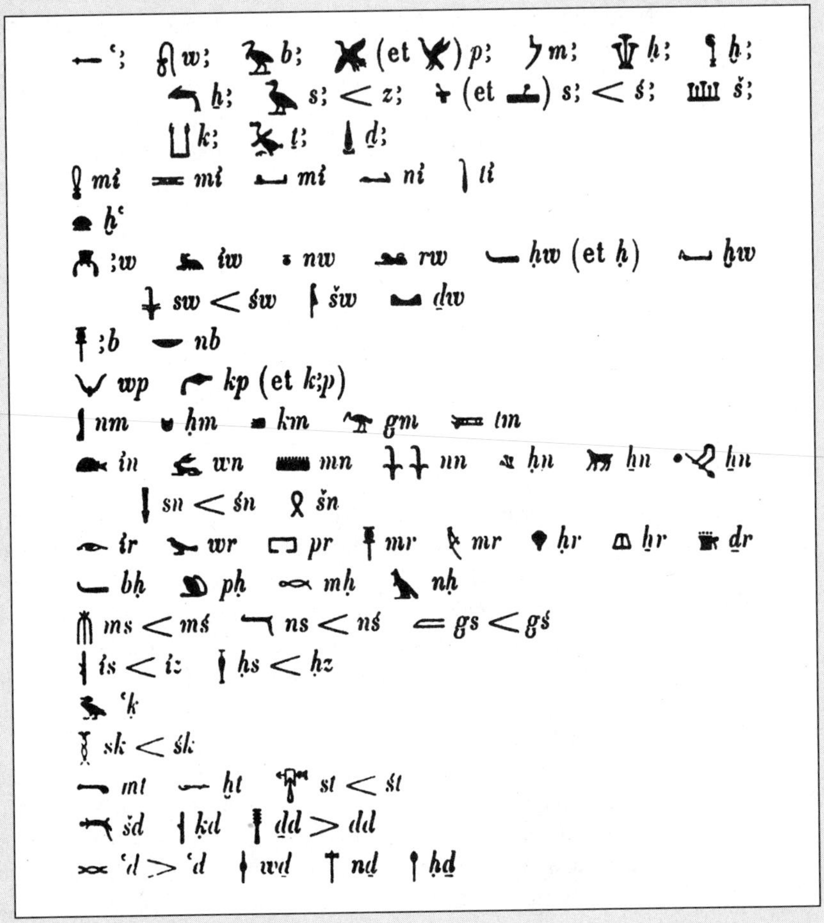

Source: Gelb 1963 (Because this figure comes originally from a French language source, the French word *et* 'and' appears in several lines.)

The Mesopotamian syllabic system may have been the model for several other systems. The ancient Egyptians, who had their own ideographic system, may have borrowed from the Sumerians and Akkadians the idea of representing spoken syllables with graphic symbols. In any case, around 3000 B.C. the Egyptians began using their ideograms to represent different sound combinations. These Egyptian written symbols are the famous *hieroglyphics* (see Figure 12–3). Like cuneiform writing, hieroglyphic writing is basically syllabic, and it had the same complexity and shortcomings as cuneiforms. Thus the hieroglyph for 'house' ▭ (third sign from the left in the thirteenth line of Figure 12–3) stood for several syllables in which the consonants /p/ and /r/ were coupled with any permitted vowel, such as /per/ and /par/.

There is nothing inherently cumbersome in syllabic systems of writing. The difficulties of the Mesopotamian and Egyptian systems can be attributed to the fact that they continued to bear traces of their ideographic origins. In the nineteenth century, an efficient syllabic system was devised by Sequoya, a Cherokee Indian. Shown in Figure 12–4, the 84 symbols of Sequoya's syllabic system are based on the Roman alphabet, and they were used by missionaries and the Cherokee people themselves in writing Cherokee.

Figure 12-4

The Cherokee Syllabary

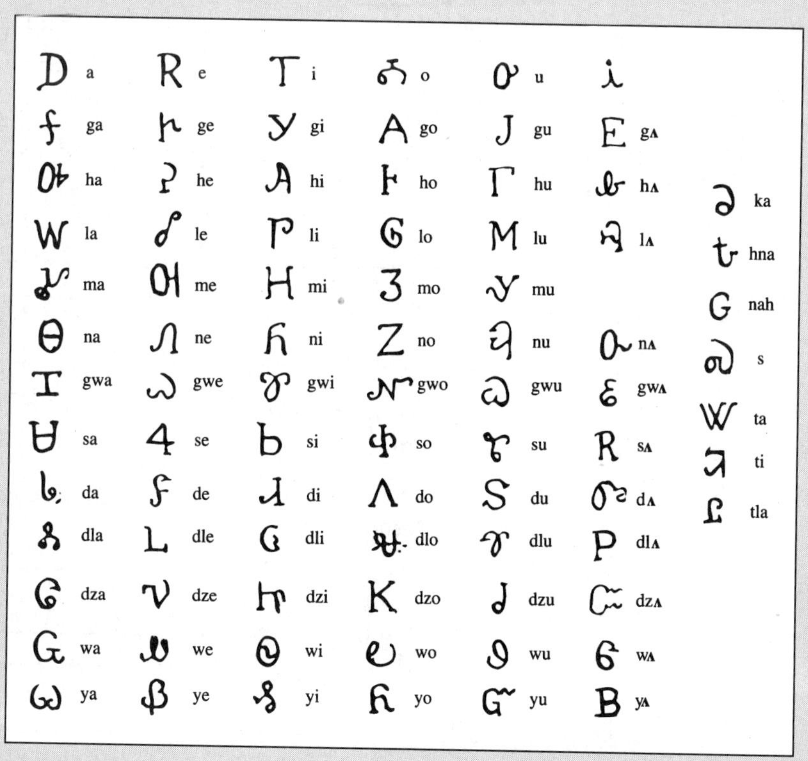

Source: H. A. Gleason 1961. *An Introduction to Descriptive Linguistics,* rev. ed. (New York: Holt, Rinehart and Winston).

Figure 12-5

The Vai Syllabary

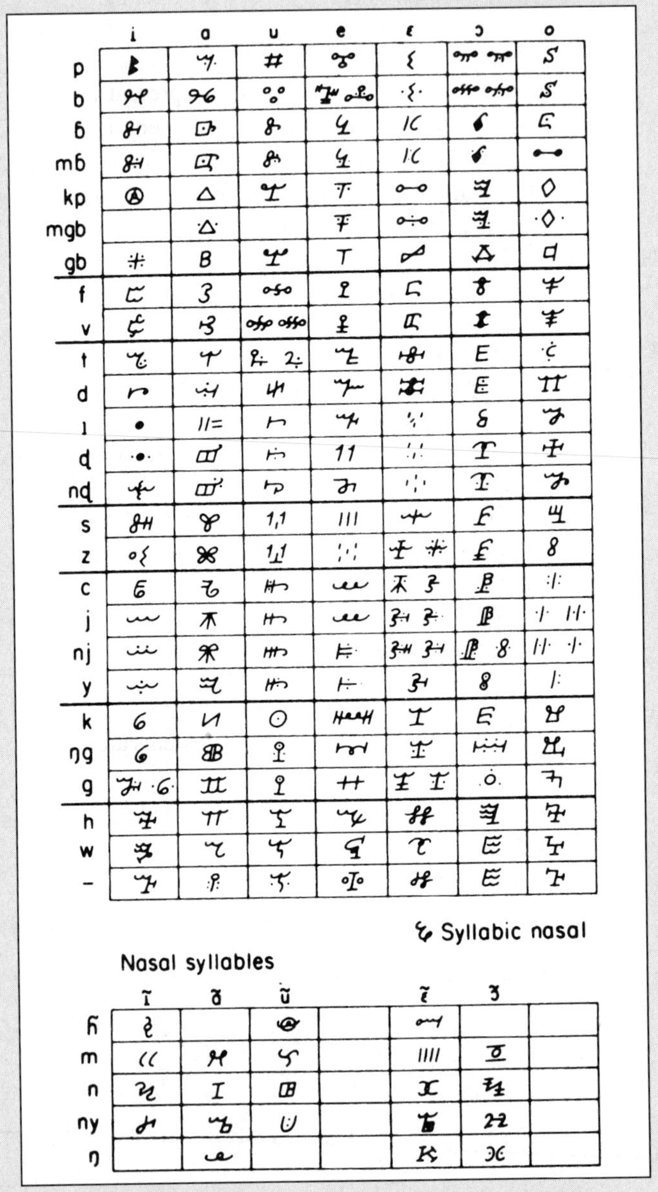

	i	a	u	e	ɛ	ɔ	o
p							
b							
ɓ							
mb							
kp							
mgb							
gb							
f							
v							
t							
d							
l							
d							
nd							
s							
z							
c							
j							
nj							
y							
k							
ng							
g							
h							
w							
–							

ɤ Syllabic nasal

Nasal syllables

	ĩ	ã	ũ	ɛ̃	ɔ̃
ɦ					
m					
n					
ny					
ŋ					

Source: Sylvia Scribner and Michael Cole 1981. *The Psychology of Literacy* (Cambridge: Harvard University Press).

Around the same time as Sequoya created the Cherokee syllabary, another syllabic system was devised by the Vai, an ethnic group of about 12,000 people in western Liberia. The Vai system, which is still in use, has one graph for each of the approximately 200 syllables in the language. With relatively few syllables, the Vai writing system is well adapted to the Vai language. The Vai syllabary is given in Figure 12–5.

Syllabic writing is also used to represent various languages of India. Tamil, spoken in the southern tip of the subcontinent, is written with a syllabic system of 246 graphic symbols, which you can see in Figure 12–6 on page 428. The Tamil syllabic system is highly regular. Each vowel has two graphic representations. One is an independent graph used at the beginning of a word; the other is used elsewhere in a word when the vowel combines with a consonant. For example, in initial position /aː/ is represented by ஆ, but it appears as ா when it combines with consonants, as in /kaː/ கா, /ḍaː/ டா, and /taː/ தா.

To represent a consonant sound alone, the graph used to represent that consonant as it appears with /aː/ is used, but a dot is placed above the symbol to mute the vowel. Thus, except for the dots, the graphs of the first column in the figure are identical to those of the second column. In the first row across the top of the syllabary are the written vowel symbols and their phonemic values; next to each graph of the first column is its phonemic value. You can readily see that one part of the symbol represents the consonant, the other part the vowel. Learning this system amounts to learning the different parts of symbols and their possible combinations. The simplicity and regularity of the Tamil system make it easy to learn.

Syllabic systems thus have the potential of being highly regular, with a one-to-one correspondence between syllables and graphs. Furthermore, the shape of the graphic symbols can be such that their pronunciation is retrievable by decomposing the graph into different parts. Such systems are best adapted to languages with a limited number of possible syllables. Syllabic systems need only as many symbols in a word as there are syllables. A regular syllabary like the Vai or Tamil systems is easily learned and simple to handle.

Logographic Writing

Around 4000 years ago in China, a new writing system was developed that used symbols to represent *words,* not *syllables.* Such a **logographic writing** system differed fundamentally from the Sumerian-Akkadian syllabic system. Partly for this reason, it is believed that the Chinese did not borrow the idea of writing from the Mesopotamians but developed it on their own.

Like the ancient Middle Eastern syllabic writing, the Chinese logographic system originated in ideograms. From archaeological records, we know that ideograms like those in Figure 12–7 on page 430 were used to represent objects and ideas such as 'cow,' 'river,' and 'below.'

Figure 12-6

The Tamil Syllabary*

		அ a	ஆ a	இ i	ஈ ı	உ u	ஊ u
க்	k	க ka	கா	கி	கீ	கு	கூ
ங்	ŋ	ங ŋa	ஙா	ஙி	ஙீ	ஙு	ஙூ
ச்	ç	ச ça	சா	சி	சீ	சு	சூ
ஞ்	ɲ	ஞ ɲa	ஞா	ஞி	ஞீ	ஞு	ஞூ
ட்	ḍ	ட ḍa	டா	டி	டீ	டு	டூ
ண்	ṇ	ண ṇa	ணா	ணி	ணீ	ணு	ணூ
த்	t	த ta	தா	தி	தீ	து	தூ
ந்	n	ந na	நா	நி	நீ	நு	நூ
ப்	p	ப pa	பா	பி	பீ	பு	பூ
ம்	m	ம ma	மா	மி	மீ	மு	மூ
ய்	y	ய ya	யா	யி	யீ	யு	யூ
ர்	r	ர ra	ரா	ரி	ரீ	ரு	ரூ
ல்	l	ல la	லா	லி	லீ	லு	லூ
வ்	v	வ va	வா	வி	வீ	வு	வூ
ழ்	ṛ	ழ ṛa	ழா	ழி	ழீ	ழு	ழூ
ள்	ḷ	ள ḷa	ளா	ளி	ளீ	ளு	ளூ
ற்	r	ற ra	றா	றி	றீ	று	றூ
ன்	n	ன na	னா	னி	னீ	னு	னூ

*A dot beneath the phonetic representation indicates a retroflex sound (one in which the tip of the tongue is curled up and back, just behind the alveolar ridge). Note that there are two graphic symbols for /r/ and two for /n/.

Toward the end of the Bronze Age (around 1700 to 500 B.C.), these ideograms came to represent not concepts but words. Today, in the three characters (or logographic symbols) that denote the modern Chinese words *niú* 'cow,' *chuān* 'river,' and *xià* 'below' (see Figure 12–8, page 430), we can recognize the ideograms that originally represented these three notions.

From a very early stage, ideograms were combined to represent abstract ideas and other notions that are difficult to represent graphically. Figure 12–9(a), for example, is made up of two ideograms placed one on top of the other. The lower part

Figure 12-6 (Continued)

எ e	ஏ e	ஐ ai	ஒ o	ஓ o	ஔ au
கெ	கே	கை	கொ	கோ	கௌ
ஙெ	ஙே	ஙை	ஙொ	ஙோ	ஙௌ
செ	சே	சை	சொ	சோ	சௌ
ஞெ	ஞே	ஞை	ஞொ	ஞோ	ஞௌ
டெ	டே	டை	டொ	டோ	டௌ
ணெ	ணே	ணை	ணொ	ணோ	ணௌ
தெ	தே	தை	தொ	தோ	தௌ
நெ	நே	நை	நொ	நோ	நௌ
பெ	பே	பை	பொ	போ	பௌ
மெ	மே	மை	மொ	மோ	மௌ
யெ	யே	யை	யொ	யோ	யௌ
ரெ	ரே	ரை	ரொ	ரோ	ரௌ
லெ	லே	லை	லொ	லோ	லௌ
வெ	வே	வை	வொ	வோ	வௌ
ழெ	ழே	ழை	ழொ	ழோ	ழௌ
ளெ	ளே	ளை	ளொ	ளோ	ளௌ
றெ	றே	றை	றொ	றோ	றௌ
னெ	னே	னை	னொ	னோ	னௌ

represents a type of dish used in divination ceremonies; the upper part represents a tree upon which the divination dish was suspended. This complex ideogram was modified over the centuries to become a character that in modern Chinese represents the word *gào*, which means 'to announce, to proclaim.' As Figure 12–9(b) shows, the modern character with this meaning bears a resemblance to the ideogram from which it originates. Such similarities between modern-day characters and ancient ideographs are uncommon, however, and the shapes of most modern Chinese characters have lost all traces of the original ideograms from which they come.

Modern Chinese Characters In an ideal logographic system, each word of the spoken language would be represented by a different graphic symbol. To a certain extent, the modern Chinese system has this characteristic, in that a portion of its vocabulary is represented by individual characters, as illustrated by Figure 12–10.

Figure 12-7

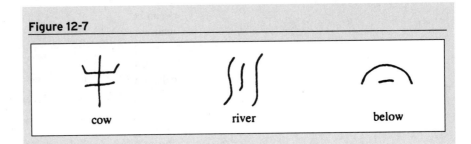

cow   river   below

Figure 12-8

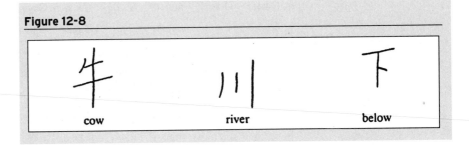

cow   river   below

Figure 12-9

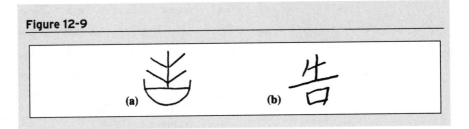

(a)   (b)

Figure 12-10

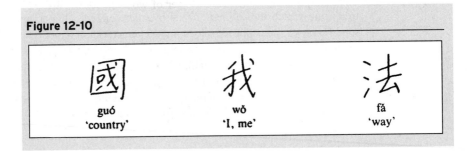

guó   wǒ   fǎ
'country'   'I, me'   'way'

Most modern Chinese characters can be decomposed into two elements. One is called the *radical* (or *signific*) and can sometimes hint at meaning. The other, of which there are many types, can sometimes give a clue to pronunciation and is known as the *phonetic*. Most radicals can also be used alone as characters, and some dictionaries are organized according to radicals, of which there are 214. The signific that traditionally corresponds to the character for the word *wéi* 'enclosure' occurs as the radical of many characters, some of which have a meaning related to 'enclosure' and some of which have little to do with the meaning of the radical (see Figure 12–11). In modern Chinese, the radical for 'enclosure' is not used as an independent character

Figure 12-11

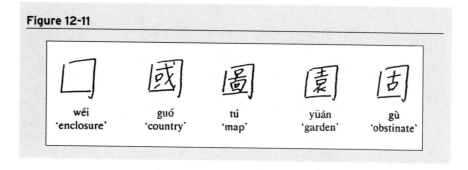

wéi	guó	tú	yüán	gù
'enclosure'	'country'	'map'	'garden'	'obstinate'

and has been replaced by the more complex character ▢ —which has the same meaning and pronunciation.

It's difficult to know exactly how many characters the Chinese logographic system contains, just as it's virtually impossible to count the number of words in any language. It's estimated that you must be able to recognize about 5000 characters (and have a good command of spoken Chinese) in order to read a Chinese newspaper. To read a learned piece of literature, you would need to be familiar with up to 30,000 characters. Compared to the number of words needed for similar tasks in English, these numbers are relatively modest. The reason can be found in the morphological structure of Chinese. In Chinese, morphemes (which are always one syllable long) can combine with each other to form compounds that together denote a new idea whose meaning is more or less clearly related to the meaning of the parts. Of course, this is reflected by corresponding compounds in writing. The word for 'bicycle,' for example, is made up of three morphemes that together mean 'self-propelled vehicle'; the three characters corresponding to these three morphemes are used to represent 'bicycle' in writing. Similarly, the word for 'grammar' is a compound that means 'language rule' (see Figure 12–12).

Figure 12-12

自行車　　　語法

zi xíng chē
'bicycle'

yǔ fǎ
'grammar'

Though compounding greatly reduces the number of characters needed in common use, learning to read and write the Chinese logographic system is a formidable task, considerably more difficult and time consuming than learning the Vai or Tamil syllabary or the English alphabet. Bear in mind that since modern characters provide a reader little information as to the pronunciation or meaning of the words they represent, learning to read and write Chinese involves learning the shape of characters as well as their meaning and pronunciation. Though several transcription systems have been devised for Chinese (some of which use the Roman alphabet, others a type of syllabary), the logographic system continues to survive after 4000 years.

You might wonder why such a seemingly impractical and complex system would endure for so long. Well, the Chinese logographic system has a number of important advantages. The first stems from the fact that though there are many homophonous words in Chinese, they usually have different written representations—as illustrated by the five characters in Figure 12–13, each of which represents a word that is pronounced [dʒīn]. Thus, the Chinese character system provides a way of distinguishing in writing among different words that a syllabic system or an alphabet could not provide. (Compare the unusual distinction in English of homophones like *cite, site,* and *sight* or *read* and *reed* with the more common orthographic merging of examples like river *bank* and savings *bank)*. A logographic system compensates for homophony.

Figure 12-13

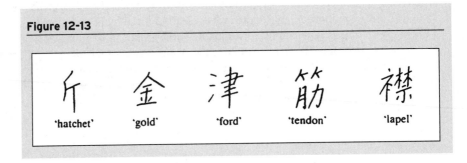

斤　　金　　津　　筋　　襟

'hatchet'　'gold'　'ford'　'tendon'　'lapel'

The second major advantage of the Chinese logographic system is peculiar to the Chinese situation. Chinese is actually a set of spoken dialects, some of which are mutually intelligible, some of which are not. Fortunately, in written communication all these dialects use the same set of characters. A character may be pronounced one way in one region of China and another way in another region, making spoken communication complicated, but the *meaning* of the character remains the same throughout the country. For example, the character 我 is read [wǒ] in the Beijing dialect, [gòa] in the Taiwan dialect, [wà] in the Minnan dialect (spoken in south China), [ŋɔ́] in the northwestern dialect of Shanxi, [ŋō] in the southern dialect of Hunan, and [ŋú] in the Shanghai dialect. In all dialects, it means 'I' or 'me.' Furthermore, since the syntax of most Chinese dialects is similar, any dialect can be more or less understood *in writing* (though not in speech) by speakers of other dialects. The character system thus has a unifying force for a nation that comprises many ethnicities speaking many different language varieties. The Chinese logographic system meets two important objectives: the need to distinguish between homophones and the need to communicate across dialect boundaries.

In the course of history, many nations of the Far East have borrowed the Chinese logographic system. The Vietnamese modified certain Chinese characters to create their own writing system, which was essentially logographic as well. (Today the Vietnamese no longer use this system.) The Koreans and the Japanese borrowed the Chinese character system very early, and in time each developed several subsidiary systems. Koreans now write their language with the help of an alphabet and the original Chinese characters. Similarly, several systems are combined for use in modern Japan: two syllabic systems known as *hiragana* and *katakana* are used alongside Chinese characters, called *kanji* (a word borrowed from the Chinese compound *hànzì* 'character'). Both written Korean and written Japanese are curious in that symbols from different systems can appear within the same sentence and even within the same word. Today the Chinese remain the only people to make exclusive use of a logographic system.

Alphabetic Writing and Orthography

An **alphabet** is a set of graphic symbols, each symbol of which represents a distinctive sound. Alphabetic writing thus differs from syllabic writing (whose graphs represent syllables) and from logographic writing (whose graphs represent words). In the view of some scholars, the first true alphabet was developed by the ancient Greeks from a North Semitic writing system that they had borrowed, probably from the Phoenicians, probably about 900 B.C. The claim that credits the Greeks with inventing the first true alphabet rests on one interpretation of how to evaluate the so-called consonantal scripts, which came into use in about 1700 B.C. Consonantal scripts are writing systems that represent only the consonants, not the vowels, of a language, and it was just such a script that the Greeks borrowed from the Phoenicians.

It is not surprising that a consonantal script should have been developed to represent Semitic languages. Recall from Chapter 2 that Semitic morphology builds upon tri-consonantal roots such as Arabic /k-t-b/. In languages such as Arabic and Hebrew, vowels are interdigitated with tri-consonantal roots to produce words such as /kitaːb/ 'book,' /kutub/ 'books,' /kaːtib/ 'writer,' and /kitaːba/ 'writing'—all of which contain the same tri-consonantal root. The paramount role of consonants in such a system led, perhaps inevitably, to a consonantal script. The graphs used for writing Semitic languages can be viewed in one of two ways: as representing *only* the consonants (which would be a kind of alphabet, though lacking in vowel graphs) or as representing the consonants plus any vowel (which would be a kind of syllabary, albeit an unusual one). In the first view, a graph would represent a single consonant, say /k/; in the second view, the same graph would represent /k/ plus any permissible vowel: /ka/, /ki/, /ku/, and so on. The first view of consonantal writing would incline one to credit a Semitic origin of the alphabet. The second view would incline one to credit a Greek origin, for it was the Greeks who viewed graphs as representing a single sound and therefore assigned specific symbols (those not needed to represent Greek consonants) for representing vowels. Whatever interpretation one is inclined to, it is clear that the Greeks had a true alphabet and that around 600 B.C. the Romans borrowed it (via the Etruscans) and developed the basis of today's familiar Roman alphabet.

The Roman alphabet is not the only alphabet currently in use. The Greeks still use an alphabet of their own, as do the Russians, Ukrainians, Bulgarians, and Serbs. These alphabets are based on the same principles as the Roman alphabet, differing only in the shape of certain letters. The alphabet currently in use for Russian, called Cyrillic in honor of Saint Cyril, an early Christian missionary to the Slavs, is partly given in Table 12–1.

An alphabet is matched as closely as possible to the sound system of the language it represents. The system used to achieve this match is the **orthography**, or spelling system. In an ideal orthography, each phoneme of the spoken language would be represented by a different graph, and each graph would represent only one phoneme. Spanish orthography comes close to this ideal: there is a virtual one-to-one correspondence between letters of the Roman alphabet and the phonemes of the language, and it is this match that students of Spanish have in mind when they say that in Spanish "every letter is pronounced." By contrast, English and French do not have close matches between letters and phonemes.

English Orthography   As we saw in Chapter 4, the number of distinctive sounds in English includes 24 consonants and between 14 and 16 vowels and diphthongs. With only 26 letters of the alphabet, English orthography falls short of the ideal one-sound~one-graph model. Because there are not enough letters to provide a symbol for each phoneme, some phonemes must be represented by a combination of letters (for example, the phoneme /i/ is represented by a double <e> in *meet,* while /θ/ is represented by the two letters <th> as in *thin).* In addition, English orthography has remained relatively stable over the centuries, while its pronunciation has changed continuously. Dramatic examples include words with letters for sounds that are no longer pronounced in those words, as with <k> and <gh> in *knight.* On the other side of the coin, a given sequence of letters may represent a diverse spectrum of sounds, as with <ough> in *cough, tough, though, through, trough, thorough, bough,* and *hiccough.*

Table 12-1

Cyrillic Alphabet as Used in Modern Russian (printed lowercase letters)

CYRILLIC LETTER	RUSSIAN PHONEME REPRESENTED	CYRILLIC LETTER	RUSSIAN PHONEME REPRESENTED
а	a	п	p
б	b	р	r
в	v	с	s
г	g	т	t
д	d	у	u
е	jɛ	ф	f
ё	jo	х	x
ж	ʒ	ц	ts
з	z	ч	tʃ
и	i	ш	ʃ
й	j	щ	ʃtʃ
к	k	ы	ɨ
л	l	ь	(y)
м	m	э	e
н	n	ю	ju
о	o	я	ja

A common response to the chaos of the English orthography is to call for spelling reform, as George Bernard Shaw did early in the twentieth century. But for a language that is used around the globe—for an international lingua franca such as English—an orthography that accurately attempted to represent pronunciation would have to sacrifice the high degree of uniformity that currently exists across national varieties. Spelling reform would also raise another set of problems, owing to the considerable morphophonemic variation of English (which we discussed at the end of Chapter 4). Recall that a morpheme such as PHOTOGRAPH has different stress patterns and different phonological realizations: [ˈforəɡræf] versus [fəˈtʰɑɡrəfər]. The three vowels in *photograph* [o ə æ] differ from the first three in *photographer* [ə ɑ ə]. An orthography aiming to represent actual sounds would represent the vowels and consonants of *photograph* and *photographer* differently, perhaps as "fodagraef" and "fataagrafar." Given their different pronunciations, even the plural inflection of *dogs* and *cats* would require different spellings, perhaps as <dogz> and <kats>, obscuring the fact that <z> and <s> represent the same morpheme. Similarly, the morpheme MUSIC would sometimes have to be spelled <muzak> (as in *muzakal* 'musical') and sometimes <muzish> (as in *muzishan* 'musician'). You can assess for yourself whether you think an English orthography with a closer match between sounds and letters would ease or complicate the task of reading.

In a few instances, as you recognize, English spelling does assign a given morpheme different spellings in different words, generally representing pronunciation more closely, as with *wife* and *wives,* both containing the morpheme WIFE. English has few such examples, which are for the most part in common words like *wife ~ wives.* If English had many instances of variant spellings for the same morpheme, especially in less familiar words, the English spelling system would likely be regarded as less good than it now is.

Try it yourself: Cite as many examples as possible of English words containing different spellings of the same morpheme, as with *knife ~ knives.* Examine both lexical and inflectional morphemes, and don't overlook certain common prefixes whose spellings vary.

So far we've considered different spellings of the same morpheme. The flip side involves spelling different morphemes differently even when they are pronounced alike. Without compromising basic principles, a system that aimed for spellings that reflected pronunciations would be unable to distinguish homophonous words such as *there* and *their, here* and *hear, I* and *eye, bore* and *boar, holy* and *wholly, wood* and *would, sea* and *see, quaffed* and *coiffed, night* and *knight,* and *to, too,* and *two.*

Advocates of English spelling reform may overlook or minimize the advantages of the current orthography, which places a premium on visual similarity across allomorphs of a morpheme. What ranks most highly in English orthography is morpheme recognition. In general, English tends to assign the same spelling to a given morpheme, irrespective of its pronunciation in a particular word, and for a language that has as much morphophonemic variation as English does, that makes a good deal of sense. Just as the Chinese logographic system is well adapted to the situation in which it functions, English orthography is well adapted both to its phonology and its widespread use.

Developing Writing Systems in Newly Literate Societies

The twentieth century witnessed an astonishing increase in communication among regions, countries, and continents. Oceans and mountains, challenging obstacles only 100 years ago, are now easily overflown. There is probably not a single inhabited area of the world that has had no contact with the outside. This is a remarkable fact, given that as recently as the 1950s large inhabited areas of Papua New Guinea, Amazonia, and the Philippines remained completely isolated from the rest of the world.

One consequence of this communications boom is that many people who had never seen writing a few decades ago are now literate. When a language is written down for the first time, a number of important questions arise: What kind of writing system should be used? How should the system be modified or adapted to fit the shape of the language and the needs of its speakers? Who makes these decisions?

Literacy has often been introduced to a people along with a new religion. For example, literacy was first imported into Tibet from India in the seventh century, when the Tibetans converted to Buddhism. Today literacy is commonly introduced to preliterate societies by Christian missionaries. What links religion and literacy is the fact that the reading of religious texts is an important doctrinal element of many religions. When literacy is introduced by missionaries, their foreign writing system is usually adopted by the incipiently literate society for writing its language. Today, newly literate societies commonly adopt the Roman alphabet because English-speaking and other Western missionaries are the most active promoters of literacy in many regions of the world.

At times a society may change from one writing system to another. Vietnam, for example, was colonized by the Chinese around 200 B.C. and remained colonized for about 12 centuries. During that time, Chinese was used for writing, while Vietnamese remained unwritten. After the end of Chinese domination, the Vietnamese began to use a syllabic writing system adapted from Chinese logographic writing for their own language. Then, at the beginning of the seventeenth century, Jesuit missionaries devised an alphabetic system for Vietnamese, which the Vietnamese gradually adopted, partly under pressure from the French colonial government. Today the system devised by the Jesuits is the only one in use for Vietnamese, and you can see a small sample of it in the photograph at the bottom of page 4, third example from the bottom.

One thorny problem that newly literate societies face is developing a standard orthography that everyone will agree to use. Ideally, an orthography must be regular, so native writers will be able to spell a word that they have never before seen in writing. The orthography must also be easy to learn and to use. Finally, it must be well adapted to the phonological and morphological structure of the language. As we saw in our discussion of English orthography, it's tough to satisfy all those requirements. A system that looks complex at first blush can have hidden advantages. Devising a standard orthography can be such a difficult task that a few Western nations (including Norway) have not yet done so, even after centuries of literacy.

Language-related concerns are not the only factors involved in devising orthographies. An important factor is social acceptance. An orthography that, for any reason, rubs users the wrong way is unlikely to be successful. If the orthography is imposed by an outside political or religious body, it may carry negative associations and never succeed. For several decades, the U.S. Bureau of Indian Affairs (BIA) hired linguists and anthropologists to devise orthographies for Native American languages, but because the Indians viewed the BIA and its activities with suspicion they never really accepted its orthographies.

Likewise, at the end of the nineteenth century, Methodist and Catholic missionaries devised different orthographies to transcribe Rotuman, the language of the South Pacific island of Rotuma. Since then, with relations between Methodist Rotumans and Catholic Rotumans strained, both orthographies have survived, and there is little or no prospect of either group adopting the other's orthography. Similar situations can involve not only orthographies but writing systems. In Serbia and Croatia, a single language is used, but the Serbs use a Cyrillic alphabet similar to that used for Russian, while the Croats use the Roman alphabet. Even when they were united in a single country, both groups adamantly kept their own alphabets as a symbol of social identity. Clearly, social acceptance is extremely important to the development of a standard orthography.

Computers and Writing

In connection with writing, computers have mostly served highly technical functions—some of them related to space travel and the most advanced space-age technologies. For example, by using software developed at the Jet Propulsion Laboratory (JPL) in Pasadena, California, computers have helped enhance the images of the writing in the Dead Sea Scrolls. They have also been used to retrieve writing that had been erased from manuscripts and even written over. Perhaps the most familiar use of computers in connection with writing is to enable images to be transmitted over the Internet, including transmitting writing systems strikingly different from the Roman alphabet. You may not be familiar with all the writing systems available on the Internet, but some of your classmates may read newspapers written in Chinese logographs or Japanese kanji or any of several other scripts. Ask a volunteer to show you how it works.

A few words about the Dead Sea Scrolls: In 1947 a 12-year old shepherd in Palestine discovered a number of leather scrolls in a cave in Qumran near Jerusalem. These scrolls were composed in the period overlapping Old and New Testament times and are of extraordinary interest to Christians, Jews, and Muslims, who have given the discovery and the linguistic recovery of the texts worldwide attention. Written in Hebrew, Aramaic, and Greek, the scrolls have provided substantial additions to the corpus of Jewish texts and genres from around the time of Christ.

Now the computer connection. The previously invisible lettering of certain scrolls was made distinguishable by advanced "multispectral" imaging techniques originally developed at JPL for remote sensing and planetary probes. Researchers were able to view the Dead Sea Scrolls in wavelengths beyond the sensitivity even of infrared film. Other technologies originally devised by JPL's team of image analysts to help read images sent from the Hubble Space Telescope and the Galileo planetary probe have been used by the National Archives to monitor deterioration in documents such as the original U.S. Constitution, the Bill of Rights, and the Declaration of Independence.

SUMMARY

- Writing is a relatively recent invention that developed from pictograms, which became writing when the pictograms began representing sounds rather than objects and concepts.

- There are several types of writing systems in use today: syllabic, logographic, and alphabetic.

- In syllabic writing, symbols represent syllables.

- In logographic writing, symbols represent morphemes or words.

- In alphabetic writing, symbols represent phonemes.

- The system that dictates how the letters of the alphabet are used to represent the phonemes of a language is called its *orthography.*

- The writing system used for English utilizes the Roman alphabet, and English orthography is strongly influenced by morphological considerations.

- Devising orthographies for hitherto unwritten languages is a difficult task that must take into account both linguistic and social factors.

WHAT DO YOU THINK? REVISITED

❖ *Persian script.* Ira's right. Persian and Arabic are not related languages and both use Arabic script, but there are a few differences, primarily because Persian has several consonants in its phonemic inventory that Arabic doesn't have. To represent the sounds /p/, /tʃ/, /g/, and /ʒ/, Persian places three dots over the Arabic symbols for /b/, /dʒ/, /k/, and /z/. For example, the Arabic and Persian letter for /z/ is < ز > and this same symbol is written with three dots above it (instead of one) to represent Persian /ʒ/, as in the word /ʒærf/ 'deep,' written < ژرف >. Persian, like Arabic, is written from right to left.

❖ *Jan and Japanese menus.* Other than Western spellings for *sushi, sashimi,* and so on, a Japanese menu contains no "letters" for individual sounds. Japanese orthography uses *kanji,* based on Chinese characters, and two syllabaries called *katakana* and *hiragana.* Of course, coincidentally the syllabaries have symbols for vowel sounds that are syllables.

❖ *Rose and the Rosetta Stone.* Because the Rosetta Stone contained the same piece of text in three different scripts, including hieroglyphs and Greek, it enabled scholars finally to decipher Egyptian hieroglyphics.

❖ *Naturalist Nate.* Sequoya invented a writing system for Cherokee in which each symbol stood for a syllable. For a language like English with a large number of syllables, a syllabic writing system would not be ideal. Sequoya needed only 84 symbols to represent the syllables of Cherokee.

❖ *Curious Caitlin.* Written symbols are independent of the spoken language they represent. In principle, any language can be represented by any writing system. If the system is linked to sounds, though, the phonological structure of the language may make some systems preferable. Independently, a community may choose a form of writing for its cultural associations, including religious ones. Vietnamese is written in a system devised by French missionaries familiar with alphabetic systems. A given language can also be written in different scripts. Turkish was written in Arabic script until the beginning of the twentieth century and then in the Roman alphabet. Chapter 3 contains a photograph (p. 84) in which Uyghur appears in Arabic script, but prior to 1987 it was written in the Roman alphabet, and it has also been written in Cyrillic.

❖ *Nerdy Nan.* The pronunciation of English morphemes can vary from word to word, but those pronunciation variants are seldom represented in spelling (compare the vowels of METAL in *metal* and *metallic*). A few morphemes have different spellings (compare KNIFE in *knife* and *knives*). If Nerdy Nan reads visual symbols directly for meaning (without "silent pronunciation"), uniform representations of the same morpheme is useful. In comparison with English, Spanish has uniform pronunciations of a given morpheme. Readers already acquainted with English find a genuine advantage in having each morpheme spelled the same way no matter how it's pronounced. But for someone learning English and wanting to know the pronunciation of a word from its printed form, the spelling is often less helpful.

EXERCISES

12-1 **a.** Identify two invented sign systems besides writing, and briefly evaluate their importance relative to writing.

b. Identify what you judge to be two of the most important human inventions of all time, and evaluate their importance in comparison to writing.

c. Specify two or three of the central criteria you used in evaluating "importance" in a and b above.

12-2 Discuss the relative merits and disadvantages of logographic, syllabic, and alphabetic writing systems. In your discussion of each type of system, address the following questions:

a. How easy is it to learn the system?

b. How easy is it to write the individual graphs?

c. How efficiently can one read the graphs?

d. What kinds of problems does the system present for printing?

e. How adaptable is it to computer technology such as word processing?

f. How easy is it to represent foreign names and new borrowings from other languages?

g. What sociological and historical factors might interact with the preceding questions in evaluating the appropriateness of each system to particular situations? (Be concrete by considering a particular situation you are familiar with.)

12-3 **a.** Using the Tamil syllabic symbols given in Figure 12–6 (pp. 428–429), transcribe the following Tamil words into Roman script:

தொழில்	'work'	ஏழு	'seven'
மூக்கு	'nose'	புலி	'tiger'
அவன்	'he'	ஆடு	'goat'
வாழைப்பழம்	'banana'	மரம்	'tree'

b. Briefly describe the general patterns that are used in forming syllabic characters in this script. For example, how is the symbol for /ke/ formed from the symbols for /k/ and /e/? How are word-final consonants and word-initial vowels represented?

12-4 The following table (adapted from Sampson 1985) is a partial representation of the inventory of graphs used in writing Korean consonants. "Tense" means (in part) that the sound is held for a longer period of time than normal, and "lax" means that the sound is held for the normal duration. The tenseness is represented in phonetic symbols with an apostrophe, as in [p'].

  a. What principles govern the shape of graphs in this system?

  b. What are the advantages of such a system over an alphabetic system such as the Roman system, in which the shape of graphs is completely arbitrary?

	Bilabial	*Dental*	*Palatal*	*Velar*
Lax nasals	ㅁ m	ㄴ n		
Lax fricatives		ㅅ s		
Lax stops/affricate	ㅂ p	ㄷ t	ㅈ c	ㄱ k
Tense aspirated stops/affricate	ㅍ p^h	ㅌ t^h	ㅊ c^h	ㅋ k^h
Tense fricative		ㅆ s		
Tense unaspirated stops/affricate	ㅃ p'	ㄸ t'	ㅉ c'	ㄲ k'

Especially for Educators and Future Teachers

12-5 English is often said to have a phonemic orthography (approximating one graph for each distinct sound). To some extent this is true in that English orthography distinguishes between, say, /b/ and /p/ but not among [p], [pʰ] and [p˥]. In light of this claim, examine the following typical sets of words and compare their orthographic representation with their pronunciation: cats/dogs/judges; history/historical; wharf/wharves.

  a. Is English orthography phonemic? Explain.

  b. In what sense would it be more accurate to describe the English orthographic system as morphophonemic?

  c. To what extent would it be fair to say that English is logographic in representing such sets of homonyms as the following: *meet/meat/mete; leaf/lief; seize/sees/seas?*

  d. What is the nature of such graphic symbols as <&>, <301>, <$>, and <%>? Can they be called logographic? Explain.

12-6 Suppose you were devising a syllabic writing system for English. What steps would you take to make such a system as simple to learn as possible? To what extent does the phonological and morphological structure of English present problems for syllabic writing?

12-7 What implications for teaching reading do you see in the character of English orthography?

OTHER RESOURCES

- **Rosetta Stone at the British Museum:**
  http://www.thebritishmuseum.ac.uk/egyptian/ea/gall/rosetta.html
  This Web site introduces you to the Rosetta Stone and discusses its importance. Many other sites are dedicated to the Rosetta Stone and its decipherment.

- **Dead Sea Scrolls: http://www.flash.net/~hoselton/deadsea/deadsea.htm**
  At this site you can view Dead Sea Scroll fragments and read descriptions of them.

SUGGESTIONS FOR FURTHER READING

- **Peter T. Daniels & William Bright, eds. 1996.** *The World's Writing Systems* (New York: Oxford University Press). The most complete reference work on writing systems. Contains articles by scores of scholars. Abundant illustrations. A superb reference work.

- **Albertine Gaur. 1984.** *The Story of Writing* (London: The British Library). A readable and lavishly illustrated history of writing.

- **J. T. Hooker, ed. 1990.** *Reading the Past: Ancient Writing from Cuneiform to the Alphabet* (Berkeley: University of California Press/British Museum). Six excellent booklets, each by a distinguished author, have been gathered into this book and introduced by the editor. Among other topics, it treats cuneiform, Egyptian hieroglyphs, and the early alphabet.

- **Roger Woodard. 1996. "Writing Systems."** In *The Atlas of Languages*, Bernard Comrie, Stephen Matthews, & Maria Polinsky, eds. (New York: Facts on File), pp. 162–209. In a lavishly illustrated book, this is a singularly accessible chapter-length source of scholarly information about the development of writing.

ADVANCED READING

Gelb (1963) is a classic study of the development of different writing systems in antiquity. Linguistically oriented surveys of writing systems can be found in Sampson (1985) and Coulmas (1989). The story of the decipherment of ancient scripts is told in Gordon (1982). Diringer (1968) discusses the discovery and development of alphabetic writing through the centuries. Interesting hypotheses about the influence of literacy on thinking and on culture are advanced in Goody (1977) and in Ong (1982). These hypotheses are constructively criticized by Street (1983).

REFERENCES

- Coulmas, Florian. 1989. *The Writing Systems of the World* (Cambridge, MA: Blackwell).
- Diringer, David. 1968. *The Alphabet* (London: Hutchinson).
- Gelb, I. J. 1963. *A Study of Writing,* 2nd ed. (Chicago: University of Chicago Press).
- Goody, Jack. 1977. *The Domestication of the Savage Mind* (Cambridge: Cambridge University Press).
- Gordon, Cyrus H. 1982. *Forgotten Scripts: Their Ongoing Discovery and Evolution,* 2nd ed. (New York: Basic Books).
- Ong, Walter. 1982. *Orality and Literacy* (London: Methuen).
- Sampson, Geoffrey. 1985. *Writing: A Linguistic Introduction* (Stanford: Stanford University Press).
- Street, Brian V. 1983. *Literacy in Theory and Practice* (Cambridge: Cambridge University Press).

Language Change, Language Development, and Language Acquisition

Part Three combines Part One's focus on language structure with Part Two's emphasis on language use. Here we'll investigate three topics that are perennial favorites:

- ❖ how languages change over time;
- ❖ how languages are related to one another;
- ❖ how children and adults learn languages.

You know that French and Spanish are related languages in that they derive from the same historical source. You also know that the English of Shakespeare's time differs from today's English. In Part Three you'll learn how languages change and develop, which languages are related to one another, and which ones are isolates, with no known relatives.

You'll also investigate language acquisition, by both children and adults. For children acquiring a first language and for anyone interacting with them during that process, a child's first words and early utterances prompt wonder and tickle listeners' imagination. In contrast to the frolicsome time children have acquiring their first tongue, adolescents and adults often must exert strenuous efforts to learn a second language. For kids, success with a native language is guaranteed. For adults, learning a second language can be a challenge and is not always successful. You'll see why.

Chapter 13

Language Change over Time: Historical Linguistics

WHAT DO YOU THINK?

❖ Pre-med Melanie conjectures that English must have come from Latin because It contains so many Latin words. What can you tell her about the relationship between Latin and English?

❖ On a field trip to Chinatown in Los Angeles with your sixth-grade class, a colleague from Taiwan accompanies you. When she tries to buy some inexpensive pieces of jade from a Chinese street vendor, it becomes apparent that, though they both speak Chinese, they cannot understand one another and must enlist help from a translator. Afterwards your colleague explains that she speaks only Mandarin dialect, while the vendor spoke only Cantonese dialect. Your students claim that if speakers of Mandarin and Cantonese cannot understand one another, they must be speaking different languages. What reasons can you offer them for considering Cantonese and Mandarin dialects of a single language?

❖ A few students are examining an atlas of the Middle East and notice that many places in Iraq have names beginning with *al, an,* or *as* (*Al Fallūjah, Al Ḥillah, Al Baṣrah, An Najaf, As Sulaymānīyah*) but those in neighboring Iran don't. Instead, many Iranian places have two-part names linked by *e* (*Dasht-e Kavīr, Posht-e Kūh, Torbat-e Jām, Naft-e Safīd*). None of the Iraqi names have that form. The students are surprised because they thought the Persian spoken in Iran was related to the Arabic of Iraq, an impression they have from knowing that the writing systems look the same. What can you tell them about the relationship between Persian and Arabic? Between speech and writing? Between writing and culture?

❖ Some students in a geography class are examining place names in Oklahoma and note two distinct kinds—those represented by transparent names like *Sweetwater, Stillwater, Sand Springs, Willow, Granite, Grove, Beaver, Commerce,* and *Mountain View* and those represented by *Okmulgee, Oktaha, Chickasha, Comanche, Chattanooga, Manitou, Cherokee, Arapaho,* and *Wynona,* which don't have independent meanings in English. They recognize that the second set contains Native American names and ask whether those names are also English words. What can you tell them about languages in contact with one another and how place names come to be?

DO LIVING LANGUAGES ALWAYS CHANGE?

It's no secret that languages change over the years. They may change dramatically, especially in times of social and political upheaval. Although usually the changes are subtle, all of us can recognize differences between the speech patterns of our parents and our friends and of our grandparents and our friends. Usually the most noticeable differences between generations are in vocabulary. What one generation called *hi-fi, car phone,* and *studious young man or woman* a younger generation calls *stereo, cell phone* or *mobile phone,* and (in some instances) *nerd.* Your grandparents may not have used the terms *tank tops, six packs, sitcoms,* or *cyberspace* in their youth, nor referred to certain verbal actions as *bad-mouthing, dissin,* or *dumping on* someone. Your great-grandparents may have kept food in an *icebox* instead of a *fridge* and played music on a *record player* instead of a *stereo.* Until recently none of us had heard of a *Segway* or *SARS.*

Pronunciation changes too, sometimes in individual words and sometimes in a whole class of words with a particular sound. For example, the pronunciation of the word *nuclear* may be changing. A few decades ago, the word was commonly pronounced [nukliər], but today you can often hear "nukular" [nukjələr]. In the same vein, *realtor,* formerly pronounced "re-al-tor" [riəltər], is increasingly pronounced "real-a-tor" [rilətər] or [rɪlətər]. Sound changes that affect individual words are called **sporadic sound changes.**

Regional accents and dialects change as well. As you saw in Chapter 12, in much of Canada and especially in the western United States, the vowel sounds in the words *cot* and *caught* are pronounced identically, so that these words—and all other similar pairs like *Don* and *Dawn* and *wok* and *walk*—are no longer distinguished, although in other regions of the United States these pairs remain distinct in their pronunciation. Sound changes that affect all the words in which a particular sound occurs in a particular sound environment are called **regular sound changes,** and regular sound changes may be conditioned or unconditioned, as we'll see below.

Sometimes a sound change affects the sound only when it occurs in particular linguistic environments. That's not the same as saying it affects the sound only in particular words. Here we are talking about sound change that affects a sound in every word where it occurs, provided the sound occurs within some specifiable phonological environment. In some dialects of the American South, for example, the vowels /ɪ/ and /ɛ/ are merging, but only when they occur before the nasal consonants /n/ or /m/. In those dialects, *pit* and *pet* are distinct in pronunciation, but *him* and *hem* sound the same. This kind of regular sound change is called **conditioned sound change.** (In order to distinguish *pin* from *pen* in those dialects that have experienced this conditioned sound change, a *pin* must be called a *safety pin* and a *pen* an *ink pen.*) We also saw in Chapter 12 that extensive shifting of vowels is occurring in the United States in the so-called Northern Cities Shift and the Southern Shift. These sound changes are **unconditioned sound changes:** they affect every word in which the particular sound appears.

The meaning of terms can also change. About 1000 years ago, the English verb *starve* (Old English *steorfan*) meant simply 'die' (by any cause). Today, it refers principally to deprivation and death by hunger (or, by metaphorical extension, to 'deprive of affection'). Until recently, the adjective *natural,* which has been used in English for over 700 years, did not have the meaning 'without chemical preservatives,' which it commonly has today, as in *all-natural ice cream.* The meanings of *joint, bust, fix, high, hit,* and many other words have been extended, in these cases by their use in the world of drugs. To take a final example, if you check the meaning of the expression *to beg the question,* you'll find that the *Oxford English Dictionary* defines it as 'take for granted the matter in dispute,' but among your friends and on radio and television you'll notice that it often means simply 'lead to the next question.' When enough people in enough contexts are recorded by the Oxford lexicographers using it in this way, the new definition will be added to the existing one in the *OED.*

There can also be grammatical differences in the speech of different generations. *Goes the king hence today?* is what Shakespeare wrote in *Macbeth.* Today, the same inquiry (were there occasion to use it) would more likely be *Is the king going away today?* The simple fact is that certain grammatical features of seventeenth-century English are no longer in use. To cite a more recent development, in many parts of the American South, double modals have come into use, and it's not uncommon to hear people using them in sentences such as *I might could do it.* Whether these "double modal" constructions will spread remains to be seen, but they have a certain appeal.

Linguistic alterations often prompt comment, especially from people who fear that language change is equivalent to linguistic corruption. Many people have commented on the pronunciation of *nuclear* as "nukular" among high-ranking politicians. Sometimes depending on what side of the political fence they sit, newspaper editors may opine that such pronunciations seem, well, unseemly in a U.S. president or presidential candidate, for example. But going back at least to the presidency of Republican Dwight D. Eisenhower in 1952 and the candidacy of Democrat Walter Mondale in 1984, "nukular" has been commented upon in newspapers; it is hardly a pronunciation invented by George W. Bush in 2000. Still, many people regard it as less than good English, less than educated English. For some people, the best language is language that has stood the test of time. Others relish the taste of linguistic innovation.

Generalizing from one's own linguistic experience may be risky, but it is safe to say that the common experience of noticing linguistic differences between one generation and another reflects the simple fact that languages do not stand still. Languages are always in the process of changing.

Try it yourself: Decide whether you believe you say "nu-ku-lar" or "nu-cle-ar" and which of the two you think your parents and your friends say. Then listen attentively over the next few days to see whether your beliefs match the facts. Afterwards, check one or more dictionaries to see whether the pronunciation you've actually heard people using is recorded in the dictionary or not. Should it be?

LANGUAGE FAMILIES AND THE INDO-EUROPEAN FAMILY

One result of ongoing language changes is that a single language can develop into several languages. The early stages of such development are apparent in differences among Australian, American, Canadian, Indian, and Irish English dialects, all of which have sprung from the English spoken in Britain. Whether these national varieties should be considered different languages or dialects of the same language is worth thinking about. In order for different dialects to develop into separate languages, groups of speakers must remain relatively isolated from one another, separated by physical barriers such as impassable mountains and great bodies of water or by social and political barriers such as those drawn along tribal, religious, racial, or national boundaries.

You've probably heard it said that French, Spanish, and Italian come from Latin. That statement is true, provided that by "Latin" one understands the different dialects spoken throughout the Roman Empire, not the written variety of classical Latin studied in school. The "Vulgar Latin" spoken in parts of the Roman Empire lives on in today's French, Italian, Spanish, Portuguese, Rumanian, Catalan, Galician, and Provençal, all of which are its direct descendants. On the other hand, the classical Latin of Cicero, Virgil, Caesar, and other Roman writers is "dead," and the written varieties of French, Spanish, and Italian are based on the modern spoken languages, not the classical written language.

You may also have heard it claimed that English comes from Latin. That claim is false. English and Latin are indeed related, but Latin is not an ancestor of English. Both come from a common ancestor, but they traveled along different paths. During the Renaissance, English borrowed thousands of words from Latin, creating striking lexical parallels, especially in the sciences and humanities. English is descended from Proto-Germanic, a language spoken about the time of classical Latin as well as a few centuries earlier, a language that ultimately gave rise not only to English but to German, Dutch, Norwegian, Danish, and Swedish (among others). Thus, as Latin is the parent language of French and Spanish, so Proto-Germanic is the parent language of English and German.

Except for a few carved runic inscriptions from the third century A.D., Proto-Germanic (unlike Latin) has left no written records. Modern knowledge of

Proto-Germanic has been inferred from the character of its daughter languages through comparative reconstruction, a technique explained in this chapter. Proto-Germanic and Latin are themselves daughters of Proto-Indo-European, another unattested (unrecorded) language. In a simplified manner, we can represent the situation by the family tree in Figure 13–1, which has two branches.

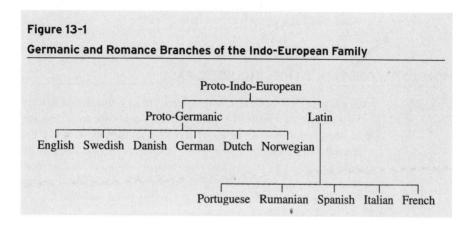

Figure 13-1

Germanic and Romance Branches of the Indo-European Family

While the notion that languages change and give rise to new languages is familiar to modern readers, it is a notion that was postulated clearly only two centuries ago. In 1786, while he was serving as a judge in Calcutta, Sir William Jones addressed the Royal Asiatic Society of Bengal about his linguistic experience.

> The Sanskrit language, whatever be its antiquity, is of a wonderful structure; more perfect than the Greek, more copious than the Latin, and more exquisitely refined than either, yet bearing to both of them a stronger affinity, both in the roots of verbs and in the forms of grammar, than could possibly have been produced by accident; so strong indeed, that no philologer could examine them all three, without believing them to have sprung from some common source, which, perhaps, no longer exists: there is a similar reason, though not quite so forcible, for supposing that both the Gothic and the Celtic, though blended with a very different idiom, had the same origin with the Sanskrit; and the old Persian might be added to the same family . . .

Today linguists would avoid such judgmental statements as Sanskrit having a "more perfect" structure than Greek and being "more exquisitely refined" than Latin, but Jones recognized that languages give rise to other languages. Indeed, Sanskrit, Latin, Greek, Celtic, Gothic, and Persian *did* spring from a "common source" that "no longer exists": Jones had made an important discovery. The common source of Latin, Greek, Sanskrit, Celtic, Gothic, Persian, and many other languages (including English and its Germanic relatives, and French and Spanish and their Romance relatives) is Proto-Indo-European. A parent language and the daughter languages that have developed from it are collectively referred to as a **language family,** and the family that

Jones recognized is called the **Indo-European** family. While there are no written records of Proto-Indo-European itself, a rich vein of inferences about its words and structures can be mined from the inherited linguistic characteristics of its daughter languages.

The working assumption of historical linguists is this: a feature that occurs widely in daughter languages and whose presence cannot be explained by reference to language typology, language universals, or borrowing from another tongue is likely to have been inherited from the parent language.

HOW TO RECONSTRUCT THE LINGUISTIC PAST

There is evidence of massive migrations from Central Asia to Europe about 4000 B.C. by a people who probably spoke Proto-Indo-European. There are no written records to document these earlier migrations, but archaeologists have found buried remains from the daily life of people who inhabited particular parts of the globe. Combined with what we can reconstruct of ancestral languages, archaeological records enable researchers to make educated guesses about where our ancestors came from and where they migrated to, as well as how they lived and died.

When scholars reconstruct an ancestral language, they also implicitly reconstruct an ancestral society and culture. Every culture lives on the lips of its speakers, so words ascribed to a prehistoric group represent artifacts in their culture and facets of their daily social and physical activities. In this chapter, we concentrate not on Indo-European culture and the Indo-European homeland but on the Polynesians, whose linguistic development presents another interesting case of reconstruction of a protolanguage and the culture of its speakers. (At the end of this chapter you'll find references for similar reconstructions of the Indo-European family and the Algonquian family.)

Polynesian and Pacific Background

On land, the only physical obstacles to sustained contacts between people are insurmountable mountains and wide rivers, which are in fact not very common. Boundaries between different languages and cultures therefore are often blurred. In contrast, once people settle on an isolated island, contact with inhabitants of other islands is difficult and limited, and languages and cultures develop in relative isolation. Islands thus offer an opportunity to study what happens when a protolanguage evolves into distinct daughter languages. Because the South Pacific region consists of small islands and island groups isolated from one another, it provides an almost ideal "laboratory" for researchers interested in the past.

The South Pacific is home to three cultural areas—Polynesia ('many islands'), Melanesia ('black islands'), and Micronesia ('small islands')—whose approximate boundaries are shown in Figure 13–2. Among other things, each area is distinguished by the physical appearance of its inhabitants: Polynesians are generally large, with olive complexions and straight or wavy hair; Melanesians typically are dark-skinned,

Figure 13-2

Cultural Areas in the Pacific

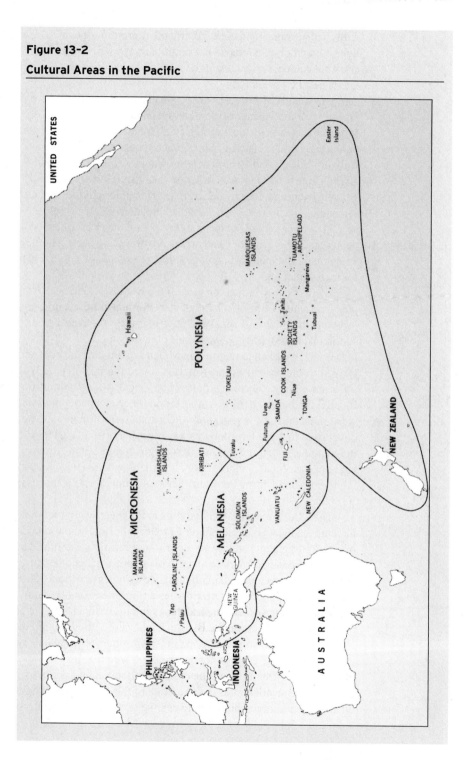

with smaller frames and curlier hair; and Micronesians tend to be slight of frame, with light brown complexions and straight hair. We will concentrate on Polynesians and ask what can be learned about their origins and their early life in Polynesia from the languages they speak today.

The islands of Polynesia vary greatly in size and structure. The main island of Hawaii and the islands of Samoa and Tahiti are comparatively large land masses formed through volcanic eruptions. Other islands are tiny atolls, little more than sand banks and coral reefs that barely reach the surface of the ocean; typically, one can walk or wade around an atoll in a few hours. Atolls are found in Tuvalu, the Tuamotu Archipelago, and the northern Cook Islands. Some coral islands in Tonga and elsewhere have been raised by underground volcanic activities and are medium-sized and often hilly, in contrast to atolls, which are utterly flat.

No written records exist to aid in tracing the Polynesians' cultural and linguistic development because they had no system of writing before literacy was introduced by Westerners. But modern languages and the archaeological record provide useful tools for reconstruction.

There is every indication that all the islands of Polynesia were settled by a people who shared a common language, a common culture, and a common way of dealing with the environment. We know that they traveled by sea from west to east, settling islands on their way, because the languages of Polynesia are clearly related to languages spoken to the west in Melanesia but have no connection with languages spoken to the east in South America. In addition, Polynesian cultures have many affinities with Melanesian cultures but virtually none with those of South America. Finally, the human bones, artifacts, and other archaeological remains found on the western islands of Polynesia are older than those found on the eastern islands. The conclusion that western Polynesia was settled prior to eastern Polynesia contradicts the hypothesis that the Polynesians originated in South America, a theory popularized by Norwegian explorer Thor Heyerdahl, who in 1947 reached Polynesia in a raft after setting sail from Peru and who subsequently told his story in a book called *Kon-Tiki*.

The oldest archaeological records in Polynesia were found in western Polynesia: in Tonga, Samoa, Uvea, and Futuna (see Figure 13–2 on page 451). Consisting mostly of pottery fragments similar to those found farther west in Melanesia, these records date to between 1500 and 1200 B.C. This implies that people moved from somewhere outside Polynesia and settled on these western islands about 3500 years ago. No pottery has been found in eastern Polynesia (the Cook Islands, Tahiti and the Society Islands, the Marquesas Islands, and the Tuamotu Archipelago), but other archaeological remains indicate that these eastern islands were settled around the first century A.D. The most recent remains are found in Hawaii and New Zealand. That these two island groups were settled last is not surprising, given that they are the most remote from other islands of the region. The earliest artifacts found on these islands suggest that the ancient Hawaiians and the ancestors of the New Zealand Maoris first arrived on their respective island homes between the seventh and eleventh centuries A.D.

Polynesian Languages and Their History

We said earlier that all of Polynesia was settled by the same people or by groups of closely related people from a single region. Linguistic evidence can help us determine the original homeland of the Polynesians. In Table 13–1 you can see some striking similarities among words in five Polynesian languages. These and other widespread similarities of expression for equivalent content demonstrate that the languages of Polynesia are related. Not finding similar close correspondences in vocabulary between the languages of Polynesia and any other language, we can safely say that Polynesian languages form a language family. In other words, all the Polynesian languages are daughter languages of a single parent language, the ancestor of the 30 or so Polynesian languages and of no other existing language. Known as Proto-Polynesian, the parent language was spoken by the people who first settled western Polynesia between 1500 and 1200 B.C.

Table 13-1
Common Words in Five Polynesian Languages

TONGAN	SAMOAN	TAHITIAN	MAORI	HAWAIIAN	
manu	manu	manu	manu	manu	'bird'
ika	iʔa	iʔa	ika	iʔa	'fish'
kai	ʔai	ʔai	kai	ʔai	'to eat'
tapu	tapu	tapu	tapu	kapu	'forbidden'
vaka	vaʔa	vaʔa	waka	waʔa	'canoe'
fohe	foe	hoe	hoe	hoe	'oar'
mata	mata	mata	mata	maka	'eye'
ʔuta	uta	uta	uta	uka	'bush'
toto	toto	toto	toto	koko	'blood'

In Table 13–1, the word *manu* 'bird' is exactly the same—in form and sense—in all five languages. The other words have the same vowel correspondences (where one has /a/, all have /a/) and differ slightly from one another in some of the consonants. The Polynesian words in each line of the table are **cognates**—words that have developed from a single, historically earlier word. In examining other words, you'll find the consonant correspondences between the different languages to be strikingly regular. On the basis of many word sets in addition to the nine in Table 13–1, it can be seen that in words where the phonemes /m/ and /n/ (as in *manu)* occur in one Polynesian language, they tend to occur in all. On the other hand, Tongan, Samoan, Tahitian, and Maori /t/ corresponds to /k/ in Hawaiian, as in the words for 'forbidden' and 'eye.' We can represent these *sound correspondences* as in Table 13–3 on page 455.

Table 13-2

Cognates in Five Polynesian Languages I

TONGAN	SAMOAN	TAHITIAN	MAORI	HAWAIIAN	
toki	toʔi	toʔi	toki	koʔi	'axe'
taŋi	taŋi	taʔi	taŋi	kani	'to cry'
taŋata	taŋata	taʔata	taŋata	kanaka	'man'
kafa	ʔafa	ʔaha	kaha	ʔaha	'rope'
kutu	ʔutu	ʔutu	kutu	ʔuku	'louse'
kata	ʔata	ʔata	kata	ʔaka	'to laugh'
moko	moʔo	moʔo	moko	moʔo	'lizard'

If we examine still other words, these sound correspondences are maintained, and additional **correspondence sets** can be established. As the words in Table 13–2 reveal, Tongan and Maori /k/ corresponds to a glottal stop /ʔ/ in Samoan, Tahitian, and Hawaiian, while Tongan, Samoan, and Maori /ŋ/ corresponds to Tahitian /ʔ/ and Hawaiian /n/. We can thus establish regular sound correspondences among modern-day Polynesian languages.

Try it yourself: The words for 'rope' in Table 13–2 provide sufficient information for two correspondence sets of consonant sounds. The final line in Table 13–3 gives k-ʔ-ʔ-k-ʔ as one of those correspondence sets. What's the other one that can be proposed from the words for 'rope'?

In comparative reconstruction, it is important to exclude all *borrowed* words, because the only words that can profitably provide sounds for use in a correspondence set are those that have descended directly from the ancestor language. For example, because Proto-Polynesian *s became /h/ in Tongan (but remained /s/ in some daughter languages), Tongan has very few words with /s/—among them *sikaleti,* meaning 'cigarette.' While *sikaleti* was obviously borrowed from a language outside the Polynesian family, words borrowed from other languages within the same family may not be so easy to spot.

Comparative Reconstruction

The method just illustrated is known as **comparative reconstruction.** It aims to reconstruct an ancestor language from the evidence that remains in daughter languages. Its premise is that, borrowing aside, similar forms with similar meanings across related languages are *reflexes* of a single form with a related meaning in the parent language. This commonsense approach is at the foundation of the comparative method and, indeed, of historical linguistics.

Table 13-3

Sound Correspondences in Five Polynesian Languages

TONGAN	SAMOAN	TAHITIAN	MAORI	HAWAIIAN
m	m	m	m	m
n	n	n	n	n
ŋ	ŋ	ʔ	ŋ	n
p	p	p	p	p
t	t	t	t	k
k	ʔ	ʔ	k	ʔ

When we examine correspondence sets such as m-m-m-m-m and t-t-t-t-k in Table 13–3, it seems reasonable to assume that *m and *t existed in the parent language and that /m/ was retained in each of the daughter languages, while /t/ was retained except in Hawaiian, where it became /k/. Such assumptions are the everyday fare of historical linguistics. When we assume the existence of a sound (or other structure) in a language for which we have no evidence except what can be inferred from daughter languages, that sound (or structure) is said to be reconstructed. Reconstructed forms are "starred" to indicate that they are unattested. We can represent the reconstructions from correspondence sets this way:

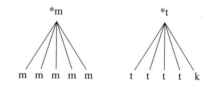

In describing the development of Hawaiian from Proto-Polynesian, we would postulate a historical rule of the form: *t > k. (A shaftless arrow indicates that one form developed into another form over time.) A sound change in which one sound (*t) develops into two or more sounds (t and k) is called a **split.**

Instead of *t, we could have reconstructed a *k in Proto-Polynesian. We would then say that *k was retained in Hawaiian and became /t/ in *all* the other languages. But we posit *t because experience with many languages has led historical linguists to prefer reconstructions that assume the *least* change consistent with the facts, unless there is good reason to do otherwise. In this instance, reconstructing *t assumes fewer subsequent changes than would a reconstruction of *k. You can think of this as the majority rule.

Now let's inspect the reconstruction of *m a little more closely. To postulate that /m/ existed in the protolanguage and was retained in all the daughter languages is the simplest hypothesis but not the only logical one. You could hypothesize some other sound in the protolanguage that independently became /m/ in each daughter language.

Try it yourself: Given that /m/, the sound in all the daughter languages of Table 13–3, is a bilabial nasal, which other two sounds would make good candidates as the sound from which /m/ might have developed in the five daughter languages represented in the table?

Because /m/ is a bilabial nasal, both the bilabial /b/ and the nasal /n/ would be other likely candidates for this reconstruction because they share phonetic features with the /m/ found in all the daughter languages. On the other hand, Polynesian languages generally lack the phoneme /b/, so it seems more reasonable to assume that the parent language also lacked /b/. Alternatively, you could reconstruct an /n/ that changed to /m/ in all the daughter languages independently of one another. But there are two reasons to reject this hypothesis. First, it is not a minimal assumption; and, second, the daughter languages have an /n/ that also requires a source in the parent language. We thus postulate Proto-Polynesian *m and *n, which were retained unchanged in all the daughter languages.

Let's examine one other correspondence set: ŋ-ŋ-ʔ-ŋ-n. We have just postulated Proto-Polynesian *n as the reconstructed earlier form (technically, the **etymon**) of the correspondence set n-n-n-n-n. It's interesting to compare this reconstruction with one for the correspondence set ŋ-ŋ-ʔ-ŋ-n, for which the most likely reconstruction is *ŋ.

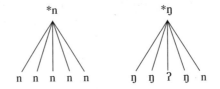

Given these reconstructions, *ŋ was retained in Tongan, Samoan, and Maori but became /ʔ/ in Tahitian and /n/ in Hawaiian. As a result, the distinction between *n and *ŋ that existed in Proto-Polynesian and is maintained in Tongan, Samoan, and Maori does not exist in Hawaiian, where *n and *ŋ have merged in /n/. Hawaiian /n/ therefore has two historical sources. When two sounds merge into one, that sound change is called a **merger**. We can represent this historical merger either in rules (*n > n; *ŋ > n) or schematically.

Merger

Subgroups   On the basis of lexical and structural characteristics, it is apparent that some Polynesian languages are more closely linked than others. As shown in Table 13–4, Tongan differs from other Polynesian languages in at least two respects: It has initial /h/ where other languages do not have anything; and it has nothing where other languages have either /l/ or /r/. Niuean, another Polynesian language, shares these and certain other characteristics with Tongan. On the basis of such evidence, Tongan and Niuean can be seen to form a **subgroup,** or *branch,* of Polynesian. This implies that Tongan and Niuean were at one time a single language distinct from Proto-Polynesian and that Proto-Tongic, as that language is called, developed certain features before splitting into Tongan and Niuean. The retention in both languages of these features (those that developed after Proto-Tongic split from Proto-Polynesian but before Tongan and Niuean split into separate languages) constitutes the characteristic shared features of the Proto-Tongic branch of the Polynesian family.

Table 13-4

Cognates in Five Polynesian Languages II

TONGAN	SAMOAN	TAHITIAN	MAORI	HAWAIIAN	
hama	ama	ama	ama	ama	'outrigger'
hiŋoa	iŋoa	iʔoa	iŋoa	inoa	'name'
mohe	moe	moe	moe	moe	'to sleep'
hake	aʔe	aʔe	ake	aʔe	'up'
ua	lua	rua	rua	lua	'two'
ama	lama	rama	rama	lama	'torch'
tui	tuli	turi	turi	kuli	'knee'

In the meantime, the other branch of Proto-Polynesian also evolved independently after its speakers lost contact with speakers of Proto-Tongic. As this second branch, called Proto-Nuclear-Polynesian, developed its distinctive characteristics, it emerged as a separate language that gave rise to still other languages. Except for Tongan and Niuean, all modern Polynesian languages share certain features inherited from Proto-Nuclear-Polynesian. In turn, Proto-Nuclear-Polynesian has two main subgroups: Samoic-Outlier and Eastern Polynesian. The evolution of Polynesian languages can be represented in the family tree shown in Figure 13–3 on page 458. Such family trees usefully represent the general genalogical relationships in a family of languages, although they inevitably oversimplify the complex facts of history, especially by excluding borrowings and other influences that languages can exert on one another.

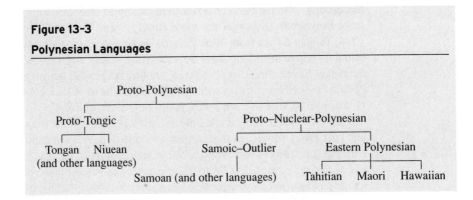

Figure 13-3

Polynesian Languages

Reconstructing the Proto-Polynesian Vocabulary

On the basis of the evidence provided by modern-day Polynesian languages, we can reconstruct the sound system and vocabulary of Proto-Polynesian (and make educated guesses about its grammatical structure). In turn, reconstructed linguistic information can tell us a good deal about the people who first settled Polynesia more than 3000 years ago.

A word can be reconstructed for Proto-Polynesian if we find **reflexes** of it—that is, cognates—in at least one language of each major subgroup (Tongic, Samoic-Outlier, and Eastern Polynesian; see Figure 13–3) and are confident that the cognates are not borrowed words. (If we reconstructed a lexical item for Proto-Polynesian based simply on evidence from Tongan and, say, Samoan, we would run the risk of having found a word that existed originally only in Tongan—after Tongan became a separate language—and that was borrowed by the early Samoans. You can see from the map in Figure 13–2 on page 451 that Tonga and Samoa are geographically close enough to have had contacts in prehistoric times.)

For example, since cognate words for 'bird,' 'fish,' and 'man' are found in all major subgroups of the Polynesian family (as shown in Tables 13–1 on page 453 and 13–2 on page 454), we can reconstruct a Proto-Polynesian form for each word. According to regular sound correspondences and the most plausible reconstructed sounds, these words are *manu, *taŋata,* and *ika. In contrast, the word for a 'night of full moon,' which in Maori and Tahitian is *hotu* and in Hawaiian *hoku,* cannot be reconstructed for Proto-Polynesian because there is no cognate in any Tongic or Samoic-Outlier language. Similarly, an etymon for the Tongan and Niuean word *kookoo* 'windpipe' cannot be reconstructed for Proto-Polynesian because there is no reflex in any Samoic-Outlier or Eastern Polynesian language.

Using the comparative method of historical reconstruction just outlined, the lexical items in Table 13–5, all referring to the physical environment, can be reconstructed for Proto-Polynesian. From Table 13–5, you can see that the Proto-Polynesian people had words for ocean-related notions (the left-hand column) and for topographic features typically found on large volcanic islands (the right-hand column). As it happens, there are no waterfalls, precipices, mountains, or lakes on coral atolls, and only rarely are they found on raised coral islands.

Table 13-5

Reconstructed Terms in Proto-Polynesian I

*awa	'channel'		*hafu	'waterfall'
*hakau	'coral reef'		*lanu	'fresh water'
*kilikili	'gravel'		*lolo	'flood'
*peau	'wave'		*mato	'precipice'
*sou	'rough ocean'		*maʔuŋa	'mountain'
*tahi	'sea'		*rano	'lake'
*ʔone	'sand'		*waitafe	'stream'

In interpreting such results, linguists make the sensible assumption that the presence of a word for a particular object in a language usually indicates the presence of that object in the speakers' environment. (There are exceptions to this rule, as we will see, but they are few and far between.) In particular, complete landlubbers will not normally have an elaborate native vocabulary for the sea and for seafaring activities, barring the possibility of a recent move inland from a coastal area. We thus surmise that the early Polynesians inhabited a high island or a chain of high islands but lived close enough to the ocean to be familiar with the landscape and phenomena of the sea.

Table 13-6

Reconstructed Terms in Proto-Polynesian II

*maŋoo	'shark'		*kulii	'dog'
*kanahe	'mullet'		*puaka	'pig'
*sakulaa	'swordfish'		*moko	'lizard'
*ʔatu	'bonito'		*kumaa	'rat'
*ʔono	'barracuda'		*ŋata	'snake'
*ʔume	'leatherjacket'		*fonu	'turtle'
*manini	'sturgeon'		*peka	'bat'
*nofu	'stonefish'		*namu	'mosquito'
*fai	'stingray'		*lulu	'owl'
*kaloama	'goatfish'		*matuku	'reef heron'
*palani	'surgeonfish'		*akiaki	'tern'
*toke	'eel'		*moa	'chicken'

In Table 13–6, we reconstruct other Proto-Polynesian names for animals and make the assumption that the ancient Polynesians were familiar with them. Names of many other reef and deepwater fish and other sea creatures can be reconstructed besides those listed in the left-hand column. In contrast, we can reconstruct only a handful of names for land animals: a few domesticated animals (dog, pig, chicken) and a few birds and reptiles. We surmise that the Polynesians' original habitat was rich in sea life but probably relatively poor in land fauna—that the Polynesians originally inhabited coastal regions and not island interiors. The character of the land fauna offers pointed information about the Proto-Polynesian homeland. Since the Proto-Polynesian terms *peka* 'bat' and *lulu* 'owl' can be reconstructed, we can exclude as possible homelands Tahiti, Easter Island, and the Marquesas, where these animals are not found.

Furthermore, snakes are found only east of Samoa. Though we find reflexes of Proto-Polynesian *ŋata* 'snake' in many languages, we find no snakes west of Samoa. Had the Proto-Polynesians inhabited an island west of Samoa, they would very likely have lost the term *ŋata* over the centuries. Similarly, we know that pigs (for which the word *puaka* can be reconstructed) are not native to Polynesia, but Europeans first arriving between the sixteenth and nineteenth centuries found them everywhere except on Niue, Easter Island, and New Zealand. These three regions are thus unlikely homelands.

Words for some animals have undergone interesting changes in certain Polynesian languages. For example, New Zealand is much colder than the rest of Polynesia, and its native animals are very different from those found on the tropical islands to the north. Upon arrival in New Zealand, the ancient Maoris encountered many new species to which they gave the names of animals they had left behind in tropical Polynesia; thus, the following correspondences exist.

PROTO-POLYNESIAN		MAORI	
*pule	'cowrie shell'	pure	'bivalve mollusk'
*ŋata	'snake'	ŋata	'snail'
*ali	'flounder'	ari	'small shark'

Names for other animals were either dropped from the Maori vocabulary or applied to things commonly associated with the animal.

PROTO-POLYNESIAN		MAORI	
*ane	'termite'	ane	'rotten'
*lupe	'pigeon'	rupe	'mythical'

Other changes are more complex. The word *lulu* (or *ruru*) refers to owls in languages such as Tongan, Samoan, and Maori, which are spoken in areas where owls are found. On some islands, such as the Marquesas and Tahiti, owls do not exist, and the reflex of Proto-Polynesian *lulu* 'owl' has either disappeared from the language, as in Marquesan, or been applied to another species, as in Tahitian. Owls inhabit Hawaii, but the Proto-Polynesian term *lulu* has been replaced by the word *pueo* there.

Why would the early Hawaiians replace one word with the other? In the Marquesas, as we noted, there are no owls, and the language spoken there has no reflex of *lulu. Apparently the ancient Polynesians settled the Marquesas and stayed there for several centuries, during which they lost the word *lulu for lack of anything to apply it to. When they subsequently traveled north and settled Hawaii, they encountered owls, but by that time the word *lulu* had been forgotten, and a new word had to be found.

The linguistic evidence argues that the ancestors of the Polynesians were fishermen and cultivators. Here are a few of the many terms that refer to fishing and horticulture.

*mataʔu	'fishhook'	*too	'to plant'
*rama	'to torch fish'	*faki	'to pick'
*paa	'fish lure'	*lohu	'picking pole'
*kupeŋa	'fish net'	*hua	'spade'
*afo	'fishing line'	*maʔala	'garden'
*faaŋota	'to fish'	*palpula	'seedling'

By contrast, hunting terms are limited, with three words apparently exhausting all possible reconstructions for verbs related to hunting: *fana 'to shoot with a bow,' *welo 'to spear,' and *seu 'to snare with a net.' It is probably safe to infer that the major source of food for the ancient Polynesians was not the bush but the sea and garden.

One field with a notable array of vocabulary is canoe navigation, with the following reconstructions: *folau 'to travel by sea,' *ʔuli 'to steer,' *fohe 'paddle,' *fana 'mast,' *laa 'sail,' *kiato 'outrigger boom,' *hama 'outrigger.' That the speakers of Proto-Polynesian were expert seafarers comes as no surprise, given that they traveled enormous distances between islands (2000 miles stretch between Hawaii and the closest inhabited island).

Historical Linguistics and Prehistory

Linguistic evidence combined with archaeological evidence leads to the following hypotheses, which are summarized (and can be tracked) in Figure 13–4 on page 462.

1. The speakers of Proto-Polynesian inhabited the coastal region of a high island or group of high islands.

2. This homeland is likely to have been in the region between Samoa and Fiji, including the islands of Tonga, Uvea, and Futuna.

3. The ancient Polynesians were fishermen, cultivators, and seafarers.

4. Around the first century A.D., the ancient Polynesians traveled eastward from their homeland, settling eastern Polynesia: Tahiti, the Cook Islands, the Marquesas, the Tuamotu, and the neighboring island groups.

5. Then, between the fourth and sixth centuries, Easter Island, Hawaii, and New Zealand were settled from eastern Polynesia.

Figure 13-4

The Settlement of Polynesia

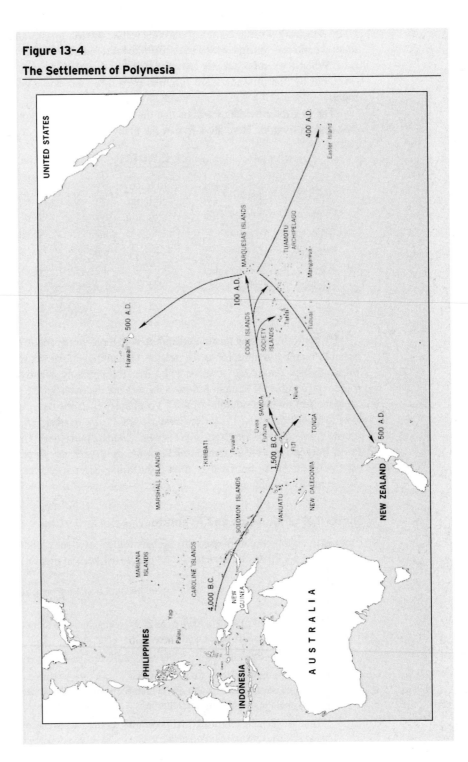

Our discussion has focused on Polynesian origins and migrations. By judiciously combining linguistic evidence with evidence from other disciplines, we have constructed a probable picture of an ancient people, the environment they lived in, and the skills they developed for survival. These same methods have been used for other peoples and to reconstruct other migration patterns, including the Indo-Europeans and the Algonquian Indians.

WHAT ARE THE LANGUAGE FAMILIES OF THE WORLD?

The comparative method that is used to trace the historical development of languages can also be applied to determine which languages are related within families. In this section we survey the major language families of the world, paying particular attention to those with the greatest number of speakers and those that include the most languages.

Counting Speakers and Languages

It is not easy to determine with certainty how many people speak languages such as English, Chinese, and Arabic. Nevertheless, these and a few others stand out for the sheer number of people that claim them as a native language. Of the world's several thousand languages, almost a dozen are spoken natively by 100 million individuals or more.

Chinese	1 billion
Hindi-Urdu	365 million
English	350 million
Spanish	250 million
Bengali	205 million
Portuguese	175 million
Russian	165 million
Arabic	150 million
Malay	150 million
Japanese	125 million
German	100 million

Of these, Chinese, English, Spanish, Russian, and Arabic are, along with French, the working languages of the United Nations.

Equally difficult to estimate is the number of languages currently spoken in the world. It is difficult to determine, in many cases, whether particular communities speak different dialects of the same language or different languages. Furthermore, little is known about many of the world's languages. In Papua New Guinea, a nation of only 3 million people, as many as 800 languages are spoken, although we have descriptions of a mere handful. Many Papuan languages are spoken in remote communities by only a few hundred speakers, or even a few dozen.

The discussion below is arranged by language family, beginning with Indo-European, Sino-Tibetan, Austronesian, and Afroasiatic, which together are the four most important families in terms of numbers of speakers and numbers of languages. The three major language families of sub-Saharan Africa are then discussed together, followed by other language families of Europe and Asia, including important isolated languages such as Japanese. Finally, we discuss the native languages of the Americas, Australia, and central Papua New Guinea. Pidgins and creoles are discussed at the end after a brief discussion of the proposed Nostratic macrofamily.

The Indo-European Family

To the Indo-European language family belong most languages of Europe (which are now spoken natively in the Americas and Oceania and play prominent roles in Africa and Asia), as well as most languages of Iran, Afghanistan, Pakistan, Bangladesh, and most of India. Of the 11 languages with more than 100 million native speakers, 7 belong to the Indo-European family. Yet Indo-European languages number only about 150, a small fraction of the world's languages. The extensive spread of Indo-European languages is shown in Figure 13–5.

The Indo-European family is divided into several groups. Figure 13–6 on page 466 is a family tree showing a few languages for each group.

Germanic Group   Modern-day Germanic languages include English, German, Yiddish, Swedish, Norwegian, Danish, Dutch (and its derivative Afrikaans), and a few other languages such as Icelandic, Faroese, and Frisian. The closest relative to English is Frisian, spoken in the northern Netherlands. As Table 13–7 illustrates, Germanic languages bear striking similarities to one another in vocabulary, and similarities in phonology and syntax are also numerous. Some Germanic languages are mutually intelligible, and all bear the imprint of a common ancestor.

Table 13-7
Common Words in Seven Germanic Languages

ENGLISH	GERMAN	DUTCH	SWEDISH	DANISH	NORWEGIAN	ICELANDIC
mother	Mutter	moeder	moder	moder	moder	móðir
father	Vater	vader	fader	fader	fader	faðir
eye	Auge	oog	öga	øje	øye	auga
foot	Fuss	voet	fot	fod	fot	fótur
one	ein	een	en	en	en	einn
three	drei	drie	tre	tre	tre	þrír
month	Monat	maand	månad	måned	måned	mánaður

Swedish, Danish, Norwegian, Icelandic, and Faroese—the North Germanic group—are more closely related to each other than to the other languages of the

Figure 13-5

Location of the Major Indo-European, Dravidian, Caucasian, Uralic, and Turkic Languages

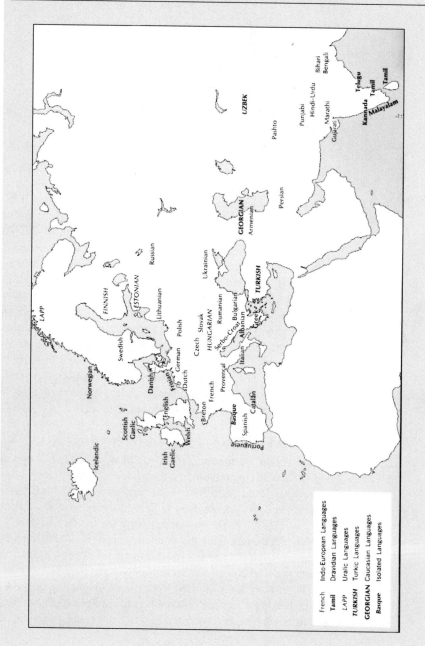

Figure 13-6

Partial Tree of the Indo-European Language Family

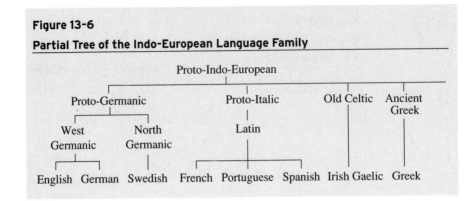

Germanic group. They descended from Proto-North-Germanic, which evolved as a single language for a longer period of time than the West Germanic subgroup that includes English, German, Frisian, and Dutch. We also have written records of Gothic, which was spoken in central Europe but disappeared around the eighth century. Gothic alone forms the East Germanic subgroup. Figure 13–7 is the family tree for the Germanic group (with Gothic in parentheses because it is extinct).

With about 350 million speakers, English is native to the inhabitants of the British Isles, the United States, most of Canada, the Caribbean, Australia, New Zealand, and South Africa. In addition, there are numerous bilingual speakers of English and another language on the Indian subcontinent, in eastern and southern Africa, and in Oceania. To these we must add the countless speakers of English as a second language scattered around the globe. English is the second most populous spoken language in the world after Chinese, but it is unrivaled in terms of its geographical spread and popularity as a second language. German, which has not spread as much as English, is still one of the world's most widely spoken languages. It claims about 100 million native speakers, mostly in central Europe.

Italic Group and Romance Subgroup   The Romance languages include French, Spanish, Italian, Portuguese, and Rumanian, as well as Provençal (in the south of France), Catalan (in northern Spain), Galician (in the Autonomous Region of Galicia in northwest Spain), and Romansch (in Switzerland). The Romance languages are closely related to each other, as witnessed by the sample of vocabulary correspondences in Table 13–8. The Rumanian words for 'mother,' 'father,' 'foot,' and 'month,' which are not derived from the same roots as those in the other Romance languages, illustrate the type of historical change that hinders communication between speakers of closely related languages. Such examples are particularly common in Rumanian, which is geographically isolated from other Romance languages.

The languages of the Romance family are descendants of Vulgar Latin. Because the Romance languages have remained in close contact over the centuries, subgroups

Figure 13-6 (Continued)

Partial Tree of the Indo-European Language Family

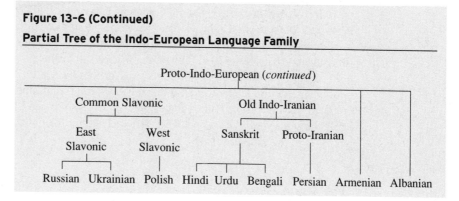

Figure 13-7

Germanic Languages

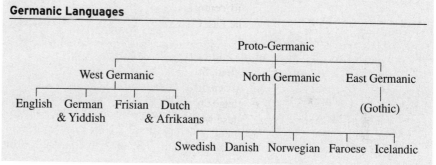

Table 13-8

Common Words in Six Romance Languages

FRENCH	ITALIAN	SPANISH	RUMANIAN	CATALAN	PORTUGUESE	
mère	madre	madre	mamă	mare	mãe	'mother'
père	padre	padre	tată	pare	pai	'father'
œil	occhio	ojo	ochiu	ull	ôlho	'eye'
pied	piede	pie	picior	peu	pé	'foot'
un	uno	uno	un	un	um	'one'
trois	tre	tres	trei	tres	três	'three'
mois	mese	mes	luna	mes	mês	'month'

are more difficult to identify than for Germanic languages. Latin is one descendant of Proto-Italic. Oscan and Umbrian, the other principal descendants, were once spoken in central and southern Italy but are now extinct and little is known about them. Spanish, with approximately 250 million native speakers in Spain and the Americas, is the third most populous language. Portuguese is spoken by nearly 175 million people, principally in Portugal and Brazil. French has almost 100 million native speakers in France, Canada, and the United States, as well as many second-language speakers, particularly in North Africa and West Africa. The tree for Italic and Romance languages is shown in Figure 13–8.

Figure 13-8

Italic Languages

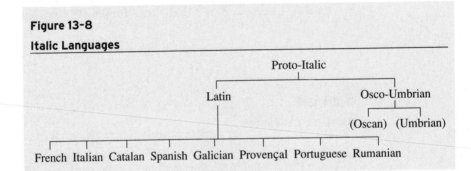

Slavonic Group   Slavonic languages are spoken in eastern Europe and the former Soviet Union. The Slavonic group can be divided into three subgroups: East Slavonic, which includes Russian (spoken in Russia), Ukrainian (spoken in Ukraine), and Belarusan (spoken in Belarus); South Slavonic, which includes Bulgarian and Serbo-Croatian; and West Slavonic, which groups together Polish, Czech, Slovak, and a few minor languages. All are derived from Common Slavonic (see Figure 13–9). Even more so than the Germanic and Romance languages, Slavonic languages are remarkably similar to each other, especially in their vocabulary (see Table 13–9).

Figure 13-9

Slavonic Languages

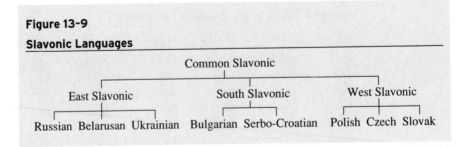

Table 13-9

Common Words in Six Slavonic Languages

RUSSIAN	UKRAINIAN	POLISH	CZECH	SERBO-CROATIAN	BULGARIAN	
mat'	mati	matka	matka	mati	mayka	'mother'
otec	otec'	ojciec	otec	otac	baʃtʃa	'father'
oko*	oko	oko	oko	oko	oko	'eye'
noga	noga	noga	noha	noga	krak	'foot'
odin	odin	jeden	jeden	jedan	edin	'one'
tri	tri	trzy	tři	tri	tri	'three'
mesjac	misjac'	miesiac	meʃíc	mjesec	mesec	'month'

*Russian *oko* 'eye' is archaic; the more modern word is *glaz*.

By far the most widely spoken Slavonic language is Russian, which is spoken natively by 150 million people and as a foreign language by an additional 65 million. Ukrainian has 50 million speakers, Polish 35 million, Serbo-Croatian 17 million, Czech 10 million, and Belarusan 10 million.

Indo-Iranian Group At the other geographical extreme of the Indo-European family is the Indo-Iranian group, subdivided into Iranian and Indic (see Figure 13–10 on page 470). Persian (or Farsi) has 35 million speakers in Iran, and Pashto has 11 million speakers in Afghanistan and northern Pakistan. Indic languages include Hindi-Urdu, spoken by about 365 million people in India (where it is called Hindi and is written in Devanāgarī script) and Pakistan (where it is called Urdu and uses the Arabic script). Other Indic languages include:

Bengali	205 million	India and Bangladesh
Marathi	65 million	Central India
Gujarati	44 million	Western India
Punjabi	40 million	Northern India and Pakistan
Bihari	25 million	Northeastern India

Many of these languages are also spoken by ethnic Indian populations in Southeast Asia, Africa, the Americas, Great Britain, and Oceania. The parent language of the modern Indic languages is Sanskrit, the ancient language of India immortalized in the Vedas and other classical texts.

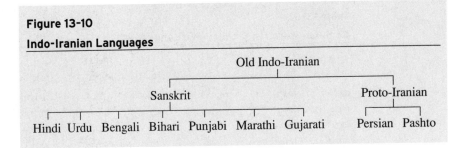

Figure 13-10

Indo-Iranian Languages

Table 13–10 presents sample vocabulary correspondences among a few Indo-Iranian languages. Not all the words with one meaning are cognates because some have sources other than a common parent language.

Table 13-10

Common Words in Six Indic Languages

HINDI	BENGALI	MARATHI	GUJARATI	PERSIAN	PASHTO	
mã:	ma	ma:	ma:	madær	mo:r	'mother'
ba:p	ba:p	baba:	ba:p	pedær	pla:r	'father'
ã:kʰ	cókʰ	dola	a:nkʰ	tʃæʃm	starga	'eye'
pã:w	pa:	pa:	pa:g	pa	pṣa	'foot'
ek	ak	ek	e:k	jek	jaw	'one'
ti:n	ti:n	ti:n	tra:n	se	dre:	'three'
mahi:na:	mas	mahi:na:	mahi:no	mah	mia:ʃt	'month'

Note: c represents a voiceless unaspirated palatal obstruent; ṣ represents a voiceless retroflex fricative.

Hellenic Group   The sole member of the Hellenic group is Greek. Certain languages, while belonging to a major language family, were isolated early enough that they do not bear any particularly close affiliations to other languages of the family. Such is the case with Greek, which evolved through the centuries in relative isolation. Greek stands out from other isolated Indo-European languages because of its relatively large number of speakers (10 million) and its historical importance in Indo-European linguistics owing to the fact that early written records of Ancient Greek have survived.

Other Indo-European Language Groups   Of the other Indo-European groups, Celtic includes Irish Gaelic, Scots Gaelic, Breton, and Welsh, which together are spoken by fewer than one million people today. Baltic includes Lithuanian, with 3 million speakers, and Latvian, with 1.5 million. Tocharian and Anatolian (including Hittite) are now extinct. Armenian and Albanian, each with more than 5 million speakers, form two additional groups.

The Sino-Tibetan Family

Included in the Sino-Tibetan family are about 300 East Asian languages, many of which remain relatively unexplored. This family is divided into a Sinitic group and a Tibeto-Burman group.

The Sinitic group includes a dozen named varieties (Mandarin, Cantonese, and so on). Most are structurally similar and are regarded by their speakers as dialects of a single language. With more than one billion speakers, this is the world's most populous language; it is, of course, Chinese. Five dialect groups can be identified. The Mandarin group includes the Běijīng (Peking) dialect, which serves as the official language of the People's Republic of China; the Yuè dialects include the dialect of Guǎngzhōu (Canton), which is spoken by the greatest number of overseas Chinese.

By comparison, the Tibeto-Burman group includes many different languages, each with relatively few speakers. The only members of this group that have more than a million speakers are Burmese (22 million) and Tibetan (1 million). Figure 13–11 maps the major Sino-Tibetan languages.

Figure 13-11

Location of the Major Sino-Tibetan, Mon-Khmer, and Tai Languages, and of the Major Isolated Languages of Asia

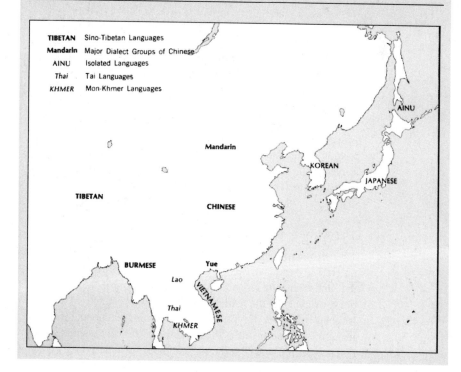

The Austronesian Family

The Austronesian family has up to 1000 languages scattered over one-third of the Southern Hemisphere. It includes Malay, spoken by about 150 million people in Indonesia and Malaysia; Javanese, with 75 million speakers on the island of Java in Indonesia; Tagalog or Pilipino, the official language of the Philippines, with 15 million speakers; Cebuano, another language of the Philippines (15 million speakers); and Malagasy, the principal language of Madagascar (10 million speakers). Most other Austronesian languages have fewer than one million speakers each, and many of them are spoken by only a few hundred people.

Table 13-11
Common Words in Six Austronesian Languages

MALAY	MALAGASY	TAGALOG	MOTU	FIJIAN	SAMOAN	
ibu	ineny	inâ	sina	tina	tinaa	'mother'
bapa	ikaky	amá	tama	tama	tamaa	'father'
mata	maso	mata	mata	mata	mata	'eye'
satu	isa	isa	ta	dua	tasi	'one'
tiga	telo	tatló	toi	tolu	tolu	'three'
batu	vato	bato	nadi	vatu	fatu*	'stone'
kutu	hao	kuto	utu	kutu	ʔutu	'louse'

*Samoan *fatu* actually means 'fruit pit,' a meaning closely related to 'stone.'

The Austronesian family contains several groups. The most ancient division is between three groups of minor Formosan languages spoken in the hills of Taiwan and all other Austronesian languages; the latter group is called Malayo-Polynesian. The most important split divides Western Malayo-Polynesian (languages spoken in Indonesia, Malaysia, Madagascar, the Philippines, and Guam) from Oceanic or Eastern Malayo-Polynesian (extending from the coastal areas of Papua New Guinea into the islands of the Pacific). Fijian and the Polynesian languages are Oceanic languages. Table 13–11 gives a sample of vocabulary correspondences between representative Austronesian languages. Figure 13–13 on page 474 is a simplified family tree, and the distribution of Austronesian languages is illustrated in Figure 13–12.

The Afroasiatic Family

The Afroasiatic family comprises about 250 languages scattered across the northern part of Africa and western Asia. It includes Arabic, dialects of which are spoken across the entire northern part of Africa and the Middle East; Hebrew, the traditional language of the Jewish nation and revived in the twentieth century as the national language of Israel; Egyptian, the now extinct language of the ancient Egyptian civilization; and Hausa, one of Africa's major languages, spoken natively by about 24 million people in Chad, Nigeria, and neighboring nations (see Figure 13–14 on page 475).

Figure 13-12

Map of Austronesian Languages

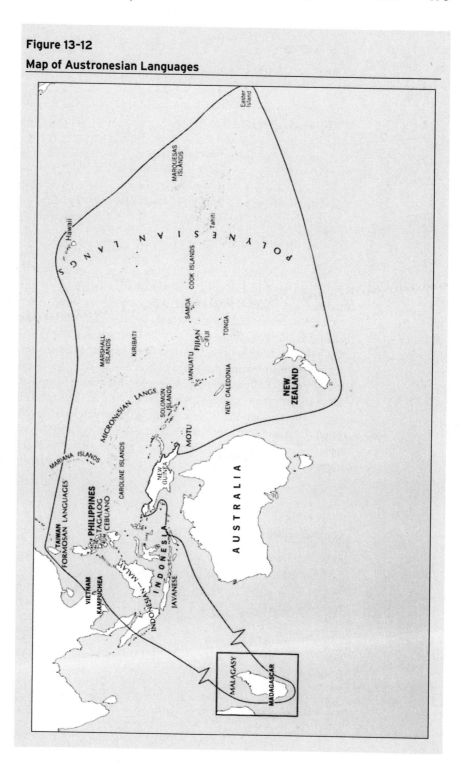

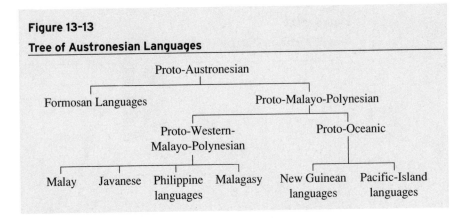

Figure 13-13
Tree of Austronesian Languages

Hebrew and Arabic form the Semitic group, to which also belong Amharic, the official language of Ethiopia, and Akkadian, a language of ancient Mesopotamia (modern Iraq), which is now extinct. Akkadian appears to have been the first language ever written, but it was replaced largely by Aramaic, which is also Semitic. Aramaic dialects include Palestinian Aramaic, the language Jesus spoke, and Modern Syriac, spoken by Christians in Iran, Iraq, and Georgia (in the former Soviet Union).

Somali, the principal language of Somalia, is one of about 40 languages of the Cushitic group. Kabyle and other languages that belong to the Berber group (with 10 million speakers) are scattered across North Africa. Hausa and perhaps close to 200 other languages form the Chadic group, all of which have developed tone systems. Ancient Egyptian forms a separate Afroasiatic group; Coptic is used as a liturgical language of the Coptic Church, but there are no native speakers. Table 13–12 is a comparative vocabulary for representative members of the Afroasiatic family.

Table 13-12
Common Words in Six Afroasiatic Languages

ARABIC	HEBREW	AMHARIC	KABYLE	HAUSA	SOMALI	
um	ɛm	annat	jemma	inna	hoojjo	'mother'
ab	av	abbat	baba	baba	aabe	'father'
ʕain	ajin	ajn	allen	ido	il	'eye'
ʔeʒer	rɛgɛl	agar	aḍaṛ	k'afa	ʕag	'foot'
waḥad	ɛxad	and	waḥed	'daya	hal	'one'
ṭalaṭa	ʃloʃa	sost	tlata	uku	saddeħ	'three'
ʃaher	xodɛʃ	wár	eccher	wata	bil	'month'

Note: ħ is the symbol for a voiceless pharyngeal fricative and ʕ for its voiced counterpart; ʃ is pronounced like *sh* in English *ship* (represented in some transcriptions by š); ʒ is the voiced counterpart to ʃ and is pronounced like the *s* in *measure* (represented in some transcriptions by ž).

Figure 13-14

The Language Families of Africa

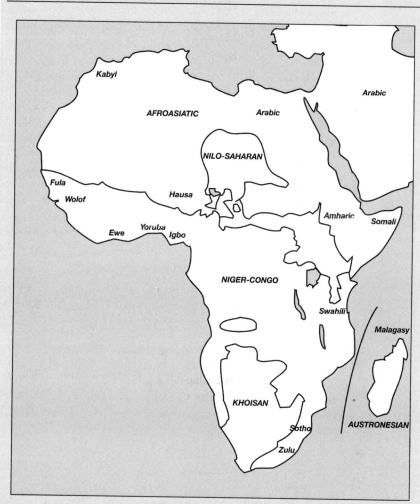

Source: Adapted from Gregersen, Edgar A. 1977. *Language in Africa: An Introductory Survey* (New York: Gordon & Breach).

The Three Major Language Families of Sub-Saharan Africa

Besides the Afroasiatic family spoken north of the Sahara Desert, Africa is home to three other language families: the Niger-Congo (or Niger-Kordofanian) family, with perhaps 1000 languages spoken by about 150 million people in a region that stretches from Senegal to Kenya to South Africa; the Nilo-Saharan family, with almost 200 languages spoken by 10 million people in and around Chad and the Sudan; and the Khoisan family in southern Africa, with 35 languages spoken by fewer than 75,000 people altogether. The Khoisan family, traditionally associated with the Bushmen of the Kalahari Desert, is the only language family in the world that has click sounds (discussed in Chapter 3). The boundaries between these language families are shown in Figure 13–14.

Most of the better-known languages of sub-Saharan Africa belong to the Niger-Congo family. These include Akan, spoken by 7 million in Ghana; Congo, spoken by about 3 million, with about 1 million each in Angola and the Democratic Republic of Congo; Fula (also called Fulani and Fulfulde), spoken by 2 million speakers in Guinea and Senegal; Wolof, with 3 million speakers principally in Senegal and others in Gambia, Guinea, and elsewhere; Yoruba, spoken in Nigeria by almost 19 million; Éwé, spoken by 1.6 million in Ghana and Togo; Igbo, with 18 million speakers in Nigeria; Swahili, with approximately 5 million first-language speakers and perhaps 30 million second-language speakers, chiefly in East Africa; and other Bantu languages of southern Africa such as Zulu (9 million speakers) and Sotho (6.5 million speakers).

Other Language Families of Asia and Europe

Scattered throughout Asia and Europe are a few smaller language families and a few languages that are not genealogically related to any other language family, so far as linguists can determine, and are therefore called *isolates*.

The Dravidian Family   Languages of the Dravidian family are spoken principally in southern India (see Figure 13–5 on page 465). The four major Dravidian languages are Tamil (60 million speakers), Malayalam (34 million speakers), Kannada (33 million speakers), and Telugu (73 million speakers), all of which have been written for many centuries. All Dravidian languages have been somewhat influenced by the Indic languages spoken to their north.

Try it yourself: Compare the words for 'month' in the four Dravidian languages given in Table 13–13 with the words for 'month' in the six Indic languages of Table 13–10 on page 470. Which Dravidian language appears to have borrowed the word for 'month' from an Indic language? Which Indic language has the word for 'month' most like the one borrowed by the Dravidian language?

The Mon-Khmer Family   The Mon-Khmer family includes about 100 languages spoken in Southeast Asia (Vietnam, Laos, Kampuchea, Thailand, and Myanmar). The most important of these is Cambodian or Khmer, the official language of Cambodia, spoken by nearly 8 million people (see Figure 13–11 on page 471). The Mon-Khmer languages may be related to other minor families of the same region.

Table 13-13

Common Words in Four Dravidian Languages

TAMIL	MALAYALAM	KANNADA	TELUGU	
amma:	amma	awwa	amma	'mother'
appa:	a:tʃtʃan	tande	na:nna	'father'
kaṇṇu	kaṇṇu	kaṇṇu	kannu	'eye'
ka:lu	ka:l	ka:lu	ka:lu	'foot'
onru	oru	ondu	okaṭi	'one'
mu:nru	mu:nnu	mu:ru	mu:ḍu	'three'
ma:sam	nela	tingaḷu	tinglu	'month'

The Tai Family   The best-known languages of the Tai family are Thai (20 million speakers) and Lao (3 million speakers), the official languages of Thailand and Laos respectively (shown in Figure 13–11 on page 471). There are about 50 other members of the Tai family scattered throughout Thailand, Laos, Vietnam, Myanmar, eastern India, and southern China, where they intertwine with Sino-Tibetan languages, Mon-Khmer languages, and Vietnamese. Tai languages may be related to a number of languages spoken in Vietnam, with which they may form a Kam-Tai family. It has also been suggested that Tai languages may be related to Austronesian, but the evidence supporting that hypothesis is scanty.

The Caucasian Family   With about 30 languages, the Caucasian family is confined to the mountainous region between the Black Sea and the Caspian Sea in Turkey, Iran, and what was part of the former Soviet Union. Spoken by about 5 million people altogether, Caucasian languages typically have complex phonological and morphological systems. The best-known Caucasian language is Georgian (see Figure 13–5 on page 465).

The Turkic Family   This family comprises about 60 languages, all of which are quite similar. The better-known members are Turkish, spoken by 59 million people, and Uzbek, with 18 million speakers in Uzbekistan. Most Turkic languages are spoken in Turkey and central Asia (see Figure 13–5). Some scholars include Turkic in a larger Altaic family.

The Uralic Family   With about 30 members, the Uralic family is thought by some to be related to the Turkic family, though this link is tenuous. The better-known Uralic languages are Finnish (6 million speakers) and Hungarian (15 million speakers); also included are Estonian and Lapp (see Figure 13–5).

Japanese   Japanese, with 125 million speakers, does not have any universally agreed-upon relatives, although many scholars regard it and Korean as belonging to an Altaic family, along with Turkic. Ryūkyūan, spoken in Okinawa, is a dialect of Japanese, and Ainu, spoken by about 15,000 people in the north of Japan, may also be related. Japanese has absorbed considerable influence from Chinese, to which it is *not* related (see Figure 13–11 on page 471).

Korean   Korean is spoken by about 75 million people. Many scholars regard Korean and Japanese as related members of the Altaic family, but this hypothesis remains unproven. Like Japanese, Korean has been greatly influenced by Chinese over the centuries (see Figure 13–11).

Vietnamese   Vietnamese, the language of the 65 million inhabitants of Vietnam and neighboring areas, does not have any clear genealogical relationships, although it may be a distant relative of Mon-Khmer languages (see Figure 13–11).

Other Isolated Languages of Asia and Europe   Of the remaining isolated languages of Eurasia, Basque is the best known. It is spoken by almost 600,000 inhabitants in an area that straddles the Spanish-French border on the Atlantic coast (see Figure 13–5 on page 465).

Native American Languages

Compared to the Old World, the linguistic situation in the New World is bewildering, with numerous Native American language families in North and South America. While proposals for the genealogical integration of these languages have been made, solid evidence for a pan-American link is lacking. Below are listed a few of those families and some of their members. You can see the approximate locations of some of these languages in Figure 13–15.

Eskimo-Aleut   In North America, we distinguish the Eskimo-Aleut family (whose speakers are *not* genetically related to Amerindians) from other language families. Inuit has 21,500 speakers across northern Canada and Alaska, and Yupik has about 16,000 speakers in Alaska and several hundred in Siberia.

Algonquian   Among the Algonquian languages are Cree (with 67,000 speakers in Canada and Montana) and Ojibwa (with more than 50,000 speakers living in Ontario, Manitoba, Michigan, Minnesota, and North Dakota). Represented by fewer speakers are Arapaho (1000 in Wyoming), Blackfoot (9000 in Montana and Canada), Cheyenne (1700 in Montana and Oklahoma), Kikapoo (850 in Kansas, Oklahoma, and Coahuila, Mexico), Malecite-Passamaquoddy (1500 in Maine and New Brunswick), Micmac (with 7000 in Maritime Canada and 1000 in Boston), Potawatomi (300 spread across Wisconsin, Michigan, Kansas, Oklahoma, and Ontario), and Shawnee (with 200 in Oklahoma).

Muskogean   Related to the Algonquian languages are the Muskogean languages. The largest language is Choctaw-Chicasaw, with 9200 speakers in Oklahoma, Mississippi, and Louisiana. Also Muskogean are Koasati, with 300 speakers in Louisiana and Texas, and Alabama, with 250 speakers in Texas.

Figure 13-15

Native american languages

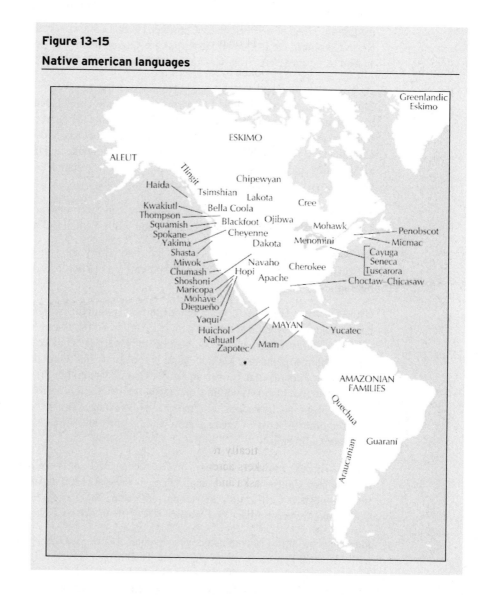

Athabaskan   In the Athabaskan family, some varieties of Apache are becoming extinct, but Western Apache has 12,700 speakers in Arizona, and Mescalero-Chiricahua Apache has 1800 speakers, chiefly in New Mexico. Navaho has 150,000 speakers in Arizona, Utah, and New Mexico. Chipewyan has 4000 speakers in Alberta, Saskatchewan, Manitoba, and the Northwest Territories. Often included with the Athabaskan languages in a group called Na-Dene are Tlingit and Haida, both spoken in Alaska and British Columbia.

Iroquoian   Excepting principally Cherokee (with 22,500 speakers in Oklahoma and North Carolina), the Iroquoian languages are spoken mainly in Ontario and Quebec, as well as upstate New York. Cayuga has 370 speakers; Mohawk 2000; Oneida 250; and Seneca 200.

Siouan   Located mainly in the upper midwest of the United States and in Canada, the Siouan family includes Dakota (20,000 in Minnesota, Montana, Nebraska, and the Dakotas, as well as Manitoba and Saskatchewan). Crow has 5500 speakers in Montana, and Lakota has 6000 in Nebraska, Minnesota, Montana, and the Dakotas, as well as Manitoba and Saskatchewan. Winnebago has fewer than 1000 in Nebraska and Wisconsin, while Omaha has 85 speakers in Nebraska.

Penutian   The Penutian family includes Tsimshian (500 speakers mostly in British Columbia), Yakima (3000 in Washington), and Walla Walla (100 in Oregon).

Salishan   Among the languages of the Salishan family are Shuswap (500 speakers in British Columbia), Spokane (50 in Washington), and Thompson (500 in British Columbia).

Uto-Aztecan   The Uto-Aztecan language family remains robust. Varieties of Nahuatl are spoken by about 1 million people in central and southern Mexico. On a much smaller scale, Huichol has 12,500 speakers in Nayarit and Jalisco, and Papago-Pima has 15,000 in Arizona and Mexico. Hopi is spoken by 5000 in Arizona and Yaqui by 17,000 near Phoenix and Tucson and in Mexico. Shoshoni has 3000 speakers in California, Nevada, Idaho, Wyoming, and Utah, while Ute-Southern Paiute is spoken by 2500 speakers in Colorado, Utah, Arizona, and Nevada. Comanche has 500 speakers in Oklahoma. Also Uto-Aztecan are Cahuilla (50) and Luiseño (100), spoken in Southern California.

Hokan   Hokan includes Kumiái, or Diegueño (320 speakers in Baja California and Southern California), Havasupai-Walapai-Yavapai (1200 in Arizona), Karok (100 in northwestern California), Maricopa (150 near Phoenix), Mohave (700 on the California-Arizona border), and Washo (100 on the California-Nevada border).

Mayan   The largest Mayan language is Yucatec, whose 940,000 speakers live mostly in the Yucatán Peninsula. Mam has about 400,000 speakers, most in Guatemala. The Mayan family also embraces Kekchi (with perhaps 365,000 speakers), Quiché (with perhaps 600,000), Cakchiquel (with perhaps 400,000), and about two dozen other languages.

Quechua   Quechua was the language of the ancient Incan Empire. Today it has 6 million speakers in the Andes and is the most popular indigenous South American language; its genealogical affiliation is unclear.

Tupi   The Tupi family includes Guaraní, with about 4 million speakers in Paraguay (where it is an official language) and southwestern Brazil.

Oto-Manguean   Members of the Oto-Manguean family include Zapotec (with almost half a million speakers), Mixtec (about 250,000), and Otomi (100,000), all spoken in central and southern Mexico.

Totonacan   Totonacan includes Totonaco, with about 250,000 speakers in Mexico.

Extinct and Dying Amerindian Languages   Scores of indigenous languages of the Americas have fallen silent over the past few decades. Red Thunder Cloud, the last speaker of the Siouan language Catawba, died in 1996 in Worcester, Massachusetts. The last speaker of Tillamook, a Salishan language, died in 1970, eight years after the last speaker of Wiyot, related to the Algonquian languages. Algonquian has also lost Miami, spoken in Indiana and Oklahoma, and Massachusett (also called Natick and Wampanoag). Also now extinct are Huron (or Wyandot) of the Iroquoian family, and the Hokan languages Chumash, from Santa Barbara, California, but extinct since 1965, and Salinan, from the central coast of California. Other extinct Amerindian languages include Chinook, of Washington and Oregon; Natchez and Tonkawa, both of Oklahoma; and Mohegan-Montauk-Narragansett, spoken earlier in Wisconsin and from Long Island to Connecticut and Rhode Island; and Iowa-Oto of Oklahoma, Iowa, and Kansas.

Amerindian languages are disappearing in the face of mounting pressure for younger speakers to adopt English, Spanish, or Portuguese, and many native languages are known only to a few older speakers. Besides several varieties of Apache, here is a list of some additional languages with fewer than 50 speakers each; the family name is given in italics.

Abnaki-Penobscot (Maine and Canada)—*Algonquian*

Coeur d'Alene (Idaho), Squamish (near Vancouver)—*Salishan*

Cupeño (Southern California)—*Uto-Aztecan*

Menomini (Wisconsin), Delaware—*Algonquian*

Osage (Oklahoma)—*Siouan*

Wichita (Oklahoma)—*Caddoan*

Miwok, Yokuts (both California), Coos (Oregon)—*Penutian*

Pomo, Shasta (both California)—*Hokan*

Tuscarora (formerly North Carolina, now near Niagara Falls, New York, and in Ontario, Canada)—*Iroquoian*

Try it yourself: In many places in the world, including the United States, Canada, Australia, Latin America, and South America, indigenous languages are still spoken, sometimes by very few speakers, most of whom may be old. Use the Internet—for example, the on-line *Ethnologue*—to discover which endangered language is geographically closest to you and how many speakers remain. See, too, whether there are efforts being made to record or preserve it.

Languages of Aboriginal Australia

Before settlement by Europeans in the eighteenth century, Australia had been inhabited by Aborigines for up to 50 millennia. It is estimated that at the time of first contact with Europeans about 200 to 300 Aboriginal languages were spoken. Today many have disappeared, along with their speakers, decimated by imported diseases and sometimes (as on the island of Tasmania) by genocide. Today, only about 100 Aboriginal languages survive, most spoken by tiny populations of older survivors.

Virtually all Australian languages fall into a single family with two groups: the large Pama-Nyungan group, which covers most of the continent and includes most Aboriginal languages, and the Non–Pama-Nyungan group, which includes about 50 languages in northern Australia.

Papuan Languages

Papuan languages are spoken on the large island of New Guinea, which is divided politically between the nation of Papua New Guinea and the Indonesian-controlled section called Irian Jaya. While the inhabitants of coastal areas of the island speak Austronesian languages, about 800 of the languages are not Austronesian languages. Referred to as Papuan languages, most are not in any danger of extinction, though many are spoken by small populations. They fall into more than 60 different families, with no established genealogical link among them. Little is known about most of these languages.

Nostratic Macrofamily

Recent years have seen renewed focus on linking certain language families within larger "macrofamilies." The proposed Nostratic macrofamily has received attention even in the popular press. Some scholars have proposed that several language families that are generally regarded as distinct should be viewed as having a common source further back in time. The languages hypothesized to belong to Nostratic differ slightly from scholar to scholar, but most scholars espousing this theory include Indo-European, Afroasiatic, Uralic, Altaic, Dravidian, and Eskimo-Aleut. Assuming that detailed comparative reconstruction confirmed this hypothesis, the Nostratic macrofamily would then make distant cousins of English (Indo-European); Hebrew, Arabic, Somali, and Hausa (Afroasiatic); Finnish and Hungarian (Uralic); perhaps Korean and Turkish (Altaic); Tamil (Dravidian); and Inuktitut (Eskimo-Aleut).

Although the links among these far-flung languages are not widely accepted among scholars, the hypothesis is provocative in an important way. As demonstrated in this chapter, the principal method for establishing genealogical relations among languages is by comparative reconstruction, whereby the forms of a parent language are hypothesized and the forms of the various daughter languages are derived by regular rules. Before any comparative reconstruction can be attempted, there must be hypotheses about which languages are and are not related. Without such hypotheses, just which languages would constitute the bases for establishing the sound correspondences that make the stuff of comparative reconstruction? With the Nostratic hypothesis in mind, you may find it thought provoking to reexamine the tables of common words for those Nostratic languages illustrated in this chapter: Tables 13–7 through 13–10 for four Indo-European groups, 13–12 for Afroasiatic, and 13–13 for Dravidian. Bear in mind that the sound correspondences among these languages would not be between the sounds of the daughter languages directly but between the sounds of the reconstructed parent languages, so any immediate correspondences that you might spy may be deceptive.

LANGUAGES IN CONTACT

At no other time in history have there been such intensive contacts between language communities as in the last few centuries. As a result of the exploratory and colonizing enterprises of the English, French, Dutch, Spanish, and Portuguese, European languages have come into contact with languages of Africa, Native America, Asia, and the Pacific. These colonizing efforts put members of different speech communities in contact with each other. For example, the importing of slaves from Africa to the Americas forced speakers of different African languages to live side by side. Several language contact phenomena can take place when speakers of different languages interact.

Multilingualism

Bilingualism   The first of these phenomena is **bilingualism** or multilingualism, in which members of a community acquire more than one language natively. In a multilingual community, children grow up speaking several languages. Use of each language is often compartmentalized, as when one is used at home and another at school or at work. Multilingualism is such a natural solution to the problem of language contact that it is extremely widespread throughout the world. In this respect, industrialized societies such as the United States and Japan, in which bilingualism is not widespread, are exceptional. In the United States, bilingualism is mostly relegated to immigrant communities, whose members are expected to learn English upon arrival. This adaptation is one-sided in contrast to what is found in most areas of the globe, where neighboring communities learn each other's languages with little ado. In central Africa, India, and Papua New Guinea, it is commonplace for small children to grow up speaking four or five languages. In Papua New Guinea, multilingualism is a highly valued attribute that enhances a person's status in the community.

Nativization   A possible side effect of multilingualism is **nativization,** which takes place when a community adopts a new language (in addition to its native language) and modifies the structure of that new language, thus developing a dialect that becomes characteristic of the community. That is precisely what has happened with English in India, where Indian English is recognized as a separate dialect of English with some of its own structural characteristics. Indeed, it has become one of India's two national languages (along with Hindi, the most widely spoken indigenous language) and is used in education, government, and communications within India and with the rest of the world.

Pidgins   Another process that may take place in language contact situations is pidginization. Although it is probably derived from the word *business,* the origin of the word **pidgin** is unclear, but the term refers to a contact language that develops where groups are in a dominant/subordinate situation, often in the context of colonization. Pidgins arise when members of a politically or economically dominant group do not learn the native language of the people they interact with as political or economic subordinates. To communicate, members of the subordinate community create a simplified variety of the language of the dominant group as their own second language. These simplified varieties then become the language of interaction between the colonizer and the colonized. Pidgins are thus defined in terms of sociological and linguistic characteristics. They are based on the language of the dominant group but are structurally simpler. They have no native speakers and are typically used for a restricted range of purposes.

Pidgins have arisen in many areas of the world, including West Africa, the Caribbean, the Far East, and the Pacific. Many pidgins have been based on English and French, the languages of the two most active colonial powers in the eighteenth and nineteenth centuries. Portuguese, Spanish, Dutch, Swedish, German, Arabic, and Russian, among others, have also served as a base for the development of pidgins. Today, most pidgins have given way to creole languages.

From Pidgin to Creole   At some point, a pidgin may begin to fulfill a greater number of roles in social life. Instead of using the pidgin language only in the workplace to communicate with traders or colonizers, speakers may begin to use the pidgin at home or among themselves. Such situations frequently arise when the colonized population is linguistically diversified. Members of that community may find it convenient to adopt the new language as a **lingua franca**—a means to communicate across language boundaries. As a result, small children begin to grow up speaking the new language, and as greater demands are put onto that language its structure becomes more complex in a process called creolization. A **creole** language is thus a former pidgin that has "acquired" native speakers. Creoles are structurally complex, eventually as complex as any other language, and they differ from pidgins in that they exhibit less variability from speaker to speaker than pidgins do.

The boundary between pidgin and creole is often difficult to establish. Creolization is a gradual process, and in many places pidgins are undergoing creolization. In such situations, there will be much variability from speaker to speaker and from situation to situation. For some speakers and in some contexts, the language will clearly be at the pidgin stage; for speakers whose language is more advanced in the creolization process, or in contexts that call for a more elaborated variety, the language will be structurally more complex. Furthermore, as a creole gains wider usage and becomes structurally more complex, it often comes to resemble the language on which it is based. For example, in the Caribbean and in Hawaii, English-based creoles are very similar to standard English for many speakers. Typically in such situations we find a continuum from speaker to speaker and from situation to situation—from a nonstandard dialect of the parent language to a very basic pidgin.

Figure 13–16 shows the location of the more important creoles in the world. Note that in common parlance many creoles are called pidgins. Such is the case with

Hawaiian Pidgin and Papua New Guinea Tok Pisin (from 'talk Pidgin'), both of which are actually creoles.

Figure 13-16

Location of Major Pidgin and Creole Languages

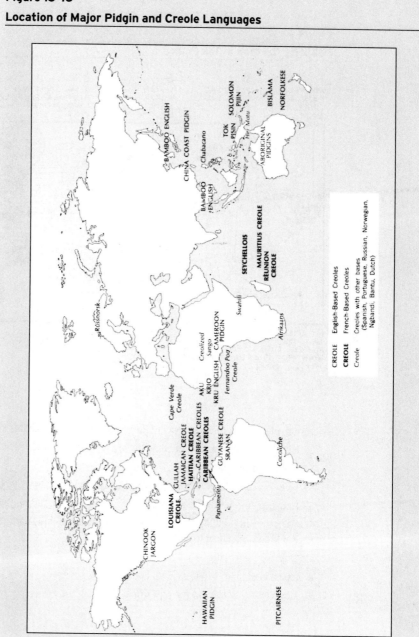

Some creoles have low status where they are spoken. Hawaiian creole, or Da Kine Talk, is often referred to as a "bastardized" version of English or as "broken English." The fact is that Hawaiian creole has its own structure, different from that of English, and you could not pretend to speak Da Kine Talk by speaking "broken" English.

Figure 13-17

Publicity Cartoon in Tok Pisin

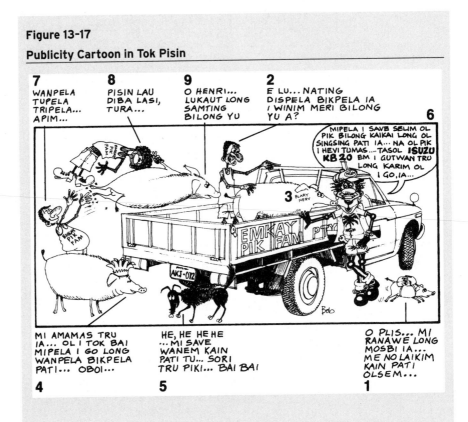

1. Oh, please. I'm running away to Port Moresby. I don't like this kind of party.

2. Hey, Lu! It's not for nothing that this big fat one beats your wife (in size).

3. The bloody nerve!

4. I am so happy. They all say that we are going to a big party. Oh, boy.

5. Hee, hee, hee, hee. I know what kind of party too. Very sorry, Piggy. Bye bye.

6. We frequently sell pigs for eating at dance parties. But pigs are very heavy so Isuzu KB20s are excellent to carry them all away.

7. One, two, three, up . . .

8. (speaking in Hiri Motu) Friend, I don't speak Tok Pisin.

9. Hey, Henry! Watch out for your things.

In contrast, in many areas of the world creoles have become national languages used in government proceedings, education, and the media. In Papua New Guinea, Tok Pisin is one of the three national languages (along with English and Kiri Motu, also a creole) and has become a symbol of national identity. Some creoles have become the language of important bodies of literature, particularly in West Africa. Elsewhere, creoles are used in newspapers and on the radio for various purposes, including cartoons and commercials. Figure 13–17 is a publicity cartoon in Papua New Guinea Tok Pisin; the English translation of the captions is given underneath. Tok Pisin is even used to write about linguistics, as illustrated by the following discussion of relative clause formation in Tok Pisin; it begins with three example sentences.

1. Ol ikilim pik bipo.
2. Na pik bai ikamap olosem draipela ston.
3. Na pik *ia* [ol ikilim bipo *ia*] bai ikamap olosem draipela ston.

Sapos yumi tingting gut long dispela tripela tok, yumi ken klia long tupela samting. Nambawan samting, sapos pik istap long (1) em inarapela pik, na pik istap long (2) em inarapela, orait, yumi no ken wokim (3). Tasol sapos wanpela pik tasol istap long (1) na (2), em orait long wokim (3). Na tu, tingting istap long (1) ia, mi bin banisim insait long tupela banis long (3), long wonem, em bilong kliaim yumi long wonem pik Elena itok en.

[Translation]

1. They killed the pig.
2. The pig looks like a big rock.
3. The pig [that they killed] looks like a big rock.

If we think carefully about these three sentences, we can obtain two interpretations. First, if the pig of sentence (1) is one pig, and the pig of sentence (2) is another pig, then we cannot construct (3). However, if the pig in (1) and (2) is the same, then we can construct (3). Thus, I have bracketed in (3) the meaning corresponding to (1) with two brackets, because it has the purpose of identifying for us which pig Elena [the speaker who produced these sentences] is talking about. [Gillian Sankoff, "Sampela Nupela lo Ikamap Long Tok Pisin," in McElhanon, 1975.]

In short, creoles can fulfill all the demands that are commonly imposed on a language.

The structural similarities among creoles worldwide are striking. Many creoles, for example, lack indefinite articles and a distinction between the future and other tenses, and many have preposition stranding (as in the English expression *the house I live in*). Such similarities have led some researchers to propose that the development of pidgins and creoles follows a "program" that is genetically innate in humans. There are, however, many differences among the world's creoles, in which the imprint of various native languages is clear. In many South Pacific creoles, for example, a distinction is made in the pronoun system between dual and plural and between inclusive first-person dual and plural and exclusive first-person dual and plural (see Chapter 7, page 229 where the Tok Pisin pronoun system is given). These distinctions are not found in West African creoles, and their presence in South Pacific creoles reflects the fact that many languages spoken in the South Pacific make these distinctions. In Nigerian creole, on the other hand, we find honorific terms of address (*Mom* and *Dad*) that are used when addressing high-status individuals. These honorifics are not found in any other creole; again, they are transferred from local languages. Thus there is both homogeneity and heterogeneity among the creoles of the world.

Computers and the History of Languages

 In the study of historical linguistics and language change, computers have been particularly helpful in their ability to manipulate large quantities of data accurately and efficiently. Several major historical corpora have been compiled over the past couple of decades, and their ability to aid researchers in tracing lexical, morphological, semantic, and syntactic change in language has proven impressive and interesting.

Among the influential historical corpora is the Helsinki Corpus of English Texts: Diachronic and Dialectal (called the Helsinki Corpus for short). Here we concentrate on the historical (diachronic) part. Compiled by researchers at the University of Helsinki, this corpus contains texts of English from the Old English period (starting at about A.D. 800) and continuing through the early eighteenth century in the period known as Early Modern English. Unlike the LOB and Brown corpora, which contain 2000-word extracts of texts, the Helsinki Corpus contains texts varying in length from 2500 to almost 20,000 words. Altogether, there are 242 text files totaling about 1.5 million words of running text. Like many corpora, for each text the Helsinki Corpus includes information about the author's name, sex, education, origin, and social status, as well as information about the date of composition and the genre of the text (which is related to what we have been calling register). Using the Helsinki Corpus, researchers have been able to investigate patterns of development with certain genres across time, across genres within a given period of time, between male and female writers, and between British and American English, to mention just some of the dimensions along which it is possible to explore.

ARCHER (A Representative Corpus of Historical English Registers) includes ten registers over the centuries from 1650 to 1990, broken into half-century periods. For the periods 1750 to 1799, 1850 to 1899, and 1950 to 1990, it contains parallel British and American texts; for the other periods, only British texts. The ten registers include written (such as fiction, legal opinions) and speech-based registers (fictional conversation, drama, sermons). All told, ARCHER contains over 1000 texts and about 1.7 million words.

SUMMARY

- Languages are always changing.
- All levels of the grammar change: phonology, morphology, lexicon, syntax, semantics, and pragmatics.
- From one language many other languages can develop in the course of time if groups of speakers remain physically or socially separated from one another.

- The method of comparative reconstruction enables linguists to make educated guesses about the structure and vocabulary of prehistoric peoples and to infer a good deal about their cultures from the nature of the reconstructed lexicon.

- The thousands of languages in the world can be grouped for the most part into language families whose branches represent languages that are genealogically closer to one another than to other languages of the family.

- When speakers of different languages come into contact, bilingualism may develop, with speakers commanding two or more languages.

- In some circumstances—usually when a dominant and a subordinate group are in contact— a pidgin may spring up for very limited use, usually in trade. Over time, if the pidgin comes to be used for other purposes and children learn it at home as a first language, the process of creolization starts.

- Creolization is a process of expansion in terms of both uses and structures.

WHAT DO YOU THINK? REVISITED

❖ *Pre-med Melanie.* Both English and Latin are descended from Indo-European, but English has come down through the Germanic branch and Latin through the Romance branch. It is the fact that English borrowed so many thousands of words from Latin during the Renaissance that sometimes gives the impression that English comes from Latin, but it does not.

❖ *Chinatown jade.* Mandarin and Cantonese derive from the same historical sources and are regarded by their speakers as dialects of the same language. In addition, using a set of Chinese characters, speakers of both dialects can comprehend a given text, though if they read it aloud it would not be understood by speakers of the other dialect. There is no precise point in the historical development of languages at which linguists can say two varieties that have descended from a common source language have become different *languages* as opposed to different *dialects* of the same language.

❖ *Iraqi and Iranian place names.* The *al, an,* and *as* in Iraqi place names such as *Al Baṣrah, An Najaf,* and *As Sulaymānīyah* is the Arabic definite article in one or another of its variants. (It also appears in words that English has borrowed from Arabic, such as *algebra* and *alcohol.*) The language of Iran is Persian, an Indo-European language distantly related to English. The **e** that often links two parts of Iranian expressions (*Dasht-e Kavīr* and *Posht-e Kūh*) is characteristic of Persian but not of Arabic. Persian and Arabic both use forms of Arabic script, in part as a consequence of their both being Muslim countries with a Muslim culture and history.

❖ *Oklahoma.* Oklahoma place names such as *Okmulgee, Comanche, Chattanooga, Manitou, Cherokee, Arapaho,* and *Wynona* have no independent meaning in English other than as the names of particular towns or cities. Such names are now English words; because they have been "naturalized," speakers of English pronounce them as English words. Languages in contact often borrow from one another, and it is not uncommon for newcomers to inquire about the name of a place and incorporate that name into their own language.

EXERCISES

Based on Languages Other Than English

The Amara data used here are taken from an unpublished Amara lexicon by Bil Thurston; the Hiw, Sowa, Mota, and Raɣa data from Darrell Tryon, *New Hebrides Languages* (Pacific Linguistics, C, 50, 1976); the Waskia data from Malcolm Ross and John Natu Paol, *A Waskia Grammar Sketch and Vocabulary* (Pacific Linguistics, B, 56, 1978); the Lusi and Bariai data from Rick Goulden, "A Comparative Study of Lusi and Bariai" (McMaster University M.A. thesis, 1982).

13-1 The following is a comparative word list from seven languages spoken in the South Pacific. (β represents a voiced bilabial fricative and ɣ a voiced velar fricative.)

Hiw	Waskia	Motu	Amara	Sowa	Mota	Raɣa	
yoŋ	utuwura	lai	akauliŋ	laiŋ	laŋ	laɲi	'wind'
en	laŋ	miri	olov	on	one	one	'sand'
βət	maŋa	nadi	epeiouŋo	βət	βət	fatu	'stone'
yə	didu	matabudi	opon	tariβanaβi	uwə	afua	'turtle'
eyə	wal	gwarume	ouŋa	ek	iɣa	iya	'fish'
noɣa	kasim	namo	ovinkin	tapken	nam	namu	'mosquito'
yo	nup	lada	serio	se	sasa	iha	'name'
moɣoɣe	kulak	natu	emim	dozo	natu	nitu	'child'
suɣe	buruk	boroma	esnei	bo	kpwoe	poe	'pig'
tø	kemak	tohu	elgo	ze	tou	toi	'sugarcane'

a. Identify which languages are likely to be related and which are not, and justify your claims.

b. Of the languages that appear to be part of the same family, which are more closely related? Justify your answer.

13-2 The following is a comparative word list from Lusi and Bariai, closely related languages spoken on the island of New Britain in Papua New Guinea.

Lusi	Bariai		Lusi	Bariai	
βaza	bada	'to fetch'	βua	bua	'Areca nut'
kalo	kalo	'frog'	niu	niu	'coconut'
ɣali	gal	'to spear'	uβu	ubu	'hip'
ahe	ae	'foot'	rai	rai	'trade wind'
zaŋa	daŋa	'thing'	oaɣa	oaga	'canoe'
tazi	tad	'sea'	mata	mata	'eye'
tupi	tup	'to peek'	zoɣi	dog	a type of plant
tori	tol	'to dance'	hani	an	'food'
ɲiɲi	ɲiŋ	'to laugh'	aŋari	aŋal	a type of bird

a. List the consonant correspondences between Lusi and Bariai.

b. Identify which vowel is lost in Bariai and give a rule that states the environment in which it is lost.

13-3 Table 13–3 on page 455 provides some correspondence sets among five Polynesian languages. We noted that Tongan had lost a phoneme /r/ from its inventory, which was kept as /r/ or became /l/ in the other four languages. Furthermore, Tongan has kept a phoneme /h/ in certain words, which has been lost in all other Polynesian languages. The following cognates illustrate these two changes.

Tongan	Samoan	Tahitian	Maori	Hawaiian	
hama	ama	ama	ama	ama	'outrigger'
ama	lama	rama	rama	lama	'torch'

a. On the basis of this information and the following words, complete the table of consonant correspondences for Tongan, Samoan, Tahitian, Maori, and Hawaiian.

Tongan	Samoan	Tahitian	Maori	Hawaiian	
leʔo	leo	reo	reo	leo	'voice'
ʔuha	ua	ua	ua	ua	'rain'
lili	lili	riri	riri	lili	'angry'
hae	sae	hae	hae	hae	'to tear'
hihi	isi	ihi	ihi	ihi	'strip'
huu	ulu	uru	uru	ulu	'to enter'
fue	fue	hue	hue	hue	type of vine
afo	afo	aho	aho	aho	'fishing line'
vela	vela	vera	wera	wela	'hot'
hiva	iva	iva	iwa	iwa	'nine'

b. Using your table of consonant correspondences and assuming that vowels have not undergone any change in any Polynesian language, complete the following comparative table by filling in the missing words.

Tongan	Samoan	Tahitian	Maori	Hawaiian	
kaukau	___	___	___	___	'to bathe'
___	mata	___	___	___	'eye'
___	tafe	___	___	kahe	'to flow'
laʔe	___	___	___	___	'forehead'
laŋo	___	___	___	___	'fly'

c. Reconstruct the Proto-Polynesian consonant system on the basis of the information you now have; take into account the genealogical classification of Polynesian languages discussed in this chapter. (*Hint:* The protosystem has to be full enough to account for all the possible correspondences found in the daughter languages. No daughter language has innovated new phonemes, but all have lost one or more from the protosystem.)

d. Reconstruct the Proto-Polynesian words for 'outrigger,' 'rain,' 'to enter,' 'strip,' and 'nine.'

13-4 Below is a list of Modern French words in phonetic transcription with the Vulgar Latin words from which they derive. (Notice that word-initial /k/ in Latin becomes /k/, /ʃ/, or /s/ in Modern French, depending on its environment.)

Modern French	Vulgar Latin	
koœd	korda	'rope'
ʃɑ̃	kampus	'field'
sɛdʁ	kɛdrus	'cedar'
kʁaʃe	krakkaːre	'to spit'
ʃamo	kameːlus	'camel'
sɛʁkl	kirkulus	'circle'
kuʁiʁ	kurrere	'to run'
ʃaʁ	karrus	'carriage'
kle	klavis	'key'
sitɛʁn	kisterna	'tank'
kɔlɔ̃b	kolomba	'dove'
ʃa	kattus	'cat'
ku	kollum	'neck'

a. Provide a rule that predicts which of the three French phonemes will appear where Latin had /k/. (Address only the initial consonant of words.)

b. Consider the additional data below.

Modern French	Vulgar Latin	
ʃov	kalvus	'bald'
ʃɛn	katena	'chain'
ʃo	kalidum	'hot'
ʃɛʁ	karo	'flesh'

At first glance, these forms are problematic for the rule you stated in (a). Note, however, that in Modern French these four words are spelled *chauve, chaine, chaud,* and *chair,* respectively. Given the fact that French orthography often reflects an earlier pronunciation of the language, explain in detail what has happened to the four words in the history of the language.

13-5 Consider the following Proto-Indo-European reconstructions. Conspicuously, no word for 'sea' can be reconstructed for Proto-Indo-European.

*rtko	'bear'		*peisk	'fish'
*laks	'salmon'		*sper	'sparrow'
*or	'eagle'		*trozdo	'thrush'
*gʷou	'cow/bull'		*suː	'pig'
*kwon	'dog'		*agwʰno	'lamb'
*mori	'lake'		*sneigʷʰ	'snow'
*bʰerəg	'birch'		*grano	'grain'
*yewo	'wheat'		*medʰu	'honey'
*weik	'village'		*sel	'fortification'
*seː	'to sow'		*kerp	'to collect (food)'
*yeug	'to yoke'		*webʰ	'to weave'
*sneː	'to spin'		*arə	'to plow'
*ayes	'metal'		*agro	'field'

a. Describe in detail what these reconstructions (or lack of reconstructions) tell us about the activities and environment of the Proto-Indo-Europeans.

b. Based on these reconstructions and on what you know about the current distribution of Indo-European languages, which area or areas of the world would be the best candidates as the homeland of the Proto-Indo-Europeans? Defend your claim.

13-6 The following is a list of Proto-Indo-European reconstructions. Cite a Modern English word that contains a reflex for each one of them; ignore the question as to whether the Modern English word is itself a borrowing or not.

*akwaː	'water'	*agro	'field'
*kwetwer	'four'	*bʰugo	'ram, goat'
*bʰreu	'to boil'	*pel	'skin'
*reg	'to rule'	*gel	'to freeze'
*wen	'to strive for'	*gʰans	'goose'
*med	'to measure'	*yeug	'to join together'
*ped	'foot'	*genə	'to give birth'

Especially for Educators and Future Teachers

13-7 Think about conversations you've had with your grandparents and their peers and identify three or four words or expressions that you regard as old-fashioned and no longer in use by you and your peers. Are there any characteristic pronunciations that identify a speaker as belonging to an older generation? Are there any characteristics of your speech that you think your students may regard as old-fashioned? Do you hold any particular views of language use that your students may regard as old-fashioned?

13-8 Given that languages typically change within a lifetime, teachers need to be attentive to such changes and consider whether usages that they may have been taught as correct remain correct or remain the only correct form. Identify two prescriptive rules you have been taught as correct but that you believe may reflect older, now outdated usage. Check a good usage handbook or dictionary to see what they report about current usage for those linguistic features.

OTHER RESOURCES

- **Ethnologue: Languages of the World: http://www.sil.org/ethnologue/search**
  The *Ethnologue* is a catalog of the world's languages, an extraordinary source of information about all languages—where they are spoken, by how many people, and to what family they belong. It is the source of much of the data about speakers and locations presented in this chapter. The Ethnologue Web site, which is maintained by the Summer Institute of Linguistics, provides an electronic version and includes a language name index and a language family index. A typical entry is given below:

  UTE-SOUTHERN PAIUTE [UTE] 1,984 speakers including 20 monolinguals (1990 census), out of 5000 population (1977 SIL), including 3 Chemehuevi (1990 census). Ute in southwestern Colorado and southeastern and northeastern Utah; Southern Paiute in southwestern Utah, northern Arizona, and southern Nevada; Chemehuevi on lower Colorado River, California. Uto-Aztecan, Northern Uto-Aztecan, Numic,

Southern. Dialects: SOUTHERN PAIUTE, UTE, CHEMEHUEVI. Most adults speak the language but most younger ones do not. Literacy rate in first language: Below 1%. Literacy rate in second language: 75% to 100%.

- **Sample of Spoken Navaho:**
  http://www.teleport.com/~napoleon/navaho/sample.html
  At this Web site you can hear a sample of spoken Navaho.

- **Alphabetical Language Index:**
  http://www.teleport.com/~napoleon/alphabetical.html
  Contains links to sites for dozens of languages, many of which provide a substantial spoken sample, including Basque, Frisian, Italian, Korean, Maori, Tamil, and even the artificial language Esperanto.

Video

- **In Search of the First Language**
  Part of the NOVA video series, this fascinating exploration was first broadcast in 1997. It includes discussion by prominent linguists on a wide range of topics related to language change and language families, including the controversial Nostratic hypothesis. (To order this video, visit NOVA's Web site at http://www.pbs.org/, where you can also find leads to a transcript of the broadcast.)

SUGGESTIONS FOR FURTHER READING

- **Jean Aitchison. 1991.** *Language Change: Progress or Decay?,* 2nd ed. (Cambridge: Cambridge University Press). Combines traditional historical analysis with sociolinguistic insights.

- **Bernd Heine & Derek Nurse. 2000.** *The Languages of Africa* (Cambridge: Cambridge University Press). An excellent introduction to the languages of Africa, written specifically for undergraduate students. Contains chapters on each of the families and on the phonology, morphology, and syntax of African languages, along with chapters on comparative linguistics, language in society, and language and history, all within an African context.

- **Calvert Watkins. 2000. "Indo-European and the Indo-Europeans."** *The American Heritage Dictionary of the English Language,* 4th ed. (Boston: Houghton Mifflin). Conveniently appended to the dictionary, this article describes Indo-European and the cultural inferences that can be drawn from the reconstructed lexicon. The article provides an introduction to a dictionary of Indo-European roots, with cognates in several languages.

ADVANCED READING

There are many good textbooks treating historical linguistics, among them McMahon (1994), Trask (1996), Crowley (1998), and Campbell (1999). Lehmann (1967) contains many of the original documents of historical work from the nineteenth century, including the speech of Sir William Jones quoted on page 449. Bellwood (1979; 1987) and Jennings (1979) survey research on Polynesian and Austronesian migrations, including extensive discussion of language history. Pawley and Green (1971) discuss the linguistic evidence for the location of the Proto-Polynesian homeland. Bomhard (1992) and Kaiser and Shevoroshkin (1988) discuss the Nostratic macrofamily.

A convenient reference work treating about a dozen language families and forty of the world's major languages is Comrie (1987), with a list of references for each family and language. In addition, there is the Cambridge Language Survey Series, which includes volumes on lesser known areas and language families by Comrie (1981), Dixon (1980a), Foley (1986), and Suárez (1983), and on major languages, such as Shibatani (1990). The languages of China are succinctly surveyed in Ramsey (1987), Native North American languages in Mithun (1999), Amazonian languages in Derbyshire and Pullum (1986), and South American languages in Manelis Klein and Stark (1985). An excellent chapter-length treatment of Native American languages is Yamamoto and Zepeda (2004), and Hinton (1994) has delightful and informative chapters on Native American languages in California. A proposal that all Amerindian languages can be classified into three families appears in Greenberg (1987). Using a method like the one used to determine the Proto-Polynesian homeland, Siebert (1967) discusses the original home of the Proto-Algonquian people. Buck (1949) is a compilation of Indo-European roots with the reflexes in various languages. Baldi (1983) is a useful overview of the Indo-European language family.

Nativization is discussed in Kachru (1982). Good surveys of the structure and use of pidgins and creoles include Mühlhäusler (1986) and Romaine (1988). A provocative hypothesis about pidginization as an innate program is advanced by Bickerton (1981). Ruhlen (1986) lists the languages of the world and their genealogical affiliation.

REFERENCES

- Baldi, Philip. 1983. *An Introduction to the Indo-European Languages* (Carbondale: Southern Illinois University Press).

- Bellwood, Peter. 1979. *Man's Conquest of the Pacific: The Prehistory of Southeast Asia and Oceania* (New York: Oxford University Press).

- Bellwood, Peter. 1987. *The Polynesians: Prehistory of an Island People,* rev. ed. (London: Thames and Hudson).

- Bickerton, Derek. 1981. *Roots of Language* (Ann Arbor: Karoma).

- Bomhard, Allan R. 1992. "The Nostratic Macrofamily (with Special Reference to Indo-European)," *Word* 43:61–83.

- Buck, Carl D. 1949. *A Dictionary of Selected Synonyms in the Principal Indo-European Languages* (Chicago: University of Chicago Press).

- Campbell, Lyle. 1999. *Historical Linguistics: An Introduction* (Cambridge, MA: MIT Press).

- Comrie, Bernard. 1981. *The Languages of the Soviet Union* (Cambridge: Cambridge University Press).

- Comrie, Bernard, ed. 1987. *The World's Major Languages* (New York: Oxford University Press).
- Crowley, Terry. 1998. *An Introduction to Historical Linguistics,* 3rd ed. (Oxford: Oxford University Press).
- Derbyshire, Desmond C. & Geoffrey K. Pullum, eds. 1986. *Handbook of Amazonian Languages,* 3 vols. (New York: Mouton).
- Dixon, R. M. W. 1980a. *The Languages of Australia* (Cambridge: Cambridge University Press).
- Dixon, R. M. W. 1980b. *The Rise and Fall of Languages* (Cambridge: Cambridge University Press).
- Foley, William A. 1986. *The Papuan Languages of New Guinea* (Cambridge: Cambridge University Press).
- Greenberg, Joseph H. 1987. *Language in the Americas* (Stanford: Stanford University Press).
- Hinton, Leanne. 1994. *Flutes of Fire,* 2nd ed. (Berkeley, CA: Heyday).
- Jennings, Jesse D., ed. 1979. *The Prehistory of Polynesia* (Cambridge: Harvard University Press).
- Kachru, Braj, ed. 1982. *The Other Tongue: English across Cultures* (Urbana: University of Illinois Press).
- Kaiser, M. & V. Shevoroshkin. 1988. "Nostratic," *Annual Review of Anthropology* 17:309–29.
- Lehmann, Winfred, ed. 1967. *A Reader in Nineteenth-Century Historical Linguistics* (Bloomington: Indiana University Press).
- Manelis Klein, Harriet E. & Louisa R. Stark, eds. 1985. *South American Indian Languages: Retrospect and Prospect* (Austin: University of Texas Press).
- McMahon, April M. S. 1994. *Understanding Language Change* (Cambridge: Cambridge University Press).
- Mithune, Marianne. 1999. *The Languages of Native North America* (Cambridge: Cambridge University Press).
- Mülhäusler, Peter. 1986. *Pidgin and Creole Linguistics* (Oxford: Blackwell).
- Pawley, Andrew & Kaye Green. 1971. "Lexical Evidence for the Proto-Polynesian Homeland," *Te Reo* 14:1–35.
- Romaine, Suzanne. 1988. *Pidgin and Creole Languages* (London: Longman).
- Ramsey, S. Robert. 1987. *The Languages of China* (Princeton: Princeton University Press).
- Ruhlen, Merritt. 1986. *A Guide to the World's Languages* (Stanford: Stanford University Press).
- Sankoff, Gillian. 1975. "Sampela Nupela lo Ikamap Long Tok Pisin." In K. A. McElhanon, ed., *Tok Pisin i Go We?* (Ukarumpa: Linguistic Society of New Guinea).
- Shibatani, Masayoshi. 1990. *The Languages of Japan* (Cambridge: Cambridge University Press).

- Siebert, Frank T. 1967. "The Original Home of the Proto-Algonquian People," *Bulletin No. 214* (Ottawa: National Museum of Canada), pp. 13–47.

- Suárez, Jorge A. 1983. *The Mesoamerican Indian Languages* (Cambridge: Cambridge University Press).

- Trask, R. L. 1996. *Historical Linguistics* (London: Arnold).

- Yamamoto, Akira & Ofelia Zepeda. 2004. "Native American Languages." In Edward Finegan & John R. Rickford, eds., *Language in the USA* (Cambridge: Cambridge University Press).

Chapter 14

Historical Development in English

❖ You and your friend Scott visit Ye Olde Coffee Shoppe, where Scott reads on the back of the menu that the word "Ye" in the shop name should *not* be pronounced "yee." The menu says *Y* is a variant of an older letter pronounced like *th* and the name of the shop is really *The Old Coffee Shop.* Scott scoffs and says that's hogwash. What do you say?

❖ In looking at maps of the United States, your sixth-grade geography class notices that many cities in California and the Southwest have names such as San Diego and Santa Monica that include the words "San" or "Santa," and they ask why those names don't occur elsewhere in the United States. What do you tell them?

❖ Gerry, a fellow secondary-school teacher of modern languages, wonders why English has so few inflections on its nouns when its close relative German has so many. What's your answer?

❖ Isabelle, an international student, asks why some English nouns such as "sheep" and "deer" do not have ordinary plural forms like most English nouns. Besides the fact that they are "irregular," what explanation can you offer her?

A THOUSAND YEARS OF CHANGE

Nearly every secondary school student in the English-speaking world has studied the writings of Shakespeare and Chaucer. You may recall that when you read Shakespeare's plays, some lines were opaque, as with these opening lines of *1 Henry IV:*

So shaken as we are, so wan with care
Find we a time for frighted peace to pant
And breathe short-winded accents of new broils
To be commenced in stronds afar remote.

The English spoken in and around London four centuries ago is sometimes subtly and sometimes strikingly different from the English spoken there and throughout the English-speaking world today. Still, much of it is accessible and very little of it is so foreign that it eludes us completely. Many of the words in the brief passage just cited are familiar enough, although some are used in ways that strike a modern reader as peculiar. While the words of the opening line are familiar and can be sorted out syntactically as poetic English, the second line is a bit tougher, even though all the words except *frighted* exist in Modern English in exactly the same forms. (The line means 'Let us find a time for frightened peace to catch its breath.')

As the many worldwide Shakespearean productions testify to, reciting Shakespeare's plays with their sixteenth-century vocabulary and syntax but with a modern pronunciation enables audiences today to follow the plays with little difficulty. With the support of costumed actors interacting with one another and stage props, there is not much in *Romeo and Juliet, Henry IV,* or *King Lear* that modern audiences fail to grasp.

Far more difficult to understand is Middle English, the language of Chaucer, who lived in London two centuries earlier. Chaucer's *Canterbury Tales,* whose opening lines follow, was the first major book to be printed in England. William Caxton published it in 1476, almost a century after it was written and well after Chaucer's death in 1400.

Whan that Aprill with his shoures soote
The droghte of March hath perced to the roote,
And bathed every veyne in swich licour,
Of which vertu engendred is the flour . . .
Thanne longen folk to goon on pilgrimages.

Although Chaucer's fourteenth-century pronunciation of these words differed dramatically from ours, quite a few of them still have the same written form as they did then.

Try it yourself: Examine the opening lines of the *Canterbury Tales* above and identify ten words besides *that* and *with* that appear exactly the same as Modern English words. Then see if you can spot five others that appear almost, but not exactly, the same as Modern English words.

Several other words in the passage can be recognized, although their Modern English counterparts differ a bit: *droghte* is 'drought,' *perced* 'pierced,' *veyne* 'vein,' *vertu* 'virtue, strength,' and *flour* 'flower.' Others are more opaque, such as *soote*, which is 'sweet'; *swich*, which is 'such'; *thane*, which is 'then'; and the verbs *longen* 'to long' and *goon* 'to go.' As a whole, the Chaucer passage is harder to grasp than the one written by Shakespeare. In the two centuries between Chaucer's death in 1400 and Shakespeare's in 1616, English changed—as languages always do. Chaucer understood language change and the arbitrariness of linguistic form for accomplishing the goals of language, as he indicates in these lines from *Troilus and Criseyde* (II, 22–26), with a modern version on the right.

Ye knowe ek, that in forme of speche is chaunge	You know also that in speech's form (there) is change
Withinne a thousand yeer, and wordes tho	Within a thousand years, and words then
That hadden pris, now wonder nyce and straunge	That had value, now wondrously foolish and strange
Us thinketh hem, and yet thei spake hem so,	To us seem them, and yet they spoke them so,
And spedde as wel in love as men now do.	And fared as well in love as men now do.

The English spoken in Chaucer's time is far enough removed from today's English that students often study the *Canterbury Tales* in "translation"—from fourteenth- into twenty-first-century English. We're not yet so estranged from Shakespeare's language that we require a translation, but published editions of his plays have abundant glosses and footnotes to help explain his language to speakers of Modern English.

If we now examine the language of the epic poem *Beowulf,* written down almost four centuries before Chaucer lived, we are struck by its utterly foreign appearance. Indeed, speakers of Modern English cannot recognize *Beowulf* as English, and it seems as far removed from Modern English as today's Dutch and German are. We don't know the identity of the *Beowulf* poet, but he composed his grim epic about 600 years before Chaucer, who would have found its language about as unintelligible as modern readers do. Here are the first three lines from a *Beowulf* manuscript transcribed around the year A.D. 1000, with a rough word-for-word translation on the right:

Hwæt wē Gār–Dena in geārdagum	What! We of Spear-Danes in yore-days
þēodcyninga þrym gefrūnon,	People's-kings glory have heard,
hū ðā æþelingas ellen fremedon.	How the nobles heroic-deeds did.

A more colloquial rendering might be: *Yes, we have heard of the might of the kings of the Spear-Danes in days of yore, how the chieftains carried out heroic deeds.*

Old English seems "foreign." Scarcely a word in the passage is familiar (although when you have finished reading this chapter, a few may seem not quite so strange). Even certain letters are different: Modern English no longer uses <æ>, <þ>, or <ð>. Still, an imaginative inspection may reveal that some function words remain in present-day English (*wē = we, in = in,* and *hū = how*). Perhaps you also suspected that *hwæt* is *what,* but it is not easy to recognize *geārdagum* as *yore* plus *days* or *cyninga* as *kings.* Even knowing these words, you would find the passage far from transparent. You would need to know the meaning of the nouns *þēod, þrym,* and *æþelingas* (none of which survives in Modern English), the verbs *gefrūnon* and *fremedon,* and the adjective *ellen* (here used as a noun). And given all that lexical information, the syntax of Old English would still be elusive.

WHERE DOES ENGLISH COME FROM?

Where does English come from, and for how long has it been spoken in England? What are its principal ancestors and its closest relatives?

Before the beginning of the modern era, Britain was inhabited by Celtic-speaking peoples, ancestors of today's Irish, Scots, and Welsh. In 55 B.C., Britain was invaded by Julius Caesar, but his attempt to colonize it failed, and the Romans conquered Britain only in A.D. 43. When, subsequently, the Roman legions withdrew in 410, the Celts, who had long been accustomed to Roman protection, were at the mercy of the Picts and the Scots from the north of Britain. In a profoundly important development for the English language, Vortigern, king of the Romanized Celts in Britain, sought help from three Germanic tribes. In 449 these tribes set sail from what is today northern Germany and southern Denmark. When they landed in Britain they decided to settle, leaving the Celts only the remote corners—Scotland, Wales, and Cornwall.

The invaders spoke closely related varieties of West Germanic, the dialects that were to become English. The word *England* derives from the name of one of the tribes, the Angles: thus England, originally *Englaland,* is the 'land of the Angles.' The Old English language used by the early Germanic inhabitants of England and their offspring up to about A.D. 1100 is often called Anglo-Saxon, after two of the tribes (the third tribe was named Jutes). We have no written records of early Anglo-Saxon. The oldest surviving English-language materials come from the end of the seventh century, with an increasing quantity after that, giving rise to an impressive literature, including *Beowulf.*

Once the Anglo-Saxon peoples had settled in Britain, there were additional onslaughts from other Germanic groups starting in 787. In the year 850, a fleet of 350 Danish ships arrived. In 867, Vikings captured York. Danes and Norwegians settled in much of eastern and northern England and from there launched attacks into the kingdom of Wessex in the southwest. In 878, after losing a major battle to King Alfred the Great of Wessex, the Danes agreed by the Treaty of Wedmore to become Christian and to remain outside Wessex in a large section of eastern and northern England that became known as the Danelaw because it was subject to Danish law. After the treaty, Danes and Norwegians were assimilated to Anglo-Saxon life, so much so that 1400 English place names are Scandinavian, including those ending in *-by* 'farm, town' (*Derby, Rugby*), *-thorp* 'village' (*Althorp*), *-thwaite* 'isolated piece of land' (*Applethwaite*), and *-toft* 'piece of ground' (*Brimtoft, Eastoft*).

Attacks from the Scandinavians continued throughout the Viking Age (roughly 750–1050) until finally King Svein of Denmark was crowned king of England and was succeeded almost immediately by his son Cnut in 1016. England was then ruled by Danish kings until 1042, when Edward the Confessor regained the throne lost to the Danes by his father Æthelred. The intermingling between the Anglo-Saxon invaders and the subsequent Scandinavian settlers created a mix of Germanic dialects in England that molded the character of the English language and distinguishes it from its cousins. (You can visit an Anglo-Saxon map of England at http://www.georgetown.edu/cball/oe/oe-map.html.)

English Is a Germanic Language

We noted in Chapter 13 that West Germanic is distinguished from two other branches of the Germanic group of Indo-European languages: North Germanic (which includes Swedish, Danish, and Norwegian) and East Germanic (including only Gothic, which has since died out).

During the first millennium B.C., before Germanic had split into three branches but after it had split from the other branches of Indo-European, Common (or Proto-) Germanic developed certain characteristic features that continue in its daughter languages, setting them apart as a group from all other Indo-European varieties. Among these characteristics are features belonging to every level of grammar: phonology, lexicon, morphology, and syntax.

Consonant Shifts   The most striking phonological characteristic of the Germanic languages, including English, is a set of consonant correspondences found in none of the other Indo-European languages. In 1822, Jacob Grimm, one of the Brothers Grimm of fairytale fame, formulated these correspondences in what is now called "Grimm's Law." Grimm described the sound shifts that had occurred within three natural classes of sounds in developing from Indo-European into Germanic.

Grimm's Law

1. Voiceless stops became voiceless fricatives:

   $p > f$ $t > \theta$ $k > h$

2. Voiced stops became voiceless stops:

   $b > p$ $d > t$ $g > k$

3. Voiced aspirated stops became voiced unaspirated stops:

   $b^h > b$ $d^h > d$ $g^h > g$

The impact of these changes can be seen in Figure 14–1 by examining the shift of voiceless stops in Indo-European to voiceless fricatives in Germanic. We illustrate this shift by citing English words that have inherited the sounds /f θ h/ from Germanic as in part 1 of Grimm's Law and by contrasting them with corresponding words in Romance languages, which (like all the other branches of Indo-European) did not undergo these sound shifts.

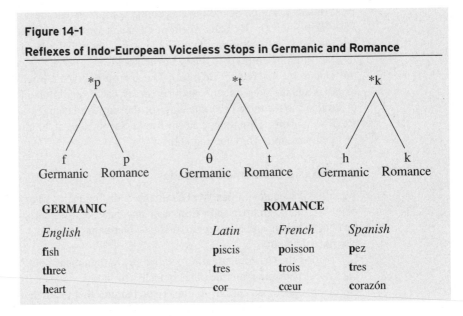

Figure 14-1

Reflexes of Indo-European Voiceless Stops in Germanic and Romance

GERMANIC	ROMANCE		
English	*Latin*	*French*	*Spanish*
fish	piscis	poisson	pez
three	tres	trois	tres
heart	cor	cœur	corazón

Stress Shifts   Another important phonological development of Common Germanic was a shift in stress patterns. Indo-European had variable stress on its words, so that a morpheme could be stressed on a particular syllable in one word but elsewhere in a different word. But in Common Germanic, stress shifted systematically to a word's first or root syllable, where it remained, irrespective of the word in which the morpheme occurred. Compare Modern English 'father, 'fatherly, un'fatherly, and 'fatherless, all of which have stress on the root syllable in the Germanic fashion, with the Greek borrowings 'photograph, pho'tographer, and photo'graphic, which have variable stress in the Indo-European fashion.

Vocabulary   The pattern of consonant shifting described by Grimm's Law set apart the pronunciation of the Germanic vocabulary from that of other Indo-European languages (as seen in the Romance examples in Figure 14–1). In addition, the Germanic languages have a set of words found nowhere else in Indo-European. Once the Germanic tribes separated from the rest of the Indo-European peoples, any words borrowed from speakers of a non-Indo-European tongue or innovated would be distinctively Germanic within Indo-European. Among the English words found in other Germanic languages but not in any other Indo-European languages are the nouns *arm*, *blood, earth, finger, hand, sea,* and *wife;* the verbs *bring, drink, drive, leap,* and *run;* and the adjectives *evil, little,* and *sick.* Here are the strictly Germanic nouns from English and German (to illustrate the similarity among Germanic tongues) and from French (to illustrate the striking contrast between Germanic and Romance languages).

ENGLISH	GERMAN	FRENCH
arm	Arm	bras
blood	Blut	sang
earth	Erd	terre
finger	Finger	doigt
hand	Hand	main
sea	See	mer
wife	Weib	femme

These Germanic words could have existed in Indo-European and been lost in all the daughter languages except Germanic, but that isn't likely, so we can assume they were not inherited from Indo-European but innovated during the Common Germanic period or borrowed from a now-lost source at that time.

Morphology and Syntax in Indo-European

Indo-European—at least at some stages—was a highly inflected language. In fact, Sanskrit, one of the oldest attested Indo-European languages, had eight case inflections on nouns, so it is possible that Indo-European itself had eight cases (although, alternatively, case distinctions absent from Proto-Indo-European could have arisen in the Indic branch to which Sanskrit belongs). If we assume that the rich inflectional morphology of Sanskrit reflects the complexity of Indo-European, then Indo-European nouns would have had eight *cases,* three *numbers* (singular, dual, plural), and three *genders* (masculine, feminine, neuter). Verbs were also highly inflected, probably for two *voices* (active and a kind of passive), four *moods* (indicative, imperative, subjunctive, optative), and three *tenses* (present, past, future). In addition, verbs carried markers for *person* and *number.*

The Indo-European system of indicating verb tenses was principally word internal (as in English *sing/sang/sung).* While this internal sound *gradation* (sometimes called *ablaut)* is typical of Indo-European languages, the typical English inflection for the past tense, pronounced [-t] (*kissed)* or [-d] (*judged),* is characteristically Germanic. Thus the two-tense system, with past tense marked by a dental or alveolar suffix, sets the Germanic group apart from all its Indo-European cousins.

Periods in the History of English

Because languages change continuously, any division into historical stages or periods must be somewhat arbitrary. Scholars have nevertheless divided the history of English into three main periods representing different stages of the language. We now refer to the language spoken in England from the end of the seventh century to the end of the eleventh century (700–1100) as Old English or Anglo-Saxon. The English spoken since 1450 or 1500 is called Modern English. The language spoken in between— roughly from 1100 to 1450 or 1500—is known as Middle English. Thus *Beowulf* is written in Old English, the *Canterbury Tales* in Middle English, and *Henry IV* in (early) Modern English.

OLD ENGLISH: 700-1100

The Angles, Saxons, and Jutes who began to invade England in 449 settled in different parts of the island, and four principal dialects of Old English sprang up: Northumbrian in the north (north of the Humber River); Mercian in the Midlands; Kentish in the southeast; and West Saxon in the southwest (see Figure 14–2). Because Wessex was the seat of the powerful King Alfred, its dialect, West Saxon, achieved a certain status; it forms the basis of most surviving Old English literature and of the study of Old English today.

Like the classical Latin of Roman times and today's German and Russian, Old English was a highly inflected language. It had an elaborate system of inflectional suffixes on nouns, pronouns, verbs, adjectives, and even determiners. Only traces of these inflectional forms survive in Modern English.

Figure 14-2
The Old English Dialects

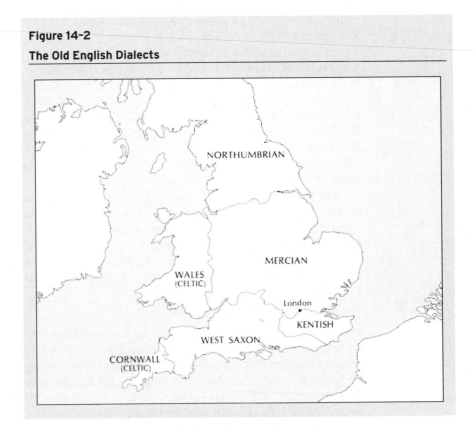

Old English Script

Only a few Old English graphs, or letters, differ from those of Modern English, but they occurred in some of the most frequently used words, giving Old English an exaggerated air of strangeness. Among the graphs no longer used in English are <þ> (called thorn), ð (eth), <ƿ> (wynn), and <æ> (ash). Editors usually let the graphs <þ>, <ð>, and <æ> remain in modern texts but substitute <w> for wynn.

Thorn <þ> and eth <ð> (and their respective capitals <Þ> and <Ð>) were alternative spellings for the sounds [θ] or [ð], which were allophones of a single phoneme in Old English. Scribes did not assign one graph to the sound [θ] and the other to [ð] because, being allophones of a single phoneme, these sounds were not perceived as different. Old English speakers were no more aware of the difference between [θ] and [ð] than Modern English speakers are aware of the different *p* sounds in *pot* and *spot*.

The graph <æ>, rarely used in Modern English, represented a pronunciation in Old English much like the vowel of *hat*. The Old English vowel combinations <ēo> and <ēa> represented the diphthongs [eːɔ] and [ɛːə] respectively. The letter sequence <sc> is equivalent to Modern English <sh> [ʃ], so that Old English *scip* was pronounced just like Modern English *ship*. The letter <c̄> represented one of two sounds: [k] as in *c̄ypmenn* or [tʃ] as in *æðellīce*. The letter <g> represented three sounds: it was pronounced as [j] word-initially when it preceded a front vowel (as in *gelamp* and *gȳt)* and word-finally when it followed one (as in *Rōmānabyrig); else-where it was pronounced as [g] or [ɣ]. The letter <y> was always the high front rounded vowel [ü]. The letters <j> and <q> were not used in Old English, and <k> was rare (hence *folc* 'folk'), although the sounds they represent today did exist as in *cwēn* 'queen' and *cēpan* 'keep.' The letter <x> was an alternative spelling of <cs>, pronounced [ks], as in *axode* [ɑksɔdɛ] 'asked.' Finally, we might mention that <⁊> 'and' was the customary representation in original manuscripts of the Old English equivalent of an ampersand sign <&>.

Old English Sounds

A good deal could be said about the Old English sound system. We'll make only a few comments about some patterns that have implications for the development of Modern English.

Vowels   Old English had long and short vowels and diphthongs, although in late Old English the diphthongs tended to become simplified by being monophthongized. (A similar simplification occurs today in American dialects of the South, in which words such as *time* /tajm/ tend to be pronounced [tʰam]; throughout the United States the pronounciation of *I* is simplified from [aj] to [a] in a phrase such as *I'm gonna* [amgʊnə].) Over the centuries the short vowels have remained relatively constant so that many words are pronounced today much as they were pronounced in Old

English: *fisc* 'fish,' *æt* 'at,' *þorn* 'thorn,' *benc* 'bench,' and *him* 'him.' By contrast, the long vowels have undergone marked changes. Suffice it to say that Old English long vowels had their "continental" values, as in the following words: *stān* [staːn] 'stone,' *sēon* [seːɔn] 'see,' *sōðlice* [soːðliːtʃɛ] 'truly,' *būton* [buːtɔn] 'without, except,' and *swīðe* [swiːðɛ] 'very.'

Consonants Old English permitted certain word-initial consonant clusters that Modern English does not allow; hence /hl/ in *hlud* 'loud,' /hr/ in *hring* 'ring,' and /kn/ in *cniht* 'knight.' Three pairs of sounds whose members are distinct phonemes in Modern English were allophones of single phonemes in Old English: [f] and [v]; [θ] and [ð]; and [s] and [z]. The voiceless allophones [f θ s] occurred at the beginning and end of words and when adjacent to voiceless sounds within words; between voiced sounds, however, the voiced allophones occurred. Thus in the nominative case of the word *wīf* [wiːf], <f> represented the allophone [f], but in the genitive case it represented the allophone [v]: *wifes* [wiːvɛs] (note the final [s], too). The phonemes /s/ and /θ/ figure prominently in the history of English because they occur in so many inflections and function words.

Try it yourself: Using the description given in the paragraph above, determine the allophone of /f/ or /θ/ that occurs in each of these words: *fōt* 'foot,' *līf* 'life,' *heofon* 'heaven,' *stæð* 'shore,' *stæðe* 'shore (dative singular form),' *ōþer* 'other,' *oð* 'until,' *oft* 'often,' *hwæðer* 'whether,' *hǣðen* 'heathen.'

Old English Vocabulary and Morphology

Compounds Old English writers were fond of compounding. The three lines of *Beowulf* cited earlier contain three compounds: *Gār-Dena* meaning 'spear Danes,' *geār + dagum* meaning 'yore days,' and *þēod + cyninga* meaning 'nation kings.' Others from *Beowulf* include *seglrād* 'sail road' and *hrōnrād* 'whale road' for *sea* and *bānhūs* 'bone house' for *body*.

Noun Inflections Old English had several inflections for noun phrases, depending on their grammatical and semantic role in a sentence. Four principal cases could be distinguished: *nominative* (usually for subjects), *genitive* (for possessives and certain other functions), *dative* (for indirect objects and certain other functions), and *accusative* (for direct objects and objects of certain prepositions). Each noun carried a grammatical gender, which occasionally reflected natural gender; *guma* 'man' and *brōðor* 'brother' were masculine, while *brȳd* 'bride' and *sweostor* 'sister' were feminine. But usually gender had little to do with the natural sex of a noun's referent. For example, the nouns *mīl* 'mile,' *wist* 'feast,' and *lēaf* 'permission' were feminine; *hund* 'dog,' *hungor* 'hunger,' *wīfmann* 'woman,' and *wīngeard* 'vineyard' were masculine; and *wīf* 'woman, wife,' *manncynn* 'mankind,' and *scip* 'ship' were neuter. Grammatical gender is simply a category that determined the way a noun was inflected and the inflections on adjectives and other constituents of the noun phrase.

Table 14–1 shows the paradigms for the nouns *fox* 'fox,' *lār* 'learning, lore,' *dēor* 'animal,' and *fōt* 'foot.' From the Old English *fox* declension (*declension* is the name for a noun paradigm) come the only productive Modern English noun inflections: the genitive singular in *-s* and all plurals in *-s*. The *dēor* declension survives in uninflected modern plurals such as *deer* (whose meaning has been narrowed from 'animal') and *sheep,* but new words never follow this pattern. The *fōt* declension has yielded a few nouns (such as *goose, tooth, louse, mouse,* and *man*) whose plurals are signaled by an internal vowel change rather than by the common *-s* suffix. Modern English phrases such as *a ten-foot pole* are relics of the Old English genitive plural ('a pole of ten feet'), whose form *fōta* has yielded *foot.* Over the centuries, most nouns that had been inflected according to other declensions have come to conform to the *fox* paradigm, and new nouns (with the exception of a few loanwords such as *alumni* and *phenomena)* are also inflected like it. Irregular forms of words tend to be relics that have been inherited from earlier regularities.

Table 14-1
Four Old English Noun Declensions

	MASCULINE 'FOX'	FEMININE 'LEARNING'	NEUTER 'ANIMAL'	MASCULINE 'FOOT'
SINGULAR				
Nominative	fox	lār	dēor	fōt
Accusative	fox	lār-e	dēor	fōt
Genitive	fox-es	lār-e	dēor-es	fōt-es
Dative	fox-e	lār-e	dēor-e	fēt
PLURAL				
Nom./Acc.	fox-as	lār-a	dēor	fēt
Genitive	fox-a	lār-a	dēor-a	fōt-a
Dative	fox-um	lār-um	dēor-um	fōt-um

Articles The Modern English definite article *the* has a single orthographic shape with two standard pronunciations, [ði] before vowels and [ðə] elsewhere. In sharp contrast, the Old English demonstratives—forerunners of today's definite article— were inflected for five cases and three genders in the singular and for three cases without gender distinction in the plural (see Table 14–2 on page 510). The fifth case, the instrumental, was used with or without a preposition to indicate such semantic roles as accompaniment or instrument ('with the chieftains,' 'by an arrow'). It's instructive to compare the Old English demonstrative in Table 14–2 with the Modern German definite article in Table 2–10 on page 65. The similarities are striking.

As with Modern English indefinite plural noun phrases (*She writes novels),* Old English indefinite noun phrases frequently lacked an explicit marker of indefiniteness. But sometimes *sum* 'a certain' and *ān* 'one' occurred in the singular for emphasis and were inflected like adjectives.

Table 14-2

Old English Declension of Demonstrative 'that'

	MASCULINE	SINGULAR FEMININE	NEUTER	PLURAL ALL GENDERS
Nominative	sē	sēo	þæt	þā
Accusative	þone	þā	þæt	þā
Genitive	þæs	þǣre	þæs	þāra
Dative	þǣm	þǣre	þǣm	þǣm
Instrumental	þȳ	þǣre	þȳ	þǣm

Adjective Inflections   Old English adjectives owe their complexity to innovations that had arisen in Common Germanic and consequently do not appear in other Indo-European languages.

Old English adjectives were inflected for gender, number, and case to agree with their head noun. There were two adjective declensions. When a noun phrase had as one of its constituents a highly inflected possessive pronoun or demonstrative, adjectives were declined with the so-called weak, or *definite,* declension. In other instances, such as predicative usage (*It's tall*), when indicators of grammatical relations were few or nonexistent, the more varied forms of the strong, or *indefinite,* declension were required. Table 14–3 gives the indefinite and definite adjective paradigms for *gōd* 'good.' Notice that Old English has ten different forms, as compared to the single form *good* in Modern English.

Table 14-3

Old English Declensions of the Adjective 'good'

	SINGULAR MASC.	FEM.	NEUT.	PLURAL MASC.	FEM.	NEUT.
INDEFINITE						
Nom.	gōd	gōd	gōd	gōd-e	gōd	gōd
Acc.	gōd-ne	gōd-e	gōd	gōd-e	gōd	gōd
Gen.	gōd-es	gōd-re	gōd-es	gōd-ra	gōd-ra	gōd-ra
Dat.	gōd-um	gōd-re	gōd-um	gōd-um	gōd-um	gōd-um
Ins.	gōd-e	gōd-re	gōd-e	gōd-um	gōd-um	gōd-um
DEFINITE				*All genders*		
Nom.	gōd-a	gōd-e	gōd-e	gōd-an		
Acc.	gōd-an	gōd-an	gōd-e	gōd-an		
Gen.	gōd-an	gōd-an	gōd-an	gōd-ra (gōd-ena)		
Dat.	gōd-an	gōd-an	gōd-an	gōd-um		

Nothing remains of the Old English inflectional system for adjectives. Today all adjectives occur in a single shape such as *tall, old,* and *beautiful* (with comparative and superlative inflections, as in *taller* and *tallest).* For any gender, number, or case of the modified noun, and for both attributive functions (*the tall ships*) and predicative functions (*the ship is tall),* the form of a Modern English adjective remains invariant.

Personal Pronouns Modern English personal pronouns preserve more of their earlier complexity than any other word class. The Old English paradigms are given in Table 14-4, alongside their modern counterparts. As you can see, besides singular and plural pronouns Old English had a dual number in the first and second persons to refer to exactly two people ('we two' and 'you two'). The dual was already weakening in late Old English and eventually disappeared. So did the distinct number and case forms for the second-person pronoun (*þū* 'thou'/*þē* 'thee' and *gē* 'ye'/*ēow* 'you' are all now *you*) and the distinct dative case form for the third-person-singular neuter pronoun.

Table 14-4

Old English and Modern English Pronouns

			OLD ENGLISH				MODERN ENGLISH			
	FIRST	SECOND	THIRD PERSON			FIRST	SECOND	THIRD PERSON		
			MASC	FEM	NEUT			MASC	FEM	NEUT
SINGULAR										
Nom.	ic	þū	hē	hēo	hit	I	you	he	she	it
Acc.	mē	þē	hine	hie	hit	me	you	him	her	it
Gen.	mīn	þīn	his	hiere	his	mine	yours	his	hers	its
Dat.	mē	þē	him	hiere	him	me	you	him	her	it
DUAL										
Nom.	wit	git								
Acc.	unc	inc								
Gen.	uncer	incer								
Dat.	unc	inc								
			All Genders					*All Genders*		
PLURAL										
Nom.	wē	gē	hīe			we	you	they		
Acc.	ūs	ēow	hīe			us	you	them		
Gen.	ūre	ēower	hiera			ours	yours	theirs		
Dat.	ūs	ēow	him			us	you	them		

Relative Pronouns In Old English, an invariant particle *þe* or *ðe* marked the introduction of a relative clause, though *þe* was often compounded with the demonstrative *sē, sēo, þæt,* as in *sē þe* (for masculine reference) and *sēo þe* (for feminine reference) 'who, that.' Forms of the demonstrative *sē, sēo, þæt* could also occurr alone as relatives:

ānne   æðeling sē   wæs Cyneheard hāten
a   prince   Rel   was   Cyneheard   called
'a prince who was called Cyneheard'

Old English relative clauses were also sometimes introduced by *þe* and a form of the personal pronoun; as in this example with *þe* and *him.*

Nis   nū   cwicra nān   þe ic him mōdsefan mīnne durre āsecgan.
(there) isn't now alive no one Rel I him mind   ' my   dare   speak
'There is no one alive now to whom I dare speak my mind.'

As this example shows, Old English relativized indirect objects (*him*). According to the relative clause hierarchy that we examined in discussing universals in Chapter 7, Old English should also have relativized direct objects and subjects—and in fact it did.

Verbs and Verb Inflections   Like other Germanic languages, Old English had two types of verbs. The characteristically Germanic ones have a [d] or [t] suffix in the past tense (and are called "weak"). The traditional Indo-European ones are called "strong" and show a vowel alternation (as in *sing/sang/sung*). Old English had seven patterns for strong verbs. Table 14–5 lists the principal parts (the forms from which all other inflected forms can be derived) of these seven classes. All the illustrative strong verbs in Table 14–5 survive as irregular verbs in Modern English, but many others have developed into regular verbs in the course of time. For example, *shove, melt, wash,* and *step* followed strong patterns in Old English but are regular in Modern English.

Table 14-5
Seven Classes of Old English Strong Verbs

INFINITIVE	PAST SINGULAR	PAST PLURAL	PAST PARTICIPLE	
1. rīdan	rād	ridon	geriden	'ride'
2. frēosan	frēas	fruron	gefroren	'freeze'
3. drincan	dranc	druncon	gedruncen	'drink'
4. beran	bær	bǣron	geboren	'bear'
5. licgan	læg	lǣgon	gelegen	'lie'
6. standan	stōd	stōdon	gestanden	'stand'
7. feallan	fēoll	fēollon	gefeallen	'fall'

Two tenses (present and past) and two moods (indicative and subjunctive) could be formed from a verb's principal parts. Table 14–6 gives a typical Old English regular verb conjugation for *dēman* 'judge, deem' (*conjugation* is the name for a verb paradigm). Note that the present-tense indicative had three singular forms and one plural, but the present-tense subjunctive had only one singular and one plural form. In contrast to the twelve distinct forms of an Old English weak verb paradigm, the Modern English regular paradigm has only four distinct forms (*judge, judges, judged,* and *judging*) and does not include any distinct subjunctive forms.

Compared to its elaborate Indo-European ancestors and some of its even more elaborate cousins, Old English had a simple verbal system. Old English verbs were inflected for person, number, and tense in the indicative mood and for number and tense in the subjunctive mood; the subjunctive was used more frequently in Old English than in Modern English.

Table 14-6
Conjugation of 'judge, deem' in Old English

	INDICATIVE MOOD	SUBJUNCTIVE MOOD
PRESENT TENSE		
Singular		
first person	dēm-e	
second person	dēm-st (or dēm-est)	dēm-e
third person	dēm-þ (or dēm-eþ)	
Plural		
first, second, and third	dēm-aþ	dēm-en
PAST TENSE		
Singular		
first person	dēm-d-e	
second person	dēm-d-est	dēm-d-e
third person	dēm-d-e	
Plural		
first, second, and third	dēm-d-on	dēm-d-en
GERUND	tō dēm-enne (or dēm-anne)	
PRESENT PARTICIPLE		dēm-ende
PAST PARTICIPLE	dēm-ed	

Inflections and Word Order in Old English

Having a rich inflectional system, Old English could rely on its morphological distinctions to indicate the grammatical relations (subject, object) of nouns (and, to a lesser extent, their semantic roles). Noun phrases had agreement in gender, number, and case among the demonstrative/definite article, the adjective, and the head noun. Adjectives were declined, either definite or indefinite, as already described. Using some of the declensions provided in Tables 14–1, 14–2, and 14–3 on pages 509–510 and two other adjectives, we can form the following Old English noun phrases. Note that in each instance the adjective and demonstrative article *agree* with the noun (that is, they have inflections that match the noun in gender, case, and number).

sē gōda fox	'the good fox' (masculine nominative singular)
gōd dēor	'good animals' (neuter nominative/accusative plural)
þā gōdan fēt	'the good feet' (masculine nominative/accusative plural)
langra fōta	'of long feet' (masculine genitive plural)
þǣre micelan lāre	'of/for the great learning' (feminine genitive/dative singular)

The rich inflectional system operating within Old English noun phrases could indicate grammatical relations and certain semantic roles without having to rely on word order the way Modern English does. Word order was therefore more flexible in Old English than in Modern English. Still, by late Old English, word order patterns were already similar in many respects to those of Modern English. In main clauses, both Old English and Modern English show a preference for SVO order (subject preceding verb preceding object). Modern English prefers SVO in subordinate clauses as well. Old English (like Modern German) preferred verb-final word order (SOV) in subordinate clauses.

As in Modern English, the order of elements in Old English noun phrases was usually determiner-adjective-noun: *sē gōda mann* 'the good man.' Far more frequently than in Modern English, genitives preceded nouns, as in the following:

folces weard	'people's protector'	
mǣres līfes mann	'splendid life's man'	('a man of splendid life')
fōtes trym	'foot's space'	('the space of a foot')

Old English generally had prepositions, although when used with pronouns they often occurred in postposition (that is, after the pronoun), as in this example:

sē	hālga Andreas	him	tō	cwæþ . . .
the	holy Andrew	him	to	said . . .

'St. Andrew said to him . . .'

Like Modern English adjectives, Old English adjectives almost uniformly preceded their head nouns (*sē foresprecena here* 'the aforesaid army'), although they could sometimes follow them:

wadu	weallendu
waters	surging

'surging waters'

As they do in Modern English, relative clauses generally followed their head nouns.

ðā	cyningas	ðe	ðone	onwald	hæfdon
the	kings	who	the	power	had

'the kings who had the power'

COMPANIONS OF ANGELS: A NARRATIVE IN OLD ENGLISH

Figure 14-3

Old English Narrative Written Around the Year 1000

1 Ðā gelamp hit æt sumum sæle, swā swā gyt for oft dēð,
Then happened it at a certain time as yet very oft does,

2 þæt Englisce cȳpmenn brōhton heora ware tō Rōmānabyrig,
that English traders brought their wares to Rome

3 ⁊ Grēgōrius ēode be þære stræt tō ðām Engliscum mannum,
and Gregory went through the street to the English men,
heora ðing scēawigende.
their things looking at.

4 Ðā geseah hē betwux ðām warum cȳpecnihtas gesette,
Then saw he among the wares slaves seated

5 þā wæron hwītes līchaman ⁊ fægeres andwlitan menn, ⁊ æðelīce gefexode.
who were of white body and of fair countenance men, and nobly haired.

6 Grēgōrius ðā behēold þæra cnapena wlite,
Gregory then saw the boys' countenances.

7 ⁊ befrān of hwilcere þēode hī gebrōhte wæron.
and asked from which people they brought were.

8 Ðā sæde him man þæt hī of Englalande wæron,
Then said to him someone that they from England were,

9 ⁊ þæt ðære ðēode mennisc swā wlitig wære.
and that that nation's people so handsome were.

10 Eft ðā Grēgōrius befrān, hwæðer þæs
Again then Gregory asked, whether that

11 landes folc crīsten wære ðe hæðen.
land's people Christian were or heathen.

12 Him man sæde þæt hī hæðene wæron. . . .
Him someone told that they heathen were. . . .

13 Eft hē āxode, hū ðære ðēode nama wære þe hī of cōmon.
Later he asked, how the people's name was that they from came.

14 Him wæs geandswarod, þæt hī Angle genemnode wæron.
To him was answered that they Angles named were.

15 Hwaet, ðā Grēgōrius gamenode mid his wordum tō ðām naman ⁊ cwæð,
Well, then Gregory played with his words on the name and said,

16 "Rihtlīce hī sind Angle gehātene, for ðan ðe hī engla wlite habbað,
"Rightly they are Angles called, because they angels' countenances have.

17 ⁊ swilcum gedafenað þæt hī on heofonum engla gefēran bēon.
and for such it is right that they in heaven angels' companions be.

The Old English passage in Figure 14–3 originates in Bede's *Ecclesiastical History of the English People,* which was completed in A.D. 731 and subsequently translated from Latin into English, perhaps by Alfred the Great during his reign as king of Wessex (871–899). The passage here is a slightly edited version of a later translation by the English abbot Ælfric (c. 955–1020). The story tells how Gregory the Great, who reigned as pope between 590 and 604, first learned of the English people as he walked through a marketplace in Rome and saw boys being sold as slaves. The passage seems as foreign as any language written in the Roman alphabet and more so than some, given its unfamiliar letters. (Don't be shy about reading it aloud, at least in private.)

Vocabulary in the Narrative

There is greater difference between Old English and Modern English in nouns, verbs, and adjectives than in function words.

Function Words   Focusing on prepositions, demonstratives, and pronouns, you'll see notable similarities between the Old English passage and Modern English: in the prepositions *æt* 'at,' *tō* 'to,' *betwux* 'between, among,' *of* 'of, from'; in the conjunction <⅂> 'and,' which occurs more than half a dozen times in the passage; in the conjunction *þā* 'then,' used frequently to introduce sentences. The subordinator *þæt* (lines 8 and 17) was used as it is in Modern English. Some of the personal pronouns functioned exactly as they do in Modern English: *hit* 'it,' *he* 'he,' *hi* 'they,' *him* 'him.' (Note that some of the demonstratives in the passage differ slightly in spelling from those in Table 14–2 on page 510, as with the dative plural *þām* in lines 3 and 4 as compared to *þǣm.*)

Content Words   Some of the unfamiliarity of nouns, verbs, and adjectives is due to inflections (*mannum,* the dative plural of 'man') and much of it to spelling differences or pronunciation rather than to loss or gain of words themselves. Thus you can see earlier forms of the nouns *English, street, thing, men,* and *name* in *Englisce, strǣt, ðing, menn,* and *nama.* In *brōhton, behēold, sǣde,* and *wǣre* are the etymons of the modern verbs *brought, beheld, said,* and *were.* You can see in the verb *to be* the singular past-tense inflection -*e* (*wǣre*) and the plural past-tense inflection -*on* (*wǣron*). Among other words that still exist today are *hwæðer* 'whether,' *hū* 'how,' *crīsten* 'Christian,' and *hǣðen* 'heathen.' Not quite so transparent are a few others that can trigger a flash of recognition once the link is pointed out: *rihtlīce* 'rightly,' *cwæð* 'quoted,' *heofonum* 'heaven,' *engla* 'angel.'

Grammar: Syntax and Morphology in the Narrative

While there was a preference for SVO in main clauses, other orders also occurred. For example, the verb appeared in second position after an introductory adverb such as *þā* (*þā gesēah he,* line 4; note also lines 1 and 8). In subordinate clauses, the verb tended to occur in final position (*þæt hī hǣðene wǣron,* line 12, and 1, 7, 9, 13, 14, and 17). As in Modern English, noun phrases had the order adjective-noun (*sumum sǣle* 'a certain time') or article-noun (*þǣre strǣt* 'the street'), and prepositional phrases had the order preposition-(article)-(adjective)-noun (*æt sumum sǣle, be þǣre strǣt*).

There happen to be no negatives in the passage, but Old English had negative concord (double negative) as in *Nis nū cwicra nān . . .*, the example on page 512.

Text Structure of the Narrative

One striking characteristic of Old English writing was the strong preference for linking sentences with <⅂> 'and' and *þā* 'then,' much as in Modern English oral narratives. Subordinators that made explicit the relation between one clause and another (*because, since, until, when*) existed in Old English but their frequent use in writing was a later development. More typically in Old English writing (as in Modern English conversation) clauses are introduced with 'and' or 'then' as in lines 1, 3, 4, 8, and 17. In addition to the relative clauses, the passage contains a few other examples of subordination: *swā swā* 'as' in line 1, *hwæðer* 'whether' in line 10, and *for ðan ðe* 'because' in line 16.

MIDDLE ENGLISH: 1100–1500

Middle English is a term used to refer to a period of great variation and instability in the history of English.

The Norman Invasion

In the year 1066, William, Duke of Normandy, sailed across the Channel to claim the English throne. After winning the Battle of Hastings, he was crowned king of England in Westminster Abbey on Christmas Day, and with that coronation Anglo-Saxon England passed into history. Thus was a Norman kingdom established in England, and for generations the king of England and the duke of Normandy would be one person. The Norman invasion would reshape England's institutions and exercise a profound effect on its language.

The Norman French spoken by the invaders quickly became the language of England's ruling class, while the lower classes still spoke English. Following the invasion, English had a recess from many of the duties it had previously performed. In particular, it was relieved of many of its functions in the affairs of government, the court, the church, and education; all these important activities were now conducted in French. Indeed, for two centuries after the conquest, the kings of England could not speak the language of many of their subjects, and English-speaking subjects could not understand their king. Richard the Lion-Hearted, the most famous king of this period, was in every way French. During his ten-year reign (1189–1199), he visited England only twice and stayed a total of less than ten months. Eventually the middle classes became bilingual, speaking to peasants in English and to the ruling classes in French.

After 1200 the situation began to change. In 1204 King John lost Normandy to King Philip of France, and on both sides of the Channel decrees were issued commanding that no one could own land in both England and France. Cut off from its Norman origins, the force that had sustained the use of French in England began to collapse.

Middle English Vocabulary

A hundred years later, at the beginning of the fourteenth century, English came to be known again by all inhabitants of England. Not surprisingly, though, the English that emerged was strikingly different from the English used prior to the Norman invasion. The vocabulary of Middle English was spiced by thousands of Norman French words as speakers learning English used French words for things whose English labels they no longer knew. Based on calculations by Otto Jespersen, it has been estimated that approximately 10,000 French words came into English during the Middle English period, and most of them remain in use today. Especially plentiful were words pertaining to religion, government, the courts, and the army and navy, although many borrowings relate to food, fashion, and education—those arenas in which the invaders and their successors had wielded great influence in England.

Once English had been reestablished as the language of the law, the residents of England found themselves without sufficient English terminology to carry on the activities that had been conducted for centuries in French. Hence a good many French legal terms were borrowed, including even the words *justice* and *court*. To discuss events in a courtroom today, the following words—all borrowed from French during the Middle English period—are used: *judgment, plea, verdict, evidence, proof, prison,* and *jail*. The actors in a courtroom now have French names: *bailiff, plaintiff, defendant, attorney, jury, juror,* and *judge*. The names of certain crimes are French, including *felony, assault, arson, larceny, fraud, libel, slander,* and *perjury,* and so is the word *crime* itself. We have cited examples only from the law (a word that derives from Old English *lagu*) and by no means all of them. Extensive lists of French borrowings could also be provided for the other arenas in which the French were socially and culturally influential.

Middle English Sounds

There was considerable change in some vowels and consonant patterns between Old English and the end of Middle English.

Vowels   Most long vowels of Old English remained unchanged in Middle English. But the Old English long vowel /ɑː/ in words like *bān, stān,* and *bāt* became long /ɔː/ (and in Modern English /o/) as in *boon* 'bone,' *stoon* 'stone,' and *boot* 'boat.' Many diphthongs were simplified in late Old English and early Middle English. Thus the vowels of *sēon* 'see' and *bēon* 'be' were monophthongized to long /eː/, a sound that later became [i] in Modern English.

Short vowels in unstressed syllables, which had been kept distinct at least in early West Saxon, tended to merge in schwa [ə], usually written <e>.

Consonants and Consonant Clusters   The Old English initial consonant clusters /hl-/, /hn-/, /hr-/, and /kn-/ were simplified to /l/, /n/, and /r/, losing their initial /h/ or /k/: *hlāf* 'loaf,' *hlot* 'lot,' *hnecca* 'neck,' *hnacod* 'naked,' *hrōf* 'roof,' *hræfn* 'raven,' *hring* 'ring,' *cnīf* 'knife,' *cnoll* 'knoll,' *cniht* 'boy, knight.' Of considerable consequence was the merging of word-final /m/ and /n/ in a single sound (/n/) when they occurred in unstressed syllables (*foxum > foxun*). Significantly, unstressed syllables included *all* the inflections on nouns, adjectives, and verbs. By the end of the Middle English period even this /n/ was dropped altogether (*foxun > foxen > foxe*), and the final *-e* was also eventually dropped.

Middle English Inflections

Three of the phonological changes just mentioned had a profound effect on the morphology of Middle English.

1. -m > -n
2. -n > Ø
3. a, o, u, e > e [ə] (when not stressed)

Figure 14–4 shows how, as a consequence of these few sound changes, certain sets of Old English inflections merged, becoming indistinguishable in Middle English and being further reduced or dropped altogether in early Modern English. As a result of these mergers, the Old English noun and adjective paradigms became greatly simplified in Middle English, and grammatical gender disappeared altogether (see Table 14–7 on page 520).

Figure 14-4

The Historical Reduction of English Inflections

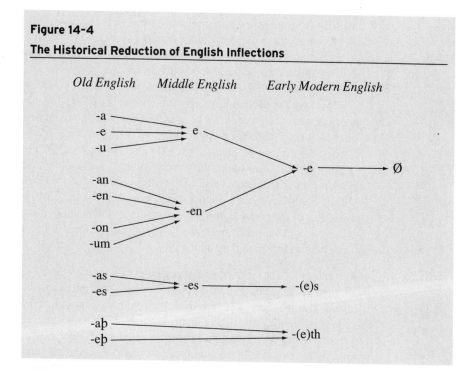

Table 14-7

Four Middle English Noun Declensions

	'FOX'	'LORE'	'ANIMAL'	'FOOT'
SINGULAR				
Nom./Acc.	fox	loor	deer	foot
Genitive	foxes	loor(e)	deeres	footes
Dative	fox(e)	loor(e)	deer(e)	foot
PLURAL				
Nom./Acc.	foxes	loor(e)	deer	feet
Genitive/Dative	foxes	loor(e)	deer(e)	foot(e)

Nouns   The frequently used subject and object noun phrase forms (nominative and accusative cases) established the nominative and accusative plural form *foxes* (and the *-es* inflection for other nouns in general) throughout the plural. They also established the nominative and accusative singular throughout the singular except that the genitive in *-s* was maintained. Thus the Middle English paradigm for a noun such as *fox* came to be what it is in Modern English: *fox* and *foxes* in the singular (*foxes* is now spelled *fox's*) and *foxes* throughout the plural (possessive *foxes'*).

In some other noun paradigms, damage to the morphological distinctions caused by the merging of unstressed vowels was even greater. Old English *dēor* was reduced to three forms (*deer/deeres/deere*), while *lār* was reduced to two (*loor* and *loore*), with a distinction that was then lost when final inflected *-e* vanished about 1500.

We have the Modern English forms of the word *deer* (*deer* and *deer's*) from the nominative and accusative singular inflection, which were extended throughout the singular (except that the ending in *-s* has been kept in the genitive). The parallel nominative and accusative plural form extended throughout the plural (except that by analogy with all other nouns the genitive plural adds *-s* to the form of the nominative plural). From the *foot* declension, the origin of the Modern English forms are clear: Middle English nominative and accusative *foot* was extended throughout the singular, with the *-s* of the genitive form *footes* maintained; the nominative and accusative plural *feet* was extended throughout the plural (and, as usual, the inflected genitive is formed by adding *-s* to the nominative).

Adjectives   The merging of distinct inflections that collapsed the noun declensions also had a drastic effect on adjectives. The only indefinite forms to survive the phonological change from Old English were *goodne* (masculine accusative singular), *goodes* (masculine and neuter genitive singular), and *goodre* (feminine genitive, dative, and instrumental singular, and genitive plural). Then *good* became the universal form for the singular. In the plural, the nominative, accusative, and dative forms for all genders became *good,* and by analogy the genitive plural also became *good*. That left *good* as the only form in the singular and plural, which yielded Modern English *good* as the invariable form of the adjective (comparative and superlative forms aside).

In the definite declension, the only forms to survive were *good* and *goodre.* Then *goodre* was re-formed to *good* by analogy (whereby one form takes on the shape of other forms in the same or another paradigm), thus leaving only a single definite adjective form, which was the same as the indefinite. Astonishingly, a few simple phonological changes (and some analogical adaptations) reduced the complexity of Old English adjectives to the striking simplicity of today's.

Middle English Word Order

Much could be said about Middle English syntax, but the language changed so thoroughly during the four centuries of this period that a good deal of provision would have to be made for intermediate stages. Since we have described Old English and Modern English syntax, suffice it to say that Middle English was a transitional period, especially with respect to the change from relying on inflection to relying on word order for a considerable amount of information about grammatical relations. As the inflections of Old English disappeared, the word order of Middle English became increasingly fixed. The communicative work previously accomplished for nouns by inflectional morphology still needed doing, and it fell principally to prepositions and word order to perform these tasks. We have already said that Old English preferred SVO word order in main clauses and SOV in subordinate clauses. The exclusive use of the SVO pattern emerged in the twelfth century and remains part of English today.

WHERE MEN AND WOMEN GO ALL NAKED: A MIDDLE ENGLISH TRAVEL FABLE

You can now see how some of these features of morphology and syntax came together in Middle English prose. Figure 14–5 on page 522 is a passage from *The Travels of John Mandeville.* It's a translation of Mandeville's French work by an unknown English writer in the early fifteenth century (about the time of Chaucer's death in 1400). These popular travel fables survive in several hundred manuscripts. In our passage, Mandeville describes a fabulous place called Lamary.

We analyze the passage with a view to how English of the early fifteenth century differs from today's. First of all, the passage is intelligible, although you can note a few marked differences (and some subtle ones) between it and today's English.

Vocabulary in the Fable

Not a single word in the passage will be unknown to you, although a few (such as *lond* 'land,' *hete* 'heat,' *ʒeer* 'year,' *byʒen* 'buy,' and *hem* 'them') might not be instantly recognizable. (The graph <ʒ>, called *yogh,* was pronounced [j], like <y> in *you.*) Not all the words borrowed from French during the Middle English period immediately took their current form, but most are nevertheless transparent: *custom, strange, clothed, nature, comoun, clos, contradiccioun, contree, habundant, marchauntes.*

Figure 14-5

A Travel Fable Written in Middle English around the Year 1400

1 In þat lond is full gret hete,
   In that land is very great heat,

2 and the custom þere is such þat men and wommen gon all naked.
   and the custom there is such that men and women go all naked.

3 And þei scornen, whan thei seen ony strange folk goynge clothed.
   And they scorn, when they see any strange folk going clothed.

4 And þei seyn, þat god made Adam and Eue all naked
   And they say, that God made Adam and Eve all naked

5 and þat no man scholde schame him to schewen him such as god made him;
   and that no man should shame himself to show himself such as God made him;

6 for no thing is foul þat is of kyndely nature . . .
   for no thing is foul that is of natural nature . . .

7 And also all the lond is comoun; for all þat a man
   And also all the land is common; for all that a man

8 holdeth o ȝeer, another man hath it anoþer ȝeer,
   keeps one year, another man has it another year,

9 and euery man taketh what part þat him lyketh.
   and every man takes what part that him pleases.

10 And also all the godes of the lond ben comoun, cornes and all oþer þinges;
   And also all the goods of the land are common, grains and all other things;

11 for no þing þere is kept in clos, ne no þing þere is vndur lok,
   for no thing there is kept in a closet nor no thing there is under lock,

12 and euery man þere taketh what he wole, withouten ony contradiccioun.
   and every man there takes what he wants, without any contradiction.

13 And als riche is o man þere as is another.
   And as rich is one man there as is another.

14 But in þat contree þere is a cursed custom:
   But in that country there is a cursed custom:

15 for þei eten more gladly mannes flesch þan ony oþer flesch.
   for they eat more gladly man's flesh than any other flesh.

16 And ȝit is þat contree habundant of flesch, of fissch,
   And yet is that country abundant with flesh, with fish,

17 of cornes, of gold and syluer, and of all oþer godes.
   with grains, with gold and silver, and with all other goods.

18 Þider gon marchauntes and bryngen with hem children,
   Thither go merchants and bring with them children,

19 to selle to hem of the contree; and þei byȝen hem.
   to sell to them of the country; and they buy them.

20 And ȝif þei ben fatte, þei eten hem anon; and ȝif þei ben lene,
   And if they are fat, they eat them at once; and if they are lean,

21 þei feden hem till þei ben fatte, and þanne þei eten hem.
   they feed them until they are fat, and then they eat them.

22 And þei seyn, þat it is the best flesch and the swettest of all the world.
   And they say, that it is the best flesh and the sweetest of all the world.

Morphology in the Fable

In the fable, only a few inflections remain from Old English that have not survived in Modern English. For example, third-person singular present-tense verbs end in *-(e)th: holdeth, hath, lyketh, taketh,* and plural present-tense verbs end in *-n* or *-en: gon, scornen, seyn, ben, eten, bryngen, byȝen,* and others. This *-n* or *-en* is not the direct reflex of the Old English plural form *-aþ* but was apparently introduced from the subjunctive plural (see Table 14–6 on page 513) so as to maintain a distinction between the singular and the plural, which otherwise would have been lost when the unstressed vowels of the singular *-eþ* and the plural *-aþ* merged to give Middle English *-eth* for both forms (see Figure 14–4 on page 519). As shown in line 3 of Figure 14–5, Mandeville's translator alternates between the spellings *þei* and *thei* for the third-person plural subject pronoun, but the *þ/th* forms of the objective case do not yet appear in this passage, which instead shows the objective form *hem* (lines 19, 20, and 21). Otherwise, several of the Modern English inflections have their current form (after slight spelling adjustments): *goynge* 'going,' *clothed, godes* 'goods,' *þinges* 'things,' *marchauntes* 'merchants,' and *swettest* 'sweetest.' Even certain words that had kept their exceptional forms from Old English are the same or nearly the same in 1400 and today: *men, wommen, folk, children,* and *best.* Being among the more common words they were more likely to maintain their unusual forms than were less frequently used words.

Syntax in the Fable

One notable difference in syntax occurs in the first line. Where Modern English requires a so-called "dummy subject" (one without a referent), Middle English did not: *In þat lond is* . . . . But note the dummy *þere* in line 14: *But in þat contree þere is* . . . . Another feature is the negative concord (double negative) *ne no þing* 'nor nothing' in line 11.

There are marked word order differences. In line 13, compare this word-for-word equivalent with its current English version (which follows the slash): *And as rich is one man there as is another/And one man there is as rich as another.* Note, too, that the adverbial phrase *more gladly* (line 15) follows its verb instead of preceding it as it would in Modern English. Finally, note the relic of Old English verb-second word order in line 18 (*Thither go merchants*) and the prepositional phrase *with hem* in the same line, which in Modern English would follow the direct object *children.*

Among subtler syntactic differences is the use of *scorn* as an intransitive verb (that is, without a direct object) in line 3. In Modern English, *scorn* requires a direct object: you must scorn something or someone. Note, too, the use of the nonreflexive pronoun *him* in line 5. You can note another difference in line 9, where the object form *him* complements the verb *lyketh* (in a benefactive semantic role); *him lyketh* literally translates *to him (it) likes* 'it pleases him.' Since Old English times, this "impersonal" construction had not required a subject but a dative (or, later, objective) case form of the pronoun. It resembles the French *s'il vous plait* 'if it you pleases,' which may have influenced the now archaic formulation *if it please you* or *if it please my lord.*

We may overlook some of the syntactic differences between this passage and current English because we are accustomed to finding relatively conservative syntax in such places as the King James Bible and certain formal prose styles such as legalese. Still, this Middle English passage, now six centuries old, is obviously English and surprisingly transparent.

MODERN ENGLISH: 1500–PRESENT

Chapters 2 through 6 of this book examined the structure of twentieth-century English in detail, and there is no need to recapitulate that material here. This section focuses instead on what changes occurred in the earliest stages of Modern English to move the language from the forms of Middle English to those we know today.

Early and Late Modern English

As our analysis of Mandeville's travel fable shows, by the beginning of the fifteenth century Middle English had developed many of the principal syntactic patterns we know today. The complex inflectional system of Old English had been simplified ("destroyed" may be a more accurate description); and today's system, with fewer than ten inflections, had emerged. Most nouns that had been inflected in Old English according to various patterns now conformed to the *fox* pattern. By the time of Shakespeare, third-person plural pronouns with *th*- instead of *h*- (*they, their,* and *them*) had been in general use for a century; Chaucer and the Mandeville translator had used *they,* but both still used the older possessive form *her* (*their*) and objective form *hem* (*them*). In addition, word order had become more fixed, essentially as it is in Modern English.

The language of the late 1400s is in most ways Modern English—although we should be mindful that a dramatic shifting of English vowels took place sometime between 1450 and 1650, when all the long vowels markedly changed their quality, as we'll see. That phonological change is not apparent simply because the modern spelling of English vowels had essentially been established by the time of William Caxton, who founded his printing press in the vicinity of Westminster Abbey in 1476, before the shift had progressed very far. Caxton's spellings disguise the fundamental alteration that has occurred in the system of English vowels.

Phonology: The English Vowel Shift

In the Mandeville travel passage, certain words are easily recognized by their similar spellings to Modern English. In particular, the words *gret, hete, schame,* and *foul* are similar to their modern counterparts. The written similarity, however, disguises the fact that the words as *pronounced* in Chaucer's time would not likely be recognizable by a modern listener. Sometime during the two centuries between 1450 and 1650, all the long vowels of Middle English underwent a systematic shift. Each long front vowel was raised and became pronounced like another vowel higher in the system, and each long back vowel was raised and pronounced like the vowel next higher in the vowel chart. Thus /ɔː/ came to be pronounced /oː/, /eː/ came to be pronounced /iː/, and so on. The two highest long vowels, /iː/ and /uː/, could not be raised any farther and instead were diphthongized to /aj/ and /aw/ respectively. Thus Middle English *I* /iː/ became /aj/, *hous* /huːs/ became /haws/ 'house,' and so on. We can represent the situation as in Figure 14–6.

Figure 14-6
The English Vowel Shift

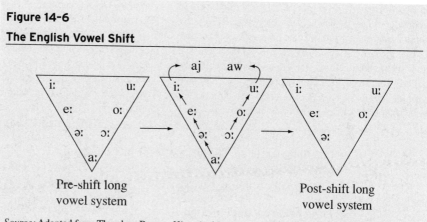

Pre-shift long
vowel system

Post-shift long
vowel system

Source: Adapted from Theodora Bynon, *Historical Linguistics* (Cambridge: Cambridge University Press, 1977), p. 82.

Modern English Morphology

Verbs   Of the hundreds of strong (irregular) verbs in Old English, relatively few survive in Modern English. Of those that do, many are now inflected as regular verbs. One tally suggests that of the 333 strong verbs of Old English, only 68 continue as irregular verbs in Modern English. Among those that have become regular over the centuries are *burned, brewed, climbed, flowed, helped,* and *walked.* By contrast, slightly more than a dozen weak verbs have become irregular in the history of English, including *dive,* which has developed a past-tense form *dove* alongside the historical form *dived.* You may also have heard *drug* for *dragged,* as its use seems to be increasing. Among other verbs that are now irregular but were formerly regular are *wear, spit,* and *dig,* with their newer past-tense forms *wore, spat,* and *dug.*

Definite Article   The initial consonant of *sē* and *sēo,* the Old English masculine and feminine nominative singular demonstrative, differed from all other forms, which began with [θ] (orthographic <þ>). *Sē* was reshaped, apparently by analogy with forms having initial [θ]. By Middle English, *þe* had become the invariant definite article in the north of England, and its use soon spread to the other dialects. Chaucer uses only *the,* pronounced [θə], not [ðə]. The voicing of the initial consonant as we know it today occurred because the customary lack of stress on *the* encouraged assimilation to the vowel nucleus, which is voiced.

Ye Olde Book Shoppe

In the early fourteenth century some English writers merged the runic letter <þ> and the Roman letter <y> in their manuscripts, setting the stage for readers to confuse the two graphs. In the fifteenth century, the use of <þ> decreased, but even Chaucer, who died in 1400, generally used <th> where earlier writers had used <þ>. Some writers and printers of the time used yᵉ, yᵗ, yᵉⁱ, yᵐ, yᵘ to represent the words *the, that, they, them,* and *thou,* and such abbreviations (or *compendia,* as they are called) continued in manuscripts into the eighteenth century. In books printed as late as the sixteenth century you can find yᵉ for *the* (sometimes with <e> superscripted directly above <y>) and yᵗ for *that* (also sometimes with <t> appearing directly above <y>). Among the citations listed in the *Oxford English Dictionary* are these from eighteenth-century letters: "I am to inform you yt ye Duchess continues as well as can be, and ye Babe too" and "He told yᵐ yt ye French was landing in the Marsh." Certain of these shorthand forms continued into nineteenth-century correspondence as well. As for current use of <y> for <th>, the *OED* characterizes it as "pseudoarchaic" and gives as examples Lewis Carroll's "Ye Carpette Knighte" and shop signs like "Ye Olde Booke Shoppe."

Indefinite Article   The history of the indefinite article *a/an* is also remarkable, for while Old English did not use an indefinite article, *a/an* is among the top ten most common words in English today.

Personal Pronouns   Although the personal pronouns retain more of their Old English diversity than any other part of speech, our earlier comparison of Old and Modern English pronouns (Table 14–4 on page 511) indicates that the dual number was lost entirely (starting at the beginning of the Middle English period). During the early Modern English period, the distinction between the second-person singular and plural forms—between singular *thou* and *thee* (Old English *þū* and *þē*) and plural *ye* and *you* (Old English *gē* and *ēow*)—disintegrated.

Under the apparent influence of French, speakers of English began using the plural forms *ye, your,* and *you* as a sign of respect or formality, much as happens with French *vous,* which is grammatically plural but is used to show respect and deference when addressing a solitary stranger, elder, or social superior. Among the upper social classes in England, the historical plural form *you* came to be used as a mutual sign of respect even in informal conversation between equals. In time, the singular forms all but disappeared, along with the distinction between the plural subject and plural object forms *ye* and *you.* Thus, from the sixfold distinction found in Old English and much of Middle English, Modern English has only a twofold distinction—between *you* and *yours.*

Many Modern English speakers find it difficult to get along without a distinct second-person plural pronoun, and some varieties have created new plural forms. These forms are regionally marked (*y'all* in the American South) or socially stigmatized (*youse,* pronounced [juz], [jɪz], or [jəz] in New York City and parts of Ireland and England, and *y'uns,* pronounced [jənz] or [jɪnz] in western Pennsylvania and the northern Ohio valley). Standard English has no way to mark the second-person pronoun for plurality, although of course one can say such things as *you two* or *you all.* Increasingly heard as an informal plural, at least in American English, is *you guys.*

Modern English Word Order

Deprived of its earlier inflectional signposts to meaning, Modern English has become an analytical language—more like Chinese than Latin. With nouns inflected only for the possessive case (and for number), word order is now the chief signal of grammatical relations such as subject and object. Pronouns preserve more case distinctions than nouns, but even pronouns are subordinate to the grammatical relations that word order signals, so that *Him and me saw her at the party,* though not standard, is not confusing in any way as to subject and object.

Why English advanced farther than its Germanic cousins along the path to becoming an analytical language (rather than remaining an inflected one) is not altogether clear. Possible explanations may be found in the thoroughgoing contact between the Danes and the English after the ninth century, in the French ascendance over English for numerous secular and religious purposes in the early Middle English period, and in the preservation of the vernacular chiefly in folk speech and therefore without the conservationist brake of writing for several generations in the eleventh and twelfth centuries. The influence of the Danes is particularly important. When they invaded England in the eighth and ninth centuries, they spoke varieties of Germanic that must have been quite similar to the dialects spoken in England, but their varieties had different inflections. It's easy to imagine that children exposed to parents using different inflectional suffixes and to friends whose inflectional suffixes were not uniform might look for other means to signal the differences indicated by these competing inflections.

In any case, decades before the Norman Conquest in 1066, those inflectional reductions started that became apparent when English reemerged. Doubtless they had advanced further in speech than the written texts of the day indicate. Thus phonological reductions undermined the inflectional morphology, and, as inflection grew less able to signal grammatical relations and semantic roles, word order and the deployment of prepositions came to bear those communicative tasks less redundantly. Gradually, the freer word order of Old English yielded to the relatively fixed order of Modern English, in which linear arrangements of words are the chief marker of grammatical functions.

Spurred by an almost total absence of inflections on nouns, Modern English syntax has evolved to permit unusually free interplay among grammatical relations and semantic roles. With nouns marked only for possessive case and pronouns marked for possessive and objective cases, Modern English exercises minimal inflectional constraint on subject noun phrases, which are consequently free to represent an exceptionally wide range of semantic roles (as illustrated in Chapter 6 on page 209).

Modern English Vocabulary

As in the course of the Middle English period, when English supplanted French and borrowed thousands of French words, so in the course of early Modern English, as English came to be used for functions Latin had previously served, a great many words were borrowed from Latin (and through Latin from Greek). The borrowed words are learned words, reflecting the arenas in which Latin was used. Even with these borrowings, English found itself in need of many more words as it spread into every sphere of activity. The *Oxford English Dictionary* records loan words from about fifty different languages borrowed during the first century and a half of Modern English (1500–1650) when the vernacular replaced Latin in nearly every learned arena.

Among the Latin borrowings of this period are the following nouns (we limit ourselves to some beginning with the letter *a):*

allusion	*appendix*
anachronism	*atmosphere*
antipathy	*autograph*
antithesis	*axis*

Among the adjectives are *abject, agile,* and *appropriate;* among the verbs, *adapt, alienate,* and *assassinate.* Some of these words, although introduced to English from Latin, came originally from Greek. During the Renaissance, some other words were borrowed directly from Greek, including these:

acme	*idiosyncrasy*
anonymous	*lexicon*
catastrophe	*ostracize*
criterion (and *criteria*)	*polemic*
tantalize	*tonic*

Not everyone in England appreciated borrowed words, and writers who used these then-strange terms were sometimes criticized for their "inkhorn" words. Not every borrowed term survived.

How Computers Track Change in English

A project of major importance for the study of the history of English is the digitizing of the *Oxford English Dictionary* (*OED*). The *OED* is a mammoth multivolume dictionary recording every word that has appeared in English printed materials since the Old English period. Or perhaps we should say *nearly* every word, for the *OED* was compiled during Victorian times and not *every* word of English was allowed free access to its Victorian pages. Among words you won't find in the original *OED* are the infamous four-letter "Anglo-Saxonisms" familiar to everyone. The *OED* took half a century to complete, and by time the final volume was published in 1928, a good deal more

had been learned about the words at the beginning of the alphabet, which had appeared in the earliest volumes. That new information required a large supplemental volume. In the 1970s a further supplement was again needed, and it ballooned into four large volumes, so much had the language changed since the previous supplement in 1933. Then, in 1989, the original twelve volumes were digitized with the five supplemental volumes incorporated, creating a second edition of this grand dictionary, which appeared in twenty large volumes weighing 137 pounds and taking up nearly four feet of shelf space. The second edition of the *OED* was made available on a compact disc, not only smaller and less expensive but much easier to use and more efficient. With access to the CD-ROM, you can readily search through a thousand years of English language history and find citations for any word that interests you, along with information about the author, date, and source for each citation. You can determine the date of a word's first recorded use; you can limit your search to any time period or author. The CD-ROM makes it possible to discover all the words that entered the language in a specified time period or all the words borrowed from a particular language—say, Japanese or French or Hindi.

Several major historical corpora of English have been compiled in recent years. In the previous chapter, we discussed the Helsinki Corpus and ARCHER. Corpora such as these have made possible previously unknown information about the history of English. Accessibility to these corpora has given researchers an opportunity to explore the history of particular structures or words.

SUMMARY

- English belongs to the West Germanic group of the Germanic branch of the Indo-European language family. It is *not* descended from Latin, but both Latin and English are members of the Indo-European language family and are descended from Proto-Indo-European.

- In the course of its history, English has been greatly enriched by thousands of loan words from more than 100 languages—most notably French, as the descendants of the Norman invaders started using English in the thirteenth century, and Latin, when the vernacular came to be used during the Renaissance in arenas previously reserved for the classical language.

- *Beowulf* is an epic poem of the Old English period (700–1100). Chaucer (1340–1400) wrote during the Middle English period (1100–1500). Shakespeare (1564–1616) wrote early in the Modern English period (1500–present).

- Old English was a highly inflected language, but sound changes subsequently eroded most of the inflectional morphology.

- As a result of the erosion of inflections in the Middle English period, Modern English is an analytical language, relying principally on word order to express grammatical relations that were formerly marked by inflections.

WHAT DO YOU THINK? REVISITED

❖ *Ye Olde Coffee Shoppe.* Scoffing Scott is wrong, and the information in the menu is right. "Ye" in the shop name is a misinterpretation of the letter thorn Þ or its lower case variant þ as it appeared in the word "the." Far from being hogwash, this use of "Ye" underscores the tentative relationship between a sound and its representation in writing.

❖ *San Diego and Santa Monica.* Many cities in California and the Southwest carry names given them by the Spaniards when they first established missions there. These are names of saints: *San* is the masculine form in Spanish and *Santa* the feminine form of 'saint.' Place names elsewhere reveal the cultural contacts of the settlers in those places.

❖ *English and German inflections.* About 1000 years ago, German and English had about the same number of inflections on nouns, and those inflections have remained relatively constant in the course of the history of German. In contrast, as English developed, a few sound changes in unstressed syllables led to the merging of various endings. Once that happened, their usefulness was greatly reduced and they faded from use.

❖ *Irregular English plurals.* In Old English, nouns including *sheep* and *deer* belonged to a group that had different endings (that is, belonged to a different declension) from those nouns that became the modern-day ones ending in *-s*.

EXERCISES

14-1 Any Modern English word that was borrowed from Latin or Greek does not show the influence of Grimm's Law, which affected only the Germanic branch of Indo-European. For many such borrowed words, English also has a word that it inherited directly from Indo-European through Germanic. Of course, any such inherited word would have undergone the consonant shifts described by Grimm. For each *borrowed* word below, cite an English word that is related in meaning and whose pronunciation shows the result of the consonant shift. For this exercise, focus only on the initial consonant of each word.

Example: Given *pedal,* you would seek a word like *foot,* which has a related meaning and begins with [f] (because Indo-European [p] became [f] in Germanic).

cardiac	paternal	plenitude	cordial
dual	pentagon	dentist	canine
capital	piscatory	triangle	decade

14-2 This exercise is like the preceding one, except here you're given English words that have undergone the Germanic consonant shift. You must provide another English word that is likely to have been borrowed because it has a closely related meaning but does *not* show the results of Grimm's Law. Bear in mind that Latin and Greek borrowings tend to be more learned or technical than the related ones inherited directly from Indo-European. Focus only on the boldfaced consonant.

Example: Given *foot,* you would seek a word that begins with [p] such as *podiatrist* 'foot doctor.'

tooth	**lip**	**fire**
ten	**hound**	**eat**

14-3 You know that, by the effects of Grimm's Law, Indo-European $*b^h$ became [b] and Indo-European $*g^h$ became [g] in Germanic. Not being a Germanic language, Latin did not undergo these consonant shifts. Instead, in Latin, Indo-European $*b^h$ became [f] and $*g^h$ became [h]. We represent these facts in the following correspondences:

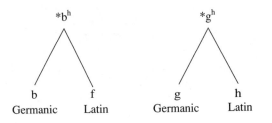

Given this information, provide an English word inherited directly from Indo-European for each of the following words, which are all borrowed from Latin, sometimes via French or another Romance language. Focus on the initial consonant, bearing in mind that other changes may have affected the remainder of the word.

fraternity	flame
fundamental	hospitable
fragile	fracture

14-4 Indicate which allophone of /f/, /θ/, or /s/ was pronounced in each of the following Old English words (use the description of the allophonic distribution given on p. 508 to help you determine the correct answer): þæt, sēo, his, ūs, wæs, æðeling 'prince,' frēosan 'freeze,' dēmst 'judge,' līfes 'of life,' þā 'then,' drīfan 'drive,' wulfas 'wolves,' hræfn 'raven,' bosm 'bosom,' seofon 'seven,' bæþ 'bath,' sceaft 'shaft.'

14-5 a. Identify the grammatical gender of the following Old English nouns and give the genitive singular and nominative plural forms for each of them.

sē stān	'the stone'
þæt word	'the word'
sēo wund	'the wound'

b. For each of these Old English noun phrases, provide the Old English pronoun that would be used in the space given.

Sē stān, _____ is gōd.	'The stone, it is good.'
Ðæt word, _____ is gōd.	'The word, it is good.'
Sēo wund, _____ nis gōd.	'The wound, it isn't good.'

14-6 Compare the Old English passage on p. 515 with the Middle English passage on p. 522 and identify ways in which Middle English differs from Old English in orthography, vocabulary, morphology, and word order. Provide an example from the passages to illustrate each point.

14-7 You have seen several words in this chapter whose meaning has changed from Old English to Modern English. One example is *dēor*, which meant 'animal' in Old English but has narrowed its meaning to 'deer' in Modern English. Among several other ways, words can change their meaning by becoming more specialized, as with *deer*, or by becoming more generalized. Examine the Old English words and meanings that follow and note what each word has become in Modern English. State whether each word's meaning has become more specialized or more generalized in the course of its development.

Old English	**Modern English**
steorfan 'die'	starve
berēafian 'deprive of'	bereave
hlāf 'bread'	loaf
spēdan 'prosper'	speed
spellian 'speak'	spell
hund 'dog'	hound
mete 'food'	meat
wīf 'woman'	wife
dōm 'judgment'	doom
sellan 'give'	sell
tīd 'time'	tide

14-8 Nearly all of the words listed below were borrowed into English from other languages. Keeping in mind the character of the word and what it signifies, make an educated guess as to the likely source language for each word and the approximate date of borrowing using half-century periods such as 1900–1950. Then, for each word, look up its origin in a good dictionary, noting for borrowed words the actual source language and the date of borrowing. For which words has no source been identified? (The source language will be identified in most good dictionaries; the date of borrowing may not be. *Webster's Ninth New Collegiate Dictionary* and *Merriam-Webster's Collegiate Dictionary,* tenth edition, do supply dates. It may be useful for different students or student groups to tackle different columns of words and then to compare their findings.)

barf	duffel	hummus	tandoori
zilch	mai tai	tortilla	ginseng
kibble	moped	nosh	glitch
bummer	jeans	ginger	schlock
dinosaur	disco	giraffe	kvetch
leviathan	dude	ciao	glasnost
tae kwon do	sphere	karate	kayak
piña colada	taffy	kimono	shtick
kerchief	dim sum	kung fu	moussaka
teriyaki	cadaver	paparazzi	whiskey
catsup	denim	taffeta	karma
hunk	algebra	falafel	caucus
honcho	alarm	mutton	caddie
macho	a la mode	klutz	goober

14-9 Go to a Web site at which you can find an image of the beginning of the *Beowulf* poem (one site is identified as "Hwæt we Gar-Dena" under "Other Resources" below). Carefully compare the beginning of the manuscript version with the transcription given in this chapter on page 501. Then, on the basis of the correspondences between the Old English orthography and the Modern English transcription, provide the transcription for another three lines.

OTHER RESOURCES

Internet

- **Old English Pages: http://www.georgetown.edu/cball/oe/old_english.html**
  This award-winning Web site supplies easily accessible information about Old English and links to other fascinating views of the period; includes a link to the British Museum, where artifacts from the Sutton Hoo Burial Ship can be found; provides access to electronic texts, translations, manuscript images, art, history, and the language itself; also contains useful references to Old English fonts, sound files, CD-ROMs and cassettes, instructional software, and—for those with wondrous ambition—access to a forum for composition in Old English. A linked audio page at **http://www.georgetown.edu/cball/oe/oe-audio.html** will lead you to recordings of "The Battle of Brunanburh," "The Funeral of Scyld Scefing," "The Lord's Prayer," "Cædmon's Hymn," "Deor," and *Beowulf*.

- **Hwæt we Gar-Dena: ftp://beowulf.engl.uky.edu/pub/beowulf/129rcol.nu.jpg**
  To see an Old English manuscript containing the words from *Beowulf* given on page 501, visit this site. For an enlargement and for Exercise 14–9, visit **ftp://beowulf.engl.uky.edu/pub/beowulf/129r.jpg**. (Note that both these addresses begin with *ftp,* not *http.*)

- **The Oxford English Dictionary Online: http://www.oed.com/dictsframe.html**
  At the time of writing, the *OED* is not available online, but this Web site promises that it soon will be. It will be a great boon to anyone interested in the development of English.

Video and Audio

- **The Story of English**
  A highly recommended video series hosted by Robert MacNeil. Two videos treat the development of English—"The Mother Tongue" and "A Muse of Fire." Readily available in libraries and video rental outlets.

- **The Chaucer Studio**
  Perhaps the best source for audiocassettes of Old and Middle English. See the Web page at **http://english.byu.edu/factftt-z/thomasp/chaucer/index.htm.** You can hear spoken samples from the General Prologue of the *Canterbury Tales,* the Knight's, Summoner's, and Nun's Priest's tales, and some of *Gawain and the Green Knight* at: **http://www.millersv.edu/~english/homepage/duncan/chaucer/audio.html.**

SUGGESTION FOR FURTHER READING

- **Tim William Machan and Charles T. Scott, eds. 1992.** *English in its Social Contexts: Essays in Historical Sociolinguistics* (New York: Oxford University Press). Accessible essays aiming to contextualize changes in English within the social contexts of their times. Also contains chapters on current British, American, and Australian English, and on the spread of English around the globe.

ADVANCED READING

There are several excellent general histories of the English language. Baugh and Cable (1993)—from which we took our examples of French borrowings in Middle English, Latin and Greek borrowings in early Modern English, and regular and irregular verbs—is superb on the external history of the language. Pyles and Algeo (1993), from which we have borrowed a few examples, is balanced between internal and external history and complements Baugh and Cable (1993) by being stronger on the internal history. Millward (1990) and Bolton (1982) are also very good. Smith (1996) takes a refreshing approach, integrating internal and external history in systematically explanatory ways. Algeo (1993) is a rich workbook. Hughes (2000) focuses on the lexicon. A useful and easy to use Old English grammar is Quirk and Wrenn (1957), from which several of our examples are taken. Especially valuable for Old English syntax and reliable as a pedagogical grammar is Mitchell and Robinson (1986). Burrow and Turville-Petre (1992) provides Middle English texts and discussion. For the early Modern English period,

Barber (1976) is good on language structure, on attitudes toward borrowing and correctness, and on semantic change in the lexicon. Görlach (1991) is also useful, especially on writing and spelling. Denison (1993) is a corpus-based treatment of historical syntax, somewhat advanced. Dillard (1992) treats American English.

Background information about Indo-European is conveniently found in Philip Baldi's "Indo-European Languages," in Comrie (1987) and about Germanic in "Germanic Languages," by John A. Hawkins in the same volume. Two excellent sources about life in Anglo-Saxon Britain are Campbell et al. (1982) and Wood (1986), with photographs of artifacts, ruins, and manuscripts; Wood's book was written to accompany a BBC series. The lavishly illustrated Evans (1986) describes the treasures evacuated at the site of a burial ship for a seventh-century king of an Anglo-Saxon kingdom. Highly readable is Laing (1982), with a bias toward the archaeological.

The Cambridge History of the English Language (CHEL) is a multivolume reference work that aims to synthesize what is known about the history of English. Designed for an educated general audience rather than a professional one, some chapters are nevertheless written at a level not easily accessed by students whose principal prior exposure to the history of English is what is available in this book. But other *CHEL* chapters are accessible, and instructors will find *CHEL* useful in providing additional insight into most matters related to historical English. Volume 1 treats "The Beginnings to 1066," Volume 2 "1066–1476," Volume 3 "1476–1776," Volume 4 "1776–Present Day," Volume 5 "English in Britain and Overseas," and Volume 6 "English in North America." For *CHEL*, see Hogg (1992–2001) below.

REFERENCES

- Algeo, John. 1997. *Problems in the Origins and Development of the English Language,* 4th ed. (Boston: International Thomson).

- Barber, Charles. 1976. *Early Modern English* (London: Andre Deutsch).

- Baugh, Albert C., & Thomas Cable. 1993. *A History of the English Language,* 4th ed. (Englewood Cliffs, NJ: Prentice-Hall).

- Bolton, W. F. 1982. *A Living Language: The History and Structure of English* (New York: Random House).

- Burrow, J., & T. Turville-Petre, eds. 1992. *A Book of Middle English* (Oxford: Blackwell).

- Campbell, James, Eric John, & Patrick Wormald. 1982. *The Anglo-Saxons* (Oxford: Phaidon).

- Comrie, Bernard, ed. 1987. *The World's Major Languages* (New York: Oxford University Press).

- Denison, David. 1993. *English Historical Syntax: Verbal Constructions* (London: Longman).

- Dillard, J. L. 1992. *A History of American English* (London: Longman).

- Evans, Angela Care. 1986. *The Sutton Hoo Ship Burial* (London: British Museum Publications).

- Görlach, Manfred. 1991. *Introduction to Early Modern English* (Cambridge: Cambridge University Press).

- Hogg, Richard M. 1992–2001. *The Cambridge History of the English Language,* 6 vols. (Cambridge: Cambridge University Press).

- Hughes, Geoffrey. 2000. *A History of English Words* (Oxford: Blackwell).
- Laing, Lloyd & Jennifer. 1982. *Anglo-Saxon England* (London: Paladin).
- Millward, C. M. 1990. *A Biography of the English Language* (Boston: International Thomson).
- Mitchell, Bruce, & Fred C. Robinson. 1986. *A Guide to Old English: Revised with Prose and Verse Texts and Glossary* (New York: Blackwell).
- Pyles, Thomas, & John Algeo. 1993. *The Origins and Development of the English Language,* 4th ed. (Boston: International Thomson).
- Quirk, Randolph, & C. L. Wrenn. (1957). *An Old English Grammar* (New York: Holt).
- Smith, Jeremy. 1996. *An Historical Study of English: Function, Form and Change* (New York: Routledge).
- Wood, Michael. 1986. *Domesday: A Search for the Roots of England* (London: BBC Books).

Chapter 15

Acquiring First and Second Languages

❖ Your friend Brenda brags that her two-and-a-half-year-old daughter has an amazing command of English. Says Brenda of her daughter: She doesn't use vocabulary she hasn't heard, but she's always uttering sentences she hasn't heard before. Brenda wonders how that's possible. What do you tell her?

❖ At a nursery school where you work part-time, a parent mentions that she read in a Sunday newspaper that all children acquire the grammatical parts of their language in approximately the same order. "I don't believe it!" she confides. What do you say?

❖ At a family picnic, your brother Brad notices how consistently young cousin Kevin says "maked" and "breaked" and "runned" for *made, broke,* and *ran.* "Where do kids learn such words!" Brad exclaims. "They don't hear them from adults, so where do they get them?" What's your reply?

❖ Working part-time with you at a bilingual nursery school is your friend Frank, who is frustrated because he's having a tough time mastering Spanish when it's obviously so easy for young kids to master it. He's curious why it's so tough for him. What do you tell him?

INTRODUCTION

The language of children, even very young ones, is remarkably rich. Early in life children reveal mastery of the phonological, syntactic, and semantic systems described in earlier chapters, as well as a high degree of communicative competence in the appropriate use of language. As early as age five, children playing with hand puppets demonstrate productive control over a range of registers, including aspects of the characteristic talk between doctors and patients and doctors and nurses. Language acquisition seems so natural and effortless that parents, elated with the addition of each successive word, take it for granted that children will acquire their native language without a hitch. It seems obvious to everyone who has interacted with children that the process of acquiring a first language is relatively automatic, although it is subject to certain predictable missteps. Still, if the apparent ease with which a child accomplishes this magnificent achievement tickles parents, it baffles researchers. In this chapter you'll see why language acquisition intrigues and puzzles linguists and psychologists and why not everyone agrees about the nature of a child's task.

For much of the twentieth century, it was widely thought that language learning was essentially a process of induction, much like other learned behavior. A child would generalize about linguistic patterns from the language samples it heard in its interactions with parents, siblings, and other caretakers. Rather than resembling such bodily systems as digestion and respiration (which do *not* require learning), language was thought to be different. Because languages vary from culture to culture, it was thought that children must *induce* the patterns of their language from the speech of those around them. In this respect, language learning appeared to resemble other forms of cultural behavior like brushing your teeth, tying your shoelaces, or doing addition and subtraction.

Try it yourself: "Children master the intricacies of their native language before they are able to tie a knot, jump rope, or draw a decent-looking circle," writes William O'Grady. Given what you know about the great complexity of language systems as discussed earlier in this book, what do you think the likelihood is that children could learn all they know about language by imitating what they hear when adults talk?

In a dramatic shift of perceptions, the view of first-language learning as similar to other forms of learning is now regarded as implausible, and language acquisition is viewed as an inductive process only in limited respects. Indeed, rather than focusing on differences in languages, some linguists and psychologists focus on the similarities across languages (the linguistic universals of Chapter 7) and explain their universality as innate structures of the human mind that do not require learning. Other linguists and psychologists view the similarities across languages as the result not so much of uniform mental *structures* as of uniform mental *strategies* or dispositions for analyzing and acquiring language. In either case, there is now intense interest in characterizing what psycholinguists call the *language-making capacity* and grammarians call the *language acquisition device*.

ACQUIRING A FIRST LANGUAGE

You know that acquiring a language entails more than learning the meaning of various expressions. A child acquiring a language must learn a system that can generate countless sentences (few of which have been heard before) and deploy them appropriately in conversations and the other social interactions of everyday life. Language acquisition also entails the ability to understand both new and familiar utterances of those around us and to interpret them appropriately in their social contexts.

Besides the words of their language and a range of meanings for virtually every word, children must master morphological, phonological, syntactic, semantic, and pragmatic patterns. Every child must know when to speak and when to listen, when and how to interrupt, when and how to greet, when to tease and how to recognize teasing from its contextualization cues, and so on. All children must learn how to make utterances achieve their intended objective and how to understand under what circumstances a particular utterance serves different functions—for example, to offer food to someone (*Do you like chocolate? Have you ever tasted a kumquat?*) or request information (*Do you like chocolate? Have you ever tasted a kumquat?*). In other words, every child must learn the grammar of its language and the effective and culturally appropriate use of its grammar in diverse social situations. Acquiring a language entails mastery of the full range of grammatical and communicative competence.

There is evidence to suggest that at least some (and perhaps a good deal) of what children know about language structure could not have been learned from the data surrounding them. To the extent that certain language structures cannot be inferred from the data available to children, it is reasonable to hypothesize that the human language capacity provides those structures at birth or through natural development. The issue can be framed in terms of "nature" versus "nurture," what is inborn versus what must be learned, what is prewired into the brain at birth ("hardware") versus what must be programmed by interaction with adult language ("software"). The challenge is to determine the nature and degree of the contributions made by biology and by socialization.

Alternatively, some psychologists and linguists suspect not so much that children share particular language structures as that they share strategies for analyzing language. In Chapter 4, we discussed how difficult it would be for a child to sort out the continuous string of sound in adult speech into the distinct sounds that constitute the phonological inventory of its language. Children appear to arrive at the task of language learning already in possession of the "knowledge" that language consists of distinct sounds. They are "preprogrammed" to analyze a continuous string of vocal sounds for its individual phonological segments. In the same way, then, children seem naturally endowed with certain strategies for analyzing other aspects of language, and it is this set of *operating principles* for analyzing language that would contribute to the similarity of acquisition patterns across languages. As illustrations of such operating principles, children are thought to pay attention to the order of words in utterances, to the order of morphemes in words, to pay attention particularly to the ends of words (where inflections are found), to focus on consistent relationships between form and content, and to look for generalizations.

Operating Principles in First-Language Acquisition

Pay attention to the order of words in utterances.

Pay attention to the order of morphemes in words.

Pay particular attention to word endings (inflections).

Focus on consistent relationships between expression and content.

Look for generalizations.

Many linguists and psychologists are convinced that language is not acquired by imitation—certainly not solely by imitation and probably not principally—although exposure to a particular language is, obviously, an essential ingredient in the process of its acquisition. Still, children have an undeniable capacity to be creative with language and certainly don't need to hear a particular sentence before saying it. They often utter sentences they haven't heard before, and they know intuitively which sentences are possible and which are not, although all children go through periods when they make predictable mistakes. While they may say *He eated my candy* or *Oh! Hurt meself* or *Where did you found it?* they don't say "Mine is candy that" or "Candy my eated he" or countless other conceivable but nonoccurring sentences. In fact, the errors children make are of a very limited sort. English-speaking children can be heard overgeneralizing that the past tense of all verbs is formed by adding an *-ed* ending and making the other mistakes noted previously. Because adult native speakers of English don't say *eated* or *did you found* and because even children who lack contact with other children do say such things, errors such as these cannot arise from mimicry. Whatever is involved in language acquisition, it is certainly a robust process that goes beyond inducing the correct generalizations on the basis of forms that have been heard.

Principles of Language Acquisition

Two aspects of general maturation are crucial to a child's ability to acquire a language: *the ability to symbolize* and *the ability to use tools*.

Maturation and Symbolization   As a system of symbols, language is an arbitrary representation of other things—other entities, experiences, feelings, thoughts, and so on. In order to acquire language, a child must first be able to hold in mind a symbolic realization of something else. Even if it is no more than a mental picture of an absent object, such symbolization is a prerequisite to language acquisition.

Using Tools   The second ability—wider-ranging than its application to language—is the ability to use tools to accomplish goals. Language is a tool made up entirely of symbols, and among other characterizations it can be seen as a system of symbols that gets work done. From an early age, children routinely use language to get fed, changed, handed a toy, and all the other things they can't do for themselves. Such purposeful activity is called tool use, and language is an effective tool for accomplishing work of many sorts. Given their extremely limited ability to achieve their goals physically, children's motivation to develop this powerful symbolic tool must be extraordinarily strong (and may be influential in the evolution of the human species).

All Languages Are Equally Challenging   Every child who is capable of acquiring a particular human language is capable of acquiring any human language. There is no biological basis—in the lips or the brain—that disposes some children to learn a particular language. Children find all languages about equally easy to acquire, although particular features of one language may be more difficult to acquire than equivalent aspects of a different language. For example, as you saw in Chapter 2 (see Table 2–10, page 65), German definite articles have several different forms representing three genders, two numbers, and four cases. Children acquiring German need more time to master its definite articles than English-speaking children need to learn the form *the* that English uses for any gender, number, and case. (English speakers use *the* in the phrases *the boy, for the daughter,* and *to the lions,* whereas the German definite article would have different forms in those phrases, reflecting different cases and genders: *der, die,* and *den,* respectively). On balance, though, when considered in their entirety, all languages are about equally easy (or equally challenging) for a child to learn.

By the age of six, barring severe mental or physical impairments, children the world over have acquired most of what they need to know to speak their language fluently. By the time a child arrives in school, perhaps 80% of the structures of its language and more than 90% of the sound system have been acquired. "Doubtless the greatest intellectual feat any one of us is ever required to perform," Leonard Bloomfield remarked of language acquisition. Fortunately, it is a feat that human beings are gifted at. This universal success has convinced linguists and psycholinguists that infants come to the task of acquiring a language with a genetic predisposition to do so and with certain analytical advantages that facilitate the process. There is little doubt that, at the very least, children are born with certain mechanisms or cognitive strategies that help in the task of language acquisition, and certain structures or kinds of structure may be innate as well.

Adult Input in Language Acquisition

Stating that language acquisition is not a process of imitation doesn't diminish the crucial importance of exposure to linguistic input in acquiring a language. Acquisition requires interaction with speakers of the language being acquired. As witness to the necessity of adult input, there is the case of Genie, a child who was not exposed to any language while she was growing up. Genie's parents locked her away for the first 13 years of her life and seldom spoke to her. When she was discovered, she was unable to speak. Linguist Susan Curtiss tried teaching her English, but the attempts were not altogether successful. Deprived of linguistic input in the first few years of life, Genie's capacity for language acquisition had become impaired.

On the other hand, parents do not generally teach language to young children directly. Instead, children spontaneously acquire language on the basis of the input they receive. Conscious attempts to teach correct linguistic forms to children lead nowhere, for children simply ignore instruction and go on acquiring a native tongue at their own pace. In ordinary settings, parents rarely correct young children's grammatical mistakes, although they do correct utterances that are inaccurate or misleading. A child who says *Kitty's hands are pink* may be told *No. Kitty doesn't have hands: Kitty has PAWS.* But if a child asks *Where Kitty go?* (for 'Where did Kitty go?'), adults are not likely to correct the utterance. To a very great extent, then, children acquire the grammar of their language without direct instruction from adults.

Of course, certain aspects of language use *are* deliberately taught to children. In cultures around the world, children are engaged in conversation with adults almost from the start. In Western cultures, parents often treat baby noises (and not only vocal ones) as openings to conversations. From their first few months children are socialized into interactional routines of turn taking, where even their burps, hiccups, and sneezes are regarded as opening turns to which parents respond as though they were weighty proclamations. Children are socialized so effectively that the turn-taking patterns of school-age children have been pretty much established since age one. Later, when young children go trick-or-treating at Halloween (to take the example of a context in which politeness becomes a salient aspect of interaction), they may not produce the appropriate utterances unless prompted (*Say "thank you"! What do you say?*). So children need consciously to learn certain rules of language use, and adults typically provide instruction for these politeness rules.

Baby Talk: How Adults Talk to Children   Even when adults are not explicitly teaching children the rules of language use, they frequently modify their speech, adapting it to what they think children will readily understand and acquire. You have probably witnessed parents and siblings using *baby talk* (some people call it "motherese" or "infant-directed speech") in addressing babies.

- Ooohh, what a biiig smiile! Is Baby smiling at Mommy?
- Baby is smiling at her Mommy? Yeess!
- Is Baby happy to see Mommy?
- Is Baby hungry? Yeess? Oopen wiiide . . .
- Hmmmm! Baby likes soup. Yeess!
- Wheere's the soup? All gone!

This example, uttered slowly and with exaggerated intonation, is typical of the kind of linguistic input that English-speaking parents and other caregivers provide to young children.

Baby talk differs from talk between adults in characteristic ways. When addressing babies, adults' voices frequently assume a higher pitch than usual. Adults also exaggerate their intonation and speak slowly and clearly. Repetitions and partial repetitions (*Is Baby smiling at Mommy? Baby is smiling at her Mommy?*) are frequent in baby talk. Sentences are short and simple, with few subordinate clauses and few modifiers. Personal names like *Baby* and *Mommy* are preferred over pronouns like *you* and *I*. Compared to adult talk to other adults, baby talk has more frequent content words (nouns, verbs, adjectives) and fewer function words (subordinators, determiners). Utterances addressed to very young children frequently include special baby-talk vocabulary—words such as *doggie, horsie, tummy,* and *din-din,* which are more easily perceived or pronounced but do not normally occur in adult talk—and the choice of baby-talk words is more restricted than in ordinary speech. Baby talk is typically concrete and refers to items and actions in the child's immediate environment and experience. It also includes a high proportion of questions, particularly for young children (*Is Baby hungry?*), and of imperatives (*Oopen wiiide*). These modifications may serve to hold a child's attention or to simplify the linguistic input it hears, possibly making utterances easier to perceive or analyze. Especially in repetitions and shorter expressions addressed to young children, adults chunk their speech by constituent structure, a practice that could provide useful syntactic insight to learners. Baby talk features are summarized below.

Characteristics of Talk to Babies

Higher than usual pitch	Concrete, immediate referents
Frequent questions	Exaggerated intonation contours
Frequent repetitions	Slow and clear enunciations
Frequent imperatives	Baby-talk words (*doggie, tummy*)
Few modifiers	Frequent content words (nouns, verbs)
Few function words	Personal names instead of pronouns (*Mommy,* not *I*)
Few subordinate clauses	Chunking by constituent structure

At a somewhat more advanced stage, when children start producing utterances, parents and other caretakers have been observed to echo those utterances in a fuller form than the child offered. Sometimes the intonation of the caretaker's expansions confirms what the child has said; sometimes a questioning intonation seems to be seeking clarification. The following examples are illustrative.

Adult Expansions of Children's Utterances

CHILD	ADULT
Baby highchair	Baby is in the highchair.
Mommy eggnog	Mommy had her eggnog.
Eve lunch	Eve is having lunch.
Throw Daddy	Throw it to Daddy.

Expansions occur far less frequently when parents and other caretakers are alone with children than when other adults are present (including researchers), and such expansions may be intended as "translations" of the baby's speech, more for the aid of the observer than for the benefit of the child.

Features of baby talk are found in cultures far and wide. When the Berbers of North Africa address babies, they simplify their language in some of the same ways that Americans do; the same is true of the Japanese. Not all cultures modify speech to children, but modification is widespread. Children themselves acquire baby talk very early in life, and four-year-olds can be heard using features of this register when addressing younger children, while even two-year-olds use it with younger siblings.

The extent to which baby talk helps children in acquiring language is difficult to assess, but in cultures where baby talk is absent (as it is in Samoa, parts of Papua New Guinea, and among the Kipsigis of Kenya, for example) children acquire their native language at the same rate as children exposed to baby talk. So we must conclude that baby talk is not essential to successful language acquisition.

Still, baby talk does serve some functions. First, it exposes small children to simple language, and simple language may be helpful in the task of unraveling constituent structures and certain grammatical operations. Since children have to figure out so many different grammatical features, selective input (fewer words, fewer complex sentences, and repetitions) facilitate their task. In addition, considering English, the unusually high percentage of questions that caregivers address to infants has the effect of exposing them to a greater number of auxiliaries (*Did Baby fall?*) than would the use of declarative sentences (*Baby fell*). Baby talk may also inculcate certain rules of language use, particularly the rules of conversation (see Chapter 9). By asking many questions of small children, adults help socialize them into the question-answer sequences and into the alternating turn-taking patterns of conversation. From the earliest stages, adults alternate their utterances with a baby's babblings, and the implicit message is to alternate one's utterances with one's interlocutor's. Interactional patterns between caregivers and children can thus provide a framework within which utterances can be situated and acquisition of grammar can take place.

Stages of Language Acquisition

Babbling   Whatever the nature of the input they receive, children go through several stages in the process of acquiring their native language. At the babbling stage, which starts at about six months of age, children first utter a series of identical syllables such as *ba-ba-ba* or *ma-ma-ma*. A couple of months later, as the vocal apparatus matures, this reduplicated babbling blossoms into a wider range of syllable types such as *bab-bab* and *ab-ab*. These early babblings are similar the world over and occur with or without others present. When some babbled sounds stabilize for a child and are linked to a consistent referent or appear to be used with a consistent purpose (for example, to be handed something), they are called *vocables* or protowords. A child may use a vocable such as *baba* to indicate it does not want something while *mama* serves to indicate it does want something.

One-Word Stage   Starting around a year old, when children take their first steps, they are also heard uttering words such as *mama, dada,* and *up.* These early words are of simple structure and typically refer to familiar people (mother and father), toys and pets (teddy bear and kitty), food and drink (cookie and juice), and social interaction (as in *bye-bye).* By this stage children already use vocal noises to get and hold attention socially and to achieve other objectives.

Often, the same word is used to refer to things that have a similar appearance, as when a child learns the word *doggie* for the family dog and then extends it to all dogs. Children are thus inclined to generalize word meanings and even to overgeneralize, as when *doggie* is applied to cats as well as dogs, or even to all animals.

Observation of utterances at the one-word stage suggests that children are not rehearsing simple words but expressing single words to convey whole propositions. A child uses the word *dada,* for example, to mean different things in different contexts: 'Here comes Daddy' (upon hearing a key in the door at the end of the day); 'This is for Daddy' (when handing Daddy a toy); 'That is where Daddy usually sits' (when looking at Daddy's empty chair at the kitchen table); or 'This shoe is Daddy's' (when touching a shoe belonging to Daddy).

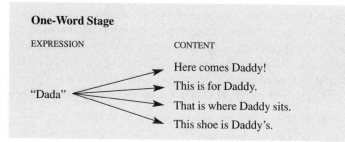

One-Word Stage

EXPRESSION   CONTENT

"Dada"   Here comes Daddy!

This is for Daddy.

That is where Daddy sits.

This shoe is Daddy's.

In different contexts, a child may give the same word different intonations. Holding a shoe and uttering *Dada,* a child is not merely naming the object of its focus but is using a relatively simple expression to communicate relatively complex content.

Two-Word Stage   From the one-word-utterance stage, children move on to utterances such as *Daddy come, Shoe mine,* and *Apple me.* The transition from the one-word stage to the two-word stage occurs at about 20 months of age, when the child has a vocabulary of about 50 words. At this stage, utterances show a preference for combining a nounlike element with a predicatelike element, and children tend to verbalize in propositions—to name something and then say something about it: *Daddy, [he is] com[ing], Shoe, [it's] mine; Apple, [give it to] me.* Other forms also occur, as in *More juice* and *There Daddy,* in which the predicatelike element precedes the noun. One striking fact about the two-word-utterance stage is that children from different cultures appear to express basically similar things in their propositions at this stage.

Two-Word Stage

EXPRESSION	CONTENT
"Daddy come"	Daddy, he is coming.
"Shoe mine"	The shoe, it's mine.
"Apple me"	The apple, give it to me.
"More juice"	I want more juice.
"There Daddy"	There is Daddy.

We don't know whether the disposition to verbalize in propositions is a tendency of the language process itself or is tied to aspects of perception. But from the start children seem to be trying to convey propositions, even when the expression is a mere word. If this interpretation is correct, children at the two-word stage are not attempting to communicate more content by using two words instead of one but to *express* more of the content than at the one-word stage. As the child masters its language system, it will learn to balance *expression* and *context* so as to communicate *content* efficiently and effectively.

Beyond Two Words   Beyond the two-word stage, distinct three-word and four-word stages are not recognized. Instead, progress is typically measured by the average number of morphemes (or sometimes words) in a child's utterances. Between about two years (2;0) and two-and-a-half years (2;6) of age, a child's expressions become considerably more complex. Utterances contain several words representing single clauses.

Consider these single-clause utterances from a boy of two years and five months:

1. Mimo hurt me. [about a past action by his brother]
2. Yeah, that money Neina. ('Yeah, that money is Zeina's.')
3. Me put it back. ('I'll put it back.')
4. No do that again! [to an adult whispering in his ear]
5. Oh! hurt meself. [upon bumping his arm into a door]
6. That's mine, Uncle Ed. [showing a toy to an uncle]

Try it yourself: To make these utterances, the boy must have considerable knowledge of English, even if his knowledge does not exactly match the linguistic knowledge of an adult. Examine the six utterances and spell out in as much detail as possible just what linguistic knowledge the boy must have to say them in the contexts described.

To utter such sentences, the boy must have a good deal of information about English vocabulary, syntax, and pragmatics. Obviously, he knows such English words as *money, mine,* and *that's*. Saying those words entails knowing what sounds they contain and in what order. That the words are used in appropriate contexts indicates that he knows what the words refer to and in what situations they are appropriate. He knows the lexical categories (the parts of speech) of these words and how to combine them with other categories, both morphologically (*me, meself, mine*) and syntactically (*Mimo hurt me* and *Me put it back*). Possibly he knows which form of the copula BE agrees with the demonstrative subject *that* and how to contract *is* to *'s* and attach it to *that,* although *that's* may be an unanalyzed unit for him at this stage. The child has also mastered basic SVO word order, as in *Mimo hurt me* (although pronominal subjects are not yet obligatory, as a comparison between *Me put it back* and *Hurt meself* shows). He also shows knowledge of declarative and imperative sentence structures and of negative imperatives.

The phrase *that money* (in 2) indicates knowledge that *money* belongs to the category of nouns—the category that takes determiners such as *that* and *the*. Given the contexts in which the utterances occur, it is also apparent that the child is uttering propositions, although some are incompletely encoded or differ from adult formulations. More noteworthy than the matches between some of these utterances and those of an adult grammar, as with 1 and 6, is the fact that the child is using language in a systematic fashion. The structured utterances are governed by rules of grammar that stay constant from utterance to utterance: subjects precede verbs; verbs precede objects and other complements; and adverbs (*back* and *again)* follow objects.

Of course, there are many other forms of the adult grammar that the child has not yet fully mastered, including syntactic and morphological matters. Syntactically, no subject is expressed in 5, no verb in 2, and no auxiliary in 3, all of which would be required in well-formed adult utterances. Morphologically, the possessive marker is not fully mastered: it appears in *mine* but is lacking in *Neina;* the adult subject form of the first-person pronoun *I* and the adult reflexive form *myself* have not yet been acquired.

By around three years of age, utterances containing multiple clauses appear, at first coordinating two clauses, as in *There's his face and he's Mister George Happy.* Later, children subordinate one clause to another with subordinators like *'cause, so,* and *if* in the early stages and then *why* and *what: Me don't know where box is now. Why did you give to her when her been flu?*

How Do Children Acquire Morphology and Grammar?

Interestingly, the morphemes and grammatical structures of language are generally acquired by children in a set order, with variation from child to child usually slight. This pattern suggests that there is an internally regulated sequence for grammatical acquisition. Psychologist Roger Brown examined the order in which 14 morphological and grammatical morphemes were acquired by three English-speaking children and found that they were acquired in the order given below:

Acquisition Order for English Morphemes

1. Present progressive verb (with or without auxiliary): (*is) playing, (are) singing*
2–3. Prepositions *in* and *on*
4. Regular noun plural: *toys, cats, dishes*
5. Irregular past-tense verbs: *came, fell, saw, hurt*
6. Possessive noun: *Daddy's, doggie's*
7. Uncontractible copula: *Here I am, Who is it?*
8. Articles: *a* and *the*
9. Regular past-tense verbs: *played, washed, wanted*
10. Regular third-person singular present-tense verbs: *sees, wants, washes*
11. Irregular third-person singular present-tense verbs: *does, has*
12. Uncontractible auxiliary: *She isn't crying, He was eating*
13. Contractible copula: *That's mine, What's that?*
14. Contractible auxiliary: *He's crying*

Although the children acquired these forms basically in the same *order,* they did not acquire them *at the same speed.* Between acquisition of the present progressive (the earliest acquired) and the contractible auxiliary (the last), anywhere from 6 to 14 months elapsed. One child acquired the contractible auxiliary by 2;3, while another took until 3;6.

The order tracked among Brown's young "consultants" basically replicated the order other linguists and psychologists had tracked with other children, and the slight variations reported probably have to do with the criteria used for judging "acquisition." For example, Brown judged a feature to be acquired only when a child used it correctly in 90% of the required cases in three successive sampling sessions. Other researchers used different criteria, such as the first time that a correct use was observed.

What Determines Acquisition Order?   As to what determines the order of acquisition, it would seem reasonable to suppose that the frequency with which a child hears a form from adults will influence the order of acquisition. In fact, however, Brown was unable to correlate frequency of parental use with the order of acquisition. The most frequent of the 14 morphemes in the parents' speech was the articles, which appeared eighth in the order of child acquisition. The prepositions, on the other hand, were acquired second by children, although they were used relatively little by parents. In determining the order of acquisition, what seems more influential than frequency is relative complexity. Morphemes that encode several semantic notions and those that are syntactically more complex tend to be acquired later than those that encode a single semantic notion and are syntactically simpler.

Exceptions and Overgeneralizations   No doubt you have observed that children tend to overgeneralize the patterns of inflectional morphology. You've heard kids say things like "eated" for *ate* and "foots" for *feet.* There are some sixty-odd irregular verbs in English, and among those that get overgeneralized are the ones listed below.

Overgeneralization of Past-Tense Verbs

eated	ate	doed	did
maked	made	speaked	spoke
finded	found	breaked	broke
hitted	hit	goed	went
falled	fell	runned	ran

English has far fewer nouns like *foot* that form their plurals irregularly; among those that children overgeneralize are those listed below.

Overgeneralization of Noun Plurals

foots	feet	mans	men
tooths	teeth	mouses	mice
childs	children	peoples	people

Evidence from several languages suggests that children tend naturally to overgeneralize or "overregularize" the morphological rules they acquire.

Sentence Structure   The sentences of the 29-month-old (2;5) boy (given on page 546) contain single clauses only. Before that boy was five years old, negative sentences were under control, as in *That isn't yours* and *That doesn't belong to you,* and sentences incorporating more than one clause were commonplace, including imperatives (*Guess who's visiting me*) and interrogatives (*Do you know what I did at school today?*). Even at age five, though, relative clauses were not fully acquired, although certain kinds of relatives are understood by children even at three years of age. When children first produce relative clauses, they attach them to object noun phrases, as in *You broke the one that I found.* Attaching relative clauses to subjects (as in *The one that I found is red*) represents a later stage of acquisition, and attaching them to other grammatical relations comes later still.

Negation   Every language has ways of expressing negation. At first, children express negation by the simple utterance *no,* either alone or preceding other expressions: *No. No want. No that. No do that.* At a somewhat later stage, by three years of age, more complex expressions incorporate negations, as in these: *Can't get it off. Don't know. It doesn't go that way. That not go in there.*

Questions   Every language also has ways of asking questions. Some do so simply by adding a question word to the end of a statement. English has a relatively complex way of forming questions, and mastery of its question-formation rules takes time. In the early stages, interrogative utterances have the same syntax as declaratives, as in *That mine.* Sometimes, though not always, the intonation of questions differs from that of statements. By three years of age, children have mastered most aspects of question formation, as in these questions from a three-year-old girl named Sophie:

Information Questions	Yes/No Questions
What is he called?	Is this a box?
What goes in this hole?	Do it go this side?
Why didn't me get flu?	Can me put it in like that?
Why's he so small?	
Where are you Mummy?	

How Fast Do Children Acquire Vocabulary?

At the start of the two-word stage, around 20 months (1;8) of age, a child knows approximately 50 words. Mostly they are nouns referring to concrete, familiar objects (*shoe, clock, apple, baby, milk, nose*) or expressions for salient notions in the child's environment (*more, no, bye-bye, oh, walk, what's that*). By age five, the child's vocabulary is increasing by about 15 or 20 words a day. Estimates of the number of basic words known by schoolchildren of age six run about 7800, even counting a word set like *cat, cats, cat's, cats'* or *walk, walks, walked, walking* as a single word. If you count derived forms such as *dollhouse* as a third word besides *doll* and *house,* then 13,000 words would be a reliable figure. Astonishingly, two years later, by age eight, a child's vocabulary has increased to 17,600 basic words (or 28,300 words including derived forms). This represents an average increase of more than 13 basic words (or 21 words and derived forms) *each day.* Of course, a word isn't acquired in its semantic fullness on a single occasion; rather, a full range of meanings for any word is generally acquired only by stages over a period of time. Indeed, this phenomenon, like the acquisition of vocabulary itself, continues well into adulthood, though at a drastically reduced rate.

How Do Children Acquire the Sounds of Language?

You have probably listened to a child uttering words and expressions that you could understand within their context even though the pronunciations did not match your own. "Neina" /nenɑ/ for *Zeina* /zenɑ/ in the speech from the boy of two years, five months is one illustration. Other examples might be "poon" or "bude" for *spoon,* "du" for *juice,* and "dis" or "di" [dɪ] for *this.* Such pronunciations suggest that a child masters certain aspects of a word before others. In these cases, the context indicates that the child knows the word's lexical category and certain semantic information (such as its referent); the child also knows some of its phonological content, although mastery of the pronunciation is incomplete. Here we examine certain patterns of phonological acquisition among English-speaking children and draw some cross-linguistic comparisons.

From as early as two months, infants react differently to different speech sounds, and they can recognize individual voices—their mother's, for example. (We know this from changes in the rate of sucking when voices alternate.) Prior to their production of recognizable utterances at about twelve months of age, infants go through a lengthy babbling stage, during which they appear to be rehearsing a wide range of sounds, extending beyond the sounds spoken around them and therefore beyond the phonological inventory needed for their own language.

Early babbling consists of simple syllable-like sequences of a consonant followed by a vowel: *ba-ba-ba.* Repetitions of CV syllables are then followed by sequences that juxtapose different CV syllables (*bamama),* first yielding CVCV patterns and then CVC patterns (such as *bam* and *mam,* which lack the vowel of the second CVCV syllable). These early babblings reveal a preference for voiced stops and nasals [b d g m n] and a dispreference for fricatives [f v θ ð s z] and liquids [l r]. Not surprisingly, sounds that are relatively rare among the world's languages tend to be acquired later than sounds that are common. By eight or nine months of age children are able to mimic adult intonation patterns to a striking degree. Unlike the sounds of babbling, these intonation patterns differ from language to language.

Consonant Sounds of Babbling						
PREFERRED				DISPREFERRED		
b	d	g		v	ð	z
m	n			f	θ	s
				l/r		

Try it yourself: What generalization can you make about the preferred sounds of babbling as compared to the dispreferred sounds? Think in terms of phonological features or natural classes.

Before the first recognizable words are produced around age one, the list of speech sounds actually shrinks (and a few children even go through a silent period), after which the inventory of sounds belonging to the adult language is gradually and systematically acquired. Full phonological development takes several years, and the last sounds may not be acquired before age six or so.

Between 12 months and 18 months of age, a child learns to produce about 50 words (which is only about a fourth of those it can recognize). The range of sounds and of syllable types needed to give voice to so small a lexicon is relatively limited (5 vowels and 10 consonants would generate 50 monosyllabic words of CV type). At about 18 months of age, however, children typically experience a "word spurt," and for this larger lexicon the previous inventory of sounds and syllables is inadequate, and an expansion of the system is necessary.

Around 24 months (2;0) of age, an English-speaking child typically has acquired the following consonant sounds, although not all of them can be produced in every position in which adults produce them:

Inventory of English Consonants at Age Two				
Nasals	m		n	
Stops	b		d	g
	p		t	k
Fricatives		f	s	h
Approximants	w			

A year later, at about 36 months (3;0), the child has added /j/ and /ŋ/ to its inventory, although [b], [d], [g], and [k] still remain elusive in word-final position.

Consonant clusters (as in *spilled* [spɪld], *stopped* [stɑpt], and *asked* [æskt]) present children with particular challenges. In fact, of the wide range of clusters that adults use, the three-year-old may have mastered only final /ŋk/, as in *pink* and *sink*.

By around four years of age, the inventory of consonants has expanded significantly and stands approximately as given here.

Inventory of English Consonants at Age Four					
Nasals	m		n		ŋ
Stops	b		d		g
	p		t		k
Fricatives		f	s	ʃ	h
		v	z		
Affricates				tʃ	
				dʒ	
Approximants	w	l/r		j	

At this stage the voiced fricatives /v/ and /z/ may be present only in medial position (as in *over* and *dizzy*), but the child may not yet be able to produce them in word-final or word-initial position. Recall that the 29-month-old (2;5) boy whose utterances we analyzed earlier substituted the nasal [n] for initial [z] in the name *Zeina,* presumably influenced by anticipation of the [n] to follow, as commonly happens with children. The interdental fricative sounds /θ/ and /ð/ (as in *thin* and *then*) have yet to be added to the four-year-old's inventory in any position, as has the relatively rare /ʒ/ (as in *measure*). Thus, between the ages of four and six, an English-speaking child may still lack /ʒ/, /v/, /θ/, /ð/, and /z/, at least in some positions. And still ahead lies mastery of the morphophonemic rules that account for variation between underlying forms and surface forms (as in the [t]/[ɾ] alternation of *late* [let] and *later* [leɾər] or the [d]/[ɾ] alternation of *dad* and *daddy*). Mastery of the more complex syllable structures and consonant clusters also lies ahead.

Substituting and Omitting Sounds   Can you imagine that, until a child mastered the phonological inventory of its language, it would skip the sounds not yet learned, producing pronunciations such as *oo* [u] for *shoe* and *juice?* As you know, of course, that isn't what happens. Instead, children generally attempt to pronounce all the sounds in a word, although they manage it by various simplifications. The principal ones in early pronunciations involve substituting easier sounds for harder ones, as in these processes:

Stopping: fricatives and affricates pronounced as stops

Devoicing: final obstruents devoiced

Voicing: initial obstruents voiced before vowels

Fronting: velars and alveopalatals pronounced as alveolars

Gliding: liquids pronounced as approximants (i.e., as glides)

Vocalization: liquids replaced by vowels

Denasalization: nasals replaced by oral stops

Processes of Substitution in Child Language

STOPPING	v → b	van → [bæn]
	ð → d, n	that → [dæt], there → [nɛr]
	dʒ → d	jack → [dæk], jam → [dæb]
	tʃ → d	check → [dɛk]
DEVOICING	b → p	knob → [nɑp]
	-d → t	bad → [bæt]
	-g → t	dog → [dɑt]
	-v → f	stove → [duf]
VOICING	p- → b	pot → [bɑt]
	t- → d	toe → [do]
	k- → d	kiss → [dɪ]
FRONTING	k → t	duck → [dɑt]
	g → d	gate → [det]
	θ → f	thumb → [fʌm]
	ʃ → z	shoes → [zus]
	ʒ → z	rouge → [wuːz]
	tʃ → ts	match → [mæts]
	dʒ → dz	cabbage → [tæːbədz]
GLIDING	r → w	rock → [wɑt], sorry → [sɑwɑ]
VOCALIZATION	l → u	table → [dubu]
DENASALIZATION	m → p, b	lamb → [bæp], broom → [bub], jam → [dæb]

(After Ingram 1989, pp. 371–72)

Actually, besides the substitution processes described above, some omission also takes place. For example, as illustrated below, young children typically delete unstressed syllables from trisyllabic words (as in *nana* for *banana)* and sometimes the unstressed syllable of a disyllabic word; they sometimes omit final consonants; and they often reduce consonant clusters.

Processes of Omission in Child Language

Deletion of syllable	banana → [nænə], kitchen → [kɪtʃ], pocket → [bɑt]
Deletion of final consonant	doll → [dɑ], far → [fɑ]
Reduction of consonant clusters	

stop + liquid → stop	glass → [dæs], bread → [but]
s- + stop → stop	star → [dɑ]
s- + nasal → nasal	snake → [nek]
nasal + voiced stop → nasal	hand → [hæn]

Determinants of Acquisition Order   It isn't entirely clear what determines the order in which sounds are acquired. If it would seem reasonable to assume that the more frequently a child heard a particular sound, the sooner it would be acquired, the facts point elsewhere. Consider that the most frequent English consonant sounds are the fricatives [s], [d], [z], and [v]. Either [s] or [z] occurs in the plural forms of most nouns, the possessive form of every noun, the third-person singular present-tense form of all verbs (*eats, does, is),* certain common pronouns and possessive determiners (*his, hers, yours),* and some other common words (*was* and *some).* In light of such frequency, it is not surprising that [s] is acquired relatively early (by about 24 months). But, perplexingly, [z] is not acquired until four years of age and then usually only in medial position. Consider also that [ð], although it occurs in extremely frequent words such as *this, that,* and *the,* is acquired very late, while [v], even at four years of age, is produced in medial position but not initially or finally, where it is common in such words as *very, have,* and *of.* Clearly, frequency of occurrence in adult speech is not the sole determinant in the order of acquisition.

Of greater influence than frequency is the functional importance of a sound within its phonological system. A sound is said to have a high functional load if it serves to differentiate many words (or words that are very frequent), and high functional load seems to promote early acquisition. Thus /tʃ/ is acquired much later by children learning English than by Guatemalan children learning the Mayan language Quiché. The reason appears to be that in Quiché /tʃ/ contrasts with other sounds in many more words than it does in English, and the high functional load of the /tʃ/ sound in Quiché fosters early acquisition. By contrast, the low functional importance of /tʃ/ in English tends to bump it towards the end of the acquisition line.

Phonological Idioms   Before acquiring all the sounds in the inventory of its language, a child may be able to produce some sounds as part of fixed phrases or phonological "idioms." In much the same way that adults have semantic idioms (*kick the bucket)* and syntactic idioms (*the sooner the better),* so children may produce unanalyzed words containing sounds that they have not yet added as separate units of their phonological inventory. They have learned to pronounce the word as a whole but haven't mastered all the individual sounds as such. The child can thus make a lexical contrast without yet having the contrasting sounds in its phonological inventory.

HOW DO RESEARCHERS STUDY LANGUAGE ACQUISITION?

Studies of child language and language acquisition have most commonly been naturalistic, or observational, studies. At regular intervals researchers have tape-recorded ordinary interactions between adults and children or among children and transcribed those results for analysis. There have also been diary studies (carried out by parents who were themselves linguists or psychologists) that record a child's utterances, the age at which they occur, and the situational context surrounding them. Depending on the focus and goals of the observer, diary studies represent different degrees of detail, ranging from ordinary orthography to a narrow phonetic transcription. Quite naturally, then, observational studies of child language have focused on the *production* of words and sentences.

Receptive Competence and Productive Competence

So far we haven't said much about a child's *receptive* mastery, or understanding, nor drawn a distinction between what a child's *grammatical competence* might allow but its *production apparatus* be unable to utter. After all, a child could have the grammatical competence to generate adult pronunciations but remain unable to utter them because of physiological immaturity in the vocal apparatus.

"FIS" Phenomenon   An oft-repeated story tells of a child who pronounced *fish* as *fis* [fɪs] but objected to an adult imitating the *fis* pronunciation. "This is your *fis?*" the adult asked. "No," said the child: "my *fis*." When the adult repeated the question, the child again rejected the *fis* pronunciation. When the adult eventually said, "Your *fish?*" the child concurred: "Yes, my *fis*"! The child could hear the distinction between *fish* and *fis* and recognized *fis* as an incorrect pronunciation. But in attempting to say *fish* the child produced a word that replicated the *fis* it knew to be wrong. We should be careful interpreting such data, however. It may seem that the child knows and recognizes the difference between [fɪʃ] and [fɪs] while being unable to pronounce [fɪʃ] because of limitations in the vocal apparatus, but there are other possible explanations. Consider the case of the child who consistently pronounced *puddle* as *puggle:* the obvious hypothesis that the vocal apparatus was not yet capable of pronouncing /d/ intervocalically was belied by the fact that the child systematically pronounced *puzzle* as *puddle*.

Big Bigs   In saying a word like *pig* or *tug,* the voicing required in pronouncing the vowels is anticipated by adults in such a fashion that /p/ and /t/, though they begin without voicing, become voiced just preceding the onset of the vowel. It is almost as if the pronunciation were [pbɪg] and [tdʌg]. The key to an adult's distinguishing initial /p/ and /b/ before vowels is *how long* the voicing is delayed, not whether it is present or absent. A child may be perceived as failing to distinguish voiced from voiceless initial stops, pronouncing *tug* and *Doug* alike as [dʌg] or *pig* and *big* alike as [bɪg]. But laboratory analyses indicate that some children systematically distinguish initial /t/ from /d/ and initial /p/ from /b/ by delaying the voicing onset time for the voiceless stops (/t/ and /p/) for a longer period than they delay voicing for the voiced stops (/d/ and /b/). The delayed voicing is detectable by laboratory instruments but not by the human ear. This would indicate that the child has heard the voiceless and voiced stops and internalized the difference between them in its lexicon but has not yet learned to delay the onset of voicing long enough to be detected by adults.

There is general agreement that receptive mastery of language outpaces production, but it is not clear that this is so at all stages of language development and in all respects. Still, children generally seem able to understand more than they can produce—that is, their lexical and syntactic repertoire is greater than their production reveals. At about 18 months of age, as we mentioned above, a child understands about 200 words although only about 50 appear in its speech. In attempts to analyze the language competence of children, then, naturalistic observation alone may offer an incomplete picture, so researchers have had to invent ingenious ways to get at receptive competence.

Wugs and Other Experimental Techniques

One experimental technique elicits utterances that children would not otherwise have occasion to say. In one study, children were shown drawings of an imaginary bird or animal and told, for example, "This is a wug." The next drawing would depict two such birds or animals, and the child would be suitably prompted to offer a plural form: "Now there is another one. There are two of them. There are two _____?" (See Figure 15–1.) This technique can uncover how much morphophonemic variation of the plural morpheme the child has mastered. Alternatively, pictures of people carrying out novel actions such as "ricking" can be used to elicit past tenses and progressive forms of verbs. With another technique, children using hand puppets speak in the voices of their puppets to another puppet that is given voice by the researcher. In a third technique, children are asked simply to repeat words or sentences (to display their progress for repetition of sounds, syllable structures, and grammatical forms). In a fourth technique, designed to gauge understanding, children playing with dolls are asked to act out such sentences as "The horse pushed the cow" and "The horse was pushed by the cow," which would test their understanding of the meaning of passives.

Although child language and first-language acquisition are important to many aspects of linguistic theory, a good deal about the processes of acquisition remains unclear or uninvestigated. The interaction between physiological and mental limitations, on the one hand, and the nature of the internalized grammar, on the other, makes interpreting child language data challenging. Given the complexities of interpreting child language data, the most reliable findings and theories will be those that emerge from using a variety of investigative methodologies, both naturalistic and experimental.

Figure 15-1

A Test for Plural Allomorphs

THIS IS A WUG.

NOW THERE IS ANOTHER ONE.
THERE ARE TWO OF THEM.
THERE ARE TWO _____ .

Source: Jean Berko (Gleason). 1958. "The Child's Learning of English Morphology," *Word* 14:154.

ACQUIRING A SECOND LANGUAGE

Besides your first language, you have probably acquired at least the rudiments of a second language, perhaps Russian, Spanish, German, French, Japanese—or English. The term *first language* refers to the language one acquires in infancy. A second language is *any* language that is acquired after one's first language; it may well be a third or fourth "second language." When we speak of second languages in this chapter, we focus on those acquired as adults.

First and Second Languages

There are two common situations in which adults learn a second language. Some may study a foreign language in school or college. As with English taught abroad, such situations often provide relatively little opportunity for experience with the spoken language outside the classroom. In this sense, the study of French in the United States could be called "French as a foreign language," paralleling the "English as a foreign language" studied in Jiddah, Tokyo, Taipei, and elsewhere. Indeed, we talk of foreign-language requirements for graduation from college, and it is useful to bear in mind that studying a foreign language typically involves activities that differ significantly from those surrounding first-language acquisition and the acquisition of a second language in a community where it is spoken natively and widely. When people acquire a language in a community in which it is spoken natively, they can participate in a range of communicative activities in the target language.

When populations of Poles, Italians, Germans, Norwegians, and others migrated to America in the nineteenth and early twentieth centuries, they settled in a land that was largely English speaking, although many immigrants initially lived in neighborhoods where their first language could be used with neighbors and shopkeepers as well as at home. The migrations of the present day, from Asia and Latin America, for example, represent a similar situation, although the communities in which immigrants now settle often have large enough immigrant populations to maintain the "foreign" language in newspapers and in radio and television broadcasting, as well as in shops, churches, and homes. In some metropolitan areas, dozens of locally broadcast "foreign" languages can be heard on the radio every day, and cable networks regularly broadcast news and entertainment in languages other than English. In Los Angeles, for example, television news is broadcast in Korean, Mandarin, Spanish, Persian, and Tagalog every day, and there are soap operas and variety shows in these languages and several others. Daily newspapers are also published locally in several languages and sold at newsstands side by side with English-language dailies. For elections, sample ballots in Los Angeles typically include a full-page notice informing registered voters: "Under federal law, voter information pamphlets are available in English as well as the following languages." Five brief paragraphs follow, each in a different language, giving telephone numbers for obtaining pamphlets or alternative-language ballots in Chinese, Japanese, Vietnamese, Tagalog, and Spanish. (See the photo in Chapter 1 on page 4.)

Staff members at many bank branches in Los Angeles are bilingual in English and another language spoken in the neighborhood, and many other commercial and professional establishments routinely provide bilingual service. As a result of such interwoven linguistic networks in some North American communities and communities around the globe, the distinction between second language and "foreign" language is not altogether tidy.

Comparing First- and Second-Language Acquisition

Typically there are significant differences between first- and second-language learning. To begin with (and by definition), first-language acquisition involves an initial linguistic experience, while a second language is mastered only by someone who already speaks another language. However blank the language slate may be at birth, it is certainly not blank after first-language acquisition is completed.

Additionally, a first language is usually acquired in a home environment by an infant in the care of parents and other caretakers, with many activities—linguistic and otherwise—jointly focused on the child. In such circumstances, language use is closely tied to the immediate surroundings and the context of language use. Caretakers use language in reference to objects in the immediate environment (objects that can be seen or heard by the infant), and language content reflects ongoing activity in which child and caretaker are participating as actors (as with eating or bathing) or as observers (of activities within sight or earshot). In contrast, second-language learning is seldom so context bound. Ordinarily an adult speaking a second language in a class-room is using it to discuss imaginary or decontextualized events removed from the learning situation.

A third difference has to do with the adaptability and malleability of learners as a consequence of age and of social identity. Infants have not yet developed strong social identities as to gender, ethnicity, or social status, factors that can be an important part of the social identity and self-awareness of adolescents and adults. Since language use reflects (and helps create) social identity, as you saw in Chapter 11, the social-psychological experiences of first- and second-language acquisition can differ greatly. For many second-language learners, the language variety being studied is emblematic of a different social status or different ethnicity from that represented by their first language, and for nearly all learners it represents new and different cultural values. For infants, this is not the case, of course, so such factors do not come into play in first-language acquisition. Ordinarily, acquisition of a first language and of a social identity go hand in hand and are inseparable.

A fourth difference is that second-language learners ordinarily have linguistic meta-knowledge that is lacking at least in the early stages of a first language. That is, with a second language, speakers may already possess a vocabulary for referring to language structures and language uses. They will certainly be aware that words and sounds differ from language to language, that some sounds are more difficult to make than others, that languages differ grammatically, and that speakers can be recognized as native or nonnative by their speech patterns. Naturally, such meta-knowledge is lacking for the first-language acquirer, who plays with language spontaneously and unselfconsciously.

Even when second-language learners haven't been exposed to such terms as *noun, verb,* and *sentence,* they are aware of certain linguistic phenomena—the existence of words, the notions of regional, social, and foreign accent, the existence of well-formed and ill-formed sentences, and so on. For many other second-language learners, phonological terms such as *consonant* and *vowel* and grammatical terms such as *verb* and *subject* are familiar. Just what influence knowledge of such categories may have on second-language acquisition is not known. Some investiga-tors believe that conscious knowledge of grammar can facilitate acquisition for some learners, but to what degree and in what ways is not well understood.

Motivation's Role in Second-Language Learning

Among the things that clearly affect mastery of a second language is the kind of mo-tivation that a learner has. People learn another language for many reasons, from va-cationing abroad where you may need to seek directions in the local language to taking up permanent residence in a locale where it is the sole means of communica-tion. For some American students the principal reason for second-language study is to meet a graduation requirement. Motivations for second-language learning can be grouped under the headings of instrumental and integrative.

Instrumental Motivation   An **instrumental motivation** is one in which knowledge of the target language will help achieve some other goal: reading scientific works, singing or understanding opera, graduating. For such uses, only a narrow range of registers (or even a single register) is necessary, and little or no social integration of the learner into a community using the language is desired.

Integrative Motivation   Integrative motivation is fundamentally different from instrumental motivation. When you take up residence in a community that uses the target language in its social interactions, **integrative motivation** encourages you to learn the new language as a way to integrate yourself socially into the community and become one of its members. Integrative motivation typically underlies successful acquisition of a wide range of registers and a nativelike pronunciation, achievements that usually elude learners with instrumental motivation.

Teaching and Learning Foreign Languages

Of the several methods of foreign-language instruction in use, you are probably familiar with pattern drills, translation, composition, listening comprehension, and a few others. Some methods are grounded in the behaviorist assumption that language mastery is a matter of inducing the right habits, much as first-language acquisition was earlier assumed to be. Other methods, aiming to be more "naturalistic," attempt to emulate the kinds of language experience children have when acquiring a first language. With naturalistic methods the emphasis is on interactional use, especially conversation, focused on matters close at hand; noninteractional use aims to provide abundant input that is nearly fully comprehensible to the learner because of its familiarity.

Contrastive Analysis   For decades, learning a second language was viewed as a matter of knowing and practicing the well-formed utterances of the target language. Learning a second language was approached as a matter of drilling grammatical patterns, and drill focused on patterns that differ from those of the first language. To prepare teaching materials, researchers carried out a **contrastive analysis** of the phonological and grammatical structures of the native and target languages, producing a list of morphological, grammatical, and phonological features that could be expected to prove difficult for learners because they differed from those of the first language.

For various reasons, teaching materials based on contrastive analysis have not proven very effective. A number of problems have been uncovered, among them the recognition of an asymmetry between learners acquiring one another's language. Contrastive analysis predicts that when two languages contrast, the difference between them should prove equally challenging for speakers of both languages. In fact, however, difficulties typically prove asymmetrical. Rather than English and Chinese speakers having equivalent difficulties learning one another's language, there are great differences in various parts of the grammar. A distinction such as English makes between masculine and feminine singular pronouns (*he* versus *she*) proves difficult to master for speakers of Chinese, which makes no such distinction, whereas it is easy for English speakers to ignore the distinction. Similarly, Chinese doesn't express the copula BE in many places where English requires it. It is relatively easy for English speakers to omit BE in such sentences but very challenging for Chinese speakers to express it where it is required in English. Likewise, English speakers find it tough to learn the Chinese tone system, while Chinese speakers find it easy to adapt to the absence of a tone system in English. Contrastive analysis also suggests that certain differences in structure should warrant considerable attention, whereas in practice learners avoid the structure altogether, substituting alternative means of expression in the target language.

Interlanguage   Some researchers view second-language learners as developing a series of interlanguages in their progression towards mastery of the target language. An **interlanguage** is that form of the target language that a learner has internalized, and the interlanguage grammar underlies the spontaneous utterances of a learner in the target language. The grammar of an interlanguage can differ from the grammar of the target language in various ways: by containing rules borrowed from the native language, by containing overgeneralizations, by lacking certain sounds of the target language, by inappropriately marking certain verbs in the lexicon as requiring (or not requiring) a preposition, by lacking certain rules altogether, and so on. A language learner can be viewed as progressing from one interlanguage to another, each one approximating more closely the target language.

Fossilizing   For various reasons, often related to the kind of motivation a learner has, the language-learning process typically slows down or ceases at some point, and the existing interlanguage stabilizes, with negligible further acquisition (leaving aside new vocabulary). When such stabilization occurs, the interlanguage may contain rules or other features that differ from those of the target language. This **fossilization** underlies the nonnative speech characteristics of someone who may have spoken the target language for some time but has stopped the process of learning. In other words, many second-language learners fossilize at a stage of acquisition that falls short of nativelike speech. Fossilization then is at the root of a foreign accent when, for instance, certain sounds have not been acquired or their allophonic distribution in the fossilized interlanguage does not match that of native speakers of the target language. The pronunciation of English *thin* and *then* as *sin* and *zen* by native speakers of French may reflect fossilization at a stage before the English sounds /θ/ and /ð/ (which do not occur in the French inventory) have been acquired. Likewise, the language of the English speaker who pronounces the French words *pain* 'bread' and *Pierre* with the aspirated [pʰ] that English has in word-initial position (instead of the unaspirated [p] of French) may have fossilized before the distribution of the French allophones was mastered.

Grammatical fossilization is manifest in expressions such as those below, which come from a native speaker of Mandarin.

1. I want to see what can I buy.
2. Where I can buy them?
3. What you gonna do on Tuesday?
4. I will cold.
5. Where did you found it?
6. Why you buy it?
7. How you pronounce this word?
8. Oh! Look this.

Such sentences reflect the speaker's current interlanguage grammar; for a speaker whose acquisition of English has ceased to develop, the utterances would represent fossilization.

The Role of Attitudes in Second-Language Learning

Language attitudes can have a profound effect on your ability to acquire a second language, especially beyond adolescence. *Studying* a foreign language is parallel to learning math or history; a body of information must be mastered, certainly including much vocabulary and perhaps including terms such as case, tense, (subjunctive) mood, and (subordinate) clause. This kind of foreign-language learning differs not only from first-language acquisition but also from second-language acquisition in immersion situations in which you can acquire a language in a fashion approximating (however inadequately) the environment normally surrounding first-language acquisition. Because the language variety you acquire becomes part of your social identity, the acquisition of a second language must be seen not just as an intellectual exercise but as an enterprise that affects or alters one's social identity.

Your attitude toward the second language and your motivation can have a profound effect on the success of acquisition. In acquiring a foreign language, your efforts are mediated by what linguist Stephen Krashen has called an affective filter—a psychological disposition that facilitates or inhibits your natural language-acquisition capacities. Krashen maintains that if there is sufficient comprehensible language use surrounding a learner, the acquisition of a second language, even by an adult, can proceed as effortlessly and efficiently as first-language acquisition, provided that the affective filter is not blocking the operation of these capacities.

The learning of a second language in school is increasingly viewed not as an intellectual or educational phenomenon but as a social-psychological phenomenon. One social psychologist describes this perspective as follows:

> In the acquisition of a second language, the student is faced with the task not simply of learning new information . . . which is part of his *own* culture but rather of *acquiring* symbolic elements of a different ethnolinguistic community. The new words are not simply new words for old concepts, the new grammar is not simply a new way of ordering words, the

new pronunciations are not merely 'different' ways of saying things. They are characteristics of another ethnolinguistic community. Furthermore, the student is not being asked to learn about them; he is being asked to acquire them, to make them part of his own language reservoir. This involves imposing elements of another culture into one's own lifespace. As a result, the student's harmony with his own cultural community and his willingness or ability to identify with other cultural communities become important considerations in the process of second language acquisition. (R. C. Gardner, "Social Psychological Aspects of Second Language Acquisition," in Howard Giles and Robert St. Clair, eds., *Language and Social Psychology* [Oxford: Blackwell, 1979], pp. 193–94.)

Computers and Language Learning

 In recent years, computers have been playing increasingly important roles in the study of first-language acquisition. The question of nature versus nurture—addressing the likelihood that language is either partly innate or entirely learned—has invited researchers to create models of how language would be acquired given one set of assumptions or another. Computers have proven essential to such complicated modeling as language acquisition entails, and while no agreement exists about what the facts of acquisition are, computational modeling is a strong ally in answering the question.

On another front, data collection and analysis have been the bedrock foundation of many of the best studies of child language acquisition, so it is not surprising that corpora of children's language have been compiled. Collecting copious data of children's language is technically challenging and time consuming, as well as difficult and expensive to transcribe for research purposes. In order to pool resources and make available to a wide spectrum of researchers the data that have been collected, researchers at Carnegie Mellon University have spearheaded an impressive project that goes by the name of CHILDES (Child Language Data Exchange System). CHILDES makes its database and software programs available via the Internet to scholars worldwide. The collection of child language data gathered and transcribed to agreed-upon standards by researchers around the globe is accompanied by a set of software programs nicknamed CLAN. With CLAN, researchers have explored the vast resources of the CHILDES database and have made a major impact on the ways in which research into first-

language acquisition is carried out. (For more information about CHILDES or for access to the files, see the CHILDES Web site, cited in the "Other Resources" section at the end of this chapter.)

Besides first-language corpora like those in the CHILDES project, corpora of second-language learners are now being compiled. They, too, give promise of providing researchers with previously unimagined access to high-quality data in great abundance. For example, the compilers of the *Longman Active Study Dictionary of English* relied on the "Longman Learner's Corpus of Students' English" to write over 250 new usage notes.

Computers have for some decades been used in language laboratories to help students studying foreign languages. An entire field has sprung up that goes by the nickname of CALL, the acronym for computer-assisted language learning. You are almost certainly familiar with some of the language teaching methods that have been facilitated by CALL. Among the most familiar ways in which computers have assisted language learners are by making CD-ROMs available for listening to language lessons. Of course, in some sense CD-ROMs have simply replaced audiocassette recordings, but more importantly they enable much freer interaction with the foreign-language materials. They also enable multimedia language lessons, including not only audio but also visual presentations. Programs that one can find on CD-ROM are sometimes accompanied by interactive teaching and testing.

Other uses of the computer are even more innovative, though not everyone is convinced of their efficacy. In one interesting application, CD-ROM audio programs are accompanied by voiceprints of native speakers and a microphone for use by the learner. Using the microphone and a relatively advanced speech recognition technology, learners of Spanish, German, French, and English, for example, can practice their pronunciation until it matches the pronunciations of the native speaker voice. (If you're interested in finding out more about these programs, you can search the Internet for "globalink," a company that already has such products in shops.)

There is no doubt that computers will enable researchers to test their hypotheses more efficiently and more definitively than has been possible before. There is also no doubt that microcomputer technologies are revolutionizing the way that learners can tackle a foreign language. What the future holds in these respects can hardly be imagined.

SUMMARY

- Children do not acquire their native language through instruction by adults or through mere imitation of what they hear adults say.

- While a child must receive some linguistic input in order to acquire language, input is not the sole factor and may not be the chief factor that accounts for the development of grammatical competence and the ability to produce and understand language.

- There is considerable evidence that children are born with the mental capacity to acquire language, probably with a disposition to acquire certain kinds of structures, and perhaps with additional specifications as to the kinds of grammar that are eligible for acquisition.

- Various stages of language acquisition can be identified, distinguished by the amount of content a child is able to express in an utterance vis-à-vis an adult's expression in equivalent circumstances.

- Even before children utter their first interpretable words, they use language socially, for example, by engaging in turn-taking expressions with caregivers.

- Adopting a second-language variety—whether a standard variety of one's first language or a foreign language—is not merely an intellectual exercise but an experience fraught with emotional overtones.

- The study of a foreign language cannot be equated with the study of history or math because, more than understanding, it involves adapting to certain customs of a different social group.

WHAT DO YOU THINK? REVISITED

❖ *Bragging Brenda.* Kids learn vocabulary only by hearing it. But they intuit syntactic processes as abstract patterns that apply to broad categories and use those patterns to produce sentences they've never heard.

❖ *Nursery school parent.* It's true! Although there's some variation, children acquire the grammatical parts of their language in approximately the same order.

❖ *Cousin Kevin.* Kids don't hear anyone say "maked," "breaked," or "runned" for *made, broke,* and *ran,* but they often overgeneralize the patterns they do hear for creating grammatical forms. The fact that they overgeneralize suggests that they don't imitate what they hear but apply intuited patterns, sometimes even to words that are exceptions.

❖ *Frustrated Frank.* Once a first language is acquired, it may "interfere" with acquisition of a second language and contribute to a "foreign accent." Obviously, there's no interference acquiring a first language. In addition, Frank's social identity is intertwined with his first language, as with everyone else, and acquiring a second language may require adaptation to the social identity represented by the other language. That's also something that's not true of first language acquisition. A great deal of the process of acquiring a first language is automatic and not consciously learned. Likewise, the process of acquiring a second language is not altogether a conscious activity and not altogether under one's conscious control.

EXERCISES

15-1 Make a list of baby-talk vocabulary in your first language. Identify the kinds of referents baby-talk vocabulary has, the lexical categories most frequently represented, and the phonological form of such vocabulary. If there are different first languages represented in your class, compare the characteristics of baby-talk terms cross-linguistically as to kinds of referents, lexical categories, and phonological form.

15-2 **a.** Explain in what ways the use of personal names such as *Baby* and *Mommy* could be easier for a young child to perceive and analyze than personal pronouns such as *I* and *you.*

b. Explain in what ways the use of content words (nouns, verbs, adjectives) could make baby talk easier for a child to analyze and understand than function words such as conjunctions and articles.

15-3 Tape-record a brief passage of talk between an adult or older child and a young child. Transcribe 45 seconds of the recorded talk and identify an example of each feature of baby talk discussed in this chapter. Organize your list into features of phonology, vocabulary, syntax, and discourse. (Television shows for children may provide access to such samples.)

15-4 On the basis of what you know about overgeneralizations of morphological rules, what forms would you predict children might use for each of the adult words below? In each case identify the rule that is being overgeneralized.

Verbs				*Nouns*	*Adjectives*	*Pronouns*
hurt	told	took	threw	geese	better	I
ate	came	bled	broke	sheep (pl.)	beautiful	myself

15-5 The utterances below (taken, slightly adapted, from Fletcher [1985]) were spoken by an English child named Sophie on three separate days over the course of about a year. Examine them closely and characterize the progress of Sophie's language acquisition across the three occasions with respect to the following features:

possessive determiners (*my, your*)	yes/no questions
the copula BE (*is, are*)	prepositions
adverbs (*down, there*)	interrogative word order
declarative word order	negative sentences
clauses per utterance	information questions
auxiliary DO	auxiliaries other than DO
contractible copula	regular noun plurals

Example: Personal pronouns—Based on this sample, Sophie, at 2;4, displays second-person *you* and first-person singular *me; she* uses *me* for both subject and oblique grammatical relations. At 3;0 she uses *her* for subject and oblique relations. At 3;5, the adult forms *I, you,* and *we* occur as subjects, *me* as object, and *it* as subject and object, but *her* appears as the subject form instead of *she.*

Age Two Years, Four Months

   (1) Me want your tea.

   (2) Where's the doll house?

   (3) Mary come me.

   (4) Me want Daddy come down.

   (5) That your turn.

   (6) That's a mess.

   (7) You play "Snakes and Ladders" me?

Age Three Years

   (8) Shall me sit mon my legs?

   (9) Can me put it in like that?

 (10) That not go in there.

 (11) Why did Hester be fast asleep?

 (12) What this one called?

 (13) What did her have wrong with her?

 (14) What is that one called?

 (15) Daddy didn't give me two in the end.

Age Three Years, Five Months

 (16) This isn't a piano book.

 (17) I don't know what to do.

 (18) Where my corder?

 (19) Can you take off my shoes?

 (20) How did that broke?

 (21) You won't let me play a guitar.

 (22) If you do it like this, it won't come down.

 (23) While Hester at school we can buy some sweets.

 (24) When her's at school I'll buy some sweeties.

 (25) I want to ring up somebody and her won't be there tomorrow.

15-6   Compare the nonnative adult English sentences on page 562 with the native English sentences of the child Sophie given in Exercise 15–5 above. List as many features as you can that are shared by both sets of data; list as many features as you can that belong only to one set or the other. Which features seem easier for the young Sophie to learn than for the adult nonnative speaker, and which seem easier for the nonnative speaker than for Sophie? What explanation can you offer for why certain features might be harder for Sophie or harder for the nonnative speaker to learn?

15-7 List four reasons that make it more difficult to gather language data from preschoolers than from schoolchildren and adults, and identify several technological advances (beginning with the tape recorder) that can help overcome those difficulties and increase the quantity or quality of data for research into first-language acquisition.

Especially for Educators and Future Teachers

15-8 Reflect on your own experience in learning a second language. Were you generally successful at it? If so, what contributed to that success? If not, what made it difficult for you? Were there others—perhaps fellow students—who found it much easier or much harder than you to learn a second language? If you have learned more than one second language, were they equally easy or equally difficult? If they weren't, what could account for the difference? Did your attitude toward the people whose language you were learning influence your success at all?

15-9 What implications for second-language teachers do you see in the discussion of identity and attitudes in this chapter?

OTHER RESOURCES

Internet

- **CHILDES: http://poppy.psy.cmu.edu/childes/index.html**
  A rich source of information about research in child language acquisition, this Web site also offers data and software.

- **LTG Helpdesk: http://www.ltg.ed.ac.uk/helpdesk/faq/index.html**
  A useful Web site providing a series of frequently asked questions (FAQs) and answers as well as many links to a variety of language technology projects. Among the FAQs: Does anyone know of a corpus containing data on second-language learning? Can you tell me where to find Arabic texts? Persian texts? Do you have any information on automatic translation software? What Web-based resources are there for learning of natural languages?

Videos

- **Acquiring the Human Language: "Playing the Language Game"**
  One of four videos in *The Human Language Series,* an award-winning set of videos originally broadcast on PBS in 1995. This 55-minute video explores how children seem to acquire language spontaneously and without instruction. It asks, "Do people imitate those around them or is grammar inherited?" (Available for rent or purchase from Transit Media, 22-D Hollywood Avenue, Ho-Ho-Kus, NJ 07423 / Tel. (800) 343–5540.)

- **The Human Language Evolves: "With and without Words"**
  Part of the same series as the previous entry, this excellent 55-minute video explores the reasons human beings acquired language while chimpanzees and other species did not; includes fascinating discussion of animal and human gestures.

- **Baby Talk**
  An interesting and informative video about first-language acquisition beginning even in the womb, produced by NOVA for public television and first broadcast in 1985.

- **Secret of the Wild Child**
  An Emmy-winning video in the NOVA series; explores the troubled history of Genie. You can get NOVA videos from many video rental stores. For information about purchasing NOVA videos, contact WGBH NOVA Videos / P.O. Box 2284 / South Burlington, VT 05407–2284 / Tel. (800) 255-WGBH. Or visit WGBH's Web site at http://www.pbs.org/wgbh/nova/novastore.html. To read an online transcript of this video, visit http://www.pbs.org/plweb-cgi/fastweb?search and click on "Secret of the Wild Child."

- **English-Speaking World**
  From *The Story of English* series with host Robert MacNeil, this video discusses English around the world and offers insight into instrumental motivations for second-language acquisition.

SUGGESTIONS FOR FURTHER READING

- **Gerry T. M. Altmann. 1997.** *The Ascent of Babel: An Exploration of Language, Mind, and Understanding* (Oxford: Oxford University Press). Written by a psychologist, this wide-ranging treatment of the cognitive aspects of first-language acquisition, though written in nontechnical language, requires some effort but is worth it.

- **Roger Brown. 1973.** *A First Language: The Early Stages* (Cambridge: Harvard University Press). An accessible classic, now available in paperback. Our examples of adult expansions of children's utterances and the list of 14 morphemes ordered by sequence of acquisition come from this book.

- **Alison J. Elliot. 1981.** *Child Language* (Cambridge: Cambridge University Press). Another good follow-up to the present chapter; highly accessible.

- **Rod Ellis. 1986.** *Understanding Second Language Acquisition* (Oxford: Oxford University Press). An accessible and comprehensive textbook about how second languages are acquired.

- **Jean Berko Gleason, ed. 1989.** *The Development of Language,* 2nd ed. (Columbus: Merrill). A good next step after the present chapter, with separate chapters on phonology, syntax, semantics, and pragmatics, among others.

- **Wolfgang Klein. 1986.** *Second Language Acquisition* (Cambridge: Cambridge University Press). An accessible and comprehensive treatment of second-language acquisition.

- **Robert E. Owens, Jr. 1996.** *Language Development: An Introduction,* 4th ed. (Boston: Allyn and Bacon). A detailed, accessible treatment attending to both social and psychological concerns.

ADVANCED READING

The most comprehensive treatment of first-language acquisition is in the set of articles in Fletcher and MacWhinney (1995). In some instances, these chapters may rely on more background than students who have read only this textbook will possess, but they are useful overviews for instructors. Chapter 4 of Slobin (1979) is highly accessible. Goodluck (1991) provides a clear introduction to aspects of child language acquisition that bear closely on current grammatical theory. O'Grady (1997) is a well-balanced treatment of syntactic development, offering analysis from various theoretical points of view.

Curtiss (1977) recounts the story of Genie, the child who received virtually no language input. Schieffelin and Ochs (1986) contains fascinating descriptions of socialization into linguistic and social roles in diverse cultures, including those of Samoa, Papua New Guinea, Lesotho (in southern Africa), and Japan. Andersen (1990) describes preschoolers' mastery over the registers associated with social roles such as father, mother, and child in middle-class American homes, as well as teacher and doctor. The socialization of children into gender roles is explored in Swann (1992). Gleason (1980) describes observations of adults teaching children politeness rules for Halloween trick-or-treating, an example of consciously prescriptive input. Slobin (1985) provides a wealth of information on language acquisition around the globe. Peters (1983) investigates the strategies that children use to analyze linguistic input and ways in which baby talk may help that process.

Wanner and Gleitman (1982) lays out the state of knowledge in language acquisition from diverse vantage points; we have relied for some of our discussion on the overview chapter by the editors and on Slobin's chapter, "Universal and Particular in the Acquisition of Language." Ingram (1989), on which we have relied for the stages of phonological acquisition, offers detailed discussion of the research on first-language acquisition. Fletcher (1985) contains four samples of Sophie's language at six-month intervals between 2;6 and 4;0; we have borrowed several examples from these transcriptions. Our discussion of vocabulary acquisition follows M. C. Templin's *Certain Language Skills,* as reported in Miller (1977).

For second-language acquisition, Krashen and Terrell (1983) presents an integrated approach emphasizing naturalistic ways of experiencing comprehensible input. Ryan and Giles (1982) discusses the empirical study of language attitudes and address the role of attitudes in second-language acquisition. Gardner and Lambert (1972) discusses attitudes and motivation in second-language acquisition.

REFERENCES

- Andersen, Elaine Slosberg. 1990. *Speaking with Style: The Sociolinguistic Skills of Children* (London: Routledge).

- Curtiss, Susan. 1977. *Genie: A Psycholinguistic Study of a Modern-day "Wild Child"* (New York: Academic).

- Fletcher, Paul. 1985. *A Child's Learning of English* (London: Blackwell).

- Fletcher, Paul, & Brian MacWhinney. 1995. *The Handbook of Child Language* (Malden, MA: Blackwell).

- Gleason, Jean Berko. 1980. "The Acquisition of Social Speech: Routines and Politeness Formulas," in Howard Giles, W. Peter Robinson, & Philip M. Smith, eds., *Language: Social Psychological Perspectives* (New York: Academic).

- Goodluck, Helen. 1991. *Language Acquisition: A Linguistic Introduction* (Oxford: Blackwell).

- Ingram, David. 1989. *First Language Acquisition: Method, Description, and Explanation* (Cambridge: Cambridge University Press).

- Krashen, Stephen D., & Tracy D. Terrell. 1983. *The Natural Approach: Language Acquisition in the Classroom* (Hayward, CA: Alemany).

- Miller, George A. 1977. *Spontaneous Apprentices: Children and Language* (New York: Seabury).
- O'Grady, William. 1997. *Syntactic Development* (Chicago: University of Chicago Press).
- Peters, Ann M. 1983. *The Units of Language Acquisition* (Cambridge: Cambridge University Press).
- Ryan, Ellen Bouchard, & Howard Giles, eds. 1982. *Attitudes towards Language Variation: Social and Applied Contexts* (London: Edward Arnold).
- Schieffelin, Bambi B., & Elinor Ochs, eds. 1986. *Language Socialization across Cultures* (Cambridge: Cambridge University Press).
- Slobin, Dan I. 1979. *Psycholinguistics,* 2nd ed. (Glenview, IL: Scott Foresman).
- Slobin, Dan I., ed. 1985. *The Crosslinguistic Study of Language Acquisition.* 2 vols. (Hillsdale, NJ: Erlbaum).
- Swann, Joan. 1992. *Girls, Boys and Language* (Oxford: Blackwell).
- Wanner, Eric, & Lila R. Gleitman, eds. 1982. *Language Acquisition: The State of the Art* (Cambridge: Cambridge University Press).

Glossary

This Glossary characterizes important terms used in this book. When first discussed in the text, such terms are printed in **boldface** to indicate their importance. Within the Glossary, *italicized* terms with an asterisk have their own entry. For further discussion of a term, consult the index.

Absolute universal   A linguistic pattern at play in all languages of the world without exception. Example: "Any language with voiced stops also has voiceless stops."

Accent   The pronunciation features of any spoken language *variety.*

Acronym   An abbreviation formed by combining the initials of an expression into a pronounceable word. Examples: *NATO, SARS, radar, yuppy, scuba* (but not *USA, UK, EU, UN, PC, BBC, ATM,* whose pronunciations merely voice the names of the letters, as in B-B-C).

Adjacency pair   A set of two consecutive, ordered turns that "go together" in a conversation, such as question/answer sequences and greeting/greeting exchanges.

Adjective   A lexical category of words that serve semantically to specify the attributes of nouns (as in *tall* ships) and that can represent degrees of comparison morphologically (*taller*) or syntactically (*most beautiful*); adjectives can have *attributive* function (*those tall ships*) or *predicative* function (*those ships are tall*).

Adverb   A lexical class with wide-ranging functions and no inflections. Many English adverbs are derived from adjectives with the *derivational morpheme* -LY (as in *suddenly, quickly* from *sudden, quick*), but the most common adverbs have no distinguishing marks (*soon, very, today*).

Affective meaning   Information conveyed about the attitudes and emotions of the language users toward the content or context of their expression; together with *social meaning*, affective meaning is sometimes called *connotation*.

Affix   A *bound morpheme* that attaches to a root or stem *morpheme* (called the *root* or *stem*). *Prefixes* and *suffixes* are the most common types of affixes in the world's languages; less common are *infixes* and *circumfixes*.

Affricate   A sound produced when air is built up by a complete closure of the oral tract at some *place of articulation* and then released and continued like a *fricative*; also called a *stop fricative*. Examples: English [tʃ], as in *chin* and [dʒ]) as in *gin*; German [ts] as in *Zeit* 'time.' In American practice, [tʃ] is sometimes written as [č] and [dʒ] as [ǰ].

Agreement   The marking of a word (as with an *affix*) to indicate its grammatical relationship to another word in the sentence. Thus, a verb that *agrees* with its *subject* in *person* and *number* has a form that indicates that relationship; an adjective may agree with a noun in *gender*, *number*, and *case*.

Allomorph An alternant realization (i.e., phonological form) of a morpheme in a particular linguistic environment. For example, the English 'PLURAL' morpheme has three allomorphs: [əz] (as in *buses)*, [z] *(twigs)*, and [s] *(cats)*.

Allophone A phonetic realization (i.e., a pronunciation) of a *phoneme* in a particular phonological environment. Example: In English, unaspirated [p] and *aspirated* [pʰ] are allophones of the phoneme /p/, and they occur in *complementary distribution*.

Alphabet A writing system in which, ideally, each graphic sign represents a distinctive sound (i.e., a *phoneme)* of the language.

Alveolar A sound articulated at the alveolar ridge, the bony ridge just behind and above the upper teeth.

Alveo-palatal A *place of articulation* in the oral cavity between the alveolar ridge and the palate. Example: The English sound [ʃ] (sometimes written [š]) represented by <sh> in *shoe* is articulated in the alveo-palatal region.

Ambiguous A term used to characterize an expression that can be interpreted in more than one way as a consequence of having more than one *constituent structure (John or Jack and Bill)* or more than one *referential meaning (river <u>bank</u>, savings <u>bank</u>)*.

Antonymy A term used in *lexical semantics* to denote opposite meanings; word pairs with opposite meanings are said to be *antonymous,* as with *wet* and *dry*.

Appropriateness conditions Conventions that regulate the interpretation under which an *utterance* serves as a particular *speech act,* such as a question, promise, or invitation.

Approximant A sound produced when one articulator approaches another but the vocal tract is not sufficiently narrowed to create the audible friction that typically characterizes a *consonant*. Examples: [w], [j], [r], [l]. See *liquid*.

Argot The specialized vocabulary of a group, often an occupational or recreational group; unlike *slang,* argot is not limited to situations of extreme informality.

Argument A noun phrase occurring with a verb as part of a proposition. For example, in *Alice washed the car* the verb *wash* has two arguments—a *subject (Alice)* and a *direct object (the car)*. (Some analysts do not treat subjects as arguments.)

Aspect A grammatical category of verbs, marking the way in which a situation described by the verb takes place in time, for example, as continuous, repetitive, or instantaneous.

Aspirated A term for sounds produced with an accompanying puff of air; represented in phonetic transcription by a following raised [ʰ].

Assimilation A phonological process whereby a sound becomes phonetically similar (or identical) to a neighboring sound. Examples: In Korean, underlying /p/ is pronounced as [b] between vowels; that is, /p/ assimilates to the voicing of the neighboring vowels.

Attributive adjective An adjective that is syntactically part of the noun phrase whose head it modifies (*a <u>spooky</u> film);* distinguished from a *predicative adjective (The film is <u>spooky</u>)*.

Auxiliary verb A verb used with (or instead of) the main verb to carry certain kinds of grammatical information, such as *tense* and *aspect*. In English, the auxiliary verb is inverted with the *subject* in yes/no questions (<u>Can</u> *Lou fail?*) and carries the negative element in contractions (*Lou <u>can't</u> sing)*.

Bilabial A *place of articulation* involving both lips; a sound produced there.

Bilingualism   The state of having *competence, both grammatical and communicative, in more than one language.

Bound morpheme   A *morpheme that cannot stand alone as a word. Examples: -MENT (as in *establishment*), -ER (*painter*), and 'PLURAL' (*zebras*). See *free morpheme.

Case   A grammatical category associated with nouns and pronouns, indicating their grammatical relationship to other elements in the clause, often the verb. Example: The pronoun *I* is marked for common case, *me* for objective case, while *book* is said to be unmarked or to be marked for common case. In some languages, adjectives agree in case with nouns.

Circumfix   A discontinuous morpheme that combines a *prefix and *suffix in a single *morpheme occurring on both ends of a root or stem.

Clause   A constituent unit of syntax consisting of a verb with its *argument noun phrases; a clause can stand alone as a simple sentence or function as a *constituent of another clause.

Click   A *stop *consonant defined by its *manner of articulation and pronounced at various *places of articulation; clicks such as the alveolar click used in English to express disapproval, as in *tsk-tsk* or *tut-tut,* function as phonemes in some Bantu languages, such as Zulu and Xhosa.

Coda   The term for any consonants that follow the *nucleus in the *rhyme of a *syllable; for example, in the syllable [pɛn], [n] is the coda.

Cognates   Words or *morphemes that have developed from a single, historically earlier source. Example: English *father,* German *Vater,* Spanish *padre,* and Gothic *fadar* are cognates because all of them have developed from the same reconstructed Proto-Indo-European word (*pəter*). The term *cognates* is also used of languages that have a common historical ancestor, as with English, Russian, German, Persian, and the other *Indo-European languages.

Collocation   Word pairs or sets that habitually co-occur (i.e., occur near one another) in *texts.

Communicative competence   See *competence.

Comparative reconstruction   A method used in historical linguistics to uncover vocabulary and structures of an ancestor language by drawing inferences from the evidence remaining in several daughter languages. See also *cognates and *correspondence set.

Competence   The ability to produce and assign meaning to grammatical sentences is called *grammatical competence;* the ability to produce and interpret utterances appropriate to their context of use is called *communicative competence.*

Complementary distribution   A pattern of distribution of two or more sounds that do not occur in the same position within words in a given language. Example: In English, [pʰ] does not occur where [p] occurs (and vice versa).

Complex sentence   A sentence consisting of a matrix *clause and at least one embedded (i.e., subordinate) clause.

Conditioned sound change   A *regular sound change that occurs only in a particular, specifiable sound environment, but not in all environments in which the sound appears. Example: The merger of the vowels in *pin* and *pen* in Southern American English is a conditioned sound change because the merger occurs only before nasals; thus, *pit* and *pet* are distinguished from one another, but not *him* and *hem.*

Conjugation   See *paradigm.

Conjunction   A closed class of words that serve to link clauses or phrases; coordinating conjunctions conjoin expressions of the same status, as with clauses (*She went but he stayed*) or noun phrases (*Alice and I*); subordinating conjunctions embed one clause into another (*Leave when you're ready*).

Consonant   A speech sound produced by partial or complete closure of part of the vocal tract, thus obstructing the airflow and creating audible friction. Consonants are described in terms of *voicing, *place of articulation, and *manner of articulation. Abbreviated C.

Constituent   A syntactic unit that functions as part of a larger unit within a sentence; typical constituent types are verb phrase, noun phrase, prepositional phrase, and *clause.

Constituent structure   The linear and hierarchical organization of the words of a sentence into syntactic units.

Content   Information conveyed or communicated by linguistic *expression as interpreted in a particular *context.

Content word   A word whose primary function is to describe entities, ideas, qualities, and states of being in the world; *nouns, *verbs, *adjectives, and *adverbs are content words; content words are contrasted with *function words.

Context   One of three main elements (context, *expression, *meaning) in a speech situation. Context typically refers to those aspects of a speech situation that affect the expression and enable an interpretation of the context.

Contractions   Spoken or written expressions that represent a fusion of two or more words in a single word. Examples: *can't/cannot; she'll/she will; could've/could have; wanna/want to; gonna/going to.*

Contrastive   A term used in *semantics of a noun phrase that is marked as being in opposition to another noun phrase in the same *discourse.

Contrastive analysis   A method of analyzing languages for instructional purposes whereby a native language and target language are compared with a view to establishing points of difference likely to cause difficulties for learners.

Converseness   The term for a reciprocal relationship between two words, as in *husband* and *wife* or *buy* and *sell.*

Cooperative principle   Four maxims that describe how language users cooperate in producing and understanding utterances in context: *quantity, quality, relevance, orderliness.*

Coordinate sentence   A sentence that contains at least two *clauses, neither of which functions as a *constituent of the other. Example: *John went to England, and Mary went to France.*

Coordinating conjunction   A category of *function words that serve to conjoin expressions of the same status, such as *clause (*He spoke and I wept*), *adverb (*slowly but surely*), or noun (*Thelma and Louise*).

Corpus   A representative collection of texts, usually in machine-readable form and including information about the situation in which each text originated, such as the speaker or author, addressee, or audience.

Corpus linguistics   The activities involved in compiling and using a *corpus* to investigate natural language use.

Correspondence set   A set of sounds in different languages, all of which derive from a single sound in a historically earlier language.

Creole   A contact language, a former *pidgin,* that has "acquired" native speakers.

Cuneiform   A written sign developed by the Sumerians and Akkadians in the Middle East around 3000 B.C.; characterized by the wedgelike shape that results from its being written on wet clay with a stylus.

Declension   The term used for a noun *paradigm.*

Deep structure   See *underlying structure.*

Definite   A noun phrase that is marked to indicate that the speaker believes the addressee can identify its referent; contrast with *indefinite.* In English, definiteness and indefiniteness can be marked by the choice of determiner (e.g., *the* versus *a).*

Degree   A grammatical category associated with the extent of comparison for *adjectives* and *adverbs;* positive degree (as in *speedy);* comparative degree (*speedier* or *more speedy);* superlative degree (*speediest* or *most speedy).*

Deixis   The marking of the orientation or position of entities and situations with respect to certain points of reference such as the place (*here/there)* and time (*now/then)* of utterance.

Derivation   In morphology designates a process whereby one lexical item is transformed into another one with a related meaning but belonging to a different lexical class. Example: The adverb *slowly* is derived from *slow* (an adjective) by suffixing the *derivational morpheme* -LY.

Derivational morpheme   A *morpheme* that serves to derive a word of one class or meaning from a word of another class or meaning. Examples: -MENT (as in *establishment)* derives the noun from the verb *establish;* RE- (*repaint)* changes the meaning of the verb *paint* to 'paint again.'

Dialect   A language variety characteristic of a particular social group; dialects can be characteristic of regional, ethnic, socioeconomic, or gender groups.

Diphthong   A vowel sound whose production requires the tongue to start in one place and move to another. Examples: the vowels in *lied, loud,* and *Lloyd.* See also *glide.*

Direct object   A kind of grammatical relation; one of two kinds of objects; the noun phrase in a *clause* that, together with the verb, usually forms the verb phrase *constituent;* the object NP is immediately dominated by the VP. Example: *She drove a truck.* See also *indirect object.*

Discourse   Spoken or written language use in particular social situations; discourse is a broader term than *text* in that it includes context and the intended and actual interpretations.

Etymon   The linguistic form from which a word or *morpheme* is historically derived.

Expression   Any bit of spoken, written, or signed language; the audible or visible aspect of language use that conveys particular *content* in a given *context.*

Family   See *language family.*

Flap   A *manner of articulation* produced by quickly flapping the tip of the tongue against some *place of articulation* on the upper surface of the vocal tract, commonly the *alveolar ridge,* as for <t> in the American pronounciation of *metal* [mɛɾəl].

Fossilization   A term used to refer to a final form of *interlanguage* that falls short of the target language; the stage of second-language acquisition where a learner has ceased making substantial progress toward the target language.

Free morpheme   A *morpheme* that can stand alone as a word. Examples: ZEBRA, PAINT, PRETTY, VERY. See *bound morpheme.*

Free variation   A term used to characterize *allophones* of a given *phoneme* that can occur in the same position in a word without altering the word's meaning, as in the final sound of the English word *step,* which can be released [p] or unreleased [p˥].

Fricative   A consonant sound made by passing a continuous stream of air through a narrowed passage in the vocal tract thereby causing turbulence, such as that created between the lower lip and the upper teeth in the production of [f] and [v].

Function words   Words such as determiners and *conjunctions* whose primary role is to mark grammatical relationships between *content words* or structures such as *phrases* and *clauses.*

Gender   A system in which all the nouns of a language fall into distinct classes. Example: German has a gender system of three noun classes (masculine, feminine, and neuter) whose inflections and associated determiners and *adjectives* vary in form for *number* and *case* in *agreement* with the gender class of the noun.

Given information   *Context* already introduced into a *discourse* and therefore presumed to be at the forefront of a hearer's mind; also called old information.

Glide   A transition from a vowel of one quality to the vowel of another quality. In [iᵊ], the superscript schwa represents a glide from the high front position of [i] to the mid central position of [ə]. Glides can be offglides, with the peak on the first element (as in [iᵊ]), or onglides, with the peak on the second element (as in certain pronunciations of *spoon* [ɪᵘ]). See also *diphthong.*

Glottis   A narrow aperture between two folds of muscle (the vocal cords) in the *larynx.*

Grammatical competence   See *competence.*

Grammatical relation   The syntactic role that a noun phrase plays in its *clause* (for example, *subject* or *direct object*).

Homonymy   The term used for the state of having identical expression but different meanings (*book* a flight and buy a *book*); homophonous is sometimes used with the related sense of 'sounding alike' but not necessarily having the same written form (*see* and *sea)* or meaning.

Homophony   The term used in semantic analysis to refer to words that are pronounced alike but have different meanings, as in *two, to, too; see, sea.*

Hyponym   A term whose *referent* is included in the referent of another term. Example: *Blue* is a hyponym of *color; sister* is a hyponym of *sibling.*

Iconic sign   See *representational sign.*

Illocution   The intention that a speaker or writer has in producing a particular utterance. Example: The illocution of the utterance *Can you pass the salt?* is a request that the salt be passed and not (as the structure would indicate) an inquiry about the addressee's *ability* to pass the salt.

Implicational universal   A universal rule of the form "If condition P is satisfied, then conclusion Q holds."

Indefinite   See *definite*.

Indirect object   One of two *grammatical relations* known as objects, the other being a *direct object*. Indirect objects usually occur in English before the direct object (*He gave the clerk a rose*).

Indirect speech act   An *utterance* whose *locution* (or literal meaning) and *illocution* (or intended meaning) are different. Example: *Can you pass the salt?* is literally a yes/no question but is usually uttered as a request or polite directive for action.

Indo-European   A *language family* all of whose members are descendants of an ancestral language called Proto-Indo-European, spoken probably in Central Asia about 5000 years ago.

Infinitive   The basic form of a verb, expressed in English sometimes with the particle *to*, as in *to see*.

Infix   A *morpheme* that is inserted within another morpheme.

Inflectional morpheme   A *bound morpheme* that creates variant forms of a word to mark its syntactic function in a sentence. Examples: The suffix *-s* added to a *verb* (as in *paints*) marks the verb as agreeing with a third-person singular *subject*; *-er* (*taller*) marks *adjectives* for comparative *degree*.

Information structure   The level of structure at which certain elements in a sentence are highlighted or backgrounded according to their prominence in the discourse. See also *pragmatics*.

Instrumental motivation   A term used for the kind of motivation one has in acquiring a second language so as to be able to use it for any purpose other than becoming a participating member of the social community that speaks the language.

Integrative motivation   A term used for the kind of motivation one has in acquiring a second language in order to become a socially functioning member of the community speaking that language.

Interdental   A *place of articulation* between the upper and lower teeth. Also used of sounds produced at that place. Examples of the sound: <th> as in English *thin* [θ] and *then* [ð].

Interlanguage   The term used for the form of a second language that a learner has internalized at any point in the acquisition process and which therefore underlies the learner's spontaneous utterances in the target language.

Intransitive verb   A verb that does not take a *direct object*. Examples: *She smiled. Joyce died in Zurich.*

Isogloss   The geographical boundary marking the limit of the regional distribution of a particular word, pronunciation, or usage.

Language family   A group of languages that have all developed from a single ancestral language.

Larynx   The part of the windpipe that houses the vocal cords; also called the voice box or Adam's apple.

Lexical item   A unit in the *lexicon;* the notion of lexical item includes all inflected forms; thus, *child, child's, children,* and *children's* constitute the lexical item CHILD.

Lexical semantics   The branch of *semantics* that deals with word meaning.

Lexical variety   An index of the number of different words in a text, usually expressed as a fraction of the number of different words divided by the number of running words. Example: *He told her he loved her* would have an index of 0.66, representing four different words in a total of six running words.

Lexicon   The list of all words and *morphemes* stored in a native speaker's memory; this internalized dictionary includes all nonpredictable information about *lexical items.*

Lingua franca   A language *variety* used for communication among groups of people who do not otherwise share a common language. Example: English is the lingua franca of the international scientific community.

Linguistic repertoire   The set of language *varieties* (including *registers* and *dialects*) used in the speaking and writing practices of a speech community; also called verbal repertoire.

Liquid   The name sometimes given to [r] and [l] in order to distinguish them from other *approximants.*

Locution   The literal meaning of an *utterance.* Example: The locution of the utterance *Can you close the window?* is a question about the hearer's ability to close the window.

Logographic writing   Writing in which each sign represents a word. Examples: <8> 'eight' and <$> 'dollar' are logographic signs, as are Chinese characters and Japanese kanji.

Low back merger   The term used to characterize the result of a sound change in which the two formerly distinct vowels [ɑ] and [ɔ] came to be pronounced identically, such that in some North American English dialects the members of the pairs *hock* and *hawk* and *cot* and *caught* are not distinguished.

Manner of articulation   How the airstream is obstructed in the vocal tract in the production of a sound.

Marked   The elements of a *lexical field* with less basic meaning. Usually, more marked elements have more precise meanings than less marked elements, can be described in terms of less marked elements, and are less frequent in natural speech. Example: *Cocker spaniel* is more marked than *dog.*

Meaning   The term used to refer to the senses and referents of expressions, including words, phrases, clauses, and sentences.

Merger   The term used for the historical process in which two distinct sounds evolve into a single sound, as exemplified in the *low back merger.*

Metaphor   An extension of a word's use beyond its primary meaning to include referents that bear some similarity to the word's primary referent, as in *eye of a needle.*

Minimal pair   A pair of words that differ by only a single sound in the same position. Examples: *look/took; spill/still; keep/coop.*

Modality   A grammatical category of *verbs marking speakers' attitudes toward the status of their assertions as factual (indicative), hypothetical (subjunctive), and so on; also called *mood.* While some languages mark modality by inflection on the verb, English uses *modal* verbs (e.g., *must, may,* and *can,* as in *must begin, may arrive, can talk),* which lack typical morphological inflections such as *-s* and *-ing.*

Modes   Channels of linguistic expression: speaking, writing, and signing.

Mood   See *modality.*

Morpheme   The smallest unit of language that carries meaning or serves a grammatical function. A morpheme can be a word, as with *zebra* and *paint,* or part of a word, as in *zebras* and *painted,* which contain two morphemes each (ZEBRA and 'PLURAL'; PAINT and 'PAST TENSE').

Nasals   A class of sounds (including the consonants [m] and [n]) produced by lowering the velum and allowing air to pass out of the vocal tract through the nasal cavity.

Nativization   The process through which a speech community adopts another speech community's language as its own and modifies the structure of that new language, thus developing a new dialect that becomes characteristic of the adopting community.

Natural class   A set of speech sounds that can all be characterized by one or a few phonetic features and that includes all the sounds of a given language that are characterized by those phonetic features. Example: /p t k/ form the natural class of voiceless stops in English because the class includes all the voiceless stops in the language and no other sounds.

Neutralized   The localized loss of a distinction between two *phonemes that have identical *allophones in a certain environment. Example: In American English, /t/ in *metal* and /d/ in *medal* are neutralized in that both are pronounced [ɾ] (i.e., intervocalically following a stressed syllable).

New information   *Content introduced into a *discourse for the first time. See *given information.*

Noun   A lexical category of words that function syntactically as heads of noun phrases and semantically as *referring expressions;* nouns can be characterized morphologically by certain inflections and syntactically by their distribution in phrases and clauses; in traditional terms, a noun is defined semantically as the name of a person, place, or thing.

Nucleus   In a *syllable,* that part of the rhyme that is the peak; usually a *vowel, but sometimes a *sonorant;* the nucleus is the sole essential element of a syllable. Example: In the English syllable [pɛn], [ɛ] is the nucleus.

Number   A grammatical category associated with *nouns and *pronouns and indicating something about the quantity of referents. Example: *Car* and *he* are marked for singular number, while *cars* and *they* are marked for plural number. Number can also be marked on verbs, usually in *agreement with subjects, as in singular *He* <u>sleeps</u>, plural *They* <u>sleep</u>.

Object   See *direct object.*

Oblique   A noun phrase whose *grammatical relation* in a *clause* is other than *subject*, *direct object*, or *indirect object;* oblique usually marks semantic categories such as location or time.

Obstruent   A cover term for *stops*, *fricatives*, and *affricates*, three classes of consonant sounds that impede or obstruct the airflow by constricting the vocal passage.

Offglide   See *glide*.

Onset   One or more consonants that precede the *rhyme* in a *syllable* constitute the **onset;** [p] is the onset in the syllable [pɛn]; [sp] in [spɛnt]; [str] in [strɛtʃ].

Orthography   A system of spelling used to achieve a match between the sound system of a language and the alphabet representing it.

Paradigm   The set of forms constituting the inflectional variants of a particular word; see also *declension* and *conjugation*.

Participle   A term used to refer to -ING and -ED/-EN forms of the verb, as in *is walking, had kicked* or *had been stolen*. (It does not refer to past-tense forms as in *they walked* or *she swam);* traditional terminology calls the -ING form the present or progressive participle and the -ED/EN form the past or perfective or passive participle.

Person   A grammatical category associated principally with pronouns marking reference to the speaker (first person), the addressee (second person), a third party (third person), or a combination of these; verbs in a clause are sometimes marked for person *agreement*, usually with their *subject*.

Phoneme   A distinctive and significant structural element in the sound system of a language. A phoneme is an abstract element (defined by a set of phonetic features) that can have alternative manifestations (called *allophones)* in particular phonological environments. Example: The English phoneme /p/ has several allophones, including aspirated [pʰ], unreleased [p̚], and unaspirated [p].

Phonetics   The study of sounds made in the production of human speech.

Phonological rule   A rule that specifies the *allophones* of a *phoneme* and their distribution in a particular language.

Phonotactic constraints   Rules that specify the structure of *syllables* permitted in a particular language.

Phrase   The term used to refer to syntactic *constituents* smaller than a *clause* and, usually, larger than a word—thus noun phrase, adjective phrase, prepositional phrase.

Phrase-structure rule   A rule that describes the composition of *constituents* in *underlying structure;* also called rewrite rule. Example: S ➔ NP VP is a phrase-structure rule stating that a sentence is made up of a noun phrase and a verb phrase in that order.

Pictogram   A symbolic drawing that represents an object or idea independently of the word that refers to that object or idea, such as highway signs that pictorially indicate dangerous curves or merging traffic without the use of words.

Pidgin   A contact language that develops in multilingual colonial situations, in which one language (commonly that of the colonizer) forms the base for a simple and usually unstable new variety; pidgins are restricted in use and not spoken natively by anyone.

Place of articulation   The location in the mouth cavity where the airstream is obstructed in the production of a sound. Example: *Alveolar* sounds such as [t] and [s] are produced by obstructing the airstream at the alveolar ridge.'

Polysemy   The term used to refer to multiple related meanings for a given word or sentence; a word with more than one meaning is said to be polysemic.

Possessor   A *grammatical relation* between two nouns that are closely associated, often by virtue of having a possessive relationship. Examples: _Luke's_ harp, the _book's_ cover, _arm's_ length.

Postposition   A category of words that serve syntactically as heads of postpositional phrases and semantically to indicate a relationship between two entities; except that they follow their complements, postpositions are like prepositions. Examples: Japanese *Taroo _no_* 'of Taro' and *hasi _de_* 'with chopsticks.'

Pragmatics   The branch of linguistics that studies language use, in particular the relationship among *syntax, *semantics,* and interpretation in light of the context of situation.

Predication   The part of a *clause* that makes a statement about a particular entity. Example: In the clause *Lou likes ice cream,* the predication made of Lou is *likes ice cream.*

Predicative adjective   An *adjective* that serves syntactically as a complement to the verb in a *clause* and predicates something of the *subject* (*The soup is _cold_*); contrasted with *attributive* adjective (*the _cold_ soup*).

Prefix   An *affix* that attaches to the front of a word stem.

Preposition   A category of words that serve syntactically as heads of prepositional phrases and semantically to indicate a relationship between two entities. Examples: _to_ school, _with_ liberty, _in_ the spring. See also *postpositions.*

Pronoun   A term used for several closed categories of words. Traditionally defined as taking the place of nouns (or more accurately noun phrases), personal pronouns, such as *it, me, he, she, they,* and *you,* are the most familiar type. Other types include relative pronouns (*who, whose, which, that*), demonstrative pronouns (*this, that, those*), interrogative pronouns (*who, which, whose*), and indefinite pronouns (*anyone, someone*).

Prosody   The term used to refer to variations in the volume, pitch, rhythm, and speed of speech.

Redundancy   The term used to refer to repeated information in a linguistic expression. Example: An expression like *those books* represents the plurality of the noun phrase in both its words, as contrasted with *the books,* which represents it only on the noun.

Reduplication   A morphological process by which a morpheme or part of a morpheme is repeated, creating a word with a different meaning or a different lexical category. Example: Mandarin Chinese *sànsànbu* 'to take a leisurely walk' is formed by reduplicating the first syllable of *sànbu* 'to walk.' Unlike reduplication, repetition (as in English *very, very tired*) does not create a new word.

Reference   A semantic category through which language provides information about the relationship between noun phrases and their *referents.*

Referent   The real-world entity (person, object, notion, situation) referred to by a linguistic expression.

Referential Said of a noun phrase that refers to a particular entity; *a good piano teacher* is referential in *Tom knows a good piano teacher* but not in *Tom wants to find a good piano teacher*.

Referential meaning The meaning that an *expression* has by virtue of its ability to refer to an entity; referential meaning is contrasted with *social meaning* and *affective meaning* and is sometimes called denotation.

Referring expression An *expression* that refers to an entity or situation.

Reflex A term used in historical linguistics for a linguistic form that derives from an earlier form called its *etymon*; reflexes of the same etymon are called *cognates*.

Register A language *variety* associated with a particular situation of use. Examples: baby talk, legalese.

Regular sound change A sound change that affects all the words in which a particular sound occurs in a particular sound environment. Example: Regular sound change may be *conditioned sound change* or *unconditioned sound change*. See *sporadic sound change*.

Relative clause A *clause* syntactically embedded in a noun phrase and semantically serving to modify a noun. The modified noun is the head of the relative clause. Example: In *This is the book that I told you about,* the relative clause *that I told you about* modifies the head *book*.

Repair A sequence of turns in a conversation during which a previous *utterance* is edited, corrected, or clarified.

Repertoire See *linguistic repertoire*.

Representational sign A sign that is basically arbitrary but nevertheless bears some resemblance to its referent or some feature of its referent. Example: *III* 'three'; *trickle, meow*.

Rhyme That part of a *syllable* comprising the *nucleus* and the *coda*. Example: In the syllable [pɛn], [ɛn] is the rhyme.

Semantic field A set of words with an identifiable semantic affinity. Example: *angry, sad, happy, exuberant, depressed*.

Semantic role The way in which the *referent* of a noun phrase is involved in the situation described or represented by the *clause*, for example as agent, patient, or cause.

Semantics The study of the systematic ways in which languages structure meaning, especially in words, phrases, and sentences.

Sequence constraints See *phonotactic constraints*

Sibilant A member of a set of *fricative* sounds made by passing a continuous stream of air through a narrowed passage in the vocal tract, thereby causing hissing, such as that created between the blade of the tongue and the back of the *alveolar* ridge in the production of [s] and [ʃ], as in *sis* and *shush*.

Sign An indicator of something else, for example of an object or event, as smoke is a sign of fire and <8> is a sign of the number 'eight.' See also *representational sign*.

Simple sentence A sentence that contains only one *clause*.

Slang   A language *variety used in situations of extreme informality, often with rebellious undertones or an intention of distancing its users from certain mainstream social values; slang also refers to particular expressions of extreme informality.

Social dialect   A language *variety characteristic of a social group, typically socioeconomic groups, gender groups, or ethnic groups, as distinct from regional groups.

Social meaning   Information that linguistic *expressions convey about the social characteristics of their producers and of the situation in which they are produced; together with *affective meaning, social meaning is sometimes called connotation.

Sonorant   A class of *consonant sounds comprising *nasals and *liquids.

Speech act   An action carried out through language, such as promising, lying, and greeting.

Speech situation   A situation in which members of a community interact linguistically on one or more topics, for a particular purpose, and with awareness of the social relations among the interlocutors.

Split   The term used in historical linguistics to characterize a historical development in which a single sound changes into two sounds, one of which may be the original sound. Example: Proto-Indo European *p became f in Germanic and p in Romance.

Sporadic sound change   A sound change that affects one or a few individual words, but not all words in which the sound occurs or even all those words that share a particular linguistic environment. Example: The pronunciation of nuclear as "nu-cu-lar" is a sporadic sound change. See *regular sound change.

Standard variety   The language variety that has been recorded in dictionaries and grammars and serves a speech community especially in its written and public functions.

Stop   A speech sound created when air is built up at a *place of articulation in the vocal tract and suddenly released through the mouth; sometimes called oral stops when nasals are excluded.

Style   The term sometimes used to refer to situational variation; what in this book has generally been called register variation.

Subcategorization   Information about the types of clause structure that each *verb permits in the verb phrase. For example, a verb may permit one or two noun phrases, or none; as in He burned the rice, She sold him the book, and He fell, respectively.

Subgroup   The term used to refer to a set of languages that belong to the same *language family and developed as a single language for a period of time after other subgroups had become separate languages. Examples: Romance and Germanic are subgroups of *Indo-European; West Germanic is the subgroup of Germanic to which English belongs; also called a branch.

Subject   A noun phrase immediately dominated by S in a phrase structure.

Subordinating conjunction   A word that links clauses to one another in a noncoordinate role, thus marking the boundary between an embedded clause and its matrix clause; also called a subordinator. Example: I think that he fell.

Suffix   An *affix that attaches to the end of a word stem.

Surface form A word's actual pronunciation; generated by the application of the *phonological rules* of a language to the *underlying form;* sometimes also said of sentences (see *underlying structure).*

Surface structure The *constituent structure* of a sentence after all applicable operations or *transformations* have applied.

Syllabic writing Writing in which each graphic *sign* represents a *syllable* rather than a word or a sound.

Syllable A phonological unit consisting of one or more sounds, including a peak (or *nucleus)* that is usually a *vowel* or *diphthong;* frequent syllable types are CV and CVC.

Synonymous The term used in *semantics* to refer to words or sentences that mean the same thing.

Syntax The term used to refer to the structure of sentences and to the study of sentence structure.

Tense A category of the *verb* that marks time reference, for example past *(walked)* or present *(walk).*

Text A unitary stretch of *expression* created in a real-world social situation; usually but not always longer than a sentence *(Smoking Not Permitted; Closed; Gesundheit);* more commonly used in written than in spoken or signed expression but applicable to any mode; sometimes used for a piece of text rather than an entire text. Examples: a novel, a personal letter, a classified advertisement, a screenplay, song lyrics, a scholarly or scientific article, a (transcribed) conversation.

Topic The main center of attention in a sentence; what the sentence is about.

Transformation A syntactic operation (or rule) that changes one *constituent structure* to another in a systematic way.

Transitive verb A verb that takes a *direct object,* as in She <u>found</u> the book.

Trill A *manner of articulation* characterized by the rapid vibrating of one articulator against another articulator (but not including vocal cord vibration).

Turn A basic term in the analysis of conversation, which comprises a series of turns among interlocutors.

Typology A field of inquiry that seeks to classify the languages of the world into different types according to particular structural characteristics.

Unconditioned sound change A *regular sound change* that affects every word in which the sound occurs. See *conditioned sound change.*

Underlying form The form of a *morpheme* that is stored in the internalized *lexicon;* sometimes also said of sentences (see *underlying structure).*

Underlying structure The abstract structure of a sentence before any *transformations* have applied; also called deep structure.

Universal A linguistic pattern at play in most or all of the world's languages. See also *absolute universal* and *universal tendency.*

Universal tendency   A linguistic pattern at play in most, but not all, of the world's languages. Example: Most (but not all) verb-final languages place adjectives before the nouns they modify.

Utterance   *Expression* produced in a particular context with a particular intention.

Variety   Any language, *dialect*, or *register.*

Velar   A *consonant* sound whose *place of articulation* is the velum, that is, a consonant produced by the tongue approaching or touching the roof of the mouth at the velum.

Verb   A category of words that syntactically determine the structure of a *clause*, especially with respect to noun phrases; that semantically express the action or state of being represented by a clause; and that morphologically can be marked for certain categories (not all of which are realized in English): *tense* (present: *walk*/past: *walked*), *mood*, *aspect* (*walk/walking*), *person* (first: *walk*/third: *walks*), and *number* (singular: *walks*/plural: *walk*).

Voicing   The vibration in the *larynx* caused by air from the lungs passing through the vocal cords when they are partly closed; speech sounds are said to be *voiced* or *voiceless.*

Vowels   One of two major classes of sounds (the other being *consonants*); vowels are articulated without complete closure in the oral cavity and without sufficient narrowing to create the friction characteristic of consonants. Abbreviated V.

Index

Separate indices for languages, Internet sites, and videos follow this general index. Terms followed by an asterisk (*) are defined in the Glossary, on pages 571–585. The abbreviation "ex" following a number refers to an exercise.

Index of Languages

Index of Internet Sites

Index of Videos

CREDITS

Thanks are due to the following authors, publishers, and agents for permission to use the material indicated.

British Library. Figure 12–2: "Evolution of Cuneiform Writing From Pictograms" by Albertine Gaur from *History of Writing.* Copyright © 1984. Reprinted by permission of the author.

Cambridge University Press. Cover of *English Today,* October 1987. Reprinted by permission of Cambridge University Press.

Cambridge University Press. Figure 13–2 "Cultural Areas in the Pacific" and Figure 13-4 "The Settlement of Polynesia" from *Prehistory in the Pacific Islands: A Study of Variation in Language, Customs, and Human Biology* by John Terrell. Copyright © 1986. Reprinted by permission of Cambridge University Press.

Friends of Washoe. Photo of Washoe. Reprinted by permission of Friends of Washoe, Chimpanzee and Human Communication Institute (CHCI).

Harvard University Press. Figures 11–7, 11–8, 11–9, 11–22, 11–23, 11–24, and 11–25 from the *Dictionary of Regional English, Volumes I-II,* edited by Frederic G. Cassidy, Cambridge, MA: The Belknap Press of Harvard University Press. Volume I, A–C, Copyright © 1985 by the President and Fellows of Harvard College. Volume II, D–H, Copyright © 1991 by the President and Fellows of Harvard College. Reprinted by permission of the publisher.

Harvard University Press. Figure 12–5 "The Vai Syllabary" from *Psychology of Literacy* by Sylvia Scribner and Michael Cole, Cambridge, MA: Harvard University Press, p. 33. Copyright © 1981 by the President and Fellows of Harvard College. Reprinted by permission of the publisher.

Houghton Mifflin. Entries "husky" and "junior" from *The American Heritage Dictionary of the English Language,* Third Edition. Copyright © 1996 by Houghton Mifflin Company.

Mouton de Gruyter. Figure 11–13: "Urban Dialect of the United States, Based on Pronunciation" from *Atlas of North American English* by William Labov, Sharon Ash, and Charles Boberg. Reprinted by permission of the author.

New Guinea Motors. Figure 13–17: New Guinea Motors publicity cartoon in Tok Pisin by Bob Browne.

Thomson Learning. Figure 12–4 "The Cherokee Syllabary" from *An Introduction to Descriptive Linguistics*, revised edition by Henry A. Gleason. Copyright © 1961 by Holt, Rinehart and Winston, and renewed by H.A. Gleason, Jr. Reproduced by permission of Thomson Learning.